Praise for Elmer Kelton

"One of the g[reatest] ... gifted of W[estern] ...
—Historical ...

"Elmer Kelton is a Texas treasure."
—*El Paso Herald-Post*

"Voted 'the greatest Western writer of all time' by
the Western Writers of America, Kelton creates
characters more complex than L'Amour's."
—*Kirkus Reviews*

"Kelton writes of early Texas with
unerring authority."
—*Fort Worth Star-Telegram*

"You can never go wrong if . . . you pick up
a title by Elmer Kelton."
—*American Cowboy*

"One of the best."
—*The New York Times*

"A splendid writer."
—*The Dallas Morning News*

"A genuine craftsman with an ear for dialogue
and, more important, an understanding
of the human heart."
—*Booklist*

Forge Books by Elmer Kelton

SONS OF TEXAS

— AND —

THE RAIDERS: SONS OF TEXAS

Elmer Kelton

FORGE®

A TOM DOHERTY ASSOCIATES BOOK | NEW YORK

NOTE: If you purchased this book without a cover, you should be aware that this book is stolen property. It was reported as "unsold and destroyed" to the publisher, and neither the author nor the publisher has received any payment for this "stripped book."

This is a work of fiction. All of the characters, organizations, and events portrayed in these novels are either products of the author's imagination or are used fictitiously.

SONS OF TEXAS AND THE RAIDERS

Sons of Texas copyright © 1989 by Elmer Stephen Kelton Estate

The Raiders: Sons of Texas copyright © 1989 by Elmer Stephen Kelton Estate

All rights reserved.

A Forge Book
Published by Tom Doherty Associates
120 Broadway
New York, NY 10271

www.tor-forge.com

Forge® is a registered trademark of Macmillan Publishing Group, LLC.

ISBN 978-1-250-22120-9

Our books may be purchased in bulk for promotional, educational, or business use. Please contact your local bookseller or the Macmillan Corporate and Premium Sales Department at 1-800-221-7945, extension 5442, or by email at MacmillanSpecialMarkets@macmillan.com.

First Edition: March 2020

Printed in the United States of America

0 9 8 7 6 5 4 3 2 1

CONTENTS

SONS OF TEXAS

PART 1

MEN OF
THE CANE

TENNESSEE, 1816

1

For many years, mention of Texas sent a chill shuddering down Michael Lewis's spine. He remembered it as a wondrous place, new and immense and mysterious, shining in the sun. He remembered it also as a place of cruelty and cold terror, for it was there, when he was sixteen years old, that he saw his father's brains blown out by a Spanish officer who left the boy wounded on an open prairie to die alone in a wild and alien land.

He knew but little of his forebears, for the Lewises and their kin were by and large a restless people who looked forward, not to the past. They were busy fighting and building and planting, then moving and fighting and building again; they had scant time to do more in the nature of keeping family records than to scrawl laboriously the names and dates of birth, marriage, and death in the front leaves of an ancient family Bible. Even the Bible, more often than not, was passed down only to the firstborn, along with the land and whatever other meager material possessions the elders' frugality, tenacity, and courage had managed to bind together.

So it was natural that Michael had no knowledge of the first of his Scotch-Irish ancestors who had turned their backs upon troubled Ireland and ventured boldly onto some treacherous seafaring craft which pointed its bowsprit westward toward a dark and little-known continent. They had been told that in this land a man could do as he wanted and think as he wished and worship God after his own lights, answering to no one except that God. Michael was but dimly aware that some of his earliest ancestors had landed in Pennsylvania when that had been a raw and forested wilderness, its rich dark soil stained again and again by the spilled blood of red man and white. The inhabitants changed faces, changed races, continuing an age-old combat for the right to claim the land's bounties.

He knew but dimly, from stories heard at his grandfather's knee, about his family's struggles to gain a foothold at the eastern base of the Allegheny barrier; of restless men whose contempt for authority and the pretensions of tidewater settlements kept pushing them southward and westward, finally up and over the mountains, then down onto the dark and bloody battlegrounds of Kentucky and Tennessee. They were a land-hungry people, the Lewises and their kin, each generation plunging westward in its own turn onto new and challenged ground; fighting, registering their claims more often by the grave markers they erected than by ink scratchings on parchment records in some courthouse far to their rear. Even in the old countries, they had been borderers for generations that stretched back into antiquity, so that strife was in their blood.

They were—sometimes with contempt—called *men of the cane*, these Lewises and the buckskin-clad westerers journeying with them, leatherstocking men who pushed relentlessly through the canebrakes and the forests, always straining the western bounds of a new country. They were regarded by the book-learned and fashionable people far behind them as but little more civilized than the red men with whom they battled for elbow room. They knew ax and plow, but they loved the rifle more. They had learned from the agricultural tribes of Indians to grow corn, squash, and beans, but their preference ran more to game, more to the hunt than to the field. As the game thinned, and as courthouses moved west and slick-handed lawyers quibbled over such petty legalities as land titles, the Lewises and their kind, long accustomed to putting such niceties behind them, pressed on into places where no quality-bred lawyer or judge dared go.

Thus it was that the year 1816 found Michael Lewis in western Tennessee—a boy as some reckoned the years but a man in responsibility—slipping out of his blankets in the dark hour before dawn with a rifle that stood almost as tall as he did. He moved quietly to avoid awakening his older brother Joseph. He would rather go to the woods and hunt fresh meat for the family than join Joseph and the younger boys plowing and hoeing the field or chopping wood for their mother's fireplace. He always justified his abdication of more mundane responsibilities by reasoning that his was the best shooting-eye in the family, better even than that of his father Mordecai. He wasted little powder and lead in his self-imposed duty of keeping meat hanging in the open dog-run between the two sections of the Lewis cabin. If there was game to be found, Michael Lewis would find it. He seldom failed to bring it down with the old Pennsylvania rifle passed to him by his grandpa on his mama's side. Even Joseph would admit, however reluctantly, that Michael had the keenest eye and the steadiest hand, and that he should not waste such a talent on ax or plow at times when the larder was thin.

"He's cut in his father's likeness," Patience Lewis would say. Her eyes would turn wistfully to the open cabin door as if she expected Mordecai Lewis to appear there, where she had watched him leave months ago. Even in his own short life, Michael had helped his father build three cabins, each farther west than the one before it; but it seemed Mordecai stayed hardly longer than was necessary to put Patience in a family way. Then he was off again on some extended mission, some duty to General Jackson such as the fight against the English or the war against the Creeks or a campaign against the Seminoles. There was always, it seemed, some higher duty to be met than staying home to plow the fields and tend the stock, to patch the cabin, or to meet the debts that kept building up. The boys were old enough to take a man's part, he would explain each time he packed his possibles and made ready to leave. Michael would watch the departure reluctantly, for he wished he could know his father better. There was no one after whom he would more gladly pattern himself. In many ways Mordecai Lewis was a stranger to him, more akin to the wild things of the forests than to his own family.

Mordecai seldom seemed to see what was right

before him, for his eyes were always fixed on far horizons, his questing spirit seeking places others had not seen and had not had an opportunity to spoil. He knew no hesitation, showed no fear except that by his explorations he opened the way for others to begin the spoiling. He could only keep moving farther west, trying to stay ahead of those who leveled the forests and broke the primeval sod.

Materially the Lewises seemed to fare well enough without Mordecai, for Joseph was a good farmer and Michael an accomplished hunter. But Michael was troubled by the longing he often saw in Patience's eyes as she stood in the open door at dusk, looking toward the dark forests into which her husband had last disappeared. There were some needs her sons were powerless to fill.

Folks said Michael was already the image of his father, except for the twenty-odd years' difference in their ages and six inches' difference in their height. The height would be made up in due time, for Michael was still in the midst of that fast growth and change which comes upon a boy in his middle teens. He had his father's earnest and unwavering blue eyes, the same stern set to a jaw just beginning to show occasional need for the razor.

Dawn lighted Michael's way as he moved carefully into the woods, alert for quick movement, for sudden sound. The region was generally regarded as cleared of hostile Indians, but some still occasionally visited old hunting grounds, not yet resigned to their irrevocable loss. Children were taught to be wary of red men in the forest just as they were taught to watch for snakes that lurked in the weeds and thick grass. A major difference was that the snake never attacked but struck only in self-defense, whereas the Indian went out of his way to avenge old blood and retake what he regarded as his own. The settlers who had displaced him indulged in no introspection, no guilt, no need to justify their conquest. That would come later, from generations who had the safety and the leisure that allowed for such contemplation. These first invaders accepted what God had wrought and considered themselves His instruments for bringing Christian settlement into a heathen wilderness. They saw no need to question His judgment and they did not want to risk His wrath by doing so.

Michael looked up toward a rustling sound in a tree. He raised the long, heavy barrel of the rifle, then let it sag as a squirrel skittered across a branch, scolding him for his trespass. He would settle for squirrel later, if the day gave him no opportunity to level his sights on better game. A squirrel now would be small reward for a gunshot that might frighten larger quarry away. Squirrel made good eating; one just didn't provide enough to go around for the seven children Mordecai and Patience's love had produced.

Michael came at length to a small clearing where fallen trees had left a tangle of rotting deadfall timber. A series of violent earthquakes a few years earlier had knocked down vast stretches of timber, had changed the courses of streams and created lakes where there had been none before over much of this region west of the mountains. The Lewises had lived farther east then, and Michael had been shaken out of the loft where he had slept with his brothers over the dog-run. The earth's violent convulsions had left the cabin leaning dangerously and had flung his mother's old family Bible out upon the dirt floor, breaking its fragile spine. Patience had accepted this as a bad omen and reentered the cabin only to remove from it what was salvageable. With the help of her small boys and a couple of neighbors, she had built a new one. As usual, Mordecai had been absent. He had taken a large bundle of tanned hides to the settlement to trade for necessities, then neglected to return home until he had spent seven weeks searching the western territory for a likely spot to take up a new and "lasting" home. He had exhausted the necessities on the trip, so the family did without. That experience was hardly new.

Michael made his way over and through the deadfall timber, pausing often to stand stone-still and watch. Such little clearings were a likely place for deer to feed upon the re-growth shrubbery and the green grass, within a few swift bounds of heavy timber and its protection.

He heard a rustling noise behind him and turned quickly, bringing the rifle to his shoulder. A stone's hard throw away, a boy in a ragged homespun shirt and leather britches labored through the fallen timber. Michael lowered the rifle and let his anger build to a useful level while he waited for his younger brother Andrew to catch up with him.

"Andrew Lewis," he declared, "you are a vexation and a pain, follerin' after me thisaway. You've made enough racket to run off every critter in three mile."

Andrew, at fourteen still half a head shorter than Michael and spare in build, met his gaze with the unwavering blue eyes of all the Lewis clan, eyes that betrayed neither trepidation nor remorse. "Two of us can find more game than one."

"Two can sure enough *run off* more than one." Michael knotted a fist with his left hand—the right one had all it could do to hold the heavy rifle—and set it upon his left hip with all the assumed authority of the older brother. In his father's absence he took upon himself the welfare of his younger brothers and sisters when they were away from Mama and the house. Older brother Joseph had enough other responsibilities to fret him, worrying about the crops and livestock. "What if you was to run into a bear out here, or even Injuns? You ain't got a gun or nothin'."

Andrew gave no ground. Grinning, he drew from its scabbard a crude hunting knife his father had forged for him. "I'm armed."

Michael gave a long sigh of resignation. Self-doubt had never been an attribute of his father Mordecai, nor of the sons growing up in Mordecai's tall shadow. He declared dryly, "It's nothin' to be joshin' about. Now I wish you'd turn around and go back so I can find some meat for the table."

"I can help you look."

"I can find it without your help."

Andrew had a quiet and sometimes irritating way of laughing to himself. He could find something funny in an earthquake. "You ain't doin' too good a job of it." He pointed with his chin.

On the far side of the clearing a fleshy doe ventured out of heavy timber and into the edge of the grassy glade, pausing in midstride to look around, jerking her head from one position to another. She warily surveyed the clearing, gauging it for danger. Michael held still as two days dead and hoped Andrew was doing the same. He could not afford to look back, for even that slight movement of his head might grab the animal's attention.

The doe relaxed her vigilance enough to take a bite of grass, then jerked her head up again to glance around once more. Each time she bent, Michael eased his lanky frame downward and raised the rifle a little until he was on one knee, the end of the long barrel resting upon a fallen tree. He cocked the hammer, took a long breath, then a careful bead, and squeezed the trigger.

Through the black powder smoke he saw the doe drop to her knees, so he knew he had hit her. Then, quickly, she was back on her feet and bounding off into the timber.

"You missed her!" Andrew shouted with gleeful accusation.

"No, I hit her, but not through the heart. Come on, we got to trail after her." It occurred to him that in saying *we* he had accepted Andrew's unwelcome company. Well, when they gutted the doe the boy could help him pack the carcass home. Then maybe he would wipe that smart-aleck look from his face. Michael took time to reload the rifle, ramming a fresh ball into the barrel. Papa had once strapped him good for setting off into the forest without his rifle primed and ready for whatever came. Michael took to book-learning with some reluctance and difficulty, but a lesson a boy learned from the hot side of a leather strap would stay with him into manhood.

When they reached the spot where the doe had fallen, he pointed silently to a splotch of blood and took satisfaction from the quick nod of Andrew's head. There were times when spoken words were dead weight. Following the trail was easy at first because of the blood, but that thinned and disappeared after a while, and he had to rely on tracks. There came a point in the heavy timber that he could not find even a track. He stopped in frustration.

Andrew pointed. "This way," he said.

Michael hesitated. "How do you know?"

"Yonder the grass is bent a little, and there's a broken twig on that tree. Anybody can see that."

Michael had not. He frowned at his brother, wondering if Andrew's eyes were that much sharper. "Luck," he said.

"How do you think I found *you*?" Andrew demanded. "Papa showed me a right smart about how to foller a trail."

"All right, you find that doe."

Andrew went about it eagerly. Sometimes Michael could see what the younger boy found; sometimes he couldn't. He followed Andrew out of curiosity and a considerable amount of faith in his father's teachings. Andrew might not be quite the marksman Michael was, but he was a Lewis, and every Lewis seemed to have something he was particularly good at. The beginnings of Mordecai's rugged features already showed plain in his freckled face, as they showed in Michael's and Joseph's. The Lewis financial legacy might be slight, but the blood legacy was formidable.

A shot echoed through the woods, and Michael halted abruptly. A chill shuddered through his thin frame. He saw his own misgivings mirrored in his brother's widened eyes. His first thought was of Indians. Some had rifles, given them a few years ago by English agents when that country tried to reclaim the land George Washington and some of Michael's forebears had wrested from the crown. Michael did not have to signal for Andrew to drop to his knees and hide in the dense undergrowth.

He held his breath, listening. After a minute he heard a shout. "Come on a-runnin', you-all! Don't be so damned slow!"

No Indians talked like that. Michael pushed to his feet, suspicion building like a slow fire. He thought he knew who that voice might belong to. They were fixing to steal his deer.

"Hurry up," he said to Andrew, "if you want fresh venison before the buzzards get it."

They broke out into a clearing, and he had a clear view of the buzzards. They were named Blackwood, and three of them stood over his deer. One had just cut her throat to bleed her out and casually wiped the blood across the thigh of leather britches almost black with grease and dirt and God knew what all. Another nudged him, and he turned to look at the approaching Lewis boys with a frown that evolved quickly into a dark scowl.

One of the Blackwoods was a year or two older than Michael, about a match for Michael's older brother Joseph. Another was Michael's age, and a third was between Michael and Andrew. Michael had pegged them for sneak thieves as soon as one of the Lewis family's chopping axes disappeared from its block just two days after the Blackwood family started clearing a cabin spot two miles from where the Lewises lived.

Like Michael, the Blackwoods were frugal with conversation and offered none. They seemed to sense Michael's intentions and came together shoulder to shoulder in a ragged, dirty line. Michael thought a man would probably have to travel a long way to find three faces that had gotten uglier in such a short number of years. He said, "That's my doe."

Only the older Blackwood boy carried a rifle. He did what little talking there was. "I shot her."

Michael moved close enough to touch the carcass. He pointed to the wound in the neck. "That's my bullet hole. Where's yours?"

"My second one will be in your ass if you don't get it back into them woods where you come from."

Michael walked around the fallen doe. He saw only the one bullet hole. He reached down, grasped the thin forelegs and turned her over. There was no wound on that side. Finis Blackwood had missed. He said, "You-all backin' off, or have me and Andrew got to whup you?"

Finis Blackwood snickered. "Andrew? Is that the baby's name? He don't look much like Ol' Hickory Jackson."

Andrew took the insult with a shout and charged into the big boy like a small pup after a bear, catching him unready and hitting him where it garnered Finis's undivided attention. The middle brother grabbed Andrew and pulled him off, but Andrew had already compromised Finis's fighting ability. Finis sagged to his knees and bent over, letting his rifle slide to the ground.

Michael might criticize his little brother's judgment but never his nerve. He leaned his own rifle against a tree and went at the other two Blackwood brothers in a rush that forced them to drop Andrew and concentrate on the larger problem.

Nobody had ever taught Michael how to fight. Certainly, nobody had ever suggested that there were any rules to it except to hit the other man firstest, mostest and try one's damndest to come out the winner. When one of the Blackwoods tried to hit him over the head with a piece of tree limb as big around as Michael's arm, Michael leaned into the other brother and took the blow across his shoulder, then kicked his immediate opponent in the groin and turned to grab the limb with both hands. He wrestled for possession, got it, and brought the limb up under Luke Blackwood's chin with enough force that he thought he heard lower and upper teeth strike smartly together. He turned to see if Finis was back on his feet and looking for another helping of Andrew's medicine. Andrew had gotten a limb of his own and brought it across Finis's ear with an authority beyond his years.

"Now," Michael said, heaving for breath, "this is my doe. If you-all want to argue about it some more, we're ready."

Finis Blackwood sat glaring at Andrew and the limb he held ready for further use. Luke Blackwood was rubbing his sore jaw. Isaac Blackwood, youngest of the three, hunched over with his hands between his legs.

A thin line of blood trickled from Andrew's nose down his upper lip. But Michael took satisfaction in the fact that the Blackwoods looked worse.

He took a razor-sharp knife from a belt scabbard and gutted the doe, saving the liver and the sweetbreads. He hoisted the deer up onto his shoulder and motioned for Andrew to carry his rifle. They started back in the direction of home. His skin prickled with the knowledge that the Blackwoods could shoot him in the back and were probably toying with the notion. But he went on the faith that they lacked the courage. They were a counterfeit lot in his judgment, from their shiftless daddy Cyrus on down to the littlest one he had seen callously squash a turtle's shell with a rock. The whole mess wasn't worth more than the price of the tallow that could be rendered out of them.

A rock sailed past Michael and disappeared into the tall grass. The youngest Blackwood, Isaac, was swinging his arm for another throw.

Andrew said indignantly, "He's chunkin' us."

"Ignore him," Michael advised. "He's a poor shot anyway."

Chunking rocks! That was a pretty fair gauge of the whole family's narrow caliber, he thought. He hoped no Indians came prowling through these woods, for the Blackwood family would be of no use to anybody else and precious little to themselves. They would probably not stop running till they crossed back over the mountains to whatever poor backwater they had come from.

He made up his mind not to look over his shoulder again, for they might take it as acknowledgement that they worried him. Isaac scored a lucky hit with a stone against the small of his back. Andrew shouted in anger and picked up the stone, hurling it at Isaac. "They ain't whupped good enough yet," he declared.

"Leave some for another day." Michael frowned, his back stinging where the rock had struck. "Mama ain't goin' to like your bloody nose. You oughtn't to've follered after me."

"You couldn't've whupped all three of them by yourself. Me bein' there, it evened the whole thing up."

Michael knew his brother had a point, but he could not afford to compromise the authority of his two extra years. "Just the same, ask me next time."

"I can't. You always tell me *no*."

When they were well beyond range of Isaac's rocks, Michael stopped and cut off a tree branch about five feet long. He tied the doe's feet and swung her from it. He and Andrew carried the deer home between them.

They neared the field where their oldest brother Joseph, a smaller brother James, and sisters Heather and Annie hoed corn. A rock just missed Michael, and he turned in surprise. Isaac Blackwood had followed them all the way home. The boy leaned down and picked up a good-sized stone, putting a strong shoulder behind the throw. Michael had to step quickly aside, or it would have struck him. He saw no sign of the two older Blackwood boys.

"Well," he said, "Isaac's got more gumption than the whole rest of the litter. He may amount to somethin' someday." He shouted, "We don't want to whup you, Isaac. Go home!"

The boy did not move, but he did not stoop for another rock.

From the field, little Annie, eight, hollered out her indignation and shook her fist at Isaac. She was inclined to be violently protective of her brothers. Heather, more mature at eleven, touched her shoulder and bade her to silence. Heather had stronger notions of a lady's obligations to dignity. James, who was six, just stared at first one and then another.

Joseph came to the end of the row to meet Michael, his face creased in rebuke. "It's a good thing you brought some meat home, or you'd catch it for slackin' off from the field work." He shifted his attention to Andrew. "Boy, you better wash that blood off of your face before Mama sees you. What you mean, runnin' off thataway?"

Michael lied, "He didn't run off. I taken him."

Joseph frowned, unconvinced. He repeated, "It's a good thing you brought meat."

Annie had dropped her hoe. She hurried to the end of the row, a small girl with a dusty, freckled face and eyes that looked as big and blue as the old china saucers Mama had brought with her from the other side of the mountains. Those eyes stared with admiration at Michael. He was the brother most like Papa, and she adored Papa. "Did you shoot the deer, Michael?"

Michael glanced back at Andrew and felt generous. "It taken us both." Andrew looked surprised but accepted the acknowledgement with a grin.

Michael jerked his head. "Come on, Andrew. We got to skin this doe." He reached out to pat the top of Annie's head and brought a wide smile to her face. Heather stood back without comment. The older and wiser sister, she would probably counsel Annie not to let such a small gesture from a boy— even a brother—go to her head.

Patience Lewis stood in the open dog-run, holding the baby girl Dora and watching. She was a medium-tall woman—skinny, some would call her. The hard work and sometimes skimpy vittles on a small frontier farm gave no one much chance to run to fat. Michael had always adjudged her a handsome woman, though he had only the vaguest idea what men in general considered handsome. She pleased Mordecai Lewis, and that was enough. Nobody had any business making judgments about Michael's mother anyway.

Patience put the baby down to play on the dog-run. She gave Andrew a grave but silent scrutiny, then said, "You boys got off without any breakfast.

I'll have you somethin' fixed by the time you've skinned that doe and hung her up to drain and cool out." She glanced at a row of metal hooks firmly fixed to a rafter over the dog-run. They called it dog-run because it was an open space where the breeze could move through between the two sections of the cabin, and thus was a favored place for dogs to loaf or to run. Dogs liked staying there anyway when meat was hanging where they could get the scent of it. Michael always made sure it hung high enough that neither they nor any stray varmints were likely to jump up and get their teeth into it.

Patience turned toward the kitchen door, then paused. Her blue eyes were accusatory. "You boys look kind of bloodied up. You fall out of a tree or somethin'?"

Michael glanced at Andrew. "Somethin' like that."

"I hope you wasn't fightin' each other. I won't tolerate that kind of behavior in this family."

"No ma'am. We never fight . . . each other."

By the time he and Andrew had the doe hanging in four quarters, the welcome smell of fried meat and corn dodgers reminded him of his hunger. His mother made the two go wash the blood and grease from their faces and hands before she let them into the kitchen.

They were almost finished eating when a man's voice boomed, "Hello the house!" and a tall frame blocked most of the light from the doorway.

Papa! Michael thought. His heart jumped a happy beat. But he blinked and slumped back upon the rough-hewn bench. Uncle Benjamin was Papa's oldest brother, and sometimes they looked so much alike that it made a body catch his breath. Benjamin was two years older and considerably more prosperous. Only his britches were of leather; the shirt was of cloth. And he owned six horses, the last count Michael had taken.

Michael glanced at his mother and thought she must have mistaken Benjamin for Papa too, for gladness sparked her eyes. She moved halfway across the little room to meet him. She reached out as if to touch him but stopped herself. She said, "Come on in, Benjamin, and welcome."

"I brought meat. Looks like somebody's already been out and fetched his own, though." He gave Michael a smile that spoke of family pride. "Ain't Mordecai got home yet?"

Patience shook her head. Her smile went quickly to a frown. "You have reason to think he should've?"

Benjamin leaned his long rifle in a corner. "Joel Bacon said he seen him four days past, down the trace towards Miller's Crossin'. Said he was on his way home."

Concern crept into Patience's voice. "I don't know why he's takin' so long, then."

Benjamin replied, "You know how it is with Mordecai. He's got to stop and bide by all his friends, and he ain't got an enemy in the world, hardly."

"He's got a family." She shrugged off the momentary resentment. "I expect you're hungry. Michael and Andrew don't need to eat all this truck that I fixed for them."

Michael thought she was being almighty generous without asking him what *he* thought about it. Uncle Benjamin relieved his mind. "My daughters fixed for me before I left the house, but obliged just the same. You boys better finish all that's on the table. Looks like there's a-plenty of work waitin' for you out in the field."

Patience said, "It's a blessin' and a comfort that you've got your children around you, Benjamin. Otherwise, that place would seem dreadful lonely now that Nancy's gone."

Benjamin's smile left him. "It's lonely anyway."

Michael's Aunt Nancy had taken sick during one of the coldest spells last winter. Spring and its warm sunshine had lifted her out of similar slumps in the past, but they had failed her this time. She was a Carolina tidewater woman, small and poorly, and folks said she never should have been exposed to the rigors of childbearing and homemaking on this harsh frontier. They said it was a wonder she had lived as long as she did. But Michael's own mother was just as thin. Hard work and mean times never seemed to put an intolerable strain on her. She took the work in her stride, and she got angry rather than bitter at the hard times, as if they were a personal affront to be met head on, like varmints in the corn-patch.

Benjamin said, "Michael, your cousin Frank came along with me for company. He stopped off down at the field to help Joseph and the young'uns."

Michael decided he had had enough to eat. To be able to visit with cousin Frank was a treat made the more pleasant for its rarity. Frank was one of those boys who could read books nigh as well as a school-master, yet could still knock a squirrel out of a tree at a hundred long paces. That combination was not often come by. A body could be proud to have kin-folk like that.

He left what remained of his breakfast. "Come on, Andrew," he said to his surprised brother. "We better get down to the field and go to work."

He had gotten halfway there, Andrew trudging

barefoot behind him, when he remembered he had left his rifle in the kitchen. Papa had counseled him never to venture far from the house without a firearm. "You go on," he told Andrew. "I'll catch up."

He trotted into the dog-run and stopped abruptly at the kitchen door.

His mother and Uncle Benjamin were in each other's arms.

2

Michael pulled back into the dog-run, his face burning. His mother and uncle had not seen him. Stung by embarrassment and confusion, he walked a little way from the cabin and considered returning to the field without the rifle. But his father's teaching had been drilled into him too firmly: trouble came quickest to a man unprepared for it. He turned back and started whistling to give notice he was coming. He spoke loudly to the baby Dora, spraddled contentedly in the dog-run. As he stepped up to the kitchen door he saw his uncle busily putting fresh wood into the fireplace. His mother stood beside the table, hands twisted in her apron, her face flushed the color of a wild rose.

Michael said uneasily, "I forgot the rifle." He fetched it and hurried out. Turning back once, he saw his uncle standing in the kitchen doorway. When Michael turned again a minute later, Uncle Benjamin was not in sight.

He tried not to think about what he had

interrupted. He tried to force his mind to the work, but the image persisted like an unwelcome dream, stirring a resentment he could not totally analyze, even a guilt because he had seen something not meant for his eyes. He felt a strong sense that what he had witnessed was a betrayal of his father. But he realized also that his mother and his uncle were lonely people. Uncle Benjamin was going to have to find himself another wife one of these days. And Papa ought to be at home, not forever on the roam from one adventure to another while his wife and family stayed behind to shift for themselves. Michael had only the vaguest notion of what a woman's needs might be, but whatever they were, Mordecai Lewis was not seeing to them. Michael was not sure whom to blame, so he blamed everybody. He walked by his favorite cousin with barely more than a nod, picked up a hoe, and went off by himself while Frank stared after him in puzzlement. Michael took out his frustration by chopping weeds from the corn with the same violence he had loosed on the Blackwood boys.

Older brother Joseph walked over after a time and calmed him a little. "You're doin' fine on the weeds, but you're also choppin' out some of the corn. One of these days you'll be wishin' you had it to eat."

Michael admitted, "I was thinkin' about somethin' else."

Joseph did not smile easily upon his younger brothers and sisters, for in a strong sense he was taking their father's place as head of the family. A father was supposed to be an advisor and firm taskmaster, not a playmate. But Joseph smiled. "Andrew told me what you-all done to them Blackwood brothers. But this corn crop is ours, not theirs."

Joseph had misread the source of Michael's dark mood, and it was just as well. Michael's tension eased.

Joseph said, "Frank's afraid you're mad at him about somethin'. I told him it's just them Blackwoods on your mind."

Michael could see cousin Frank watching him uneasily from down the corn row. He looked enough like Joseph and Michael and Andrew to be a brother instead of a cousin. Old Grandpa Lewis had put a powerful mark on his descendants. "I'll tell him. That's all it is, just the Blackwoods."

Frank Lewis could always lift Michael's spirits with some good story he had read or heard, or just telling what he had learned observing a bug or a bird or a bear. He also seemed to have an uncommon store of information about girls, which he was willing to share with little encouragement. Michael had only a limited knowledge on that subject, for his exposure to girls outside his own family was seldom and short. But for some reason lately he had found his curiosity growing, so he welcomed enlightenment. Working alongside his talkative cousin, Michael felt the burden begin to slip from his shoulders, and he was able finally to laugh. Laughter felt good, but it had never come as easily to him as it did to younger brother Andrew.

Sisters Heather and Annie brought their hoes up close to the boys, and Michael felt obliged to shoo them away. What Frank was talking about, no girl ought to hear. And no six-year-old boy like James, either. Heather seemed to understand and retreated without argument, taking her smallest brother with her. But little Annie stubbornly stood her ground until Heather returned to pull her away. "If Michael can hear it, so can I," she argued.

Frank broke off in the middle of a story to say, "Looks like somebody comin' yonder."

Michael leaned on his hoe and squinted. A mule plodded at a slow and deliberate pace, a man hunched slouchily on its bare back. "Aw hell," he declared. "It's Ol' Cyrus Blackwood."

Joseph had seen him too. He joined Michael and Frank, his face furrowed. "Michael, you'd better git to the house before he does. No tellin' what kind of a yarn he'll tell Mama about you and them boys of his."

Michael glanced toward the cabin. He could think of another reason to get there before Blackwood did. That whiskey-soak was known to be a bigger gossip than any old woman within twenty miles. He said, "Frank, you watch out for my rifle." Michael dropped his hoe and set off at a trot. He hollered several times to give his mother ample notice of his coming. She stepped out of the cabin, closing the door behind her. She stood in the sun and shaded her eyes with one hand. He did not see Uncle Benjamin.

Patience appeared calm and at peace with the world. Perhaps she did not recognize the man on the mule. Michael told her Cyrus Blackwood was coming.

She asked, "And why should he not? He's our neighbor."

Michael caught his breath, then said, "Mama, you know he'll lie to you."

"We'll do him the courtesy of hearin' him out."

"You won't hear no truth from him."

Only as Blackwood drew near did Michael see a small girl riding behind him on the mule. She leaned out to look around him with half-frightened eyes. Blackwood said, "Slip down, Florrie." The girl, her skirt pushed way up to show skinned and skinny legs past the knee, got off opposite Michael and his mother and peered shyly around the mule's hindquarters without coming closer.

Mordecai Lewis always said you could tell something about a man's character by the way he sat a horse, and the way he got on and off. Michael supposed that held for mules as well. Cyrus Blackwood dismounted in a slow and careless manner lacking in any grace. He was a lanky, loose-jointed man with a beard that looked like a piece of bearskin except that it was matted in places by streaks of tobacco juice; some wet, some old and dried. He avoided looking a person in the eye for more than a moment. While he talked, he would look everywhere but toward the recipients of his wisdom.

He gave Michael the briefest of glances, then touched the fingers of his right hand to the sagging brim of an old black hat. He said unnecessarily, "Miz Lewis, I come to talk to you."

She replied flatly, "I presumed as much, Mister Blackwood."

His gaze went to the four quarters of fresh venison hanging in the dog-run. "I suppose you've heard there was some difference of opinion this mornin' as to the right and proper ownership of a certain young, fat doe."

"I heard my sons say there was no question about the rightful ownership."

Blackwood gave Michael another resentful glance. "Now, ma'am, there's another side to that story which you ain't heered. My boy Finis, he had a claim on that doe too. Your boys beat him out of it."

Michael declared, "There wasn't but one bullet in her, and that bullet was mine."

Petulantly Blackwood said, "When grown folks are talkin', young'uns mind their tongues."

Patience said sternly, "Michael is of an age to take a man's responsibility, Mister Blackwood. He is old enough to speak his mind."

Michael declared again that Finis might indeed have fired at the doe, but he had missed her. Therefore he had no claim.

Blackwood said, "My boys tell it different, so I reckon we'll never know whose bullet taken that deer. Seems to me like there's grounds here for some give on both sides. Since my boy and your boy both shot at her, looks to me like the only fair thing is to share the meat."

Patience said nothing.

Blackwood called to his daughter. "Florrie, you come on around here and say howdy to Miz Lewis. Come on now, don't be shy." The girl hesitantly moved into sight from the off side of the mule, but not very far. Michael would guess her to be eight or ten years old, with a thin face and hungry looking eyes. He could not help comparing her to Annie, and Florrie came off a pathetic second. Cyrus's poorly tended fields didn't put much food on the family table.

Blackwood said, "I got a bunch more at home like this 'un, and there ain't a bite of meat in the house, hardly. Just seems to me like fair's fair, Miz Lewis."

Michael saw his mother weakening as she stared at the hollow-eyed girl. He knew Blackwood had brought her along for just that purpose. "Mama," he protested, "they got no claim."

She motioned for him to be still. "Your Uncle Benjamin brought us two sides of cured ham. I reckon we can spare half of your doe. Go help yourself, Mister Blackwood."

Cyrus Blackwood rarely moved with alacrity, but he did so now as if fearing she might change her mind. "You're a woman of true Christian charity, Miz Lewis." He lifted down two hindquarters. Fairness would have dictated that he take a hindquarter and a foreshoulder, but he strained the quality of mercy. He looked out beyond the cabin where Michael and Joseph had stretched the deerskin for tanning. He said, "If you-all don't need that hide, my missus could make mighty good use of it."

Patience did not forbid him, so he took it. He got onto the mule with his load, then motioned to his daughter. "You come on now, Florrie. We got our work to tend to, and so do these good folks. Good day to you, missus." He heeled the mule into a trot as if afraid someone might decide to take his spoils from him.

Michael's resentment boiled over. "He didn't have nothin' comin' to him, Mama! He taken advantage of your good nature."

"Cast your bread upon the waters, son."

Michael replied disgustedly, "And all you'll do is lose your bread."

He did not have to explain anything to his brothers and sisters in the field. They had seen Blackwood carrying away more than he had brought. Michael picked up his hoe and attacked the weeds again, even more fiercely than before. Frank joined him, and he had talked his way through the Creek war and the battle of New Orleans before Michael's anger ebbed.

Michael sometimes fantasized about his father

coming home one day in triumph with a bagful of gold coin and a cluster of well-wishers proclaiming him a hero, but usually he returned as he did this time, afoot, hidden by the night. He brought no sugar, no flour, no coffee, nothing except a bottomless hunger and a gray-bearded old man even hungrier than Mordecai was. Michael heard them coming. He was down from the sleeping loft and out before anybody else. Mordecai stood before the cabin in the moonlight, looking bigger and taller than life, half reality, half a product of Michael's worshipful imagination. Michael threw his arms around his father, who hugged him so hard that the breath went out of him.

Mordecai pushed Michael to arm's length. "My, but you've growed." Michael doubted that he had, at least not enough to notice. Mordecai just never stayed home long enough to remember. "I'd intended to bring you a new horse, son. Had one, but I was obliged to trade him for vittles."

"I've *got* a pony, Papa." That was true, up to a point. He had a horse named Blaze, the same age as Michael. If Blaze hadn't been so old, Papa would probably have traded him off like he had swapped away every other good horse he had ever acquired. The Lewises were lucky to have a mule for the plowing and a couple of old horses they could ride when there was a need. Papa had left here on horseback. That he came back afoot did not bode well for the family's fortune.

That was of no matter for the moment. Joseph and the younger children clustered around him, and Mordecai gave each a moment of his attention, especially the teary-eyed Annie, before turning finally to the woman who stood in the dog-run, holding a lamp. She was smiling. However difficult the long days and nights of loneliness had been, they were set aside now, and her eyes were aglow with welcome.

Mordecai stared at her a moment without moving. The light of Patience's lamp fell full upon his tall, gaunt frame, deepening the lines in a square-jawed face which was ruggedly handsome but hard-etched by a lifetime willingly, even joyously, spent exposed to hot sun and bitter cold winds. It was a strong, determined face that often appeared to be chiseled from stone. But the deep blue eyes could go soft, and they seemed to melt now as he looked upon the woman who so long had shared one side of his life but had been excluded from the other. His lips formed the word, though Michael could not hear him speak it: "Patience."

She held out the free hand, and Mordecai took it. She turned back into the kitchen. He followed.

The children would have gone in behind them, but the old man stepped into their way and raised his hands. He had a friendly grin as wide as a wagon hoop. "Now, young'uns, there's a time when a man and a woman don't need nobody but one another. You-all give them a spell to say their howdies."

Michael studied the jovial gray-bearded face. He could not remember ever having seen it before. The man said, "My name's Eli Pleasant. I met up with your papa out west a ways."

Mordecai was always bringing friends home with him, old friends as well as new ones who would *become* old friends. He had a way of gathering the rootless ones like some people had of gathering stray dogs, and usually they were just as hungry.

They were kin to him in spirit. It was always up to Patience to make them feel that they were blood kin as well.

Michael asked, "Where you come from, Mister Pleasant?"

"Lots of places. Alabama, Kentucky, Missouri, Louisiana. You ever hear of Texas?"

Michael nodded. The word had floated around these hills. It had a strange and exotic sound to it, like some foreign country way across the big water. Texas was the other side of the Mississippi River somewhere, which for all Michael knew was as far away as Europe.

Eli Pleasant said, "I been to Texas too. I'll tell you about it. But right now I see your papa standin' in the door, wavin' us in. He 'lows as how your mama knows her business with the cookin' vessels. Him and me, we ain't et since early mornin', and I'm drawed a little lank."

Pleasant had understated the case. Between him and Papa they put away one of the venison fore-shoulders Cyrus Blackwood had not taken. Michael sat on a bench in silence and stared, first at his father because he was such a rare and welcome sight, and then at Eli Pleasant because *he* was simply a sight. His gray beard hid much of his face, but it did not hide all of a leathery skin. It did not hide quick eyes that looked like flint and seemed to see everything that moved, like those of an animal in the woods. Andrew asked him how many Indians he had killed. Pleasant avoided an answer by saying he had never learned to count past ten. Everything about him bespoke one of those border men always pushing past the limits of what was commonly regarded as civilization, a man of the cane if Michael had ever seen one. It was natural that Mordecai would ally himself with one like this; they had so much in common.

At last Pleasant pushed his bench back from the table and held up his hands. "Miz Lewis, I always said that when it come my time to die, I wanted it to be from overeatin' at a good woman's table. I swear I've nigh about done it tonight."

"There's a-plenty more," Mordecai said.

If so, Patience would have to return to the hearth. Eli Pleasant spared her. "I'm afraid I'd get spoilt and never want to leave the settlements again. It was most elegant, ma'am."

Patience responded to the compliment with a faint smile. Most of the time when she had not been busy cooking or fetching she had kept her eyes on Mordecai. For the first time in weeks Michael saw happiness in them like a reflection of sunrise. But at odd moments something else crept in, fear perhaps, or doubt. Michael could almost hear her asking: *How long will he stay this time?*

Joseph and Michael stood back while Andrew and the younger children gathered around their father, once he had finished his supper. Little Annie clung with her arms around Mordecai's neck while he told of a big black bear he had killed, and a splendid red stallion he had seen, a wild one that ran faster than a deer. "I almost had him once," he said. "If I'd caught him, I'd've brung him home for you-all to ride. But there's more like him out yonder, a lot more. Next time I'll catch a horse for every one of you."

Michael tried to contain himself but could not. "Next time? When you goin' back, Papa, and where?"

"West. A long ways west. Maybe I'll tell you about it tomorrow, but now I'm tired, and Eli's tired, and I believe your mama is ready for bed too."

While Papa had been away the girls had slept in the room with their mother and the baby Dora. Now they were shunted off to sleep on the kitchen floor. Heather seemed to understand, but Annie put up some argument, not wanting to leave her father. Eli Pleasant climbed up into the loft over the dog-run to bunk down with the boys. Michael noticed that he did not take his clothes off. He simply spread his one ragged old woolen blanket on a thin corn-husk mattress and lay down, wrapping one end of it around him.

Michael asked, "Were you with Papa when he nearly caught the horse?"

"I was," the gravelly voice replied. "But it's much too late to be talkin' about it tonight." The man was snoring almost immediately. Michael lay awake a long time, wondering what adventures Papa had been through this time.

Once he heard a sound like his mother crying out. He supposed she was almighty glad to have Papa home.

Mordecai Lewis had never been one to keep his enthusiasms to himself. His feelings on any subject had always been free and open for the world to see and hear, if the world wanted to. Before breakfast was finished, Michael knew the futility of his mother's hope that this time her husband was home to stay a while.

"I never had it in mind to travel so far," Mordecai said to the family gathered around him at the table, "but the farther I went the farther I had to go." His eyes were shining with the telling. They were deep blue eyes that sometimes could not focus on the reality of the moment but could always see the distant dream with great clarity. "I tell you, Patience, it's a land like nowhere you've been. It's a place where a man could grow up with the country and be rich before he's too old to take pleasure in it all. It's bigger out yonder than you can ever imagine, and free for the takin', just about."

Michael probed eagerly, "Where, Papa? Where-all did you go?"

Mordecai leaned across the table. The excitement in his voice was infectious. "I went past the Mississippi, and on across Louisiana, and—boys, you won't believe this—I even rode over into the Texas country itself. I been in Texas!"

The word had always had a foreign sound to Michael and aroused more curiosity than enthusiasm. But the way his father spoke it sent a thrill tingling up his back. Instantly he formed an image in his mind of a vast open land, shining golden like ripe wheat in the sun.

Patience frowned. "It ain't a part of America even, is it? Don't it belong to France or one of them other foreign countries?"

"To Spain," Mordecai replied. The way he said it was almost like shrugging it off. "They ain't hardly usin' it. Most of it, in fact, they ain't even seen. It's just settin' out there waitin' for somebody to come along that knows what to do with it."

Eli Pleasant had been too busy eating to say anything, but he put in seriously, "Now, you know, Mordecai . . . just because they don't use it don't mean they've left the door open for anybody that wants to come in and take it. They're jealous of what belongs to them, whether they need it or not."

"I wasn't thinkin' about takin' it, not yet, anyway. But I *am* thinkin' of the wild horses runnin' free, and the price they'd bring if we was to fetch them back here to sell. Tennessee farmers need horses. Texas has got them, more than enough for everybody. They're there for the takin'."

Michael put in, "Why didn't you take some of them while you was there, Papa?"

Mordecai glanced quickly at Eli. Some secret lay between them. Mordecai said, "I didn't have enough help. There was just me and Eli. We need us a good-sized party of men, a dozen or so, maybe. I figure I can find them around here, men that want to get ahead in the world. One bunch of horses . . . we could pay off all we owe and have money to bury besides."

Patience appeared almost ready to cry. "Mordecai, you've just gotten home."

He placed his huge farmer hand against her cheek. He could be incredibly gentle at times, Michael thought, when it came to Patience or the girls. "I ain't fixin' to leave right off. It's liable to take me a week or two to find the right men, and get us some horses to ride."

Michael said, "I've got Ol' Blaze."

Mordecai smiled. "I'm afraid it'll take somethin' younger and faster than Blaze to catch wild horses."

Patience showed a faint surge of hope. "You've got nothin' to buy a horse like that with."

"My brother Benjamin's got horses. I expect he'll lend me a couple if I promise to bring him half a dozen in return."

Michael could see Patience's hope fade. Uncle

Benjamin did not agree with many of the things Mordecai did, but Michael could not remember a time Benjamin ever failed to support him. That was the way things were in the Lewis family.

Michael tried to curb his eagerness but could not. It sounded like a wondrous place, the way his father described it. "I want to go with you, Papa."

He saw foreboding leap into his mother's eyes. She did not wait for Mordecai to reply. She said, "No, Michael. Isn't it enough that *one* man is always gone someplace?"

Mordecai gave her a quick study, for the brittleness in her voice was not to be overlooked. He said, "Your mama's right. She needs a man like you here at home."

"I ain't much punkin at the field work. Joseph's a lot better, and so is Andrew."

Mordecai pointed his chin at his empty plate. "That venison me and Eli just put away . . . your mama said you fetched it in."

Michael admitted, "Yes sir, I did."

"You've got a keen eye down a rifle, son. It's needed here to keep meat in the house."

"Andrew's almost as good a shot as me, and better at trackin'."

"A man serves where he's needed most. You're needed here, son, so we'll say no more about it."

Michael's face warmed. Disappointment soured his stomach like a long drink of bad water.

Mordecai said, "You'll be seein' Texas soon enough. The whole family will, some day before you know it. I can feel it in my bones."

Michael did not know how, but he was going to see Texas a lot sooner than that.

He felt that in *his* bones.

He found Eli Pleasant's flint eyes boring into him. He had an uncomfortable feeling that Pleasant was reading his mind.

"There's time, boy," Pleasant said. "There's time enough."

Michael kept his eye on his father when Mordecai and Eli Pleasant walked out onto the dog-run to smoke cigars roughly rolled from tobacco leaves raised in a corner of the garden. It was in Michael's mind to pose his question again, discreetly, if the right moment arose.

He heard Eli ask quietly, "Are you forgettin' about Rodriguez?"

Rodriguez. Michael did not know what the word meant, a place perhaps, or somebody's name. It had a strange, intriguing sound, a hint of faraway places, exotic peoples.

Eli asked, "Do you think it's fair not to tell them about the danger, Mordecai? This ain't no tidewater turkey-shoot we're fixin' to go to. We just got away from that hellhound and his troops by the skin of our teeth."

"We got careless, is all. Texas is bigger'n all creation. Them Spanish won't find us the next time."

Pleasant's voice was dark as midnight. "If they was to, we'd never see Tennessee again!"

3

Sergeant Elizandro Zaragosa warily circled the cabin of logs on his black horse, musket primed and ready. The place appeared deserted, falling into the ruin which nature provided for all man-made things left untended. Still, there was but one way to allay all doubt. He dismounted and handed the reins to a tense young private just sent north to the small Nacogdoches garrison from recruitment in San Antonio de Bexar and not yet tested by fire. Zaragosa cradled the musket in his arms and moved cautiously toward the door, walking almost on tiptoe. He could not shake off a nagging uneasiness, for this place had been home to one Guadalupe Lucero, high on Lieutenant Armando Rodriguez's priority list for execution. Many of these rebels fought to the death rather than surrender and be stood against the wall for their disloyalty to the Spanish crown. Zaragosa glanced back with poorly concealed resentment at the officer who waited a safe hundred long paces in the rear with most of his military detail.

Lieutenant Rodriguez would not weep salty tears into his wine if Zaragosa were shot in the line of duty. His pleasure in dispatching the perpetrator would outweigh any short-term inconvenience over the death of a sergeant who walked too often on the dangerous edge of insubordination.

"*Cabrón!*" Zaragosa muttered under his breath, and paused at the open, sagging door of the cabin. He moved inside, the musket's stock against his shoulder. He swung the muzzle in a swift half circle, eyes searching. He relaxed then, for the wind had blown leaves and other debris through the open door to eddy into a pile against the wall. The house appeared to have known no guests for weeks, perhaps months.

Its former occupants had fled eastward into Louisiana after Lieutenant Rodriguez had forced the head of the household, Felipe Lucero, to dig his own grave. Rodriguez then shot the helpless man and kicked his body into the gaping hole. It was known that the fugitive oldest son, Guadalupe, had tendered aid and comfort to the insurrectionists who had rallied after Padre Miguel Hidalgo y Costilla's cry in Dolores for Mexican revolt against the repressions of Spain. After that rebellion had been put down with fire and blood, the younger Lucero was known to have helped the dissidents and the *americano* adventurers of the Gutierrez-Magee invasion. Those *piratas*—defeated only at a heavy cost in lives by both sides—had attempted to wrest Texas from Spanish rule and set it up as an independent land, perhaps to be annexed to the *Estados Unidos*. Such a scheme could not be tolerated, Rodriguez had declared. If all Mexico could not break free, certainly this far-flung province known as Texas with its miserable little huddles of mud and stone and log villages could not be allowed to escape the wrath of the crown and its protectors.

The elder Lucero was not known to have taken part, but it was only to be expected that if his son was a rebel, the father must harbor similar tendencies. And even if he did not, his summary execution would stand as a warning to others that the punishment for dissension was swift and terrible. Sergeant Zaragosa had argued at the time that the old man should at least be taken to Nacogdoches for trial. "We have no proof, only suspicion," he had said.

Rodriguez had stood firm for immediate reprisal. During the Inquisition, he reminded the sergeant, suspicion of heresy had been enough to satisfy God. Surely suspicion of treason should be enough for the crown. In such a time of turmoil, trials were a luxury. When no man was to be trusted, the only certainty was that the dead would never rebel again. They would rise only when called to face the final judgment and to be cast into that special eternal Hell reserved for those infidels who did not believe the crown ruled Spain and all its possessions by the grace of God.

Zaragosa looked up at the ceiling. The sun peeped through tiny holes and cast sparkling beams of light down through the dusty gloom to the dirt floor. Gradually the rains and the wind would bludgeon this rude cabin back to the earth, and it would crumble into its original dust like the hope of freedom that had brought so much of northeastern Texas to abandonment and ruin.

A waste, Zaragosa thought, an unholy waste of

labor and resources and dreams, for nothing more than the vanity and power of the ruling class, for the pure-blood *gachupínes* like that damned Rodriguez.

He heard a faint scraping sound and went stiff, jerking the musket back to his shoulder as he turned quickly on his heel. It seemed to have come from a corner, where an abandoned cornhusk mattress lay brown and dirty atop a crude bed frame ax-cut from pine. Uneasily Zaragosa bent to look under the bed. He saw frightened eyes staring up at him. They were the eyes of the old Lucero whom Rodriguez had killed. But that could not be.

Zaragosa knew instinctively that this was the Guadalupe Lucero they sought. The lieutenant would be pleased.

The brown eyes continued to stare at him. Lucero was frightened, but he did not beg. He did not speak at all. Zaragosa started to call out to the recruit to notify the lieutenant, but he held back. He had no taste for this man's blood. Rodriguez would almost certainly spill it right here, or hang Lucero from a nearby tree. There would be no wait, no trial.

Zaragosa took a long, deep breath, then brought his fingers to his lips for silence. He lowered the musket and made a silent signal for Lucero to remain where he was. He walked back out into the sunshine and jerked his head, motioning for the recruit to bring his black horse. He glanced involuntarily at the grave of the elder Lucero, dug as the final act of a hard life that had known few comforts. The place of rest was marked by a crude cross constructed of two tree limbs bound together by rawhide. Suicide, Rodriguez had termed his death, the natural consequence of rearing a traitorous son.

Sergeant Zaragosa rode back to the waiting lieutenant and studiously avoided saluting him. They had ridden together since dawn, and such a gesture seemed superfluous to Zaragosa. He knew it did not seem so to the lieutenant, who frowned over the blatant omission.

Zaragosa said, "There is no one, sir."

Rodriguez had the blue eyes which marked his descent from a long line of pure Spanish forebears careful in their marital alliances. The lieutenant half closed those blue eyes and growled, "You took so much time that he could have escaped the cabin and gone two miles before you entered the door. A stiffer backbone would do you credit, sergeant."

Zaragosa felt heat rise into his face, but he was careful not to respond in kind. He suspected the lieutenant was trying to bait him into a moment of foolishness and provoke a pretext for punishment. "The house does not appear to have had a visitor for weeks, perhaps months, sir."

Rodriguez spat, then glared at the cabin. "He has to be *somewhere*. My informant said Lucero had returned to gather the cattle his family left behind in its flight, and to drive them back to Louisiana."

"The Luceros were poor people," the sergeant said, "like most here. If they owned a dozen cattle I would be much surprised."

"What is important is that he has returned to this district. He has placed himself where I could reach him if I were not saddled with *mestizo* incompetents and cowards, scum from the jails of Mexico."

"These men have obeyed your every command, as have I."

"With inefficiency and insolence." Rodriguez frowned. "Sometimes, sergeant, I wonder about your loyalty."

Zaragosa stiffened. "I am a soldier, sir. My service proves my loyalty."

"You talk of loyalty, but sometimes I see your eyes saying something else. You should be most cautious not to arouse your superiors to doubt. We are all here to serve Mother Spain."

"My only mission in life, sir."

Zaragosa had never seen Spain, nor, of course, had Rodriguez. Many generations had passed since their ancestors had sailed to the New World in flimsy galleons, and the umbilical cord had stretched thin. The dark shade of Zaragosa's skin showed that some of his ancestors had been here since antiquity. He had but the vaguest notion of what Spain must be like, and little save the language to give him any real tie to it.

Rodriguez said, "If memory serves me well, the *rancho* of Lucero's cousin lies some distance in that direction." He pointed with his chin.

Zaragosa nodded. "That is as I remember it, sir." He thought the word *rancho* sadly overblown for the realities of this isolated and impoverished region.

Rodriguez said, "You may lead the way, sergeant."

May lead the way. Rodriguez made it sound as if it were a privilege, but the point position carried the greatest hazard. Zaragosa saluted in an exaggeration of the best military style. "Yes, sir." His eyes sought the new recruit, and he jerked his head as a sign for the nervous young man to ride by his side.

He looked back once and saw Rodriguez ride up to the grave, slip his foot from the stirrup, and catch his toe beneath the horizontal bar of the wooden cross. With a jerk of his leg Rodriguez uprooted the cross and let it fall to the ground.

Zaragosa gritted his teeth and turned his face

to the trail. It would be God's justice if Rodriguez should be struck down somewhere and had neither grave nor marker but fed the wolves and the buzzards and the ants.

The young recruit asked worriedly, "If we find this Lucero, I suppose the lieutenant will hang him?"

"Or shoot him. Whatever comes into his mind."

The young man's eyes had a haunted look. "They have shot or hanged many at Bexar because of the rebellion. No one is above suspicion, not even the priests."

Zaragosa clenched a fist. How many more must die before this insanity ran its course?

He heard the bawling of cattle before he broke out of a heavy wood and saw a small farm in a clearing just above a narrow creek. In a nearby field, newly risen corn stood green, waving in the soft southern wind. A woman and several children labored in a modest garden. A man and two large boys had a dozen or so cattle caught up in a pen. By the look of it, they were branding several new spring calves. Light gray smoke rose from a small fire beside the log corral. He heard the frightened bawling of a calf at the hot touch of the branding iron.

He remembered the place, for he had ridden by more than once during their first search for Guadalupe Lucero. The farmer here had stoutly proclaimed his loyalty and denounced all traitors with a fervor that should have pleased even Rodriguez. Zaragosa rode a few paces into the open, then waited for the rest of the patrol to come up. He saw no threat from either house or corral, but he suspected Rodriguez would send him ahead as a target to test the danger. He waited only for confirmation of his expectation, and it was not long in coming.

Rodriguez demanded, "Why do you wait, sergeant? Proceed, and determine the intentions of those people."

This time the sergeant saluted with purpose. On the slender chance that someone might be waiting in ambush, he saw no reason not to make it clear who was in authority and therefore most suitable for assassination.

The man in the branding pen halted the work and climbed over the fence. Fear was etched in his brown face as his gaze went beyond the sergeant and the young recruit to the horsemen waiting behind them. The coming of the military in these mean times was always reason for fear, even among those who had remained faithful through the troubles.

Zaragosa gave the corral a quick scrutiny and saw no weapons more fierce than an intricately designed branding iron which glowed red in the small fire. He turned in the saddle and gave the lieutenant a signal to come ahead.

The two boys, one ten or twelve, the other some years older, remained inside the corral with the cattle. Their attention was riveted to the horsemen who rode in behind the sergeant. Zaragosa saw the same fear in their eyes as in their father's.

The man removed his hat. "In what way may I serve you?"

The lieutenant's voice was heavy with accusation. "Your name is Lucero?"

The man shook his head. "My name is Moreno."

"But you are related to the family named Lucero."

The man hesitated. "I once had a cousin by that name. He is dead."

"He was a traitor and I killed him. He had a son

named Guadalupe Lucero. We are informed that he has been seen."

Sweat broke across Moreno's forehead and ran down his face. "He is not here."

"But has he *been* here? And where is he now?"

Moreno wiped a dirty sleeve across his face. "I have no knowledge of him."

Rodriguez tried staring him down, then called to the boys. "You two. Come out here!"

Moreno pleaded, "They are but boys. They know nothing."

Rodriguez directed a menacing gaze at first one, then the other. "To lie to me is treason. Do you know the whereabouts of Guadalupe Lucero?"

The youngsters stood mute, trembling with fear. Again the father protested that they were but boys and knew nothing of politics or treason or Guadalupe Lucero.

Rodriguez signaled the patrol to dismount. He ordered two of the largest men to throw the elder Moreno to the ground. Moreno cried out that he was a patriot and that he loved Spain. Rodriguez commanded, "Pull off his boots and sit on his legs."

He walked to the fire and gingerly lifted the branding iron from among the red coals. The stamp end of it shimmered with a blistering heat. "The Inquisition taught us that there is nothing like fire to give faith and loyalty their severest test." He lowered the heated end of the iron. "Tell me about Lucero."

Moreno's eyes were wide and desperate, his voice shrill. "I know nothing of him."

Rodriguez walked past the three men who held Moreno tightly to the ground. He jammed the blazing iron against a bare foot. Moreno screamed.

Rodriguez paused a moment. "How is your memory now?"

Sergeant Zaragosa looked away, but he could not escape the nauseating stench of burned flesh. He saw shock and anger in the faces of the other soldiers. If the fugitive Lucero were to appear now and attempt to murder the lieutenant, Zaragosa thought he would face little resistance from the soldiers.

Rodriguez applied the iron to the other foot. Moreno screamed again.

The older of the two boys rushed forward. "Stop! Stop! I will tell you."

Rodriguez stepped back, holding the iron like a weapon. "Be quick, then."

The boy spoke rapidly and in desperation. "He came looking for his cattle but could not find any. We do not know where he is now."

Rodriguez turned his hard stare to the younger boy. "Is this true?"

The boy's fear would not let him bring out words, but he nodded quickly.

Rodriguez turned back to Moreno and ordered the three men to turn him loose. "So! You lied to us."

Moreno wept. He brought his legs up and gripped one foot in agony.

Rodriguez drew his sword from its sheath.

Sergeant Zaragosa protested, "This man is known as a patriot, sir. He was only being loyal to those of his blood."

"In these times a man can have but one loyalty." Rodriguez raised both arms with his sword. Moreno's eyes bulged. The sword flashed in the sun and made a sickening sound as it struck his neck.

The younger boy cried out, "Papa!" He dropped to his knees beside his dying father, unmindful of the blood. The older one stood silent, more than a little frightened. But mixed with the fear in his eyes was a defiance and a hatred that once kindled would be there for life.

Zaragosa knew the same hatred must be evident in his own eyes, but at this moment he did not care. "The man was a patriot," he repeated.

Rodriguez gave him a look that invited him to insubordination. Zaragosa recognized the trap and drew back from it.

Rodriguez knelt and wiped the blood from his sword onto the dying man's pants leg. He said, "The next time I ask one of these *mestizo* peasants a question, he will be eager to answer, and with the truth."

The day will come when they will answer you with a sword, Zaragosa thought.

Rodriguez mounted his horse and turned back to the two boys. "Spread the word," he shouted. "This is what awaits any traitor, and any invader who sets foot in my district. Death, swift and certain!"

His eyes were like blue fire as he swung his gaze to Zaragosa. "Now, let us go and find Lucero."

The sergeant remounted stiffly. He touched spurs to his horse and set him into a trot, eager to leave this place where the woman and the other children now came running from the garden, crying with fear and grief.

He gave the officer a glance that carried black anger. *Someday, Rodriguez. Someday.*

4

Michael Lewis was hesitant about riding to Uncle Benjamin's farm with Papa because of the worrisome secret he possessed about his mother and his uncle. He feared that through a look or a word let slip, he might betray his uneasiness to Mordecai and be hard put to explain. He loved his father too much to lie to him, though on occasion, when silence seemed appropriate, Michael had neglected to tell everything he knew. Silence seemed highly appropriate in this case.

But he saddled Old Blaze and went, for it was not often he was granted an opportunity to ride in the splendid shadow of his father. Besides, he had always enjoyed his uncle's place. Its fields were larger because Benjamin Lewis stayed home and tended to them, breaking out new ground as time allowed, whereas Mordecai seemed always to have interests elsewhere and left the day-to-day responsibilities to his sons. Uncle Benjamin had even built two cabins, a small one a few paces away from the larger so his growing sons would have a sleeping place apart from their elders as well as from their sisters. Benjamin had strong notions about the right of things . . . certainly where his children were concerned. Papa, by contrast, never seemed to bother himself with such details; his mind was on the hills and the forests. Bringing the children up proper was a mother's place.

Going to Uncle Benjamin's usually provided Michael a welcome visit with cousin Frank, who always knew a good story to tell or had something new worth showing off. Today he was bubbling about a colt, but Michael could spare no time for such diversions. Papa had come to see Uncle Benjamin on a matter of urgency. Michael wanted to hear him tell again about Texas, for the name had begun to arouse a thrill, an image of a golden land huge and open; the Tennessee that Michael knew was steep hills and narrow valleys, noisy settlements and deep forests in which the sun did not shine. If the moment came when the climate seemed right, Michael intended to put in a few words of his own.

Uncle Benjamin looked much like Mordecai except more solidly built, with several more pounds on his tall, sturdy frame. Papa was on the thin side. He seemed always to be on the move and took his vittles when providence smiled upon him. For days at a time she turned her face away.

Mordecai and Uncle Benjamin hunched on rough benches beneath the great umbrella of an oak tree while Michael and Frank sat cross-legged on the ground, near enough to hear the conversation but not close enough that they were likely to be sent away on some fool's errand to get them from underfoot. Uncle Benjamin was mending a broken piece of harness leather. Even when he rested, he liked to busy his hands with useful endeavor.

Mordecai said, "Sure, it's a gamble, Ben. Everything we ever done was a gamble. Comin' out here into western Tennessee warn't no certain thing, but we done it because we thought we'd better ourselves. And we have, ain't we? Look here at this place of yours."

Benjamin Lewis had the stressed expression of a man who had caught one foot in a bear trap and the other in a bear's mouth. Clearly, he was reluctant and looking for a way out. "Texas is to the edge of the whole earth, almost."

"But I already been there. I tell you, except for the distance there ain't no more risk in Texas than right where we're at, hardly. I never heard one word about bad Injuns. They ain't got none where me and Eli was at. Them that's there, they're friendly."

"But it ain't even the United States."

"It ain't *nothin'*, to speak of. Spain claims some kind of a hold on it, but it's so far from the rest of their country that they don't do much. Just a handful of soldiers and a little old court there in Nacogdoches, is all I heard tell of. If a man'll take roundance on Nacogdoches, just pass her by, he can go anywhere he's of a mind to, pretty near."

Benjamin vigorously shook his head. "Sounds too easy to me. I never found nothin' easy that was worthwhile."

"There's a fortune, Ben, waitin' there for the reachin' and takin'. You know what horses'll fetch in this country. There's horses out yonder free for the catchin', enough to plow out every canebrake from here to the tidewater. We just got to go catch them and fetch them back."

A dark frown cut Benjamin's face. "You've got a fortune *here,* Mordecai, if you'd just stop lookin' off into the distance all the time and see what's right under your feet. Other men would kill for what you already have. You've got a good place if you'd stay home and tend it. You've got a bunch of good young'uns, and the finest wife . . ." Pain came into his eyes. Aunt Nancy had lain since last winter beneath a roughly chiseled stone marker beneath a small rail fence at the edge of the woods. Watching his uncle now, Michael just about convinced himself that all he had seen was his mother comforting Uncle Benjamin in his loneliness.

Mordecai argued, "But I got a chance to make it better."

"Seems to me like you're always lookin' for a big chance, and it's always somewheres else. The biggest chance you'll ever have is right here, where you're at." Benjamin's gaze shifted to Michael for a moment. "If it was your boy Michael achin' to find new country, I'd understand. *We* did, when we were as young as him. But there's gray in your hair now. It's time you stayed home with Patience and thanked the Lord for the blessin's you've already got."

Mordecai nodded eagerly. "Soon's I get done with this last trip. This is the one I been lookin' for all my life. It's my chance to pay off debts instead of makin' them bigger. It's my chance to be somebody of my own and not just the younger brother of Benjamin Lewis."

Benjamin gave him a long and critical study. "I didn't know you felt like that about it."

"Ain't your fault, Ben. But from the time we was little, I always stood in your shadow, seemed like. Whatever we done that was good, Pap give you the credit for it. Whatever we done wrong, it was always me. There wasn't nothin' for me but to run off to the woods, and I done it time after time. I spent my whole life tryin' to catch up to you, and I ain't been able. But you just wait till I bring back a big bunch of fine horses to sell. It'll be different then."

"It won't be different. First thing you know you'll be wantin' to drag your whole family off to Texas."

Mordecai looked quickly away. Michael knew that thought had been in his father's mind. Uncle Benjamin had read him like cousin Frank would read a book.

Benjamin said, "It'll be just like when we came here. This was the place you'd been lookin' for all your life; you said you could stay here forever."

"But it changed, don't you see? That's always been the trouble. Everywhere I went, people follered after like I'd blazed the trail just for them, and people always spoiled it for me. I want to find a place that'll stay the way it is when I first lay eyes on it. No change, no people, just me and mine."

"A dream, Mordecai, a hopeless dream. There's no such place, not this side of the moon."

"There's got to be one, and I'll find it. This time I'll find it."

Michael could see his uncle giving in. He had never been able to keep saying no to Papa.

Benjamin said, "Just what is it you want me to do?"

"It'll take good horses to catch good horses. You know I ain't got nothin' fit for the job."

Michael put in eagerly, "I've got Ol' Blaze."

His father acknowledged the interruption with a sharp look. Michael had interrupted the flow of his well-calculated argument. "You've got some good horses, Ben. You lend me and Eli one apiece, and maybe throw in an extry to take along, just in case. I promise you'll get them back and have your pick of the catch to boot."

Benjamin flinched and cut a piece of leather completely in two. He stared at it in dismay. His voice had a snap to it. "You was ridin' a good horse the last time you left here. You came home afoot." He dropped the harness to the ground in resignation. "I couldn't mount a whole expedition. What about the other men you're figurin' to take with you?"

"They'll furnish their own. That's part of the agreement."

"Except you and Eli Pleasant. *I'm* furnishin' for you-all."

"A loan, Ben, that's all it is. You'll be repaid with interest."

Benjamin finally shrugged, as Michael had known all along he would. "All right, Mordecai. You can take that sorrel of mine, Big Red. He's the fastest thing I ever rode. He ought to catch up to your wild horses. Red's got a runnin' mate that he always stays with, Ol' Jug. Pleasant can have him. Jug ain't as fast, but he's hog stout. He can hold anything you and Red can catch."

Mordecai's gratitude was genuine; it always was, every time Ben gave him something. "I'm much obliged. And you won't be sorry, not for a minute. You just wait and see what we come back with." He glanced at Michael. "It grieves me, of course, to go off and leave the young'uns and Patience again. You'll look in on them now and again, won't you? Kind of watch out for them?"

Benjamin nodded, as he always did when this question came up. "Sure I will."

Michael knew it was time to speak, if he was ever

going to. "I don't know if Ol' Blaze is fast enough to catch wild horses."

Mordecai laid his heavy hand on Michael's shoulder. His voice held sympathy, but it also held resolve. "It don't matter. He ain't goin', and neither are you."

"Papa, when you left in the spring you said you'd take me with you next time."

"I didn't mean to Texas."

"But I could help. I'm a good shot; you've always said so yourself. I can keep the camp in meat so you and the others won't have to be frettin' with it."

"I know you're good with a rifle. That's all the more reason your mama needs you here to keep the house supplied."

Michael reverted to an old argument that had done him no good the last time. "Andrew's purty near as good a shot as I am, and better at follerin' tracks. And Joseph takes good care of the field work."

His father resolutely shook his head, his blue eyes firmly declaring the subject closed. Michael's throat went tight in disappointment.

Cousin Frank Lewis punched Michael in the ribs. "Why don't you come out with me and look at my new colt? Time he's full growed, me and you'll go to Texas ourselves."

Mordecai and Uncle Benjamin had turned away and were talking earnestly about Papa's plans. Michael felt shut out. He swallowed hard. "Sure, Frank. Let's go see him."

All the way home with Papa and the three borrowed horses, Michael kept thinking of a more effective way he could have broached the subject. He wished Papa were as easy to talk into things as Uncle Benjamin was. But at least Michael was riding beside Papa now; that was consolation of a sort. Astride the big handsome sorrel, Papa fulfilled every image Michael had built in his mind. Michael kept looking at his own shadow on the ground, measuring it against Papa's and wondering how much longer it would be before he was as tall. One thing about Papa: folks might say he had a rover's restless foot and all that, but they had to look up to him just the same.

Papa seemed to have a way of sensing things. "You'll be growed before you know it, son."

"I wish I already was, so I could go to Texas too."

"You'll go to Texas, probably sooner'n you think. I have a notion we'll all go together once I get home from this trip."

"Is it really as fine a place as Eli says?"

"Ol' Eli ain't got the words to tell it," Mordecai declared, his eyes shining as he talked. "These little ol' cramped-up hills and woods of Tennessee . . . they ain't nothin' to what's out yonder. You ride over a hill and you can see into the middle of next week. You ride over the next one and it's more of the same. Ain't nothin' I ever seen that's a particle as big. And rich soil? They say if you drop a seed on the ground you better step back quick to keep from bein' hit in the face by the plant comin' up."

Michael thought Papa might be exaggerating just a little bit, but all the same, it sounded like a place he had to see.

It won't be in no few years, either, he promised himself.

They rode by the field and saw Eli Pleasant out in the middle of the standing corn with Joseph and Andrew. He was making broad gestures, probably relating some of his adventures. He had a whole bag of them. Andrew would be listening, holding his breath, but Joseph would have his mind on some way to make the corn grow bigger ears. He was turned more like Uncle Benjamin than like Papa. Business came before pleasure. In fact, business *was* his pleasure.

Riding up to the cabin with his father, Michael saw a mule tied to a post. Mordecai asked with his eyes. Michael said with no attempt to hide his displeasure, "That's Ol' Man Blackwood's mule. He's probably come to beg somethin' off us again."

Mordecai said with mild reproach, "Now, son, it ain't meant for us to speak ill of our fellow man." He was still feeling good about getting the horses from Uncle Benjamin. "Surely Ol' Cyrus must have some good points."

"The only good one I know is that he don't come around very often." *Only when he wants something,* he thought, but he held that back. Papa ought to be able to read character for himself, especially when it was as plain as yesterday's tobacco juice in Cyrus Blackwood's beard.

Blackwood was lying on the ground in the shade of a tree while his mule stood hitched in the sun. The man got up and stretched himself and slowly followed Mordecai and Michael and the horses down to the pole pens. "Howdy, Mordecai," he said. "I see you got home."

That, Michael thought, was about as intelligent as the conversation was likely to get.

"I'm here, Cyrus," Mordecai replied pleasantly. "What can I do for you?"

Damn, Michael thought, *you shouldn't have asked him that! He'll be an hour telling you what-all.*

But Cyrus came directly to the point, almost. "I

hear you're a-fixin' to go out west and catch you some horses."

Mordecai's face betrayed a beginning of doubt. "I been talkin' to some folks about it."

"I was hopin' you'd see fit to let me ride along with you."

Mordecai frowned now. "You, Cyrus? Why on earth would you be wantin' to make a trip such as that?"

"Same reason as you, I reckon. I . . . my family could sure use some money. I'd guess that a bunch of horses would fetch a right smart price."

Michael could see his father begin casting about for a way to get out of this. "I ain't takin' nobody but single men and one widower that ain't got nobody. You got family needin' you."

Michael thought the argument was beginning to sound much like Uncle Benjamin's. And it was having about as much effect.

Cyrus said, "I got boys big enough to see after things here. The boys are better at farmin' than I ever was; Isaac anyhow. Missus, she acts like she's happier when I ain't around too much. Name's Charity, you know. Ain't got much charity about her when it comes to me."

Mordecai began to tell things he had not mentioned to Uncle Benjamin. "It's a long ways, and there ain't no tellin' what-all could happen. We got Injun country to go through. And when we get to Texas we won't be protected by no American laws. Them Spanish, they could do just about anything they was of a mind to with us, and there wouldn't be nobody we could look to for help."

Nothing swayed Cyrus Blackwood. He kept arguing need until Mordecai ran out of counter arguments.

Finally Mordecai was down to one last reservation. "All I see is that mule, Cyrus. He won't be no good to you in the job we got cut out for us."

"Now," Cyrus said, "don't you fret none about that. I know where I can lay my hands on a real good horse, the match of anything you just brought in. When did you say we was leavin'?"

"Day after tomorrow mornin', first light. The boys'll be gatherin' here tomorrow so we can make an early start."

"I'll be here," Cyrus said. He grabbed Mordecai's hand and shook it violently. "I'm much obliged to you, Mordecai. You don't know what this'll mean to my family."

Mordecai stared helplessly after him as Cyrus untied the mule, wriggled up bareback and rode the animal away in a long, splay-footed trot. He said, "I never did tell him he could go."

Michael observed, "He'll probably get tired after a day or two and turn back. Especially if he's got to do any work."

Mordecai shrugged. "One more pair of hands might make a difference somewhere down the line."

Michael knew Cyrus better than Mordecai did. He knew the whole family. "You'll have to be watchin' him all the time. When he *does* turn back he'll steal whatever he can get his hands on."

Mordecai frowned at his son. "I don't know where you get your dark ways of lookin' on people. It don't come from me."

After supper Mordecai and Eli Pleasant huddled together in the kitchen, talking plans. Papa was going to ride to the settlement the next day and sell pelts that Michael and Andrew had put together after Mordecai had left the last time and before warm weather spoiled the trapping. That money would go for supplies. Mordecai always traveled light, relying upon his ability to live mostly off the land, and Michael supposed from the gaunt look of him that Eli was used to doing the same. But powder and lead and coffee and flour were things they couldn't find in the woods.

Listening to their talk, Michael felt a tingling sensation from his rump halfway up his back. The longer he considered, the more the thought of staying behind made his stomach feel sour.

An idea had come to him during the night after Papa had first mentioned his plan. It had been just a wild notion in the beginning, but he had kept sifting through it for whatever parts of it might serve reality.

Papa was in for a surprise.

The men began to gather as the next day wore on. With each new addition the air became more electric, like before a spring thunderstorm. There was Old Man Wilson from down on Buck Holler, who had gone with Papa and Uncle Benjamin the time they followed Andrew Jackson off to fight the British. There were the two Macklin brothers from over on Muddy Branch. The sheriff would be tickled to see them leave the country for a while; they were always starting a scrap down at the settlement, fighting each other if they couldn't get somebody else to mix into it. There was a book-learned man named Judkins some said had come from a wealthy planter family over in Virginia but had been turned out on his own because he couldn't leave the whiskey alone. Michael figured he'd get precious little of it on *this* trip. Papa liked the jug as well as anybody when he was home, but he didn't hold with it on the trail. It put a man at too much disadvantage, he always said, like wearing his left boot on his right foot. Nature provided enough to confound a man without him making it worse on his own account.

Other men were strangers to Michael, but Papa seemed to know them well enough. They were his kindred spirits, men of the cane. By suppertime there were nine, not counting Papa and Eli Pleasant. They were buckskin men, for the most part, carrying long rifles, long knives. A couple wore pistols in leather holsters. They were a rough-looking bunch all in all, Michael thought, capable of riding into the biggest hostile Shawnee camp that ever was and making a smoking ruin out of it. That was the kind of men Mordecai had always seemed to gather around him, men who took more glory in the challenge than in the accomplishment.

And their horses . . . Rarely had Michael seen so many likely animals in one place, though he thought none were as good as the sorrel Uncle Benjamin had loaned Papa.

When this bunch lights into them wild ones, he thought, *it'll be a sight to see.*

There was a lot of laughing and joking and loud talking around the cabin that afternoon and evening, but none of it came from Mama. Michael had not heard her say ten words all day except whatever was necessary to get the work done and the family and the newcomers fed. She kept looking at Papa with eyes that were sometimes sad and sometimes angry.

Little Annie clung to her father's neck as much as he would tolerate when he was sitting, or to his leg when he was standing. Heather, because she was eleven and nearly grown, was more reserved and held her distance. But her blue eyes were as sad as Mama's.

Darkness came, but Cyrus Blackwood did not. Michael was afraid to mention his name for fear that the old reprobate would appear. *Speak of the devil* ... He saw Papa look hopefully in the direction of the Blackwood place a couple of times. He couldn't tell whether Papa wanted Cyrus to show up or wished he wouldn't.

Eli Pleasant had already voiced his opinion in no bashful terms. He had sized up Cyrus Blackwood and declared that he would as soon ride to Texas with a boil on his butt.

The men rolled out their blankets and slept on the ground, all except Mordecai, who spent his last night at home where a married man should, in bed with his wife. Instead of sleeping with the boys up in the loft, as he had done these past several nights, Eli Pleasant carried out his one blanket and joined the rest of the men. But not before he took Michael aside for a little quiet counsel.

"Now, young feller," he said earnestly, "I know you're disappointed, but long as you live under your papa's roof you got to stand by him and do as he says."

Michael argued, "When Papa was sixteen he was travelin' with a bunch, makin' a trail over the mountains."

"You're old enough, I don't question that. But your daddy ain't told it all. There's more risk than he's let on to your mama about, a heap sight more. A man don't win high stakes without he bets high stakes, and Mordecai is bettin' his life. But he ain't bettin' *yours*." Pleasant laid both hands heavily on Michael's shoulders. "You got a lot of your papa in you. I seen that right off. You'll pretty soon be off chasin' the wild geese like me and your papa, and more than likely leavin' some good woman behind to cry just like your mama."

"You think Papa'll ever catch them wild geese?"

"No. It's the chasin' he lives for, not the catchin'. He sows, but other men reap. I'm afraid you've got that look about you too. I hope I'm wrong, because it's a sickness without a cure."

Michael lay awake long after everybody went to sleep. When he thought he was reasonably safe he rolled his blanket and climbed quietly down from the loft. He paused in the dog-run to lift a ham from a hook, then went to the shed for his bridle, blanket, and saddle. As he expected, he found Blaze standing outside the pen, fraternizing with the horses on the inside. Blaze made no fuss as Michael walked slowly to him and slipped a loop around his neck. Michael put the saddle on Blaze's back and led him a little way into the wood. There he dumped everything on the ground behind a screening of underbrush, tied Blaze at the end of the rope, and hung the ham from a limb high enough that no varmint was likely to steal it during the night.

He patted Blaze on the neck before he left him. "Sorry, old boy, but you're goin' to have to wait here till I'm ready."

He worked his way carefully back to the cabin and up the ladder to the loft. He lay on the straw and hoped no one would notice in the morning that his blanket was gone.

The men began stirring in the yard long before any sign of daylight appeared in the east. Michael was the first to climb down from the loft. He bumped into Mordecai, who came out of the sleeping side of the double cabin. "Up already?" Mordecai asked cheerfully. "That's what I like to see, a lad so full of ambition that he wakes up the roosters. You go in the kitchen and kindle a fire for your mama so she can start breakfast. We'll be wantin' to travel as quick as we can."

Heather and Annie, sleeping in the kitchen, awakened when Michael started bumping the firewood around. Annie asked fearfully, "Is Papa gone already?" She looked relieved when Michael told her he was not. Heather did not speak, but her eyes said she was trying hard to act grown and not cry.

By the time Patience came into the kitchen, Michael had a good blaze going in the hearth. He thought she might offer some compliment, but she said brusquely, "You've put on too much wood. You want me to burn everything up?" Her eyes had a hollow look. She had been crying, and he doubted she had slept much.

"It'll be all right," he offered tentatively. "Papa'll be back before you know it, hardly."

She grimaced. "And stay maybe a week. Here, grind up some coffee. Wouldn't want them startin' a long trip without even a cup of coffee."

His sisters got dressed while Michael's back was turned, and he gladly relinquished the women's work to them. He wanted to get out of the kitchen before he made some mistake that would put Mama in an even worse mood. He heard a familiar voice, loud in the early-morning darkness, and felt disgust. Old Man Cyrus Blackwood was telling the bunch what-all he was going to do with any Indians they might run into on the way, and how he was going to spend the money when they got back with those horses. A new rifle, a new steel plow like the big planters had, several store-bought suits of clothes so he could have a change any time he wanted one, whether the old woman had done her washing or not. Maybe even a new chopping ax for his wife; she was having a hard time keeping a sharp edge on the one she had.

Well, Cyrus would probably tire quickly and turn back. Or the men would tire of him and chase him back.

Breakfast finished, Mordecai bid his children good-bye one by one, lingering longest with the sobbing Annie, who would not let go of his neck until he forcibly pried her loose. He hugged and kissed Patience, then got on his horse and shouted, "Let's be on our way," like he couldn't wait to get started. It was still so dark that Michael could not tell what color horse Blackwood was riding. At least it wasn't that old mule.

Patience stood in the dog-run and watched until Mordecai and the other riders disappeared into the darkness. She rubbed a hand across her eyes and said, "All right, let's not be lettin' the Lord and the daylight catch us idle."

Michael went out to milk the cow, then picked up a hoe and walked to the garden. Every so often he felt compelled to glance toward the place where he had staked Blaze and cached his traveling outfit.

A couple of hours after daylight, two men named Thomas rode up to the garden where Michael and his brothers were working. Their faces looked grim. The older of the pair asked, "You-all seen any strangers come by this mornin'?"

Michael and Joseph and Andrew glanced at one

another. James, being just six, stared in silent curiosity at the men. Because Joseph was the oldest, he did the answering. "No, sir. Ain't been no strangers come this way."

Thomas said, "Somebody stole a horse out of our pen durin' the night. Black horse, he was, with a snip nose and a star on his forehead. Stockin' on the right foreleg."

Andrew put in, "Maybe it was Injuns." He sounded almost eager about it. Very little exciting ever happened around here.

Concern leaped into Joseph's eyes. "Come to think of it, Ol' Blaze ain't been around this mornin'."

Michael saw trouble coming and quickly headed it off. "Ol' Blaze was here just a little while ago. I seen him." Joseph appeared satisfied, and Michael eased.

Thomas shrugged. "Well, if you-all see anything of my horse, I'd be obliged if you let me know." The two men rode away.

Michael suspected he knew why Cyrus Blackwood had been able to leave the mule at home.

5

Controlling his impatience was like skinning a bear with a dull knife, but Michael had to give Papa and the others a head start. Often as not, Mordecai forgot something the first time and had to come back. If Michael were caught trailing after him, Papa would not give him a second chance. So he stayed in the garden and worked like he was being paid for it. That came dangerously near arousing his older brother's suspicion.

Joseph stared at him in disbelief. "I ain't seen you put in so much sweat since I don't know when. I figured you'd crawl up into the loft and sulk when Papa didn't take you."

Michael hoped his eyes did not betray the excitement which had his body tingling. "That wouldn't change anything."

"No, but I figured you'd take it a lot harder. I swear, you may make a farmer in spite of yourself."

A while after the Thomas brothers left, Michael became convinced Papa had not forgotten anything and was not coming back. It was time. He pointed toward the woods. "Looky yonder, Joseph. Did you see that?"

His brother glanced up from the hoeing and frowned. "See what?"

"A big fat doe just come out of the timber. Right yonder."

Joseph squinted, trying hard to see. "If she did, she's gone now."

"She was there. She'd look mighty good quartered and hung up in the dog-run."

"You're just tired of the hoe."

"I'll go fetch her." Michael gave Joseph no opportunity for argument. He walked briskly to the cabin for his rifle. He filled the shot pouch and powderhorn with all they would hold. Patience Lewis watched with curiosity, hands on her slender hips. "You fixin' to go to war?"

"I just seen a big fat doe."

"How many shots you figure it'll take?"

Michael tried to cover his nervousness. "I like to always go prepared."

Patience placed one hand on top of his head. The last year or two he had grown tall enough that she had to look up to him, almost like she did Papa. "I saw you out there beatin' the ground to death with that hoe. I know how disappointed you are."

"It'll be all right," he said, trying to shrug it off.

His mother's gaze was steady and penetrating, as if she could read what was in his mind. It made him uncomfortable. She said with regret, "You've got eyes just like your papa's, and they're always lookin' off into the distance, like his. I'm afraid they'll never be at peace. They'll never see a place they're content to settle on."

He started toward the door, then paused. He turned to see his mother still watching him. He felt himself compelled to go back to her. "Mama . . ."

"Yes?"

"Nothin', just . . ." He leaned down and kissed her, then turned quickly away. He walked hurriedly toward the woods. He turned once to look back. She was watching him from the dog-run, a hand shading her eyes.

I believe she knows. The thought shook him for a moment, and he half expected that she would send Joseph to catch him. But she did not. If she knew and made no move to stop him, he reasoned, it meant she realized it was time to cut the string, to let him seek his own destiny. Papa had been on his own younger than this.

He turned once again as he entered the timber. His brothers were still in the garden. Joseph was working, but Andrew had stopped, his gaze following Michael. Andrew was always the one quickest to laugh, but now his shoulders were slumped. He had an uncanny way of sensing things. *He knows too,* Michael thought. *Somehow they both know.*

He went directly to the place where he had left Blaze tied and his saddle stashed. Blaze's ears pricked forward. He hadn't had much chance to graze, for grass was scant amid this heavy pine timber that blocked off the sunshine, and the rope had left him only a little room to move around. Well, he'd just have to make do. He could drink when they crossed the creek a little ways down the trail, but he would have to put off grazing until Michael decided to stop.

Michael saddled him and tied the rolled blanket behind. He retrieved the ham he had left hanging high in a tree and set out through the woods at a fast trot. He wanted to make as much early distance as possible in case his mother began to have second thoughts and sent somebody out after him. A couple of miles farther on he cut into the trail that travelers and hunters used going west. The tracks of the horses were fresh and deep and easy to see. He might wish later that he had Andrew's ability at tracking, but so long as Papa left this clear a trail, he should have no trouble following.

The afternoon was well along when he came upon a place where the remnants of a campfire still smouldered. The horse hunters evidently had nooned here, boiling coffee, frying venison. Michael became aware of his own hunger. He had no utensils for cooking, but he rekindled the fire with fresh wood. He loosened the saddle's girth and staked Blaze at the end of the rope to allow him to graze. He sliced off a cut of ham and wrapped it around a stick, then held it over the fire. The meat came undone and fell into the coals. He retrieved it with the point of the stick, dusted most of the ashes and dirt off onto his pants leg and tried again. His impatience did not allow the ham time to cook through. The result was barely passable, but he was hungry enough to get it down despite the clinging ashes and the gritty sand. There had been no opportunity to sneak bread out of the cabin. He had done well to get away with a supply of powder and shot.

His skin prickled with the need to be on the move, but he could tell that the men had rested their horses a while. To do less would be to risk overrunning them. He stretched out on the ground and tried to nap; he had not slept much last night. But the nervousness and excitement had his blood pumping too strongly. Before long he tightened the girth, coiled the rope, and resumed his journey.

Increasing freshness of the horse manure warned him late in the afternoon that he was pressing too closely. Caught now, he would almost certainly be sent home.

He stopped before dark and struck a small fire with flint and steel, cooking another piece of the ham. If it had tasted poor at noon, it was even less appealing now. He could see where he was going to become almighty tired of existing on ham, augmented by a few berries he managed to pick along the way. It occurred to him that he had not planned this trip as carefully as he might.

Well, his father had told him of living on water and air for days at a time. A man was not so easily killed as was commonly supposed, Mordecai had said. Determination was not to be discounted.

At dark Michael spread the blanket, lying on half of it and pulling the other half over him. He listened to the sounds awakened by the night—the birds, the crickets, the occasional distant howling of a prowling predator. He had slept in the woods many times, hunting with his father, but this was his first time alone. He found more thrill in it than threat. Mordecai had taught him that a man had little to fear so long as he understood the woods and its creatures and met them on their own terms. The concern, if there was one, was with the human animals, and with oneself. More than anything else, Mordecai had told him, a man had to come to terms with himself, smothering both his pridefulness and his self-doubts.

"A man has got to know what he can do and what he can't," Mordecai had counseled. "And bein' by yourself is somethin' some just can't stand for long at a time. If you ain't your own best company, the woods'll leave you crazy or dead."

At dawn Michael moved Blaze to give him a fresh patch of grass to graze upon before they set out again. He shot a rabbit feeding on the underbrush, trusting that his father and party were far enough ahead not to hear, or if they heard would not be curious enough to come back and investigate. After all, they were traveling through a partially settled country. He roasted the rabbit on the end of a stick, glad to give the ham a rest. His hunger did not let him wait for the meat to be done. He ate part of it still pink in color while the rest finished cooking over the shimmering coals. He knew he should save part of it for noon, but he felt too hungry. When he kicked dirt over the fire to smother it, nothing was left of the rabbit but hide, innards, and a scattering of small bones.

Once during the morning he encountered a few minutes of confusion and wished for his younger brother Andrew. A set of tracks pulled out of the main trail and branched off to the south. He struggled over his decision, whether to follow those or remain with the larger trail and the tracks that continued upon it. He decided there probably were not enough horses in the split-off group to be his father's bunch. Still, a lingering doubt pestered him through the day. During his noon stop for rest he was unable to nap for worrying.

He found little comfort in an adage of his father's: when you make up your mind to something, stay with it and don't let doubts lead you astray. Mordecai had always added with a grin that it probably wouldn't make much difference in the long run anyway; chances were that either choice would be wrong.

He saw a couple of deer and considered shooting fresh meat, but concern over the tracks left him no patience for it. Toward evening he made another decision. The only way to set his mind at ease was to sneak up on the horsemen's camp. Darkness dropped down hurriedly over the dense woods. He could not see the tracks anymore. He had to go on faith that the horsemen still followed the old wagon trace.

Thinking he smelled woodsmoke, he stopped. The notion passed, and he was about to ride on when the smell came again. In the distance he saw a faint point of firelight. Blaze raised his head, catching the scent of the smoke or perhaps of other horses. If Michael rode closer, Blaze was likely to whinny and give him away. He tied the horse and moved on afoot.

He saw figures moving casually around the fire, as men would when cooking up a mess of vittles. The smoke brought an aroma of coffee, of roasting meat, that reminded him he had taken no supper. The ham was becoming tiresome, cooked on a stick without salt or any of the other seasonings his mother and sisters used to give it flavor. He thought he was moving silently, but suddenly he came upon a large dark shape and heard a snort of alarm. He had almost walked into the horses, tied along a picket line.

A voice at the fire said, "Somethin' spooked a horse. Could be a catamount prowlin' around. We better go take a look."

Michael retreated back into the timber and dropped behind the black curtain of underbrush.

He held his breath as footsteps crunched the fallen mat of old leaves. A man said, "I don't see nothin', Mordecai."

His father's voice replied, "It was probably that dun horse of Ol' Wilson's, bitin' at one of the others. He's been tryin' for two days to take a chunk out of my sorrel."

Michael took comfort in knowing this was Mordecai's camp. But being so near his father brought him a feeling akin to homesickness. He wanted to rise up and announce himself, especially when his stomach growled and the smell of food tantalized him wickedly. But he had not traveled far enough yet. Mordecai would probably send him home.

With regret that went all the way to the bone, he pushed himself to his feet and walked back to Blaze. He backtracked in darkness a mile or so. He dared not build a fire and risk its being seen. He made a dry, hungry camp, then spent a restless night with little sleep. He woke to see three deer browsing in plain sight and knew he could not afford to shoot one so near his father's camp.

Texas, he thought, had better be one hell of a grand place.

His fifth evening, he still had half the ham left, and the sight of it was enough to set him gagging. He had seen no game all day fit to kill, though late in the afternoon he had managed to bag a small rabbit. He made camp at dusk, skinned the rabbit and built a fire. He had the rabbit about half done at the end of a stick when he heard a rustling in the undergrowth and a grunt he took to be human. Heart skipping, he propped the rabbit and stick against a log, grabbed his long rifle, and jumped to his feet. "Who's out there?" he demanded.

A reply came from behind the vegetation. "Now, don't you get excited and pull that trigger, young feller. It's just me and Ol' Quint. Ain't no harm in neither of us."

Michael's first thought had been of Indians. But he decided to judge for himself about the potential harm. He had heard enough stories to know that all the wild things in the woods were not animal. He held the rifle ready. He tried to make his voice sound deeper and older than it was. "You-all come on out where I can see you."

The brush crackled, and two men stepped into the trail. Each carried a rifle and a small pack of possibles. Both were lanky and bearded and looked as if they had not been out of the woods since Christmas. As they approached, they smelled that way too.

The one who had spoken had a patch where one eye was supposed to be. That did not lend to his beauty. He said, "We smelt your fire."

Suspiciously Michael asked, "How come you-all out yonder instead of on the trail?"

"We wasn't sure but what you might be Injuns. Me and Quint, we ain't got along too good with Injuns lately, you might say." Patch-eye nodded toward Michael's rifle. "I sure wish you'd lower that thing. Rifles make Quint awful nervous, especially from the business end. They kind of bother me too."

Michael lowered the muzzle a little, but not so much that he could not bring it up again in a hurry.

Patch-eye shifted his attention to the tiny campfire. "I see you was fixin' you some rabbit. Me and Quint, we ain't et nothin' since yesterday. We'd be much obliged if you seen your way clear to share some of that with us."

The fact that they asked gave Michael some relief. They could have rushed him and taken it if they wanted to. He lowered the rifle more. "The rabbit's kind of small, but I got a ham." He motioned toward it. "You-all might find that to your likin'."

Patch-eye glanced at his partner and grinned. "Ham. You hear that, Quint? Why, we've forgot what hog tastes like. The Lord hisself must've set you down here for us to find."

The one called Quint whipped a long knife from his belt. Instinctively Michael stepped back and raised the rifle again, but Quint attacked only the ham. Almost in a frenzy he cut off a slice and jammed it into his mouth raw. It was smoked, and Michael knew people sometimes ate it without cooking, but such a thing struck him as savage. He supposed these men must be on the edge of starvation. Patch-eye wrenched the ham from Quint and cut off a piece for himself, eating it as Quint had, with near-desperation.

Patch-eye said, "You ain't got a pot or a skillet?"

Michael told him he had nothing in the way of utensils, that he had been doing all his cooking on a stick.

Patch-eye said, "That ain't quite civilized, but it'll do, I reckon." He cut another slice of the ham and impaled it on a stick as Michael had done to the rabbit. Quint followed his example. The two men shared Michael's fire. Piece by piece, they reduced the ham to bone.

Michael shrugged. He was sick of the ham anyway; but now the two visitors had left him no choice. He would have to join Papa tomorrow and take his chances. Surely, as far as he had already come, Mordecai would not send him home.

Patch-eye said, "I wish you had some coffee. Or better still, some whiskey. But I reckon you ain't got nothin' like that."

Michael shook his head. "All I had was that ham." That and the rabbit. Watching the pair decimate the ham, he had wolfed down the rabbit in self-defense, lest they take part of it too. He had seen Papa come home hungry many a time, but not *that* hungry.

When nothing was left to eat, the two men relaxed. Across the campfire, Michael could feel Patch-eye's one good eye studying him. The man said, "What you doin' out here all by yourself? You are by yourself, ain't you?"

Caution made Michael hedge. "Papa's camped on down the trail a piece. I'll be catchin' up to him tomorrow."

Patch-eye did not seem to believe him. "You ain't too well fixed for travelin'. Looks to me like you might've left home sort of sudden. Like maybe you had somebody after you?"

Michael did not want anyone thinking he was a fugitive. But he figured what he was doing here was his business. "Ain't nobody after me."

Patch-eye said, "Me and Quint, we know what it's like to not want to be found. We come out of Kentucky. There's some folks there who'd sure like to see us again, but we ain't atall anxious to see *them*. Eh, Quint?"

Quint just grunted. Michael had not heard him speak three intelligible words.

Patch-eye continued, "We been three days throwin'

some Creek Injuns off our trail. We couldn't tell at first but what you might be one of them yourself."

Michael's interest quickened. "How come there's Injuns after you?"

"A misunderstandin', you might say. We was doin' some tradin' amongst them, had us a prime bunch of skins to take back to the settlements. Then a little disagreement come up over a girl."

Quint grunted and nodded. Patch-eye said, "Purty little thing she was, for an Injun. When a man's been away from the settlements for a long time, you'd be surprised how good-lookin' them Injun girls can be. Well, this one they was savin' back to marry off to some young chief or somethin', keepin' her pure and unspoilt, you might say. Seemed like an awful waste, savin' stuff like that for some greasy Injun.

"The night me and Quint left camp, we sort of borryed that girl, you might say. We didn't do her no real harm. We turned her loose after a couple of days so she could go home, but she wasn't quite so pure and unspoilt no more, was she, Quint?"

Quint grunted and grinned, shaking his head.

Patch-eye said, "You'd think them redskins'd be grateful we didn't kill her. We'd've been justified, the way she kept fightin' us like a catamount. But they dogged our trail for three days. We lost our pack horses and the pelts and everything to them. Hard to understand how an Injun thinks."

Michael's father had fought Indians since his boy-hood, and Michael had never questioned the right-ness of it. But this story filled him with revulsion. He was impelled to speak his mind. "You wouldn't do a thing like that in the settlements, not to a white girl."

"But she was just an Injun. The way them redskins come after us, you'd've thought she was white."

Michael said, "I suppose they got the same feelin's as white folks have when it comes to their women-folk."

Patch-eye's voice took on a tone of reproach, even of threat. "You ain't one of them Injun-lovers, are you, boy?"

"Papa was in the Blackhawk war, and some other fights too."

"Then you oughta know that in the end it'll be them or us. The world'll be better off when the last of them red devils has gone back to Hell where they come from."

Michael had learned a long time ago that it was useless to argue with somebody whose mind was nailed shut. To do so only brought aggravation and sometimes a fight, which settled nothing more than the argument had. He asked, "Where you-all figurin' to go from here?"

Patch-eye asked suspiciously, "What do you want to know for?"

"Just askin'." Michael became a little defensive. He was wishing they had not found his camp, and he wondered how Papa would have met a situation like this. "I don't mean nothin'."

Patch-eye said, "Me and Quint, we just sort of take things as they come. Man goes to makin' too many plans, he gets all tied up to where he can't move when he wants to."

Michael spread his blanket, trying to put some distance between himself and his visitors, for their aroma did not improve with familiarity. Their manner kept him uneasy. Patch-eye and Quint huddled together, talking in low tones that he could not hear though he strained himself in the effort. The longer he considered, the more troubled he became. He tried once in the middle of the night to get up and slip out of camp without waking them, but Patch-eye must have slept with that one good eye open. Michael was hardly upon his feet before Patch-eye was standing in front of him, rifle in his hands.

"Oh, it's you, is it, boy? I like to've shot you for an Injun. You better lay back down and be still. We'd all be a lot less nervous."

Michael stretched out again, more agitated than before. He laid his hand on his rifle and made up his mind not to sleep. But sometime in the early morning his best intentions came to naught, and he nodded off.

Blaze snorted, waking Michael with a start, as dawn was breaking. He raised up on his elbow and saw Quint throwing Michael's saddle on the horse. Michael reached for his rifle, but it was gone. He jumped to his feet, flinging the blanket aside. "What're you doin' with my horse?"

Patch-eye stood with a rifle in each hand. One of them was Michael's. He said, "Sorry we woke you up, boy. We was hopin' to just leave you a-sleepin'."

Anger came with a rush. "You-all let my horse alone!" Michael took a long stride toward Blaze.

Quint gave him a silent look that spoke of murder. The ferocity of it caused Michael to pause and ponder his odds. They looked poor.

Patch-eye said, "Now, boy, you just stand back so we won't have to hurt you. We need this horse more'n you do. You said your pap is just a ways ahead. You can catch up to him afoot if you'll push yourself. But we ain't got no pap to see after us."

"You've got no right!" Michael's outrage overcame his caution. He made two more strides toward

Quint before something struck him from behind
and knocked him flat on the ground. His head felt
cracked open. He lay stunned, but not so much that
he did not hear Quint speak. "You better hit him
again."

Patch-eye replied, "Next time might bust this
good rifle."

Quint said, "You don't have to use no rifle." He
picked up a heavy piece of tree limb, broken off
by some high wind. It came to Michael suddenly
that Quint intended to kill him. He wanted to cry
out, but no sound came. He tried to move aside
but could not. The impact was like an explosion
in Michael's head. Lights wheeled and darted and
danced. He felt that some force he could not resist
was pushing his body into the ground.

Patch-eye said, "We'll ride and tie. You ride the
horse a ways, then tie him and go on. I'll trot along
behind you and pick him up where you leave him."

Quint replied, "All right. Hand me that boy's shot
pouch and powderhorn. The way I hit him, he'll
never get up from where he's layin'."

Patch-eye said, "Damnfool button. Serves him
good and proper."

Michael tried pushing himself up but was unable
to do more than raise his head a little. Through the
painful haze he saw Patch-eye moving along afoot,
back toward the settlements. Ahead of him, on
Blaze, rode the man called Quint. Michael cried
out in pain and rage, but he did not know if the sound
got past his constricted throat.

He heard a scream and thought it must be his
own voice. Blaze jumped. Quint tumbled backward
to the ground. Michael wondered in anger what
cruelty the man had committed to make Blaze act

that way. Then he heard voices yelling, and a shot. Through the red haze he saw Patch-eye wheel and run back toward him, crying out in panic. Several men burst from the timber. They grabbed Patch-eye and roughly wrestled him down, smashing his face against the ground. Patch-eye cried and cursed and begged.

Michael blinked away the haze. His heart pounded. Indians! Fear shook him, raw cold fear, for he was sure they would come to get him next. He tried desperately to push himself up. He was helpless. He collapsed, exhausted, eyes burning so badly he had to close them. He lay with the side of his head on a mat of leaves and struggled for breath. He heard soft footsteps and opened his eyes. He saw two leather moccasins inches from his face. Forcing himself to turn onto his side, he looked straight up at what seemed the tallest man he had ever seen, a leather-clad Indian holding a steel headed tomahawk. Michael held his breath, expecting that blade to come crashing into his skull. The man spoke, but the words were alien to Michael. He supposed they meant death. His stomach was like ice.

Another Indian came up to stand beside him. Strong hands grasped Michael's arms and lifted him to his feet. His heart hammered. He tried to stand, for he had been taught that Indians respected a man who faced his fate bravely. His legs betrayed him. The two Indians caught him before he hit the ground and eased him back to his knees. One man kept talking to him in words that seemed without form. He could hear Patch-eye blubbering and crying for mercy. He doubted that the Indians understood the words. Even if they did, it was not likely to make any difference. They had come for revenge on Patch-eye and Quint. It was Michael's bad luck that he had been found with them.

His head threatened to burst. Blood trickled into one eye, setting it afire. To his surprise, one of the Indians spoke gently to him while another rubbed some kind of pungent grease on the wound. It burned for a moment, but he sensed that its purpose was medicinal. He blinked in confusion, looking up at first one of the dark-skinned men, then the other. It seemed strange that they would treat his wounds if they intended to kill him.

He knew little about identifying Indian tribal connections, but he thought this was probably Creek country. For one wild moment he wondered if they somehow knew that his father had once fought against them. He decided that was far-fetched. He managed to say, "I don't know what you-all want with me. I never saw them two before last night."

The tallest Indian spoke briskly to his comrades and made a motion with his hand. They dragged the terrified Patch-eye up in front of Michael, twisting his arms behind his back and forcing him down on his knees. The Indian made a strong demand that Michael did not understand, but evidently Patch-eye did. He sobbed, "They think we set out to do you harm, boy. In God's name, tell them it's all a mistake. Tell them we're old friends. Tell them me and Quint ain't the ones they been after."

"You tried to knock my brains out," Michael accused.

"I'll make it up to you, I promise. I'll give you back everything we taken off of you."

"*They*'ve got it all now."

"Boy, have some charity. Help me or I'll end up dead as Ol' Quint yonder."

Michael could see Quint lying twisted, where an arrow had taken him. His scalp hung fresh and bloody from an Indian's waist. Michael had seen scalps before, brought back by the veterans of Indian battles, but they had always been cured and dried, so time had somehow blunted the specter of death. He had not seen the open, sightless eyes of the victim before. His stomach crawled, though he managed not to lose last night's supper. Mordecai had told him Indians despised a show of weakness.

Patch-eye bleated, "Please, boy . . . you don't know what they're fixin' to do to me."

"No worse than you was fixin' to do to me, I reckon." He supposed he should try to help Patch-eye. After all, he was white. But Michael saw not one thing he could do. He would be lucky to come out of this thing himself. He said, "I ain't goin' to lie for you."

The tall Indian spoke gravely, and the others dragged Patch-eye away, still crying for Michael to help him.

The Indian said in plain-enough English, "Good. Boy does not lie for that man. Boy can take horse and go."

Michael stared in surprise as one of the other Indians fetched Blaze to him. The two who had helped him to his feet boosted him up into the saddle. They handed him his shot pouch and his powderhorn. It took a minute for him to realize they were actually setting him free. Relief washed over him, though he did not really understand.

A momentary argument arose between the tall Indian and one who held two rifles, Michael's and Patch-eye's. But the tall Indian prevailed. He pointed at the rifles. "One is yours?"

Michael indicated the weapon that had belonged to Grandpa. The tall Indian handed it to him, though the other man plainly did not relish giving it up. He said, "You must go now."

Michael hesitated. He pointed his chin at Patch-eye. "What you fixin' to do to him?"

The Indian shook his head grimly. "This is very bad man. You do not want to see."

Papa had told Michael some things about the Creek war, things on both sides which could turn a strong man's stomach to clabber. The warriors had torn Patch-eye's clothes from him, leaving him naked. His skin was as white as the belly of a catfish. They had taken the patch, exposing the empty eye socket like something long dead. Patch-eye pleaded and cried while they tied him against a tree, legs spread apart.

The tall Indian again gave Michael the sign to ride on, with a special firmness this time. Michael thought he had best comply before they took a different notion. He put Blaze into a healthy trot. Far down the trail, he could still hear Patch-eye's screams.

At length he had to get down and vomit.

His emotions were a confused turmoil of anger and fear and relief. Never before had he come so near death that he could feel its bony hand on his throat. The closest had been a time in the forest when he inadvertently placed himself between a sow bear and her two cubs. She had come at him with a roar that meant murder and struck him one hard blow that slammed him against a tree. But she had not followed up the attack. She had taken her young and disappeared, grumbling loudly.

Michael had been in fights before, though always with boys more or less his own age, and usually about nothing of more moment than his recent scrap with the Blackwoods over the ownership of the downed doe. Never before had he confronted someone who made a serious effort to kill him. He had always been conscious that such things happened—they had happened to Papa—but Michael had been emotionally unprepared to have it happen to *him*. Even after he had emptied his stomach, the queasiness remained.

He stopped an hour or so later as he came upon a stream. He washed away the dried blood the best he could, though the Indian grease still clung. He knew by the feel of it that his face was swollen, and a knot of some size had risen on the back of his head. He did not tarry long at the water, fearing that when the Indians got done with Patch-eye they might forget their generous natures and come after him too.

He heard a horse on the trail ahead. Fear constricted his throat, for it might be more Indians, or trail vultures like Patch-eye and Quint. He looked desperately to both sides of the trace for cover heavy enough to hide him and Blaze.

A familiar voice calmed him. Eli Pleasant rode up on the horse Jug, borrowed from Uncle Benjamin. He raised his hand in greeting. "Howdy, boy. Your pa decided I ought to come back and fetch you. He thought we've let you trail behind us long enough."

Michael said incredulously, "You knew?"

"For the last two, three days. Your pa thought you'd give up and go home. And if you didn't, it'd add considerable to your learnin' was you to make your own way a while longer." Pleasant squinted critically. "Good Lord, young'un, you look like you been in a scrap with a bear. What does the other feller look like?"

Michael gritted his teeth. "By now, I expect he looks dead."

6

Mordecai tried to be stern. When Michael and Eli rode up to the picket line where the horses were tied, Mordecai strode briskly out from the campfire to meet them. He looked seven feet tall, his brow furrowed and his voice severe. "Now, Michael, you heard me declare more than once that you wasn't goin' with us." Then he saw Michael's swollen face, bruised a dark blue. His resolve melted like April snow. His jaw dropped in dismay. "God almighty, son, what went and got ahold of you?"

Michael was so choked with emotion at the sight of his father that he could hardly speak. While the rest of the party gathered around, he clung to Mordecai as if he had not seen him in a year. Eli recounted what Michael had told him about the two land-pirates and the Indians. Mordecai looked as if he had been kicked in the stomach. He placed heavy hands on Michael's shoulders and stared remorsefully into his son's eyes. "My God, boy. I had no idea, or I wouldn't've let you hang back there all by yourself. I'd've carried your blood on my soul plumb to the grave." He put his strong arms around Michael and gave him a hug that left Michael gasping for breath.

Michael managed, "I don't want to go back home, Papa."

"What you done was foolish, son, but I done worse, leavin' you back there. I reckon you've earned the right to stay. Come on now, put some warm vittles in your belly. You'll feel better."

"I don't know if I can hold it down." He admitted with some shame, "I threw everything up."

"That's no disgrace. We've all done the same, one time or another. It's almighty mean, the first time you have to watch a man die hard. I was younger than you. You look like you stood it better than I did."

Michael still nursed a lingering doubt. "That patch-eyed feller, he kept a-cryin' for me to do somethin' to help him. I didn't do a thing, Papa. I just stood there."

"What would you have done, get yourself killed for the likes of him? He deserved whatever they done to him."

"But they was Injuns, and he was white. You've fought Injuns yourself, Papa, lots of times."

"I had to. But I wasn't always proud of it. My side was chosen for me the day I was born; I was given no choice. Maybe it'll be different for you." His hand on Michael's shoulder, he led his son to the campfire. "Now you get somethin' in your belly. It'll put the strength back into you."

Cyrus Blackwood spat tobacco, some of it trailing into his matted black beard. "Just a minute, Mordecai. You mean you're lettin' this boy stay?"

Mordecai stiffened against the challenge. "I believe he's shown he can handle whatever comes. He's a Lewis, and my son."

"Maybe so, but he's not a full-growed man yet. I don't see it's fair to give him a man's share of the horses we catch. That'd take away from the rest of us."

Mordecai reddened. "My boy come near gettin' killed, and all you can think about is horses we ain't even caught yet?"

Cyrus looked around for support but found none in the faces of the other men. Clearly, they sided with Mordecai and Michael. Eli clenched his fists and moved toward Cyrus as if he had violent intentions. Cyrus put his hands up defensively and backed off, declaring, "I'm just thinkin' about my family."

Mordecai gave him a withering glare. "Michael come without permission, so any share he gets will be out of mine, not out of yours or anybody else's. That satisfy you?"

Cyrus flushed, for he had been made to look little and mean. "Satisfied."

Michael glanced at the picket line. There stood a black horse that had a snip nose and a star on its forehead. "That your horse, Cyrus?"

At Michael's age his upbringing would have dictated that he address the man as *Mister Blackwood*, but he would gag on that.

Cyrus seemed surprised by the question. "That's him. Why?"

"A while after you-all left, some fellers named Thomas come lookin' for a black horse. Suspicioned that somebody stole it."

Cyrus swallowed a little of his tobacco. "There's lots of black horses."

"They said theirs had a snip nose and a star on its forehead. Like yours. Said it had a stockin' on the right foreleg. Like yours."

Cyrus looked around quickly, trying to gauge the reaction of the other men. "That horse was a stray, come up eatin' my feed. I didn't know who he belonged to."

Dryly Eli said, "I don't reckon you asked around too much."

Cyrus turned and stomped away.

Michael said with disgust, "He's a thief and a liar, Papa. You ought to send him home."

Mordecai said, "I ought to send you both home. But I reckon we've come too far. We'll make do the best we can with what we've got."

In many ways the long trip to Texas was like a festive hunting and fishing party. The traveling was paced to be easy on the horses, which made it easy also on the men. Mordecai usually went into camp early to allow time for the men to fish if they stopped beside a likely stream, or to fan out and search for meat. Few days went by without one or more deer being brought to ground, and more than once a good fat bear that yielded grease enough to fry up more venison than the party could eat. Game birds added to the variety.

Michael could not help visualizing what the trip might have been like had Uncle Benjamin been in charge; they would already be in Texas hunting horses. Mordecai Lewis might interrupt business for pleasure, but he did not often interrupt pleasure for business.

Michael could not remember that he had ever

been this close to his father for so long at a time. He cherished the opportunity to get to know the man who had been something of a mystery to him, as much myth as reality. Mordecai had always seemed to be gone somewhere, or just getting back, or fixing to leave. Michael knew him as much by the stories people told about him as from his own personal relationship, and the stories had made Mordecai seem eight feet tall. Close up, Michael began to see that this was a man of flesh and blood, not a legend. He was a man in middle age, hard used by the outdoor life he had lived by his own choice. His hair was graying, his face furrowing, his eyes in a hard squint much of the time because he no longer could see the world around him in the sharp focus of his youth. He was a long way from being frail, but he was far short of eight feet tall.

Evenings, on a creek bank with their fishing lines in the water, Michael and Mordecai might sit together for an hour without either saying a word. Or if Mordecai was in a talking mood, he might recount old stories about adventures on his way to a war or on his way home from one. Of war itself he talked little, and Michael had little success in drawing him out. Mordecai's face would cloud as some painful memory came to him, and he would shift to more pleasant subjects. "War," he said, "is a mean, hard thing. It makes men do the best that's in them, and the worst. Since the British gave up and went home the second time, maybe we're finally through with it for good in this country."

Where Michael enjoyed his father's company most was on the hunt, for there Mordecai could give full rein to his restless, questing spirit. He could find a track where Michael could not see the least sign of one. Michael would have to admit that his younger brother Andrew had been a better pupil in that regard. But Michael's eye was keen when it came to spotting game, keener now than Mordecai's.

Michael was the one who first saw the buck browsing in a tangle of underbrush some three hundred yards away. The wind was wrong. Michael suspected it carried a little of their scent, for the buck seemed increasingly suspicious, nervously jerking its head around, looking intently in their direction, taking another bite, then looking again.

Mordecai said softly, "We'll never get close enough for a clean shot at him." He leveled his long-barreled rifle across a limb to steady it. He blinked, trying to clear the haze, then lowered the rifle. "It'd be a waste of good lead."

Michael said confidently, "I can hit him, Papa."

"From here?" Mordecai frowned. "It can't be done."

"Let me try anyway." Michael braced his rifle barrel upon the same limb his father had used. He allowed for windage and the long distance, took a deep breath, let some of it go, closed one eye, and slowly squeezed the trigger. The pan flashed and the rifle roared, shoving back hard against his shoulder. Through the black smoke he saw the buck leap high, then collapse, kicking.

Mordecai stared. "I'll be damned."

Michael said, "It wasn't so far." He felt like bragging a little, but it was more seemly to act modest.

Mordecai clapped him on the shoulder, hard enough that it hurt. Yet, at the same time it felt good. He said, "There ain't much more I can teach you, son. The student has got better than the teacher. I just wish Eli could've seen that."

Michael was only glad that his father had seen it. From now on perhaps he would no longer harbor reservations about Michael's audacity in coming along.

The trail Mordecai followed was plain enough but not much traveled. The Tennesseans sometimes rode for days without meeting a stranger. Now and again they came upon a clearing and a small farm recently broken to the plow. The settlers, who did not often have an opportunity to enjoy company, would almost invariably insist that the party stay and share whatever provender the land had yielded. Mordecai Lewis would examine their crops admiringly, running his hands through their soil and declaring it rich. More than once, some of the party suggested they had gone far enough, that this would be a good place to put down stakes. But always Mordecai found something lacking about the location. Better land always lay somewhere ahead, across the Mississippi, then across the Red or the Sabine. He would trade fresh venison or bear meat or hides for corn or coffee or whatever the settlers could spare that would make the night encampments more pleasurable. Then he would move on.

Beyond the Mississippi they came more often than not upon people who spoke a strange tongue that fell pleasantly if confusingly on the ear. Old Eli identified it as French. He knew a fair smattering of it, though Michael sensed that his usage was awkward. Children covered their mouths with their hands to hide their laughter, but their eyes betrayed them. Eli laughed with them and put them at ease.

This land, long the property first of France, then

of Spain and then again of France, had been sold to the United States in 1803, all the way west to where it abutted Spanish territory, Eli explained. That border had long been the subject of dispute between France and Spain and now was a matter of delicate diplomacy between Spain and the United States. Spain had done relatively little to develop its northernmost lands, but she had remained jealous of their possession. She now watched fretfully an increasing population of aggressive Americans in the vast territory so recently acquired by purchase from France against the Spanish will. Americans were notorious for always wanting more, for wanting to advance beyond what rightfully belonged to them. The Indians had learned about that.

Michael had always regarded his father as being immune to ordinary human frailties, and it came as a saddening revelation to discover that Mordecai suffered from rheumatism. He had never owned up to it at home, but on the trail it was not to be denied. On evenings when riding had set the rheumatism to hurting more than usual, Mordecai would forego the opportunity to fish or hunt, preferring to rest in camp. At such times Michael liked to ride out with Eli Pleasant or to sit with him on a riverbank while they waited patiently for fish to strike the bait. Eli had a storehouse of remembered experiences and could recite them for hours without repeating a story. However, Michael pressed him again and again to relate his adventures hunting horses in Texas. Texas by now had taken on the aura of a golden land in Michael's mind, a golden promised land for the adventuresome, the breakers of new trails.

Eli obliged him with tales of a bold Irishman

named Philip Nolan, who had first crossed into Spanish territory before the turn of the century to trade in wild or half-broken horses, driving them east to sell to American settlers. Pleasant's voice went harsh as he talked of Nolan's last expedition. Eli had broken a leg trying to tame a wild young stallion and was unable to go along, a misfortune which probably saved his life. The Spanish had become suspicious—with justification, it seemed—that Nolan's plans included the acquisition of much more than horses. He had cast covetous eyes upon the rich soils of eastern Texas and had speculated aloud that God and mankind would be better served if the land were attached to the United States. The Spanish military took the precaution of shooting him and carrying his men away to captivity deep in Mexico.

Eli said, "Them Spaniards, they can take a likin' to you and give you the moon. Or they can take a *dis*likin' to you and cut your throat before you can find the door. A man don't ever want to quit watchin' behind him when he's in their country."

Michael replied with short-lived concern, "They may not like *us* bein' there, then."

"The trick is to not let them find out."

The first few nights after joining his father's party, Michael did not sleep well. He would awaken with a start in the darkness, seeing the man named Quint lying in his final death throes, an arrow in his back, and hearing Patch-eye scream as his own slow death was just beginning. Michael would sit up in a cold sweat and look around in confusion until he remembered where he was. A couple of times he awakened to the sound of his own voice crying out.

Mordecai was always there, his manner gentle

and reassuring. "It'll pass," Mordecai told him. "You'll see worse, and you'll be better fixed to stand up to it for what you've already gone through."

Michael shuddered. What kind of a future offered worse than he had already seen?

Eli had been patient and easy-moving, but as the party skirted Louisiana's deep-shaded swamps and crossed its rich black farming lands, nearing old Natchitoches, he became dissatisfied with the slow pace of travel, with Mordecai's early making of camp in the afternoons. He finally came to blows with Cyrus Blackwood, who had been a constant irritant to the party, as Michael had known all along that he would. Blackwood was relentlessly discontented, complaining about the food, about the campsites, about having to stand guard at night when everybody knew there was nothing out there to stand guard against. The only person who had seen an Indian the whole trip was Michael, and Cyrus declared his suspicion that Michael had imagined it all.

One night Cyrus was supposed to relieve Eli on guard duty at the picket line and did not. When Eli shook him in his blankets, a sleepy Cyrus cursed him. By the time Eli finished administering retribution, Cyrus was not fit for guard duty. One eye was swollen shut, and the other had only a thin slit left open, just enough that Cyrus could see to get out of Eli's way.

Eli angrily told Mordecai, "You'll be wishin' you'd sent him home."

Mordecai tried his most soothing manner. "We'll be needin' all the men we got."

"You got no man there. And he'll keep one good man out of useful service just a-watchin' the son of a bitch."

"We come too far to send him back."

"Well, you tell him to stay out of my way. I got all the patience in the world with a man who tries but can't. I ain't got three minutes to waste on one who don't even try."

The rest of the way to Natchitoches, Cyrus Blackwood made it a point to trail along in the rear, well out of Eli's reach. That did not prevent his grumbling about one thing or another, but it kept the others from having to listen.

7

Mordecai remarked upon sighting Natchitoches that it was not a large town, as towns went. It looked large to Michael, but he had not seen many towns in his life. The place seemed an oasis after such a long trip across lands so sparsely settled. Most of it lay on the west side of a river which Eli said was called the Red. Across its gently flowing waters Michael saw tree-lined streets and many houses of a curious style, single-story for the most part, their roofs higher-pitched than the cabins he had known. He saw boats on the river, small steamers up from New Orleans, flatboats carrying off their cargoes of farm produce to a waiting world. There was a bustle and a busyness about the place which made his pulse quicken. There was far too much to see all at one time. Too many glittering curiosities competed for his attention.

Eli Pleasant rode up to a house where a man stood waiting at the front door. Recognition came, and the man rushed off the porch with his arms outstretched as Eli swung down from his saddle, betraying none of the weariness to which his years would have given him just claim. The two men conversed in the language which Michael had come to recognize easily as French. Then the man approached Mordecai, right hand extended in greeting. He spoke a heavily accented but understandable English. Calling him Baptiste Villaret, Eli patiently introduced him to everybody except Cyrus Blackwood. The man looked at Cyrus with a question in his eyes, but Eli ignored it. He put his arm around Baptiste's shoulder and turned him away. Michael could not miss the resentment that leaped into Cyrus's face. Cyrus got down from his horse, led him out to a shed and relieved himself against the log wall without concern over whether Baptiste had womenfolk who might be offended. The gesture was typical of his attitude toward most of the people they had encountered along the way, especially the French. Cyrus had declared it his solemn belief that this country ought to be reserved for good Americans, and people who spoke some devilish foreign language ought to be shipped back where they came from. Or perhaps just shot.

Eli pointed out to Michael, but felt no obligation to explain to Cyrus, that this country had belonged to the United States for only a dozen or so years. Anybody born here earlier was likely to be French or Spanish, or a mixing of the two. Or, of course, a slave.

Michael found that his father had met Baptiste before, though his acquaintance with the voluble Frenchman had been casual and short compared to Eli's. Baptiste offered Mordecai's company the hospitality of his house. The structure was too small for all or even most of the men to sleep indoors. Mordecai acknowledged the offer with grace but suggested that the men had been used to sleeping under the stars. He saw no point in spoiling them now, especially in view of the fact that they would soon again be back in the wilderness. However, they would appreciate the opportunity to roll their blankets beneath the sheltering roof of his broad porch in event of rain.

Baptiste *did* have womenfolk, Michael soon learned. He had a Spanish wife, a woman of dark complexion, small but possessed of enough energy for three. There were four daughters, the oldest a lithe and lively girl named Marie, who reminded Michael of nothing so much as a doe fawn. Darker in complexion than her father but lighter than her mother, she was a couple of years younger than Michael, about Andrew's age. She was glorified by flashing black eyes unlike any he had ever seen. He listened to the music of her voice though he did not understand the words, and he glanced often at her as she bustled about the kitchen helping her mother prepare a meal for the Tennesseans. More than once he found her gaze upon him. His cheeks would warm, and he would try to put his mind to work on what his father and Eli and Baptiste were saying.

Baptiste spoke rapidly, his hands in constant motion. From his manner and Eli's, Michael knew he told of dark and troubling matters. The name Rodriguez kept coming into the conversation. More than once Eli had to slow him down and get him to repeat. At length Eli turned to Mordecai.

"I'd hoped somebody might've killed that damned Lieutenant Rodriguez by now, but he's still goin' strong. Baptiste's been tellin' me about a friend of

his by the name of Lucero, from over on the Spanish side of the Sabine. Seems he's a rebel. Got hisself
on the losin' side of a fight agin the Spanish government. He escaped over here just barely ahead of
Rodriguez and a firin' squad. He snuck back to get
some stock he left behind, and Rodriguez found out.
He tortured a cousin of Lucero's and then killed him
for revenge. Baptiste says we'd better stay out of
Texas for a while. Rodriguez is watchin' the river."

Mordecai frowned. "We didn't come this far to
turn back."

"That's what I told him. I said Texas is a big
enough country that we ought to be able to keep
them soldiers from findin' us. Just the same, Baptiste's advice is: don't go."

Mordecai cast an uneasy glance toward the rest
of the men, resting out on the porch. "I'd as soon we
didn't say nothin' right now where they can hear it.
Time enough to worry them when we find out for
sure how bad the situation is."

Eli nodded darkly. "They'll be wantin' to cut loose
and celebrate a little—put a little whiskey under their
belts, and maybe find them a woman for company.
No use us takin' that pleasure away from them." He
asked Baptiste something in French, and Baptiste
nodded, amplifying his spoken reply with a pointing
of both his chin and his finger.

Eli said hesitantly, like a boy caught smoking tobacco behind the barn, "Fact is, there's a widder
lady of my acquaintance that I had sort of set my
hopes on seein'. Baptiste says she's still a widder. I
don't reckon, bein' a married man, you'd care for
that kind of diversion, Mordecai?"

Mordecai shook his head and glanced at Michael.
"I ain't been the best husband in the world, but I'm

better than *that*. A little somethin' wet to warm my stomach and lighten my soul . . . that'll be all I need."

Eli grunted his approval. "Well, then, I'll point the boys in the direction they'll be wantin' to go, and the rest of it they can work out for theirselves." He stood up and, with a few words to Baptiste, started for the door.

Mordecai said, "Better leave Cyrus Blackwood here. He's a married man, like me."

Eli paused, disgust in his eyes. "There ain't one thing about him that's like you."

Michael followed Eli to the door. Mordecai said, "You'd best stay here with me, Michael. There's things out yonder that you'll learn about bye and bye. Tonight's too soon."

Michael figured he already knew a lot more than his father suspected, thanks partly to living with sisters and in no small part to long discussions with his cousin Frank. But he stopped at the door and watched the men gather eagerly around Eli, excited over a chance to vent some of the steam that had built up on the long trail. Even Old Man Wilson seemed as exuberant as the young bachelor Macklin brothers. Michael thought the grizzled veteran should be content to try and wear the rockers off of a chair on the porch, but the old man had never once lagged behind on the trip, or failed to carry his share of any load. The book-learned Judkins had suffered some at first, deprived of the whiskey to which his system had become overly accustomed, and Michael suspected that when the celebration in Natchitoches was done he would have a lot more whiskey to sweat out of his pores.

As the group started down the tree-shaded street

toward the main part of town, Cyrus Blackwood was out in front, turning and motioning for the others to walk faster.

Michael said, "Eli's right, Papa. Cyrus Blackwood ain't noways the same as you."

Dusk came down upon the old French town. Michael sat on the porch, listening to his father and Baptiste Villaret. The conversation ranged from crops and the sad state of the farm economy to Villaret's strong confidence that sooner or later Texas must become part of the United States. The Spaniards would never do much with it, he contended. The government was in constant strife with the native citizens of Mexico, resentful over being exploited for the enrichment of the pureblood *gachupínes* who held the political and military power. The king lived far away across the great waters and perhaps did not know, or even care, what was happening to his subjects in the New World so long as a goodly portion of their labors delivered gold into his treasury.

"One day," he prophesized, "there will be revolt, and he will lose all of Mexico. Then perhaps Mexico will sell Texas to the United States, as France sold Louisiana."

Mordecai drew deeply on a home-rolled cigar. An old dream was in his eyes, the dream of faraway places that had kept him moving, searching, since he was Michael's age. "And if they don't want to sell it . . ."

Villaret glanced sharply at him, fathomed his meaning and nodded agreement. "Their army would be small, for it is a poor country."

Michael could hear music rising and falling on the soft evening breeze, fiddles like the ones he heard back home in Tennessee, though the style of playing was somehow different. He guessed music was a language all people could understand, no matter where they came from.

He wearied of sitting on the edge of the porch and listening to talk of politics. He got up, stretched himself, then went wandering around the house. Villaret had some sheds and pens out back. He heard a horse squeal and decided to investigate. He found Old Man Wilson's dun horse fighting the others back from a rack of hay. That animal, he thought, was a little like the Spanish king they were talking about, a selfish tyrant. He had challenged every horse in the bunch and established his dominance over most of them. He seemed to have a particular dislike for the black horse Cyrus rode and would bite it at any opportunity.

A girl spoke behind Michael. He turned from the wooden fence and saw Marie Villaret. She said something, but it was in French, and he did not understand a word. He knew only that it must be a pleasantry, because she smiled.

He asked, "Don't you speak any English?"

The reply was in French, so he supposed she didn't. She pointed into the pen and asked him something. When he stared in confusion, she pointed to him, then to the horses. He decided she was trying to ask which was his. He pointed to Blaze, by all odds the oldest animal in the pen. Her response seemed complimentary, the best he could tell. He decided she didn't know much more about horses than she knew about English.

She moved close beside him, looking into the pen at the animals. He felt suddenly a little flustered, for he had never been at ease around girls except for his own sisters, and sometimes not them either. He felt like moving away, but he did not. He found that despite his uneasiness, there was something pleasurable about the nearness of her. He fancied she smelled a little like sweet soap.

Old Man Wilson's horse made a lunge at the big sorrel Papa had borrowed from Uncle Benjamin. The sorrel wheeled and kicked the aggressor in the belly, hard enough that the Wilson horse broke wind. The girl laughed and shouted something that Michael took for approval. The sorrel moved up to the hayrack and began to feed, while the Wilson horse backed off and looked frustrated, as if plotting its next treachery.

"Can you ride a horse?" he asked Marie.

She shrugged, not understanding.

The Wilson horse made a run at the sorrel, which turned and defended itself with sharp teeth. Both horses smashed against the fence. The girl fell back against Michael, and instinctively he caught her. For a moment she remained in his arms, embarrassed and uncertain, but no more so than he was.

Her cheeks flushed, she said something and hastily retreated to the house. She stopped at the door and turned to look back at him before she disappeared inside. He stared at the door long after she was gone, his face unaccountably warm. He fancied he could still smell her sweet fragrance. He felt both elated and frustrated. More than either, he felt confused.

He spent the next day walking around, watching the busy hoof and wheel traffic, the boats large and small loading and unloading their varied cargoes at the wharves. He learned that Natchitoches was the head of navigation, because a short distance to the north the Red was blocked by a huge natural raft of driftwood, built up over the ages, that prevented boat passage. He listened to a dazzling mixture of languages, for this town had been founded by the French a hundred or so years ago as they sought to spread their influence in the New World. The Spanish, in reaction, had founded the town of Nacogdoches a day's ride to the west, attempting to counter any French expansion in that direction. For generations the two governments had sparred and quarreled from afar while their soldiers and their settlers fraternized peacefully, smuggled and traded and even intermarried. Baptiste Villaret's family was evidence enough of that. From little things he picked up, mostly from Eli, he deduced that the merchant Villaret had long done clandestine business west of the Sabine, smuggling goods to Spanish settlers in Texas, trading for or buying contraband from them in defiance of the law. It seemed to Michael that the Frenchman had reason to wish for a change in the government which ruled Texas.

Sometimes when Michael was around the house he would get a strong feeling that he was being watched. Often as not, when he turned he saw the girl Marie, her dark eyes fixed on him. She would quickly busy herself at some task or move out of his sight.

The boldest she ever got was to go to the horse pen in the evening when he was putting out hay and watch him through the fence. She seemed to be trying to work up courage to say something. He knew it was futile; he would not understand her anyway. But she surprised him. She pointed to him, then to herself, and asked in measured, painful English that

she obviously had worked to memorize: "You . . .
like . . . me?"

He could only nod. "I guess so," he replied hesitantly. "But I don't hardly know you."

She stared blankly, not understanding. She tried
again, pointing first to herself, then to him. "I . . .
like . . . you." Before he could say anything in reply,
she turned and ran to the house.

He almost forgot to finish forking hay to the
horses. He thought he might ask Eli how hard it was
to learn French.

Mordecai intended to remain in Natchitoches
several days, resting the horses as well as the men.
But the stay was cut short when the Macklin brothers got into a fight over some local beauties and left
a couple of flatboatmen whittled up a bit. It seemed
expedient to cut the visit short and be gone.

Mordecai had conversed at length with a grim-
faced Guadalupe Lucero through Baptiste, whose
ability to switch back and forth from English to
Spanish and French left Michael in awe. Lucero
was a dark-faced, muscular man with black eyes
that simmered and crackled in bitterness and hatred
as he related his experiences. He would speak for
a time in broken English, then become dissatisfied
with the slowness of it and revert to Spanish.

"I will go back one day," Villaret interpreted for
Lucero, "and when I do, I will not be hunting for
horses!" Lucero made a quick slicing motion across
his throat.

Villaret said, "That Rodriguez is the devil. Lucero
will see one day if the devil can be killed."

Lucero drew a rough map for Mordecai, showing
how he might enter Texas well south of Nacogdoches and be most likely to avoid contact with the

small military troop which operated out of there. He was on hand to see the Tennesseans off in the cool of dawn, along with Baptiste and his family. Michael lifted a hand in quiet farewell to the girl whose dark eyes had said things he readily understood though the words she spoke to him in French remained a mystery.

As the men rode away, Michael looked back. He saw Marie watching him, her face sad. And he saw Lucero make the sign of the cross.

8

Cyrus Blackwood complained from the start. Mordecai had been obliged to drag him out of a warm bed in which he was not alone. Cyrus protested, "I don't see why we had to be in such a damned rush just on account of them Macklins. I tell you, Mordecai, it ain't often a man finds him somebody who wants it as bad as that little Creole woman. There weren't no quit to her."

Mordecai glanced at Michael, then grabbed a handful of Cyrus's shirt. For a moment Michael thought his father would drive a fist into those filthy whiskers and see if he could find the chin. Mordecai loosened his hold but declared in the harshest tone Michael had heard him use on the whole trip: "This boy don't need to be hearin' that kind of trashy talk. You shut the hell up, Cyrus, or get the hell back to Tennessee!"

Cowed, Cyrus pulled away and ducked his head. "I didn't mean no harm. I got boys of my own . . . good boys."

Mordecai frowned darkly. "You got a wife too, if you ain't forgot."

Cyrus let his gaze drift over the other men as if looking for someone to take his part. He found none; he never had. He slowed his horse and let the men ride past him. They all made a point of not giving him a glance. Michael looked back hopefully, thinking Cyrus might indeed turn eastward toward Tennessee. He was disappointed. Cyrus took a place at the rear of the ragged column.

Guided by Eli's memory of the country, augmented by the rough map Guadalupe Lucero had provided, Mordecai led his group across the span between the Red and the Sabine rivers, good farming land by the look of it, though much was not yet taken up or broken out. Mordecai gave it but brief attention, for his blue eyes held to the west. At the bank of the Sabine he halted and stared a long time at the heavy trees which lined the opposite side. He crooked his finger and beckoned Michael up beside him. "Your eyes are better'n mine, son. You see anything over yonder?"

Excitement coursed through Michael like the electricity he sometimes felt in a spring storm. "I see Texas. That *is* Texas, ain't it?"

"It's Texas. But that wasn't my meanin'. You see anything that could be people . . . like soldiers, maybe?"

Michael squinted. The only movement he saw was the trees, their branches swaying gently in the wind that roved along the river. In a break between the trees he could see the land stretching far beyond, far westward, a sea of tall green grass that waved as he had always imagined the ocean would wave.

"No sir, I don't see a thing. We're goin' on across, ain't we?"

Mordecai shook his head. "Not we. Just me and Eli. We'll go have ourselves a look-see. Everybody else'll rest on this side of the river till we make sure there's no trouble waitin' for us yonder."

Michael's rump prickled with impatience to put this river behind him and set his feet upon the land he had anticipated so long. Texas! Yonder it stood, so near he thought he could skim a rock across the water's surface and hit it.

"Let me go with you, Papa. You can use my eyes."

Mordecai shook his head. "Your eyes are fine, but Ol' Blaze's legs ain't as good. If it come to a horse race with Spanish soldiers, you might not finish." He responded to Michael's disappointment by placing his big hand on Michael's arm. "Like as not we'll find everything clear, and you'll be goin' over soon enough."

Eli grinned. "I promise you, boy, we won't try to catch no wild horses till you get there."

Cyrus Blackwood waited until Mordecai and Eli had pushed their horses into the river and out of hearing before he said testily, "In my day a button didn't open his mouth till he was told to, and he didn't say nothin' except what he was asked."

Michael's face warmed. He sensed that Cyrus was trying to pick an argument with him. He sensed also that Cyrus was afraid of Mordecai, so picking on Mordecai's son was an indirect form of retaliation. Michael wanted to oblige the reprobate, but his father would say that only a hog gets down into the mud to wrestle another hog. He turned awkwardly away without giving answer.

Cyrus said, "I was talkin' to you, boy."

Old Man Wilson rode up beside Cyrus. His dun horse wickedly took advantage of the opportunity and sank its teeth into the hide of Cyrus's black. The black horse squealed and made a lunge that tumbled Cyrus out of the saddle. Cyrus rolled on the ground and scrambled desperately to get out of his panicked horse's way. He glared angrily at Old Man Wilson. "You done that on purpose. That horse of yours needs a whip taken to him."

Wilson, who never spoke except when it was necessary, and then always in a quiet voice, said, "You ever try it and you'll eat that whip, handle and all." He turned to Michael. "That ol' pony of yours needs a rest, son. Why don't you take the saddle off of him and let him graze a spell?"

As always, Cyrus swallowed his pride and turned away. He caught his black horse and led it apart from the others. He sat on the ground, in the horse's shadow, and sulked.

Wilson said to Michael, "Don't you pay him no mind, son. Him and his whole family ain't worth a bucket of cold spit. The only opinion you need to be concerned about is your papa's, and your own."

"My own?"

"Sure. Always be at peace with yourself. Then you can go to sleep at night justified."

Mordecai and Eli returned after a couple of hours, satisfied that soldiers were nowhere around. "All right, boys," said Mordecai with a broad smile, "let's go to Texas."

The water was colder than Michael expected. It took his breath. He found himself shivering as he followed his father's lead and slipped out of the saddle to make it easier for his horse to swim. He held on to Blaze's mane, for he was not much of a swimmer himself. The trees on the Texas bank seemed to bob up and down in rhythm with the horse's movement.

As he found shallow ground, Michael caught Blaze's reins and led the horse up onto dry land. Blaze shook himself like a dog. Michael wondered if his old leather saddle could stand the punishment, for the stirrups swung wildly, and Cyrus Blackwood had to step back to avoid being struck. He muttered something under his breath and gave Michael a hard glance.

Michael refused to let Cyrus's sourness spoil his exhilaration. Texas! They had finally reached it. He stood trembling from the cold as the wind searched through the wet cotton shirt stuck to his body. Or perhaps it was not altogether from the cold. He looked up the bank past the trees at the expanse of rolling prairie stretching to the horizon. He thought the air here smelled differently from that on the Louisiana side, though he knew this was wild imagination.

"Beautiful!" he declared to whoever might be listening.

Eli Pleasant said, "Looks pretty much like the other side. But I reckon it's like the Bible says: the forbidden fruit always tastes the sweetest."

Michael asked, "Is it really all that forbidden?"

"You'll know it is if we run into an officer by the name of Rodriguez. Come on, Michael, and help me wipe out these tracks."

Each of them broke a small limb from a tree. As the others moved up over the riverbank and into the shelter of the timber, Michael and Eli dragged the branches across the horse tracks and boot prints on the wet soil. They were only partially successful in making the ground look as smooth as before. But Eli said, "Time it's dried and the wind has worked on it a while, it'll be all right."

Michael pointed into the timber. "What about up there?"

Eli shook his head. "Any patrol that comes along'll work the riverbank. If they don't find nothin' here, they ain't apt to look further. Come on now, boy, or we'll get left."

As Mordecai had promised, eastern Texas was a broader, more open land than Michael's old home country in Tennessee. It was alternately forest land and rolling prairie, the latter covered by dense stands of tall grasses that rubbed against Michael's stirrups. The seedheads of some types reached up to his shoulders as he sat on Blaze's back. Even when the riders traversed the open prairies, they were almost always within sight of forest lands.

Michael could not see sign that anyone else had ever been here. It was as if they were the first human beings to set foot upon this endless land. The thought of it raised bumps on his skin and made him tremble, chilled though the sun was warm.

Mordecai stayed close to the timber when he could, like a deer which tries always to be within a few bounds of cover. The timber was often dense pine, not unlike that which Michael knew at home. Other times it was a mixture of species tall and short, and sometimes it was moss-covered oaks. Mordecai paused often for a long and cautious look around. Not until they had traveled for three days did he finally become emboldened by their failure to see any sign of soldiers, or even of civilians.

Eli explained, "The Spanish, they don't scatter out as much as we-uns when they settle. They had a-plenty of hell in the early days from Injuns here-abouts, so they always stayed pretty close together. Even yet, you'll find most of the Spanish livin' in clusters like at Nacogdoches, and way south at San Antonio de Bexar and La Bahia. All out in the middle is vacant country, just beggin' for somebody to come and make use of it."

Michael gloried in the size of the country. The fourth day he asked Eli, "Are we still in Texas? Seems like we ought to've passed plumb through it and into somethin' else."

Eli grinned. "We ain't hardly even started yet."

"There's so much of it," Mordecai enthused. Michael had been able to tell that the land had taken hold of his father as it had himself, from the minute they swam their horses across the Sabine and let them drip off on the Texas side. "Just look at what them Spanish are lettin' go to waste. I believe a man could grow just about anything in this soil."

"Texas ain't all like this," Eli warned. "Some of it is rocky and thin, and a lot of it is choked up with canebrakes a man has got to cut his way across. There's places where it don't rain hardly atall."

"But the waste! There's people in Tennessee would give their lives for a country like this. Ol' Hickory could come in here with a hundred or two good men and take it from one end to the other. Wouldn't be a patch on the fight we had with the British at New Orleans."

Eli made a dark frown. "The takin' would be the easy part. The holdin' might be a lot tougher, when them Spanish bring their army up from the south. There was some filibusters a few years ago named Gutierrez and Magee. They come in here with a *thousand* or so and thought they had the whole country won. But when they stretched theirselves all the way down to Bexar, it was like a cannon blowed up in their faces. The killin' ain't stopped even yet."

A glow was in Mordecai's eyes, a glow Michael had seen every time they picked up and moved to "better" land. "There never was nothin' worth the havin' that didn't take a fight."

Eli's frown bit deeper. "We come here for horses."

Michael had studied Lucero's map. It indicated where Lucero thought Mordecai's party would be most likely to find horses running wild. Michael was fairly sure his father was not taking them in that direction, at least not yet. After several days he began to sense that Mordecai was surveying the land, running an inventory of sorts. He made notes on the map, adding things to it like streams and rivers and forests, and especially open deep-soil areas that he thought would be good farming country.

It was the grumbling that finally brought Mordecai back to his original purpose. Cyrus Blackwood had complained from the first, of course, and Mordecai paid no attention to him. But when it started coming from Old Man Wilson and the Macklin brothers, and finally even from Eli Pleasant, he led the party out of the canebrakes and pine forests, moving southwestward onto the open, rolling prairie.

One day the Tennesseans sat on their mounts atop a small hill and looked down toward a tree-lined stream where a large band of horses watered, a big blood-bay stallion standing watch over his harem. Michael found himself holding his breath, for the thrill hit him hard. He did not remember that he had ever seen so many horses in one place, certainly not running wild and free. He declared to Mordecai, "Papa, it must have looked this way to

God when He finished His work and rested on the seventh day."

Mordecai nodded, caught up in the splendor of the horses. "I'd not be surprised, son. A finer sight I've never seen."

Eli was the only man in the group who had any experience with wild horses. He said, "If this was a mountain country, a man could fence off a canyon and trap them in it. But out here in the open, about the best you can do is chase them till you run them down, then take one of these rawhide reatas we got in Natchitoches and work a loop over their heads. Then you got you a horse, if you can keep him."

Mordecai looked over the eager faces of his men, then winked at Michael. "Well, then, let's go get us a horse."

He charged down the hillside with a reata in his hand. Michael heeled old Blaze into the best run he could muster, but his father kept widening the gap with Uncle Benjamin's good sorrel horse. The stallion tossed its head and gave an alarm. The wild horses flushed like a covey of quail from the banks of the stream and broke into a desperate run across the rolling prairie. Unencumbered by riders and saddles, most of them soon widened the distance between themselves and the horsemen, just as Mordecai widened the distance between himself and the rest of his group. The only animal which did not was an old mare so heavy with foal that she seemed likely to give birth at any minute. Michael watched his father ride alongside her and try several times to work the loop around her neck before he finally managed. The mare fought the rope, then bared her teeth and charged at Mordecai. He retreated a little and let her get some slack in the reata. As she hit the end of it, the rawhide broke, and she ran free. She would have gotten away if the Macklin brothers had not followed in wild pursuit and tossed another loop over her head.

Eli and Michael and the others chased the main body of horses a while until Eli called a halt and declared the effort hopeless. Their mounts were lathered with sweat and breathing heavily as they returned to Mordecai and the Macklin brothers and the mare. She still struggled on the end of the reata, slowly choking herself to the ground.

Mordecai pointed his chin toward her and said ruefully, "At least we got two of them, countin' the foal she's fixin' to have."

Eli said, "We got to do better than just charge after them like a pack of hounds. We got to have us a system."

Over the next few days the system evolved a little at a time as the men became increasingly experienced. They ran the horses in a wide circle, part of the riders waiting and resting their mounts while two or three kept the circle going. Those rested would take up the chase as the circle came around, and the others would drop out. The wild horses were kept running until they were ready for collapse. Then the riders could pick the ones they wanted, the younger mares and the stud colts not yet old enough for the old stallion to have run them out of the harem. A man would drop a rawhide loop around a neck and fight the animal to a standstill. The caught horse would be thrown to the ground and one foot tied up, to be left that way sometimes for days. When they became reasonably tractable, that treatment would be replaced by hobbles that prevented their running. Michael found exhilaration in the chase, in the fight, in the captures.

Slowly, ever so slowly, it seemed, the number of caught horses increased . . . a dozen, two dozen, three. For every horse taken, a man suffered a bruise, a knot, miscellaneous abrasions and contusions. Cyrus Blackwood declared it a man-killing operation, though he always held back and let someone else take the punishment. When a big colt got him down, stepped in the middle of his back, and then dragged him a hundred feet across the grassy prairie, he was ready to quit.

"We got horses enough to make us all some money," Blackwood argued. "I say it's time we start back."

Mordecai granted him but brief hearing, for it was clearly the consensus of the group that they wanted to stay and take more horses. Eli Pleasant spoke for them all. "Ain't no use settlin' for sowbelly when a man can have the whole hog."

Mordecai began to worry, however, when a couple of Spanish settlers rode down into camp one day and quietly looked over the crude set of brush pens in which the captured horses were being confined at night. Through Eli, who knew some Spanish as well as French, they said they were looking for a couple of their mares that had been stolen by a wild stallion. They did not find them among the ones the Tennesseans had caught.

Eli's face furrowed as he watched the pair ride away. He told Mordecai, "They may not report us to the soldiers, but they'll talk to their friends about us. Sooner or later, it's apt to get back to the military."

Mordecai shrugged. "I don't know what we can do about it."

Cyrus Blackwood suggested darkly, "Dead men won't tell nobody nothin'."

Mordecai shook his head. "They probably wouldn't do us any harm on purpose. We got no right to hurt them."

"It's us or them," Blackwood argued. "I say we go and kill them." He started for his horse.

Eli Pleasant moved after him, but Mordecai pushed him aside and caught up to Cyrus himself. He flattened him with one good swing of his fist, then stood over him with his face an angry red. "Cyrus, you've whined and raised hell ever since we left Tennessee. Now you shut your goddamned mouth, or I'll neck you to one of them wild colts and let him teach you to lead!"

When Cyrus looked as if he would make some heated reply, Mordecai grabbed him by the shirt and shook him like a dog would shake a rabbit, then threw him to the ground again. He stood over him, tall and strong and trembling in righteous anger. "Not a word, Cyrus. Not one damned word!"

Michael had never felt prouder of his father.

Cyrus looked around in vain for sympathy. He bowed his head and rubbed his hand across his mouth and stared mutely at the thin smear of blood he brought away.

That night he failed to awaken Michael to take his place on guard watch. Michael awoke and went on his own.

He found that Cyrus Blackwood was gone.

Mordecai was considerably agitated. "The damned fool, he'll never make it back to Tennessee alone. He'll die someplace and never be heard of again."

Eli Pleasant took some pleasure in that thought. But another worried him. "What if the soldiers was to catch him? He'd lead them to us, like as not. He'd trade us all to save hisself."

Grave doubt came into Mordecai's face. He walked down to the horse pen and stared a while at the catch. The rest of the men slowly followed him. Mordecai turned, after a bit, his decision made.

"I wanted to take back more horses than this. We come a long ways and earned the chance. But every day we stay, the bigger the risk gets. So we'll give thanks to the Lord for what He's let us have, and we'll start east right now."

The Macklin boys were inclined to stay a while longer and gamble. Eli and Old Man Wilson sided with Mordecai, and after some argument they brought the rest around to their thinking. The outfit ate breakfast, then broke camp. The horses were let out of the brush pen as they had been for many days, when Michael loose-herded them to graze while the rest of the men went horse-hunting. Most had gentled enough to remain together and respond to herding. Those animals still inclined to break for freedom were hobbled as a handicap.

Mordecai decided to try driving them without hobbles, for the horses could move considerably faster that way. A couple of the big colts and one mare tried to run. They had to be overtaken, snared, and choked into submission. These Mordecai tied onto a long rope, and the Macklins took turns leading them behind the main bunch. Their noses were sore from the halters, and they resisted but little.

Mordecai pushed hard the first day, purposely tiring the horses to lessen the chances of losing them all. Toward nightfall Eli rode ahead and located a natural gully, its walls too steep for the horses to climb. Brush was piled behind and in front of the mustangs to prevent their escape in the night.

The second day went easier, and Mordecai decided to accept a slower pace. Evenings when no suitable natural trap could be located, it was necessary to catch the horses one by one and tie them to trees. Supper would be prepared hastily and the fire snuffed out so it would not betray the camp after darkness.

Mordecai said nothing, but Michael could see a growing uneasiness in his father's face, and the contagion among the other men was considerable. Eli Pleasant kept looking back over his shoulder.

One night Mordecai sat spraddle-legged on the ground, laboriously wrapping and securing a patch of sorts around the toe of a disintegrating leather boot. This expedition had left the men in rags and all but barefoot. "Son," he said, "I never did tell you how proud I was, the way you snuck off and follered after us. Showed a lot of nerve, even if it was not very good judgment. I done pretty much the same thing once, follered after my pap and my Uncle Simeon when they went off to fight Injuns. Pap threatened the lickin' of my life, but he let me stay. Later on, I wished he'd whipped me and sent me home. We fell into the damndest Injun fight you'd ever want to see." He cut a leather string with his sharp hunting knife and threaded it through a tiny hole in the patch while the tip of his tongue stuck out one corner of his mouth. "I'm wishin' now that you was still home with your mama."

Michael said, "We're doin' all right."

"We got a ways to go before we reach the Sabine.

I ain't told the others—it ain't good for them to see the leader fret—but I'm gettin' a real dark feelin'."

Michael could have told him they all sensed it, but he saw nothing to be gained by adding to his father's burden.

Mordecai looked around carefully to be sure no one was within earshot. "If anything was to happen that you got back and I didn't, I'd want you to tell your mama that I love her. I ain't been the kind of husband she deserves, but I've loved her from the first time ever I laid eyes on her. I ain't never once betrayed her."

"She knows that, Papa."

"Well, you tell her anyway." Mordecai set the boot down and stared at Michael in the near darkness. "I been lucky. I not only had me a good wife, but I had me a bunch of young'uns that done me proud. Joseph, he's like your Uncle Ben, and you're like me. Andrew, he's a little like all of us, and yet he's not really like any of us. That's probably to his everlastin' credit. But you're all Lewises; that's what counts. Don't you ever forget who you are, and what you come from."

"I won't forget, Papa."

Mordecai hugged him. Surprised, Michael returned the hug without shame. He did not care whether anyone saw or not.

The men were up at daylight, fixed a quick breakfast, and began untying the wild horses from the trees. Eli Pleasant had freed a young stud and was holding him while he loosed another. The stud suddenly wheeled and knocked Eli down, stepping on him. The other big colt broke free. Together the two loose horses lifted their tails and took off to the

south as hard as they could run, trailing their rawhide halter ropes.

Cursing, bleeding, Eli jumped into his saddle.
"You-all go ahead," he shouted to Mordecai. "I'll
catch up to you." He was gone in a minute, spurring
Jug over a low hill where the two young animals
had disappeared.

Big Red nickered and had to be restrained from
following after him. The two horses had been in-
separable.

Michael wanted to follow and help, but Mordecai said Eli could take care of himself. The rest of
the bunch was set to moving. Michael looked back
several times and saw no sign of Eli. Mordecai assured him, "He'll be catchin' up to us in his own
good time. Won't hurt to keep a-watchin' for him,
though."

Thus it was that Michael was the first to see the
Spanish soldiers closing up rapidly behind them in
a hard gallop. For a moment his throat was so tight
he could bring out no sound. Then he managed to
shout urgently, "Papa!" and point.

Mordecai turned in the saddle. "Godalmighty!"
He yelled, "Push 'em hard, boys! Let's make for that
timber yonder!"

The Tennesseans began hollering, waving their
hats, and slapping them against their legs, putting
the captured horses into a run. But it was futile. The
soldiers were gaining, some already moving past the
Tennesseans in a strong bid to surround them. Mordecai shouted, "Let the horses go."

It was already too late. The soldiers began firing.
Michael heard an angry buzz, like a hornet, as a
slug passed his face. One of the Macklin brothers
brought up a rifle and fired back. It was a useless

gesture, for the long barrel bobbed up and down with every stride his horse made.

A powerful force struck Michael in the shoulder and drove him forward over Blaze's neck. Instinctively he grabbed a handful of mane and tried to hang on. His shoulder began to burn like the fires of Hell. He gasped for breath but could not find it. He felt himself sliding off the running horse, helpless.

A strong hand caught and held him. He heard Old Man Wilson's voice. "Mordecai! Your boy's hit!"

Mordecai Lewis cried, "Michael!" He reined over quickly and encircled Michael with a powerful arm just as Blaze pulled away. Michael felt himself bounced against his father's body. His feet dragged the ground as Mordecai tried desperately to hold onto him. Mordecai got Big Red stopped and swung down from the saddle, easing Michael onto his back on the ground. Old Man Wilson stopped and dismounted beside Mordecai. The teacher Judkins saw their predicament and reined up, turning back to join them. The others raced on, unaware.

Gasping for breath, Michael managed to rasp, "Go on, Papa. Don't stop." But Big Red jerked free and ran away in a panic after Blaze, the stirrups flopping. Mordecai knelt over Michael and tore at his shirt. "Hush, son," he whispered.

Michael could hear a rattle of gunfire ahead. Old Man Wilson said huskily, "God help us, Mordecai. They're killin' them all!"

9

Lying on his side while his father tried anxiously to stop the bleeding with cloth torn from his own rough-spun shirt, Michael gritted his teeth against a blazing fire that brought tears to his eyes. Even through the tears, he could see that soldiers had surrounded the little huddle of Tennesseans—him, his father, Old Man Wilson, and Judkins. A dark fear all but smothered him as he listened to the distant firing of guns. Even more fearful was the silence that followed.

He heard Judkins say in a trembling voice, "It's just us now. God in heaven, Mordecai, what do we do?"

His father was silent. There was no answer to give.

In a while the main body of soldiers came straggling back. Through a reddening haze, Michael saw that they had caught the horses and were bringing them along, the wild ones augmented by those the Tennesseans had ridden. The soldiers who had remained behind to guard the four Americans were joined by two dozen more. Michael soon discerned which was the leader. The man snapped orders in a voice which bespoke absolute authority. His soldiers were quick to respond, showing more apprehension of him than of the men they had surrounded.

Mordecai and Wilson and Judkins still had their guns, but Mordecai counseled gravely, "We can't shoot our way out of this. Best we can do is try to bargain."

"Bargain with what?" asked Judkins.

Again, Mordecai had no answer. His face was frozen as if chiseled from stone.

The officer rode up close. He studied the captives only a moment before he instinctively chose Mordecai as the leader. Michael's father had always had that look about him, tall and imposing. The Spaniard spoke sharply in his own language but elicited no response. The only man who could have understood was Eli, and Eli had gone chasing after runaway horses.

The officer shifted to a heavily accented English. "Is there one among you who speaks Spanish?"

Mordecai quickly shook his head. "Ain't nobody can."

The officer was of somewhat lighter complexion than his men, and his eyes were blue. Eli had told Michael that many pure-blood Spaniards were fair-skinned and blue-eyed, that they looked with contempt upon their dark-skinned and dark-eyed countrymen. The officer wore a uniform of a much better cut than those of his men, though it was dusty and wrinkled. He had been on the trail for some days, by the look of him. He was plainly tired and out of sorts. He barked commands in Spanish to one of his men whom Michael took to be a junior officer of some kind. He said a word which Michael took to mean *sergeant*.

The sergeant, a darker-skinned man, detailed a young soldier to gather the Tennesseans' weapons.

Mordecai resisted, raising his rifle. "You've got no right. We're Americans."

The officer leaned forward in the saddle and slashed Mordecai's face with a quirt, bringing blood and leaving a welt that rapidly began to turn purple. Michael cried, "Papa . . ." and tried to raise up. He dropped back weakly, the pain racking him. Mordecai held stubbornly to the rifle until the officer slashed him again, wresting the weapon from his hands and giving it to the hesitant young soldier with a rebuke. He snarled, "Tell the others to surrender their guns."

Mordecai gave no such order, but Wilson and Judkins saw the futility of resistance. The soldier collected their weapons. Michael's long rifle, the one Grandpa had given him, had fallen when Michael was hit. He did not know if the soldiers had found it. At the moment it didn't matter.

Mordecai said urgently, "My son's been wounded. He needs help."

The officer made no acknowledgement. He centered his attention on Mordecai. "Now, *americano,* this is New Spain. Why are you here?"

Blood trickled from the cut on Mordecai's face. He gave the officer a long, defiant stare. "You can see for yourself. We come to catch wild horses. Now, you goin' to help my boy?"

The officer slashed at him a third time, the quirt

lashing Mordecai's arms as he raised them to protect his face. "You lie. You are spies."

Mordecai gave him a look of hatred that would be fatal if looks had been able to kill. "We just come huntin' horses. You goin' to sit there and let my boy bleed to death?"

The officer turned in the saddle and crisply gave an order. A soldier on horseback prodded another horseman with the muzzle of a rifle. Blinking, Michael recognized the black horse, and he knew who the rider had to be.

Mordecai let go a long breath. "Cyrus Blackwood. Somehow I knew."

Cyrus cried, "It weren't my fault, Mordecai. They whipped me somethin' shameful. You ought to see my back."

Mordecai turned away from him in disgust. "All those men . . . I don't even want to see your *face*."

Old Man Wilson crimsoned, and he cursed in words that would scorch the hide of a wild hog loose in the woods. When he took a step toward Cyrus, the officer shouted an order, and most of his troops raised rifles to their shoulders.

Michael gritted his teeth and braced himself for the impact of another bullet. He thought of his mother, who would never know what had become of him. She would have wanted him to say a prayer, but in the turmoil his brain seemed numbed.

Wilson stepped back beside Mordecai, but he was not through with Cyrus. "May you burn in Hell for a million years!"

The officer leaned forward again in his saddle, staring hard into Mordecai's face. "Do you know who I am, American?"

Mordecai said with gravel in his voice, "I'd bet your name is Rodriguez."

A cruel smile crossed the officer's face. "It is good that you Americans have heard of me. You know I will do what I say."

Mordecai said, "What about my boy?"

Wilson and Judkins still held their horses. Rodriguez gave a sharp order, and a soldier took both animals, turning them in with the others.

Rodriguez gave Michael a moment's scrutiny. No sympathy showed in his pale blue eyes. "You are in pain, young man?"

Michael groaned for an answer.

The officer said, "Soon you will feel nothing."

Mordecai stiffened. "What're you sayin'?"

"The penalty for trespass upon the king's land is death!"

Mordecai staggered as if he had been hit in the stomach. Mordecai looked down hollow-eyed at Michael and whispered, "Jesus." He turned his face back to Rodriguez. "You got to give us a trial."

"A trial is for *your* country. You should have remained in your country." Rodriguez's gaze roved contemptuously over the Tennesseans. "Here there is only military law. Here I say who lives. I say who dies."

Mordecai looked gravely to either side of him at the two comrades who stood in stunned silence. He said in a quiet voice, "I'm sorry I brought you to this."

Old Man Wilson said, "We all knowed the risk. You didn't drag none of us here against our will."

Mordecai knelt beside Michael, touching him with a gentle hand. "My son is not of age," he pleaded. "And these other men, they ain't responsible neither.

Whatever we've done, it was my say-so, and mine alone. Take me and let the others go, please."

Rodriguez dismounted and handed his reins to a nearby soldier with a nod that said to take the horse aside. He shouted an order to the sergeant, who relayed it to the men. Half a dozen dismounted and formed a line. The sergeant delegated other men to hold their horses. A heavy muzzle-loading pistol in his hand, Rodriguez began to back away from the Americans. Michael swallowed hard, knowing what the move meant. He thought his heart had already stopped beating.

The sergeant said something which, by the tone of it, sounded like a protest. The officer responded in sharp anger. The sergeant then pointed to Michael. He seemed to be pleading Michael's case. The officer railed at him, and the sergeant shrugged, bowing his head.

Rodriguez turned once more to face Mordecai. In a cutting voice he declared, "You wanted our land. Very well. You may stay here forever!"

He gave an order, and the soldiers aimed their muskets.

Michael had never seen his father stand so straight, so tall. Mordecai shouted, "They're fixin' to kill us. At least let's die a-fightin'!"

He gave a shout of defiance and charged toward Rodriguez with his hands outstretched. Surprised, the officer took a step backward. He was slow in bringing up his pistol. Mordecai's hands were on Rodriguez's throat when the pistol's pan flashed and powder belched from the muzzle. Mordecai stumbled in midstride and staggered back. He pitched to the ground beside Michael. His brains were blown out.

The muskets roared. Michael's heart was in his throat as he rolled over toward his fallen father. He heard Judkins scream as bullets tore into him. Horses squealed in terror and jerked and fought and pitched. Old Man Wilson, though hit, managed to grapple with a soldier. Another soldier brought the butt of his rifle up and clubbed the old man in the back of the head, then dropped to one knee, whipped a long knife from his belt, and slashed Wilson's throat. Wilson thrashed on the ground.

Michael cried, "Papa!" and reached out to touch his father. He stared in horror at Mordecai's sightless eyes, at the spilling blood, the jagged pieces of skull smashed by the officer's bullet.

Rage overwhelmed his fear and his pain. He shouted in fury and tried to push to his feet. The soldier who had killed Wilson smashed the butt of his rifle into Michael's back. The ground rushed up and slammed Michael in the face. His shoulder was afire like the furnaces of Hell. He gasped in vain for breath.

Judkins was still twitching. Rodriguez reloaded his pistol, and coldly fired it point-blank into Judkins's head. Then he saw that the firing had set the captured horses into a wild run. He waved his arms and shouted, moving quickly toward his own horse. He swung into the saddle and gave an angry order to the sergeant. He pointed at Michael and at Cyrus.

Cyrus began weeping uncontrollably. "No. No, you promised. You promised me!"

The officer gave him a look of contempt and spurred off after the scattering horses.

Only the sergeant remained, and the young soldier who had been reluctant about taking the Tennesseans' rifles. The sergeant motioned for Cyrus to dismount. Cyrus blubbered and pleaded and fell to his knees, his trembling hands clasped. "Oh God! He promised he'd let me go. Oh God! Please!"

Michael managed to roll onto his back and defiantly stare up at the sergeant, though he saw him only through a red blur. He tried to lick his lips, dry as leather, and found his tongue just as dry. He wanted to tell Cyrus to shut off his crying and act like a man, but he could not speak. He willed himself to die with dignity, as his father had.

The sergeant said something to the young soldier. The soldier fired his musket into the air. The sergeant aimed his pistol above Cyrus's head and squeezed the trigger. Cyrus screamed and slumped to the ground, terrified. Scornfully the sergeant poked him with the hot, smoking muzzle. "Get up. I do not shoot you, *cobarde*."

Cyrus pushed onto hands and knees, shaking in terror. He would not look directly at the sergeant. The dark-skinned man said, "I leave your horse. You help this boy." He pointed in the direction the officer and the other soldiers had ridden. His English came slowly, as if he were thinking the words out one at a time. "Rodriguez must not see. You wait. Later you take boy, and you go." He pointed eastward.

The sergeant looked sorrowfully at the fallen Tennesseans, especially at Mordecai. He shook his head. *"Triste. Muy triste."* He knelt and gently turned Michael onto his side to examine the wound in his shoulder. He motioned to Cyrus. "You come. You help."

Cyrus did not move. The sergeant's voice went

sharp, and he drew his hand across his throat with a message that was unmistakable. "You help this boy."

Cyrus's body was racked with his sobbing, but he crawled over to Michael. Reluctantly he took hold of the bloody piece of shirt that Mordecai had torn and pressed it against the wound. Michael ground his teeth as the pain intensified. The sergeant looked down with pity. He made the sign of the cross and mounted his horse. He glanced back once before he and the young soldier rode off after the others.

Michael caught the pungent smell of urine. Cyrus, in his terror, had wet himself.

Cyrus stopped his whimpering after a bit. He stood up, turning the cloth loose and letting Michael roll onto his back. Michael bit off a cry as a stabbing pain grabbed him.

The black horse stood where the sergeant had left him, tied to a small shrub. Cyrus walked shakily toward the animal. Weakly Michael called, "Cyrus! Cyrus!"

Cyrus swung into the saddle. Michael summoned strength to call, "Don't leave me."

Cyrus seemed to have a hard time making himself turn around. He did, finally, and rode back. The black horse snorted, uneasy at the smell of blood. Cyrus gripped the reins up short. "I got to go, boy, don't you see that? They're liable to come back. I got to go."

"Cyrus, don't . . ."

"If there was any hope for you, boy . . . but there ain't. I got to think of my ownself . . . I got to think of my family."

He turned quickly and rode off toward the nearest timber. In a minute the soft thud of the horse's hoofs was gone. The only sound Michael could hear was the buzzing of flies, drawn to the blood. And he heard his own voice crying . . .

"Papa! Papa!"

10

Though Michael's eyes were closed, the sun seemed to penetrate the lids and sear them. He lay half-conscious, paralyzed. Perhaps he was dead. Perhaps this was the sensation that came when life left the body. He could not move his arms and legs. He felt as if someone held a flaming torch against his shoulder, pinning him to the ground. He tried to open his eyes but was forced to close them against the harsh brilliance of the sun. Through a loud roaring in his ears he became conscious of flies walking across his face, and of someone groaning. He realized the sound came from his own tortured body.

Surely, he thought, he could not be dead, for the dead were not supposed to feel pain.

Dazed, he was unable for a time to remember where he was, or how he came to be in such a condition. Then it began rushing back to him like a relentless flood tide. He remembered his father's cry, the desperate shouting, the musket fire, the screams of mortally wounded Judkins. He remembered his own smothering fear as he had awaited the final bullet that would kill him. He remembered his father falling beside him.

He gave way to a moment of panic. *Papa! What's happened to Papa?*

The rest of it came back to him. He tried to raise up, to look around, to see where Papa lay. He could not move. He strained until he was exhausted, but he roused no response from his arms or legs. He gave up in despair, wondering why he had not died with the others. Grief and anger and hurt took hold of him together, and tears burned the eyes he was unable to open.

He became aware, after a while, of new sounds, of horses moving in the deep grass. He heard the creak of saddle leather as a rider dismounted. *They've come back to kill me!* he thought, and strangely felt no fear. Death might come now as a blessing. He heard a voice repeating over and over, "My God! My God!"

Through the pain and the burning glare of the sun, it came to him that he knew the voice. He tried to speak the name, but he could not bring it out. All that came was a moan.

"Michael! Michael, boy!"

He felt hands touching him, gripping his shoulder, bringing the pain to a sudden new high. He cried aloud in reaction to it.

Eli Pleasant said, "Praise the Lord, boy. It's a miracle you're alive."

If I'm alive, why can't I move? Michael thought. *Why can't I speak?*

The sun no longer burned against his closed eyes. He realized Eli was blocking it. With a determined effort he brought his eyes open for a second or two.

He sensed more than saw Eli's bearded face. "Eli. Eli." He heard the sound of the words and knew he had managed to say them aloud. "Eli . . . Papa?"

After a moment of hesitation, Eli said, "I'm sorry, boy. He's dead. They're all dead. God knows why *you* ain't. Now you hold still."

Eli tore Michael's shirt and in doing so moved him a little. Michael cried out at the burning.

Eli said, "I know it hurts, boy. You just go ahead and cry. If cryin' didn't help, the Lord wouldn't of fixed us to where we could." His hands probed. Michael sternly made up his mind not to cry out again. He ground his teeth together as Eli examined the wound.

Eli said, "The longer the ball stays in there, the worse it'll get. I got to cut it out of you now, else you're most apt to foller off after your papa."

Michael managed to hold his eyes open a little longer. He saw three horses, Eli's and the two wild ones Eli had ridden off to pursue. Eli had tied the two captured animals to a scrub pine tree and his own horse to another. Eli walked back with a quirt from his saddle. He said, "I wish there was some whiskey to give you first. Best I can do is let you bite down on this."

He placed the quirt in Michael's mouth. "Now you clamp down tight. This is fixin' to hurt like all hell."

Eli had always been a man of his word, and never more so than now. As the knife blade punched into the wound, Michael's body went stiff. He tried to suppress the scream but could not. It was the last thing he heard before he sank deeply into the ground, into a darkness which had no bottom.

Consciousness returned by fits and flickers, like

a lantern lighted, blown out, and lighted again. He felt as if someone had driven a white-hot poker into his shoulder and left it there. He raised his right hand, seeking the spot, and remembered that it was in the back where he could not reach. It occurred to him, when his mind cleared a little, that he had been unable to move the hand before. He forced his eyes open a bit at a time and found Eli seated on the ground, gazing anxiously at him.

"Good boy," Eli said. "I was afeered you wouldn't come out of it atall."

Consciousness brought the terrible memories rushing back. He asked plaintively, "Papa?"

"You're the only one come through it. How they overlooked you, I ain't got the slightest idee."

They hadn't overlooked him. Michael remembered the sergeant who had been left behind to dispatch him but had spared him instead. And he remembered there had been someone else.

"Cyrus," he said weakly.

"How's that?" Eli demanded.

"Cyrus. He was here." He could see the confusion in Eli's eyes, and he strained to get the words out. "He gave us away. He just rode off and left me."

He saw doubt in Eli's eyes. Eli probably thought this was a product of Michael's delirium. Eli said, "Not even Cyrus Blackwood is that low . . ." But he began to reconsider. "And then again . . ."

Tears scalded Michael's eyes as he thought of his father. "I wish they killed me too."

"Don't question the Lord and His gifts, boy. There's a purpose in all that He does."

Eli stiffened suddenly, and his hand darted toward the rifle he had leaned across Mordecai's body. He crouched, staring. Michael heard something. It sounded like a horse's hoofs, pounding softly in the grass. He thought, *They're coming back*.

"Run, Eli," he said. "Get away."

Eli put his finger to his lips in a sign for silence. After a moment he raised up, surprise in his face. "It's your papa's horse, Big Red. He must've got loose from them."

The horse nickered, then trotted up to Eli's mount.

Eli said, "God bless him, he come back lookin' for Jug." He pushed to his feet and walked cautiously toward the sorrel, careful not to startle him into running again. He caught the reins and led the animal up to Michael. "The Lord's sent him for a good purpose, son. Them two wild horses ain't fit to ride, and I been wonderin' how I was goin' to get you out of this place before them Spanish maybe circle back and finish the job."

Michael looked at his father's body. "What about Papa? You're not leavin' him just layin' here . . ."

"I got no choice, boy. I got nothin' to dig with, and there ain't no rocks hereabouts to cover him and the others. The dead are in the Lord's hands. I got to think of the livin'."

Michael cried out against leaving his father unburied, but Eli made no further answer. He lifted Michael up with considerable difficulty and got him into Mordecai's saddle. Michael thought the pain would bludgeon him back into unconsciousness, but it ebbed after he had sat slumped on the sorrel horse for a minute.

Eli asked, "Think you can stay on, or had I ought to tie you in the saddle?"

Thinking came with difficulty, but Michael said, "Tie me."

While doing so, Eli said, "Them two wild horses'll

be a right smart of trouble. I'd sooner turn them loose. But we'll be needin' cash money when we get to Natchitoches. Maybe they'll fetch enough to where we can pay our way."

Eli mounted Jug. Leaning from the saddle, he untied the two horses and led them. He had already jerked them around enough that the rawhide halters had made their noses sore, so they responded to his pull on the long leather reins. They followed, for resistance hurt too much.

Michael went along because he was too weak for resistance. He turned his head and looked back as long as he could see the place where his father and the other men lay sprawled in death.

"I don't want to leave him there," he cried. "Papa!"

Michael lapsed into unconsciousness off and on. It was well that he was tied to the horse. He had no idea how long they traveled before Eli came to a halt. He heard Eli mumble to himself, then say aloud, "You're about done, boy. We got to take the risk."

Michael had no idea what Eli was talking about until he became aware of a log hut, of a youth working with an ox team in a small field, pulling the animals to a halt as Eli rode out of the timber and moved toward him, leading Big Red and the two wild horses. The lad was little older than Michael, but he had the same dark brown face as the soldiers who had opened fire so suddenly. Michael felt hatred rise up through the pain.

Eli asked, "You speak English, friend?" The response was but a shrug of the shoulders. Eli spoke then in Spanish. The lad made a reply which Eli seemed to accept as favorable. Eli talked in a broken, halting manner. Whatever he said, the youth seemed to grasp it, and his brown eyes were sympathetic as he studied Michael, slumped and tied in the saddle. "*Pobrecito*," he murmured. He left the oxen standing and trotted toward the hut, leading the way.

Eli said, "He told me he hates the damned soldiers too. We got no choice but to trust him."

Michael lost consciousness when they lifted him from the saddle. He was vaguely aware of being carried into the hut and placed on a crude and lumpy cot. He was aware of a woman washing the wound clean and pouring something over it that seared like the iron hinges of Hell. Michael dropped away. When he finally came around, he saw the woman sitting in a rough, hand-made chair near his bed. Shadows from a small open fire danced against the mud-daubed log walls. He realized he had slept through the day, and it was dark outside.

"Eli!" he called, not seeing Pleasant anywhere.

The woman pushed quickly to her feet and came to his side. She said something he did not understand and pointed toward the door. She made motions like a horse in movement and gestured again, indicating distance. Michael understood only that Eli had gone off somewhere and left him in a strange place, with dark-skinned people he did not understand and could not like.

The grief and the loss and the burning pain threatened to overcome him, but he did not cry. He felt that nothing he might ever go through again could be as shattering as this awful day. He was done with crying. He made up his mind that he would never cry again.

The woman fed him some kind of broth, which threatened to come back up. He summoned determination to hold it down. Whatever it was, it helped, for in a while he felt stronger. He watched the woman feeding her children . . . four by his count . . . no, five. He blinked, because his eyes kept blurring. Sight of that family made him think of his own, back in Tennessee. They made him think of Mama, waiting now for Mordecai and Michael to come home.

Mordecai never would. And Michael was not sure *he* would either. He felt nearer to death than to life.

The hand-hewn wooden door swung open, and the dark-faced Spanish youth came in, followed by Eli Pleasant. Eli walked directly to the rough cot on which Michael lay. His eyes were anxious, but the anxiety faded when he saw that Michael was awake. "I was afeered I'd have to bury you too," Eli said.

"Too?"

"Me and Carlos Moreno here, we went back. We buried your papa and them." It was plain that he was exhausted.

Michael mustered a strong effort not to cry, for he had made himself a vow. "Thanks, Eli." Michael looked at the Spanish lad and tried to feel gratitude, but somehow the dark face got in the way. He said, "I ought to tell *him* thanks too, but I can't. He's one of them."

Eli blinked, not comprehending. "He ain't a soldier."

"He's Spanish, like the soldiers."

"You're seein' the outside of him. What's inside is all that really counts." Eli spoke in Spanish, and the lad nodded at Michael, smiling. Plainly, Eli had conveyed thanks that Michael had not expressed.

Eli said, "Found something." He swung his arm around from behind his back. He held Grandpa's old rifle. "I don't know how the soldiers come to miss it."

Eli and Carlos Moreno evidently had talked a lot. Eli said Lieutenant Rodriguez, in command of the soldiers at Nacogdoches, was a most cold-blooded *gachupín* whose sense of duty to the crown was of an order most extreme. He had come north from Bexar, killing those he found to be or even suspected of being in sympathy with the recent aborted rebellion. He had harassed outlying farmers like the Moreno family, seeking any excuse to punish them for transgressions real or imagined. Just recently, at this very place, he had murdered Moreno's father with his sword. Young Moreno had always heard the king was a just man, but he seemed to send the most unjust to do his work. Small wonder that embers of rebellion smouldered all over the land.

Michael's feelings against young Moreno eased a bit. His father too had been murdered by the officer named Rodriguez. Michael began to see through Moreno's brown skin to the loss they shared, and the anger.

Eli decided the next day to remain longer at the Moreno place, for Michael's pain and fever became worse, and he babbled deliriously at times. When Michael had lucid periods, he sensed that Eli was as nervous as a man tied on an anthill, going out of the hut often to look around. Eli did not speak of his fears, but they showed in his eyes.

They were justified. Just at dusk, Carlos rushed into the hut, pointing excitedly. *"Soldados!"*

Eli grabbed up his rifle from a corner and took two long strides toward the door. He seemed about to rush out, then pulled back. "Too late. They're already here." He flattened himself against the wall and waited, the rifle raised.

Michael licked dry lips and held his breath as the door slowly pushed open. A uniformed man cautiously stepped inside. In the dim light, it was a moment before recognition came.

The sergeant!

Eli poked his rifle into the sergeant's back. The surprised man raised his hands and turned slowly.

Eli said in a quiet fury, "You son of a bitch, I ought to kill you."

Michael raised his hand. "Eli, he's the one saved me . . . the sergeant I told you about."

Eli demanded something in Spanish. The sergeant gave him an answer, holding up one finger. Eli said, "He claims there's just one soldier outside." The sergeant turned back to the door and called to the trooper who waited in the yard with the horses. When the soldier came in, Michael recognized the youth who had remained with the sergeant at the killing ground under orders to finish the executions. He told Eli, "He was there too. Fired his rifle into the air."

Eli remained suspicious. He interrogated the sergeant vigorously. "He says he follered our tracks. Wanted to see if you was still alive and if you was goin' to make it across the Sabine." Eli's brow furrowed. "I thought you dreamed that stuff about Cyrus. But he says it was real."

"Told you," Michael said defensively. "Cyrus went off and left me to die."

Eli cursed under his breath. The sergeant moved close to the cot and knelt over Michael. He placed his palm against Michael's forehead, feeling for fever and finding it. He talked a moment to the woman, evidently giving her suggestions for more effective treatment. He took Michael's hand and squeezed it gently. He said something in Spanish.

Eli translated. "He says he's got a brother about your age. Says he seen you layin' there wounded, and all he could think of was his own brother."

The sergeant nodded and struggled for the English. "You go home, boy. You go home."

Michael stared up at the sergeant with contradictory and confusing feelings. The sergeant had been part of the detail that slaughtered Mordecai and the others. Michael did not know if he could forgive him that. But there had been compassion in the man.

Michael said, "Ask him what the officer would do if he was to find out they didn't kill me."

The sergeant replied in Spanish. Eli said, "He'd send the sergeant packin' off to prison. Might even shoot him."

The sergeant looked questioningly at Eli, who had lowered the rifle but had not set it down. Eli nodded and motioned toward the door.

Michael said, "Wait." He wished he knew the words. "Eli, I can't forget what they done to Papa and the others. But tell him I said thanks."

"He knows."

"Tell him I'd like to remember his name."

The reply was, "Elizandro Zaragosa."

Michael said, "Thanks, Zaragosa."

Zaragosa beckoned to the young soldier. Eli stood

at the door, watching the pair leave. Michael heard hoofbeats trailing away.

Eli kept vigil a while, then turned back to Michael. "There's good folks amongst the Spanish. Even amongst the soldiers. But if Zaragosa can find us, so can others."

By morning Michael's fever had broken. The pain remained fierce, but he sat up in bed and took some nourishment, a broth of some kind, and a thin, flat bread made of cornmeal. Eli went out frequently "to see about the horses."

He came hurrying into the hut, finally, his face flushed with anxiety. "Michael, boy, we got no choice. Moreno's neighbor just come. He says soldiers are headed this way. Ready or not, you got to ride."

He helped Michael to his feet. The dark little woman, Moreno's recently widowed mother, extended her hands, and Michael accepted them without having to force himself. He managed, "I'm much obliged," knowing she would not understand the words.

"*Vaya con Dios,*" she said.

Carlos and a younger brother had the horses ready. Eli and the youth lifted Michael into the saddle, and Eli swung up onto Jug, taking the reins to Michael's sorrel and the two wild horses.

"*Mil gracias,*" Eli said to the pair. Carlos shook Eli's hand vigorously. He reached for Michael's. Michael held back a moment, then accepted, ashamed for the hesitation. Eli thumped Jug's ribs with his heels and moved into a trot, leading Big Red and the two captured horses.

Michael looked back. The Moreno brothers were using small branches from a pine tree to smooth out the horse tracks. Eli moved quickly into deep grass where tracks would be less easily seen.

He said, "I'm glad you seen your way clear to shake that boy's hand. Them people put their necks up next to a noose for us."

"I know, Eli. But you saw what the Spanish done to Papa and them. The Morenos are Spanish too."

"Them two pirates that tried to kill you on the trail a ways back . . . they wasn't Spanish. They was Americans. You begrudge all Americans for what they done?"

"You know I don't. There's too many good Americans."

"Well, now you met some good Spanish."

Michael rode hunched, his body numb except for the fire in his shoulder. The passage of time meant little beyond the continuing pain. They rode until full dark, ate from a small sack Mrs. Moreno had given Eli, slept a little, and were traveling again by first light. Over and over, the massacre played through Michael's mind until every detail of it was burned into his memory too deeply ever to be erased or even blunted. He saw again and again his father's defiant rush against Rodriguez in the instant before the bullet struck him. He saw his father's head blasted apart, eyes that were open but did not see. Michael had memorized the cruel face of Rodriguez. He knew every feature, every line. He wanted to cry out in his grief and his pain and his anger, but he would not, not now, not ever again.

They came, finally, to the river. Eli paused only a moment, looking back over his shoulder as if expecting pursuit. None was in sight, but he proceeded as if it were. He put the horses into the water. Red followed eagerly after Jug. The wild ones resisted but little because the halters bit into noses sore and swollen.

The horses slipped and slid as they climbed the eastern bank. They reached the top, and Eli stopped to look back at the river. Michael looked too, remembering the day they had first crossed it. Texas had seemed a golden land, shining with promise. Now the Sabine was the boundary between sanctuary and Hell.

"Boy," Eli said, "we made it. We're out of Texas."

Out. Yes, they were out of it, but they had left much behind. Michael's throat swelled. His eyes scalded. "Texas owes me, Eli."

"Some debts a man just has to set aside. He can't collect them all."

"I don't know when and I don't know how, but some day I'm comin' back. Some way, *I'll* collect it all."

Eli grunted and set the horses into an easy walk, putting Texas behind them.

11

The people in Natchitoches were amazed to see Eli Pleasant ride in, leading two wild horses and a big sorrel with a half-delirious Michael tied in the saddle. Dark news had already spread about the massacre of the Tennesseans. Baptiste Villaret and his sons rushed down from the porch to help Eli untie Michael. Michael tried but could do little to help himself. He could not even focus his gaze on the people who lifted him down from the saddle and carried him gently through the door that a wide-eyed Marie Villaret held open for them. He saw her as if through a clouded glass, but he could hear her weeping with joy that he was still alive. Mrs. Villaret hovered over him, giving crisp orders to husband and offspring alike.

The Villarets put one of the smaller boys out of his bed and onto a pallet on the floor. In lucid moments Michael realized from the searing heat and the throbbing pain of the wound that it had become infected, that he stood in some danger of dying here in this strange place so far from Tennessee. He cared little, at first. Death would bring an end to the pain and to the constantly recurring nightmare of the fusillade, the death cries, the shattering sight of his father's face at the moment the Spanish bullet struck him. Mordecai's blood was a crimson stain that burned itself into Michael's soul and would remain there long after the clothing had been washed clean.

Again and again Michael awoke, crying out in the midst of a fevered dream. Usually he found the girl Marie sitting beside his bed, dark eyes soft in sympathy, her hands gripping his, trying to pull him up from the abyss and back to the reality of the moment. The olive color of her face would remind him that she too carried Spanish blood like the men who had murdered his father. At times he wanted to turn away from her, but he could not.

Once he dreamed his mother had kissed him. He reached for her, and his eyes came open. He saw Marie's face, inches above his own. She kissed him again, and he knew it had been only half a dream.

Little by little, the fever drained away. The swelling subsided. He had only the vaguest idea how many days it had been. Eli sat on the edge of Michael's narrow bed and said, "I'll soon be able to take you home to your mama and family."

That thought brought Michael a mixture of joy and dread. He would be glad to leave this alien place, he thought, this land where most people spoke in languages he did not understand and so many of them by the darker hue of their skin were a constant reminder of the terrible thing he had endured. But he dreaded facing his mother, his brothers, and sisters, having to tell them the brutal circumstances of his father's death. He was haunted by a recurring sense of guilt that the others had died and he had lived. It was as if by surviving he had somehow betrayed Mordecai and Old Man Wilson, the Macklins and the rest.

He tried to tell Eli, but Eli did not understand. Eli said, "It's every man's duty to survive if he can. He owes it to them that didn't, so he can keep on a-fightin' in their name."

Michael tried to tell the girl Marie. Her eyes watched him intently as he spilled out all his angers and doubts and fears. He realized she did not understand a tenth of what he said, for English was not her language.

Now that his mind was clear, he made it up that he would learn at least some French. He was stung by frustration when he tried to tell her about Tennessee and knew she did not comprehend. She would sit at his bedside and talk to him for an hour at a time, smiling, often laughing. He felt a strong sense of loss because he did not know what she was saying. But he enjoyed the music of her voice. It made him forget that her skin was darker than his own, dark like that of the soldiers in Texas.

He would point to his hand and ask her what the French word for it was.

"*Main,*" she would tell him, and he would point to his eye. "*Oeil,*" she would say.

"What's the word for *mouth*?" he would ask.

"*Bouche.*"

He would try to repeat and get the words for hand and mouth confused, and she would go into a fit of gentle laughter. He would tell her the words in English. She would repeat them until she had them down solid. She never seemed to mix them up; she always remembered.

"You're smarter'n I am," he would admit, glad she did not understand him. A thing like that could go to a woman's head.

By the time he was up and walking out onto the porch to take in the sun and the fresh air, he knew probably fifty French and Spanish words, mostly for the necessities such as food and the like. He had not learned how to string them together in any logical manner that would even approach normal conversation. Often he had trouble remembering which language a word belonged to, French or Spanish.

When Marie talked to him now he could pick out many stray words, though sometimes not enough to follow her full meaning. The words did not matter. He could read meaning in her eyes, in the tone of her voice. As he strengthened, as he became able to walk to the river and back unassisted, and without having to rest every few minutes, he could see a worry in her eyes that betrayed the forced levity in her conversation.

The day came when they stood on the bank together, watching flatboats drift on the Red's easy current. He heard a muffled sound and turned to find her crying softly. He asked anxiously, "What's the matter?"

She struggled to find the English. "Soon you go. Too soon."

"I have to," he said, wondering if she understood. "I got to let Mama know I'm alive. And I got to tell her about Papa."

"I wish . . . I wish . . ." She could not finish in English, so she spoke in French. He did not know the words, but he thought he knew what she meant.

"I know," he said. "In some ways I'm goin' to hate to leave. But I got to be goin' home."

She clung to his arm as if she feared to let go, lest he leave her now. "You will remember? You will not forget?"

He shook his head. "I couldn't forget."

She raised up on tiptoe and kissed him. He flushed, for he felt sure people were watching, but he did not resist or pull away. She broke free suddenly and ran, crying, leaving him there on the riverbank to make his slow way back to the house alone. He was flustered, uncertain, warmed in a manner he had never been before.

He could not understand exactly why, but something changed between them that day. No longer was he confined to the bed most of the time, and no longer did Marie come and sit in the chair beside him. If anything, he had the feeling that she began avoiding him purposely, though often he caught her watching him with sad eyes that she cut away as soon as he looked at her.

Cousin Frank had always told him there was something mysterious about women that a man was not supposed to understand. It must be true, for he did not understand Marie.

The day came soon when Eli saddled Jug and Big Red for the journey home. Michael did not see Marie at the breakfast table and asked Baptiste about her. Baptiste only shrugged.

"She does not feel well. She does not come."

An emptiness settled over Michael. "I'd at least like to tell her good-bye."

Baptiste avoided his eyes. "I will tell her you asked."

Walking out to the shed where Eli waited, Michael looked in vain at the window of the room where Marie slept. He saw no sign of her. Eli took a last tug at the rope that tied a pack on a third horse. He had managed to trade the two halfbroken wild horses for one old pack horse and enough of the necessaries to see them home, provided the hunting stayed good all the way. Eli asked, "You about ready, Michael?"

Michael had noticed that Eli no longer called him *boy*.

"I reckon so. I've said my good-byes. To 'most everybody, anyway."

He was still sore and weak, and Eli gave him a boost up into the saddle. Then Eli swung onto Jug's back and tugged on the long rope attached to the pack horse's halter.

The Villaret family was lined up on the porch, waving; all except one. Michael swallowed, waving back.

They had gone a little way up the street when he heard a welcome voice calling desperately, "Michael! Michael!"

He swung down from the saddle, needing no help. Marie ran to him, and he swept her into his arms. They clung for a moment. Tears streamed down her cheeks as she pulled away to arm's length. "Michael . . . I love . . ."

She turned and ran back toward the house, her head down. Michael stood slump-shouldered, watching until she disappeared through the door.

Eli waited a minute or two, then cleared his throat. "It's a long ways to Tennessee," he said.

The old man set an easy pace eastward, following the route they had taken coming west toward Texas. The traveling days were short at first, lengthening as

Michael gained strength and was able to ride longer without rest. Big Red had a comfortable gait and infinite patience. Michael could well understand why Uncle Benjamin had put so much stock in the horse, and why Mordecai had liked the animal.

Michael slept little the final night out, visualizing his home-coming, trying to compose in his mind what he should say to his mother and the family. It all evaporated when they broke out of the woods and came upon the field where the corn was ripening, its matured leaves rustling dryly in the wind. Michael's eyes brimmed as he saw his brothers and sisters working, harvesting the ears with knives, dropping them into sacks they dragged along the rows.

All work stopped suddenly as the youngsters turned to stare in disbelief. Michael's older brother Joseph and younger brother Andrew came to the pole fence, their blue eyes wide in wonder. Heather, Annie, and little James moved up uncertainly behind them.

Andrew spoke first, his young voice unsteady. "Michael? You ain't a ghost?"

Michael's throat was tight. "No, it's me . . . what's left of me."

The girls climbed the fence, joyfully shouting his name. He stepped down from the sorrel horse and hugged them, Heather first, then Annie, long and fiercely, while little James wrapped both arms around Michael's legs. He felt Annie's tears wet and warm against his cheek. They reminded him of tears he had felt in Natchitoches, and they mixed with his own.

Joseph kept staring. "But how? Cyrus said . . ."

Michael straightened, glancing up at Eli. "I'll be almighty interested in hearin' what Cyrus said. But later."

The field work was abandoned. All the young Lewises followed afoot as Eli and Michael rode to the cabin. Michael smelled the woodsmoke and looked at the rock chimney. There had always been something warmly reassuring about smoke rising from the chimney and curling upward into invisibility against the blue sky.

He swung stiffly to the ground, favoring his arm and shoulder. Andrew held out his hand to take the reins and silently pointed his chin toward the kitchen door. Michael took a deep breath and stepped inside.

Patience bent over the fireplace, stirring something in a blackened pot hanging low over the bright red coals. The baby Dora was asleep on a blanket on the floor.

"Mama?" Michael spoke.

She went stiff. She let the metal spoon slide into the pot and rubbed her hand against her apron. She turned slowly, almost painfully, her eyes full of hope and fear, of joy and despair. She spoke in a doubting whisper. "Michael?"

"Yes, Mama."

They stared at each other across the width of the room for a long moment, then both moved at once, into each other's arms. There were no words, not for a while.

Finally Patience drew back and stared at him, her eyes awash in tears. "Then Cyrus was wrong about you. Maybe about your papa too . . ."

Michael shook his head. "Not about Papa. They killed him. They killed them all except me and Eli."

She hugged him again, and cried a little. Eventually she said, "Joseph, you hurry over to your Uncle

Benjamin's. He'll want to know. They'll all want to know."

Joseph nodded. "I'll tell everybody."

Michael turned. "Don't tell Cyrus Blackwood." He glanced a moment at Eli, standing like a dark shadow in the doorway. Michael's voice went heavy and deep and sounded like Mordecai's. "Me and Eli, we'll want to tell Cyrus ourselves."

They came upon Cyrus by surprise. He was sitting on the ground with his back against a tree, watching his wife and sons and daughters harvesting corn from their poor, rocky little field. He shouted at one of the boys, "You, Isaac, you watch what you're doin' now. You're missin' some of them ears."

The boy Isaac was the first to see Michael and Eli. He dropped his sack and stared. Cyrus shouted at him, "Boy, don't you be goin' lazy on me now. Everybody's got to tote his share of the load."

Isaac kept staring until Cyrus finally turned. He seemed to blanch. He blinked, and his hands began to tremble. His right hand went to his ratty beard. It took a minute for him to recover sufficiently to push to his feet. He swayed, his mouth sagging open.

"No," he rasped. "You're dead. You're both dead."

Michael tried to speak but found his throat tight with pent-up anger. Eli spoke for him. "If we're dead, it was you got us killed, Cyrus. It was you that played the Judas." Cyrus sputtered and stammered. His trembling built until his whole body was shaking. "I had no choice. I didn't know they'd kill everybody."

Eli glowered. "They didn't kill Michael. You went off and left him to die."

"I didn't know." The voice was thin and barely audible. "I thought he was dead when I left."

Michael said in a building fury, "That's a lie. I was callin' for you not to go. You heard me."

Eli had not let Michael fetch his rifle over here. Now he knew why, for he felt his hands begin to tremble uncontrollably. If he had his rifle in them now he would probably kill Cyrus in the sight of his family. He felt an overwhelming urge to kill him anyway, without the rifle. He raised the shaking hands and reached toward Cyrus's throat.

Eli's fingers firmly gripped Michael's good shoulder. "That's enough, son, enough for now. Let's be goin' along."

Cyrus leaned against the tree to steady himself, and he managed a belated show of bravado. "All that's a lie, boy. I never done no such of a thing. You go tellin' people a lie like that and I won't stand for it, you hear me?"

Michael fastened Cyrus with a gaze that simmered in hatred. "I'll tell everybody who'll listen. I'll tell them you're a coward and a Judas. And if you come lookin' for me, bring a gun. I'll be damned easy to find! Come on, Eli, let's go home."

PART 2

THE
WESTWARD
TRACE

TENNESSEE, 1821

12

Michael Lewis felt a sharp tug against the pack mule's lead rope and turned to find the animal had tried to go around the opposite side of a tree from the horse he was riding. "Damn you, Jethro!" He regarded the move as stubbornness rather than stupidity. The mule had stoutly resisted bearing the heavy weight of Michael's winter fur catch and had given in only to a determined will more stubborn than its own. Twenty-one now and going on twenty-two, Michael could respect a strong will, for he had one by inheritance from his father Mordecai. But he had made up his mind that when he sold his pelts he would sell the mule along with them. Respect and acceptance were not the same.

Michael was done growing. At six feet he was as tall as his father had been, and sometimes people who had known Mordecai reacted with startled eyes at the sight of Michael. They swore he had become the image of Mordecai Lewis, rangy and strong, his face beginning to take on the stone-chiseled edges, the stern jaw that had been the mark of his father, though at the moment it was hidden by a winter's growth of whiskers. His blue eyes could be severe and unyielding, yet had the same faraway look sometimes, as when Mordecai had dreamed of distant places yet unseen. But people remarked that there was more pain in Michael's, and occasionally a quicker flare of anger. Considering what those eyes had witnessed, they said there was good reason.

With the first sharp cold spell of the winter, the field work finished, Michael had gone off by himself deep into the woods as had been his custom the last several years. He had slept in a tent sometimes. Other times, when he expected the camp to last a while, he would throw up a rude log shelter against the snow and the bitter winds, running his traplines in wild country where white men's boots had seldom trod. He had encountered other men only three times all of this past winter. They were like himself; eager for a brief visit with their own kind, for the sound of kindred voices, then just as eager to set off again, alone. They were solitary men who accepted loneliness as the price of putting behind them the noisy demands of other humankind, the clang and clatter of so-called civilized life.

Michael no longer wondered what had drawn his father so often to the woods and had kept him so long from home. He knew. A man could think, and no one would ask what he was thinking. He could talk to himself, and no one would interrupt to ask what he meant. He could listen to the voices of the forest, speaking in a thousand tongues, and learn to understand them all.

When old memories and old fears threatened to

smother him in the dark of night and he awoke shouting and fighting, there was no one to question or blame or pity. He could confront his private torments in his own way, and no one else would know.

Restless, his older brother Joseph said of him, but Michael was only restless at home, on the farm, or in the settlements. Except when the dark dreams came, he was not restless on the trail, in the forests, or camped on the rivers. There he could find a measure of peace, of contentment that escaped him where people lived in clusters.

Like his father, his mother said, and Michael accepted that as a compliment, though he was not sure Patience always meant it to be one. She had been taken hard by the death of Mordecai Lewis. She had been fearful of it for years because Mordecai had not been one to seek out the safe and easy path or long abide one if he happened across it. She had worn the widow's black a respectable period while Uncle Benjamin had watched over her family as if it was his own. When he and Patience decided a proper time had passed, he had made the two families one, taking Patience to bring warmth back into a home left cold by the death of Aunt Nancy. And, in due course, the combined family grew once again with the addition of a baby boy named Jonathan.

Now the boy was three years old, and still Michael could not quite bring himself to call him *brother.* It was a hell of a thing, he knew, to blame a child so young, so unaware, but Michael could not help it. He could not quite accept this final affront to his father's memory, this symbol that his mother had accepted a place in the bed of another man, even his own uncle. He had moved back from Uncle

Benjamin's farm to the old claim, ostensibly to help brother Joseph keep up the place. Ownership had passed to Joseph, the eldest, as was the custom. Joseph had taken excellent care of it, as he had from the time he was old enough to handle a mule and a plow by himself and take on the responsibilities that should have been Mordecai's. A hard worker, Joseph was, a man who knew what he wanted from life and believed the way to get it was to irrigate the growing-ground with sweat. Michael found no fault with him, but his interests were often different from Joseph's. Michael understood Joseph's ways better than Joseph understood Michael's. They came to disagreement at times, never in a bitter manner but never quite finding a compromise agreeable to them both.

Late last year, when the crops were laid by, Joseph had taken himself a wife, a farmer's daughter from down on Buck Holler, a niece of Old Man Wilson who had died with Papa in Texas. She was a dandy girl, good-looking, handy with the pots and the skillet, but she and Joseph had no need of anyone except each other right now. Michael had been glad to light out for the woods with the winter's first chill. His brother Andrew, nineteen, going on twenty, and fully able to hold up his end on any problem that might arise, had wanted to go with him. But Michael had preferred to spend the winter alone to sort out his thoughts, to see if he could arrive at some plan for the future. He could not see spending another spring and summer on the old farm where everything brought back his father's memory. He no longer felt there was a real place for him there, compromising the privacy of the newlyweds. And though he loved his mother and respected his uncle, the larger farm was not for him either. Now the grass was rising, the birds were finding their way north, and the shape of the future remained as elusive as when he had set out months ago to find it.

Ahead of him, Michael saw a fork in the trail. He knew he must soon make a decision about another fork in another trail, and he had no idea which direction he might take.

For now he took the right-hand fork that would lead him to Miller's Crossing. Sizemore Miller had been a friend of his father's and now was a friend of Michael's, running a little trading post where a man could buy a few necessaries for the trail or get a jug of decent-enough squeezings or even sell a mule-load of pelts if he did not fancy going all the way back to the settlements where prices tended to be higher.

The mule brayed when the log structure came in sight around a bend in the trail, and from a pen somewhere in back another mule answered him in a raucous voice. A man came out onto the small porch and stood waiting, wiping his hands on an apron tied around his middle. Michael knew at a glance that this was not his friend Miller; this was a stranger. The place was littered with trash. Sizemore Miller had always been as fussy as an old woman about cleanliness and order.

"How do," Michael said, reining up, taking a careful look around before he stepped down. His rifle lay across his lap, and he kept his hand upon it, for not all the wolves ran on four legs. He had learned that in a bitter way on the trail to Texas some five years ago. Strangers were suspect until he had time to size them up.

"How do," came the reply, backed by a smile that

looked as false as its wooden teeth. "Git yourself down and come on in. You look like a man who ain't hefted a jug in a spell."

"Where's Sizemore at?" Michael asked suspiciously.

"Gone west. Sold me this place and lit out as soon as the grass begun to rise. Gone to seek his fortune."

Michael's jaw sagged in surprise. "He didn't say nothin' about it when I come by here last fall."

"Bound for Louisiana, so he told me. Hopin' they might open Texas up for settlement some day soon. You've heard of Texas?"

Old memories rushed back unbidden. Michael said in a strained voice, "I've heard of it."

The man on the porch motioned toward a row of posts. "Tie up your beasts and come on in and have a drink with me." He gave the mule's load a moment's study. "Would you be interested in sellin' that pelfry?"

"That's what it's for, if you're willin' to pay me fair return for a winter's work."

Michael tied the horse and mule and stepped up onto the low, narrow rough-planking porch. He paused a moment, looking up at the roof over his head. It seemed unnatural, after these long months under the sky and the trees. He followed the proprietor through the open door into the gloom of a log building that had only one window. He blinked and gave his eyes a moment to adjust themselves. He saw two men sitting on a bench and leaning against the back wall. One of them passed a jug to the other and said without enthusiasm, "Howdy, Michael Lewis."

Michael stared at him, trying to see beyond a winter's growth of ragged black beard, not unlike his own. "That you, Finis Blackwood?" He made no move to walk over and shake hands.

"It's me," Finis said. He made no move either. Studying him, Michael decided Finis was looking more like his father Cyrus all the time. One thing the world didn't need was more people like Cyrus Blackwood.

The proprietor said, "You-all are friends, then? Well, a friend of Finis Blackwood's is a friend of mine." He extended his hand. "My name's Ephraim Crow."

Michael accepted the hand with reservations. Any friend of Finis Blackwood's was automatically suspect. "How do," he said.

Crow shouted, "Fleetie! Fleetie girl! You come out here and bring us a jug of that best corn liquor, you hear me?"

Michael heard a woman's voice from somewhere in the back, mumbling something unintelligible. She came through a door that led to a shotgun-shaped set of rooms in the back. She was hardly more than a girl, barefoot, long hair hanging raggedly toward her waist, mercifully hiding part of a plain home-spun dress that lacked any semblance of color. Her face was comely enough, Michael thought, but her eyes were dull and without life. She seemed to be walking in some dream of her own; he suspected she was not of whole mind.

Somehow, seeing her carried him back to another girl, the black-eyed French-Spanish Marie Villaret, who had sat so often beside his bed while he was recuperating from his wound. He wondered why she came to his mind now; there was no comparison between her and this unfortunate creature.

Michael found Crow appraising him carefully.

Crow said, "I don't reckon you've seen a woman in a while, have you?"

"Not since fall," Michael replied. "That your daughter?"

"Naw. She's just an orphan girl I taken pity on and give a home to. Does the cookin' and the cleanin' up around here. And whatever else I tell her to."

Michael was keenly aware that the girl was watching him with something like resignation. Her eyes made him uncomfortable.

Crow pulled a corncob stopper from the jug she had brought and handed it to Michael. "Take you a snort of that, why don't you? You'll feel like you just shot a bear."

Michael lifted the jug. The whiskey burned like fire going down his throat, and kept burning all the way to his stomach. Aside from that, it was not bad.

"Made it myself," Crow declared, "so I know just whatall's in it. Have yourself another."

Michael shook his head. "One's enough. I don't believe in drinkin' till the tradin's done. You want to take a look at them pelts?"

"Ain't no big hurry about it." The girl gave Michael a look that he took for invitation and went back through the door. Crow's gaze followed her. "Tell you what: why don't you go back yonder and play with Fleetie a while? Take all the time you want. I'll look at what you got on that mule, and when you're done with the girl I'll bet you we can come to terms."

Michael frowned, looking toward the door where the girl had gone. He was stirred to resentment that Crow thought him so lacking in morality. "Sizemore never offered nothin' like that."

"I carry a fuller stock of merchandise."

Finis Blackwood spoke up. "She's better than his whiskey. I've tried them both."

Revulsion made Michael's stomach turn. The girl was a slave, or next to it, he realized. It was not that he had any strong principles against a man and a woman doing what their natures bade them do; it was just that he hated the thought of the woman having no say in the matter, or in this case perhaps not the mind to realize she *should* have any say.

Somehow he pictured Marie Villaret helplessly caught in a trap like this. The improbable image stirred him to an unexpected anger. He took a step backward, toward the door. "Much obliged for the drink. I'll be movin' on."

Crow frowned. "Fleetie's waitin' for you."

"I don't hold with such as that."

"You accepted my whiskey. Ain't you goin' to even let me make you a bid on that pelfry?"

Michael saw Finis and his companion stand up and set their jug on the floor. He sensed that they were moving to Crow's aid. He kept backing up until he reached his rifle that he had left standing beside the door. He lifted it in a manner calculated to carry a quiet warning without being an open threat. "I'll leave you a bait of venison for the whiskey. I ain't seen nothin' here that I especially like. Includin' your friends."

Finis Blackwood muttered, "You've always had a big mouth when it come to us Blackwoods."

Michael replied, "I ain't said half of what I was thinkin'." He backed out across the porch and untied his horse and mule. Crow and Blackwood and the third man came onto the porch and watched him untie a leg of venison. He pitched it to the rough pine floor at Crow's feet. "That's a lot more than I owe you."

Crow did not speak, but his eyes said the incident was not yet over. His gaze went to the pack mule, and Michael could read the calculation. It was a long way to the settlements. Many an accident might yet befall the unwary. Michael gave Finis Blackwood and the other man a quick study. He had been hearing ugly rumors about Finis for some time now. Barns had been burned. A couple of men had disappeared. In every case, Finis had had a grievance. Finis had *many* grievances. Michael decided he might just as well have one more.

He said, "I'd take it real unkindly if anybody was to foller after me." He swung into the saddle and laid the rifle across his lap, its muzzle not quite pointing at the men on the porch.

As he rode away he saw the girl standing by a back door, shading her eyes with one hand, watching him without any expression that he could discern. He wondered again why this dull-eyed drudge, traded like a piece of poor merchandise, should make him think of Marie, whose dark eyes had been full of life and energy and emotion.

So long as he kept looking behind him, he could see the three men still standing on the porch, watching him as closely as he watched them. The dim trail shortly made a turn back into the timber, and the trading post was out of sight. Michael suspected a council of war had begun there. Pulse quickening, he touched his heels to the horse's ribs and moved him into a brisk trot. The mule Jethro reluctantly stepped up its pace after a moment's stubborn resistance to the lead rope.

It occurred to him that his friend Sizemore Miller might not have left this place voluntarily. He might not have left at all. It was not beyond reason that he might be buried in some dark and hidden place out in the timber. Such things happened.

After three or four miles he came upon a shallow creek running a little higher and muddier than usual because of spring rains. He paused a moment to look back and listen. The mule pranced nervously and kept him from hearing if anyone might be coming along his backtrail. But intuition told him someone was. He led the mule out into the creek, then turned downstream and went perhaps fifty yards before he rode out again on the same side he had entered. He circled back through the woods toward the trail, dismounted, and tied the two animals where the timber would hide them. He took his rifle, his shot pouch and powder-horn, and walked back toward the trail, careful to remain behind the underbrush as much as possible. Near the trail he settled down on his heels, his rifle across his lap, and waited.

The wait was short. He heard them before he saw them, horses coming from the direction of the trading post. He crouched low but was able to see through the foliage. Crow had not come. There were just the two, Finis Blackwood and his companion, moving at a fast trot. Both carried rifles across their laps. He heard the murmur of conversation before he was able to make out the words.

As they neared, he heard the stranger saying, "I don't know as I hold with killin' somebody, Finis. Don't seem like a mule-load of furs is worth that much."

"But we can't just take the furs and leave him go. Soon's he gets home he'll have the law after me."

"Law's been after you before."

"It ain't caught me at nothin'. And it won't this time. We'll bury him where there won't nobody find him. They'll just figure the Injuns got him or some varmint did, or he froze to death durin' the winter. Crow said he'll pay us right well for them pelts and for the horse and mule."

Michael gritted his teeth, the anger rising like tainted meat trying to fight its way back up. He waited until the two men had put their horses into the water before he arose from his hiding place and shouted, "Stop where you're at!"

Finis Blackwood whirled his horse around, but his companion halted dead in his tracks and sat there as if frozen, the muddy water washing around his horse's legs. Finis's eyes were large as he stared at Michael, and at Michael's rifle pointed right where his black moustache met his nose. He stammered, "Michael! We wasn't lookin' for you here."

"But you *were* lookin' for me. Well, now you've found me. You talked mighty big about how you'd kill me and take my winter's catch. Let's see you start."

"Now, Michael, you got awful poor hearin' if that's what you think we was talkin' about. It was the farthest thing from our mind to do you any harm. Me and Bilks, we was just startin' on our way home, is all."

"My hearin' is fine. Now the first thing I want you-all to do is to drop your rifles."

Finis went slack-jawed. "In the water?"

"In the water."

Finis had his hands on his own rifle, lying across his lap. He could bring it around to bear upon Michael in the winking of an eye. He said, "There's two of us, in case you ain't counted."

"I can count."

"You can't get but one of us," Finis said. "The other one'll have you before you can spit."

Michael nodded. "I know that. But what *you* don't know is which one of you I'll kill. You might want to study on it."

Finis's companion settled the matter without studying much. He dropped his rifle. Finis had to think about it, but after a moment's further consideration of the weapon pointed at his nose, he let the rifle slip out of his lap and into the running creek. There was an instant of foam atop the brown water, then no trace. Michael reasoned that the two rifles' weight probably would not let them be carried far, but it would take a long and diligent search in ice-cold water to retrieve them. "Now your shot pouches and powderhorns," he said. "Everything."

Finis protested, "This is a wild ol' country."

"It won't be half as wild with you disarmed. Do it!"

Finis muttered but followed orders. Bilks complained about the high price of powder and lead. Michael told him, "It's gettin' on to plantin' time, and you'll be too busy to go huntin' for a while anyway. All right, you-all can ride back out of the creek. But I want you both to stop on the bank."

Bilks whimpered, "You ain't fixin' to kill us, are you?"

Finis put in, "He won't do that. Them Lewises ain't the kind that shoots unarmed men. But they'll kill a man's reputation, accusin' him, talkin' about him behind his back."

Michael said, "If you mean your ol' daddy, I ain't said anything behind his back that I ain't told him to his face. And lookin' at you, I'd say the blood is runnin' true."

Finis declared, "The Blackwood family ain't goin' to tolerate your loose talk forever, Michael."

"If you think it's just talk, you come and try me."

Finis eyed the rifle. "You got the gun."

"I have. And the gun says for you-all to get down and take the saddles off of them horses. Now!"

Finis whined as he unfastened the cinch. "You ain't fixin' to take our horses, are you?"

"I'd be afraid to show up in the settlements with them. They're probably stolen." When the saddles were on the ground he said, "Take the bridles off of them." He watched that done, then ordered, "Now whip them into a run; both of them."

Finis started to protest, but Michael stood firm. Finis cursed and struck his horse sharply across the rump with the bridle reins. Bilks was a little easier, but his horse went pounding back down the trail with Finis's in a hard lope, head held high in a manner that indicated he would not stop running until he reached the trading post.

Michael said, "Now, I figure by the time you-all find your rifles in that creek and walk back to Crow's place, you oughtn't to be interested in comin' after me again. And I sure won't be interested in seein' *you* anymore. But if I *do,* my friendly nature is about used up."

Finis Blackwood's eyes were narrowed almost to the point of being closed, but the cold anger showed through. "You Lewises are a high and mighty bunch, big landowners and all that. But the higher you climb, the farther you'll fall. You'll wish you hadn't seen me today."

"I *already* wish I hadn't seen you, today or any other time. Now, I'm fixin' to be on my way. I want you-all to stand right there where I can watch you till I'm plumb gone."

When he retrieved his horse and mule and crossed the creek, he looked back one last time. Finis and Bilks were wading in water above their knees, looking for their rifles.

13

Michael went first to the old farm because he felt more at home there than on Uncle Benjamin's place, though the farm now belonged to his older brother Joseph. He paused at a nearby creek to shave so Joseph's wife Emily would not have to look at the whiskers that had protected his face all winter. He carried with him a freshly killed fat doe so he would not be a burden at his brother's table. As he expected, he found Joseph in the field, spring planting in the newly warmed soil. Emily stood at the edge of the freshly turned rows, and Michael knew at a glance that all the planting had not been done in the field. She showed every sign of approaching motherhood.

Uncle Michael, he thought. *Damned if that won't take some getting used to.* It seemed not so long ago that he had been a small boy himself, following along after Joseph as his younger brother Andrew in turn had followed after *him. Time moves too fast anymore.*

Joseph laid the plow over on its side and walked out to the end of the row to stand by Emily, his arm around her, as Michael approached. Emily smiled. She had the same sparkling blue eyes as all the Lewis women, possibly one reason Joseph had been drawn to her. Joseph studied the mule-load of pelts. "Looks like you had a good winter," he commented.

Michael glanced at Emily's stomach, pushing out conspicuously. "Looks like you-all did too."

Emily blushed and looked down. Joseph squeezed his wife's shoulder. "The baby'll be here early in the summer, best we can tell. You ought to find *you* a wife, Michael. You don't know how much you're missin', sleepin' out in the woods."

Michael could not help thinking about the slow-moving girl he had seen at Crow's place and comparing the blank look in her face to the glow he could see in Emily's. *You're lucky people, both of you,* he thought. *But this life's not for me.* Joseph was a farmer, with his feet firmly planted on the ground, his future set right here on this place. Michael had no plans, not even an idea what his future might hold. How could a woman—any woman—understand the dark memories and dreams that haunted him and sometimes drove him away from other people?

Joseph asked, "You'll stay a while, won't you?"

"The night. Then I'd best ride on over and see about Mama and them. They all right?"

Joseph said, "Everybody's made the winter in good shape. You ought to see your little brother Jonathan. He can already ride a horse, and he can see a squirrel farther than I can."

"Poor kid is ruined for life," Michael observed. That was the way *he* had started, and probably Papa too.

Emily said, "It won't seem right, our little 'un havin' to call him *uncle,* and there won't be but four years or so of difference between them."

Uncomfortably Michael considered that Joseph had called Jonathan *brother,* but he was not . . . not a full brother, anyway. That thought still troubled him, even so many years after his mother's remarriage. In the faces of his other brothers and sisters he could see a little of Papa. In Jonathan's, he could not.

He unsaddled the horse and took the pack from the mule, staking them on grass a little way from the double cabin. He felt ill at ease sitting long in the kitchen with Emily, for it was her kitchen now, not his mother's. He drank a cup of coffee with her, then went outside, picked up the chopping ax and attacked a big woodpile that Joseph had built up during the long winter months when there was no field work to be done and when the snow was not too deep for him to drag deadfall timber out of the forest. By the time sunset brought Joseph trudging wearily in from the field, trailing behind the work mule, Michael had built up a goodly stack of wood cut to fireplace length. It was a chore no woman in Emily's condition should be expected to do for herself, he thought, and Joseph's long days in the field would make it difficult for him to find the time.

The way Emily kissed Joseph at the door, a stranger might think they had not seen each other in a month. Michael felt like an intruder and turned back to the woodpile to fetch an armload of the newly cut fuel for the fireplace. He gave the couple a little time before he walked through the kitchen door and stacked the wood neatly within easy reach of the fire. The smell of a woman's cooking could make a bachelor reassess his condition, he thought. So could the warmth in Emily's eyes as she looked at her husband. It made Michael feel lonely.

I wish it could be for me, he thought. *But it isn't.*

Joseph wanted to hear about Michael's winter. There was not much to tell, so it did not take long. Michael mentioned stopping at Miller's Crossing and finding a new proprietor there. For Emily's sake he did not mention the girl Fleetie. "Man's name was Crow," he said. "Claimed he bought out Sizemore Miller, and Sizemore went west. You reckon he really did?"

Joseph shrugged. "I ain't heard about Sizemore, but there's been stories about people goin' yonderway, tryin' for Texas."

Emily frowned. "I couldn't ever go there, not after what happened to my Uncle Amos, and you-all's daddy. I don't see how anybody could go. It must be a terrible place."

"It is," Michael agreed darkly. "And yet . . ." He could not finish expressing the thought, for it seemed a hopeless contradiction. He often remembered his exhilaration in the size and freshness of the land, how it had seemed a brand-new piece of world never touched by man, how his father had taken to it with an enthusiasm Michael had never seen. But always the idyllic part of the memory would be shattered by the intrusion of an opposite side, the fear, the sudden violence, the horror of wholesale murder.

Joseph said, "Don't worry, Emily. You're a Lewis now, and you can bet that no Lewises will ever go to Texas again."

He looked to Michael as if for support. But Michael fixed his gaze on coals that flared red, then darkened as their inner heat surged and ebbed in the fireplace. His mind carried him back to long-ago campfires far away, campfires where he had sat with his father and the others, pondering the mysteries of an immense land new to them all. Those men were like ghosts now, ghosts who walked through his fretful dreams in the night and invaded his restless mind during the day. Times, it was almost as if he could hear his father calling him.

There was no way he could explain that to Joseph, much less to Emily. He said, "It's been a long day. If you-all will excuse me, I think I'll go spread my beddin'." He added thoughtfully, "Out yonder in the shed."

He always dreaded returning to his uncle's farm. It was not that Uncle Benjamin did not greet him like a long-lost son, for he invariably did. He knew his uncle regarded him as one of his own. The problem lay within Michael himself. The rare times when he was able to look at his image in the mirror, he saw Mordecai Lewis there. It was, in a sense, as if Michael had taken over much of his father's role. But Uncle Benjamin had undertaken that role too. Try as he might, Michael could not get over the feeling that they were somehow competitors. Worst of all, though he tried never to show it, he could not reconcile himself to his mother's acceptance of Uncle Benjamin in Papa's place, especially as that acceptance was manifested in the little boy Jonathan.

Dora was no longer the baby of the family.

It was Uncle Benjamin he saw first, and he had to force himself through the pretense that he reciprocated all the good feeling he could see in his uncle's eyes. Benjamin hugged him, told him he was glad to see him home—though Michael never quite accepted his uncle's farm as home—and congratulated him on the good winter's catch carried by his mule. Michael's younger brothers came up out of the fields to greet him, Andrew breathless from running so he could be the first. James, eleven, was taking his time. He had more of Joseph's quiet reserve. Andrew, almost twenty now, threw his arms around Michael as if he had returned from the dead. He had, once, and Andrew had never quite conquered the dread of that experience.

Andrew declared, "I wish you never would go out again like that. We never know if you're ever comin' home."

"I always come home," Michael told him. But an inner voice told him he *had* no home, not anymore. *Home* was something vague, some place out yonder in the forests, or beyond the rivers, some place like his father had sought all his life and never found. Michael often wondered if *he* would ever find it.

Heather was sixteen now and filled out in the first full bloom of young womanhood. She kissed him quickly, then pulled back. Dora, edging up on seven, looked like Annie used to look, back when Papa went away. She kissed Michael as Heather had. Annie, thirteen, was still the most demonstrative in the family. She threw her arms around Michael's neck, hugged him hard, let him go, but then hugged him a second time as if once just wasn't enough. She still favored Michael, seeing Papa in him.

His mother's greeting was silent but long. She held him as if she feared to let him go, lest he not return.

She looked him up and down. "You're a poor cook, son, thin as a slab of bacon. Like your papa always was, comin' home."

"I've never starved yet," he assured her. "A few days of yours and Heather's cookin' and I'll flesh out like a hog on acorns."

He saw contentment in his mother's eyes. Gone was the anxiety of the old days when she had worried constantly over Mordecai—when he was coming home, *if* he was coming home—all the time shouldering not only her responsibilities but his. If anything, she looked younger now than she used to. Michael would have to give Uncle Benjamin credit for that. Times, before he could catch himself, he would almost get to thinking she would have been better off to have married Uncle Benjamin in the beginning instead of Papa, and to have let Papa go on roaming the way his natural bent had always led him, without anyone left behind to encumber him with guilt. Michael never let such thoughts run too far, for they seemed disloyal to his father. Had it happened that way, he and his brothers would not be here.

Except perhaps Jonathan. The boy clung to Michael's leg and repeated his name over and over, begging for attention. Michael started to reach down for him but could not complete the move. He saw the hurt in his mother's eyes. She said, "He's your brother."

"Half brother," Michael replied, then wished he hadn't.

Patience stared into Michael's eyes until he had to look away. She said with regret more than rebuke, "You're a good man, Michael. You're much like your father . . . *too* much at times. But he had one thing you seem to've lost. He had understanding. He would've understood how your Uncle Benjamin and I needed one another. Your father didn't know how to show love sometimes, but it was always there. There was a side to him that you couldn't know. Only a woman could."

Michael's face burned. He looked at the boy still clinging to his leg, begging him to go see some new kittens in the shed.

Patience said, "Maybe Texas burned that out of you. But if you can't find a way to get it back someday, you'll be a lonely man as long as you live."

Michael placed his hand on Jonathan's head and held it there a minute, then forced himself to lift the boy up into his arms. Quietly he asked, "Where'd you say them kittens are?"

At supper he announced his intention of going to the settlement the next day to see about selling his furs and the mule. Benjamin Lewis questioned him at some length about the animal. Michael guessed he was considering buying it himself and he tried to spare his uncle some grief by describing all of Jethro's worst habits.

Benjamin Lewis was a man who knew mules, so he was easy to discourage. "I've been needin' another because we've got so many hands now to help with the plantin'. If it's all the same with you, Michael, I believe I'll ride along with you and see if I can happen upon a good mule for sale."

Michael was never totally comfortable around his uncle anymore, but he knew no graceful way to decline. He put on the most pleasant face he could manage. "You'd be welcome."

They were up at daylight to load the pelts on the mule and to saddle their horses. By the time that was done, Patience and the girls had breakfast ready. Afterward Benjamin assigned all the boys to their respective jobs.

"Frank, I want you to ride out and see if you can find that old brindle milk cow. She's bound to've had her calf by now. James, you take a hoe to those weeds in your mama's garden. They're sappin' the moisture we'll be needin' to get the first vegetables up. Andrew, I wish you'd get started plantin' that south field."

As the boys hustled off to their respective jobs Benjamin Lewis watched them with satisfaction. He said something Michael had heard from him a hundred times. "Idle hands invite the devil's work instead of the Lord's."

Michael said, "I expect you're right. The Blackwood boys are proof enough if any was needed." He had not mentioned his run-in with Finis Blackwood; it would just cause unnecessary fretting by the family.

Benjamin nodded and swung into the saddle. "I can't see much sign any of them'll turn out better than their old daddy Cyrus. Drinkin' all the time . . . gamblin' . . . fightin' . . . I do believe they'd rather shed blood than sweat. Ain't one of them does any more work than he absolutely has to keep from starvin' to death. Well, maybe Isaac. He'll work a little."

Michael never saw much of Isaac, the one who had chunked rocks at him and Andrew the time they had fought over rightful possession of a doe Michael had shot. Isaac worked for wages on various farms and sent money home to help feed other family members whose ambition was not as strong as their appetites.

He said, "Last fall, before I went to the woods, I heard Isaac was in jail."

"He was. They let him out at Christmas. Isaac has a hard time holdin' a job for very long. He'll fight anybody who'll give him a reason, and he's not choosy about the reason."

Like all the Lewises, Benjamin studied the sky a lot, trying to find there some clue about the weather to come. Riding along, he looked up at the eastern sky, where the sun was already taking the spring cool from the morning air. The coolness felt good, but the crops needed warmth to grow. "Been a cold winter," he said, "but I do believe this spring is goin' to be a warm one. Good for the corn."

"I'd reckon so," Michael responded. He was unable to find much enthusiasm for the crops. He preferred the winter, and the trapping.

He felt Benjamin's eyes appraising him at much length, and he was vaguely ill at ease. Benjamin said, "There's a nice meadow over yonder that I've been wantin' to break out and put into somethin' useful. I just haven't had the time. If you'd be willin', I'd turn it over to you on the halves. I'll furnish the mule and the plow and the seed. You furnish the labor."

Again Michael began searching for some graceful way to turn his uncle down. "That'd be almighty generous of you," he said, stalling for time. "Too generous, I'm thinkin'."

"You're a grown man now, Michael, and needin' to be on your own. This'd be a chance for you to start at a profit to us both. I'd figure out some way that in a little while the land would be yours. I've got more than I can properly see to, even with so many helpin' hands."

"I'll study on it," Michael promised, trying not to frown. He felt the cool west wind at his back, and he turned to face it. He fancied he could hear a calling in it from the silence of the past. Papa maybe, way out yonder.

His uncle caught the look. "I've seen that same thing in your father's eye, many a time. He was always lookin' over the next hill for his fortune, but it never was there. The fortune is here, in the soil. It don't come easy, Michael. A man has got to grub and sweat for it. But at the end of the day he can look back on his labor and know it's good. He can sit in his own cabin of an evenin', by his own fire, and take pleasure in seein' that his woman and his young'uns are properly fed, and he can feel justified in the eyes of the Lord. There's happiness in that, happiness I don't think your father—God rest him—every really knew."

Michael had to disagree. "There was a happy side to Papa, one you probably never got to see much, because it mostly showed on him when he was out in the woods, or on the trail. I saw it on our trip to Texas. You're a farmer by nature, and happy at it, but he wasn't. He was miserable tryin' to *be* one, as miserable as you'd've been if you'd tried to be a woodsman like he was.

"Everybody is born to walk his own way. You're content with yours, and I'm glad you are. But I've got too much of Papa in me. I just ain't found yet where I belong."

Benjamin puffed thoughtfully on a corncob pipe. "Some men *never* find where they belong. They live miserable, and they die that way."

"There's got be someplace for me. If I keep lookin', I believe I'll find it."

"I hope you do. But in the meantime, there's still that meadow. And my offer stands."

"Maybe for this season. I'll do some studyin' on it."

His eye caught a movement at the edge of the woods, so quickly gone that he could not tell what it was. A deer, most likely, he thought, until a horse nickered from somewhere out of sight amid the trees, and his own horse looked quickly in that direction, its ears alert. He considered it strange, for horses did not often stray far into the woods; they found little grass in the constant shade. And a man would seem foolish to be riding through the woods when there were good beaten trails to be had, or the broad openings where Michael and his uncle rode.

He felt the first stirring of alarm, and his fingers tightened on the long rifle that lay across his saddle. He carried it always, for one never knew when meat might be had for the table. "You see anything out yonder, Uncle Benjamin?"

Benjamin had heard the nicker, but he showed no concern. He had ridden this trail a hundred times or more. "Probably just a hunter," he suggested. "He'll scare off all the game, breakin' his way through that brush on horseback."

Michael saw a flash and a puff of smoke. He heard the impact of the bullet against his uncle's body before the sound of the shot traveled the distance. Benjamin gave a cry of surprise, then slipped from the saddle and fell in a heap on the ground.

It was Texas, all over again. One shot this time instead of a volley, but Michael's reaction was instinctive, conditioned by memories lived over a thousand times in his mind. He stepped instantly from the saddle and dropped to one knee, bringing the rifle up. He saw a movement in the timber, a man on horseback, whirling about. He took aim as the rider paused a moment, evidently tangled in some undergrowth. Recognition came an instant before he squeezed the trigger.

Finis Blackwood!

The pan flashed, then the rifle roared. Through the black smoke he thought he saw the rider jerk suddenly. Whether he was hit or reacted out of fright, Michael could not know. He saw the horse break into a run, the rider bent, ducking the low limbs in headlong flight. Before Michael could begin to reload, horse and rider were out of sight.

Turning back to his uncle, he felt his lungs ache. He had held his breath from the instant he had seen Finis fire the shot.

He looked into Benjamin's glazing eyes and knew the bullet had struck him hard.

Good God, he thought. *He taken what was meant for me.*

14

Benjamin Lewis had been struck high in the chest, toward the right shoulder. His breathing was ragged, his face going gray with shock. For a moment, staring down at him, Michael could see only his father, shot five years ago in Texas. The same anger and desperation swept over him. But this time, at least, he was not helpless. He tore open his uncle's shirt. A glance told him the wound was bad. He looked around quickly, calculating the distance back to his uncle's house. A family named Baxter lived closer; he could see smoke rising from their chimney a half mile away.

"Can you hear me, Uncle Ben?" At first he saw no response, then Benjamin's lips moved. Michael thought he was trying to say *yes*. He said, "I've got to get you onto a horse. I'll take you to the Baxters'."

The mule Jethro had panicked and run away, back in the direction from which Michael and Benjamin had come. Benjamin's sorrel had run a hundred yards and stopped, but Michael's horse stood waiting where he had stopped. Michael caught the reins and led the horse to where his uncle lay. He raised Benjamin to a sitting position. "I'm goin' to put you on my horse now. Think you can help a little?"

Benjamin nodded weakly. He tried but had little strength. Michael strained and grunted, getting him to his feet, then lifted him into the saddle. He put his own left foot in the stirrup and swung up behind the cantle so he could hold onto his uncle. "This is liable to hurt like hell," he warned, "but it won't take us long to get there."

He put the horse into a walk for a minute. Then, satisfied he would not let Benjamin fall, he moved into a long trot. As he came upon the Baxters' field he saw a man and two half-grown boys working there, the man behind two mules and a moldboard plow, the boys picking up large stones the plow turned over and carrying them to the edge of the field. Michael shouted and waved his hat. The man halted the mules and stared, then comprehended that there was trouble. He unhitched a mule and jumped upon him bareback, running to catch up while Michael proceeded to the cabin.

One of the boys was sent to fetch Patience while Michael and Baxter probed the wound and extracted the bullet. Benjamin had lapsed into unconsciousness early in the operation, which Michael thought was merciful. He well remembered the time Eli Pleasant had performed a similar operation upon him, under even cruder circumstances.

For a time Michael felt little pulse and saw no sign that his uncle was breathing. A little of the old Texas feeling of helplessness came over him. It took all the strength he could muster to put it down. He did so by letting anger rise in its place.

The Blackwoods! It seemed that every time a calamity struck the Lewis family, a Blackwood was behind it. Finis had set out to take revenge upon Michael because of what had happened near Miller's Crossing. He had shot the wrong man by mischance or poor marksmanship.

Benjamin Lewis lay on a rough bunk, his face still gray, his breathing so faint as to be almost imperceptible.

Michael declared, more to himself than to his uncle, "We ain't takin' this. We ain't takin' it atall."

He heard the rattle of trace chains and the rumble of steel-tired wagon wheels. He strode to the cabin's door in time to see his brother Andrew help his mother down from the wagon. Patience rushed toward the cabin, her eyes fearful. Michael stepped out to meet her and put his arms around her. "You'd better be prepared for the worst. It don't look good."

Patience Lewis was a strong woman. She had to be, for she had raised her family and had taken care of one farm or another by herself for much of the time she had been married to Mordecai. She said, "Let's be seein' to him, then."

He thought he might have to grab her when she took her first look at Benjamin, but she was of sterner stuff. Her moment of shock was quickly past. She summoned up all the strength that years of self-sufficiency had given her. "I don't understand. Benjamin had no enemies."

Reluctantly Michael admitted, "But *I* have. That bullet was aimed at me."

"If you know who it was, let's notify the law."

Michael said grimly, "I'll take care of it." He realized his mother misunderstood his meaning, thinking he intended to notify the officials. He let her keep the comfort of that error, for she had more than enough to grieve her. He studied the deep sadness in her eyes and knew, if he had not already, how much Benjamin Lewis meant to her.

He said, "I'd best be gettin' about it."

Patience caught his hand. "Won't you stay with me until we know?"

"Andrew'll be with you. There's nothin' I could do here that he can't." He bent and kissed his mother on the forehead, then turned to summon his younger brother with a nod. Andrew followed him outside, into the sunshine of a warm spring day.

Andrew eyed him suspiciously. "You ain't really goin' to the settlement, are you?"

"I'm goin' to *make* a settlement."

He had not told Andrew who had shot Benjamin, but he felt that his brother knew intuitively. Andrew had always had an uncanny knack of sensing things. Besides, he was aware of the intended robbery at the crossing. Andrew said, "I'll go with you."

"It was me he was after. It's up to me to settle it."

"There's a bunch of them Blackwoods. I could watch your back, at least."

"You stay here and watch Mama. Worst comes to worst, she'll need you real bad."

Andrew frowned. "You be careful, then. It'd be almighty hard on her to lose two of you the same day."

"She ain't lost either one of us yet. Uncle Benjamin may be a farmer instead of a woodsman, but he's a Lewis just the same. He's a fighter."

One of the Baxter boys had caught Uncle Benjamin's sorrel and the pelt-laden mule and had brought them to the pole pen. As Michael mounted his horse he pointed his chin toward the mule. "You'd just as well take the pack off of him. I won't be gettin' to the settlement with him for a while yet."

He hunched in the saddle as he rode away, shoulders burdened by the task ahead of him.

He had shunned the Blackwood place in the years since his return from Texas, for it stirred bitter memories and pain. He could not see that it was one bit improved since the time he had come here and accused Cyrus to his face. The fields showed but little sign of spring plowing and planting. Old weeds from last year, their stems dried hard as rawhide, stood testament to the heritability of shiftlessness. Not a soul was working in the fields, though this was a time when every able body should be there.

Atop a gentle slope stood a double log cabin whose walls had not been plumb the day they had gone up, and now they swayed lazily to the north as if waiting only for a strong wind to lay them over. Chickens prowled the yard, scratching for bugs and worms. The work stock stood idle in a pen carelessly thrown together with timber of all sizes and lengths. Michael wondered if anybody had bothered to feed them.

He heard a shout and saw a young boy running toward the cabin. Cyrus Blackwood came out onto the narrow porch with a rifle in his hands. He was flanked by four of his sons, ranging in age from Luke and Isaac down to a boy of eight or ten whose name Michael did not even know. Finis should be there, he thought, for he was the oldest. Michael checked the powder in the rifle's pan, then rode boldly up to the porch. He felt hostile eyes fastened upon him, and he tried to return the look in kind.

"I've come to see Finis," he declared. "Where's he at?"

Black-bearded Cyrus took a half step forward. He jerked his head toward the cabin door. "He's in yonder."

Michael started to dismount. Cyrus brought up the rifle. Michael stopped, his leg half over the horse's back. He said, "Finis has got a-plenty to answer for."

When Cyrus did not reply, Luke declared, "So do you, you son of a bitch."

Michael stared hard into Cyrus's eyes. Cyrus tried but could not hold. He lowered his eyes and the muzzle of the rifle. Michael finished dismounting and looped his reins over a post set in front of the porch. "I'm comin' in." He walked directly toward Cyrus. Cyrus waited until Michael was almost within arm's reach, then took one step to the side. When Isaac saw his father was caving in, he stepped in front of Michael.

Michael said, "My quarrel is with Finis, not with you."

Cyrus said, "Let him go on in, Isaac. Let him see the damage he's done." His voice held more sadness than anger.

The old lady Blackwood sat in a hand-made wooden chair beside a rude bunk. She was holding a handkerchief to her eyes. In the close and choking gloom of the place Michael saw Finis Blackwood lying on the cot. He saw bloody cloths scattered on the floor, and one wrapped around the stump of Finis's right arm. Finis's face had the same gray look Michael had seen in his uncle's. Finis was unconscious. He looked as if he might even be dead.

Mrs. Blackwood's eyes smouldered with hatred as she arose from the chair. Bitterly she said, "If you come to finish the job, there ain't much left for you to do."

Cyrus Blackwood said, "His arm was shattered. We'uns had to take it off. Proud of yourself, Michael Lewis?"

Michael had come with every intention of killing Finis if he gave the least excuse. He had not come to see him butchered up like this. "Are you sure you had to? Maybe it could've been saved."

"There wasn't enough left of it. He like to've bled to death before he got home. There's still a big chance he ain't goin' to make it."

"He fired first," Michael said stiffly. "He shot my Uncle Benjamin. *He* may not make it either."

It was as if Cyrus and the others did not hear him, as if it made no difference to them what Finis had done. Cyrus said, "You been achin' to take revenge on us Blackwoods ever since what happened to your pa. But you oughtn't to've shot my boy to take out your grudge against *me*."

"I shot Finis because he shot at *us,* and not because of what you done to Papa and them."

He could tell that his explanation meant nothing. These were a people who recognized no wrong of their own and no right of anyone else. He looked once more at Finis and thought it probably would have been better had he killed him outright. If he were to say so, he would probably not leave this place alive.

He said, "I'm sorry for you, Mrs. Blackwood. The same way I'm sorry for my mother."

He saw something leap into her eyes, something beyond anger, beyond even hatred. He saw a wildness there, a stern and vengeful will that reminded him of a sow bear defending her young. He had long wondered what held this family together all these years against the shiftlessness and improvidence of old Cyrus Blackwood. Now he knew. She brought her face up so close that he could feel her breath. Her eyes crackled.

"Now you hear me, Michael Lewis. We got that boy yonder to see after right now. He may yet die. If he don't die, he'll be a cripple the rest of his life, just a part of a man. But whichever way it goes, my boys'll be comin' after you. I'll send Luke first, and if Luke don't get you, I'll send Isaac to help him. If them two don't get you, I'll send the others. If *they* can't get you, I'll kill you myself. And if any of your folks gets in the way, we'll kill them too!"

Michael felt a cold chill raise the hair on the back of his neck. Cyrus and the boys might bluster and bluff, but this old woman meant what she said.

She pointed to the door. "Git now, before I take a notion to finish it here!"

Michael moved slowly, trying to let them know he was not afraid of any of them, and he was not, except for the old lady. He felt as if he had been trapped in a den with a mama bear. He warned her, "Don't send anybody you can't do without."

He knew the warning was hollow, for chances were that when they came he would be able to do nothing. They would not face him and give him an equal chance; they would shoot at him from ambush as Finis had done. And more than likely they would do the same to anyone else near enough to be considered in the way or to bear witness before the law. He hoped the Blackwoods could not see the cold chill that ran through him and made his skin feel as if it were crawling.

He did not look behind him as he walked across the narrow porch and out to his horse. They could easily shoot him in the back, and a strong sense of dread told him they were considering it. But to let them see that dread would be weakness, he thought, and the last thing to show a Blackwood or a snarling dog was weakness. He swung up onto the horse before he stole a glance toward the cabin.

Isaac, third oldest of the Blackwood sons, had followed him partway out from the porch. Michael said quietly, "Isaac, I've always thought you had some sense. Tell her it's gone far enough. There's been blood spilt on both sides."

"It's gone beyond talkin' now. You heard her. You seen her eyes. As long as you stay in this country there'll be people killed. Maybe you, maybe us. And maybe some of your folks. I wish I could say different, but I'd be lyin' to you. So watch yourself, Michael. From now on take every breath like it was fixin' to be your last, because one of them will be."

Michael rode away, his skin still crawling. He could almost feel a rifle pointed toward his back, but he would not let himself turn and look.

He knew when he rode up to the Baxter cabin that the worst had passed. The farmer met him at the horse pen, and he was smiling. "I do believe your uncle's goin' to make it. He come around a while ago and talked a little. Seemed real pleased to find your mama there. I think that helped him more than anything *we* done."

His mother met him at the door. She hugged him briefly, out of relief, then pushed him away and looked at him. "You went to the Blackwoods', didn't you?"

He glanced accusingly at his brother Andrew. Patience said, "Andrew didn't tell me. I can figure things out for myself. I hope you didn't . . ."

He shook his head. "Wasn't no use. I'd already done about all there was to do."

"He's dead?"

"No, but he's shot up some." He thought that was enough to tell her for now. "How's Uncle Benjamin?"

"He ought to live if he don't get blood poisoning."

"If we're goin' to take him home, we ought to do it before the damp night air sets in."

She nodded. "You and Andrew get the team hitched to the wagon. I'll see if Mrs. Baxter can give us the borry of some blankets."

Andrew drove the wagon with all the competence of a professional freighter, picking the smoothest ground so he would not jostle Benjamin any more than he could help. Michael rode behind, leading Benjamin's horse and the reluctant pack mule. His mother looked back two or three times before she said, "Why don't you come up and ride alongside of us?"

Michael could not help glancing toward the woods which lay off to the left, within rifle range. His skin prickled. He doubted that any of the Blackwoods would already be trying to set an ambush for him. But if they did, he did not want his mother or Andrew or Benjamin in the line of fire. He evaded by saying, "This mule is crazy enough that if somethin' was to spook him, he might jump right up into the wagon."

They came, finally, to Benjamin Lewis's farm. Michael felt part of his burden lift, but not all. Even as he and Andrew and cousin Frank carried Benjamin into the house, he cast a glance back over his shoulder toward a dark grove of trees which could handily hide a man. The range would be long, but a good shot could do it.

Andrew gave him a searching look. "You all right, Michael?"

"Sure I'm all right. Why wouldn't I be?"

He helped carry Benjamin to his bed and saw to it that he was made as comfortable as was possible. The little boy Jonathan cried to know what was wrong with his father. The house seemed to close in on Michael, and he had to go outside. He stood in the open dog-run, staring off toward the grove, knowing he was a target but grimly determined not to let them make him a prisoner in the house.

He tensed as he heard someone come up behind him. The boy Jonathan, frightened by what he had seen inside, put his arms around Michael's leg and clung tightly. Michael looked uneasily toward the grove, then back to the boy. "Jonathan, you'd better go in to your mother."

The boy clung until Michael pulled him free and pushed him toward the door. "Go on now!" Reluctantly Jonathan went, but he looked back, hurt and disappointed.

Andrew came out into the dog-run. He glanced toward the grove and seemed to read Michael's mind. Andrew was strongly given to joking, most of the time, but he was dead serious now. "They wouldn't shoot a little boy like that."

"They might shoot at me and hit him, like Finis hit Uncle Benjamin. Next time it could be any of you."

"We can't all hide in the house. We've got to get on about our business and take our chances."

"As long as I'm here I'm a danger to all of you. Looks like I got no choice but to go."

"Where to?"

"I don't know. Someplace. Maybe I'll find out when I get there."

"I'll go with you."

"You don't even know where I'm goin'. Neither do I."

"It don't matter. If it suits you it'll suit me."

"Sometimes I'm not a pleasure to be with."

"You're my brother. I can stand it." Andrew looked toward the grove again. "I think you need the company. And if them Blackwoods trail along, you could sure use some help."

"No, Andrew. I might get you killed."

"You're not gone yet. Think on it some." Andrew went back inside. Michael's gaze turned to the west. A soft breeze had picked up, bringing with it the pleasant spring smell of the new grass and the wildflowers, the freshly turned earth with its winter-stored moisture yielding up to the wind and the sun. It brought memories, fleeting fragments at first, then whole pictures. He remembered another time, another place, when the same fragrances had stirred him.

He tried to dismiss the thought, but it would not

go away. He told himself it was the last place on earth he wanted to see again.

But the breeze was relentless, and Texas would not leave him.

15

Morgan's store was larger and enjoyed a livelier trade than Sizemore Miller's obscure place on the trail down at Miller's Crossing. Around its original log structure a settlement of sorts had grown, and with the settlement the store had expanded a little at a time, each new addition not quite fitting architecturally with those that had preceded it. This mattered not at all to the frontier clientele, whose tastes ran to utility rather than to esthetics. The first log structure was now a storage area at the back, and the store's front was built of sawed lumber, rough but sturdy, a credit to a thriving modern community.

Storekeeper Oscar Morgan spread Michael's winter catch of pelts on his front porch and studied them with a critical eye practiced to discover any flaw. But Michael felt Morgan would be honest with him, within the natural limitations of his calling.

Morgan said, "I always thought the world of your daddy. But with all due respect to him, you've got these pelts in better shape than he ever did. Morde-cai lacked your patience, I'm thinkin'."

At the moment Michael did not feel patient. His rump prickled with impatience to be about the business and gone. "You're in a good place to hear things, Mister Morgan. Do you know anything about Texas openin' up to settlement?"

"I hear there's been another try by some damn-fool named Long to take the country over. It blowed up like all the other tries. Them that didn't get killed are prisoners." His look turned quizzical. "You ain't studyin' on goin' there, are you? You, more than anybody I know of, ought to consider Texas barely one notch better than Hell."

"Just thinkin' it might be a good idea if I went *someplace*. I'd be much obliged if you wouldn't say nothin' to anybody." He helped Morgan stack some of the pelts so the storekeeper would have room to take a closer look at others.

Morgan said, "It might be a good thing if you *was* to go somewhere. Nobody's goin' to think the worse of you for it."

Michael frowned. "What do you mean by that?"

"Luke Blackwood was here a while ago. Done a lot of talkin'."

Michael looked around quickly. He had been so intent on getting the pelts sold that he had not considered the possibility of an attack by the Black-woods right here in the settlement.

Morgan said, "He bought him a jug and was gone before you come. Probably hunted him a place to lay up and get drunk." Morgan frowned. "Every-body around here knows the Blackwoods won't stand up to you. You're your daddy all over again, with the same grit he had, and they're afraid of you.

They'll strike you from ambush, like a snake. There ain't no shame in a man turnin' his back on a hopeless situation like that."

"I ain't gone anywhere yet."

"But you should. The sooner the better. Come on in and let's figure out what I owe you."

Michael took part of his pay in supplies, like powder and lead, a couple of new blankets, a pair of strong, heavy boots. Finding neither Morgan nor anyone else in the settlement much in the mood to buy or trade for his contrary mule, he packed his goods on its back. Before leaving the settlement he looked carefully for any sign of Luke Blackwood but saw none. His senses keened by Morgan's warning, he held to the open places, departing from the trail wherever it led near timber that might furnish Blackwood concealment within rifle range.

The trail crossed a place known as Buck Holler where there stood the cabin of an early settler named Wilson, father of Joseph's new wife and brother to old Amos Wilson who had died with Papa in Texas. Michael watered the horse and the mule, then rode up to a garden where the jovial Wilson was planting beans. Wilson came to the fence to say howdy and shake hands and inquire after Benjamin's health. Michael assured him his uncle would recover.

Wilson said exuberantly, "Him and me are fixin' to be granddaddies, you know."

It grated on Michael that Wilson now seemed to consider his brother Joseph to be Benjamin's son rather than Mordecai's. It was as if Benjamin had completely replaced Mordecai for everybody except Michael. Michael sidestepped the subject. "Seen anything of Luke Blackwood?"

Wilson seemed to catch the urgency behind the

question. "He come by early this morin', ridin' toward the settlement. Ain't seen him come back." The joviality was suddenly gone. "You don't reckon your trouble with them Blackwoods might spill over onto your brothers, do you? My little girl'd be caught right in the middle."

Michael did not know how to give him a satisfactory answer, so he did not try. "I'll tell Uncle Benjamin that you inquired after his health." He turned away.

Wilson waved. "If I was you, I'd go over and kill all them Blackwood boys like you'd kill out a den of snakes. That'd put an end to the trouble."

Michael said distastefully, "I'd have to kill the little'uns as well as the big'uns, because they'd get to be big'uns someday and come huntin' me." He left Wilson to his planting.

He made a wide swing around the place where Uncle Benjamin had been shot, for it seemed a likely place for the unimaginative Luke to try to set up an ambush. Michael found the farmer Baxter milking his cow. Baxter said he had not seen Luke. He made somewhat the same general suggestion about the Blackwoods that Wilson had except a little less sanguine.

"They ought to all be put in jail for the good of the community," he declared. "As for Finis, it's a damn shame you wasn't a better shot."

Michael led the mule by the cabin he had been sharing with Andrew and his cousin Frank and some of the younger boys. He dropped off the supplies there, then led the two animals down to the pen to turn them loose. Little Jonathan was playing in the barn, chunking rocks at some half-wild cats kept there to control the mice. Michael told him, "If one of them cats ever gets his claws into your butt, you'll wish you'd left them alone."

Andrew came down to the barn and watched Michael unsaddle. He pointed his chin at the mule. "Thought you was goin' to get rid of him." He smiled. "I reckon them settlement folks are good judges of a mule."

"I reckon they are," Michael admitted ruefully. "Couldn't find anybody who wanted him."

"I saw what you brought back with you. Looks to me like you're fixin' to make a trip."

The boy Jonathan caught the comment. "Where you goin', Michael? Would you take me with you? Please?"

Michael shook his head. "Ain't said I'm goin' anywhere, yet." He pushed the subject aside. "How's Uncle Benjamin?"

"Stronger today," Andrew replied. "He's tough, like Papa used to be."

Michael said grittily, "*Nobody's* like Papa used to be." He picked up his rifle and started out the gate, then turned. "You comin', Jonathan?"

The boy picked up another rock and started looking for the cats. "Mama didn't call supper yet."

"Well, you'd better be listenin' when she does. I ain't comin' out to hunt for you."

Andrew walked up to the house with Michael. He said, "That kid thinks you're the greatest man in the world, except for his daddy. You treat him like he's a stray dog instead of your brother."

"*Half* brother," Michael corrected him, then realized how narrow that sounded. He added, "I don't intend to be thataway. It's just . . ." He realized he could not articulate his feelings. He did not fully understand them himself. "The boy's all right. It's me, not him."

Andrew said pointedly, "Papa'd've been crazy about him. Jonathan's a Lewis. He's one of us."

Michael did not like feeling guilty. "I'll go fetch him when suppertime comes."

He looked first into the kitchen, where his mother and sisters and girl cousins were fixing supper. Then he went to his mother's and uncle's bedroom on the other side of the dog-run. Benjamin Lewis was propped up in his bed, a feather tick covering only the lower part of his body. His shoulder and chest were swathed in bandages not much whiter than his face. But Michael could see strength in his eyes, deep blue eyes that reminded him too much of Papa.

"Did you get everything sold?" Benjamin wanted to know. "The pelts? The mule?"

"The pelts. Not the mule. I guess I'll just have to learn to out-stubborn him some more."

Andrew put in, "Michael can do that, all right." He was still inclined to look for the humor, something Michael seemed to lack.

Benjamin smiled. It looked good on him, Michael thought.

"So what now, Michael?" Benjamin asked. "You studied any more about that meadow I offered you?"

"I've thought about it." Michael could say that with honesty. He did not want to worry his uncle with the rest of it, though. So far as he knew, nobody had told Benjamin about the Blackwood family's threat.

"Well then," Benjamin pressed, "what do you say?"

Michael knew he was going to have to tell him no. As he cast around for the best way to say it, cousin Frank pushed the door open. Urgency was in his eyes. "Michael, I've got to see you. Now!"

Puzzled, Michael told his uncle, "I'll be back," and followed Frank out into the dog-run.

Excitedly Frank said, "I was just comin' up from the field when I seen Luke Blackwood run his horse out of that grove yonder and up to the back of the barn. He's got a rifle."

Michael had propped his own rifle outside the door to his uncle's room, on the dog-run. He grabbed it. A sudden realization struck him. "The barn? Jonathan's out there."

Frank's eyes widened. "You stay here out of sight." He left the dog-run at a brisk pace, moving toward the barn. "Jonathan! Jonathan, come here to me."

A rough voice called from the barn door. "Frank, you stop where you're at! Don't you come no closer."

Michael's throat went dry. He knew the voice.

Luke Blackwood shouted, "I've got this boy here. I'll trade him to you for Michael."

Jonathan cried out, "Mama! Papa!" His voice was more angry than fearful.

Frank stopped halfway between the house and the barn and looked back over his shoulder. "He's got him, Michael. I can see them both."

Luke Blackwood shouted louder. "Michael Lewis! That you up yonder? I want you, Michael. You come on out here and I'll let this boy go."

Michael's heartbeat quickened. He had no doubt that if he went, Luke would kill him. But if he did not go, Luke Blackwood was the sort who might

very well take out his frustrations on a small boy.
Michael's breath came short, and his hand went
wet with cold sweat against the rifle. But he pondered for only a moment, for he saw no choice. He
stepped out, away from the dog-run, into the open.
"I'm comin', Luke. Let the boy go."

Luke said nothing until Michael had walked up
even with Frank. Then he shouted, "I want you to
fire that rifle into the air, Michael. Then lay it down."

Michael said, "You let the boy go first."

"No. You do what I tell you."

Michael saw the anxiety in Frank's eyes. The
whole family doted on Jonathan, except Michael.
He held the rifle tightly against his shoulder and
raised the muzzle high, then squeezed the trigger.
The report echoed across the fields. He carefully laid
the rifle on the ground, along with his powder-horn.
His eyes locked solemnly on Frank's. He could see
a promise there. Whatever happened, Luke Blackwood would not get away.

Michael walked toward the barn. He could see
Luke now, and Jonathan, between the logs that
made up the horse pen. Jonathan was struggling to
break free. Luke had a grip on the boy's arm with
his left hand. With his right he held a long rifle pre-
cariously to his shoulder.

Michael said, "Let him go now, Luke."

"I want you a lot closer, Michael. If you try anything, I'll shoot this boy."

"You can't, Luke. You've just got one shot, and if
you use it on him, you know I'll get you. I'll kill you
with my hands."

His hand was on the gate. He slid open the bar
that held it. The gate swung heavily on rawhide

hinges. He stood then, twenty feet from Luke Black-wood, and looked him in the face. He saw fear in Luke's eyes. But he also saw murder.

He said, "You won't get away from here, Luke. There's other Lewises at the house, and guns. You can kill me, but you'll never get to that grove. Turn the boy a-loose."

"This boy is what's goin' to get me away from here alive."

Michael could have argued with him, could have told him he was justified in shooting Finis, that Finis was crippled through his own doing. But such argument would be wasted, as it had been wasted at the Blackwood cabin. So he stood and looked silently into the muzzle of the rifle. He remembered another day and other rifles and felt the same dread churning his stomach.

He saw the intention in Luke's eyes a second before Luke made his move. To stabilize the rifle he had to turn Jonathan loose and bring his left hand up to the long barrel. In that moment Michael made a quick move to his right. Jonathan broke free, then turned angrily and kicked Luke on the shin. Luke vacillated in confusion, trying to watch Michael while he booted the boy away. The rifle barrel wobbled. Michael saw the pan flash and threw himself to the ground. As the rifle roared, he knew Luke had missed him.

Luke knew too. He stared a second in wild terror as Michael pushed himself to his feet. The boy clung to Luke's pants leg, trying to kick him again. Then Luke turned and vaulted across the fence, dropping his rifle as he hit the ground. Stopping to pick it up, he sprinted to where his horse was tied. Michael grabbed the top rail of the fence and swung himself over. He landed awkwardly and went down. He saw Luke's horse shy away in fright at Luke running headlong toward it. The horse broke the tied bridle rein and jerked free. Luke grabbed at what was left of the rein, swung into the saddle, and drummed his heels in panic against the animal's ribs. In his haste he had dropped his rifle a second time, and he did not stop to pick it up.

Frank Lewis came running, loading Michael's rifle as he moved. Andrew hurried from the house with another rifle, but he was considerably behind.

Jonathan angrily hurled a rock at the fleeing Luke, but it went hardly beyond the fence. He seemed unaware of the danger that had just passed him by. Michael grabbed him up and hugged him. "Little brother, you've got a lot of spunk. By God, you *are* a Lewis!"

Frank Lewis braced the rifle against a corner post and took a bead. The bullet kicked up dust just ahead of Luke's running horse. Still holding the boy in his arms, Michael said, "Frank, I think you'd better stick to farmin'."

Andrew reached there just as Luke's horse was about to plunge into the grove. He took a wild shot for luck but had none.

Michael said, "It's just as well. If you'd killed him the rest of the Blackwoods'd be after the whole family, and not just after me."

Andrew grimaced. "I'd hate to be the one has to wash his britches tonight. He won't be comin' back."

But Michael remembered the fury in Old Lady Blackwood's eyes, and the thing she had said: *"If Luke don't get you, I'll send Isaac to help him. If them two don't get you, I'll send the others. If they can't get you, I'll kill you myself. And if any of your folks gets in the way, we'll kill them too!"*

He had no doubt that she had meant every word. Luke was only the first. He saw Patience, hand over her alarmed eyes, moving quickly toward the barn to see what the commotion had been about. Michael's younger sisters followed her. He set Jonathan on the ground. "You'd better run to your mama. She's frettin' about you."

Jonathan did not go. He took Michael's hand. "Who was that man, Michael? What was he so mad for?"

"Some people are just mad all the time, like some boys are good all the time. Now, you be good and go to your mama."

Patience reached the gate and knelt, swinging Jonathan up into her arms. Her eyes asked the question; she had no need to put it into words. Michael felt a twinge of guilt even though he realized it had been none of his fault. The boy in her arms had been in jeopardy for Michael's sake.

Andrew told her, "Luke Blackwood had Jonathan. He used Jonathan to make Michael go to him."

Patience moved up close to Michael and studied him with grave concern. "I heard shots."

Michael shrugged. "Nobody's hit. That's the main thing."

She held the boy tightly. "He may come back."

Michael knew now that he had no choice. "I'll leave him no reason to."

By the stricken look in her eyes, he knew she understood his meaning. There was no need to add to the pain by putting it into words. She said tightly, "Supper's about ready."

Michael nodded. "We'll be along directly."

He watched her walk back toward the house, the boy still in her arms, the girls following. He turned to Andrew and Frank. "I can make a few miles before dark. Even if they was to come at daylight, they'd be too late. They won't know where to start lookin' for me." He glanced regretfully at the horse and mule he had turned loose in the pen a little earlier. "Looks like there'll be no rest for the weary."

Cousin Frank argued, "We could all go over to the Blackwoods' in a bunch and let them know that the Lewises stick together. Maybe they'd back off."

Michael knew better. "They stick together too. We'd just set off a family feud, and kill each other one or two at a time till there wasn't nobody left, hardly. We've known it to happen with other families. I don't intend for it to happen to this one, just because of me."

Frank offered, "Then let me and Andrew go with you."

Michael shook his head. "Frank, Uncle Benjamin won't be able to work much for a long time, and there's a-plenty to do with spring just started. You bein' the oldest, it'll be your farm someday. Your place is here helpin' your daddy."

Andrew said, "But it won't be *my* farm. I'll have to go out and find my own. Let me go with you, and we'll find us one together."

The temptation was almost overpowering. Of all his brothers, Andrew was the one most like Michael in many respects, attuned to the forest, the trail, yet he could be equally at home in the cornfield or working with the handful of cattle the family owned.

But there were too many reasons not to accept. The chance was slim, to be sure, but there was at least an outside possibility that the Blackwoods might manage to follow Michael and exact the price the old lady had set. He thought it unlikely that they would leave Andrew unharmed if he got in the way, and having all the Lewis determination, he would most certainly get in the way. Even if the Blackwoods did not find them, there was the great uncertainty about what lay ahead. One Lewis already lay buried in a faraway place. Michael did not intend for Andrew to risk the same fate.

He said, "I've always traveled best alone. And fastest." He turned toward the house, putting argument behind him.

Supper done, he went into Benjamin Lewis's room and took his uncle's hand. Benjamin had already gotten wind of Michael's plans, and he understood the reason behind them. Benjamin squeezed Michael's fingers with more strength than Michael had expected. Benjamin asked heavily, "When you goin', son?"

"I'm fixin' to leave now."

Benjamin stared at him a long, silent moment. "You'll need a better horse than the one you've got. Take Big Red."

"He didn't bring Papa any luck."

"Wasn't the fault of the horse. You'll be glad you taken him." Benjamin gave him a sad study. "You're like one of my own sons to me, Michael. You leavin', it's almost like havin' a death in the family."

Michael nodded solemnly. "But that's why I'm leavin', so there won't *be* any. Once I'm gone they'll have no reason to bother the rest of you."

"Your mother'll take this hard, like the time your daddy left and never came back."

"She's strong. She's got other family. And she's got you." He looked away, surprised that he could bring himself to say it.

Benjamin squeezed Michael's hand again. His eyes misted. "I didn't agree with your daddy about some things, but he was my brother, and I loved him. When I look at you, I can still see him, like when *he* was twenty-one. He'd be proud of you, Michael. *I'm* proud to be your kin."

Michael said with total honesty, "And I'm proud you're mine."

His mother watched while he hugged his sisters, Annie the last, then his brothers. She walked out into the yard where Andrew held the sorrel horse and the pack mule, waiting for him. All there was to say, she said with her eyes. She hugged him hard, then stepped back and let him go.

As he rode into the woods, he turned for a last glance. She was still standing there watching him go, as she had so often watched his father leave.

He rode long into the darkness, pausing only a few minutes at Joseph's place to say good-bye to his older brother and the girl who had become Joseph's wife. Having eaten supper before setting out, he had no need to stop and cook a meal, or even to build a fire when he finally decided to give the animals a rest. He slept but little and was up at first light, eating hastily and without relish, nervous to be on his way. He left the trail, striking off on his own to confound the Blackwoods should they make an attempt at following. He rode north a while, simply to confuse the issue, then dropped southwestward for some time before setting a generally westward course across forests and meadows and hills that alternated, one with the other. Any Blackwood would play hell ever catching up to him now. In a clearing in a wood, he made a fire and fixed some coffee and bacon and ate cold bread Joseph's wife had insisted he take. He slept as if he had been knocked in the head and did not awaken the next morning until the rising sun struck him in the face. He took his time fixing breakfast, watching the animals graze.

Two hours underway, he thought he heard something, and alarm tingled through him. He gripped the rifle and turned the sorrel horse around, facing back to the east. Convincing himself it was imagination, he rode on. At what he guessed to be noontime he stopped at the bank of a creek to let the animals rest and graze, and he built a small fire to broil some bacon.

It was about done when he saw his horse suddenly swing its head around, ears pointed. He heard a horse's hoofs. He grabbed the rifle and dropped onto his belly behind a tree, training the rifle toward the sound. His heartbeat quickened.

A familiar voice hailed him before he could see more than a flash of color through the trees. "That you up yonder, Michael? Don't you be shootin' me now."

Michael pushed to his feet and stepped out into the open. From the ground Andrew Lewis looked like a man fully grown, though he lacked some yet. He looked enough like Mordecai that Michael had a hard time feeling as angry as he wanted to be. Crossly he declared, "Little brother, you are a vexation and a pain. I might've shot you for a Blackwood."

Andrew grinned like a possum sucking eggs. "For a Blackwood? I'd've been mad at you for the rest of my life."

"It'd've been a damned short life. The crooked trail I left, how the hell did you follow me?"

"You know I was always the best tracker in the family. Papa taught me that."

"Then why? I said you couldn't go."

"Papa told *you* the same thing once. You trailed behind him till he couldn't send you back. Anyway, I've already said my good-byes at home. They thought it was a good idea for me to come along and watch out for you."

"Watch out for me?"

"You've got a way of gettin' in trouble when you're by yourself."

"I'll be takin' care of *you* instead of the other way around."

"You won't hardly know I'm here. I'll be quieter than a little mouse."

Michael knew the only way to make Andrew go home would be to take him there. He could not do that. "First time you make one of them bad jokes I'll ride off and leave you behind."

"No jokes." Andrew added with a wicked grin, "You never understood them anyhow."

"What's that mean?"

"Means you've got too serious a turn of mind. You ought to laugh more."

"It's a serious world, and no place for a damned fool."

"That runs in the family."

16

Sergeant Elizandro Zaragosa suspected that had the military leadership known how badly he wanted to return to San Antonio de Bexar to rejoin his wife Elvira, the company would never have been transferred south from Nacogdoches. It was not the way of the military command to recognize the wishes of the men except to deny them.

Even Lieutenant Armando Rodriguez seemed in good humor, pleased to leave the primitive pleasures and limited social climate of the little Northern Texas community for the relative comfort of the more populated Bexar. He had not captured and dispatched an insurrectionist in more than a year, despite many a diligent search and occasional hot pursuit. The sanctuary of nearby American Louisiana was too quickly reached, and those anti-royalist agitators who had survived this long were not easily caught unaware. Rodriguez had become wearied by the frustrating chore of searching out and expelling *norteamericano* squatters who stubbornly crossed the ill-marked line from Louisiana, making themselves at home on the king's soil. They thumbed their noses at authority and sprang up everywhere like weeds in a garden, declaring that land unused was a waste in the eyes of the Lord and that therefore theirs was virtually a Biblical obligation. While he was driving one out, two more would slip in behind him.

General Joaquin de Arredondo had ordered that they be relentlessly sought and evicted lest they take root and multiply, and perhaps lend motivation and strength to more filibustering expeditions out of the infernal United States. But the general was far to the south in Monterrey. He did not understand that these people infested the frontier like locusts, building their rude cabins in the edges of the pine forests, breaking out land to which they had no claim, trading in contraband goods from Natchitoches and points to the east. Not even an occasional application of the sword seemed to deter the invasion, though God knew Rodriguez had tried. He had always been an eager administrator of justice in the name of his king, especially against insurrectionists and *norteamericanos*. He had no dread of spilled blood, so long as it was someone else's.

The royal road from Nacogdoches to Bexar had the name, but it was hardly more than a crude trace, certainly not a road in the sense of those which traversed the settled portions of Mexico farther south. Travelers along its path always faced the hazard of miscreants who took advantage of the poorly defended, relieving any burden of valuable goods and possessions that might be weighing heavily upon their shoulders, and sometimes of the animals that carried them. There was also the possibility of confrontation with the wild Indians who periodically invaded from those dark and unknown regions to the west, to which they retreated with impunity after exacting their toll. But neither bandits nor Indians were likely to attack a body of soldiers armed with muskets and lances. Zaragosa rode watchfully but with confidence.

They encountered few people along the way, which in one sense he felt was a pity, for the potential of this land was limitless. It was blessed with great forests and open valleys of deep soil the Lord must have intended for the plow. Settled by the proper sort of industrious people, it could be a colonial jewel in the king's crown. But the royal government, during its years of troubles in Mexico since the first rebellion, had made it policy to encourage settlement only within regions which it could control with its military presence. People had a tendency to want to think for themselves and question authority when they were allowed to disperse too widely. Lieutenant Rodriguez had often pointed to the Americans as an example of this truth; they took a perverse pride in their independence and their ability to thrive when not fettered by what they regarded as excessive law. They seemed not to realize that the only justification for the common man's existence was to serve those born to higher station, as Rodriguez served his king, and as these misbegotten *mestizo* soldiers served *him*.

They came across a couple of cart trains carrying merchandise which the merchants said was for the settlers at Nacogdoches. Zaragosa suspected most of it was intended for contraband trade with Louisiana. Smuggling was among the region's chief enterprises; equal to, if not greater than, agriculture.

Zaragosa assumed the lieutenant was well aware of the intended transgressions, but the papers were in order, thanks to appropriate payment to the officials in Bexar in the form of the *mordida*, the "little bite." The lieutenant went through the proper procedures, inspecting the cargoes and the manifests with military correctness. Zaragosa was sure Rodriguez came out of the encounters a little richer, though the officer was too practiced in the ways of the world to let his subordinates see him accept any coin. That they all knew he did was of no matter; they had not seen him. It was a fact of life in the Spanish colonial system that the reality was easily overlooked so long as appearances remained proper.

Sergeant Zaragosa whiled away the long, weary hours on the trail by remembering the lovely face of his wife Elvira and picturing his happy reunion with her. He had sent her south to her family in Bexar as her pregnancy became advanced, for she and her child would receive better care among her own. Once there, it had been agreed that she would be well served to stay, for life was precarious in a small and backward outpost such as Nacogdoches. That had been more than two years ago. He had a son whose second birthday had already been celebrated without his being given leave to go and see him. Another reason to hate Lieutenant Rodriguez.

He had remained true to Elvira during their long separation, though to have taken himself a mistress would have been accepted, even expected. If forced to submit to inquisition he would have to admit that the opportunity for infidelity had been small in such a sparsely settled community. He had seen no woman there whose beauty approached that of Elvira. Any temptation had been transient and easily put aside.

His excitement built as they began to see the rough limestone hills that rose to the north and west of San Antonio de Bexar. The royal road skirted them, its originators having judiciously remained with gentler and less demanding terrain to the east. It was here, and south along the San Antonio River, that the government almost a century ago had settled Canary Islanders to establish its hold on this land against encroachment by France. Attempts to move west into the rough hills had always been thrown back by the fearsome Comanches and Apaches, enemies to each other but equally hostile to the settlers. Even now, Comanches occasionally rode boldly through the streets of Bexar, silently daring one and all to make a move against them. There were seldom enough soldiers to meet the challenge in force, certainly not enough to beat back Indians so fearsome. The people of Bexar pueblo fervently wished for settlers to occupy the land between them and the hills to act as a buffer against the Indians. Those occasional brave souls who tried either gave up and moved back to the fringes of the town or were buried in the soil they had tried to cultivate. The king held title, but Comanche and Apache held the land.

The Galindo family's farm lay just northeast of the town, part of the land running up to Salado Creek. The Nacogdoches road passed nearby, and Zaragosa felt the delicious agony of seeing from some distance the flat-topped stone house in which Elvira would be living with her parents, brothers, and sisters. He watched closely, hoping that by some stroke of good fortune he might see her in the yard or upon the road, but he did not. It would bring him refusal and a stern rebuke from Rodriguez if he

were to ask permission to stop, even briefly. He was
still looking back over his shoulder long after they
passed, until the lieutenant asked him sourly if he
feared an Indian attack.

Riding through the narrow, confining streets beside Rodriguez at the head of the company, Zaragosa could see little change since he had been sent
north. The small houses of stone and adobe were
the same as he remembered them. The town had not
grown. On the contrary, it had shrunk as a result of
all the troubles, the rebellions and invasions large
and small. The old mission San Antonio de Valero,
which some called the Alamo because of the cotton-
woods, was gradually crumbling into ruins. The San
Fernando cathedral had taken over its religious duties, standing across the plaza from the governor's
palace. Zaragosa wondered if Governor Antonio
Martinez watched through his window as the company rode by, and whether he took its presence as
reassurance or as a threat. Many citizens regarded
the troops as a greater menace than the Indians.
When Armando Rodriguez gave the orders, that
fear held a grim validity.

Zaragosa hoped but did not actually expect the
lieutenant to grant him leave to ride out for a reunion with his wife. In this supposition he was correct, for it was the following day before Rodriguez
finally gave him grudging permission to absent himself from the garrison. He did so then only because
the whole company except those on punishment
were freed for a night to seek the pleasures of the
pueblo and divest themselves of the meager pay which
jingled temporarily in their pockets. If the people of
the town sometimes wished for protection from the

soldiers, Zaragosa thought there were times the soldiers also needed protection from at least some elements of the town.

Dressed in the best uniform he had, every button polished, his black horse curried and brushed, Zaragosa approached the Galindo house trembling as if before the worst battle he had ever faced. He vacillated between heady anticipation and paralyzing self-doubt, wondering if he should not have sent a note by messenger to let her know of his coming. But such airs were for officers, not for soldiers of low degree, even one so fortunate as to hold the rank of sergeant.

By the standards of Mexico, the Galindos were far from wealthy. By the standards of isolated San Antonio de Bexar they were at least comfortable, for they owned fields and horses and mules and cattle, and every member of the family of an age to do so was able to read and write. This relatively high standing had once given Zaragosa reason to question whether he was being pretentious in pressing his suit of Elvira, for this presumed an equality he was not certain he could justify.

The late-afternoon sun had descended almost to the rough tops of the brooding western hills as he rode up the tree-shaded lane toward the rambling stone house. Several dogs bounded out to meet him, setting up a racket that surely must be a good defense against any surprise attack by Indians. Toward the barns he could see men unburdening work oxen and driving in cows for the evening milking. They paid him little attention, for these were hired laborers who lived in small stone and adobe hovels well away from the main house, separated from the Galindo family by both a considerable physical distance and the many-layered class distinctions that put each person in his place on the day of birth and rarely let him move in any direction except downward.

A small child played in front of the house; a boy he took to be about two years old. His heart raced with the realization that this was his son. The boy became aware of the approaching stranger and fearfully retreated inside. Evidently he had been taught about soldiers.

Zaragosa checked all his buttons and brushed his uniform with one hand. He dismounted and called, "Elvira!" He watched the door for what seemed an hour before she stood there, hesitant, more beautiful than he remembered her.

Recognition struck her, and she rushed into his arms. As her warmth smothered him, he wanted to do much more than hold and kiss her. He wanted to sweep her up into his arms and carry her straight to the bedroom. But there were proprieties. And he did not have to report back to the garrison until tomorrow. He stared into her shining olive face. "Elvira, time has been a friend to you."

"No, it has stolen too much from us." The way she stared at him, he suspected the same wild urge ran through her. But yes, there were proprieties.

She took his arm and led him into the house, much more slowly and gently than he really wanted to go. "Come," she said, leaning her head against his shoulder. "It is time you meet your son Manuel."

Time came for supper. Old Mauro Galindo, the father of Elvira and eight others, walked up from the barns with his son Nicolas beside him. Nicolas, the firstborn and a year older than Elvira, had much of the old man in his face but had something else besides, an anger in his black eyes that had been there as long as Zaragosa had known the family. It was an anger born of the first aborted rebellion against Spain, an anger that had never cooled. Because Zaragosa wore the uniform of a Spanish soldier, Nicolas had never been more than politely cool toward him.

The old man vigorously shook Zaragosa's hand and welcomed him back to the bosom of the family, as Señora Galindo had done soon after Zaragosa's arrival. But Zaragosa saw little welcome in Nicolas's eyes. Nicolas stared at the uniform, and he frowned.

The evening was long and uncomfortable, partly because of Nicolas's coldness and partly because Zaragosa wanted so badly to say his good-nights and retreat with Elvira to their bedroom. Try as Elvira and her mother might, they could not long keep the conversation deflected from politics and war. The elder Galindo professed to have no interest in politics. He declared that he had seen first one and then another authority figure come and go. "It makes no difference who is in charge of the government. They are all like apples—sweet at first, then rotten with time. Power and money, these are the spoilers of honorable men."

Nicolas argued, "'There is one good thing to be said for the *americanos*. They are greedy and grasping and want what does not belong to them, but at least they are free men. They bow to no one. It will be like that for us one day. We will not forever be slaves to the *gachupín*!" He pointed to the boy

Manuel, Zaragosa's son. "He will grow up to be a free man."

Old Mauro Galindo said gruffly, "He will grow up to work for his living like all the rest of us. Do you think it makes any difference to the horse whether the rider is a king or a peasant? Do you think it makes any difference to the seed in the ground whether the man who pushes the plow is a slave or a free man?"

Nicolas thrust his chin forward as if in challenge. "It makes a difference to the man with the plow."

Elvira begged to be excused to put the boy to bed. Zaragosa kissed him, but the boy pulled away, afraid. It would take time.

Nicolas turned to Zaragosa. "You still belong to that damned Rodriguez, I suppose?"

Zaragosa frowned. He did not like the feeling of *belonging* to anyone, least of all to Rodriguez. "I serve under him."

Nicolas's voice was bitter. "Rodriguez has the blood of many good men to answer for. He will burn in Hell."

"I do not doubt it," Zaragosa replied. "'But for the present he is much alive."

"That can be remedied."

Zaragosa waited impatiently for the old man to say goodnight and give the cue for the conversation to break up. He did, finally, plodding away with his graying wife toward their bedroom. Nicolas tarried a minute longer, his eyes burning a hole into Zaragosa. He pushed to his feet and went to the door, pausing there. "You may tell that dog Rodriguez the fire of freedom has been lighted. It will consume him one day soon, him and all his kind." His eyes narrowed. "It will consume anyone else who stands in the way."

Carrying a candle, Elvira took Zaragosa's hand and led him out into the open patio, to the door of her bedroom. He closed the door behind them. "Elvira, Nicolas puts everyone in this family in danger. If Rodriguez hears of his talk, there is no telling how far he may go."

"I will speak to him about it tomorrow. There has been enough talking for tonight." She turned eagerly into his arms, and the time for talk was past.

17

For Michael the trip west was begun with reluctance, but for younger brother Andrew it was a grand adventure to be met with a light heart and eagerness. That spirit became contagious after Michael's gradual acceptance of the necessity which had set him upon the trail west. He began to relax into the quiet contentment that always came upon him when he entered the wilderness. And after his initial resistance passed, he found pleasure in Andrew's company, something he had not expected after enjoying several winters in the solitude of the deep and silent woods. Andrew had laughed off Michael's early disapproval and his attempts at demonstrated anger. Andrew's easy smile and his quick wit squelched every objection, like soft spring rain dousing a campfire. Michael had no choice but to give in. In a sense he relived, through Andrew's wondering eyes, his own first gaining of independence.

They moved at a leisurely pace, once Michael felt relatively confident the Blackwoods could not follow. He doubted anyone in that family was Andrew's equal at finding a trail and staying on it like a hound following a scent. Andrew, more farmer than Michael and more attentive to the future, had thoughtfully brought a supply of corn tied with the rest of his possibles behind his saddle. But they were to eat sparingly of it, saving most for seed to be planted whenever and wherever they found a place to drive stakes. As Michael had usually done during his winter trapping trips, they lived mostly on whatever the land offered . . . squirrel and rabbit when pickings were lean, fish sometimes when they camped by a stream, venison when luck showed her warm side.

They encountered almost no people in the first days on the trail. Michael regarded this as a blessing, for he needed no one. Besides, a careless word by somebody whose path they crossed could betray them to the Blackwoods. Andrew became a little restive. He was more inclined toward sociability. "We've passed through some fair to middlin' country," Andrew offered one night as they sat beside a small burned down campfire, roasting venison on sticks over the glowing coals. "How come there ain't no people here to speak of?"

"This country's still the way the Lord made it," Michael replied. "Ain't had no people except Injuns since the creation. Why rush to spoil it?"

"Just seems to me like this world was made for people. Don't seem right for it to be so empty."

"Empty?" Michael lifted the sharp stick from which a juicy piece of venison dripped fat into the fire. "We found meat here, didn't we? There's plenty more where it come from. This land is full of life. Just ain't much of it human, is all. Seems to me maybe the Lord likes it thisaway, or He wouldn't've given us so much of it."

Andrew shrugged. "Everybody talks about what the Lord likes. I wonder if anybody ever asked *Him*?"

Michael shook his head. He had never thought of it that way.

Andrew observed, "We probably wouldn't like what He'd say. So most people don't ask Him. They *tell* Him instead." Andrew smiled and examined his piece of venison gingerly with his fingers, for it was sizzling hot from exposure to the coals. "One thing I'll bet He *don't* like is for us to waste what all He's given us. Been wonderin' about that seedcorn. Will we get to where we're goin' in time to plant it this season?"

Michael gave him an honest if indefinite reply. "I don't even know where we're goin', exactly. Just to wherever we find a place we like that's got room for us."

One place had been much on his mind of late, a land forbidden to him, one that had given him some of the grandest days of his life, sharing the sunshine of his father's company. It had also given him the most terrible time in his memory. He found himself speaking the name aloud, though softly, as if to test the sound on his ear and see what inner reaction it might stir. "Texas."

Nothing was wrong with Andrew's hearing. "We goin' to Texas?"

Michael was startled at himself, and at the question. "It's a closed country. They kill Americans there. You don't even want to be thinkin' about it."

"*You've* been thinkin' about it ever since you came back that time without Papa. I could always tell when it was on your mind. I could see it in your eyes. I see it there now."

Michael frowned. Andrew had a knack for perception. Maybe that was why he was such a good tracker, among his other virtues. "Like you said, I came back without Papa. I wouldn't want to go back without *you*."

"That's been years. Maybe things have changed now."

"I ain't *heard* of nothin' changed. There was a story in the settlement about some feller named Long who went in there just a while back. Them Spanish, they buried him. Don't sound like their hospitality has improved much."

"I heard he meant to take the country away from them."

"Wouldn't make any difference. They'll shoot a man for bein' an American whether he's takin' anything or not. We don't need no truck with them people."

Andrew was silent a while. Finally: "If not Texas, then where? We can't just wander around the rest of our lives like some bird that can't decide between north and south."

"It ain't a bad way to live," Michael told him. "Papa liked it." But he knew it was not for Andrew, not indefinitely. Andrew had much of Papa's look about him. Studying him in the red glow of the small fire, Michael thought he probably looked very much like Papa did at that age. He had much of Papa's manner too. But he lacked Papa's unquenchable wanderlust. Andrew enjoyed getting away from home and field a while at a time, then he was ready to return to a more structured way of living. In that respect he fitted somewhere between Michael and older brother Joseph. He liked to travel and to hunt, but he had no fear of a plowhandle. Sooner or later, Michael knew, he would have to find Andrew a home.

"Natchitoches," Michael said. "Natchitoches, Louisiana. I'm thinkin' that's where we'll go to first."

"What's at Natchitoches?"

"I don't know. Maybe Eli Pleasant."

"It's been years. How do you know Eli's even alive?"

"I don't. But I've got a feelin' in my gut that if he's still livin' we'll find him around Natchitoches. He had a likin' for the place."

"And if we do find him, then what?"

"He knows the country. Maybe he can show us where two likely young fellers can make a place for themselves."

There had always been opportunity on a frontier for bold men who welcomed a challenge. Michael had no concern for himself. He could live off the forest. Given his choices, he would prefer that style of life over the plow, though he knew in the long run it was not practical. Papa had done it, and he had gone hungry a lot. But Papa had been a happy man, after his fashion. The only pity was that he always went off and left a family behind to do for itself the best it was able. If Michael could, he would follow the same pattern as his father with one major exception: he would not marry as Papa had done and burden some unfortunate woman with the responsibility for farm and children.

Andrew asked a lot of questions about Natchitoches. Michael answered them to the best of his somewhat sketchy memory. His first visit, with Papa, had been short, and during his second stay he had been handicapped by his slow recovery from the wound suffered at the hands of the Spanish soldiers.

"Main thing I remember is that it was about as big a settlement as ever I saw, though Papa said he'd seen several that was bigger. I remember there was a lot of boats on the river, people haulin' stuff up and down and actin' like they knew what they was doin'. But I never could tell it by listenin' to them. They spoke French, most of them, instead of American. And there was Spanish too. Kept me tied up in a knot, tryin' to figure out what they were talkin' about."

Andrew mused. "I don't recollect that I ever heard folks talk any language but American. Must seem real funny."

"At first, maybe. But it's got a kind of a pleasant sound to it, once you get used to not understandin'."

"Did you learn any French?"

"Just a few words. I'm afraid I've forgot them all by now."

"Was it Marie taught them to you?"

Michael almost dropped the venison. "Who said there was somebody named Marie?"

"You did. I've heard you talkin' to her in your sleep, more than once. There was a word now and then that I didn't understand. I expect it was French." He smiled. "Pretty language, you say? Pretty girl too, I'd bet."

Michael grunted. "You must've heard me wrong. Anyway, you're too young to know about pretty girls."

Andrew's smiled broadened. "You ain't the only one who's listened to cousin Frank." He looked at the venison and seemed to decide it needed a little

more time over the fire. "How's that country look
for farmin'?"

Michael shrugged. "Fair to middlin'. Kind of
swampy, some of it. But there was good farms
around Natchitoches, some big'uns, some little'uns.
Mostly they're owned by people with French names.
They been traded from France to the Spanish and
back to France and finally to us, till they don't know
which country they belong to, hardly. Louisiana's
like some foreign country itself compared to what
we know. Me and you, we may not fit into a place
like that."

Andrew seemed intrigued, and he harbored no
doubts. "We're from Tennessee. We can hold our
own anywhere." Humor flickered in his blue eyes.
"That girl Marie . . . she got any sisters?"

The first people they met in days turned out to
be a family on its way back to the safe and known
comforts of Tennessee. They were a ragged and
hungry lot, a farmer and his wife and four children,
hollow-eyed and haggard, at first obviously frightened of Michael and Andrew. Some of that fear remained even after the two young men gave them a
fat doe they had killed.

"You-all headin' west?" the farmer asked, his
eyes showing that he assessed any such notion as a
poor idea. "We been there, plumb out past Natchitoches to the Sabine River, with Texas acrost on the
other side. I'm tellin' you, it ain't no fit place for
a Christian. The stories you hear from the people
who come across the river to get away from the
Spanish soldiers . . . And it ain't that much better on
this side, neither. Squatters, fugitives, sinners of the
meanest sort. A man's got to watch or they'll steal
the boots off of his feet while he's walkin'. They

done cleaned us out, picked us to the bone. Wagon, plow, house goods . . . All we got is what you see."

It wasn't much . . . two horses, one carrying the gaunt woman and a small girl of six or seven, the other carrying a pack too small to contain much of the world's goods. A girl in her teens and two smaller boys walked behind their father. The man said, "You'd think they'd finally leave us alone, as little as we had left, but no. Back yonder a ways we come upon some human vultures along the trail, and they taken what vittles we had left. Had to beg them not to take the horses and set the woman and the baby afoot." He glanced at his wife, who still held her distance distrustfully from Michael and Andrew. "The way they looked at Marthy and my oldest girl, I was afraid they had even worse on their minds. I'm tellin' you, boys, this trail is wicked. Was I you, I'd h'ist my tail and go back to where I come from as fast as my horse could carry me. That's what we'uns are a-doin'."

Even after the gift of the deer, the miserable little family would not stop and share camp with Michael and Andrew. With her nervous eyes the woman begged her husband to keep moving on.

Andrew watched with sympathy as they continued eastward along the dim trace. "Sounds scary the way he tells it."

Michael said severely, "It's always scary to them that shouldn't've left home in the first place. People like that ain't got the backbone for raw country. They ought to stay in the tidewater. Tennessee wasn't exactly like church when Papa and Uncle Benjamin first went into it. But you didn't see *them* turn around and go back. They was of stronger stuff."

Andrew was defensive. "I didn't mean we ought to turn around. Anywhere you go, I'm game to go with you."

"I never doubted that. If the Lewises that went before us had listened to everybody that talked scary, we'd still be on the other side of the big water, bowin' to some king. We don't bow to nobody."

But the farmer's anxiety lingered with Michael, reminding him of the time he had followed after Papa and had run onto the robbers Patch-eye and Quint. He had heard tales of terrible deeds along the old Natchez Trace. This trace from Tennessee to Louisiana was as dim, perhaps even dimmer. People had disappeared on it, lots of people. It passed through many a long stretch darkened by the dense timber, the heavy canopy of trees that shut out the sunlight and hid the deeds of cold-blooded men. Against this, Texas by Michael's recollection was a land of open sunlight. There, evil deeds were hidden not by the gloom of the forest but by the vastness of the land, the isolation.

The wind at their backs, Michael and Andrew failed to smell woodsmoke until suddenly they broke through a clump of timber and rode upon several men camped on the bank of a clear-running creek, their blankets spread in the sun to freshen and dry. A sizeable number of horses were staked on the grass, though it was but mid-afternoon. The nearest man sprang to his feet, bringing up a long Kentucky-style rifle and pointing it first at Andrew, then at Michael.

18

Michael knew immediately that he did not like the looks of this bunch. He stared down the rifle barrel at the man's suspicious eyes and got a strong message that the feeling was mutual. His hand tightened on his own rifle, though he had the good judgment not to make any threatening move.

A tall man, hunkered beside a campfire, roasting a goodly chunk of venison on a crude spit, pushed warily to a stand. He strode slowly toward Michael and Andrew, giving them a long and careful study. The other men in camp formed a wedge on either side of him, all carrying their weapons. At length the man said, "Put the gun down, Jake. These boys don't look like there'd be any harm in them."

Jake was not in a rush about it, but he complied, lowering the rifle barrel an inch at a time while he visually inventoried the Lewises' weapons. He had several weeks' growth of ragged beard and did not appear to have used the waters of this creek—or any other for some time—either to bathe himself or to wash his clothes. Neither, by the look of him, had the gangling spokesman, who said, "Where you boys come from?"

Michael remembered Patch-eye and Quint. These looked as if they might be of the same caliber, and there were far more of them. He had long since embraced a rule that the less information he gave to strangers, the better. He jerked his head toward the trail over which they had ridden. "Back yonder."

"Where you bound for?"

Michael pointed his chin westward. "Yonder-way."

The man threatened to break into a smile. He turned to Andrew. "Are you as talkative as your friend?"

"Pretty near. We're brothers."

"Shows in your faces. You-all by yourselves?"

Michael shook his head quickly. "There's a bunch just behind us." He frowned as Andrew glanced questioningly at him. "I expect they'll be catchin' up to us in a little bit."

Andrew nodded. "Just about any time now."

The man gave Michael and Andrew another minute's speculative study. His eyes indicated that he did not accept the story, but he offered no argument. "We're headed the opposite direction ourselves. Been way out past Natchitoches to the Sabine River. Traded for a bunch of young horses to peddle in the settlements."

Michael saw them, grazing near the edge of the creek. They looked like the same kind of Texas wild horses which had brought death to his father and so many others. He wondered if men had died for these. Horseflesh came at a high price sometimes.

The man said, "You mustn't think hard of Jake for bein' suspicious. Been some mean doin's on this trace, and a bunch of young horses could be a temptation to men of loose character. I can tell by lookin' that you-all ain't of that stripe. Git down and share the Lord's bounty with us, and welcome."

Michael counted six men in all. The rest looked pretty much like Jake and the tall man doing the talking. He wondered if there might be others in the timber, out of sight. Even six were too many to fight, if it came to that.

He could see the hunger in Andrew's eyes as he looked toward the venison roasting over the coals. They had encountered no game after giving theirs to the defeated family retreating to Tennessee. But Michael considered the risk too high. He said, "Thank you kindly, but there's considerable daylight left, and we'd best be usin' it."

The tall man nodded. "I reckon we *are* a hard-lookin' lot to somebody who don't know us. I don't blame you for bein' careful. If two sons of mine was on the trail, I'd want them to be just as cautious."

Andrew's eyes told Michael he would like to stay and eat. Michael frowned, silently bidding him to be quiet. He heard two of the darker-skinned men speaking softly in a foreign tongue. He thought of Texas, and the dark-faced men who had murdered his father. He shuddered from a chill that ran counter to the warm spring weather. "Much obliged, but we'll keep travelin'."

The spokesman appeared genuinely regretful. "As you wish. You-all keep your eyes open, just the same. There's people loose upon the land that Ol' Lucifer wouldn't claim."

Michael stopped his horse in the creek to let him drink, facing him toward the camp so he could keep a watch on the men there. Andrew took the cue and did likewise, though it was clear he did not share Michael's misgivings. "They're rough-lookin', sure, but I believe they're honest. I don't see where it would've hurt to've eaten with them."

Michael said curtly, "If you're wrong it might've been us that got eaten up instead of the venison."

Disagreement was in Andrew's eyes, but he accepted the older brother's judgment as he would have accepted Mordecai's were he still living. "I heard two of them talkin' in words that didn't make sense to me. Was they speakin' French?"

"French or Spanish; I don't know which."

"I wonder how they know what they're sayin'?"

Michael was glad when the horses and the pack mule were satisfied so they could put the camp behind them. Uneasiness remained with him long after the men were out of sight. At length he said, "Let's turn out into that brush yonder."

Andrew kept his questions bottled up. Michael rode over a matting of old leaves that retained little or no track. A hundred feet from the trail he dismounted, rifle in his hand. He checked the powder in the pan. "Let's set and watch a spell."

Andrew's eyebrows arched. "You don't really think they'll come after us?"

"If they do, I'd rather it was *them* got surprised."

They squatted in the heavy growth of timber and waited. Michael expected pursuit to come quickly, if it was to come at all. He remembered the day at

Miller's Crossing, when Finis Blackwood had plotted to steal his pelts.

After perhaps a quarter hour Andrew loosened up and seated himself on the ground. "I don't think anybody's comin'."

"Don't be in a rush."

But another quarter hour passed without sign of pursuit. Andrew said, "Looks to me like you saw a possum and thought it was a bear."

Michael was weakening but not yet ready to surrender. "We'll watch a while yet. You trust folks too much."

"I was taught that way."

"Out here you better teach yourself different, or somebody is apt to deliver you a lesson you won't laugh about."

Finally he conceded to himself, though not to Andrew, that his suspicions were probably unfounded. Hunting and trapping in the woods, he had seen lots of men who looked as rough as the ones in that camp, and he had thought little about it. But he and Andrew were beyond the settled country, beyond the protecting arm of the law. It was in his mind that the men might still follow, hoping to catch the Lewises in camp asleep where they would be easy picking. He decided to make a cold camp tonight well off the trail, where not even an Indian could find them.

"We'll ride on," he said. "But we'll keep eyes in the backs of our heads."

They rode a couple of hours. Michael could not get over the feeling of being followed. Once he thought he heard a sound and waited for a time afoot, listening, while Andrew held his sorrel horse at some distance so the animal's sounds and the creaking of leather would not interfere. He heard nothing more but pointed to heavy undergrowth just off the trail. "Let's go yonder and wait a spell."

"Again?" Andrew protested.

Michael's voice was firm. "Again."

Andrew's face twisted with doubt, but he followed Michael's lead, as he always had. He said, "I thought you had nerves like Papa. I've never seen you so jittered up before."

"There's a difference between bein' jittered and bein' careful. Papa was generally careful."

They had waited only a little while when they heard horses' hoofs. Michael glanced at his brother with a silent *Told you*.

He cradled the rifle in his arms so he could bring it quickly into use. Andrew, believing now, followed his example.

Michael expected the bearded horse traders, but to his surprise he saw only two men. They were not from the camp on the creek. At least, he had not seen them there. One, a huge man, was clean-shaven except for a day or two of stubble growth. The other had a moustache and short beard, more neatly trimmed than would be expected on the trail. He wore a black coat with swallowtails that split on either side of the saddle. He looked like just about every itinerant minister who had ever sought out the Lewis family over the years to take a meal or two and a night's rest beneath a roof in return for delivering the Lord's blessings. They looked in no way like that group of potential brigands camped on the creek.

He was considering whether to hail them or just let them pass on unaware when the pack mule Jethro brayed at the strangers' horses. The men reined up in surprise and looked toward the source of the sound. The larger man brought up a pistol. The black-clad rider shouted, "Who's there?" He waited a moment, then added, "We are peaceful men in the Lord's service."

Michael and Andrew glanced at one another. Michael remained suspicious but did not want to be.

Andrew said confidently, "The worst they'll want to do is maybe take up collection. We ain't got enough money on us to make much of a clatter in a tin cup." Without waiting for Michael's approval, he mounted his horse and rode out.

Michael had no choice but to follow. Well, hell, Andrew was starved for company. Maybe there was no harm in this pair. He raised his right hand to show that he meant no mischief, for he could not very well use the long rifle one-handed. "Hope we didn't scare you none. We didn't know who you might be."

The one who looked like a preacher gave him a quick study and said, "Bless the Lord, I thought for a minute we might have fallen into the hands of Philistines. But these look like a pair of good young Christian men."

His companion only nodded, his half-closed eyes unreadable. He probably approached three hundred pounds, his arms bigger than most men's thighs.

The black-clad rider extended his hand. "I am the Reverend Fairweather. This gentle giant is my friend and traveling companion, Abijah Wilkes. He was once given to the evils of drunkenness and sloth, using his great strength in brawling and bloodying his fellow man. But now he is a student of the scriptures. As, I hope, you two young gentlemen are."

Andrew accepted the handshake. "I'm Andrew Lewis. This tall, silent feller is my brother Michael.

We've had a little churchin' now and again, when a preacher come around. Not near enough, though, I'm bound to say."

"So long as the heart is in the right place and the feet set upon a path of righteousness, I am sure the Lord is pleased." Fairweather gave Michael and Andrew a long appraisal, less critical than the one they had received at the creek. "I hope you will forgive our nervousness. We came across a rather disreputable group of men back along the trail. To be honest, we feared for our lives. I feel that had God not been watching over us, we might now be in His company and our meager possessions in the hands of blackguards."

Andrew said, "We seen the same bunch. The vittles they was fixin' sure did smell good, but Michael thought they looked worrisome."

Michael said, "Out here it pays to be cautious." He thought Fairweather looked all right, but he would not have wanted to meet the big man Wilkes alone on some dark and lonely trail.

Fairweather nodded. "I suppose they saw nothing worth the taking in such a poor pair as I and Brother Wilkes. They are waiting for larger game. But I would not be surprised if they decided to follow us and catch us in camp."

"Same thought that came to me," Michael said. "That's why we went to the timber. We thought you might be *them*."

"A prudent response. I say, young gentlemen, would you mind if we ride along with you for a time? They might be less disposed to bother four of us."

Michael was hesitant. "Well . . ." He had reservations about having to listen to Brother Fairweather's preaching. Michael had sneaked out of many a prayer meeting and had taken to the woods to escape the pungent smell of hellfire and brimstone as some minister beat with all his might upon the doors of the devil's lair.

Without asking Michael, Andrew said, "We'd be tickled to have you."

Fairweather glanced behind him. "Then I'd suggest we make some distance while the Lord's good sunshine still blesses us. One never knows what mischief Satan may plant in evil minds."

They rode along at a steady pace that was not a challenge to the horses. Fairweather talked a great deal. Michael supposed he was glad to have a new audience, for Abijah Wilkes seemed not to be listening; he had probably heard all these stories too many times. Michael thought it might even be possible that Wilkes had been cheated in the matter of brains even as he had been overly blessed in the matter of size and muscle. He had seen people like that, unusually strong in body but weak in mind. Luke Blackwood, for one.

Fairweather talked of the government in Washington, of turmoil in Mexico, of Thomas Jefferson and the Louisiana Purchase by which the United States had acquired a huge block of land west of the Mississippi from the French emperor Napoleon. He declared, "It is now God's plan for Americans to go forth into this great land and multiply. It is this nation's manifest destiny to spread from sea to sea, with God's blessing to guide us."

Michael caught a questioning expression from his younger brother. He remembered what Andrew had said about people who knew just what God wanted.

Andrew asked with an air of mischief, "Have you spoken to God about this?"

"Many times," Fairweather replied firmly.

"And has He answered you back?"

Fairweather gave Andrew a sharp glance. "Not in words such as yours and mine. He speaks in whispers that do not depend upon the ear but go directly to the mind and the heart."

To shift the conversation from this touchy ground Michael asked Fairweather how much of the country he had seen. The man in black expounded at length.

"I have traveled the highways, and I have traveled the dark and narrow traces. I have found God and Satan in eternal conflict wherever I go. Sometimes it seems a most one-sided fight, weighted in Satan's favor. But we of the faith must lend our sinews to aid the Lord to final victory. Is that not so, young gentlemen?"

Michael supposed it was. Andrew asked dryly, "What do you do when Satan wins anyway?"

"Why, one does not give up. One continues to fight no matter the odds. One keeps his faith, like Jonah in the lions' den."

Andrew blinked in surprise and gave Michael a knowing look. "I thought that was Daniel."

Fairweather seemed not even to notice, for he was swept along on the strong tide of his subject. "The final victory will be that of the righteous, have no fear. It is written in the Book of Truth." He reached into his saddlebag and drew out a heavy volume bound in black leather. He slapped it soundly with the palm of his hand. "Every mystery of life is explained herein. With this as our fortress we need have no fear."

Andrew said no more. He stared a while at Fairweather, then at Wilkes, who sat slumped like a sack

of grain on his big plodding brown horse. Though
Michael was hardly a student of the Bible, he knew
Andrew was right about it being Daniel in the lions'
den; he had heard his mother use that story as an
illustration of never giving up hope. Jonah was in
some other story. A fisherman, maybe. At least, it
seemed like he had something to do with fish.

Wilkes said nothing. He stared ahead with hooded
eyes.

Andrew gradually dropped back, bringing up
the rear behind Michael and the other two. He
held his rifle across his lap as if he were watching
for a deer to make their supper. But Michael discerned that he was actually watching Fairweather
and Wilkes. It was the first time Michael had seen
Andrew looking genuinely worried since they had
started their trip.

Fairweather looked behind him often. He said he
was uneasy about the men back at the creek; they
could be following, hoping to set upon this little
group by surprise at the night's camp. He suggested
they stop before dark, fix a quick supper, then move
on farther and make a dry, cold camp well off the
trail. Michael readily agreed, for that had been his
own plan.

They managed to shoot a couple of squirrels.
These were to be their supper, along with some
hardtack that Fairweather said he carried with him.
While Michael and Andrew prepared the squirrels for cooking, Fairweather and Wilkes went out
to open their pack. Wilkes chopped wood with a
short-handled ax.

Andrew took the opportunity to say quietly,
"I made a bad mistake, Michael, invitin' them to

go along with us. That man is a liar. He's no more preacher than me and you."

Michael already had the same feeling, but he asked, "How do you know?"

"No preacher would've got Daniel and Jonah mixed up. He'd just as well've forgotten about Adam and Eve."

Michael frowned, watching the two men out by the horses. "Don't blame yourself too much. He *sounds* like a preacher, and he's got a preacher face. But he's got liar's eyes."

"I ought to've seen that a lot sooner than I did."

Michael grimaced. "You're learnin', little brother. But we're stuck with them both. Best we can do now is to keep our eyes open till we're well shed of them."

Fairweather said grace, and they had their supper. Afterward they rode on until full dark, departing from the trail a while before they stopped to camp. Fairweather was still talking as they rolled out their blankets. Andrew spread his own closer than usual to Michael's. Michael noticed that Andrew never let his gaze stray far from Fairweather and Wilkes.

Andrew *was* learning.

Michael spoke hardly above a whisper. "We'll think up some excuse to let them go their own way tomorrow. We'll tell them we want to bide a while and do some huntin'."

Andrew said dryly, "I got a bad feelin' that it's *them* doin' the huntin'."

"Then we'd better neither one of us go to sleep."

In a little while Michael thought he could hear one of the men, probably Fairweather, begin to snore softly. At another time and place that might have lulled Michael off to sleep as well, but he was wide awake. He turned in his blanket to look at his brother. Andrew's eyes were open.

Even if they were wrong—maybe Fairweather was simply not a very good preacher—Michael was glad they would part from him and Wilkes tomorrow. Michael had already had more than enough of the man's constant talk. Come to a fight with any brigands they might meet down the trail, a preacher like Fairweather probably wouldn't be much help. As for Wilkes, Michael hadn't heard the man say twenty words. His eyes seemed half closed most of the time, hiding whatever might be running through the mind that worked behind them. If there *was* a mind. Wilkes's bovine manner left room for doubt.

Michael always slept with his rifle beneath his blanket to protect it from the night dew. He lay with one hand on it, and the feeling gave him comfort.

He thought about the home he had left behind, about Mordecai and his mother, about Uncle Benjamin, about the brothers and sisters and cousins he might never see again. He thought about Natchitoches, still ahead, remembering the bustling boat town it had been the last time he saw it. Unbidden, the dark-haired, dark-eyed Marie Villaret invaded his thoughts. Grown up and married by now, likely, with two babies in the crib and another on the way.

Andrew gave him a sharp nudge.

Two vague shapes moved silently toward them in the night's darkness. The larger of the pair came to the edge of Andrew's blankets. Michael knew it was Wilkes. He saw the man raise both hands, and he saw the blade of the short-handled ax outlined against the night sky.

Michael shouted, "Andrew! Move!" He jammed

the stock of the rifle against his shoulder. There was no time to aim, nor light to see the front sight. He just brought the muzzle up and squeezed the trigger. His rifle spat a lance of flame from its long barrel.

19

Over the echoing of the gunshot through the timber, Michael heard Wilkes cry out. Wilkes dropped the ax, folded his arms across his broad belly and sank to his knees, groaning. Fairweather had a rifle, and he fired it in haste. The flash blinded Michael for a moment. He was not hit, and he surmised that Andrew was not either, for Andrew brought his own rifle to his shoulder and fired back. Michael heard a curse that should never have come from a preacher's mouth, and an angry voice calling down the wrath of the Lord. Footsteps hurried toward the place where they had staked their horses. In a moment he heard hoofbeats and a slapping of tree branches as Fairweather rode headlong through the timber, getting away.

Andrew knelt beside the fallen Wilkes and demanded half in anger, half in pity, "Why? What've we got that's worth killin' for?" His voice trembled.

Michael said brittlely, "Two horses, a mule, two

rifles. People like this ain't greedy. They'll kill you for a little of nothin'.' "

Wilkes was a while in dying, for he had taken Michael's bullet in his stomach. He spoke more words in his agony than Michael had heard from him since they had met. Most were curses called down upon Michael for shooting him and upon Fairweather for running off and leaving him. Michael found himself shaking like Andrew in the aftermath of violence. It had been too much like Texas.

Regret was in Andrew's voice. "Ain't there anything we can do to help him?"

Michael said curtly, "He was fixin' to split you wide open with that ax. Now you want to help him."

"It just don't seem right to stand here and watch him die like some animal."

"He *is* an animal. If you've got to pity somebody, think about the people he's probably already killed the way he was fixin' to kill you."

When Wilkes at last went still, Michael and Andrew retreated to the horses. Fairweather's was gone. The man's saddle lay on the ground. In his haste to get away he had ridden off bareback.

Michael considered gravely. "All he's got is his rifle and maybe his powderhorn. He'll be comin' back to get what he can."

Andrew shuddered. "I'd as soon not to be here."

"We'll make it hard for him to find us. We'll go farther into the woods." They saddled the horses, including Wilkes's, to leave as little as possible for Fairweather to find and use against them. They left his saddle, for it would have been a burden to them anyway. Andrew picked up Wilkes's ax and tied it on Jethro's pack.

They rode perhaps a half mile in the darkness. They slipped the saddles to the ground, staked the horses, and sat down to wait out the rest of the night, one facing one direction, one the other, so Fairweather would have less chance of slipping up on them. Neither had any wish to sleep. Michael's stomach was in a turmoil. The sudden flash of guns, the stench of black powder, had set loose nightmarish memories.

Andrew asked huskily, "You feelin' all right, Michael?"

"Middlin'. How about you?"

"I'm kind of poorly in my stomach. Feels like everything wants to come up."

Michael remembered his own reaction to the deaths of Quint and Patch-eye. He could empathize with his brother. "You never been shot at before."

"Does it get easier after the first time?"

"I don't expect it *ever* gets easier."

He listened all night for sounds that might be Fairweather trying to find them. All he heard was his and Andrew's breathing and occasional movement of the horses on their tethers. After the seemingly interminable darkness, he welcomed the first signs of daylight. His stomach was still unsettled, the original upset now worsened by loss of sleep.

Andrew pushed shakily to his feet. He had not slept either. He asked, "We leavin'?"

"I sure got no taste for any breakfast. I want to put this place as far behind us as we can."

Andrew frowned. "But we can't just go off and leave Wilkes layin' back yonder."

"He'd've left *us* without lookin' back. Besides, Fairweather might be there waitin' for us. Let *him* do the buryin'. And the preachin' too, if there's to be any."

Andrew shrugged, still troubled but bowing to Michael's judgment. "You reckon I hit him?"

"If you did, it didn't slow him down much."

"I kind of hope I didn't. I'd hate to have a man's blood on my hands. Don't it bother you, knowin' you killed Wilkes?"

Michael examined his conscience and found no guilt. "No more than if I'd shot a sheep-killin' dog."

Andrew went to their pack, where they had dropped it on the ground in the darkness. "We gathered up in sort of a hurry last night. Looks like we got Fairweather's saddlebags along with everything else." He lifted them for Michael to see, then opened the pouch on one side. He took out the black-bound Bible Fairweather had shown them. He opened it and silently read an inscription on the first inside page. Brow creased, he asked, "How old would you guess Fairweather to be?"

Michael pondered. "Forty, maybe. Man that old, it's hard to tell."

Andrew ran his finger along the lines, reading aloud. "Given to the Reverend Lemuel Fairweather by his loving mother and father on his twenty-fourth birthday, June the 25th in this year of our Lord 1818. May its words light the path of righteousness for him that he may faithfully serve the Lord." He looked up questioningly. "That's way too young to've been the Fairweather we met."

Grimly Michael replied, "I'd reckon there *was* a Reverend Fairweather. The man we met robbed him. Killed him too, more than likely. He took the name and played the preacher so he could put people off their guard, like he tried to do with us." He shuddered. It had worked, for a while.

Andrew said, "It's a good thing he put Jonah in the lions' den instead of in the belly of the whale. Else we might not've figured out there was somethin' wrong about him."

"*You* figured it out. I didn't know where Jonah belonged."

Andrew managed a thin smile as he patted the cover of the Bible. "That's because every time there was preachin' done, and readin' from the Book, you slipped out and went huntin'."

They saddled and packed their horses and the mule. Andrew gave Wilkes's horse a critical study. "Reckon we ought to take him along? We might come up needin' an extra one."

Michael had no compunctions against taking a dead man's horse, especially a man who had intended to kill them. But he saw a troublesome possibility. "Wilkes stole him, more than likely. May even've killed for him. If somebody was to recognize that horse it'd put us in a ticklish place."

They took what they thought they could use from Wilkes's belongings, which wasn't much, and left the rest lying on the ground. The horse followed them a while despite their best efforts to turn him back.

"Damn fool animal could get us hung," Michael gritted.

But after a time they reached a big green meadow, and the horse stopped to graze. Michael and Andrew left him there, contented. Horses had a homing instinct. This one might eventually drift back to where he had originally come from, if it was not too far. If he did not, this was as good a country as any for a horse to get along by himself.

They rode in a moody silence. Finally Michael said, "Now ain't you glad you followed after me?"

Andrew thought about it. "I'm sorry about what happened back there, but I'm not sorry I came. There's a lot I can learn from you, Michael."

A little warmth came to Michael, helping offset the sourness in his stomach. "Maybe we can learn a lot from one another."

Andrew gradually began to regain his happy demeanor. He began to take notice of the country through which they traveled. He would point out what he considered a likely place to put up a cabin, to drop a plowpoint into the sod. "There's plenty of good land here, Michael. Soil looks rich. We could do a lot worse than help ourselves to some of it before the big rush starts."

Michael was more concerned about Fairweather than about locating good farmland. "We ain't hardly even got our trip started yet."

If he had been so inclined, Michael might have admitted that Andrew was right. But some deep urge drew him westward, toward a distant land he had seen once before. Others would stop here and make this into a home, eventually. They would plow up these meadows and cut down the forests and transform the land as nearly as possible into their own personal images of the places they had come from. That, he knew, was what Andrew would do. But Michael liked it the way he saw it. It would change, probably soon, and he did not think he would care to see it then.

He said, "We'd better not go back to the marked

trail for a while. That Fairweather may hold a grudge."

Andrew did not protest, but he asked pointedly, "You sure you won't get us lost?"

"We know the general direction of the trail. Long as we travel the same way, we can always find it again by takin' a straight line to the north."

By the second day he was beginning to wonder which might be worse, running headlong into Fairweather or continuing to fight the canebrakes and the deadfall timber that taxed their animals almost to the limits of endurance. The pack mule stumbled and fell, trying to pick its way across two fallen trees. The impact broke the short handle of Wilkes's ax tied on the pack.

Andrew said dryly, "At this rate we ought to reach Natchitoches before winter. Winter of next year."

"At least we'll reach it," Michael responded sharply, "without one of us gettin' Fairweather's bullet in our back. You've already seen that this is a dangerous country. I don't understand how you can be makin' jokes."

"Beats cryin'."

By the third day both horses had their legs skinned, and the mule was putting up so much resistance Michael literally had to drag him across some rough places while Andrew rode behind him, applying the end of a rope smartly across the rump. Andrew said, "If we cripple our horses we'll never get there."

Michael grumped, "If you want to turn back . . ." But he knew Andrew was right. It was better to face the possibility of another fight with Fairweather—or whatever his name was—than to continue this hard struggle, perhaps losing their horses. Without saying anything more, he turned northward. Andrew accepted his little victory in discreet silence while Michael spoke to the recalcitrant mule Jethro in somewhat less than endearing terms.

It took longer than Michael expected to intersect the trail. The animals were worn out, the brothers were exhausted, and Michael deemed it wise to make camp.

Andrew stared at the ground. "Wagons," he said with some surprise. "Somebody's brought wagons along here."

The tracks showed wide iron rims, cutting deeply into the soft ground. The wagons were heavily loaded, possibly carrying freight. Michael commented, "I'll bet those folks've had hell. This trail is too rough for wagons."

Andrew got down and examined the tracks closely. "Maybe so, but there's two wagons, I'd make it. Fresh tracks." He nudged horse droppings with the toe of his boot. "Probably made this afternoon sometime. If we was to keep ridin', we'd probably catch up to them pretty soon."

Michael frowned. "Why would we want to do that?"

"Company. Besides, the more of us there are, the less chance there'd be of Fairweather tryin' anything."

Michael had an old aversion to dependence upon others, and it welled up stubbornly. "We've done all right by ourselves. Remember what happened when we joined up with Fairweather."

Andrew had had his say. He bowed to Michael's judgment without arguing, though his face betrayed disappointment. "They're bound to be travelin' slower than we are. We'll overtake them tomorrow."

"We'll say howdy-do, then go on our way," Michael declared. "We don't want to be held back by any slow-movin' wagons."

Gray clouds began rolling in just before dark. Smelling rain, Michael and Andrew spread a pack cover between two trees as a makeshift substitute for a tent. They ate a meager supper before the storm began, then huddled beneath the small shelter while rain pelted the canvas. It dripped through in places, and after a while runoff water began coursing around the brothers. They slept in spite of their dampened bedding, for both were bone-weary. Michael did not worry about standing guard. If Fairweather was half as smart as Michael thought he was, he would not be moving in all this rain.

The rain stopped at dawn, and the sun burst bright and warm through breaking clouds. Andrew started a breakfast of roasted squirrel over a small fire made from dry wood they had sheltered beneath their blankets through the night. Michael saw after the animals, which had enjoyed no shelter at all. He could arouse no compassion for the mule, but he felt sorry for the horses. He told Andrew, "We'll stay in camp a while this mornin'. It'll give the stock a chance to graze and our beddin' time to dry out."

"We won't catch up to the wagons."

"Muddy as it is, them wagons won't be travelin' far. Told you anyway, we'll just say howdy and go on."

"I heard you," Andrew replied crisply. "I was just thinkin' that maybe with wagons they've got somethin' better to eat than squirrel."

"A man can live all right on squirrel. I've seen the time I've done on a sight less."

They did not talk much all morning. Michael

staked the animals out to graze while Andrew spread their blankets in the sunshine. Andrew stayed in camp. Michael walked out into the woods to see if he might scare up some game. He was about to call the venture a loss when he came upon several deer grazing at the edge of a tiny clearing and brought down a doe. He gutted her and packed the carcass into camp on his shoulder. He dropped it on the ground beside his brother.

"There," he said. "You can give the squirrels a little rest."

Andrew grunted. "Now, if we just had us some bread to go with it . . ."

Michael sighed in resignation. Andrew seldom argued in any belligerent way. He just kept gnawing until a person gave up. "Your wagon people probably ain't even got squirrel. But if it'll comfort you to find out, we'll likely overtake them before dark."

It was past midafternoon when they came upon the place where the wagons had been camped overnight. Gray ashes were cold in a shallow pit, and the ruts cut by the wagons went much deeper into the muddy ground than they had the day before. Andrew got down and went over the sign with a great deal of interest. "Two wagons," he said, "just like I guessed. Can't tell for sure about the people. Three or four, I'd expect, from the looks of the tracks."

Michael let Andrew do the inspection; that was what he was best at. "Families, you reckon?"

"Footprints all look grown-sized." Andrew made a second inspection of the cold firepit and kicked something he found lying on the ground. He looked disappointed.

Michael asked, "What is it?"

Andrew answered reluctantly, "Squirrel skins."

It was the first time all day that Michael had found anything to smile about.

Deep tracks showed that the wagons and their teams were laboring heavily. Boot tracks, driven inches into the mud, told of people putting their shoulders to the rear wheels to help push the vehicles out of places where water had stood and the earth seemed to have no bottom. Michael said, "They'll get tired of this by and by, and make camp until things dry up."

Late in the afternoon they heard distant shouting. The pattern was that of men urging a team to pull. Michael's smile came back, momentarily. "Sounds like work. You sure you want to ride up and get acquainted?"

"Sounds like the folks might welcome a little help."

"And feed you squirrel for supper. But come on, let's see."

It was as he expected. He saw two canvas-covered wagons ahead. The team had been unhooked from the second and hitched onto the first wagon to augment its own. The lead wagon was mired in the edge of a creek, its front wheels out of sight in the running water, its rear wheels sunk to the hubs in the muddy bank. He saw four people. A horsebacker was beside the lead team, urging it to pull. Two men were at the rear wheels, tugging, trying to get them to turn. A heavy woman pushed against the endgate. These three were black. Slaves, Michael figured, to the man on the horse.

Michael said to his brother, "Remember, it was your idea." He stepped down and tied his horse. Andrew followed suit. The black man on the right rear wheel smiled broadly when he saw help coming. Michael judged him to be approaching middle age, or already there. The woman appeared to be of roughly the same years. The other black was a boy in his middle teens.

The rider turned just long enough to acknowledge the help, then set about urging the teams to a stronger effort. Michael gripped a wagon spoke and gave it all the push he could muster. The wheel turned just a little, then rolled back. They tried again, with the same lack of success. Michael straightened to catch his breath. The rider had left the team and was returning.

Michael said, "I'm sorry, mister, but it looks to me like we'll have to take off part of the load before it'll come out of this hole."

The reply was brusque. "The hell you say!"

Michael glanced at Andrew in surprise. His brother broke into a grin.

The horsebacker was a woman.

20

Michael blinked in disbelief at the rider. Not only was she a woman, wearing a man's trousers considerably too large for her, but she was a *young* woman. Her face was half covered by mud, spattered freely in her attempts to move the wagon. Even so, he could see enough to guess she was still in her twenties. And he could see that she did not appreciate his incredulous staring; there was work to be done. But a woman out here so far from settled country, accompanied only by three slaves . . . it didn't seem a likely thing at all.

He asked her, "Where's the rest of your bunch, ma'am?"

He sensed that he had touched a raw nerve. She said crisply, "Count us. You see all there is, right here in front of you."

Michael looked at the lead wagon, then back at the other, its tongue lowered to the ground. Its team had been unhooked and taken to help pull the first one across the creek. "You can't be here all by your-self. A woman?"

She bristled. "Why not? I've made out for myself most of my born life. Anyway, I've got Marcus here, and Nellie, and Isham can do a man's work when it's needful. We've come a long ways. We can go the rest of it."

"It just don't seem a proper thing . . ."

"For a woman to do a man's work? I *had* a man. I did my work and most of his too. I'm gettin' along real well without him, thank you. I can get along with-out you too, if you're of a mind to give advice that ain't been asked for."

Michael was caught without an answer. Grinning, Andrew said, "Ma'am, we wouldn't think of leavin' you in this fix. You just tell us what you want done, and don't pay any attention to my big brother. He got kicked in the head by a mule when he was a baby. He's still mad about it."

Andrew's humor seemed to take the edge from the woman's resentment. She said in a gentler voice, "We'll have to move some of the load off of the wagon."

Michael had suggested the same thing, but to re-mind her might only stir her to another speech. He climbed onto the endgate and untied the wagonsheet. He was surprised to see many wooden barrels, neatly stacked and lashed down with rope. "What's this? Gunpowder?"

She volunteered, "More potent than that. It's whis-key. As good as Kentucky ever sent out to a thirsty world." A little of defiance returned to her voice. "You see somethin' the matter with it?"

"I just expected household goods and such as

that. I never figured to see a woman haulin' sippin'-whiskey."

"The people that drink it, they don't care who brought it. Now, are you helpin' or watchin'?"

Michael and Andrew worked together to worry a barrel to the ground. The black man Marcus outweighed either of them by a hundred pounds and had muscles like a bull. Shortly the men and the boy Isham, big for his age, had the wagon half-emptied.

The woman said, "Maybe that's enough. Every barrel we unload, somebody's got to tote across the creek afoot."

She rode back to the lead team. The four men tugged at the rear wheels. The black woman, almost as hefty as Marcus, pushed with her shoulder against the endgate. The wheels rocked tentatively forward and back, then the horses took hold and pulled the wagon across. The men kept pushing to maintain the momentum. Michael came out on the other side soaked to the waist and spattered with mud. Big Marcus and young Isham unhitched both teams, leading them back across for the second wagon. Michael suggested they might have to unload that one too.

The woman had her own notion. "We'll try with the whole load first. We taken the other one in too slow and got it stuck. This time we'll go in a-runnin' like hell and see if we can make it across before the mud has a chance to grab ahold."

She climbed to the wagon seat, popped the whip, and squalled like a wildcat. The doubled team hit the water in a long trot. The wagon lurched once, seemed about to stop, then broke free and came up on the far bank, trailing water from the wheels and the bottom of the wagon bed. The men kept pushing until it reached level ground.

Michael slumped forward, hands on his knees, and gasped for breath. But he took satisfaction from the accomplishment. The exertion had set his blood into a rush, and it brought a peculiar exhilaration he had not expected. He laughed aloud.

The woman sawed the lines and whoaed the team. The animals heaved from the hard pull. She climbed down and took a long look at the second wagon. Standing, its wheels sank several inches into the rain-softened ground. Reluctantly she declared, "We'd just as leave stop here a day or two till the ground dries some. Else we'll be doin' this at every frogpond we come to."

Andrew offered, "It'll put more age on the whiskey."

If she found any humor in the remark, she did not show it. She had business on her mind. She told the black man, "Marcus, we got to go back and fetch them other barrels."

"Yes'm," he replied, and jerked his head at the boy Isham. They bore a considerable resemblance. Michael assumed the lad was Marcus's son.

The woman turned to Michael and Andrew. "I do appreciate you-all's pitchin' in to get the wagons over. If you was of a mind to stay, Nellie's a good cook. We'll have somethin' to eat after a while."

Michael was torn between curiosity over this woman and doubt as to whether he wanted to risk having to put up with any more of her sharp tongue. While he pondered an answer, Andrew put in, "Supper sounds real good to us. And while we wait, we got nothin' better to do than help with them barrels."

The matter taken out of his hands, Michael went

along with it. Out of the woman's hearing, however, he reminded his brother, "I thought *I* was makin' the decisions."

"You are. I just wanted to be sure you made the right one," Andrew said blandly. "I sure would admire to eat a woman-cooked meal."

"Apt to be just squirrel."

"I was fixin' to offer them that doe we shot."

"That'll put us back to squirrel tomorrow, when we go on."

"At least we'll eat good tonight. Hard work gives me a fearsome appetite." Andrew's gaze went to the woman. She was unharnessing the teams while black Nellie started a fire with dry wood she evidently had kept protected in one of the wagons.

Michael suspected his brother's interest was in more than a good meal. At nearly twenty, Andrew was noticing things, like women. Michael pointed out, "She's some older than you."

"No harm in just lookin'. She don't hurt my eyes a bit."

"That's probably what Samson said, before his haircut."

"She look anything like that girl Marie?"

"I don't know who you're talkin' about."

They stored the barrels back in the wagon they had come from. Wet to the skin anyway, Michael walked out into the stream and soaked much of the mud from his clothes. The woman ventured into the water. She washed the mud from her face and out of her light brown hair, which reached almost to her waist when she let it down. Michael could not help but stare. He had always admired long hair on a woman. She offered, "Nellie'll rinse out them clothes for you if you want her to."

Michael shook his head. "They'd be dirty again by tomorrow. Travelin' ain't much for clean."

She smiled for the first time. It was a pleasant change. "That bothered me when we first started out. But I got over it."

Looking at her now, he found her handsomer than he had first supposed, and younger. But her blue eyes hinted at long, hard experience and more than a little cynicism. He surmised that life had not offered her much in the way of comforts. For whatever it had given, it had exacted a price.

She said, "I don't believe I heard your name."

"I never had time to give it. I'm Michael Lewis. That yonder is my brother Andrew."

She stuck her hand out like a man. "I'm Sally Boone. Out of Kentuck. No kin to Daniel, that I know of."

"Daniel who?"

"Never mind. I don't reckon he's much heard of except where I come from. Where you and your brother headed?"

"Natchitoches, to start. After that, ain't much tellin'. Maybe Texas eventually, if things go right."

She considered a moment. "Folks talk like Texas is a right smart of a place. But it don't welcome foreigners."

"That's the truth," he replied, frowning as dark memories came, unwanted. "But maybe it won't always be like that."

The black woman was every bit as good a cook as Sally Boone had built her up to be; or perhaps it was that Michael had been on the trail so long, eating meat roasted on a stick and poke salads when they could find the greens for them. He hadn't eaten cornbread or pone in some time now; he and Andrew had agreed to preserve the corn for planting, if and when they found a likely place to put it in the ground.

Michael sat back in the evening's fading light and ate a second plate of beans that Nellie had made a day or two earlier and reheated by hanging the pot from a steel bar over the fire. He had a strong sense of being stared at. His gaze went to Sally Boone. He found her blue eyes fixed boldly on him, examining him critically from his head down his body and all the way to his feet. He had the uneasy notion she was sizing him up like she was buying a stud horse or a bull or some such.

She went to one of the wagons and came back with a jug. "Try this," she said, handing it to Michael. "See if I lied about the quality of them barrels."

Michael tipped the jug and took a long swallow. He gave it time to warm his stomach before he passed it over to Andrew. He wasn't sure how much whiskey his brother had ever tasted, but Andrew was a man now, pretty near. Andrew sampled it approvingly and handed the jug back to Sally. She took a small drink and offered it to Michael again. He shook his head. "One drink at a time. Too much gives a man notions he can't live up to."

She stoppered the jug and placed it back in the wagon. "Then you're different from most of the men I ever knew. My man Cephus, now, he'd've drunk up both wagons if I'd've let him." She grimaced. The memory was evidently painful. She sat down again and gave Michael another long, silent study. "You-all in a hurry about gettin' to wherever you're goin'?"

"We've got some seedcorn needs plantin'."

"By the time you get settled the plantin' season'll be over with till next year, more'n likely. I was wonderin' if you-all would want to ride along with us? Seems to me like you're both well taken with Nellie's cookin'."

Andrew put in, "It's mighty good." He looked hopefully at Michael.

Michael's gaze went to the wagons. They would be slow. And God knew how many mudholes still lay ahead. He could see himself pushing muddy wagons all the way to Natchitoches. "It's a kind offer, ma'am. But . . ."

"Nothin' kind about it. You'd be useful to us. And Nellie's cookin'd put some meat back on your bones. Way you're goin' now you'll both be lookin' like scarecrows pretty soon. A strong wind might blow you plumb back to where you come from."

Michael saw that Andrew was itching to accept the offer. But an ingrained stubbornness made him resist. He had always been most comfortable alone or with one or two he knew well, like cousin Frank or his brother. Granted that Sally Boone was not hard to look at and the black woman was a good cook, they were still strangers.

"We'll have to study on it." He tried with his eyes to tell Andrew to keep his mouth shut.

She shrugged. "I'll not beg you. I'll not even ask again."

Independent, she was. She had already told him she didn't need a man's help, almost to the point of making a challenge of it. He supposed she was trying to prove something. A man could get awfully tired being around a woman who always had to prove she was as much a man as he was. He wondered about the man she said she used to have. Life must have been a trial for him.

He said, "That Cephus you talked about . . . your husband. What did he die of?"

"I told you he was my *man*. I didn't say he was my husband."

"I just took that for granted."

"Don't ever take nothin' for granted except death and crooked politicians. Life is full of surprises, and damned few of them are good news. Especially the men."

"I've known a lot of good men."

"You never saw them from my side of the bed. Even the preachers don't always follow the Good Book."

His jaw dropped in sudden suspicion. "Preachers? How come you to mention preachers?"

"There was one came up on us yesterday. Called himself a preacher, anyway. Done a lot of talkin' about redemption. Prayed loud and long for our safe delivery. A little bit of that preachifyin' always went a long ways with me. Then he got to takin' more interest in what we had in the wagons than I thought a Bible-thumper ought to. Sanctimonious damned hypocrite, is what he was: I had to threaten him with my whip."

Michael felt his stomach start to knot. "He didn't call himself Fairweather, did he?"

She gave him a look of surprise. "Why yes, he did. You know him?"

"We had some business with him a ways back."

She seemed to read a lot into what he did not say.

She commented shrewdly, "I figured him for a fraud. Nobody hollers at the Lord that loud."

"He'd've murdered you for what's in them wagons."

Her voice went harsh. "He'd've found Sally Boone hard to kill. It's been tried."

It was difficult for him to imagine even Fairweather killing a handsome young woman like this. Those blue eyes ought to be enough to stop anybody. "Won't hurt to be watchful, in case he was to come back."

"Ain't likely. I told him if I ever seen him come up to my wagons again I'd pop his eyes out with my whip. I proved to him I could do it. I laid the business end right where his britches stretched the tightest."

She'd probably do it to me eventually, if I stayed around her long enough, he thought.

He said, "Just the same, you'll want to watch out."

As darkness came, Michael kept noticing the horses fidgeting where they were staked. It was probably just that his and Andrew's were strangers to the Boone teams. Horses tended to be clannish, often slow to accept newcomers. The pack mule barely tolerated Michael's and Andrew's mounts even after all this time and showed no inclination to meet the others on any terms except out-and-out hostility.

The fidgeting and occasional squealing continued long after Michael had crawled into his blankets. He reasoned that the trouble was simply between the horses, but there was always a chance some predator was prowling around out there and keeping the animals stirred up. Grumbling under his breath, he put on his boots and took his clothes, blankets, and rifle out where the horses were. He addressed a few quiet but stern admonitions to the animals, especially Jethro, and respread his blankets.

He lay awake, listening. If it were a bear or a panther, his presence ought to be enough to keep it away.

After a while he heard a rustle of grass. Tensing, he grasped the rifle until a woman's voice asked quietly, "They still restless?"

In the pale moonlight he saw that Sally Boone had a blanket wrapped around her, and the jug hung loosely from one finger. She said, "Seen you move out here. I been as restless as the horses."

"They've settled down," he said. "You don't need to worry."

She handed him the jug. "I wasn't worried. Just couldn't sleep. Thought we might talk a little."

"What about?"

"Don't matter. Who you are, where you come from. Anything that passes the time."

She seated herself on the edge of his blanket, holding her own blanket around her with one hand. He said, "Where I come from, there'd be plenty of talkin' done if anybody saw us together out here thisaway, in the middle of the night."

"We ain't where you come from. Anyway, people've been talkin' about me since I was fifteen years old. Talk never bruised me or broke my bones."

He sipped sparingly from the jug, then watched her raise it. She stoppered it after one drink. He could not imagine his mother ever drinking out of a jug; he could not imagine many of the women he ever knew doing so, though he had seen a few do it around the dramshops. They were not women of high repute.

He asked her straight out, "How come you to have two wagonloads of whiskey?"

"To sell and make a profit. That's what this country's all about." Defensively she added, "I didn't steal it, if that's what you're wonderin'. It's mine, bought and paid for."

"Just don't seem a likely thing for a woman, is all."

"I wasn't raised in no likely way. Wasn't raised at all, you might say. Just come up on my own."

"How so?"

"Never did know who my daddy was. Folks sort of whispered about that, like he was probably a married man or somethin'. My mother's folks, they run her off, and she was workin' for a barkeeper when I come along. She died when I was three or four years old. Her folks wouldn't have nothin' to do with me, so I got shoved off on first one and then another. Growed up around barrooms mostly, and sometimes worse, takin' what people felt like givin' me till I got old enough to take what I wanted.

"Finally wound up with an old man named Boone when I was fourteen or fifteen. Had him a dramshop . . . a good, goin' business. He also had a sick wife. Pretty good old woman . . . just a little mean. I had to take her place with the cookin' and the washin' and the cleanin' and all. After she died, and I got a little older, I commenced takin' her place in other things too."

She grimaced. "That's when I learned that talk can't hurt you if you make up your mind not to listen to it. At least I had a good roof to live under, and I was eatin' regular for the first time in my life. Them people that talked, they never went for two or three days at a time with nothin' to eat. And Boone wasn't a bad old man. He was always kind to me, long's I done what pleasured him. He even talked about marryin' me to make it all honest."

She unstoppered the jug again, took a sip, and passed it to Michael. "They say it's a man's world, but I found out real young that a woman can get by all right if she knows how to handle men. I know how to pleasure them, and I know how to run them the hell off."

Michael felt the glow of the whiskey beginning to spread. Or it might not have been altogether the whiskey. He felt the disturbing warmth of Sally Boone as she inched closer to him.

He said, "You never explained about the wagons and the whiskey."

"Ol' Man Boone finally died. He didn't have no family, and some of the local politicians was gangin' up to take everything away from me. So I sold it all and taken the money and left there before they got the chance."

"And then you bought the whiskey . . ."

"Not right off. I kept a tight hold on the money while I went about learnin' how to do for myself. I found out most men are like Ol' Man Boone in what they want out of a woman, but a lot of them don't have his kindness. Taken me a while to learn which ones to trust and which ones to walk away from. Cephus Carpenter come along, by and by. I'll have to admit, he had me goin' around in circles for a while."

"How was that?"

"He was tall and good-lookin', and he had a smile that was like the whole room lit up. He took a lot better to whiskey than to hard work, and I'd get mad enough sometimes to stomp on him. But he'd start sayin' all them nice things and touchin' me gentle, and first thing I knew I melted like butter in the sunshine." Her voice went soft in the memory. "Wasn't no man could pleasure me like Cephus. I wake up in the night reachin' for him, and he ain't there. Lord, I do miss him."

She leaned over Michael, her breath warm on his face. She touched the palm of her hand against his cheek, and heat leaped to meet it. "But *you're* here, Michael. I think we could pleasure one another."

Michael's heartbeat quickened, and he breathed faster. His sexual experience had been slight. He had lived in a country of few people, and fewer available women. His cousin Frank had not taken all of his education out of books; he had known where the pliable females were. He had matched Michael once with a girl named Amity; her father had run half-wild hogs in the woods. The experience had been cold and mechanical and too quickly finished, leaving him embarrassed and ashamed and woefully unfulfilled. He had not tried again.

Sally Boone pressed her lips to Michael's, and they burned like flame. She put her arms around him and dropped the blanket from her shoulders. She wore only a thin cotton shift. Soon even that was gone. The initial aggression was hers, and he never quite caught up. She clutched and clung with a hunger and a desperation that set him afire.

It was nothing like his experience with the girl Amity.

One of the horses stirred, but a panther could have taken him and Michael would not have interfered.

They pulled apart after a time, sticky with sweat. He propped himself on one elbow to study her peaceful face. She lay on her back, staring up at the stars. His hand resting on her breastbone, he could feel her heartbeat gradually slowing, her breathing dropping back toward normal. He thought she might say something, but all she did was press his hand against her bosom and hold it there. He asked, "Thinkin' about Cephus?"

"Who's Cephus?"

Apologetically he said, "I ain't had much experience at this."

"You do fine. You'll make some woman a good husband."

He wondered if she might be considering him for that role. At the moment he found temptation in the thought. But he remembered the neglectful kind of husband his father had been to Patience Lewis.

She seemed to read his thoughts. "I ain't lookin' for a husband. Sure, I get a yearnin' for a man every once in a while, the way I wanted *you*. That's nature. But if a man gets tiresome I want to be able to shed him like I'd get shed of a worn-out pair of shoes. I don't want no husband hangin' around my neck like a millstone."

"It's just as well. I'm afraid you might get tired of me awful quick."

She looked at him a minute, then raised up and leaned over to kiss him again. She pressed closer, her warm hand roaming over his chest, exploring his ribs, moving down tantalizingly to his thigh. "Maybe," she whispered. "But I ain't yet. I hope you're not a man who needs a lot of sleep."

Just before she smothered him under a renewal of their lovemaking, he realized he and Andrew were going to have to leave this camp come daylight. Otherwise he might not be able to pull himself away from Sally Boone at all, not until such time as she began to regard him like an old pair of shoes.

21

Regret pinched Sally Boone's blue eyes, but she said nothing as Michael and Andrew saddled their horses and packed the mule. Andrew had said more than enough when Michael had shaken him at first light and told him they were leaving. Andrew was inclined to stay with the wagons and the company and Nellie's cooking. He complained, "I don't see what we got to be in such an all-fired hurry for. I had a notion you was gettin' along with her real good."

Too good, Michael thought, wondering how much his brother knew. Andrew could always see a little and figure a lot. He had become more and more independent-minded as they went along on this trip. The signs were clear: a day would soon come when Andrew would no longer accept any judgment except his own. That was as it should be. It was Mordecai Lewis's legacy of self-sufficiency to his sons.

Michael said, "These wagons'll just tie us down." The argument was thin, but he did not feel comfortable admitting his true reason: a strong dread of becoming entrapped by his desire for Sally Boone, to a point that he might follow her around like some servile pup. He suspected the late Cephus Carpenter, for whom she still mourned, had fallen into that trap. While Michael and Sally had been at the peak of their lovemaking, she had whispered that name without seeming to realize it. He sensed that her real hunger was for the other man, not Michael. That did not diminish the fierce urgency of the moment, but it left him with a certain frustration afterward, feeling that he was no more than a substitute. He suspected the effect was much the same for her. She was simply making do.

He had no wish to be accepted only as somebody's replacement. Yet if he remained with her he might begin to accept that station as a price for sharing blankets with her.

He knew by the look in Sally Boone's eyes that she wanted him to stay, but pride would not let her speak the thought. She said, "We can spare you some coffee, and some corn for bread. It's little enough for the help you gave us."

"No need," Michael said. "We don't ask pay for a small kindness."

"A gift cheerfully offered is not considered payment. It comes from the heart."

She was not talking about coffee or corn. Michael said, "But an honest man expects to repay it in kind. I'm afraid I don't have enough to give."

"You've got no apologies to make."

"I might have, if I took advantage of your good nature. So good-bye, Sally. Good luck to you." He nodded at the three amiable but quiet black people, who stood together, and he turned westward. Andrew stayed behind for a minute or two. Michael wanted to look back for him, but that might be taken as a sign of weakness. He kept plodding along until Andrew caught up, leading the pack mule. Andrew said, "Come night, you'll be wishin' you'd stayed with her."

Michael half wished that already, but he would not say so. And anyway, what the hell did Andrew know about it? Maybe his younger brother was not so innocent as he seemed. Michael looked suspiciously at the pack mule. An extra sack was tied to the rope that held the pack in place.

Andrew shrugged but offered no apology. "A little corn, a little coffee. From the goodness of her heart."

"I ain't goin' back to thank her."

"*I* said thanks for both of us." He frowned. "I don't know how you could just ride off and leave her thataway. I couldn't if it was me."

"Go back to her yourself, if it bothers you so much."

"Don't think I ain't tempted."

That was the extent of their conversation. Andrew rode in silence that spoke of accusation. Michael kept reliving the night in his mind, in all of its blood-warming detail.

He was so engrossed in his thoughts that he would have ridden directly into the Reverend Fairweather's little band had Andrew not shouted a warning and brought up his rifle. Michael snapped out of his erotic reverie, instinctively raising his own rifle in response to Andrew's move.

Rounding a bend in the faint trail, he found himself face to face with the man who called himself Fairweather. They were no more than fifteen feet apart. Michael almost lost his breath. Fairweather had one horseman on his left, two on his right, every one of them carrying a firearm. Fairweather aimed a pistol at Michael, but the muzzle of Michael's rifle was pointed directly at Fairweather's ample stomach. Michael did not take his eyes from Fairweather to see what Andrew was doing; he had to trust that his brother was prepared for whatever might come.

Fairweather blinked, his wide mouth hanging open. Gradually he put on the preacher's smile calculated to lull his victims into complacency. "Well, young gentlemen, we meet again. The Lord has twice blessed us." He had been playing preacher so long he seemed to have taken the role at least partly to heart.

Michael's mouth was dry. "He blessed *us,* lettin' us see you first."

Fairweather's false smile widened. "You boys have a mistaken opinion of me. You misread our intentions the last time we met. You killed poor Wilkes for no reason."

"There was reason enough."

For a man who wanted to appear a preacher, Fairweather had found a rough set of companions who looked as if the only reason they would ever go into a church was to loot it. One was a cadaverous man whose long legs hung far below the belly of the scrubby little horse he rode. His trousers had ridden up to expose long thin shins above the tops of a pair of Indian-style moccasins. One was a fat little man with a ragged beard and a set of pouched little eyes that reminded Michael of a greedy pig waiting to be fed slops. The other was an overgrown boy with long, dirty, straw-colored hair that reached down to his shoulders. He was perhaps of Andrew's age, with a cruel, hard smile set aslant across wide, thin lips. Of the four, he looked the one most likely to do murder for the joy of it. Michael wondered if anybody accepted the credit for his upbringing.

Michael asked, "You come back lookin' for us, Fairweather?"

Fairweather shook his head. "No, I assumed you were far gone down the trail. I had not thought to see you two again."

The fat man suggested, "That's a decent pair of horses they're ridin'. And I wonder what's in the pack on that mule?"

Fairweather responded sharply, "Perhaps you have not noticed, but they both have rifles cocked and pointed at us."

The boy said, "There ain't but two of them. I'd give a pretty to see in that pack."

Fairweather's patience thinned. "And which two of us do you think would survive to open that pack? This is a standoff, so let it be. Anyway, we have bigger fish to catch." He cut his gaze back to Michael. "We have no interest in you or what you're carryin'. Would you back away and give us the road?"

Michael did not intend to yield them even a moment of advantage during which they might grab the upper hand. "We're settin' right where we're at. You-all go around."

Fairweather gave him a long and irritated study. "Very well. But I must say, young gentlemen, you make it difficult for a man to remember the Biblical injunction to love thy neighbor."

"You're no neighbor of ours."

Fairweather jerked his head as a signal to his companions. They rode out of the trail. As they circled around Michael and Andrew, the two brothers watchfully brought their horses about, keeping their rifles pointed toward the four. The boy stared belligerently in their direction until his party pulled back into the trail and rode out of sight.

Only then did Michael draw a full breath. His hands were sticky with cold sweat. He told Andrew thinly, "Good thing you gave a holler. My mind was off in the clouds."

"Or between the blankets," Andrew suggested.

Michael could not deny that, but he would not admit it.

Andrew frowned. "He talked about catchin' bigger fish. You know who that would be."

Michael grunted. Two wagonloads of prime Kentucky whiskey. Three blacks to carry off to some slave market. Against that, his and Andrew's two horses and pack mule would have seemed a poor compromise. Whatever his shortcomings, Fairweather had a well-developed sense of commercial values.

Andrew urged, "We can't ride on. We got to do somethin'."

"We will. I'm just tryin' to figure out what."

"We could sneak up behind them and pick off Fairweather. I expect the others would give up the notion in a hurry."

Michael gave his brother a look of surprise. "You'd do that? I remember how hard you took the killin' of Wilkes."

"I got over it. Tough times call for tough ways."

Michael pondered. "I don't hold with shootin' a man in the back, even somebody like Fairweather. We got to go around them some way and warn Sally before they get there. If they see we're ready for them, maybe they'll back off again."

"It'd be simpler to shoot Fairweather. But whatever

we do, we'd better be a-movin'. They're gettin' ahead of us."

The pack mule would slow them down. Michael led him off the trail, dropped the pack to the ground, and staked the mule on a rope that would give it grazing room. Perversely, though it had long evidenced a dislike for the horses, it brayed for them when Michael and Andrew set out in a lope, leaving it behind.

It was Michael's intention to remain in the forest only long enough to move ahead of Fairweather and his three coconspirators, then cut back into the trail and beat them to the wagons. But he did not count on running into a tangle of deadfall timber, then into a thick and choking canebrake they had to pick and fight their way through. They broke out of the canebrake, finally, and angled across to the trail.

Andrew pointed at the ground. "Fresh horse tracks. After all the hell we went through, we're still behind them."

Michael had no time to waste in either anger or despair. "All right, we'll do it your way," he told Andrew, seeing no better alternative now.

Andrew's jaw was set grimly, and at that moment he looked uncannily like his father Mordecai. "If you've got any compunctions about it, Michael, *I'll* shoot him," Andrew said.

The racketing echo of gunshots through the timber told them the point was moot; Fairweather had already reached the wagons. Michael drummed his heels against Big Red's ribs and put him into a hard run. He listened for more shots, but none came. He recognized a lightning-struck tree beside the trail and knew they were almost to Sally Boone's camp.

He raised his hand in silent signal and reined off the trail. Andrew pushed close behind.

Michael heard voices, though he could not make out words. One was a woman's, shrill in outrage. *They've got her,* he thought, a chill shaking him. He jumped from the horse and tied him. Silently Andrew followed suit. Crouching low so the underbrush would hide them, they warily approached the camp.

Dropping to his belly, carefully parting the foliage with one hand while the other gripped the rifle, Michael saw the black man Marcus and the boy Isham lying on the ground. Blood was streaked red across Marcus's black face. The tall, skinny man bent over him, raising his rifle like a club. The woman Nellie was on her knees, begging for her man's life.

Fairweather commanded, "Don't hit him again, you damnfool! A dead nigger won't fetch us a dollar."

The white youth and the fat man held Sally Boone's arms, pushing her against a wagon wheel while she lunged at them and tried vainly to break free. "What we goin' to do with *her*?" the younger of the pair asked.

Fairweather replied reproachfully, "You know what we have to do with her. Them niggers wouldn't be taken for witness, but she would."

The youth laid the palm of one hand against Sally's face and slowly moved it down the front of the man's shirt she wore. "Seems a waste. We don't have to do it just yet, do we?"

Fairweather frowned. "Boy, what you're thinkin' about is an abomination in the sight of the Lord."

"A *what*?" the youth asked.

Sally Boone's eyes were wide, but fear did not

overwhelm her anger. She struggled against the strong hands that held her. "Stealin' . . . murder . . . they're all an abomination, ain't they?"

"A regrettable necessity, dear lady. A matter of survival. The Lord helps them that helps theirselves. It is a pity that you happen to be in the way, but the Lord's will must be done." He shrugged to the youth and the fat man. "It's too muddy to move these wagons anyway, so we have time. But when you're done, I trust you know what you must do." He turned his back to them and climbed up onto one of the wagons, peeling back some of the canvas and running one hand along the barrels as if he were caressing a woman.

The youth began tearing at Sally's shirt. She cursed and cried at him. The fat man grinned, and the tall one walked away from the three black people to get a closer look. Sally's cry brought rage boiling up in Michael. He jumped from his hiding place and raced toward her, shouting in fury. The fat man turned, and instantly he had a knife in his hand.

Michael shot him in the face.

The youth turned loose of Sally and rushed to meet Michael. They collided and went down rolling in the mud. Michael had no idea what Andrew was doing, but he saw the tall man raise his rifle. The man hesitated, for he was as likely to hit the youth as Michael while they wrestled and rolled on the wet ground. He moved in closer, and Michael felt the cold muzzle of the rifle touch the back of his neck. A shot roared. The tall man buckled at the knees, pitching forward across Michael and the struggling youth. Michael saw Andrew standing there, smoke curling from his rifle.

It occurred to Michael suddenly that both their

firearms were empty now. He broke free from the youth and grabbed at his own rifle, furiously trying to reload while he looked around to determine what Fairweather was doing.

The youth was on hands and knees, crouched as if to spring at Michael. The black woman Nellie came running, screaming like a wounded wildcat and grabbing up a heavy singletree from the nearest wagon. It made a swishing sound as she swung it, and a crunching sound as it struck the youth's head with all the force she could put behind it. He fell like a shot deer.

Sally had picked up a rifle dropped by either the fat man or the youth. She pointed it at Fairweather as the man dropped down from the wagon, and she jerked the trigger. Nothing happened. The rifle had already been fired.

But Fairweather's had not. It was propped against a wagon wheel. He brought it to his shoulder and trained his sights on Michael, his eyes narrowed. "Now, everybody just stand still." Michael held his breath, for he could see the man's finger going white against the trigger, and he expected any second to see the flash of the powderpan.

Fairweather motioned with the muzzle. "Now, everybody move real slow and easy over to where them niggers are layin'."

Michael waited for Sally. She was trying to pull the torn shirt together to cover herself. Her eyes touched him with gratitude, but that gave way to anxiety as she looked toward Fairweather and the rifle. Andrew laid down his empty weapon and walked as he was bid to stand beside the prone figures of the two blacks. The boy Isham was stirring a little, but Marcus still lay unconscious, blood trickling from a cruel wound on the side of his head.

Fairweather glowered. "I swear, you two young gentlemen have become a vexation to me. What am I to do with you?"

Michael was emboldened by a realization. "Whatever you do, you've only got one shot to do it with."

Fairweather nodded. "It seems to me we were in somewhat the same situation back down the trail. You know I can only shoot one of you, but you don't know which one it'll be."

The youth with the straw-colored hair was sitting up and rubbing his head. A purplish welt was rising where the singletree had struck him. Fairweather spoke reproachfully, "You see now the position your carnal nature has placed us in? The Lord has visited his punishment upon you. Get to your feet. See if there is anything to be done for your foolish friends."

The lad managed with some difficulty to get his feet under him. He still appeared addled, unsure what had happened to him. He knelt over the tall man, almost falling, then staggered over to the fat one. He held the wagon wheel while he leaned to touch the man. "Deader'n hell," he said, "both of them." Revenge was in his eyes as he looked up, searching out Michael. "You're a dead man too, fixin' to be."

Fairweather said, "You'd better load a rifle before you invoke the Lord's vengeance. Our advantage at the moment is not strong enough to support loud talk."

The young man spilled more powder than he managed to put into the barrel of his rifle. He rammed a patch and a ball into place and seemed to have trouble drawing out the ramrod. Michael only half watched him. His attention was focused on

Fairweather and the rifle. He knew if he rushed the pseudo-preacher he would probably be wounded, perhaps killed, but his brother and Sally would have a chance.

Fairweather seemed to read his thoughts. "My young friend, what you consider would be most foolish. I would kill you before you moved two steps."

A man's voice spoke from somewhere at the edge of the forest. "You ain't killin' nobody. You raise up that gun before I blow your head off!"

Michael jerked around. He saw a lanky stranger stride out of the timber and into the opening, rifle jammed firmly against his shoulder. The man had a voice deep as doom. "You raise that rifle up and blow the powder out of the pan or I'll blow the guts out of *you*!"

Fairweather hesitated, then did as he was told.

Michael caught a movement out of the corner of his eye. The boy had dropped to his knee and was aiming his rifle, the ramrod still in the barrel. Michael rushed toward him but knew even as he started that he would not reach him in time. He heard two shots, one a half second behind the other. The boy made a gurgling sound and pitched forward onto his face. The quivering ramrod stuck in the soft ground a dozen feet in front of him.

The stranger's rifle was empty. Instantly Fairweather had his powderhorn up and was replacing the charge in the pan. He would have the rifle ready again before anyone could reach him. Michael and Andrew both ran at him anyway.

Sally Boone was quicker. From the nearby wagon seat she grabbed her long whip, swung it, and popped the end of it into Fairweather's face. He screamed and dropped his rifle, raising both hands to cover his eyes. Blood trickled between his fingers.

Andrew knelt to pick up the fallen rifle. The stranger at the edge of the wood finished reloading before he came on into camp. He glanced at the three black people, at Michael and Andrew, then turned his attention to the woman. "Sally. You all right?"

She took two steps toward him and stopped. The torn shirt hung open, but she no longer seemed to care. "Cephus! Cephus Carpenter, I thought you'd gone home." She began laughing and crying both at the same time, then ran into his open arms.

Michael's jaw dropped, his mouth hanging open and dry as cotton. He thought they stood a fair chance of squeezing each other to death, the way they clenched.

Fairweather hunched against a wagon wheel, crying in agony. Andrew nudged Michael. "What're we goin' to do with him?"

Michael said grittily, "Ought to shoot the son of a bitch while we've got the chance."

Fairweather turned, finally. He brought his hands down from his face. Michael felt his stomach turn a little. Where Fairweather's left eye had been was a mass of bleeding flesh. The man dropped to his knees and cried out for God's mercy.

Andrew grimaced. "I'd've shot him a while ago and been glad at the chance. But he's helpless now."

"Man like that ain't *ever* helpless," Michael replied. "He'll be dangerous as long as he draws breath."

He turned back toward Sally and the stranger. This morning he had willingly ridden away from her, leaving her for whoever else might come along and win her acceptance. Now, seeing her clutching a stranger, he felt a sense of betrayal, though he had no right. Jealousy was a new experience for him; he did not know quite how to accommodate it.

Sally faced him, finally. Joyful tears stained her cheeks. "Cephus, this is Michael. He saved my life once already. You came along and saved it the second time."

Michael nodded toward the kneeling, cringing Fairweather. "You done pretty good service yourself, with that whip."

Carpenter's hand, big as a side of ham, squeezed Sally's shoulder. "She always *could* knock a horsefly off of the nigh leader's ear with that thing. She's popped *me* good a time or two, when I went for the whiskey once too often."

She said, "If you want a drink now, Cephus, you just go and help yourself. I won't say a word about it."

The closer Michael stood to him, the taller and larger Carpenter appeared. He had a strong jaw that looked as if it might have been carved from an oak stump. Michael supposed women would find such a man handsome; he had no basis for judgment.

He looked questioningly at Sally. "I thought you told me he was dead."

"No, I just said he was gone."

Carpenter hugged her again. "She run me off, is what happened. She done right. I was drinkin' up the merchandise."

Sally declared, "You told me you was goin' back to Kentucky."

"I started, sure enough I did. But I didn't get far. I laid awake worryin' about how you'd make out with just Marcus and them, so I turned around and follered you afoot. I been behind you, watchin' from a distance, makin' sure nothin' happened to you."

She said accusingly, "We could've used your help gettin' the wagons over that creek yesterday."

"I was afraid you'd run me off again. I seen these fellers come along to help you, so I stayed back on the other side."

Sally glanced at Michael, and he caught a momentary worry in her eyes. She asked Carpenter, "Where'd you camp last night?"

"Back a mile or so, far enough to where you wouldn't see my fire. I was still a ways behind when the shootin' started a while ago."

Relief flickered in Sally's eyes where the concern had been. Carpenter couldn't have seen her and Michael together out by the picket line.

Carpenter said, "I ain't had a drink of whiskey since I left you. I thought it was lifesblood. I found out it ain't. You're lifesblood to me."

She cautioned him, "I ain't got any easier to live with."

Michael discerned that she was already subtly setting conditions for whatever reconciliation they might agree upon. Carpenter was going to be a lap dog, even though a big one.

Carpenter said, "I ain't easy to live with either. But I've found out it's a lot harder livin' without you than with you."

Sternly she told him, "I ain't askin' you, understand. But if you're of a mind to stay . . ."

"Woman, that's what I been tryin' to tell you." Carpenter turned away from her, toward the black family. "I'll see after Marcus. Looks like they used him pretty hard."

Sally's gaze went to Michael. She reached out to him, then quickly withdrew her hand. "It's a good thing you'd already left. I might have a hard time makin' up my mind between the two of you."

He shook his head. Cephus Carpenter was a big man, workhorse-strong, but he exhibited a gentleness in helping Marcus to his feet. "No you wouldn't. I wouldn't even come close."

He heard a horse moving through the timber and turned quickly. Fairweather was gone. Andrew stood with his hands on his hips, staring off into the woods.

Michael demanded, "You didn't let him go . . ."

Andrew shrugged. "We talked about killin' him, but when it come down to cases I couldn't do it. And I didn't want you to have to. So I put him on his horse and told him to git while the gittin' was good."

"Like as not he'll live to plague us another time."

"Maybe not. He promised we'd never see his face again. I told him if we ever did it'd be over the sights of a rifle. He blessed me and rode off."

On balance, Michael was more relieved than angered. He had wondered what in hell they could do with Fairweather. Andrew had taken a painful decision out of his hands.

Andrew motioned toward the three dead men, scattered over the campground. "Looks like we got some buryin' to do."

Michael frowned. Sally Boone stood beside Cephus Carpenter, helping him and Nellie minister to Marcus and the boy Isham. "That Carpenter's got big shoulders, just built for usin' a shovel. It'll give him somethin' to do the rest of the day."

He figured Sally and Carpenter would have no trouble finding something to do after dark.

"They don't need us anymore," he said, a little of regret coloring his voice. "We left a pack mule staked out yonder a ways. We better go see after him."

Riding away, he tried not to look back, but as they reached the lightning-struck tree he had to. Sally and Carpenter were in each other's arms again.

Andrew set him to looking westward. He asked, "Reckon how far it still is to Natchitoches?"

PART 3

THE RETURN TO TEXAS

NATCHITOCHES, 1821

22

His name was Moses—Moses Austin—and like his Biblical namesake he sought a promised land.

A Connecticut yankee, Austin had seen youthful dreams come to flower, then languish and die. He had been successful as a banker, a miner, a businessman. Then, at age fifty-four, through circumstances of a national scope far beyond his control, he went dead broke in the money panic which almost paralyzed the new country in 1818. Though American-born, he had once, by an unusual set of circumstances, been a Spanish subject, and it was to Spain that he turned in hope of recouping what he had so painfully lost.

Austin had once found a pleasant and profitable place for himself mining lead in Virginia, until that vein began to thin. He had then learned of lead deposits in Missouri when that land was still a province of Spain. He had visited the provincial capital, St. Louis, in 1797 and obtained permission to seek out and develop the lead deposits. As a Spanish citizen he founded the first permanent settlement in what would become Washington County, Missouri. He regained his American citizenship when Missouri became a part of the United States by purchase in 1804.

Like many another businessman ruined by the national panic, he could have gone back to the land and the plow, but Austin was not by nature or training a farmer. He was an entrepreneur. He was aware that Spain had become nervous about its undeveloped Texas lands, fearing for its ability to hold them against the aggressive encroachment already experienced at the hands of French and American adventurers. So in 1820 he made a long, wearying ride to Texas to offer Spanish authorities a proposition he believed was of advantage to them and to himself.

His timing could not have been worse. Spanish officialdom had been bloodied by years of internal rebellion and by filibuster incursions from outside. There had been Philip Nolan, Gutierrez, and Magee, and just recently, a nephew of Andrew Jackson named James Long. American visitors of any kind were regarded with suspicion that bordered on hostility. Austin rode eight hundred miles into Texas and entered San Antonio de Bexar only to confront an embittered veteran of several anti-filibuster campaigns, Governor Antonio Martinez. In no mood for conversation with an *extranjero americano*, Martinez ordered Austin to leave immediately. If he remained in Bexar even for the night, Martinez declared, he would be arrested.

Shocked and bitterly disappointed after the health-breaking hardships he had endured to reach that colonial capital, Moses Austin trudged wearily

across the old plaza to get his horse. Then occurred
one of those chance coincidences upon which history occasionally hinges. Someone called his name.
Turning, he saw a friendly face, an acquaintance
from the old days in Spanish Missouri. This was a
Hollander known in Texas as Baron de Bastrop. The
baron, because of his title and his aristocratic manner, had the governor's ear and his friendship, for
Martinez served in an isolated frontier settlement
where such refined company was scarce. Bastrop reacted with sympathy to Austin's plight. He took his
old friend back for a second and more cordial audience with Martinez. He argued persuasively that
Austin had once been a loyal and productive subject of Spain and wished to be so again. Moreover,
Austin could hand-pick and bring into Texas honest and reliable settlers who would set up a barrier
not only against further filibuster expeditions but
against the hostile Indians of the western frontier.
He pointed out that San Antonio citizens were occasionally terrorized by Comanche Indians who rode
in from the rugged limestone hills and paraded their
savage glory upon the streets as if they held title to
the town.

Even those Spanish officers most militant against
foreigners saw logic in the baron's argument. Put
Americans between Spanish settlers and the Indians,
they said. If the Indians must kill someone, let it be
foreigners.

His fortunes seemingly reversed, Austin left for
Missouri with a signed and sealed agreement in the
pocket of his coat, the right to settle three hundred
families on two hundred thousand acres along the
Colorado and Brazos Rivers at the head of San Ber-
nardo Bay. Texas was to be his promised land.

But promise was not enough. Robbed on the trail, set afoot without supplies in the midst of winter, Austin suffered terribly from hunger and cold. He reached home in a desperately weakened condition. Under the pressure of time, he dispatched his bachelor son Stephen, then twenty-seven, to take care of his Texas interests until he might recover enough to resume the responsibilities himself. But like the other Moses, the elder Austin would not live to see his promised land.

Stephen had been more than willing to accept the job for, like his father, he had suffered financially from the money panic and had been studying law and working as a newspaper editor in New Orleans to put bread on the family table while his father was away. Capable, energetic, he had itched for a chance once again to become something more than someone else's employee.

And so, in June of 1821, Stephen F. Austin took passage on the shallow-draft steamer *Beaver* out of New Orleans, its paddlewheel churning against the strong current of the Mississippi and then the Red River of the South, bound for the Creole town of Natchitoches, Louisiana . . . and destiny.

Marie Villaret was placing supper dishes on the long table in the dining room when her mother called from the front gallery.

"Marie, *vengas*." There was a sense of urgency in her tone. Marie set down a stack of plates and hurried out onto the broad porch which stretched the length of the house. The dark-complexioned little woman unfolded her arms to point. In Spanish she said, "Look, Marie, here comes that nice Mister Robertson riding down the street."

Feeling tricked, Marie placed her hands on her slender hips and declared impatiently, "Mama, that nice Mister Robertson rides down this street every day."

"There are other streets. I am sure he uses this one only because he hopes for a glimpse of you. The least you can do is to curtsy when he tips his hat."

This had become a long-running game between Marie and her mother, who worried that Marie had long since passed her nineteenth birthday without giving any sign that she contemplated marriage. This was despite the fact that she was considered a beauty by the young men of Natchitoches, who were bewitched by the flash in her black eyes. She had received diligent teaching in the art of snaring a prosperous husband, the born duty of every proper daughter in Natchitoches. Mrs. Villaret said, "If he stops, you should invite him in for coffee. It would give you a chance to show him how well you have learned the English."

Marie had grown up speaking Spanish with her mother and French with her father. The study of English had been a struggle. "Mother, I did not learn the English so I could flirt with every young American who comes to town. I learned so I could be of more help to Papa in the store."

"You learned it because you hoped that wild boy from Tennessee would return. But he will never be back. He probably has a wife by now, and two or three children. Or he has gone outlaw and rides with a price on his head. I have told you that twenty times."

"You have told me a hundred times, Mama, perhaps two hundred. And you may be right. But that does not mean I care to throw myself at the feet of every young man who happens to ride down this street."

"With your beauty, Marie, you do not have to throw yourself at anyone's feet. That is for them to do for you."

The young Robertson dutifully tipped his hat and smiled. Marie curtsied in return to preserve a measure of peace in the house. But she put no invitation into her smile, and Robertson did not presume that one was implied. He spoke a polite "Good afternoon," and went on his way.

Mrs. Villaret turned on her daughter in disappointment. "You should use that pretty face while you can. One day you will look in the mirror and see a frustrated, wrinkled old maid."

"I am not yet twenty, Mama. There is still time enough. Surely you have better things to do with *your* time than to stand on the gallery and look for young men to match me with."

"I came out to look for your father," Mrs. Villaret said defensively. "It is time he came home for his supper."

"He said someone was bringing in goods from the Sabine. You know how it is with Papa and that side of the business. He will come when he comes."

"Perhaps someday with a policeman close behind him."

Marie had learned years ago that there were two parts to her father's business. One was the store, in which she had begun helping him as a clerk and bookkeeper. That part was open to the world and freely acknowledged. Of the other part, the women

of the family professed no knowledge. If asked,
they would deny that it existed. It had to do with
the trade between merchants of Louisiana and the
colonists of Spanish Texas. Prohibited from the earliest days of Spanish and French settlement, it had
begun almost as soon as farmers on the Spanish side
of the Sabine River started growing crops and seeking a market nearer than the only legal one open
to them, San Antonio de Bexar, which was far, far
south down the Camino Real. It had been a barter
trade for the most part, farmers, trappers, and wild-
horse runners trading eastward for necessities they
could obtain only at ruinous prices through legal
commercial channels in the south. There had also
been, almost from the time the first intrepid Frenchman daringly set foot in Spanish territory, a quiet
but flourishing trade with the peaceful Indians of
northern Texas.

For more than a century this type of enterprise—
smuggling, the authorities called it—had continued
with mutual benefit to the people on both sides of
the Sabine. It had become legal during the years
Spain owned Louisiana, then was again branded
illicit when that vast province reverted to French
ownership and finally to the United States. Through
the long decades, some officials fought it. Others
quietly looked in the opposite direction, often with
open palms outstretched behind their backs, waiting
to receive a share of the profits. Condoned or not,
the trade went on. And Baptiste Villaret had been
involved in it since he was old enough to count furs
or weigh corn. It was a financially important ad-
junct to the conduct of his acknowledged mercantile
enterprise. The Texas trade might have been illegal,
but immoral it was not, at least in the sight of most

citizens of Natchitoches. Directly and indirectly, it was bread and butter for this old Creole community.

Now, like her mother, Marie used her father's lateness as an excuse for looking up and down the street. And as had been the case with her mother, it was not her father she sought. A thousand times, and a thousand more, she had watched that street, wishing *he* would come.

Michael Lewis would be a grown man now. She had often imagined what he would look like and wondered if she would even recognize him. Surely he would have changed much from the boy she had helped nurse back to his strength five years ago, after the Spanish soldiers had so cruelly left him for dead, along with his father and the others of their party.

An artist with the brush, she had several times painted his portrait from memory, trying to make allowances for the changes the years would have wrought upon that youthful face. Now she was no longer sure what part of the image was truly memory and what was her own invention with bristle and paint.

During the last few years her mother had contrived again and again to bring her into the company of eligible young bachelors, hoping first one and then another might find favor in her eyes. But always she compared them unfavorably to her memory of the boy from Tennessee who had awakened in her the first stirrings of young womanhood, yearnings she was a long time in fully understanding. She had set an impossible standard for other young men to meet. She recognized that her image of him was probably exaggerated beyond reality, for no man could be that handsome, that strong and forceful. But the image was there, and she could not put it aside.

Since the day Michael Lewis had ridden away toward Tennessee with old Eli Pleasant, she had not tolerated any doubt that one day he would ride back again. And if he left another time, she would go with him.

Her mother said with resignation, "Come, we must see to supper for the children. We will simply have to heat it over again when your father comes home."

"Yes, Mama." Marie turned to follow her mother through the door. She paused then, catching movement from the corner of her eye. She looked back and smiled.

"There he comes now, Mama. He brings company. We will have to set extra places."

Mrs. Villaret frowned. "I wish he would tell me . . . How many are there?"

Marie counted four, including her father. All were walking, but three led horses. She squinted. "One of them is the old man, Eli Pleasant. The others, I don't know." She started again to enter the house but could not move. A chill ran up her spine, and she shivered involuntarily.

Her mother caught it. "What is the matter with you, girl? It is too warm an evening for you to be shivering. I hope you are not coming down with the malaria."

Marie tried to answer but could only shake her head. Her throat was so tight she could not speak. Her hands trembled as she stared at the young man striding along on her father's left. It was not . . . it could not be, for this man was much taller than the young Michael Lewis she remembered. . . . She stared, and she felt her pulse quicken. She caught her mother's arm and gripped it so tightly that her knuckles turned white.

"It is *him*, Mama. As God is my witness, it is *him*!"

23

Long before they reached Natchitoches, the narrow and often-dim trace they had followed merged with a much more heavily traveled trail, even a highway as highways were judged by the standards to which Michael was accustomed. More and more he found the land settled, the better irrigable portions broken out into cultivation. There were fields of tobacco and tall sugar cane and, perhaps most of all, of cotton, mile after mile, tended by sweating black slaves and small landowners too poor to own slaves, bending to hoe out the weeds that otherwise would sap the plants' strength and leave few bolls to scratch and bleed pickers' fingers at fall harvest, fewer bales to be shipped by flatboat or shallow-draft steamer down the Red River to the Mississippi for cash on the New Orleans market.

Andrew found the land much to his liking. Michael knew he had but to suggest, and Andrew would gladly stop anywhere. The farmer instinct made him look at a piece of raw, unclaimed land

and convert it in his mind's eye to a neatly plowed field, crops growing tall and fruitful where the grass had been. Andrew asked eagerly, "How about us locatin' a piece of land that nobody's usin' and stakin' us a claim on it? This seedcorn needs to be put in the ground pretty soon if it's to make a crop this year."

Sometimes Michael wished they had eaten the seedcorn the first week on the trail so it would not be a plague on his conscience. He remembered times on that other trip to Texas when someone suggested they might already have found a good place to light, that a bird in the hand was better than a wild horse still running free on some distant prairie. Mordecai's reaction was invariably, "It's better farther west." Michael repeated his father's words to Andrew as if they were his own.

It had always been better farther west.

There were farms aplenty, and small settlements where Michael and Andrew could have bought the necessities if they had had the money to spare. They found it more difficult to live off the land, for as settlement had increased, wild game had diminished. They caught fish, and in swampy areas sometimes frogs.

Andrew said ruefully, "If a man travels with you he'd better develop a high likin' for squirrel." They had eaten plenty of it on this trip. "I get to feelin' like I want to climb a tree."

"You'd better do it pretty quick," Michael declared with a strong touch of irony, "before some new settler cuts the trees all down."

As before, Michael often found that when they rode up to farmhouses or met travelers on the road he had difficulty in conducting a satisfactory conversation. Many spoke French or Spanish, their English broken or nonexistent. He had learned a scattering of French words as well as some Spanish from Marie Villaret while he recuperated from his wounding at the hands of the king's soldiers. But he could not remember one of them now.

After an unsuccessful attempt to ask a farmer how far it still was to Natchitoches, Andrew said, "You'd think these folks've been part of us long enough to learn American."

Michael felt defensive, remembering many kindnesses shown him by the people of Natchitoches. "They been through too many hands already, and they don't know who they may belong to next. Maybe me and you had better learn a little French."

Andrew said mischievously, "Maybe I will, if you'll introduce me to Marie."

Michael tried to think of a retort but realized his brother was trying in a teasing way to bait him. "Andrew, I do believe you could find somethin' to laugh about in pneumonia."

"I'd sure look for it. Life has got to be pretty tough for anybody who can't find it in him to laugh a little."

"I laugh, now and again."

"I know. I've seen you do it at least twice since we started this trip."

The long journey had brought the two of them to respect one another's strengths and to overlook whatever shortcomings they had. Michael had decided far back on the trail that they made a balanced pair. Sometimes the weight of responsibility caused him to stretch himself too tightly. Andrew had an easy knack of offering a light-humored comment or simply making a face that relaxed the tension.

Michael tried to shift the subject to something benign. "You notice how red-colored the land has gotten since we forded that last river?"

Andrew smiled. "As red as your face gets every time I ask you about that girl by the name of Marie."

Andrew was never going to quit nudging him about Marie. He decided to lie a little. "She was an old lady who helped take care of me after I got shot, that's all."

"She didn't sound that old, the way you talked to her in your sleep."

Michael's thoughts began to stray from the land over which they were riding. Often during the long days and the long, warm nights, he remembered with a glow the night he had lain with Sally Boone. He relived in fancy the passions she had stirred. She had aroused something powerful in him, had awakened a slumbering wolf he was not sure he could put back under control.

He supposed he should be ashamed, taking pleasure from such memories, letting them run free without any effort at putting them to rest. He vaguely recalled a Biblical injunction delivered by an itinerant preacher who had sheltered beneath the Lewis roof, a solemn declaration that to sin in the mind was the same as to sin in the flesh. Michael had tried it both ways. Stimulating as the thoughts were, they did not compare with the flesh.

The realization that he was unlikely to see Sally again set him to thinking more and more about the dark-haired Marie Villaret. He was not sure why, for the differences between them were considerable. Marie was gentle-raised and mannered, Sally wild and free. He could not conceive of Marie coming

unbidden to a stranger's bed in the night and crawling between the blankets. Of course, when he had
known Marie he had been little more than a boy
and she only a young girl, both of them unsure and
shy. But he remembered that she had made him feel
some of the same emotions that Sally had later set
loose. The difference was that the emotions had
gone nowhere then; he would not have known what
to do with them.

He would know now.

"Town looks some bigger than I remember it,"
he said upon their approach to Natchitoches. "But
maybe my memory is some shy on particulars."

"Like on an old lady named Marie?"

He would not admit to Andrew that she had been
much upon his mind, that in regard to her, at least,
his memory was but little diminished.

Andrew asked, "I wonder if she's got any sisters?"

"She does." He added gratuitously, "And all ugly."

"I'd want to judge that for myself."

Michael quickly discerned a more pronounced
American presence. Not far from the place where
the Frenchman, St. Denis, had built Fort St. Jean
Baptiste a century earlier, American forces had established Fort Claiborne on two tall hills overlook-
ing the river. Seeing so many soldiers made Michael
uneasy at first because of his experience with the
Spanish. They aroused dark emotions in his subconscious though he knew on a conscious level that
these were fellow Americans; he had nothing to fear
from them.

Michael said, "At least maybe we'll find somebody

we can talk to. Sign on that store yonder has the name Smith on it. Another says Jackson. Used to be everything was French."

The first two people he approached to ask about Eli Pleasant gave him an apologetic shrug and said words he could not understand. The place was in no danger of turning fully American overnight, he decided. He could see signs that still bore names like Prudhomme and Moreau and Fontinot.

Michael and Andrew had bathed, shaved, and washed out their clothes before they rode into town. The most logical course was to go directly to the Villaret house and inquire about Eli, he knew. But the closer he came to it, the more reluctant he felt. Marie was probably married now, with a houseful of noisy children. She was probably fat and far removed from the idealized memory he had carried so long.

And why should he want to see her anyway? He had no intention of getting married, of domesticating like his Uncle Benjamin. That had not been Papa's way, though Papa had tried, and it would not be Michael's.

Deferring the disappointment, he led Andrew through town and down to the river. They sat on their horses and watched a small steamboat forging against the reddish water's current, making its way to a landing where dry wood was stacked high, waiting to serve its brief and fiery destiny in the ship's boiler. Though they had paused on the Mississippi for a whole day and had watched larger boats than these, the sights still aroused awe in the two young men from the Tennessee woods. A couple of flatboats drifted in the opposite direction, their pace slow and lazy like the river.

"They was built here," Michael said, remembering what Eli had shown him. "That one yonder looks like it's stacked high with hides of some kind. They'll float all the way down to New Orleans and sell the hides and then rip the boat apart and sell the lumber."

Andrew observed, "Kind of like makin' a trip, then eatin' your pack mule."

Michael looked back at their own, which had never displayed the servile attitude expected of a beast of burden. "That wouldn't be too bad an idea."

Andrew laughed. "He's taken several bites out of *us*."

At a second landing Michael saw another steamboat tied up, a crew of black workmen unloading its varied cargo. He touched the horse's belly with his heels and moved off in that direction for a closer look. The sorrel shied at the unaccustomed noise and activity. Michael dismounted and patted him on the neck, speaking softly to give reassurance. When Big Red quieted, Michael turned his attention back to the steamboat. The name painted on it was *Beaver*. He marveled at the engineering genius which could put such a complicated contraption together and then keep it running.

Andrew declared with enthusiasm, "Ain't nothin' like this in Tennessee."

"Ain't no place in Tennessee to float it except the Mississippi."

A quiet, pleasant voice spoke behind them. "I would assume you gentlemen have not made the acquaintance of a steamboat."

Turning, Michael faced a thin young man he would take to be just a little one side or the other of thirty. He was obviously American from his speech and from the once-nice but now travel-worn coat and breeches, and the tall beaver hat. He had striking eyes; large, brown, and intense.

Michael replied, "No sir, where we come from, a boat like this would hang up in the shallows before it went a hundred feet. We never even seen a raft till we got to the Mississippi."

"By the look of you, and your pack mule, I would judge that you have just arrived."

Michael was reticent about imparting too much information to strangers. But he sensed that there was no harm in this friendly young fellow, a natural gentleman by the look of him. Michael took him for a store clerk or a bank teller or a lawyer; he had none of the hard-handed, sunburned look of the farmer about him and certainly none of the backwoodsman. He said, "Yes sir, we just now come in off of the trace. We was about to set out lookin' for an old friend name of Eli Pleasant. By chance would you know him?"

The stranger shook his head. "I have just arrived here myself, on that boat." He extended his hand. "My name is Austin. Stephen Austin."

Michael accepted the handshake, instinctively drawn to the man on sight. Something in Austin's eyes told him that there was no guile here, no ulterior motive for his friendliness. "This here is my brother Andrew. We've come down from Tennessee."

"You plan to take up farming land, I would imagine."

"Someplace. We ain't decided yet just where to turn our horses loose."

Austin gave the two men a moment's silent scrutiny. "I wonder . . . have you given Texas any thought?"

Michael blinked. "Texas? Sure, I have. But they shoot Americans there."

"Not necessarily. *I* am about to go to Texas myself. My father has the sanction of the Spanish authorities to settle three hundred American families there. I am on my way to work out the details. The Spanish want honest and industrious farmers. You look like farmers to me. Am I correct?"

Michael was hesitant in answering. Andrew said, "That's all we ever done, our whole lives."

"And are you by chance family men?"

Michael replied, "We're both bachelors."

"Do you have any prospects of marrying?"

"We didn't come here lookin' for wives. We come lookin' for land."

"According to the agreement my father worked out in Bexar, families will receive larger land grants than bachelors. If you come across any likely young ladies, you might wish to give the matter some consideration."

Texas. Michael stared at the steamboat, and it seemed to dissolve before his eyes. He saw the Texas he had explored with his father and Eli and the others, the great open prairies, the deep green forests, the clear-running streams. He felt a tingling from his head to his heels. To see it again . . .

Austin's voice broke into his consciousness. "Are you all right, Mister Lewis?"

Michael blinked and came back to reality. "Yes. I was just rememberin' . . ." He said no more.

Andrew put in, "He was in Texas some years ago, with Papa. They were catchin' wild horses to take back to Tennessee."

Austin's interest quickened. "You have been to

Texas before? Your experience might prove useful to me."

Michael winced. "My experience wouldn't be useful for anybody. They killed Papa there, the soldiers did, him and all the others except for me and Eli Pleasant."

Austin's eyes softened in sympathy. "I am sorry I introduced such an unpleasant subject. I can imagine why you might never want to see Texas again."

"It ain't that I wouldn't want to see it; I would. The place has stayed in my head all these years, like some kind of a ghost that never quits walkin'. Maybe if I did go back I could put the whole notion to rest."

"I am supposed to meet an official Spanish delegation here and travel down to Bexar with them."

Michael felt a sudden chill. "They got soldiers?"

"Possibly. I am not sure. Perhaps you two would like to accompany me."

Andrew was about to speak up, and Michael knew from his apparent eagerness what he would say. Michael declared, "Not with soldiers." He shuddered. "I don't think I could stand the company of Spanish soldiers after what they done."

Austin nodded. "I can understand. Well, should you change your mind before I leave, look me up. I'll not be difficult to find. It was a pleasure to become acquainted." He walked up the gangplank and onto the boat.

Michael watched him, paralyzed.

Andrew was silent for a time. "Michael, you don't look like you feel none too good."

"It was the things he said . . . about goin' to Texas . . . about us maybe goin' with him. Now that we've come this far, it don't seem quite real."

"Looks real enough to me. And I know it's been on your mind for the whole last five years."

"It has. But it's been more like a dream than somethin' actual. It's been like ghosts walkin' through my head, wakin' me up in the middle of the night. Ghosts of Papa and them, all that shootin', all that blood . . ."

"I've heard you sometimes. Seems to me like the way to drive away ghosts is to rush them head-on."

"But soldiers . . . I don't want nothin' to do with soldiers." Michael turned. "We ain't gettin' it done standin' here watchin' other people work. Let's go down to Ol' Baptiste Villaret's store and see if he can tell us somethin' about Eli."

Times had been good to Villaret, Michael thought. The store had been enlarged since his last time here. The growing settlement of the country was bringing a booming business up the Red River from New Orleans. He and Andrew had passed warehouses from which emanated the odor of skins, and baled remnants of last year's cotton crop stood awaiting shipment downriver to market, little feathers of dirty-white lint fluttering in the breeze that came up from the river. Trade goods from other parts of the world were moving up and down the street by dray cart and wagon.

"Looks like we come to a lively town," he said.

Andrew replied, "I guess this is the steppin'-off place to God knows where-all. There's a lot of country out yonder, and somewhere there's a place for us in it. Maybe, like Austin said, that place is Texas."

Michael dismounted and took a long look at

Villaret's place of business. "I just hope Ol' Eli is still among the livin'."

He recognized Villaret on sight; the man looked the same as the last time, perhaps a few pounds rounder about the middle, as befitted a busy merchant in a growing town. Villaret obviously did not know him, however. He approached the brothers with a smile. "And, my good friends, how may I serve you today?"

The French accent had not lessened a whit, nor had his friendly spirit.

Michael could not help smiling in return, remembering the kindness and generosity of the old man and his family. "You've already helped me, Mister Villaret. Was it not for you, I'd probably not be alive today. Look close and see if you remember."

Villaret turned his head a little to one side, concentrating with his left eye; Michael suspected the other was weakening "The face. I know the face. You are the boy Michael, that is it. The boy Michael from Tennessee. But a boy no longer."

He grabbed Michael's hand and pumped it vigorously, then threw his arms round him. Michael was not quite prepared for such a show of emotion. He half expected Villaret to kiss him—the French had a reputation for that—but Villaret stopped short of so extreme a display. "We had not heard from you. We were afraid you might have died . . ."

"No sir, not hardly." When Villaret stepped back for another study, Michael introduced him to Andrew. Villaret accepted him warmly. "Another Looees. He was a good man, your father. I am sure you are a good man too."

Michael wanted to ask about Marie but did not

want to be obvious. "How's your family? Miz Villaret and them?"

"All fine. All fine. You will go with me home for supper. They will all be glad to see you." He winked. "Especially one."

Michael stammered. "Marie . . . she still at home?" That was a way of asking if she were married without being too blunt.

"And where else would she be? A respectable young woman, not yet with husband . . ."

Michael knew the relief showed in his face. He knew by Villaret's widening smile that the old man saw it. Villaret said, "Mama has introduced her to many young men, but she seems not in a hurry to leave us. She will be very happy to see you, I think."

A knowing grin spread across Andrew's face. "An old woman who just helped take care of you, huh?"

Michael felt his face redden. He was defenseless against Andrew's humor. He decided it was time they get down to cases. "Mister Villaret, we was hopin' maybe you could tell us somethin' about Eli Pleasant. Is he anywhere around this country?"

Villaret's smile lost some of its warmth. "Has anyone said anything to you about Eli?"

"No. Is he dead or somethin'?"

Villaret shook his head. "He is much alive. There are certain authorities who probably wish he were otherwise."

"He in trouble?"

"All his life, Eli Pleasant has been in trouble. No more now than before. We all transgress against the law a little, when we feel the law is not just. Eli's transgressions are a bit more open than some. He moves things from the Spanish side to the American side, and in the other direction as well. He does not bother with the regulations."

"He's a smuggler, then."

"The deeds are not so bad as the name. We are all smugglers here, if one wishes to read the fine detail of the law. But the laws were written thousands of miles away by people who know nothing of the realities. We live with realities."

"Is Eli hidin' out?"

"There is no need. Some of the Spanish officials would gladly shoot him on sight if they could catch him, but here he comes and goes freely. Natchitoches officials look the other way. They too live with realities."

"We'd sure admire to see him, if you could point us the way."

The smile returned in all its glory. "If you would simply turn around . . ."

Michael heard footsteps behind him. Striding toward him between the barrels and bales came the old man whose face had been burned into his memory, the man who had carried him back out through the gates of Hell.

"Eli!"

The beard was a bit grayer but no better kept. Otherwise Michael saw no change. Eli was one of those men who seemed to age only to a point, then remain forever the same. Eli squinted, recognition evading him. When it came, he rushed forward with a shout and threw his arms around Michael, his forward momentum driving Michael backward. He would have fallen had he not bumped hard against a large wooden crate.

Eli stepped back for a second look. "Boy, you're the image of your ol' daddy, I swear you are." He paused, turning to give the same close study to Andrew. "And you're one of the Lewis boys too. Your ol' daddy's stamp is mighty strong."

"I'm Andrew."

Eli pulled a dirty handkerchief from a deep pocket and wiped his eyes and nose. "I never thought to see you boys again on this earth. What brings you so far?"

Michael and Andrew glanced at one another. Michael said, "Come a time we had to set out and find a place for ourselves. We was hopin' you might have some good notions."

Eli seemed pleased that his advice was considered to have merit. "Now, we'll do some thinkin' on that, we sure will. You boys go with me out to my place on the river. We'll look at some country. There's a-plenty to look at."

Villaret put in, "But it is too far to go tonight. You will come home and have supper with my family, all of you. Time enough tomorrow for you to let this old heathen take you out to his lair."

Villaret lived near enough to his store that he customarily walked rather than ride a horse or take a carriage. Michael, Andrew, and Eli led their horses and walked beside him. Michael noticed as they went along that men tipped their hats and women curtsied to Villaret. He was obviously a man of substance and respect. He remembered that his father had always said it was easy for a man to put on a false face and fool strangers, but he could not long fool his neighbors, for they came to know all sides of his nature.

Villaret said, "I must let Guadalupe Lucero know that you have come, Michael. He occasionally asks if we have heard anything of you."

Michael only vaguely remembered Lucero. He recalled that the man was a Spaniard, a fugitive from the authorities in Spanish Texas. "Why would he be interested in me?"

"Your enemies are his enemies. They have killed many of his people, just as they killed some of yours."

Eli said, "I doubt he's in town. He was by my place a day or two ago. Didn't say if he was on his way into Texas or on his way out. And I didn't feel like I ought to ask him."

Villaret said, "These are still troubled times on the other side of the Sabine. There is revolution afoot."

Eli declared, "There's been revolution afoot down there for a dozen years. All it's come to has been a heap of killin'."

Villaret grimaced. "And there will be more. It is not a good place to be in these times."

Michael remembered the young man he and Andrew had met at the dock. "There's a feller named Austin goin' down into Texas to see about settlin' some American families."

Villaret nodded. "So I have heard. I fear he will not have a happy time."

Andrew said, "He asked us if we'd like to go with him."

Villaret missed a stride. "My advice is probably worth only what it costs you, which is nothing. But in your place, I would think a long time. Texas is not a healthy place for an American." He glanced at Eli. "Especially for one who is constantly in and out of it, like the wind in the night."

Eli shrugged. "I got friends. They take care of me."

Michael said, "But it's big and wide open and got very few people. It's got worlds of room to grow."

Villaret nodded. "And worlds of room for a man to die in."

They rounded a corner, and Michael could see the Villaret house ahead, its high-pitched roof, its long deep gallery just as he remembered them. And on the gallery he saw two women standing. One was Mrs. Villaret. The other . . .

Marie hurried down the steps and out into the street. Michael heard her mother calling, "Marie. Marie, no! A lady waits."

Marie Villaret did not wait. She rushed toward Michael, her wide skirts flaring. Michael's sorrel horse took fright and jerked the reins from his hand. Michael made no effort at retrieval. He strode forward, almost in a run, to meet Marie. They came together in the middle of the street. Wildly she threw her arms around him, and unashamedly she kissed him on the mouth, almost smothering him with her joy.

"Michael! Michael, I knew someday you would come!"

Andrew caught Big Red and stood grinning. He declared, "Prettiest old woman I ever saw."

24

Through supper, Michael could not escape the apprehension in Mrs. Villaret's eyes as she gazed at him across the table. He tried not to look at her, concentrating his attention upon Marie. She sat opposite him, where he had an unobstructed view without having to turn his head. He suspected Marie had arranged the seating that way. Hungry, he gorged himself on the kitchen-cooked food he had missed during the weeks on the trail. He felt a little ashamed of his gluttony, but not enough to keep him from refilling his plate twice. Marie ate little. Every time he lifted his gaze to her face, he found her staring at him with eyes dark and warm and wonderfully alive, eyes a man could tumble into and just keep falling.

Baptiste and Eli had many questions, but Michael held silent and let Andrew provide most of the answers. He would have sounded like a babbling idiot anyway, he thought, with his mind on Marie instead of the conversation. She had blossomed to full

flower during the years since he had last seen her,
somewhat like his sister Heather, except that there
was little about Marie's features which resembled
Heather's. Marie's eyes were black, where Heather's
were blue. Her skin was smooth and olive, where
Heather's was fair and given to blistering in the sun
if she failed to wear her bonnet. Marie was a bit
more slender than Heather; he had a notion a man
could almost reach around her waist with his two
hands and touch fingers. The thought of doing so
brought him a fleeting pleasure, then uneasiness.
The way her eyes sparkled, he suspected she might
somehow be reading his mind.

Halfway through supper he felt something nudge
his foot. He first thought one of the family dogs had
sneaked beneath the table. But Marie smiled, and he
realized she was rubbing her toes against his boot.
The sensation was erotic, for a moment bringing up
a discomforting memory of Sally Boone. Warmth
rushed to his cheeks. Laughter danced in Marie's
dark eyes. He wondered if she realized the extent
of the effect she was having on him. He glanced
about apprehensively, fearing someone might have
noticed. No one showed any sign, so he answered
Marie's gesture by rubbing his foot against hers.
He thought her face flushed a little, but perhaps he
was misled by her smile that lighted the room like a
dozen candles.

When everyone finished supper, Mrs. Villaret
stood up and began issuing orders to her children
in Spanish. Michael sensed that she was instructing
them to clear the table and put away the food—
what little the hungry visitors had left—for another
meal. Marie began stacking plates. Baptiste Villaret
stopped her. In English he said, "Marie, the others

can do this. You have a guest. Why do you not take him out onto the gallery?"

Mrs. Villaret gave her husband and her daughter that same anxious look Michael had seen before. She said something in Spanish. Marie glanced provocatively at Michael. She took his hand and led him out the front door. She seated herself on a wooden bench and patted the place beside her.

Michael hesitated. "I get a strong idee that your mother ain't a bit keen on me comin' back."

"Do not worry about Mama. It was Papa who sent us out here. Papa is French, and a romantic. Sit down."

He sat beside her, leaving the space of two hands between them. She inched up against him. The image of Sally Boone intruded again.

"Ain't you afraid your neighbors will gossip?"

"On the front porch it is all right to sit. It is our way. If we sat where we could not be seen, then they would have something to whisper."

Michael was not sure he followed her logic, but he accepted it. He puzzled about one thing. "Last time I was here we couldn't talk to one another much. I didn't speak French, and you didn't speak American. Now you talk it pert' near as good as I do."

"I have worked hard to learn the English. I have always known you would come back."

"You done real good."

"What matters is to understand. I hope you understand me, Michael Lewis. In all that time, I do not forget you. I see other men and I compare, and always it is you. Sometimes I close my eyes and think very hard, and I believe you are thinking of me too. It is like we are talking though we are many miles apart. Does that seem silly to you, Michael?"

"I never did come up with such a notion. But I wish I had."

"You have thought of me, Michael?"

"Sure I did, many a time. Kept rememberin' what you looked like, wonderin' if you'd changed?"

"And have I changed?"

"A heap. I kept rememberin' a girl, fourteen, fifteen years old. But look at you now, a grown woman."

She slipped her hand into his. "Do you know what a grown woman thinks about, Michael?"

He shook his head. "I've got no idee."

Her fingers squeezed his hand. "The same things a grown man thinks about."

The invitation was overpowering. He leaned to kiss her, thinking the neighbors be damned. But Mrs. Villaret stepped out onto the porch, and he pulled back in frustration. Marie's mother gave them a moment's suspicious glance, then walked to a chair at the far end of the gallery and sat, cooling herself with a folding black Spanish fan. She had appointed herself chaperone.

Marie squeezed Michael's hand again before she released it and placed both hands properly in her lap. Softly she said, "Mama is Spanish. She does not remember how it is when people are young."

"Maybe she does remember." He had a guilty feeling that it might be a good thing the old lady showed up when she did. He was beginning to have some Sally Boone notions. They were not appropriate, not with this girl.

Marie said, "Now that you're here, what will you do?"

"Look around the country, see if we can find a place that me and Andrew would like to settle on.

We're fixin' to go out with Eli in the mornin'. He knows some places to take us."

"Eli takes many risks. He is an old man, and he has not so much to lose. You are a young man. You would have much to lose." She leaned against him, and the warmth of her body led him to ease one arm around her slim waist. He stole a glance at Mrs. Villaret. Her fan was working more rapidly, but she held her place. If he went any further, she would put a stop to it.

Marie said, "When you find your land, you will build a house on it?"

"Andrew admires lookin' up at a roof come night-time. Me, I ain't that particular."

"You will have everything you need in the house . . . table, chairs, beds, a fireplace?"

"A house has to have all them things."

"A house needs more, Michael. It needs a woman."

Michael sensed the direction she was trying to carry the conversation. He felt a sudden caution. "Are you askin'?"

"That is for the man to do. But I was hoping you would."

He felt a nervous prickling of his skin. "Marie . . . if I was in a marryin' frame of mind, you'd be the one I'd ask. But—I don't know how I can explain this to you—Papa was always of a restless and solitary nature. Never could stay put in one place. He was always off in the woods or goin' out to hunt new country. Half the time, my mother never had any idee where he was at. Papa tried, but it just wasn't in him to be what he ought to've been to her. The hard truth is, he ought never to've got married.

"He was a good man, but he just wasn't meant for a husband. He couldn't stay in one place the way she needed him to. And I'm afraid I'm too much like him. I wouldn't want to put a woman through the miserable times my mother had, not knowin' when Papa'd ever come home, or if he'd come home . . . afraid he'd die a long ways off and she'd never see him again. When he finally did, she died a little, too. I wouldn't want that for you."

Marie took his hand in hers and pressed it firmly against her waist, out of Mrs. Villaret's sight. "But your mother never stopped loving him."

He remembered that his mother had leaned upon his Uncle Benjamin for support at times, but he could honestly say, "No, she never did."

"Then that is your answer, Michael. If a woman loved you, she would love you no matter where you lived, and how you lived. And if at times you had to travel alone, she would want to make a home that you could always come back to. If you tried to take from her that right to love you, would you make her happy?"

He could not give her a satisfactory answer. "I just wouldn't want to make you . . . her . . . unhappy."

Her fingers tightened on his hand. "You could never make me unhappy, Michael. So go, this time. Go with Eli Pleasant. Find your land, build your house. One day you will come back looking for me. However long that may be, I will be waiting."

Turning, she put her arms around him, forcefully pulled him against her soft bosom and kissed him with a ferocity that took him by surprise. Heat rolled over him like the blaze in a newly lighted fireplace.

Down the porch, Mrs. Villaret loudly cleared her throat.

Marie stood up and faced him, holding onto his

hands. He saw fire in her black eyes. "There, Michael Lewis. Forget that if you can. Forget *me* if you can."

She walked down the gallery toward her dismayed mother, then entered the house without looking back.

Michael raised one hand to his tingling lips. He would not forget . . . not if he traveled ten thousand miles.

Eli Pleasant had never been one to let the rising sun shine on his sleeping face. He and Michael and Andrew were on the trail by good daylight, leading the recalcitrant pack mule Jethro which had come over the trace from Tennessee, as well as several of Eli's. Except for a few supplies which Eli needed to restock his cabin, his pack mules carried no load. Eli hinted that they had come to Natchitoches heavily laden with goods traded from Indians on the Texas side of the river. Neither Spanish nor American authorities had taxed them, for the tax collectors went home at night. That was Eli's favorite time for traveling when his mules carried a load.

"Cooler," he explained, "and easier on the stock."

They rode through well-developed countryside at first, past plantations which sprawled across huge expanses of red soil, past small farmsteads which supported perhaps one family. "It's a rich country," Eli said, "if one's taste runs in that direction. Me, I like it better where I don't hear my neighbor's ax ring of a mornin', and where the soldiers don't hardly ever come. I get fidgety when I feel somebody lookin' over my shoulder."

Michael nodded, for he understood. A little bit

of company went a long way. He had been glad
enough to leave Natchitoches, except for one regret
which haunted him every mile. That was the good-
bye he had spoken to Marie Villaret.

She had challenged him to forget her kiss. It
would be useless to try. He entertained himself with
remembering how it had been, and his memories
would expand to include Sally Boone, except that in
a little while it was not Sally's face he saw or whose
body he touched; it was Marie's.

He felt a little guilty. Where he came from, a man
could get killed for such thoughts if they became
known. He had no intention of telling anyone. But
some of it must have shown, for Andrew said, "I
couldn't've gone off and left that girl so easy if it
was me."

"It isn't you."

"I wish it was. If you don't want her, how about
givin' her to me?"

Michael's face warmed. "You wouldn't know
what to do with a girl if you had one."

"I was always a willin' learner."

"Sometimes you're a vexation and a pain."

After many miles, Eli said, "This is where the neutral strip starts."

"The what?" Michael asked.

"It taken the Spanish and American governments
a long time to agree where the boundary line is between Texas and Louisiana. So they set up a neutral
strip from the Sabine east about halfways to Natchitoches where neither side was supposed to settle or
to send their soldiers. It pretty soon got to be an
outlaw country, and it still is. People settle here now
and some rough ol' boys have made theirselves a
home in here. If you're lookin' for somebody that

don't want to be found, chances are he's in the strip someplace. Ain't much law except what a man carries on him. Get in trouble and there ain't no officers comin' to help you out."

"*You* live here, don't you?"

"The wild ones take me as one of them. You'll see a white locust tree at my place, with Spanish daggers planted on both sides of it. That's a sign that I won't bother the boys if they won't bother me. I don't see nothin', and I don't tell nothin'. If governments could get together like the people in the strip, there wouldn't be no more war. Not much, anyway."

They came late in the day to a cabin just short of the river. Eli said, "It ain't too much for pretty, but the roof is sound. I built her far enough up from the floodline that I don't get chased out of bed by high water. Man gets to be my age, he needs his rest."

It was a single-room cabin built of logs in the most rudimentary style, with a small porch but no dog-run. Living alone, Eli didn't need much space. Michael thought the small barn and a lean-to shed out at the horse pens looked more solid than the cabin. Eli was a man who took care of his animals.

Eli said, "Had me a woman out here for a while, widder from Natchitoches. Frenchwoman, she was, and hard to satisfy. Kept complainin' about the cabin. Said I either had to build her a better one or take her back to town. The longer I studied on it, the less I could see wrong with the cabin and the more I could see wrong with *her*. So I taken her back to town. She'd already hounded one man to death. I wasn't fixin' to let her do it to me."

As Eli had said, a white locust tree stood in front of the cabin, a dagger planted on either side. Farther back, Michael had noticed a couple of other places featuring the same display, but he had thought little of it at the time. This, he decided, was self-government in a most elementary form.

They unsaddled their horses and unpacked the mule Jethro, which promptly buckled its legs and rolled over in the sand. The horses followed suit, the mule kicking at both of them while they were down. Michael regretted that he had not taken time to attempt a good trade while they were in Natchitoches.

Eli had a field of corn and some tobacco. Michael thought both needed more tending than they had received. He suspected they were only a secondary consideration; Eli's real interests were commercial. He walked out past the cabin to the slope that slanted down toward the Sabine River. His nerves tingled as he stared at the water, then lifted his gaze to the line of trees and spots of open prairie he could see on the other side.

Texas!

He found himself trembling. Old images surged back like a river in flood. His eyes misted. He remembered the other time he had come from Louisiana to this river and had waited impatiently while his father and Eli scouted the western side for danger.

"Papa!" he said under his breath, wishing he could bring back the day, wishing they *had* found danger and had turned around in time. Things might have ended differently.

But probably not. Mordecai might have delayed his plans but he would never have given them up. It had always been his way to go ahead with whatever he intended to do, no matter the odds. The eventual outcome would likely have been the same.

He stared across the river at Texas, Mordecai's golden land . . . Mordecai's dream . . . He was not sure whether it attracted or repelled him; sometimes the line between the two emotions was thin.

He heard footsteps but did not look back. Eli and Andrew joined him.

Eli seemed to read his mind. "Don't dwell on it, Michael. It don't change anything."

Michael did not take his eyes from the land on the far bank. "You spend a lot of time over yonder, don't you?"

"Enough. I got friends there, Spanish, Injuns . . . We do a right smart of tradin'."

"It'd cost your neck if you get caught, wouldn't it?"

"It's an old neck. Anyway, them soldiers ain't fixin' to catch me. Wherever they move, the word goes out ahead of them."

"How?"

"People watch where they go and spread the alarm. And often they know ahead of time, because not everybody in the army likes what's happenin'."

"You mean soldiers themselves let the word out?"

"They ain't all bloodthirsty. There's a goodly scatterin' of decent men amongst them. Remember the sergeant that was ordered to shoot you and didn't?"

Michael swallowed. "I'll remember his face till they put me in the ground."

"He does what he can to spoil Rodriguez's digestion."

"Rodriguez!" Michael stiffened at mention of the name. "That's another face I'll carry with me to the grave."

"He's still around." Eli's face darkened. "*Gachupín*, the people call him, because he's a pureblood Spaniard. It's a wonder the mixed-blood *mestizos* ain't killed him. Too afraid of him, I reckon. He's killed a good many of *them* in the name of the king. Killed his share of Americans too."

The officer's face had been burned into Michael's brain, a face he would recognize in the darkest corner of Hell. "You ever seen him?"

"From a distance. If it'd been close I wouldn't be here."

Michael shuddered. "There ain't been a day or a night that *I* ain't seen him. I wake up in a cold sweat, seein' him." He kept staring at the river. "Next trip you make into Texas, would you take us with you?"

Eli grunted. "Ain't you had enough of that place?"

"I hate it because of what happened there. But I've always known I had to go back to it someday. Maybe go find the place where it happened, where Papa is buried. Maybe that's what it'll take to clear my mind of it all."

Eli cautioned, "It might just make things worse. Seein' the place again might set more devils loose than you already got."

"I'm ready to take that chance."

Andrew was staring with interest toward the river. He raised his hand and pointed. "Seems like some of Texas is comin' to *us*. Looky yonder."

The afternoon sun hit Michael in the eyes. He lowered his chin so his hat brim would shade him. He made out three horsebackers swimming toward them from the western bank. "Friends of yours, Eli?"

Eli held one hand over his eyes. "One of them, maybe. Looks like Guadalupe Lucero. The other two . . ."

Andrew's voice went tense. "Somethin's the matter. One man looks like he's been tied in the saddle. The other two are helpin' him."

Eli struck a brisk trot that belied the gray in his hair. It was all Michael and Andrew could do to keep up with him. The riders came up out of the water before the three men on foot were able to reach the bank. One leaned over his horse's neck. He would have fallen if a rope had not held him in the saddle. One of the other men pushed quickly to his side and tried to set him aright. Andrew ran forward to help. Michael held back. He recognized a Spanish uniform, or what was left of one. An old bitterness suddenly welled up.

"Damn him, he's a Spanish soldier!"

The other two riders dismounted to let their horses breathe easier. One looked apprehensively back across the river.

Guadalupe Lucero asked an urgent question in Spanish. The man who watched the river answered "No" and shook his head. Lucero rasped something else Michael could not understand, and his face contorted with hatred.

"Who's comin'?" Eli asked. He could speak Spanish almost as well as a native, but he used English with Lucero.

Lucero declared, "Rodriguez!" He spoke the name like a curse.

Michael felt himself trembling. "*That* Rodriguez?"

Eli nodded solemnly. "That Rodriguez." He asked some questions in Spanish, then hurried to the side of the horseman slumped in the saddle. His eyes were grave. "Come here, Michael. I want you to look at this man."

It was a struggle for Michael, because the uniform stirred a remembered hatred, but he went to Eli's side. Eli spoke quietly in Spanish. The man raised his head.

Recognition struck Michael like a blow on the chin. This was the sergeant who had saved his life. What was his name? Sargosa? No, *Zaragosa,* that was it.

"It's him," he acknowledged huskily. "What's happened to him?"

Eli said, "He's in about the same shape you was the time you came back across the river. Want to guess who shot him?"

"Rodriguez."

"Lucero says Zaragosa tried to help just one poor bastard too many and got caught at it. Come on, we better get him up to the house and see what we can do for him."

Michael did not move. He kept looking across the river. "What about Rodriguez?"

"He's on their trail, been tryin' to catch them all the way up from Bexar. But this is American territory. All he can do is stop over yonder and cuss till he turns blue."

Eli went on toward the cabin with the men who had just crossed. The two riders held Zaragosa in the saddle. Michael stayed behind, watching the far bank, wondering if Rodriguez was really going to come.

Andrew started after Eli, then turned back. "Ain't you comin', Michael?"

Michael's stomach churned. "That Rodriguez . . . he's the one who murdered Papa."

"You couldn't shoot him from here. The range is too far."

"I could go over yonder and wait for him."

Andrew grabbed his arm. "Come on, Michael. You're talkin' crazy."

"Maybe you wouldn't think so if you'd been there, if you'd seen."

"I didn't come all this way just to watch you get yourself killed in Texas like Papa did." He tugged again on Michael's arm. "Come on."

Reluctantly Michael went with him, pausing a couple of times to look back. He saw no sign of activity on the opposite bank. "But what I'd give . . ."

25

The two Spaniards carefully helped Sergeant Zaragosa down from the saddle. Zaragosa choked off a groan with the stubborn pride of a soldier. The river's water had not washed away all of a bloodstain high on the sleeve of his shirt. The shirt was partially shredded, evidence of flight through clutching timber. The man's bewhiskered face was pale from shock, almost gray. His dark eyes touched upon Michael but seemed to have trouble focusing. Even with the whiskers, the drawn features, the dulled eyes, Michael did not doubt his identity.

Eli said, "We got to get the bullet out of him."

Lucero had learned a lot of English in the years since Michael had last seen him. He said, "The bullet is out, but the wound is fevered."

The wet clothes and a faint breeze made Zaragosa shiver with a sudden chill, a violent contrast to his fever. He nodded toward a bench at the side of the cabin, in the afternoon sunshine and out of the breeze. He mumbled something in Spanish. Lucero and the other Spaniard supported him as he made his way there. He sank wearily upon the bench but managed to hold himself in a half upright position.

Eli fretted, "He'd be better off inside, on a bed."

Zaragosa understood and shook his head. "The sunshine," he managed weakly. "It gives warmth. And strength."

Eli looked dubious but accepted Zaragosa's judgment. "How'd he come to get in this shape?" he demanded of Lucero.

Lucero nodded toward the other Spaniard. "This is the brother of Zaragosa's wife. He is from far south, from Bexar. His name is Nicolas Galindo." Galindo was a tall, slender young man with animated black eyes. He did not seem to know English. Lucero went on. "Galindo works much for the rebellion. He makes many speeches, too many speeches. Rodriguez decides it is time to shoot him. Zaragosa goes to make warning, and Rodriguez catches them together." He scowled. "It has been a long chase from Bexar. Some of my people helped them."

Eli clucked with sympathy and gave Zaragosa a long, approving study. "He's safe now, if the wound don't get worse." He leaned over the sergeant. "I got somebody I want you to see. Michael, come here."

Michael no longer saw the uniform. He stared in admiration at the man who had spared his life a long time ago. By all accounts Zaragosa had spared many others as well. The risk he had run was evidenced by the fact that he was here now, wounded.

Eli asked, "You remember this young feller?"

Zaragosa seemed, after some effort, to bring Michael into focus. "No, I think I do not."

Eli started to explain, but Michael pushed in. "A bunch of us was gatherin' up wild horses. Your soldiers shot everybody. Rodriguez told you to finish me off, but you let me live."

Zaragosa's jaw dropped. "You are that boy?" He blinked away a starting of tears, for they were unbecoming a soldier. "You were much hurt. I feared you would die."

"I would've if it hadn't been for you. And Eli."

"It shamed me much to leave you. But there was a man with you, an *americano* . . ."

"Cyrus Blackwood," Michael said bitterly. "He ran off and left me. Never did have the guts of a grubworm."

Andrew shouted. He had been standing at the edge of the slope, watching the river. He pointed and came running. "There's soldiers on the other side. Looks to me like they're fixin' to swim across."

Eli's eyes went angry. "They can't do that. The law says they dassn't come over."

Andrew declared, "The law better get here quick, then, because they're comin'."

Zaragosa pushed himself to a shaky stand, bracing with one hand pressed against the cabin. "A gun. A gun, please. I do not die without a fight."

Michael's heartbeat quickened. He fetched his rifle where he had leaned it beside the log structure. "You-all give me the first shot at Rodriguez."

Eli Pleasant had regained his composure. "Better nobody shoots unless it's a case of havin' to. I count ten men. All we got is six, and the sergeant ain't in a shape to do much, even if he had a gun."

Lucero cursed in Spanish. "Rodriguez has no right here. This is the United States. He has no right."

Eli said, "He's got ten guns. With that kind of advantage he don't need no rights."

Michael declared, "I say we kill Rodriguez, and the rest'll turn back."

Eli gave him a look of reproach. "Think so? One shot and all of us'll die. You think killin' Rodriguez is worth that much?"

Michael was about to say it was worth any price, but he looked at Andrew and Eli, then at the Spaniards, and he was forced to back away. Eli's logic calmed him a little.

Eli said, "I don't think even ten men'll relish lookin' into five loaded rifles. They'll worry about which five dies."

Zaragosa was unable to stand long. He sank back onto the bench and called again for a gun. Eli told him, "I'm sorry but we ain't got enough. You just stay where you're at. We ain't fixin' to let them have you."

He cut his gaze back to Michael. "You let me do the talkin'. Don't shoot unless you have to. And *if* you have to make it good. Kill the son of a bitch!"

Not even a stranger could mistake Rodriguez's importance. He rode at the head of the detail. Even trail-weary, he had observed an officer's proprieties. He had shaved, probably that very morning. His uniform was the most colorful despite the wrinkling and the dirt of a grueling pursuit. He issued crisp orders, and his men quickly formed a semicircle to cover the five who waited at the log cabin—six, counting the unarmed Zaragosa.

Michael's hand went sweaty on his rifle. Hatred

welled up like heat from a forge as he stared into the face that had haunted him in so many awful dreams. There was no mistaking the cruel eyes, the lips pulled back against white teeth. It took all the resolve he could muster not to raise the muzzle and squeeze the trigger, to blast that hated face into oblivion.

Rodriguez looked fiercely at the armed men who faced him. If some inner uncertainty made him feel like flinching, he did not allow it to show. He demanded, first in Spanish and then in English, "Who is in charge here?"

Eli Pleasant replied in a flat voice, "This is my place."

Rodriguez studied him a moment, perhaps trying to remember if he had ever encountered this old scoundrel. He nodded first toward Galindo, then at Zaragosa, who leaned heavily against the cabin's log wall. "You harbor two fugitives. I want them."

Eli stood solid as a fencepost, rifle firmly clenched in both hands. "This is the United States of America. Maybe you didn't notice that you just crossed the Sabine."

Haughtily Rodriguez said, "I saw no river." His horse was still dripping wet. "I see only the fugitives. You will give them to me."

Pleasant said, "If American soldiers was to come along and find you on this side, you'd be in one hell of a mess."

"What soldiers?" Rodriguez demanded. A cold smile curved his lips, then died. "I see no soldiers. I see no river. So far as I know this is still New Spain. I want those men."

Pleasant raised the muzzle of his rifle an inch or

so, just enough for effect. "Well now, you ain't gettin' them. All you're gettin' is back across the river. And was I you, I'd start damned quick."

Rodriguez let his calculating gaze play over the armed men who opposed him. He passed over Michael, then came back to him, a question in his eyes. Perhaps he was puzzled by the hatred in Michael's face. He asked, "Do I know you?"

Michael moved his finger away from the trigger, struggling not to shoot the man. "We met, once."

"I do not remember it." Rodriguez looked back at Eli. "You are not so many as we."

"I can't argue about that. Your men could whup us in a minute. But you wouldn't live to see it." His voice grated like a rasp. "You'd be the first one dead."

Lucero declared, "Rodriguez, you have murdered many of my people. I would kill you now like a mad dog."

Rodriguez's eyes narrowed. "I know you. There is a price on your head, Lucero."

Nicolas Galindo had trembled a little at first, awed by so many armed men. Now he was emboldened to address the soldiers on either side of Rodriguez. Michael could only guess at what he said, but the words were impassioned, the gestures broad. He heard the words *gachupín* and *mestizo*. He surmised that Galindo was urging them to turn against the officer and join the rebellion. Some appeared to be wavering.

Rodriguez did not long tolerate the speech. He cut in with one of his own, his eyes raking the men. The words were delivered like a lashing, and Michael could see some of the men flinch. Rodriguez turned his attention back to Galindo. He addressed him by name, and also called upon Sergeant Zaragosa.

Eli said, "You can't arrest them. You're off of your grounds."

The lieutenant made a chilling smile. "I have seen the sergeant's wife. A handsome woman. Think of her in prison, turned over to the pleasure of the vilest guards I can find. Think of her swollen like a cow, giving birth on a dungeon floor to a bastard child . . . if she lives that long." He repeated the words in Spanish.

Zaragosa cursed him. Galindo went crimson.

Rodriguez lost the cold smile, but not the cruelty in his eyes. "She has family. They have aided in this treason. I shall see that all of them pay."

Trembling in rage, Zaragosa tried to arise from the bench but could not remain on his feet. He sank back.

Rodriguez said something more in Spanish. Michael saw the bluster go out of Galindo. Eli's and Lucero's faces had turned grim. Rodriguez gave Eli a moment's final consideration. "I do not know you, old man, but I suspect you are one of the *americano* smugglers who traffics in our country. If ever I catch you there . . ."

Pleasant spat toward the feet of the officer's horse. "You never have yet." He waved the muzzle of his rifle. "You gave them ten minutes to make up their minds. I'm givin' you just one."

Rodriguez turned, snapped an order, and started toward the river. Michael lowered his rifle. "Ten minutes to do what?"

Eli gave Zaragosa and Galindo a look of pity. "If they don't start across the river in ten minutes, he's goin' after their families back in Bexar."

Michael felt numb. "He wouldn't."

"Like hell he wouldn't."

Two of the soldiers hung back as the rest rode down the sloping bank and into the river. They talked between themselves until Rodriguez snarled an order, then they spurred to catch up.

Eli said to Michael, "I'm proud of you. I seen your face when you was lookin' at Rodriguez. I was afraid you was fixin' to start a war any minute. Was I you, I'd've done it."

Michael's voice was strained. "It was all I could do to keep from shootin' him right where his eyes and his nose come together."

"There'd've been dead men layin' all over this place now, and most of them would've been us."

Nicolas Galindo stood before Zaragosa in dismay. The two argued. Eli explained, "Each one of them says it's *him* Rodriguez really wants. Each of them wants to go and leave the other one here."

Michael frowned. "The sergeant don't look like he could make it across the river."

Eli grunted. "That's as far as he *would* get. Rodriguez would shoot him the minute he sets foot back in Texas."

Galindo made a decision. He strode toward his horse, still half wet from the crossing. Zaragosa called desperately, "*Espere,* Nicolas," and tried to wave him back. He pushed to his feet, took one step, and sank back upon the bench. "Nicolas. Nicolas."

Guadalupe Lucero followed Galindo, arguing. It was to no avail. Galindo swung up onto his horse, took one forlorn glance at his brother-in-law, then turned the mount down toward the river. Lucero's shoulders slumped. "I tried to tell him we would trail after Rodriguez and kill him before he gets to the family. He thinks if he gives himself up Rodriguez will be satisfied."

Zaragosa struggled to his feet again. "Please. Please, take me where I can see."

Michael handed his rifle to Andrew and went to the sergeant's aid. Arm around Michael's shoulder, Zaragosa managed to move to a point that gave him a view of the river.

Galindo's horse was swimming. Zaragosa made the sign of the cross. Galindo's animal found solid footing and started out of the shallow water on the Texas side. Rodriguez rode out to the edge of the river to meet him. Michael saw the officer's hand come up with a pistol.

Lucero shouted a warning, but it was futile. The pistol flashed. Galindo buckled under the impact, grabbed wildly at the saddle, then slipped over the horse's shoulder and into the water. For a moment his arms thrashed, then he went still. The current picked him up, and his body drifted down the river, lifeless as a broken tree limb.

"Lord Jesus!" Michael said. He felt Zaragosa stiffen in shock. The sergeant cried out in helpless fury.

On the far side, Rodriguez appeared to be having problems with his troops. He drew his sword and waved it threateningly. After a bit one soldier split off from the group and started swimming his horse back across. Michael thought for a moment he might be deserting to the Louisiana side, but Rodriguez made no attempt to stop him.

Michael raised his rifle. Zaragosa cried, "No, please. That is Talamantes. He is a good boy."

The young Talamantes came out of the water and pushed his horse up the slope to the cabin. Shame was in his eyes as he approached Zaragosa. He did not dismount but spoke apologetically from the saddle.

Eli translated. "He says the soldiers didn't know Rodriguez was fixin' to do that."

Michael demanded, "What could they have done if they did?"

"Could've shot him, is about all."

"They're soldiers. They wouldn't do that."

"They will sooner or later. When the rebellion comes."

Talamantes looked at the ground while he spoke to the sergeant. Eli said, "Rodriguez sent him to tell Zaragosa that Galindo wasn't enough. He wants Zaragosa too, and right now. Otherwise he's goin' after the family just like he said he would."

Zaragosa seemed drained. His gaze went to Michael. "Please, bring my horse."

Michael did not move. "You saw what happened to Galindo. You'll never come out of that river alive."

"I have no choice," Zaragosa cried. "My wife, my child."

"Even if you was to die, Rodriguez'd go after your family, just for revenge." Michael looked to Eli and Lucero for support.

Eli said, "He's right. You know what Rodriguez is. Your blood won't be enough for him."

"What else is there for me to do?"

Lucero said in English, so all could understand, "I tried to tell Galindo. He would not listen. All the way from Bexar, Rodriguez hunted *you*. Now all the way back, we can hunt Rodriguez. Somewhere, we will have our chance."

"I have not the strength."

"*I* have the strength, and more than enough dead family to give me reason. Leave Rodriguez to me."

In the determined face of Guadalupe Lucero,

Michael could see that Rodriguez was as good as dead, unless he killed Lucero first. Lucero spoke to the soldier Talamantes in Spanish.

Talamantes looked reluctantly across the river toward the waiting officer and made a reply.

Eli explained to Michael, "Lucero told him to say Zaragosa ain't comin'. The soldier says Rodriguez'll have to figure that out for himself. Boy says next time he goes back to Texas it'll be to fight the *gachupines*."

Zaragosa nodded his approval of Talamantes's choice. "But now I have no way to send an answer to Rodriguez."

Michael strode over with arms extended, offering his rifle. "This speaks all languages."

Zaragosa was unable to raise the rifle. Michael took hold of it near the muzzle. He turned his back and laid the long barrel across his shoulder to steady it. He said, "Fire!"

The rifle cracked. A splash of water blossomed just short of the opposite edge, and dust puffed as the bullet skipped up the bank. A couple of the horses danced in excitement. Rodriguez fought for control of his own. Though his voice did not carry across the river, his brisk and angry movements gave testimony to his reaction. He rode up the bank and across the floodplain, his eight remaining soldiers strung out behind him.

Michael said, "Pity he didn't hit him."

Lucero said, "*I* will hit him. When he is safely out of sight, I will go after him."

Michael fixed his gaze on the retreating Spanish soldiers. "Not by yourself. I'm goin' with you."

Eli Pleasant objected. "It ain't your fight. One

mistake and you'll die over there the same way your daddy did."

Michael's eyes narrowed as he nodded toward Zaragosa. "I owe that man. And I owe Rodriguez. I don't intend to make no mistakes."

"We all make mistakes. Even me."

Michael remained unmoved by Eli's arguments. Eli mumbled an epithet under his breath. "You're a full-growed man with the look of your daddy in your eyes; I know I can't change your mind. So I'll make a mistake too. I'll go with you."

"That ain't necessary."

"I ain't talkin' about necessary. I'm talkin' odds. Three of us would have a better chance over there than two."

"Four," Andrew said.

Michael turned fiercely on his brother. "Not you. I'll not go home and tell our mother how I went and let you get yourself killed. You'll stay on this side of the river. The sergeant can't take care of himself. He'll need your help."

Andrew tried to argue, but Michael cut him off abruptly. "You're stayin', and that's the last I want to hear about it."

Young Talamantes looked from one to another, following the back-and-forth shuffle of the conversation but understanding none of it. Lucero told him the gist in a few words.

Eli said, "We can't take no pack mule. Can't do no huntin' over there neither, not till the job is done. Come in the cabin with me, Michael. We'll pack up a few necessaries to carry on our saddles."

Talamantes helped Zaragosa back to the bench. Zaragosa seemed shamed by his helplessness. "*I* should be the one to kill Rodriguez. I owe it to Nicolas."

Lucero said, "Galindo was right about the revolution. It is coming. Even Rodriguez knows, and he is frightened of it. You can pay what you owe Galindo by staying here until you get well and can take Galindo's place."

"But this is not my country."

"It is a good country. And someday, when the time is right, we will go home together to *our* country."

26

Michael was of a mind to start immediately after Lieutenant Rodriguez, to get on his trail while the dust still lingered behind the Spaniards' horses. Eli Pleasant counseled caution.

"Like as not he'll post a man to hang behind and watch his backtrail a while. If we was to go chasin' after him like some little feist dog after a bear, he'd turn and gobble us up. No, we need to give him time. We'll catch him nappin' and gobble *him* up."

"And just how'll we do that?" Michael demanded, looking first at Eli, then at Lucero. Lucero gave him no answer, but he was grimly rubbing the sharp edge of a knife against the leg of his trousers, a knife with a blade as long as his hand.

Eli said, "They outnumber us three to one. We got to take him by surprise and give him as little chance as we can. *No* chance'd be better."

Michael found the thought distasteful. "You're talkin' about ambushin' him."

"Son, I got to know your daddy pretty good. I

imagine he taught you about the Christian way, and never hittin' the other man first, and all such as that. I know the way he thought. But the way he thought got him killed. There ain't nothin' Christian nor fair about this Rodriguez. If we treat him like there is, he'll live to see us all dead. We got to take him any way we can. By surprise for sure, when he ain't lookin'. In the back, if we can. In his sleep would be the best. You want him dead, don't you?"

"I'd want him to know it's happenin' to him, and why. What you're talkin' about ain't fittin' and proper."

"Fittin' is whatever'll get the job done and bring us all back amongst the livin'. When Ol' George Washington and his boys whupped the British, they didn't always go out in the open and charge like a wild bull. They hit them redcoats in ambush and got the hell out of there, and come back and hit them another day. My ol' daddy was in some of that, and he told me. War ain't no Christian thing, and this is war."

Lucero nodded grimly. "We are a long way from the church."

They ate while they waited. The soldier Talamantes carefully cleaned Sergeant Zaragosa's swollen and angry arm, wrapping a fresh cloth around it. His deferential manner told Michael a great deal about his respect for the sergeant, a respect Michael assumed the other soldiers shared. It fit with his own recollection of a man who defied an officer's order and let a wounded boy live, likely at some jeopardy to himself. Michael could only hope gangrene did not develop, or Zaragosa would be buried in an alien land far from home, just as Michael's father had been.

Michael kept expecting his brother to resume the argument about going along. He was surprised that Andrew kept his peace. *Learning*, Michael thought. *He's finally found out there are situations where he can't find anything funny.*

Eli decided it was time to go. The three mounted their horses and started down toward the river. Eli suddenly raised his hand. A horseman was swimming across to meet them. His uniform showed he was one of Rodriguez's soldiers. Three rifles were trained on him as he brought his horse up out of the shallows, dripping water onto the dry bank. The soldier, about Michael's age, raised both hands to show he meant no harm. Eli and Lucero moved forward to meet him and took the *escopeta* that was the soldier's only weapon. Michael listened to the quick flow of Spanish back and forth between them and wished he could understand.

If I stay in this part of the country I'll have to make myself learn how to talk it, he told himself reluctantly. That would be a load, on top of learning the French.

At length Eli turned in the saddle. "Rodriguez left him behind to stand watch, like I figured. But he's loyal to Zaragosa. He deserted."

Michael was unsure. "Can we trust him?"

"I think so. Says the whole bunch is tired of the lieutenant's abuse. They come near to mutiny when Rodriguez shot that poor Galindo out of the saddle. If he hadn't had a sword and a loaded rifle, they'd've all left him and come to sanctuary."

Lucero approvingly clapped the young soldier on the shoulder and started to hand the *escopeta* back to him but paused to blow the gunpowder out of the pan. Trust was one thing, caution another. The soldier took no offense. He answered one more question for Lucero, then rode on up toward the cabin.

Eli explained, "Me and Lucero, we figured Rodriguez would go to Nacogdoches first. It ain't no sight of a ride, and he needs fresh horses and supplies for the long trip south. But the boy says he's headed straight for Bexar instead. Probably afraid of more desertions, or even a revolt. He wants to get far from this river, as fast as he can. You ready?"

"*Been* ready."

Michael took a final look up toward the cabin before he edged his horse into the water. Andrew stood with the young Talamantes and the newly arrived soldier, watching. Andrew raised one hand in a silent farewell. Michael only nodded in return and gave his attention to the river.

He felt his heart swell as Big Red swam toward the Texas shore. His mind went back to that first crossing with Papa and the other Tennesseans, to a time bright with hope and promise and adventure, the thrill of coming into a new and unknown land. As the horse brought him out on the other side, Michael knew a sudden wild and unexpected exhilaration. *After all these years, I am back in Texas!*

If compelled, he would admit that the land looked much the same on the Texas side of the river; the vegetation was the same, and the sweet green smell of it on the wind. But something was different, something intangible. Michael knew the difference came from within himself. The magic was not in the land, it was in the idea. But magic it was, whatever the source. He allowed his memory full rein, carrying him back to those first grand happy days, to the shining dream in his father's eyes.

The tracks of the soldiers' horses were easy to

follow, and Rodriguez evidenced no attempt to make it difficult. He probably had little fear of anyone coming after him from the Louisiana side. If he was afraid of anything, it was probably his own men. It would be obvious to him, after a while, that he had suffered another desertion, that the steel-edged discipline he had imposed upon his command was breaking down. It was, Lucero declared, indicative of the breaking of Mother Spain's long hold on colonial Mexico. Eli, old enough to remember some of it, said it was not unlike the American colonies' final break from King George and England. Rodriguez represented to Mexico somewhat the same symbol that the loyalist Tories had represented to the American colonies. And when the inevitable break finally came, he must know he would suffer the consequences.

Except that Michael, Eli, and Lucero did not intend for him to live that long.

The trail became fresher as late afternoon wore on toward dusk. Once, as the three riders topped a small rise, they sighted the soldiers far ahead. Eli halted immediately and stepped down from his horse to present less of a profile against the horizon. He led the animal to the edge of a screening grove of trees. Michael and Lucero joined him.

Michael squinted, then placed the tips of his forefingers to the corners of his eyes and stretched the skin to sharpen his vision, a trick he had seen his father use. "They haven't shown any excitement. I doubt they saw us. Best I can tell, Rodriguez is bringin' up the rear. Tryin' to keep all his men in sight so none of them can drop off behind him and make a run back for the Sabine."

Eli said, "We'll just foller along slow and easy.

Our best go is to slip into their camp tonight and see if we can catch him unawares." He gave Michael a quick and questioning glance.

Michael said nothing, though he suspected his face revealed his distaste for the tactic.

They rested the horses a while, giving Rodriguez time to travel a little farther and perhaps encourage him to some degree of complacency, at least about any pursuit. His main concern now would be to keep from losing more of his command.

As they resumed their ride Michael commented, "It may be hard to catch him in his sleep, because he ain't liable to do much sleepin'. If any more soldiers have desertion on their minds, he knows they'll take their leave as soon as he starts to snore."

Eli grumped, "If you come up with a better idee, just tell us."

Dusk deepened into darkness. The tracks were hard to see. Eli got down from the saddle and began to lead his horse. "We'll move slow and watch our step," he said. "Else we're liable to run upon them before we know it." Michael and Lucero dismounted as Eli had. They had done little talking along the trail, and now they spoke not at all. When Eli's horse stumbled and broke wind, the old man froze for a moment. He handed the reins to Michael and walked ahead so he could listen without the horses or the creaking leather handicapping his ability to hear. He came back satisfied that no harm had been done. "I couldn't hear a damned thing," he said. "They probably didn't either."

Eli grumbled when full darkness made it impossible to see the tracks.

Michael said, "We know their direction. We'll come upon them by and by."

Presently he caught the scent of woodsmoke on a light breeze from the west. Then he saw the red glow of a campfire. He tapped Eli's shoulder. "Found them," he said triumphantly.

They led their horses to within less than a hundred yards of the camp, near enough for Michael to worry that one of the animals might nicker to the soldiers' mounts and give them away. But that risk offset another; that when they had completed their mission they might be overrun afoot before they could reach their horses.

It was Michael's guess that if they killed Rodriguez and nobody else, the soldiers would give them little difficulty. They might even cheer.

The soldiers had made camp on a sparsely wooded prairie. Michael saw figures moving as black silhouettes between himself and the fire. He whispered to Eli, "How can we pick Rodriguez out from amongst the others? It's bad enough killin' him thisaway like a possum in a trap. It'd be a heap sight worse to kill some common soldier by mistake and leave that dirty bastard breathin'."

Eli said quietly, "We'll manage," and motioned for him to sit down. Lucero already had. Eli whispered near Michael's ear, "They're still up and movin' around too much. We'll wait till they've taken to their blankets."

That was no answer, but it was all Eli was going to offer. The old man stretched himself out on the ground. Michael watched him in surprise. Eli was actually going to try to catch a nap! Michael could only shake his head in disbelief. Lucero sat up, his back against a tree. He whetted the blade of his knife against his leg. It was too dark to see his face, but Michael could guess the emotions which must be tearing at him. They would be something like his own, for Eli had told him of the crimes Rodriguez had perpetrated against Lucero's family. It was easier to understand Lucero's willingness to go through with this murder—that was what it would be, murder—than to accept it on Eli's part. The old man had lived on a rough frontier so long and had seen so much of violence that he must be hardened against dread or remorse.

It was two hours, and perhaps more, before Eli finally raised up, casually stretched his arms, and gave the camp a leisurely study. Michael had not seen anyone move in some time.

Eli whispered, "You get any sleep?"

"Hell no," Michael replied. "I don't see how you could."

"In my business a man eats when he can and sleeps when he can, because he don't know when he'll get his next chance at either one." He turned to Lucero. *"Listo?"*

"Listo." Lucero pushed to his feet.

Michael's pulse quickened, and he found his lips dry. That seemed strange, because his hands were sticky wet against the long rifle. "How we goin' to know which one is Rodriguez?"

Eli shrugged and whispered, "We'll just have to look."

Michael could not remember when he had heard an answer that told him less. He gritted his teeth in frustration. He was glad Andrew was not here to witness. His brother would take no pride in what they were about to do.

Eli told him, "Me and you, we'll just leave it up to Lucero. He'll know. Our job's to help him get out of the camp alive."

Lucero had moved his rifle to his left hand. In his right he carried the long knife. Michael shuddered, thinking how that sharp cold blade would feel driving deep between a man's ribs, or into his throat.

They moved slowly, picking each step to avoid making a noise. The smell of woodsmoke was stronger now; Michael thought he could feel the campfire's warmth and realized his imagination was running away with him. He told himself he had better take a tighter grip on his nerves if he was going to tote his part of this load.

Eli tapped him on the arm. He pointed his finger toward the camp. Lucero moved away to the left, making a small semicircle to come in from a bit farther around. Eli started to move away from Michael, then paused. He whispered, "You all right?"

Michael nodded stiffly. All right might not be quite the proper description, but he had made up his mind to go along the best he could. He would feel no compunctions about shooting Rodriguez squarely in the eye if the man were looking at him. Slashing the throat of a sleeping man was something he had not come prepared for. Not even the memory of his father's murder was enough to steel him for this.

Maybe Rodriguez would be awake, fearing more desertions. Maybe he would see Lucero coming, not in time enough to stop him but in time enough to know what was about to happen to him, and while dying, know he was paying for the cruelties he had wrought upon so many. Maybe as he lay spilling his blood upon the ground, he would even remember the day he had slaughtered Mordecai Lewis and the other Tennesseans. Michael would like to think so.

That took a little of the edge from his distaste for the manner of vengeance.

There should be a guard, but he could not see one. Perhaps Rodriguez did not trust any of his men to move beyond the thin circle of firelight, lest they slip away from him. Michael tried to count the blanket-wrapped figures on the ground near the fire and came up short of the number he knew should be there. His heart was beating even faster now. Where the hell were they?

Near him in the darkness, half blinded by the glow of the fire, Eli walked into a low-hanging tree branch and bumped his head solidly. He lost his footing and staggered forward. The long barrel of his rifle struck the branch again.

From the camp came a cry, *"Quién es? Quién es?"* There *was* a guard. Or perhaps the cry came from Rodriguez himself. Michael saw the flash of a rifle or pistol; he could not tell which, and it did not matter. He dropped to his stomach as the swishing sound of the slug passed harmlessly to one side of him. He saw the awakened soldiers fling their blankets aside.

Then, in the firelight, he saw the man he had come for: Rodriguez. His instinct was to jump up and run, to save himself, but his mind told him this was his chance. Lucero's opportunity was probably spoiled anyway. Lying flat, Michael leveled the rifle and tried vainly to see its sights. He could hardly even see the barrel. He took what he hoped was good aim on the lieutenant's belly and squeezed the trigger. The flash blinded him for a second, then he knew with a sinking feeling in his stomach: he had missed. From the camp came several shots, fired in confusion and panic.

Hunched low, Eli Pleasant ran to Michael. "Let's git! I've spilt it."

Disappointment washed over Michael, overwhelming even his sense of fear. He jumped to his feet and followed Eli in a long run out through the scattered timber toward the horses. They stopped, after a little, and looked back in the direction of the camp. Michael could hear an angry voice shouting, haranguing. That would be Rodriguez.

He expected the soldiers to come spilling after them in hot pursuit. They did not. They fired a few desultory shots into the darkness, but they never ventured into it. Afraid of what might be out there, Michael thought. Or Rodriguez was afraid to let them go beyond his sight. He could still hear the man shouting angrily.

Lucero was a while in showing up. Michael worried that he might have caught one of those bullets fired in haste and panic from within the camp. But Lucero came, appearing suddenly out of the darkness, silent as a shadow. Eli explained in a shamed voice what had happened. "I'm gettin' too old for this. An old fart like me ought to be settin' on a front porch someplace with my boots off."

Lucero accepted the failure without rancor. "It is best. I chose my man. I was about to put my knife in his throat when the guard cried out. Then I saw that I had the wrong one. I would have killed him instead of Rodriguez. It is for the best."

Michael asked, "Did anybody see you?"

"They were all too excited. But I heard Rodriguez curse the men. He thinks it was one of his own who tried to kill him. He would shoot them all if he could. But he would have only two shots—one from his rifle and one from his pistol—and then they would be on him."

From the camp came sounds of horses and men

stirring around. Michael realized, "They're breakin' camp. They're movin' on."

Eli agreed. "Sure as hell. We got Rodriguez all scared up now. But he'll be so busy watchin' his soldiers that he won't be watchin' us. That'll give us a better chance for another shot at him. Let's get our horses."

The way toward San Antonio de Bexar was south. It quickly became evident that Rodriquez was traveling west.

"To Nacogdoches," Lucero said. "He fears his soldiers too much to travel with them all the way to Bexar."

Eli grunted. "Which means we'll have a lot less time for that second chance. We'd better be a-ridin'."

27

The soldiers made enough racket at first that it was easy to follow them in the darkness. But somehow the pursuers lost them after an hour or so. Though Michael listened hard, he no longer heard any horses except their own. All three men tried, one at a time, moving forward while the other two stayed back with the mounts. The only sounds were the birds of the night and the distant howling of two wolves exchanging their nocturnal greetings. Michael cursed under his breath. Though the moon had risen, the light was not enough for following tracks.

Eli and Lucero talked a few minutes in animated Spanish while Michael stood back, feeling left out because he could not understand. Eli explained, finally. "We know they're headed for Nacogdoches. We'll keep riding the same direction so they don't gain too much on us. Come mornin' we ought to cut their sign."

"And when we catch up to them, what?"

Eli grunted. "I ain't got no more notion than a one-eyed squirrel. We'll figure it out when the time comes."

Daylight found them picking their way through an area too wooded to be considered an open prairie but without enough trees to be a forest. The soldiers were neither to be seen nor heard. The three set a diagonal course generally northward for a while, then cut southward again without finding tracks. It became evident to Michael that whatever their other talents might be, neither Eli nor Lucero would ever gain recognition for their ability as trackers.

"I sort of wish Andrew was with us now," Michael said. "Papa taught him to track a bird flyin' across solid rock."

Eli pointed out, "As I recollect, it was you told him he couldn't come."

"And I was right. But just this minute we could use him. There's got to be tracks here somewhere."

Lucero frowned. "Unless . . ."

Michael turned. "Unless what?"

"Unless we have passed them. Unless they are behind us, not in front of us."

Eli brightened. "Now, that could be. If they slowed down for some reason, we could've gone on one side of them or the other and never knowed it. If we was to make us a little *vuelta* back the way we come . . ." He did not wait for concurrence; he just started riding. Lucero nodded at Michael, and they hurried to catch up to the old man.

They came upon the soldiers suddenly and unexpectedly, the meeting a jolting surprise to both sides. They gaped at each other across the space of a small clearing. Holding his breath until his lungs ached, Michael recognized Rodriguez. The officer spurred

to come around in front of his horsemen. He had
been riding behind them, keeping them all in sight
lest some of them drop away. Shouting, he pointed
his saber at the Americans. Michael leveled his rifle
at the officer and fired, but Big Red was dancing
nervously, sensing the excitement. For the second
time, Michael missed a clear shot at Rodriguez.

Eli yelled, "Dammit, boys, we've spilt it again!"
He whipped his horse about and put him into a
hard run. Michael and Lucero were but a half
length behind him. Looking back, Michael thought
Rodriguez and the soldiers might be gaining. It was
certain they were not losing any ground.

Someone fired a shot. Eli's horse stumbled, went
to its knees, then scrambled unsteadily back to its
feet. Hauling up quickly and facing back around to
help, Michael saw blood welling from the animal's
shoulder. Eli jumped to the ground. Michael freed
his left stirrup so Eli could jam a foot into it and
swing up behind him. The maneuver, though it took
but a moment, allowed the soldiers to halve the
space between them and their quarry. Lucero fired
his rifle in their direction in an effort to slow them.

The soldiers would not be long in overtaking a
horse burdened by two riders. In desperation Michael looked for some kind of protection. Ahead lay
a depression, a washout created by runoff water. It
wasn't much, but he saw nothing else. He pointed it
out to Lucero, who was trying in vain to reload his
rifle on the back of his running horse.

Eli shouted in his ear, "Drop me off there and
keep a-goin'. You can outrun them without me."

"They'll kill you," Michael protested.

"They'll kill us all if you stop."

For a wild moment the temptation for self-preservation was strong. But Michael knew he could not yield to it. Had it not been for Eli Pleasant he would have died in Texas five years ago. Now he could not abandon Eli here to die alone, even though by staying with him he might only insure that they die together.

The sorrel horse stumbled and fell as they rode down the steep wall of the washout. Michael rolled free and sprang to his feet, never losing his hold on the rifle. Eli scrambled, the horse almost stepping on him in its struggle to regain its feet. Lucero found a gentler slope and came down to join them as Michael turned to face the soldiers and furiously began reloading his rifle. Eli fired a shot that clipped the green grass in front of Rodriguez. The soldiers reined up and quickly looked for cover. Rodriguez railed at them in vain to continue the charge. But he made no effort to proceed alone.

Eli threw himself against the steep earthen wall and leveled his reloaded rifle across the top of it. He muttered, "Hold still so I can get a bead on you, you son of a bitch!" He fired at Rodriguez. Quickly reloading his own rifle, Michael saw the officer grab at his side.

Eli declared, "Finally nicked him, by God. But I didn't get him in the vitals, more's the pity."

For a moment, until Eli and Lucero reloaded their rifles, they would have been vulnerable to a charge. But the soldiers did not press it, and the moment was lost. All three men quickly had their weapons ready and waiting for a target.

Rodriguez, the target of preference, had retreated behind trees and put himself out of immediate jeopardy.

Michael had time now to survey their position.

It was poor. Though the steep bank protected them from the point where the soldiers were, a higher slope behind would leave them exposed should any of the troops work their way around. To do so would momentarily put the soldiers in the line of fire. Michael suspected that was a chance Rodriguez would sooner or later decide to take—with his men's lives, though probably not with his own.

Eli commented dryly, "If we'd had a little more time, I feel like we could've found ourselves a better place to light."

Lucero pointed out what Michael had already observed, that they were vulnerable from the rear. It would be only a question of time before Rodriguez would press for that advantage. "We will die if we remain here," Lucero said.

Michael replied, "We'll die if we try to leave."

Eli gave them both a look like a weary teacher frowning down upon a pair of dullard students. "If you ain't got somethin' useful to say, what's the use in talkin' atall?" He pointed to the wide patch of open ground between the gully and the little clump of trees where the soldiers waited uncertainly. "They ain't wantin' to charge us across there, I don't think, not into three loaded rifles. Eight to three ain't fine odds when you know that three of the eight are sure as hell goin' to die."

Michael said, "But they could work around to that high ground yonder and pick us off."

"They'll have a hard time reachin' it without us gettin' them first. They know that. So all we got to do is wait for dark and then slip out of here."

"Dark?" Michael demanded. "It's still mornin'."

"The time'll pass," Eli said confidently.

Michael remembered his mother reading something out of the Bible about people who had the faith of the mustard seed.

A little to his left, a knoll overlooked the clump of trees, much as the rising ground behind them overlooked the gully in which they had taken refuge. If one of them could reach that knoll he could make the soldiers' present position untenable. Michael pondered his chances of getting there. The odds were about those of an icicle in Hell.

The soldiers were quiet a while, occasionally firing a shot to kick up dust at the edge of the washout, just a reminder, if one was needed, that they were still there and contemplating the next move. Once voices rose in anger, the loudest of them Rodriguez's.

Eli listened. "He's tryin' to force them to make a run across that open ground. They're tellin' him to do it hisself."

Lucero nodded in satisfaction. "Perhaps he will die here at their hands and not at ours."

"That'd be fittin'," Michael said. "But I'm a lot more worried about *us* dyin' at their hands."

The sun reached its midday peak and started down on the western side of a wide-open sky. Its summer heat bore heavily upon Michael, for it was stronger here than back in Tennessee, and this gully afforded no shade other than his hat. Burning sweat worked down into his eyes. He had to keep rubbing them to see. It bothered him a little that Eli could be so relaxed. He supposed the old smuggler had been in and out of so many tight places in his life that he could be dispassionate about it. Michael had been in several, but indifference was not in his makeup.

He said, "You know they'll come at us one way or another."

Eli nodded without expression. "I expect so. Was I them, *I* would. They know we'll otherwise get away after dark."

"You ever given much thought to dyin', Eli?"

Eli shook his head. "Never was interested in it, much. Always rather think about livin'. There's more future in that."

"I come near dyin' in Texas once already."

Eli nodded toward Lucero. "So've him and me. We all have. And we're all still here. So why not take what you've got and enjoy it while you can?"

"Ain't much here to enjoy."

"Sure there is. Sunshine instead of rain. Birds singin' in the trees. A man takes his blessin's where he finds them."

During the long wait Michael took refuge from the grim present by allowing his mind to wander back to Tennessee, to Papa, to Mama, to Joseph and little Jonathan, and the other brothers and sisters and cousins he had left there. Now, facing a strong probability that he would never see the sun go down, he asked himself why he could not have been content there, why he had always had an itch to hunt for a better place. It was a restlessness he had inherited from Papa, and Papa from *his* father. It was a Lewis family curse, a restlessness that had no cure, for Papa had hunted all his life and not found a place where he could long remain content. Somewhere, there was always something better.

A better place . . . this was sure as hell not it.

He thought again of the pleasurable night he had lain in the blankets with Sally Boone, and that memory led him finally to Marie Villaret. He thought of dark eyes, of dark hair he wished he could run his hand through now, of soft lips that had pressed eagerly against his own, that had invited him to stay. Her memory came as a melancholy reminder of what he was about to lose. Yet it was also a solace of sorts, and he thought perhaps he understood why his restless father had married in spite of all the good reasons not to. No matter how long or how far Mordecai had roamed, he always knew the comfort of having a place to go home to, a woman to go home to, loving him regardless of his shortcomings, taking him for richer or poorer, mostly poorer, accepting him for what he was though this sometimes brought her more than her proper portion of pain.

Marie would be like that. And maybe for her he could change. Maybe for her he could put aside the wanderlust. Maybe, like his older brother Joseph, he could find contentment in home and hearth and settle down to being a husband and a farmer.

Thinking of Marie, of his family back home, he wondered darkly: if he died here, would they ever know? Or would they go through the years uncertain what had become of him, knowing only that he had ridden off into the Texas country and was swallowed up in its vastness, never to be seen or heard of again. The thought left him empty and cold.

He asked, "Eli, you ever been married?"

Eli pondered. "Depends on what you consider married. Never had a preacher read no words or sign no papers, but there's been women that I sort of had an arrangement with. We just taken it for granted that we was married without all the fuss and feathers. We had all the benefits without the complications. Time come when we didn't get along no more, we wasn't held by nothin' but a slipknot. Worked out pretty good."

Michael couldn't see his father and mother living

under such an arrangement. He didn't think he could see himself doing it either. "It doesn't seem like enough," he said.

Eli studied him knowingly. "You must've left a girl back yonder in Tennessee."

"No, not in Tennessee."

Eli grunted. "Then it's Marie. No, my kind of partnership wouldn't work with a girl like her. If you want to put your boots under her bed you'll have to have everything wrote up legal and proper. Ain't nothin' temporary about her kind, and there oughtn't to be. She's like your mama; she's for life."

Sadness crept into Michael's voice. "If I have any life left."

Eli shook his head. "You're too young to die, and me and Lucero are too ornery. Every bad tight I was ever in, somethin' always come along at the last minute."

Michael looked over the edge of the gully and felt his pulse pick up. "It'd better come along pretty quick."

Two soldiers had left the trees. They were trying to skirt around to cross over the gully at a shallow point and reach the higher ground behind it. Michael did not want to kill anyone except Rodriguez. He took careful aim and fired. One of the soldiers stumbled and fell, Michael's bullet in his leg. The other paused in confusion, then stopped to help him to his feet. He started back toward the trees, the wounded man's arm around his shoulder. He looked fearfully toward the gully, expecting to be cut down.

Eli said, "A damned shame to have to shoot some poor soldier that probably joined the army just to get hisself enough to eat."

Michael's conscience nagged him a little, but self-preservation was a stronger consideration. He could hear an angry voice from the trees. Rodriguez was cursing the unwounded soldier for not proceeding on his mission and letting the other one lie there.

Lucero shouted across at Rodriguez to quit sending boys out to do a job that required a man. "Come yourself if you are not seven kinds of a cringing coward!"

At least that was the translation as Eli gave it to Michael. Michael suspected Eli had not bothered with all the fine details.

Lucero held up his hand, signaling for silence. His face twisted as he tried hard to hear the words that carried across from the trees. "They come pretty soon now," he said grimly. "Rodriguez is saying he will kill the first man who turns back."

"Damn!" Eli clenched his fist. "I do hate shootin' them boys when it's *him* we come for. We'll likely never see him."

The trees became ominously silent. Michael wiped sweat from his burning eyes and from the palms of his hands. He grimly set his mind on Marie in an effort to avoid thinking about what was coming. Lucero crossed himself. Eli grunted, "Damned rheumatism was fixin' to git me anyway."

A shot echoed across the opening. Michael thought for a moment it was the signal for a charge. He heard shouting from within the trees, but it was not what he would have expected from soldiers starting a run against the enemy. It sounded more like panic.

He saw a slight movement from the top of the knoll that overlooked the trees. It came to him that the shot had originated there, not from the soldiers. And it had been directed into the trees.

After about the time it would take a man to reload

a rifle, a second shot cracked, and another shout arose from among the soldiers. Several, maneuvering to get away from this new source of danger, let themselves become exposed to the three men in the gully. But those men held their fire. They waited for Rodriguez to appear in their sights.

Eli frowned in puzzlement, staring toward the knoll. "Friend of yours, Lucero?"

Lucero shook his head. "I cannot see. I do not know who it could be."

Michael knew. Pride surged as recognition came. "That brother of mine . . . he'll follow me to his death someday."

Eli's jaw dropped. "Andrew?"

Michael nodded. "Andrew. When he was a kid he used to follow me out a-huntin' after I'd tell him he couldn't. He followed me across Tennessee after I said I was goin' alone."

Eli's smile returned. "Seems to me I remember a boy that follered after his daddy one time."

Michael heard a violent argument behind the trees. Though the language was foreign to him, he recognized cursing when he heard it. He heard a shot, a cry of pain, then a babble of furious voices. He saw a surging of men backward and forward, though he could not tell what they were doing.

A man burst out of the trees on horseback, spurring eastward. Even at the distance, Michael knew the uniform.

Rodriguez!

From the knoll came another shot, meant for the horseman. Michael fired his own rifle, though at the range it was a futile gesture. He indulged in a little cursing of his own, in the best of Tennessee American.

A soldier came out of the trees, waving a cloth that at some time had been white. Eli and Lucero glanced at each other. Lucero shouted across the opening. The soldier took a couple more uncertain steps, shouting back. Several other soldiers came out, laying down their rifles, raising their hands.

Andrew disappeared from the knoll. In a minute he reappeared on horseback. He rode up as the remaining soldiers came out into the open, all but three. One was the soldier who had Lucero's bullet in his leg. Another, older than the rest, lay on his back, dying. The third was doing what he could to tend him.

Eli and Lucero climbed out of the gully and walked forward to meet the soldiers. Michael reloaded his rifle as a precaution and followed. Andrew raised his hand in the slightest of greetings. He was grinning. "What've you fellers been doin' out in the sunshine? The shade'd been a lot cooler."

Michael was unsure whether to hug his neck or kick him where his legs joined together in the back. "Little brother, you are a vexation and a pain."

Andrew's grin did not flicker. "But handy, just the same. Looked to me like you was fixin' to have a little difficulty gettin' out of that ditch."

"How'd you find us?"

"Just followed your tracks. It wasn't no big thing."

Eli shook Andrew's hand and said he was middlin' glad to see him. Then he turned to Michael. "The boys say the wounded man in yonder is an old soldier named Sanchez. When Andrew started shootin' into the trees and broke up the charge, Rodriguez tried to make the men come against us anyway. Ol' Sanchez, he put up an argument, said there wasn't no more of them goin' to die for a *gachupín* who was fixin' to lose his head anyway soon's the revolution started. Told Rodriguez if he knowed what was good for him he'd make a run for Louisiana and take sanctuary. Rodriguez shot him.

"Rodriguez grabbed him a rifle and held off the soldiers while he got his horse. They told him he'd better head for Louisiana, because if he went to Nacogdoches or to Bexar they'd find him and kill him for what he done to Sanchez."

Michael looked toward the east. Rodriguez was no longer in sight. "That's the direction he took, all right, toward the Sabine."

Lucero said, "Then let us get him." He turned and trotted back toward his horse, still safe in the deep gully. Eli shouted, "Andrew, catch me one of the soldiers' horses."

Michael sprinted for the gully and Big Red.

28

Lieutenant Armando Rodriguez was not frightened so much as simply outraged. He slowed his horse once he was beyond sight of the soldiers he had left behind, and those *americanos* whose reason for being on Spanish soil he had not attempted to question. Smugglers, probably, or plain bandits. Either way, they should have died, and would have, had it not been for cowardice and treachery among his own men. He seethed with indignation at the mutinous behavior, and over the fact that under the circumstances he had no choice but to retreat from superior numbers. But it would be temporary. He would be back, and the bastards would hang!

What galled most of all was that he, an officer and by the right of birth a gentleman, had been forced to back away from inferior men who should deem it an honor to curry his horse. That was the natural consequence of permitting those of lower station to presume rights to which the circumstances of their births had not entitled them. The

Spanish conquistadores who first took this land for God and king had not done so with an olive branch and a gentle hand; they had conquered the savages with fire and sword, with whip and chain. Gentle words were for the mission padres, who preached of peace but cried to the military for help when they could not control their primitive charges. It was the military who knew how to contend with the recalcitrants, first among the Indians and later among the mixed-race *mestizos* who arose out of the union of lusty Spaniards with the native Indian women.

That had been the first failure of the purebloods, Rodriguez had always believed, the recognition of these mongrel hordes as citizens, granting them rights that should have been reserved for the *gente de razón,* the people of reason.

Rodriguez had often demonstrated the proper cure for rebellion: death, swift and without mercy. Show the least sign of softness and the unleashed dogs would cut him to pieces. A while ago they almost had, and all because, badly outnumbered, he had briefly brooked argument and allowed them to become emboldened. He had corrected his impropriety by shooting down that insolent old Sanchez the way he should have done a long time ago, the way he should have done the disloyal Sergeant Elizandro Zaragosa. As for the others, they would see Rodriguez again. They would die like the dogs they were, whining for mercy until the ropes choked off their cries and their faces turned black in the strangling. And their families—those who had any— would share in his righteous wrath.

He savored the image as he savored the thought of returning one day to the proper environment for a gentleman. Monclova perhaps, or even Mexico

City itself, where the wine was good, the conversation stimulating, the women beautiful and properly appreciative of an officer who had done his duty to the crown.

But now he must see to the necessities of the moment. Before yesterday he had never crossed into the territory of the United States; the thought had always been distasteful, for the Americans were a rude and greedy people, unmindful of the deference due a gentleman by his inferiors. That he was obliged to do so now, almost as a fugitive, was a humiliating circumstance for which many would be called upon to pay, and soon.

He could feel the horse tiring beneath him, its pace labored. He slowed to a walk and finally dismounted, leading the mount into deep shade beneath a large oak. He loosened the saddle to allow the animal to breathe more easily. There had been few better horses in Bexar than this one, but much had been demanded of it . . . the long pursuit after the insurrectionist Galindo and the turncoat Zaragosa . . . the aborted ride toward Nacogdoches . . . the retreat just now from the soldiers' rebellion. He probably would not find as good a one in Louisiana . . . another indignity for which he would exact a stern price from those who had wronged him.

He had rested the horse for perhaps twenty minutes when he saw riders coming. He tensed, counting them. Four. These were not his traitorous soldiers, in pursuit of him. They must be those damned Americans. He had first seen them yesterday at the cabin on the east side of the Sabine with the arrogant *mestizo* rebel Lucero who had cursed him so darkly. Running into them this morning had been unexpected, as had their fierce defense in the gully.

Americans gave up fairly easily most of the time, expecting the sort of lenient treatment they received at the hands of authorities in their own country. That was one reason they would all be defeated in the long run: they were soft, and forgiving of their enemies.

Perhaps one day Rodriguez would be so fortunate as to lead a strong Spanish force and retake Louisiana for the Spanish crown. If the government were only in the hands of the military instead of so many weak-willed civilian bureaucrats, more interested in enriching themselves than in preserving the empire . . .

He remounted reluctantly and looked around for a wooded area where he might slip out of sight until the four horsemen passed on. But it became evident as he watched that they were not behind him by happenstance; they were deliberately following his tracks. Alarm stung him like a nettle.

Why? What could this miserable rabble want of him?

He sensed that it would not be wise to stay and ask them. He called upon the tired horse to move into a gallop. When he looked back the four had put their horses into a run and were closing the distance. He tried to remember how far it should be to the river but was unsure. He spurred the horse for all the speed he could wring out of it.

The four riders kept gaining ground, pushing closer. They were within range. If one of them wanted, he could probably jump from his horse and have some chance of hitting Rodriguez with his rifle. Rodriguez swallowed hard, trying to calm his growing anxiety. He found himself on a dimly beaten trail, formed over a long period of time by the hoofs of many horses.

His pulse racing faster than the horse beneath him, he was almost ready to turn to face them for a fight when he saw the heavy line of trees that marked the river. He saw a cabin on the distant bank and realized it was the one he had visited yesterday in his quest for Galindo and Zaragosa. Those four riders—damn them!—had driven him back to it.

They were pounding hard to close the distance, trying to catch him before he could reach the water. He spurred viciously and plunged in at the place where yesterday he had shot Galindo out of the saddle.

In a moment the horse was swimming. Rodriguez had his hands full to avoid being swept away by the current. He was heavy with armament, a pistol in his belt along with a shot pouch, a saber at his side, a rifle slung over his arm, heavy boots, and spurs. It would not do to be cast off now.

He was in the middle of the stream by the time the riders reached the edge of the water. It was in his mind that when he came to the opposite bank he could turn and shoot two of them while they struggled with the river. With any luck he could reload and get the other two before they could reach him.

Almost to the bank, he lifted his gaze toward the cabin. His eyes widened, for he saw three figures standing there, halfway down the slope. All wore the uniform of Spanish soldiers.

His throat went dry as he recognized Zaragosa and the two young troopers who had deserted yesterday. He tried to shout orders for them to stand by to help him, but the words did not come. One of the soldiers handed Zaragosa a rifle, then stood in front of him to allow the sergeant to level it firmly across his shoulder. He leveled it at Rodriguez.

Rodriguez recovered his voice and shouted, but

the shout was without form. It was of surprise and anger and terror, all mixed. He tried to whip the horse around, but it floundered and almost went out from under him.

He saw the rifle flash and felt the blow take him in the chest, a blow like the strike of a broad-edged sword, searing, tearing, driving the breath from him in one long, agonized scream.

The strength dropped out of him. He let go his rifle and grabbed at the saddle with both hands but could not find it. As the animal thrashed, Rodriguez saw the four horsemen coming toward him from the Texas side, and he saw the three figures standing on the Louisiana bank . . . all this before a blazing glare blinded his eyes and he felt himself sliding . . . sliding into the water. His arms and legs felt paralyzed, though he tried desperately to move them, to fight the current that caught him. He gasped for breath, but his mouth filled with water as he went under.

In his mind he cried out for mercy, but his weight carried him down, and he made no sound except for his strangling.

Michael was unaware that he had been holding his breath until his lungs began to ache. He heard Eli gritting, "Drown, you bastard! Drown!" There was a momentary swirling of the water where Rodriguez had gone down, but most of it was caused by the panicked thrashing of the lieutenant's horse, frightened by the shot and fighting the current until its feet found solid ground. The animal went up on the Louisiana shore, dripping. It stopped and shook like a dog, rattling the wet leather of the saddle, flopping the steel stirrups.

Rodriguez never came up. Michael watched in silence until Eli said, "Well, looks like Sergeant Zaragosa taken vengeance out of your hands."

Michael could see the sergeant on the far bank with the two soldiers, still holding the smoking rifle. He knew a moment of disappointment, but it passed. "The son of a bitch is dead. And he died with his eyes open, knowin' what was happenin' to him, like Papa and so many others he killed. It don't matter much who pulled the trigger."

Andrew had drawn up beside him. "Well, the debt has been squared. Now maybe you can get Texas out of your system."

Michael turned and looked behind him at the open stretch of prairie over which they had ridden. The sun was low now, casting a golden sheen across the land. It was as he had seen it long ago, with Mordecai. He felt reluctant to cross back over to the Louisiana side.

"No, the feelin' about Texas is as strong as ever. Maybe even stronger now. I want to come back and stay. I been thinkin' about that man Austin. I wonder if he's still in Natchitoches?"

Andrew shrugged. "I reckon we'll just have to go and see."

The four riders pushed their horses out into the river, not even pausing at the place where Rodriguez had gone down.

As they approached Natchitoches, Michael stopped each person they met and inquired about Stephen Austin. The first three had never heard of him. The fourth was a French-accented farmer riding a fine black stallion, followed by a slave on a gray mule.

The farmer remembered encountering Austin in Villaret's mercantile store the previous day. He had considered Austin a most agreeable if perhaps misguided young man, whose notions about settling American families among the Spanish in Texas were regrettably unrealistic. Mexico, he said, was like a boiling pot with the lid loose, awaiting only a sufficient buildup of steam to explode into violent convulsions against the excesses of the crown and its official servants.

Michael commented, "I think the lid's already comin' undone."

"And who knows," the farmer asked, "what will remain in the pot after the fire has burnt itself out?"

Michael and Andrew watched the farmer and the slave continue on their way westward. Michael gave a sigh of relief. "At least Austin ain't left for Texas yet."

"If the Spaniards knew that we already been in Texas, and what we been up to, they might find a cozy spot for us in a dungeon someplace. Or just shoot us, like Rodriguez wanted to."

"I wasn't figurin' on tellin' them. We're just a couple of Tennessee farm boys, innocent as the day we was born."

Andrew smiled. "Not quite that innocent."

They heard the distant whistle of a steamboat as they came to the edge of town. Andrew declared, "Don't that set your back to ticklin'? Makes me think of cities I've heard of but never seen, like New Orleans and St. Louis."

"You wouldn't like them, not for long. You're a farm boy at heart, little brother. You're the kind who finds him a place and stays put."

"Ain't a thing wrong with that. I thought the whole reason for us comin' so far was to find us both a place."

"There's still a lot of Papa in me. It'll be a hard thing to fight."

"But Papa always came home by and by, because he always had somethin' to come home to. And somebody. You've got somebody, Michael. You just got to work up the courage to ask her."

"I know." The wish was strong, but so was the concern. "I remember how it used to be with Mama."

"Mama took Papa the way she found him. Sure, she got lonesome, but you remember the light in her eyes when Papa came home? She wouldn't've traded places with the richest woman in the tidewater."

They came to the river, where flatboats drifted southward, and two steamboats chuffed busily northward against the reddish current. Natchitoches was up to its elbows in commerce, and loving it from all Michael could see. If Austin succeeded in his plan, this place would become a gateway, even busier than it was now.

Just up from the riverbank he noticed a large tent with several wooden barrels stacked in front and two large wagons beside it. He recognized the young woman standing beside the tent's open flaps, next to a crude wooden sign nailed to a post freshly set into the ground. Its awkwardly formed letters read, *Pure Kentuckie whiskie, Sallie Boon prop*. Warmth rose in his face. He tried to ride past, but she whistled and hailed him.

"Michael Lewis! You fixin' to go on like you didn't even know who I was?"

Sally Boone strode a few paces out from the tent, and Michael knew no graceful way to avoid stopping to talk with her. Uncomfortably he touched his fingers to the brim of his hat. "Howdy, Sally. Glad to see you-all made it in all right."

She wore a new dress, blazing red and tight enough to be a far better advertisement than the crudely painted sign. "Wasn't no more trouble after the Reverend Fairweather got religion. We just set up shop here yesterday, and already we've sold enough to halfway pay us for comin'. I never had no idee so many folks here was thirsty for a taste of good Kentucky whiskey. You-all git down and come in for a little drink with us, why don't you? I'm tickled to see you, and I'm sure Cephus will be too."

Michael spotted Cephus working inside the tent with the big black man Marcus. He had his doubts about Cephus's joy in seeing him, especially if Sally had given him any inkling of what had passed between them one long, warm night on the trail. "I reckon we'd better be movin' on along," he said apologetically. "We got to go see a man."

It was tempting to linger. Sally's smile was infectious, and the red dress improved Michael's memory for details.

Sally casually took hold of Big Red's bridle reins, up near the bit so the horse would not move. "Business is lookin' so good we're already talkin' about Cephus goin' back with the wagons and fetchin' us a couple more loads."

"Sounds mighty prosperous."

"It'll be lonesome with him gone. Hoped maybe me and you, we might visit sometimes."

Michael's face warmed again. "I expect to be goin' over into Texas pretty soon."

Sally made no secret of her disappointment. She looked at Andrew. "How about you, little brother?"

Andrew grinned like a bear eating honey. Michael could have kicked him. Andrew said, "I'll be goin' with Michael. But it may not be today."

Sally shrugged. "Well, you both know where I'm at."

Michael said, "We sure do. And the best of luck to you."

Baptiste Villaret told him where to find Austin, down by the river at a set of corrals where he was putting together a string of horses and mules for the long trip to San Antonio de Bexar. Villaret frowned. "You would go with him?"

"If he'll take us. I've set my mind on findin' a place down there somewhere."

Villaret stared so hard into Michael's eyes that Michael had to look away. "May I ask you something, one man to another? My daughter Marie has been crying since you have been gone. Have you an interest in her?"

Michael was taken aback by the directness of the question. "Yes sir, I have."

Villaret pondered gravely. "I would hope you have no bad intentions toward her."

Michael remembered his mother; the long, lonely days and nights she had waited in vain for Mordecai to come home. He replied, "Yes sir, I have. The worst you can imagine."

He found Austin where Villaret said he would, examining some pack animals he had bought for the journey. Michael dismounted and extended his hand. "Remember us, Mister Austin? Michael and

Andrew Lewis. Down by the boat landin' the other day you asked if we'd like to go with you into Texas. Well sir, we would."

Austin seemed pleased but betrayed reservations. "It will not be an easy trip."

"Can't be no harder than what we made comin' this far. Me and Andrew, we're purty handy with animals and such like. We think we could be of help to you."

Austin nodded. "We leave at daybreak."

Michael shoved out his hand again. "We'll be here, waitin'."

As they turned the corner into the street where the Villaret house stood, Andrew reined up. Michael said, "It's just a little ways more. What're you stoppin' for?"

Andrew smiled. "I've always come trailin' after you, like your shadow. But this is one time I don't think I ought to get in your way. I think I'll go back and try that whiskey Sally Boone offered."

"Don't take too much," Michael counseled. "And be damned sure you don't take nothin' else."

The smile broadened. "Now, big brother, don't you be a vexation and a pain." Andrew turned his horse and went back in the direction he had come.

Michael touched his heels to Big Red's ribs. At the Villaret house, he saw the slender Marie standing on the big porch, her hands clasped at her breasts. He sensed that she had seen him as soon as he had turned the corner; her father must have told her he would be coming along. She watched him for a minute, then hurried down the steps and came running.

Michael dismounted as Marie ran to him, and they clung to each other in the middle of the dirt street. Michael became aware of neighbors watching, of Mrs. Villaret standing on her porch, wringing her hands in dismay. It did not matter.

He said, "Your daddy asked me if I had bad intentions for you. I told him I did."

She looked up, a flicker of disappointment in her dark eyes, but she kept her arms tight around him. "The church would frown. But whatever you want of me, you can have. Bad intentions are better than no intentions at all."

"I'm leavin' for Texas with Austin tomorrow. The worst thing I could do to you would be to ask you to marry me as soon as I get back."

She laid her head against his chest. "Then do your worst, Michael Lewis, because I will be here waiting."

THE RAIDERS: SONS OF TEXAS

PART 1

THE ALIEN LAND

1

Yesterday nature had been quarrelsome. Dark and chilly clouds had scudded ominously inland from the Gulf of Mexico, threatening a drenching cold rain across the gently rolling prairie land and dense forests that stretched westward beyond the flat coastal plain of Texas. An angry wind had lashed the trees, whipping away new leaves still the pale green of early spring. Michael Lewis had pulled his bay horse into the deep woods in search of protection, but the trees had offered only partial shelter from winter's final revolt against the changing of the season.

He had slept fitfully last night, for an old nightmare he hoped he had finally put behind him had crept back like a thief in the darkness. He had awakened wide-eyed to the sound of his own voice crying out. Afterward he had lain cold and trembling, trying to rewrap his thin woolen blanket around his shoulders in a way that would shut out the chill. But the chill came more from within than from without, and no blanket was thick enough to shield him from a memory too cruel to die.

Today Nature smiled. The skies had cleared. The sun was pleasantly warm, and he had taken off his old woolen coat, remnant of another time back in Tennessee. The wind had dropped to a soft and kindly breeze that carried the hopeful scent of new grass, the sweetness of wild flowers coming to blossom, and at times the slightest salty hint of the Gulf many long miles eastward. Michael had lived close to Nature all of his twenty-five years; he accepted her blessings with the same equanimity that he endured her torments. Nature had to be taken as she was, for nothing a man could do would change her. The works of men, however, need not be accepted without question, and Michael never had. So now he wandered here, far west of the American settlements, hoping the solitude would give him peace, would help him put down old angers, old ghosts.

Michael Lewis was a tall man, with strong arms and shoulders, though he had a gaunt and hungry look about him, as if he seldom had enough to eat, seldom got a full night's sleep. Comfort was but an occasional acquaintance, and plenty was a stranger. From the hills of Tennessee to the first American colony in Texas, his next meal had often depended upon the long-barreled rifle he carried. He seldom failed to hit what he saw over the sights, but there were times the rifle stayed cold when game was scarce and he found nothing at which to aim. The shadow of want was often upon him when he left home and hearth for the challenge of unknown lands.

Days behind him waited his French-Spanish wife Marie and a young son Michael had named Mordecai after his father, long since buried. By now Marie probably worried that he might have met with misfortune, for the few days intended had stretched to many. He knew he should be turning back. But the devils which had driven him here had come along with him, and he did not know how to shake free of their torment. It had to do with this land, this Texas, which he had visited with the first Mordecai Lewis almost a decade ago. It had been a forbidden land then, property of the Spanish crown. No longer forbidden, at least by law, it could still at times be forbidding.

This was a Texas which belonged to a newly independent Mexico but had guardedly opened its doors to limited numbers of American settlers under a young Missouri *empresario*, Stephen F. Austin. An older Austin named Moses, who had lived under Spanish rule when Spain had owned Missouri, had appealed to colonial authorities in San Antonio de Bexar. He had argued that despite its great size and potential, the interior of Texas had attracted only some two thousand Spanish inhabitants. Even these few were constantly endangered by Indian depredation. As bad or worse were nagging incursions by illegal land seekers who relentlessly pushed across the boundary from Louisiana. For a century or so these had been mostly French. Now that the Louisiana Purchase had transferred a vast region to the United States, they were American in the main. How much better it would be, Austin had reasoned, that legal immigrants be allowed to establish a deterrent to the filibusters and illegal squatters, as well as placing a buffer between the few isolated old Spanish settlements and the Indians who roamed wild and free to the west and north. To that argument he found Spanish ears receptive. If Indians had to kill someone, let it be Americans, the authorities decided.

To Austin, once wealthy but broken by a national money panic, Texas had seemed a promised land. Like an earlier Moses, he had not lived to see his promised land become reality. His son Stephen, frail in body but possessed of a dogged patience and steely determination, had taken up the lantern lighted by his father's dream. It had been a twisting, thorny path. Just as the colony was driving its first stakes into the ground, Mexico had thrown off the domination of the Spanish crown and declared itself free, as the United States had severed its ties to England two generations before. The young Austin had faced the formidable challenge of doing over with the new government of Mexico all that he and his father had accomplished with the old colonial leadership. Through nerve, statesmanship, and a stubborn refusal to accept half a loaf, he had gradually established a friendly, if sometimes uneasy, relationship with at least some of the powers in Bexar and Mexico City. He had been granted a region some one hundred twenty miles square, extending northwestward from the Gulf of Mexico. His Old Three Hundred colonists were firmly entrenched in this new land, mostly along the two major rivers, the Brazos and the Colorado. Others were gradually coming in overland and by sea, breaking the prairie sod, chopping away at the forests, transforming the wilderness into some resemblance of the places they had left behind them in the old states.

Texas was accepting more and more newcomers, some under Austin, many under other *empresarios* who followed the path Austin had blazed.

Part of what troubled Michael Lewis was this,

for he had seen the same forces at work during his youth back in Tennessee. He had loved the woods and the wild open spaces where a man afoot or on horseback could travel for hours, even days, and see no mark of another human. Little by little he had watched the woods hacked away, the open spaces surrendered to the plow, the game decimated or driven off. Now those forces were here, repeating in this virgin land the pattern of the whole western migration. And Michael, though he did not like it, had been a party to the process.

Back yonder, many days' ride behind him, he owned a grant of land, guaranteed by a paper which carried the flourish of Stephen F. Austin. Over the last three years he had gradually enlarged his field, turning under the ancient prairie sod, bringing up the rich black soil built through untold ages of nature's annual cycle: growth, decay, and regrowth. He should be at home now, plowing out the winter weeds, planting the seed for a new year's crops. He knew many would call him an idler, a shiftless leatherstocking tramping in the woods when good Christian men were at work in their fields, living up to their responsibilities.

But in Michael's veins pulsed the blood of a father who had been a leatherstocking in his own time, a product of the canebrake and wood, a man whose hands fit more easily upon the rifle than upon the plow. Mordecai Lewis had grown fitful when he spent too many days in the fields, too many nights within the confines of his cabin. His eyes would turn west toward new lands that lay somewhere beyond sight. His westering ways had brought him finally to a violent death and an unmarked grave in an alien country far from home.

Yesterday Michael had bent down over a clear-running stream for a drink of water. The angular, bearded face he saw reflected back at him did not appear to be his own; it was his father's.

That, as much as the oppressive weather, had been at the root of his nightmare; that and a small company of Mexican soldiers who had innocently ridden by Michael's farm. Their unexpected appearance had swept his mind back to another time, other soldiers. After a fruitless inner struggle to put down the ghosts, he kissed Marie and the boy good-bye and rode west up the Colorado River, looking for he knew not what. He was not sure he would even know when he found it.

He was at the edge of the wood when he saw the wolf, working a zigzag pattern through the old winter-dried grass, sniffing at the ground for scent of a rabbit or other prey. Michael's hand tightened instinctively on the long rifle that lay across his lap. Then it relaxed, for there would be no point in killing the wolf. It was too far west to be any threat to Marie's priceless little flock of chickens, or even to Michael's few calves. Here it could do no harm beyond that which Nature had appointed as its duty, controlling the increase of prey animals that otherwise might multiply beyond the ability of the land to sustain them. So Michael felt no threat from the wolf and saw no reason that he should be any threat to it.

He drew gently on the reins and stopped, his attention riveted to the graceful movement of the gray predator, its coat still winter-rough, its ribs spare of flesh because food had been scant through the cold months. The wolf caught his scent and jerked its head up, holding its nose into the breeze. Finding

Michael, it stood still as a stone for a full minute, perhaps more, watching him. This was a region in which men—white men, anyway—did not often invade. The wolf was probably accustomed to wild horses, so it saw the bay as no threat. It exhibited caution but no particular fear. Curiosity satisfied, it went on about its business of searching for a meal.

Michael felt an instinctive kinship to the wolf, for at heart he was a hunter, a creature of the wild. Circumstances forced him to take on the trappings of the civilized man, to build his cabin and farm his land, to try to be a husband to his wife and a father to his child. But beneath the surface, fighting for escape, was a man who would be grateful to live in a state of nature if circumstances would but allow.

The wolf moved on. Michael watched, hoping to see it scare up a rabbit, for he could feel its hunger, its need. He had a hunger of his own, a hunger civilization would not allow him to satisfy.

He saw the wolf pull up short again, two hundred yards away, and he thought for a moment it had found the scent it sought. But the animal watched something hidden from Michael by a jutting edge of the forest. It crouched, retreated several paces, then halted to look again.

Michael saw them as they came around the outer edge of the irregular wood; half a dozen men on horseback. At a glance he knew they were Indians. He had no idea of their tribe, for he had not seen enough of Texas Indians to have any clear notion of their tribal characteristics. It would not matter anyway if they were of violent intent. Tawakoni, Karankawa, Waco, or Tonkawa: one could kill a man as dead as another. Comanche—perhaps these were Comanche. He was far enough west to be in their hunting grounds. That horseback tribe preyed mercilessly upon the Mexican settlers around Bexar and beyond but so far had professed a wary friend-liness toward the light-skinned new American in-vaders, perhaps still trying to figure out just what manner of human they were.

It was too late to escape discovery. Michael was fifty yards beyond the forest, and a sudden move-ment back to cover would only draw their atten-tion that much sooner. Any defensive advantage the trees could give him would be temporary at best. He might just as well stand his ground.

They had seen the wolf, for they drew their horses into a line and halted, watching the animal move through the grass. As it had done for Michael, it stopped and stared at them for a moment, then changed course just enough to angle past them with-out going into actual retreat.

Proud little bastard, Michael thought. *It ain't just about to turn tail and run.*

It had no reason to run. Michael had heard it said that most Indians held the wolf in some reverence. Many thought it a guiding spirit. Few would do it harm, fearing they might run afoul of some super-natural malevolence.

The Indians watched the wolf until it had moved well past. Only then did one of them notice Mi-chael, sitting on his horse some three hundred yards away. The warrior raised a hand, and the others turned their heads. Michael trembled to a chill that ran down his back. It was a struggle not to turn and run. To do so would only insure that they would come and take him. To stand defiant would require all the nerve he could muster, from as deeply as he could reach, but it might also save his life.

The warriors clustered together, holding a quick council, then surged forward, pushing their horses into a trot. They were a wild, barbaric sight, bows in their hands, feathers in their hair jiggling up and down to the rhythm of their horses' movements. Michael lifted the long rifle enough that they would surely see it. He checked the pan to be certain it held powder to set off a shot. One shot was all he would have time for.

The Indians slowed and spread a little as they neared him. He continued to hold the rifle high but forced down a strong impulse to aim at one of the riders. He pointed the muzzle over their heads.

They halted at perhaps thirty paces. Their horses were curious about his bay, as the riders were curious about Michael, but the Indians did not move closer. They studied Michael with keen eyes, so keen that he had a feeling they knew he had eaten squirrel for breakfast. He could hear their voices as they talked about him in low tones, though he had no sense of the words or their meaning. He could not tell whether they intended to declare friendship or to kill him.

After a few tense minutes they decided to do neither, exactly. A young warrior in the center, who carried himself like a leader, rode a few feet beyond the others. He spoke words Michael had no way of understanding. It took all of his resolve not to lower the muzzle of the rifle and center it on a small leather pouch the man wore about his neck. At length the Indian raised his bow to arm's length, shouted and pulled his horse about. As he rode through the ragged line, the others turned and followed.

Michael suspected they had intentionally put him through a test of nerve, and he had passed it to their satisfaction. After a moment he felt his lungs ache and realized he was still holding his breath. He expelled it, then took several long, deep breaths to compensate. He lowered the rifle and found his hands wet, his mouth dry.

The wolf circled back toward him. Watching, he felt that kinship again. He knew the Indians had felt it too.

Brothers to the wolf. It struck him that kinship to the wolf gave him a kinship to the Indians as well.

He turned back, finally, and pointed his horse toward the settlement, days to the east. He would follow the river, and it would lead him home.

He had been far enough west, this time. There would be other times.

2

The blue-speckled ox plodded with stolid patience to the end of the row, then stopped, waiting for Andrew Lewis to give the command to turn. But Andrew laid the wooden plow over on its side and stood a moment wiping his brow, smelling the dampness of freshly turned earth, looking off across the rolling prairie toward a faraway log cabin. At this distance he could not see whether smoke curled from the stone chimney or not. It was getting on toward time for his brother's wife Marie to be cooking supper. He wondered if Michael had come home yet to eat it. He did not have to look toward his own cabin, just up the long slope from the field, to know that its chimney yielded no smoke. No one was there to build a fire or to cook anything for him.

He pondered the irony of it. Michael had somebody but would not stay home to enjoy the warmth of her company. Andrew, twenty-three now, wished for someone like Marie but had nobody. What was more, he saw no prospects. Marriageable women were scarce as gold coin in Austin's colony, and those few had bachelors lined up at their doors, handsomer and richer than Andrew Lewis. Well, richer, anyway. As to handsome, that was a matter of a woman's taste. It had been a while since one had given him any indication that he qualified, at least one who measured up to his notion of a partner for bed and board. She would need to be somebody much like his brother's wife, and he had never met anyone quite like Marie. Maybe someday, if he ever got time, he would take himself a long ride beyond the Sabine River to the old Louisiana French town of Natchitoches. That was where Michael had found Marie. Perhaps there was another like her at home, as yet unclaimed.

At least Andrew never had to worry about getting fat, eating his own cooking. Texas had lots of lanky bachelors.

Now and again when he was *really* hungry he would find an excuse to ride over to his brother's cabin and debauch himself on Marie's cooking. Being of both French and Spanish extraction, she had ways of fixing food unlike anything he had known in old Tennessee. She could make squirrel stew taste as good as roast beef, pretty near, and do things with simple garden truck that even Andrew's mother back home had never thought of.

The ox took a notion to shake itself, trying to ease the chafing of the heavy wooden yoke. Andrew said, "All right, Blue, we've plowed a right smart of ground today. We'll go to the house."

He looked around for his dog, which had wandered away in search of a rabbit and had not come back. The fool dog would trot behind him back and forth across the field all day, watching for the ox and plow to scare up some edible prey like a rabbit or a wood rat, then disappear just when it was time to send him off to bring home the milk cow. *He'll wander into a hungry Indian out in those woods one of these days, and he'll wish he'd paid a little better attention to business*, Andrew thought.

Actually, Andrew had never run into an Indian in the woods himself, though through the years since he had taken up this piece of land on the Colorado River side of Austin's colony, he had halfway expected to. Austin's people had been fortunate so far not to have had much serious Indian trouble beyond some nocturnal taking of horses and mules or the occasional ransacking of a cabin. Murder had been rare. But it was probably only a question of time. It didn't hurt for a man to have a rifle always within reach.

The dog came panting up to the cabin about the time Andrew finished unyoking the ox and giving the big beast a forkful of hay. The ox would wander off presently in search of fresh green grass, but it would be waiting here in the morning for another modest bait of dry prairie hay. Andrew had conditioned it that way to structure its habits and give him control. He saw the reddish milk cow plodding in from the edge of the wood, where the wide river ran deep and cold. The bell around her neck clanked softly to her measured steps. He had tried to condition her like the ox, but she possessed a more independent turn of mind, as if she knew how much he had had to pay for her. He called her Boss, for good reason.

At least he would not have to send the dog to fetch her this time. Boss hated the dog, which nipped at her heels when she tried to defy him. She would run at him, tossing her head and trying to dig him in the ribs with her short, curved horns. She had succeeded only once. That experience had had a salutary effect upon the dog's attention to duty. The dog and the cow eyed each other warily as she approached the pole pen where Andrew milked her morning and evening. The dog would end up getting half the milk, because Boss gave twice as much as Andrew needed for drinking or cooking. That seemed not to mellow the dog's narrow opinion of her, however. He nipped once at her heels as she entered the open gate. She quickened her step, and the bell clamored in protest.

Andrew scolded him. "Hickory, you come back away from there!" He picked up a stick as if to throw it. The dog trotted off toward the cabin, totally happy with itself. Andrew chuckled at the show of bravado and forked the cow some hay to keep her in place until he could get back from the cabin with his milk bucket.

He stopped a moment to look with a warm surge of satisfaction at his pole pens, his single-unit log cabin, his field which he had expanded bit by bit, year by year. Everything here had been built or bought with his own sweat, along with some help from his older brother Michael. He and Michael had often traded labor when one or the other had a job too large or too urgent to do by himself. Michael, being a married man, had been granted a larger tract of land than Andrew, but that was all right. Andrew's was more than large enough to meet his present needs. If he should ever find himself a wife the terms of his contract with Stephen Austin were that he could acquire more land. What he already had was far more than he could have expected to acquire in a lifetime had he remained in Tennessee instead of running off from home to tag along behind his brother. He could not imagine willingly giving this up and returning to the old country, ever. He had been gone too long for Tennessee to be home again. This was home now. He had put his sweat and blood, his heart and soul into this bit of new land. He would live here and he would be buried here. God and the Indians willing, he would be an old man when that happened.

Finished with the milking, he found the bucket nearly three-quarters full, far more than he could use or the dog needed. He remembered that Marie's best cow had dried up pending her freshening with a new calf, and the young heifer serving in her stead probably gave only about enough milk to fill a fair-to-middling coffee cup. If Andrew started now he should reach Marie's cabin just ahead of suppertime. He did not particularly relish the idea of eating his own cooking tonight anyway. A man took his excuses where he found them.

His brown horse had ambled up to the pens just behind the cow and stood waiting in the hope that Andrew might be generous with the hay kept tantalizingly out of reach behind a sturdy rail fence. Andrew slipped a bridle over the brown's head and got a sad look of betrayal. "I'll feed you when we come back, Brown," he said. "Right now you've got a little job of work to do."

He had never given the horse a better name than simply Brown, for its color. The animal was strictly utilitarian, lacking any strong individuality that might give rise to a more imaginative appellation. He did what he had to, and no more. He had even less personality than that blue ox.

Andrew saddled up. At the cabin he cut down a quarter of venison that was likely to spoil before he could get around to eating all of it anyway, and he picked up the bucket of milk. He wished he had something more practical to carry it in that would not allow half of it to slosh out on the way. But the necessities were hard to come by in colonial Texas, and luxuries like a good metal container were out of his reach. He had seen Mexicans and Indians carry water in goatskins and the paunches from cattle, but he feared those were not the proper vessels for milk. At least not if he was taking it to Marie. Though she had learned to be a good pioneering woman, able to do with a little and make it seem a lot, her Louisiana upbringing had been more refined than that.

The brown horse had an easy gait, so Andrew managed to keep most of the milk in the bucket. He lost a little of it crossing an arroyo and a little more when the brown horse took it in his head to jump a fallen tree rather than go around it.

A black and white spotted dog barked as he approached. A young woman stepped out into the open dog-run that separated the two sections of Michael and Marie's log cabin. One hand held a rifle; the other shaded her eyes. A small boy clung to her floor-length homespun skirt, peering around her in shy curiosity. Andrew felt his heart rise as he rode toward her. He had always thought Marie an uncommonly handsome woman. He always wished he had seen her first.

A glimmer of disappointment showed in her dark

eyes. She said with a noticeable accent, "From the sun you came at me, and you looked like Michael."

Impatience tugged at Andrew as he thought of his brother leaving this woman and boy here alone. If Marie were his, he would never leave her. "Hasn't he come home yet? I'd've figured he'd be back by now. Field over yonder needs to be gettin' seed in the ground."

"He was in something of—what you say?—a state when he left here."

Andrew frowned. He assumed Michael and Marie had argued. But she went on, "It was the soldiers riding by. That is what did it, I think."

"Soldiers?"

"Mexican soldiers. Their horses, they watered at the river. They were friendly; they did not seem to want anything. But just to see them, Michael was much nervous. Soon then, he was gone. We know, you and me, what is his trouble."

Andrew nodded grimly. Brother Michael displayed little fear of the world's traditional hazards. Man, beast, or weather, he took them in stride. But Andrew could remember times, when they had lived and traveled together, that Michael would awaken in the night in a cold sweat, trembling from a dream. He would seldom talk of it, but Andrew knew where its roots lay. Years ago, when Michael had been but fifteen, he had followed his footloose father Mordecai on a horse-gathering trip west of the Sabine River at a time when Texas belonged to Spain. Grasping adventurers and power-seeking fili-busters had made Americans extremely unpopular, subject to summary justice. When a troop of Span-ish soldiers caught up with the little party of horse hunters, a vengeful lieutenant ordered them slaughtered like cattle on the open prairie. The officer had blown Mordecai Lewis's brains out. Michael was wounded and left for dead.

That Michael was back in Texas a decade later, and settled down to stay, seemed remarkable to Andrew. The political climate had changed. The Mexican government was at least guardedly hospitable to American immigrants so long as they minded their own business, pledged allegiance to their new hosts, and showed no inclination toward lawlessness or rebellion. Itself having been born of rebellion, the government of Mexico was particularly sensitive to any sign of discontent among its subjects lest history repeat itself.

Michael had seemed to have no qualms about embracing that government. He held Spain, not Mexico, responsible for the killing of his and Andrew's father. But the sight of dark-skinned soldiers in uniform still opened old wounds unlikely ever to heal.

Marie smiled tentatively as she looked up at the bucket in Andrew's hand. "For strawberries, it is much too early."

Her smile could turn a man's heart to butter. "Milk," he said. "My old Boss cow is fairly spillin' over because of all this new spring grass. Thought you and the button might have some use for it, if you don't mind a little weedy flavor."

"It will taste fine. Get down. I will fix the supper."

"I wouldn't want to put you to no trouble."

"No trouble. Maybe Michael will come."

Andrew smiled. He had always liked to listen to Marie talk. Her speech betrayed her French and Spanish heritage. The accent was not enough to get in the way; it was just enough to play arrestingly upon the ear.

Leaning from the saddle, he handed her the bucket, then swung to the ground and untied the venison. She told him to put the brown horse in the pen and give it some hay while she set a pot over the fire. He took a little time, feeling awkward about being here alone with Michael's young wife when Michael was gone. It was not as if anything untoward was going to happen. Even though he was strongly drawn to Marie, to act upon those feelings was unthinkable. It was the appearance that bothered him, however innocent the reality might be. Michael would think nothing of it, but some people in the colony were given to talk. There were people everywhere who would talk, whether there was anything to talk about or not.

Little Mordecai stood on the dog-run and watched his uncle with big and curious eyes that reminded Andrew of his own small brother named Jonathan, left behind in Tennessee. The Lewis stamp had always been strong. Andrew suspected that as this boy grew older he would take on his grandfather Mordecai's gaunt and rangy look. All the Lewis male offspring did. He tousled the boy's long hair. "Another year or two, young'un, and you'll have to learn to follow a plow."

"Plow," Mordecai said, pointing toward the field. The boy was always initially shy when Andrew came over, but he never remained that way for long. He warmed quickly to company.

Andrew said, "I may have to come plow that field if your daddy don't find his way home pretty quick."

It was in his mind that some misfortune might have befallen Michael, but he regarded that possibility as remote. Their father had been an outdoorsman, never so happy as when he tramped the woods, preferably alone. Michael was in many ways his father's image and unable to change the legacy. Their mother often had taken the responsibility of organizing the farm work and parceling out the tasks to her young sons when Mordecai forgot to come home from the forests. Now Michael's Marie was following the same pattern. But little Mordecai was several years shy of being able to take on the work.

Before entering the cabin Andrew walked to the woodpile out back. The stack was large; Michael had dragged up deadfall timber from the forest during winter's lull. But only a little of it was chopped into short lengths for the fireplace. Andrew picked up the ax, looked around to be sure the boy was not in harm's way, then set to work. He took out against the ax and the wood the anger he felt against Michael. A few chips bounced violently off the log wall of the cabin. He did not stop until Marie called him for supper.

She had sliced a little of the venison he had brought, had made some cornbread and warmed up a pot of beans. He would have liked coffee, but that was a luxury. Texas settlers often parched grain as a substitute for coffee beans. To Andrew it had always been a poor replacement. He'd as soon drink plain water, and did.

After sating his first hunger he paused to tell her, "It's awful good, Marie."

"*Your* venison," she said. "For some days we are out of meat, except for ham in the smokehouse. That I take only a little, to make it last."

"If I'd known, I'd've fetched you somethin'. I'll make a little sashay out into the woods tomorrow."

"You should do your plowing while the weather is good. You should not bother about us."

No, he would agree, he shouldn't. And he wouldn't have to if Michael stayed around like a good husband. But that was Michael's way, and nothing would keep him from roaming except a crippling accident, or worse. He said, "You don't need to be worryin' about the weather. Old Man Willet is somethin' of a weather prophet. He says we're fixin' to have a good spring."

Marie wrinkled her fine little nose. "The Old Man Willet always says it will be good weather. When it is dry he says soon it will rain. When it rains he says soon the sun will shine."

Marie pushed away from the table and walked out the door to the dog-run. She stood with arms folded, brow furrowed, and stared toward the dark line of forest that lay to the west, as Michael remembered his mother doing many a time. Marie had eaten but little. Andrew was mildly ashamed for having eaten so much. One piece of cornbread remained on the plate. The boy Mordecai looked longingly at it but was too well trained to reach for it so long as someone older sat at the table. Andrew pushed the plate toward him. "You better eat this before that spotted dog comes in here and steals it." He walked out onto the dog-run and joined Marie.

Dusk was gathering. Marie's sad eyes indicated that she knew Michael was not coming.

Andrew said, "Maybe he'll be back tomorrow."

"Perhaps." Her frown deepened. "I did not want to tell you, but I should, I think. Three men came yesterday, looking for him."

Andrew had been trying to dislodge a rough-ground piece of corn from between his teeth by probing at it with his tongue. He stopped abruptly. "What men was that?"

"They did not say their names. They said they knew Michael back in Tennessee. They were a rough-looking lot of men."

Andrew began digging at the wedged corn again. A lot of men in these colonies would look rough by the standards of other places, but Marie was used to that. "Did they say *how* they knew him?"

"They said only that they were old friends and neighbors. They kept asking which way he had gone. I told them west of here is a very big country. They said they would be back."

A dark suspicion began rising in Andrew. "If they knew Michael in Tennessee, they knew me too."

"They talked about Michael only. They said they were his friends, but they made me nervous."

"What did they look like?" He was afraid he already knew.

Marie shrugged. "Tall men, thin, bearded. About the age of you and Michael."

His eyes narrowed. "Was a one-armed man amongst them?"

She blinked, remembering. "Yes, it is true. One of them *did* have a sleeve pinned up."

"Blackwood!" He spoke the name like a curse.

The name brought a flicker to her eyes. She had heard Michael and Andrew speak of them. "You think so?"

He nodded bleakly and stared toward the dark woods, wishing Michael were here. He had not thought about the Blackwoods in a long time. He and Michael had assumed they put the Blackwood trouble behind them years ago, when they left Tennessee. But that kind of trouble seemed to follow a man like a hungry wolf sniffing out tracks. "Which-away did they go when they left?"

"East, toward San Felipe. They said they look for land. They said soon they will be Michael's neighbors again."

"Like hell they will!" Andrew muttered. He picked up his rifle and started toward the pen where he had put the brown horse.

Surprised, she asked, "Where do you go?"

"To San Felipe, to see Stephen Austin. If I start now I'll be there in the mornin'." He turned to face her. His voice was grim. "If Michael gets back before I do, you tell him about the Blackwoods first thing. *Then* you can take time to kiss him."

Riding in the darkness, he startled some wild animal, which broke for the nearby brush, crackling branches as it plunged into the protective cover. Deer, he thought, though he never got a clear look at it. He found his heart thumping, his hand slick on the stock of his rifle.

It could as easily have been the Blackwoods, setting up an ambush.

That would have been their style.

3

Generations later, Texans would know them as bluebonnets, but these blue-and-white wild flowers had not yet acquired the name. Riding his brown horse toward the village of San Felipe de Austin on a trail not yet old enough to be deeply beaten-out, Andrew Lewis knew only that they were one of the most striking sights he had ever seen. Even in his weariness from riding all night, he was able to appreciate their beauty. Their early-spring splendor was like a reflection of the morning's open sky, a brilliant blue carpet spread almost solidly across the hillsides and down into the valleys, broken here and there by newly leafing trees and bushes, some of which had blossoms of their own to provide a counterpoint in color. Now and again the blue weave was interspersed by yellow buttercups and by blazing orange skeins of another wild flower similar in height. In a sense, these blue flowers were like Texas itself, new and fresh and unspoiled. They would run their course much too soon, the blossoms drying

and dropping away, leaving a coarse and nondescript weed, like a beautiful, smiling girl who turns
much too quickly into a nagging and unappealing
old crone. But while they lasted they lifted his spirit
and made him glad he had followed his brother Michael westward into Texas. It was a raw country yet,
long on hardship and privation, short on prosper-
ity and comfort. But if its weeds could bring forth
such blossoms, even for a little while, then surely
this stern and still-rugged land should be capable of
a gentle and generous side to its nature.

It had, up to now, been generous with its wildlife,
its bounty of fresh meat to help put food on families' tables until they had time to break out their
land and lay by a crop or two. Were it not for deer
and squirrel, fish and wild fowl, Andrew and Michael might not have survived their first two years.
But now, as more and more people took up parcels
of land in the region the Mexican government had
allotted for Austin's colony, Andrew sensed that the
game was thinning, killed off or scared away into
remote regions not yet familiar with the strike of the
ax, the bite of plowpoint into primeval sod.

Most settlers, including Stephen Austin, seemed
to feel that this was the way it was meant to be,
that destiny called for the wilderness and all that
went with it to be pushed steadily westward until it
ran out of room and out of existence. Andrew found
himself partially inclined toward Austin's view, that
the land was meant to be tamed, that the wild forest
was to be converted to fruitful fields, that the wild
animal was to give way to the domestic beast, that
civilized man was meant to live from his own cattle
and hogs and chickens, not by the hunt for the native white-tailed deer that multiplied and consumed

the land's bounty and too often contributed not to the welfare of man. Nature was not to be accommodated, it was to be overcome, for only thus could the multitudes be fed.

Andrew had no fear of the multitudes. It was his nature to be gregarious, to enjoy company and laughter and song.

But another side of him felt sympathy with his brother's far different view. Michael was uncomfortable wherever there were many people. He loved the forests, the unaltered prairies. He had a respect that bordered on worship for the wild things of the earth and sky, while he had what amounted almost to contempt for the cud-chewing cow, the rooting pig, the ever-dependent sheep.

Andrew saw futility in that view, even while he acknowledged the validity of it. Like it or not, people would keep coming. Their ever-expanding numbers would need fields to provide them sustenance, homes for shelter, roads to grant them passage, grass and water for the domestic livestock which provided their walking commissary. The Indian had made little demand upon the land, had altered its face virtually none at all. But the white man's way was to take whatever he found and restructure it, to bend it to his own needs, his own dreams. The Michael Lewises of this world would never stop that process of constant change. They might as well try to stop the wind.

Andrew's stomach growled, for normally by this time he had eaten his breakfast and had been at work in the field for an hour or more. He had paused only once in his journey, at the cabin of the Willet family some miles east of his own. There he had shared a

quick cup of parched-corn coffee and a story or two
with Old Man Willet before traveling on. Given congenial company such as that, he would have been
happy under normal circumstances to have spent a
day or two. It was in Andrew's nature to laugh, to
sing, something Michael had never learned.

San Felipe de Austin, some seventy miles inland
from Galveston Bay, could hardly claim to be a
town, not in the sense of towns Andrew had known
in Tennessee. Village was more like it, though if
one counted the many farms which clustered close
around, the total population would have amounted
to much more than the small settlement revealed at
first glance. In the Mexican style it boasted a small
square bearing a high-sounding name, Constitu-
tional Plaza. But the plaza had far more huisache
trees around it than buildings. Most of the stores
and houses were strung in a random manner along
a road that paralleled Palmito Creek. Timber was
plentiful here, so most were constructed mainly
of logs, American-style. A majority were built on
about the same rough utilitarian plan as those Andrew had known in Tennessee; double cabins like
Michael and Marie's, with an open dog-run in the
center and a single roof joining the two sections, or
a single cabin like Andrew's own, which could easily be expanded into a double cabin if the right girl
ever smiled at him. There was little about San Felipe to indicate that this was part of Mexico. It was
totally unlike the town of San Antonio de Bexar,
which he had found to be in sharp contrast to anything he had seen elsewhere. Bexar was unlike even
the northernmost Mexican town of Nacogdoches,
Texas. And Nacogdoches was different in many ways

from its sister city Natchitoches, across the Sabine in Louisiana, despite the similarity in names. Each had a personality uniquely its own.

San Felipe, except for the Spanish name and what passed for a plaza, appeared to be simply an extension of the old states, an American island in an alien sea. To the occasional Mexicans who visited, it must have seemed as strange as Bexar had been to Andrew. But he had found something intriguing about Bexar, almost magnetic. Perhaps Mexican visitors to San Felipe knew the same feeling. The new and unknown tended to have two sides like a coin, one bringing apprehension, the other an exotic and compelling attraction.

There was nothing about Stephen Austin's office to mark it as different or better than other structures in this village on a bluff above the wide and muddy Brazos River. There was little about Austin himself to mark him as wealthier or living any better than the colonists who depended upon him for leadership except that he had the general look of a tradesman or merchant rather than the rough and weather-worn appearance of a farmer. He customarily wore homespun to avoid giving an impression that he felt himself above those in his community who could afford no better. His double log cabin, shaded by a huge moss-strewn oak, served as both residence and working quarters.

Andrew dismounted and tied the brown horse, then walked up the foot-packed path toward the cabin. Two men burst angrily through the door and down from the dog-run. A burly young man was a step or two in the lead, a dour, gray-bearded man behind him. The young man in his haste bumped hard against Andrew, causing Andrew to falter and fall back. The man turned with blazing eyes. "Why don't you get the hell out of folks' way?" he demanded. "You seen me comin'."

He acted as if he intended to pursue the matter with his fists, and Andrew raised his own in self-defense. But the older man gripped the younger one's arm. Andrew saw thunder and lightning in the creased old face as the bearded man said, "Come on, son. Let us begone from this place." The younger one seemed inclined to stay and pursue his grievances, whatever they were, but the old man hustled him toward two tied horses.

Andrew watched them ride away. He thought the old man's back was straighter than the young one's. Whatever had made him angry had done a thorough job of it. When the pair had traveled fifty yards or so and he was sure they were not coming back, Andrew walked to a well in the yard, rocked up to about waist height. "Help yourself," a pleasant voice said. "Water is the one thing which we have in plentiful measure." Stephen Austin stood on the dog-run, watching him.

Andrew turned the windlass and studied the man as he filled the community dipper from the wooden bucket. Austin looked older than his early thirties. He was thin, almost emaciated-looking, betraying in his spare frame little of the inner strength that had enabled him to build this American outpost in the midst of an untouched wilderness, that had made it possible for him to deal on the one hand with leather-clad frontiersmen who in some instances could not write their own names on the deeds he prepared for them, and on the other to fit into the highest courts of Mexico, fighting his colonists' cause with the vigor and resolve of a missionary zealot.

Andrew and Michael had met him in Natchitoches
on the brink of his first great adventure into Texas.
Other would-be land *empresarios* had tried to duplicate what Austin had done. Most had fallen by
the wayside. Austin's eyes burned with a fire that
said he would die before he would retreat.

Andrew measured all men by his brother Michael
and by the memory of his father Mordecai. Physi-
cally, Austin stood in their shadow. But in spirit and
determination he would have put them to severe
test.

Austin shook hands. "It is good to see you, Andrew Lewis. But I would think you would be at
home, taking advantage of this fine spring weather
to get your planting done."

"Been workin' on it," Andrew acknowledged
with a nod. "But somethin' come up." He frowned.

Austin said, "Whatever it is, it will look better
over a cup of coffee."

Andrew followed the *empresario* into the office
side of the cabin, where the coals of a burned-down
fire still glowed beneath a blackened pot. Austin
poured coffee for Andrew and refilled his own cup.
Andrew blew the coffee and savored its aroma. Real
coffee was an indulgence he reserved for special
days, and there were not many of those.

He said, "Them fellers that just left here, they
weren't in too good a humor."

"I just refused them land in this colony. I do not
believe they are the sort we want."

"Who are they?"

"The old one is named Tolliver Beard, from Louisiana. The other is his son. Their reputation has
preceded them. Beard is a contentious old man who
would bring nothing but discord into this colony.

His son Jayce is just a brutal lout with no sense of propriety. I told them not to come back."

"I'd as soon not see them again," Andrew said. He studied a hand-drawn map stretched across part of the log wall. Idly he ran his finger from San Felipe past several dozen other land holdings to the pair which bore his name and Michael's. They were among those farthest west. That had been Michael's doing, a legacy from their father Mordecai. Mordecai's eyes had always been set on something farther west.

Austin said speculatively, "You indicated trouble. I hope no one is ill. Perhaps your sister-in-law is with child again?"

Andrew blinked. Such a thought had not occurred to him. "Not that I know of. I'm already an uncle once. But in a way this concerns her. There was three men come by my brother's place while he was gone. Caused Marie a mite of worry. I wonder if you've talked to some fellers named Blackwood?"

Austin pondered a moment, his eyes narrowing. "As a matter of fact, I have. Three brothers. From Georgia, they said—no, Tennessee. They asked me about taking up land." He paused, contemplating darkly. "And yes, they asked about your brother Michael. They said they knew him."

Andrew nodded solemnly. "They know him sure enough."

Austin seemed to sense Andrew's mood. "I would surmise that it is not a friendly acquaintance?"

"They're a shiftless family. Only thing they ever broke a sweat at was mischief. Reason Michael come to Texas in the first place was, he knew if he stayed he'd sooner or later have to kill one of them, or they'd kill him."

More than that, though he saw no need to burden Austin with details, had been Michael's fear that the Blackwoods in their determination to get at him would hurt others in his family. Finis Blackwood had wounded Michael's Uncle Benjamin by mistake, trying to hit Michael. Andrew thought it best not to mention that. Austin had gone to considerable lengths to avoid accepting violent men and leatherstockings among his colonists. He had probably suspected more than once that Michael belonged in that class. By extension, Andrew would also fit the category.

Andrew said, "I hope you're not grantin' them land."

Austin shook his head and almost spilled his coffee. "I made up my mind almost on sight that I would find reason to pass them by. They did not appear the sort to fit in with my Old Three Hundred. And the fact that they said your brother was a friend of theirs gave me some pause about *him*. That he is not their friend comes as a relief."

"It'd be a relief to *me* if you could chase them plumb back to Tennessee."

"Under Mexican law I am the *alcalde* here. I have considerable police and military power. But that power extends only to the borders of this colony. That is as far as I could push them. And even then I probably would not have authority to do so until and unless they break the law."

"They will, sooner or later. It's born in them, I reckon, like it's born in a fox to steal chickens."

Austin's face was creased with concern. To him, this colony was his life and the people in it were his family, even if a few became errant now and again, or resented him out of a false perception that he was becoming rich on their labor. "One of my requirements for land claimants is that they bring proof of good character, letters of reference or recommendation. The Blackwoods had none. If they appear again in San Felipe I will request that they depart this colony forthwith."

Request. Andrew wondered what Austin could do if they refused. This colony was so law-abiding that as yet there had been no necessity even to build a jail. The nearest he knew was a Mexican *calabozo* in Bexar, a long way for anybody to be obliged to ride with the Blackwoods as reluctant company.

Austin said, "If these men appear again, tell them I wish to consult with them. The problem will be out of your hands."

"They may not want to come."

"I have always suspected that your brother possesses strong powers of persuasion. I suspect that some of his determination runs in your blood as well." Austin drained his cup and smiled. "Just see that you do not spill any of that blood in the process, will you please? Violence disturbs the Mexican authorities in Bexar. And it does my digestion no good, either."

Austin did not invite Andrew to stay for dinner. By the thin look of him Andrew suspected the man might not be eating regularly anyway; the work and worry of the colony overrode his sense of comfort, or even of physical need. He was one of those people who stopped to eat only when the notion struck him. Other matters took priority, even over concern for his own health.

Andrew could put aside considerations of comfort when the need arose, but he was not immune to fatigue. The coffee had temporarily overcome his hunger, but he felt the weight of the night's long miles bearing heavily upon him. More important, he knew the brown horse did also. He followed the wagon road down to the bluff and lingered to watch the ferry which operated between the two banks of the wide and silt-laden Brazos. Sleepiness soon overcame his curiosity. He rode upriver away from the noise of human endeavor, staked the brown horse on new grass, and lay down in the benign shade of a towering oak from which the moss dangled like an old man's long beard.

He was awakened, finally, by a snuffing sound around his face. He opened his startled eyes and found himself the object of interest for a couple of lean hounds of a bluish hue, a kind favored by coon hunters back in Tennessee. One of them backed away cautiously, but the other continued to sniff at Andrew's legs, probably picking up the scent of Andrew's dog Hickory. A man's voice hailed him. "Sorry if my hounds woke you up. They got no more manners than a brush hog."

Andrew rose up and stretched, facing a farmer probably ten or fifteen years his senior. The man rode a black mule. Behind him, astride an old plow mare, came a boy of ten or twelve. He drove half a dozen cows, three with calves trotting beside them. Andrew had seen the man around San Felipe. This was probably his land.

The man said jovially, "We come out to gather up our stock. Didn't figure to gather up no company. Your name is Lewis, ain't it?"

"Andrew Lewis." Andrew extended his hand. "Rode all night. Just lettin' my horse rest a little before I start home."

The man smiled. "I always like to see a man

who watches out for the welfare of his animals." He pointed upriver with his chin. "Time we get to the barn with our cows, the woman'll have dinner ready to put on the table. We'd be pleasured to have you join us."

It would have been impolite to refuse, even if Andrew had not been so hungry. "I'd be tickled." He rode along beside the man, complimenting him first upon his strapping son, then upon the fruitfulness of his cows. Besides the three which had already calved, two more would obviously yield their increase before the bluebonnets lost all their blooms. The farmer acknowledged that five out of six wasn't bad. But the dry cow had cost him the most. A man didn't always get just what he paid for, he lamented with good humor.

The man's fields were well plowed, the rows straight as a rifle barrel, and they were pole-fenced to keep the cattle from getting in. The log house was long, three rooms at least, with a sturdy clapboard roof. The whole place showed the mark of a good and industrious manager, the kind Austin had sought for the nucleus of his colony. As they drove the cows and calves into a pen and closed the gate behind them, the woman of the house rang dinnertime by hammering a broken piece of wagon wheel against a dangling iron ring on the dog-run.

The fare was simple, all home-raised, but it was plentiful and filling. Andrew sensed the contentment of the farmer and his wife, and watching them reminded him of the missing element in his own life, of the empty cabin to which he would return. When he remarked upon the fact that the farmer had a handsome family—there were three children younger than the boy who had ridden the plow mare—the farmer replied, "That's what makes the work a pleasure, Andrew, havin' somebody to share the fruits of it with. Can't be much in it for a man who don't work for nobody except himself."

Andrew's mind drifted to Marie. "Not what there ought to be," he agreed.

The farmer said, "We've done well here in Texas. Got more land here than we could ever've gotten back in Georgia. There it was mostly all took, and too high for a man ever to buy and pay for. We've only broke out the smallest part of this so far. Time the boys come of age they can each parcel off for their own needs, and we'll still have plenty. Austin's been real good to us."

"The Mexican government's been good to us," Andrew remarked.

That was the first time he had seen the farmer frown. The man said, "But it's a foreign government, and we're Americans. That's the only thing which don't set quite right with me. They're good to us now, sure, but what if they come along some day and see what we've built and decide they want it for theirselves? They ain't our people, and we ain't theirs. They won't have any deep compunctions against tryin' to take it away from us, I'm thinkin'."

Andrew said, "They've promised us, solemn."

"The bunch that's *in* has promised us. But them people down in Mexico, they're everlastin'ly fightin' amongst theirselves. What if someday a bunch takes over that won't honor the promises? What'll we do?"

This was not the first time Andrew had heard that question asked. He had no answer.

The farmer said, "We'll fight. That's all we *can* do."

Andrew shrugged. "Maybe it'll never come to that."

The farmer slapped the flat of his hand against his

stomach. "I've got a feelin' in my gut, and it's a fair-sized gut as you can see. It will come to that. Maybe not tomorrow, maybe not next year. But someday. And not even Mr. Austin will be able to stop it."

Andrew started toward home after the best meal he had eaten in days, his stomach satisfied but his mind in turmoil. The farmer had started him thinking about questions that had risen periodically from his subconscious and that he had forcibly put aside.

It was a long way south to Mexico City. Who here could really know what was happening there, and how many men were harboring the same suspicion of the American colonists as the colonists harbored about them?

4

Lieutenant Elizandro Zaragosa sat gun-barrel straight on his finely curried, shiny black horse and stared down in painful resignation at the line of ragged men slouched before him, a dozen half-starved new recruits, all but barefoot after their long march to San Antonio de Bexar from somewhere south of the Rio Grande. The indifference in their dark and unshaven faces did not lead him to hope they would be better than the last set, now mostly scattered: deserted; jailed; killed in fights over women, whiskey, or games of no chance. He wondered from what prisons in Monclova or Monterrey these had been dredged up. It made no difference. Brilliant military minds in the interior had sent them. It was his duty to do the best he could with what he was given.

The mentality of the central government was supposed to have improved when Mexico wrested its independence from Spain, but some things never changed. The lower-level bureaucrats who sat comfortably at their desks and exacted their bribes under the benign name *mordida,* or little bite, were mostly the same men who had always been there. The outer trappings had changed, but the inner machinery of government was as corrupt as under the Spanish king. Painting the house did not rid it of the termites hidden within the wood.

He shrugged and commended the recruits to the dubious mercies of a heavyset noncommissioned officer whose generous black moustache made his dark scowl look even fiercer than it was. Sergeant Isidro Gomez had a man's work ahead of him. Zaragosa could sympathize. Now in his early thirties and looking a world-weary forty or more, he himself had once been a sergeant in this same garrison, when all of Mexico including Texas had been but an outpost of Spain. He had whipped his share of unlikely recruits into some semblance of military discipline and had suffered through his share of failures. He might still be doing so had it not been for the revolution. Or, and this was by no means unlikely, he would be dead. God knew how close he had come.

His left arm was still a little stiff and gave him pain at times when the weather changed, all because of a vengeful royalist officer's bullet. It had been Zaragosa's considerable pleasure to put a better-aimed bullet through that son of a goat and send him to his everlasting punishment in a place far hotter even than Texas.

He turned in the saddle and saw some passing citizens giving the recruits a baleful study. Soldiers were a bane of their life. Supposedly sent to protect them from Indian depredations, the soldiers themselves all too often became the predators. Underpaid, underfed, many of them taken from the prisons of

Mexico, they had on occasion burglarized homes and businesses and even openly robbed people at the point of a gun or a knife, knowing that the citizens' well-justified fear of the military would probably prevent their ever being called upon to pay for their crimes. Most citizens looked upon the soldiers as they looked upon taxes: a curse to be avoided where possible but endured with stoical resignation when circumvention was not to be.

At least, he thought, the situation was less harsh under the government of free Mexico than it had been under the royalist aristocrats. The *gachupínes* had looked upon the common people as little more than chattels, their only purpose to make life richer and more comfortable for those who possessed the power. There had been disappointments. Despite the revolution, many of the *gachupínes* remained in high positions. By and large they were more careful now in the way they wielded their power. The new government took a more benign view and exhibited some regard for the rights of even the lowliest. So far, at least. But time had not dulled Zaragosa's suspicions. Resentments still smouldered beneath the surface, both with the *gachupínes* who had lost power and with the common people who had but a tenuous hold. News drifted to Bexar from time to time about power struggles in the capital far, far to the south. First one and then another politician or military leader pushed to the fore with his own concepts of the proper way to govern Mexico. Zaragosa feared it was only a matter of time before the common people again were forced to take up arms to fight for their rights and their dignity against those who had known absolute power before and were determined to have absolute power again.

In the crowd which watched the recruits he saw two light-skinned *americanos,* one wearing a blondish beard which reminded him uncomfortably of the blue-eyed pureblood Spaniards who so long had lorded it over the mixed-blood people. He could not restrain a frown which set itself deeply into his dark features, or a sour feeling of dislike that arose. His mind told him these foreigners had nothing to do with those who so long had oppressed the majority of Mexican citizens, that the only similarity was their appearance. But appearance was enough to arouse old angers in his heart. He was glad most of the American settlers lived far enough away that he did not often have to look upon them.

A light-colored beard, a pair of blue eyes, always made him remember Lieutenant Armando Rodriguez, a pureblood, a *gachupín* of the most hated sort. It had been Rodriguez's bullet which had stiffened Zaragosa's arm, and Zaragosa's bullet which had sent Rodriguez to a watery grave in the Sabine River. But that bullet had not laid the memory to rest. Though long dead, Rodriguez still lurked in the dark corners of Zaragosa's mind, appearing unexpectedly, as now, to disturb the peace of his soul.

How many times must I yet kill him before he is finally dead? Zaragosa wondered.

From the tail of his eye he caught movement as Captain Emilio Sanchez appeared in the doorway of the *comandante*'s office. Sanchez stared a minute at the recruits, then beckoned Zaragosa with a silent jerk of his head. Zaragosa pulled the black horse around and walked him to the front of the building, dismounting and handing the reins to an orderly who stood waiting at stiff attention. The orderly saluted, and Zaragosa gave him a slack response that betrayed his weariness with the military regiment.

Captain Sanchez was a pureblood Spaniard, but Zaragosa had found him a generally tolerant man as *gachupínes* went, not disposed to flaunt his power or his station, an officer firm but generally fair in dealing with his subordinates. He was a portly gentleman, his dark brown eyes rimmed with angry red veins, testimony to his frequent excesses with wine. Zaragosa did not know whether this was a cause or an effect of Sanchez's being exiled to the isolated northern province of Texas, an obscure outpost far from the captain's old home in the interior of Mexico. He pitied Sanchez in his afflictions, the principal of these being periodic seizures of painful gout and constant harassment by a shrewish wife who felt he had betrayed her by not earning a prestigious station in Mexico City.

Each time Zaragosa encountered the vitriolic *Señora* Sanchez, he became more grateful for the quiet temperament and warmly loving attention given him by his own wife, Elvira. Captain Sanchez had a great deal more money and the command of this post, but Zaragosa would not trade places with him for as much as a minute. At night Zaragosa could look forward to going to sleep contented in the tender and willing embrace of Elvira. Sanchez could sleep only in the sodden embrace of a quart of poor wine.

Not all the *gachupínes* were favored.

Sanchez returned his salute with an indifference to which officers of his rank seemed addicted, and he seated himself behind a heavy, hand-carved wooden desk. He gestured for Zaragosa to sit in a high-backed chair he suspected was designed to be so uncomfortable that visitors would quickly state their business and be gone. Sanchez's expression was pained. Zaragosa suspected he was still under the attack of last night's wine. The captain asked, "What do you think of the new recruits?"

Zaragosa shrugged. "They look like just about all the others. We will probably get two or three decent soldiers from the lot. The others should never have been let out of jail."

The captain covered his mouth as he burped gas from last night's indulgences. Pain crossed his face, and he ran his tongue over his lips. That wine must have a sour taste indeed, the tenth time it came up. He said, "Recruits are a nuisance, but they are not the heaviest cross we are called upon to bear in this life." He burped again and made a considerable noise in clearing his throat. He asked, "How do you get along with the American settlers in our midst?"

Zaragosa was not sure how he was expected to answer. "I have no problems with them. I avoid them whenever possible."

"Would that we could all do so," Sanchez said. "How long has it been since you have visited their colonies?"

Zaragosa thought back. "I made an inspection through Austin's colony last fall. I found it peaceful and prosperous."

Sanchez nodded. "Austin's Americans have never given us much cause for concern. They apply themselves diligently to their own business and leave politics alone. But there are problems around Nacogdoches."

Zaragosa had heard rumors. "Of what sort, sir?"

"Squatters, illegal settlers, thieves, and brigands of all sorts. They steal across from the neutral strip between us and the Americans in Louisiana. They harass our people and cause unrest among the Indians. They are breaking out farms where they have no right and taking land from our own people. They seem to think that because they are Americans they are a superior race."

Zaragosa remembered. As a sergeant in the Spanish army, serving under the late Lieutenant Rodriguez, he was stationed for some years in the northern outpost of Nacogdoches. He had spent much time in the saddle, rooting out and expelling smugglers and illegal immigrants who seemed constantly working to extend the borders of the United States westward and confiscate Texas lands that were a part of Mexico. Many of these were lawless and defiant men who knew no authority except that which came at the point of a sword or from the muzzle of a rifle.

The late Lieutenant Rodriguez had taken special pleasure in obliging them with either or both, to the point of bloody excess which had sometimes turned Zaragosa's stomach. The courts were slow and overly lenient, Rodriguez had contended. On the other hand, there was no appeal from the grave.

Sanchez said, "The situation appears beyond the control of our few soldiers in Nacogdoches. You know that region, lieutenant. Therefore I am dispatching you northward with enough troops to make our presence felt. I want you to seek out those who have no legitimate purpose on our side of the Sabine River and send them back where they belong. How soon could you start?"

"Whenever you say, sir. I await your orders." He hoped he spoke with military correctness and that his misgivings did not betray themselves. Nacogdoches and its region held many unpleasant memories for him. Even more important, he knew that to take Elvira with him was out of the question. He had no idea how long this mission might require him to be separated from her.

Sanchez said, "Tomorrow, then. I will issue orders to the quartermaster to see that your troops are properly outfitted."

"Properly outfitted" meant little in the Mexican army, certainly not at this level and in such an isolated post. His men would be given little beyond arms and a modest supply of ammunition, horses, and castoff equipment that no other army post between here and Mexico City had wanted. Their rations would be of the most meager kind. For the most part Zaragosa and his men would be expected to live off of the land. As a practical matter, beyond whatever wild game they could manage to bag, that meant taking from the settlers whose lives and property it was supposed to be their duty to protect. To be sure, they would issue army scrip or requisitions in payment, but these usually were worth no more than the paper they were written upon. Small wonder then, that settlers—Mexican or American— tried to hide whatever they had that was of value when they saw soldiers.

Sanchez said, "I would expect that you will want to go home early and have time for a proper goodbye to that beautiful wife of yours, and your children."

"I would be grateful, sir." Zaragosa saluted and started for the door.

Sanchez called after him. "One more thing, lieutenant. I want you to go by the Austin colony, just for a look around."

Zaragosa frowned. That would add much distance

to the trip, for Austin's colony was east of Bexar. Nacogdoches was far to the northeast. He commented, "Austin's people are quiet, sir."

"Seeing a few soldiers once in a while should help keep them that way." Sanchez frowned under a fresh attack of biliousness. He asked, "Do you speak English?"

"Here a word, there a word. My English is poor."

"Then take Corporal Diaz with you as interpreter. He contemplates matrimony to a most devious young woman. Perhaps some time away from Bexar will afford him the opportunity to reconsider his error. He will thank me someday."

Zaragosa found little Manuel at the front of his modest adobe house, throwing a stick for a small spotted dog to run and fetch. Manuel, six, appeared surprised at seeing him, for it was still early in the afternoon, but he came running as Zaragosa stepped down from the black horse. "Papa!" he called. Zaragosa knelt for the boy to hug him. He asked, "Is the baby asleep?"

Manuel shook his head. "No, she is crawling everywhere. I came outside to get away from her for a while. Why are children such a nuisance, Papa?"

Zaragosa smiled. "That is simply their way. We just have to suffer them until they grow up like you and me." He turned to look for the dog. "You had better keep him away from the heels of that black horse. It does not like dogs."

Manuel ran off in a direction away from the mount, luring the dog after him with the stick. He joined several neighbor boys with whom he often played. Zaragosa watched a moment, taking plea-sure in the laughter of children, then pushed the heavy wooden door inward. The thick adobe walls made the room dark and cool.

Elvira stood in the kitchen doorway, her eyes wide in surprise. They were beautiful eyes, large and dark, set in a face he found so beautiful that he could never stop with kissing her upon the lips. He had to kiss each smooth cheek, the high forehead, the tip of her perfect nose. As he held her body against his and she responded by clasping her arms tightly around him, he felt the upsurge of a wanting that was never satisfied for long. Glancing toward the bed-room door, he wondered if this was a proper time to surrender to such an impulse. The baby girl crawl-ing on the floor would pay no attention, but the boy might return to the house.

They would have the night, all of the night, if he could wait.

When they pushed to arm's length, Elvira caught her breath. "Why are you home so early? Is any-thing wrong?"

He knew no easy way to tell her, but it was a thing to which a soldier's wife had to become accustomed. "I must leave for Nacogdoches in the morning."

Her large black eyes looked downward, trying to hide their dismay. "I hope it is not for anything dan-gerous." She always reacted badly when he had to leave her for any length of time.

He said, "It is only routine." He saw no reason to tell her everything. It was the lot of a soldier's wife to accept without question, just as the soldier him-self accepted without question. "But I thought while I am gone it might be well for you to go out to the

farm and stay with your father and mother so you
will not feel alone. It would be good for the boy to
be away from this town for a while too."

Her family, the Galindos, had land holdings north
of town along the Nacogdoches road. They were
considered wealthy, as wealth was measured in a
community like Bexar where no one had any excess
of the world's goods. Their wealth, if such it be, was
tied up in land and horses, cattle and sheep, not in
coin of the republic.

Elvira could not hold back a couple of tears. Ten-
derly he caught them with one finger as they trailed
down her soft cheek, and he wiped them away with
a gentle gesture. "I will be back before you have
time to miss me," he promised.

She nodded but turned her face away from him,
leaning her head against his chest. "I wish you never
had to go anywhere again. I wish you would accept
what Papa has offered you."

They had talked about this many times. Old
Mauro Galindo's proposal had been generous. He
said, "I am a soldier, not a farmer."

"You need not always be a soldier. There are
other things."

"Someday, perhaps. But let me save a little more
money first. Let me say that I had something of my
own besides just a kind and generous father-in-law."

"You have too much pride, Elizandro."

"If I had no pride, you could not love me."

She turned her face up toward him and pressed
her lips against his. Her kiss was first warm and
soft, then turned fierce and demanding as a flush
rose in her cheeks. Her hands roamed, and he let
his roam in response. She said, "I love you so much

I never want you to leave me. Not for a day, much less for a night."

She gave the baby girl a concerned glance and found she had dropped off to sleep on the floor, peacefully clutching a small glove. The child often ignored toys but could entertain herself for hours with something as lifeless as a shoe. Elvira turned toward the bedroom, tugging at her husband's hand.

He gave her no resistance. The boy would probably remain outside, playing with his friends. Even if not, there was a small wooden bar on the inside of the bedroom door.

5

Michael Lewis felt his backside prickling with anxiety as the bay horse carried him closer to home. He had been gone now more than two weeks, probably close to three; he had lost count of days after ten or so. He had not told Marie where he was going or how long he would be gone for the simple reason that he had no real idea himself, except that he would ride west. It was a legacy from his footloose father, who had never known a place he did not want to go, so long as it was westward, and never found a place where he wanted to stay. Marie would have every right not to speak to him, he thought. She would have every right to bar the bedroom door and make him sleep on the dog-run, or out in the pole-walled shed. But his mother had endured the same treatment over and over during the long and often taxing years of her marriage to Mordecai Lewis. Michael had seen her resentment rise during Mordecai's extended absences, anger enough that she attacked her housework with a determination bordering on violence. Unlucky was the hound that strayed upon the dog-run when she held a broom in her hands. But the anger usually vanished when Mordecai finally appeared. She would welcome him home like the prodigal son rather than the errant husband.

Marie had maintained the same tolerance with Michael. He had warned her before their marriage that he was his father's son and that wedlock was unlikely to cure his wanderlust. Before that, he had even vowed that he would never marry because he did not want some woman to put up with the loneliness and hardship his mother had endured. But that vow had melted like ice in July when he looked into the dark eyes of Marie Villaret. His desire for her overcame his best intentions. Each time he tested Marie's endurance with a long trip away from home, he half expected her to meet his return with an explosive release of pent-up resentment. God knew she had reason enough.

It was not just his encounter with the Indians that had turned him homeward. It was his need and hunger for her, his guilt over leaving Marie and the boy Mordecai for so long, the firewood not cut, the fields not planted. Each time he returned from one of those solitary sojourns, he promised himself he would never do it again. He avoided making that vow to Marie, however. It was forgivable to break a promise to oneself, but he would not give Marie a pledge he knew his nature would probably prevent him from keeping. Whatever his other shortcomings might be, he would not lie to her.

He could have reached home last night had he pushed to do so, but he had held back. He remembered times when his father had come in the middle of the night, as if he were sneaking in. However Michael's conscience might punish him, he would not use darkness to hide his homecoming. He would ride up to the front of the cabin in broad daylight like a man who knew who he was and what he was about. If Marie had a dose of bitter medicine waiting for him, he would stand squarely on both feet and accept the punishment due him. He had not run from the Indians. He would not turn and run from a little French-speaking woman who probably weighed no more than a hundred pounds wearing all the clothes she owned and had a waist so tiny he could reach most of the way around it with his two big, rough hands.

He brought a peace offering of sorts, meat in the form of a doe he had shot just at daylight as she edged into a clearing in search of forage.

Following the general course of the Colorado River but remaining up out of the heavy timber that bordered it, he found he was leaning forward in the saddle as if this would help him see his home sooner. He settled back and took a deep breath to steady himself. For two days he had been composing the first words he would say to Marie, speaking them aloud to himself for practice, honing them until he had given them the right combination of contrition and male authority. The trees fell back to his left, and he touched his spurs gently to the bay horse to put him up the final hill. He said the words one more time to be certain he had them down firmly. As he topped over, he saw at a glance that all was not just as he had left it. Someone had been plowing his field. Row after row, the earth had the dark look of fresh turning. His first thought was that Marie had done it. Conscience came rushing back with a vengeance at the thought of that little woman struggling with the big red ox and heavy wooden plow. Then he saw a man at the far side of the field, carrying a large stone the plow had turned up. The man dumped it a couple of paces beyond the end of the row and faced around. Michael knew him by the way he walked, the way he stood.

His younger brother Andrew was doing the work that should have been Michael's.

Aw, hell, he thought, *he didn't have to go and do that.* But that was Andrew's way. He had inherited their father's strength without so much of his wandering nature. Like their older brother Joseph, who had remained on the old farm back in Tennessee, Andrew tended to business first.

Michael pulled the horse to a stop and gathered all his resolve. He took one last long look back over his shoulder at the timber which lined the broad Colorado River. He had no idea how far west he would have to travel to find its source, how far out into mysterious lands known only to the Indians. Someday he would know. Someday he would go—

He angrily clenched his fist. *Damn you, you haven't even got home yet, and you're already thinking about going again. When're you ever going to grow up and take hold of your responsibilities?*

The morning sun was halfway to noon as he pushed the horse down the long slope and out upon the flat where he and Marie had chosen to build their cabin, within easy water-toting distance of the river. Life was tough enough for a woman on the outer edge of the settlements in a newly developing land without her carrying water in a heavy wooden bucket a step farther than necessary. In Natchitoches, where Marie had grown up, she had enjoyed some of life's little luxuries, within the limitations of a river town itself not far from the western frontier. By the standards of the time and place, her father had been relatively well-off, for he operated a mercantile business that served a wide and developing region. Some of his trade was clandestine, reaching far into Texas when it had still been Spanish and continuing now that it belonged to Mexico. Old Baptiste Villaret had provided well for his family.

Marie's life was far different out here. Sometimes Michael wondered how she stood up to its challenge. He could truthfully declare that she had never actually gone hungry. One way or another, he had always provided food for the table. There had been times at first when the next meal had been highly in doubt, and only his keen eye over the sights of the long rifle had brought them through. But she had strengths of her own; Baptiste Villaret had seen to that in her upbringing. Natchitoches was enough of a frontier town that it taught its children self-sufficiency. She had put in a log-fenced garden, enlarging it every year they had lived here. From the time of her first crop, she had seen to it that their dugout storage had a stock of food always in reserve against the lean days when no game presented itself to Michael's good aim. She and the child could subsist for a considerable time if he never came back.

He saw her in the garden, bending over a hoe, chopping the early spring weeds out of her first emerging plants. The boy Mordecai played nearby with the protective dog, which never failed to place itself between the boy and anything unusual that arose. Once last year Michael had seen the dog dragging the baby by its shirt while little Mordecai howled in protest. When Michael hurried out to reprimand the animal, he had seen that it was pulling the boy away from a coiled rattlesnake.

The dog was the first to see Michael. It moved in front of the boy and started barking. Marie turned and looked up, dropping the hoe as recognition came. The dog stopped barking and bounded forth to meet Michael, while little Mordecai turned quickly toward his mother, unsure who the horseman might be.

Marie waited outside the hip-high garden fence. A wide slat bonnet shaded her face so that he could hardly see the fine features, but memory filled them in for him. She looked little enough that he could pick her up under one arm and carry her into the cabin. But not against her will, for she had strength that did not show.

He stepped down from the horse, looking at her, trying to remember the words he had so carefully rehearsed. They had left him like brown leaves swept away by the west wind. She stood staring at him as he stared at her, then pulled the slipknot in the string that bound the bonnet beneath her chin. She slipped the bonnet from her head and took a long step toward him, her arms outstretched. He hurried into them and crushed her with joy and wanting. They held together in silence for a minute or two. Little Mordecai clung to his leg and talked rapidly in words the dog might have understood but Michael could not.

He asked Marie finally, "Ain't you teachin' that boy English?"

She smiled up at Michael. "*You* teach him English." She spoke with an accent that never failed to delight him. "I will teach him French and Spanish. Then he can talk to anybody who comes."

Michael lifted the youngster into his arms and

hugged him. "You been a good boy?" he demanded. "Been helpin' your mama?"

Mordecai nodded vigorously, arms clasped around Michael's neck. "You stay home now, Papa? You stay home?"

"I'll stay home. Got lots of work to do." He turned and looked off toward the field. "Marie, I hope you didn't ask Andrew to start my plowin' for me. He's got work enough of his own to do."

"I told him that. But he said he thought the corn should be planted, at least. We cannot eat cotton, but we can live on corn."

"I ought to've been here," he admitted ruefully. That was as near as he would come to an apology. Even that was further than his father ever went. Apology was an admission of error.

Marie took his free left arm; he held the boy in his right. She said, "You are hungry?"

He nodded toward the doe tied across his horse. "I brought meat. I could eat half of it myself, here and now."

"Hang it in the dog-run, and what you want to eat, cut it off. I will go to build up the fire."

He looked back again. "I ought to go speak to Andrew first."

She blinked. "I almost forgot. Andrew said I should tell you. Some men came—the Blackwoods."

An old cold, sick feeling spread from the pit of Michael's stomach. Blackwood. The name itself was enough to spoil his hunger. He set the boy down upon the ground and clenched his hands into fists. He glanced back at his saddle, where his long rifle hung. "You sure it was the Blackwoods?"

"Andrew said yes, they were."

"They do anything, say anything?"

"Said you were old friends. Said they wished to see you."

"Over the sights of a rifle is the way they would like it best. I thought Texas would be far enough—" His face twisted to the sour taste that rose in his mouth. His eyes narrowed as he studied her. "They didn't do nothin'—didn't touch you or nothin'?"

"They stayed on their horses. They only said I must tell you they will see you soon."

"I just hope I see them first." He turned to the horse, lifting the doe's carcass down from behind the saddle. "I'll quarter this and hang it up. Then I better go out and talk to Andrew."

"You will not eat first?"

"I've lost my appetite." He looked at the boy, then at Marie, feeling an apprehension akin to that which had come to him when he had faced the Indian hunting party. "Till we know for sure what their intentions are, you and little Mordecai better not go farther than the garden. If you see anybody comin' besides me or Andrew, skin out for the cabin and bar the door."

Her eyes widened. "They are that bad?"

"They're bad, them Blackwoods, and they're cowards. That's the most dangerous combination I can think of."

Andrew halted the big ox and laid Michael's wooden plow over on its side. Michael had built the plow himself out of timber near at hand, as he had built most of the other accoutrements on this farm. A steel plow made by a blacksmith cost more money than he could spare. From what he had read, folks had used a plow like this since Bible times. If it was good enough for the Bible, he figured it was good enough for him. Anyway, some folks argued that a steel point might somehow poison the ground.

Andrew stood with hands on his hips, frowning darkly as Michael rode up. That took Michael aback a little, for a smile fitted his brother much better than a frown. Usually he was so cheerful that Michael was now and then tempted to choke him. Sweat soaked Andrew's homespun shirt and made dirty rivulets down his dusty face. Farming was not a clean job. Michael thought he saw relief in Andrew's eyes, but it did not endure. Censure took its place. Andrew said accusingly, "You been gone long enough."

Michael saw no point in argument. "Too long, I'm afraid. I didn't figure on you doin' my work for me."

"It needed doin', and you wasn't here." Andrew gave him a moment to absorb the rebuke, then added, "Anyway, I thought I'd better stay pretty close for Marie's sake. She had company while you was off yonder roamin' around."

"She told me it was the Blackwoods."

"It was. I rode over to San Felipe and talked to Stephen Austin. He says they'll get no place in this colony, but that don't mean they can't take up in some other, or just squat somewhere the way so many do."

"They didn't come to Texas just to get land. They've come to get even. What I don't figure is why they waited so long."

"They had to work up the nerve. Sooner or later they'll come lookin' for their chance. I hope you've got eyes in the back of your head, because they'll likely be comin' from behind you."

"I don't reckon they can help themselves. It runs in the blood, like a family disease. Their old daddy Cyrus never was worth his own hide and tallow."

Andrew's gaze went to Michael's rifle. "You better keep that with you everywhere you go."

"I always do."

"Might even be a good idea if you had two rifles. We can work together; finish your field, then go finish mine."

Michael looked toward the red ox, standing stolidly in the field where Andrew had stopped him. "You'd do that? You gave me a strong notion that you were mad at me."

Andrew's voice cut like a blade. "Hell yes, I'm mad at you, goin' off the way you done, leavin' a woman and a boy that need you. But you're the only brother I've got this side of Tennessee. Be damned if I want to lose you to the likes of them Blackwoods."

6

Marie awakened earlier than usual, and she felt the warmth of her husband lying in the narrow bed close beside her. She turned slowly toward Michael, careful not to wake him. In the near darkness that preceded the dawn, she stared into the freshly shaved face that only in sleep looked totally at peace. The bed had seemed large and empty those many long nights he had been gone. She resisted a strong desire to caress his cheek. She supposed she had a right to feel hurt and angry that he had left her here with the baby, and perhaps there had been times during his absence when she had allowed herself the luxury of brief self-pity. But she had known how he was when she married him; he had made no effort to convince her he would change. If anything, she had been attracted by that sense of adventure, the hint of danger that seemed always a part of him. She would not acknowledge it now as a threat to the life they shared.

Even so, she remembered her Spanish mother's

dire warnings about the trap she was setting for herself, tied to a footloose *americano* frontiersman. That her mother had married a once-footloose French frontiersman was beside the point, the older woman argued. There was half a world's difference between Baptiste Villaret and Michael Lewis. Marie's mother had been happy and, after a time, enjoyed a relatively comfortable life in the old Louisiana town of Natchitoches. Marie was confident that a similar future was in store for her, eventually. She was young. What other people might consider hardship she counted as but inconvenience. It was a small price to pay for being able to live with a man she had loved since she had been twelve and he fifteen, brought back from Texas gravely wounded by a Spanish bullet. She had spent long hours at his bedside then, watching anxiously as he pulled back gradually from the dark precipice and regained strength enough to return to his old home in Tennessee.

His leaving her behind was nothing new. That time, he had not returned until he was a grown man.

She felt a peaceful glow as she lay looking at his quiet face. Dawn's light began to push back the darkness. It was time to be getting up and going about the day's work. She gave in to a wish and softly kissed his forehead.

He awoke instantly, his eyes wide in momentary confusion. She raised up on one elbow and kissed him again, on the end of his nose. She whispered, "It is too late for you to go out and wake up the rooster. I have heard him already."

Michael raised a big hand gently to her cheek, and she felt a stirring at his touch. She placed her hand over his and touched her lips to the tips of his fingers. "I will start a fire for breakfast," she said.

He caught her arm and held her. "I don't feel like I've had a full night's sleep yet."

She smiled wickedly. "You have not. It was not for sleep that you came to the bed."

His face turned red, and her smile broadened. She said in mock accusation, "You are embarrassed."

He brought both arms around her. "You have a shameless mind."

"Where is there shame in it? We are properly married."

"Some things a woman ain't supposed to talk about."

"It is only for men to talk? If it is all right to do something, why is it not all right to talk about it? Everyone knows what we do. Little Mordecai is the evidence."

"I've got no answer for that." Michael raised up on his elbows and looked across the room to the boy's small bed, set in a corner. The youngster had not yet stirred. "He's pretty soon goin' to have to start sleepin' someplace else. He's gettin' big enough to notice things."

"He is too small to climb a ladder to the loft. He might fall."

The cabin had only two rooms, the kitchen on one side, the bedroom on the other, with an open loft beneath the roof of the dog-run that separated the two parts.

Michael said, "I may have to build us another room. Like as not Mordecai won't be the last young 'un."

She smiled to herself. She had not told him yet. She wanted to wait until the mood was proper. Right now he had enough on his mind, getting the crops planted, worrying about the three brothers named Blackwood.

He lay back on the bed and stared up at her, his eyes soft. "By rights, Marie, you ought not to even speak to me, much less love me like you done. I'd've understood if you'd sent me out of the house to sleep in the shed with Andrew."

"But I wanted you in the house. I wanted you here, where you are."

"I ain't done right by you; I know that."

"You have made a home for me here. We have land that is ours. We have a son, and—" She checked herself before she gave the rest of it away. "With you, Michael, I am happy. No, I do not like it when you are gone from me. But when you come home, all is good again." She leaned down and kissed him.

He said, "I didn't mean to be gone so long. But you know how it is with me."

She leaned her face against his. "You do not have to say more. I know." She felt a flood of warmth as she lay against him, and she nearly gave herself to it before she pushed back. "We had better get up before Andrew comes in."

"He could as well have gone home."

"You know he stays because of those men. Come on, we should get up."

He held her arms for a moment. "Can't say as I'm ready."

"You will be ready when you smell breakfast on the hearth."

He lay watching her as she removed her gown and slipped a plain homespun cotton dress over her head for the day's work. "Seein' you thataway, I don't know how I can ever leave."

"You see me like that every morning and again every night."

"Not when I'm gone from you. Except I keep seein' you in my mind. That always brings me back."

She gave him a pleased smile. "Then never forget."

"I just wish I could provide better clothes for you. You had good clothes when you lived in Natchitoches."

"Not many women in Austin's colony have more. And no other woman in Austin's colony has you. I do not complain."

She went into the kitchen and began to stir the coals and ashes from last night's fire, slowly kindling a new fire with small pieces of straw and thin strips of pine, adding larger pieces as the flames gained strength. Michael took a wooden bucket and went out to milk the red cow Andrew had brought over so there would be plenty for little Mordecai. Marie promised herself she would also start drinking more milk, too, now that she was again providing for two bodies instead of one. She wondered if Michael would be perceptive enough to guess for himself. Probably not. Men could tell when a cow was going to calve, but they did not know half so much about women.

Andrew stood in the door, his arms full of wood cut to the proper length for the fireplace. He seldom failed to bring something when he came to a meal, even if no more than a little wood so Marie would not have to carry it herself. She smiled at him. "Good morning, Andrew."

"Mornin'." He had a shy way about him, at least around Marie. But always when she was not looking in his direction she sensed his eyes following her. Sometimes she wondered if in his own way he might not be in love with her. Or perhaps not her, exactly, but what she stood for: a home life, someone with whom to share. The thought aroused ambivalent feelings in Marie. On the one hand she was flattered that she could still attract the interest of a man other than her husband. On the other she felt a vague stirring of guilt, a fear that she might have done something to encourage his feelings. She could offer Andrew nothing except the love of a sister.

She stole a glance at him and saw him cut his eyes quickly away. It was amazing how much he resembled Michael. Even a stranger seeing them together would recognize that they were brothers. She could remember in a general way how their father, the old Mordecai, had looked the time he had stopped in Natchitoches before he made his fatal trip into Spanish Texas in search of wild horses. The two brothers had the same rangy build, the same deeply carved features. Where there was a major difference was in their blue eyes. Andrew's were lively and questing, where Michael's were often stern and troubled, haunted by terrible sights Andrew had been fortunate enough not to see.

Andrew apologized as he watched Marie bend over the hearth. "I'm sorry to be a burden to you. You got family enough of your own to feed."

"You are part of this family, Andrew. You have no one to cook for you except me."

"I do for myself most of the time."

"But you are here to help Michael finish his planting. We owe you much more than food. And to cook for one more is no extra work."

For a moment she considered the extravagance, then decided to put coffee on to boil. They took coffee as a luxury on special occasions. She decided Andrew deserved to be treated as a special guest. That finished, she turned and gave him a long, speculative study. "It is not good that you live alone. When the crops are finished this year you should make a trip. Go to Natchitoches. Go even back to Tennessee. Somewhere there must be a girl who watches for someone like you to come and carry her away."

Andrew shook his head. "I'm afraid I'd be hard to suit. I'd not want to settle for less than my brother has got, and I doubt there's another one like you anywhere around."

A pleased warmth rose in Marie's face. She watched Andrew pick up Michael's rifle and walk outside for a cautious look around. Neither he nor Michael had spoken much of the Blackwoods, but she knew the thought was never out of mind. She knew, though no one had told her, that Andrew was staying here not to help plant the field so much as to help protect his brother should the Blackwoods come again.

It would be nice if Andrew found himself a wife. It would be good to have a woman so close by that they could visit every day. But that woman would have to be special to be worthy of a husband like Andrew, she thought.

Michael brought the fresh milk, then checked the water bucket and found it nearly empty. He walked down to the river, swinging the bucket as if he had no cares. Marie noticed that he stood a long time at the bank, looking down into the water. When he returned, he set the bucket on a rough table he had built with his own skilled hands.

She said, "You were gone so long, I had some fear you had fallen in."

Michael shook his head and turned to Andrew, who had walked in behind him and set the rifle on its pegs over the fireplace above another rifle that was Marie's. "I was just lookin' at that runnin' water, thinkin' where-all it's been before it got all the way down here to us, thinkin' I'd like to go someday and see the place where it comes from."

Marie caught the look that flashed for a moment in Andrew's eyes and knew it mirrored her own. Michael had just come home yesterday. Already his mind was beginning to turn toward the next leavetaking.

"Breakfast is ready," she said, and tried to make her voice cheerful. But her mind was beginning to prepare itself for the next time Michael left her.

7

Isaac Blackwood kept turning in the saddle, looking back in disappointment at the wheel-worn ruts that were the main street of San Felipe de Austin. Wild flowers lined either side in great profusion and variety of color, their sweet scent heady. He thought this region could match beauty with the prettiest places he had ever seen in Tennessee. That made his regret even deeper, for he had not wanted to leave home in the first place. It had seemed expedient, however, perhaps even crucial. At twenty-three he could no longer plead youth as an excuse for following his two older brothers where none of them should go and into deeds none of them should do, keeping them constantly crossways with the authorities.

Finis, the oldest, rode three lengths ahead, with next oldest Luke beside him. Finis's angry voice demanded, "Spur up, Isaac. Ain't no use us wastin' any more time around this Goddamned place."

"Goddamned place," Luke echoed.

Isaac drummed his bootheels against his horse's ribs in an effort to catch up. He knew there was little to be gained by arguing with Finis when anger so crimsoned that part of his face which showed around a long, ragged growth of black beard. There was nothing to be gained by arguing with Luke at any time, because Luke looked to Finis for The Word, and Luke was sure Finis was never wrong. But Isaac contended, "Austin didn't say right out that we *couldn't* take up land around here. What he said was, we'll need to put up some money, and we'll need an endorsement of good character."

Finis's eyes had the fiery look that might have come from a jug of bad whiskey, but the whiskey had played out far back up the trail. The color was from outrage. When his temper was running loose he usually flapped his stump of an arm up and down like a rooster flapping its wings. "He'd just as well've asked us to drag the moon up to his doorstep for him. We ain't got no money, and from the looks of this place there ain't none to be had. I'll bet there ain't five hundred dollars in honest-to-God specie between here and the Sabine River.

"As for an endorsement, where the hell you think we'll get that? Ain't nobody here knows us, and if they did they wouldn't walk across the road to help us none. They never would back in Tennessee."

Luke came in like an echo, "Not in Tennessee."

Isaac said, "The Lewises know us."

Finis looked at Isaac as if he considered him the village idiot. "The *Lewises*." He spat. "Them's the last people on earth that'll give us a helpin' hand."

Luke echoed. "The last people."

Finis said grittily, "The only thing they ever gave *me* was the losin' of this arm." He raised the stump again. "I owe Michael Lewis for that. And before we leave this country, I swear I'll pay him good and proper."

Luke nodded solemn agreement. "Good and proper. Remember what we promised Maw."

Maw. Isaac grimaced, an ugly memory rising like poison. Charity was their mother's name, but she had precious little of it in her character. Charity Blackwood had spent most of the last thirty years trying to whip her sons into the men her husband never was. She had promised them, threatened them, cajoled them, beaten them. That her own people had forced her into a loveless marriage to a man without spine had festered in her soul like an open sore until it had become an obsession with her to make the Blackwood name feared.

"If we can't make them respect us, we can by God make them afraid of us," she had declared many a time. She had drilled it into her sons from the time they were old enough to understand: *Let no man laugh at you, let no insult go unavenged*. Isaac, like his older brothers, had followed her teachings, though it had exposed him to many a fight, many a brutal beating. And for what? he had begun to ask himself. It had earned him no one's respect, and certainly no one's liking. Fear? People feared a snake. For a hundred miles in every direction of their Tennessee home, people knew the Blackwood name and spoke it in deprecation. There was not a sheriff in twice that distance who did not have a Blackwood name scribbled in his little book of men to watch for and arrest if they chanced into his jurisdiction. Eventually the three oldest brothers had no choice but to leave Tennessee in the dark of night and seek new country where they were not known. It had been older brother Finis's decision to come to Texas, for Michael Lewis was here. Finis had pledged to Charity Blackwood that one way or another he would finally settle a blood debt long deferred.

Times like now, Isaac wished he had let his two older brothers go their own way. He wished he had chosen another direction to travel, up into Missouri, perhaps, to make a new start where Finis and Luke would not hang like a millstone around his neck. But he was a Blackwood. Blackwoods stood by their own.

That lesson Charity Blackwood had taught him well, even if she had driven herself crazy doing it.

Isaac said, "There's other colonies besides Austin's. And there's Louisiana. We seen a lot of good country comin' through Louisiana, country that didn't have nobody on it."

"We come to Texas," Finis said, with a strong tone of rebuke. "We'll stay in Texas!"

Isaac declared, "Not if you go and kill Michael Lewis."

Finis only grunted in reply.

Isaac had a pretty good notion where Finis was headed, but he asked anyway.

Finis grunted. "What difference does it make to you? You'll go where we go."

"Looks to me like this is the direction to the Lewis place."

"I do believe you're gettin' smarter as you get older, little brother. By God, Luke, maybe there's hope for him yet."

Luke grinned, his teeth crooked as they showed through matted whiskers that had not felt scissors or razor in months. "Yeah, there's hope for him."

Their mother had said Luke was born two months

too soon, and he had come up cheated on mental development. Isaac's suspicions confirmed, he said, "I'd like to know what you figure on us doin' when we get there."

"I ain't set in my mind yet. We'll just draw the cards as they come up. Whatever we do, it won't be somethin' Michael Lewis is goin' to like."

"I don't want no part of a killin'."

"I don't see you got any choice, if that's what me and Luke decide to do."

"If it comes to a killin', don't you be figurin' on me."

"You're a Blackwood. If we're in, you're in."

Several times on the long trip to Texas Isaac had felt sorely tempted to go off and leave them to ride into hell in their own good time without his company. He was confident he could make a better place for himself without them. He was a tolerably good farmer, when he set his mind and his shoulders to it, something Finis and Luke would never be. He was a better than average hunter and trapper. Just give him woods where he could find game, some decent pelt-bearing animals; he would make a living. If it hadn't been for his skill with the rifle on the way here from Tennessee, Finis and Luke would have starved down like a gutted snowbird. They could talk big and cuss the bark off of a stump, but neither had ever shown an ability to make a living on his own. Like Paw, they had leaned on Maw or Isaac. Now Maw was too far back east to help them any. They were Isaac's responsibility.

That was the reason he had not left them on the trail, and why he knew he would not leave them now, though the urge was so strong it fair made a fever rise in him sometimes. A man could not travel far enough to get completely away from Maw. The lessons she had drilled into him, sometimes with sugar and sometimes with a whip, would be with him to the grave.

The grave. That could be nearer rather than farther if he stayed with Finis and Luke, for they hated fiercely and never gave a moment's thought to consequences until after the deed was done. Then their main thought was to run like hell.

He shivered. After Texas, where could they run? They had already reached the end of the earth, seemed like.

The two older brothers shut Isaac out of their deliberations as they sat on their horses and looked across a gently rolling prairie toward a field and a double cabin. Luke said, "I see two fellers workin' out yonder, Finis. Didn't you say we'd catch Michael all by himself?"

"That's the way I'd figured it. It's probably that younger brother of his, that Andrew. They was always close."

Isaac frowned. He remembered one time he and his two brothers had fought with Michael over the rightful possession of a deer both Finis and Michael had shot at. Andrew had waded in fiercely, taking his brother's side with a chunk of wood as big as a man's arm. Isaac still remembered the pain.

Finis turned his narrowed eyes to Isaac. "You're the best shot, little brother. You reckon you could hit him from here?"

Isaac shrugged. "Maybe. But I ain't a-goin' to."

Finis's eyes narrowed even more. "And why the hell not?"

"Because I don't cotton to shootin' a man that

ain't even lookin' at me. If a man's worth killin', he's worth killin' with me standin' there lookin' him square in the eye."

Finis snapped, "He'll look at you right enough, right over the sights of his rifle. Way I remember it, he's a hell of a good shot."

Isaac glanced at Finis's stump of an arm. Dryly he said, "He sure is."

Finis swallowed a few times in anger and made threatening motions toward Isaac as if he intended to do him injury. But Isaac knew it was all show. If Finis ever came at him with real hostile intent, it would be from behind. What Finis usually did when he was out of sorts with Isaac was to sic Luke onto him like a dog. Sometimes Isaac could whip Luke and sometimes he couldn't. He had lost count of the occasions when they had fought each other to exhaustion, with Finis standing there cussing them both. What they should have done, Isaac sometimes thought, was to turn and whip Finis. But they both had pity for a poor one-armed man.

Isaac said, "I won't ambush him for you, so you'd just as leave forget that. But if you'll ride down yonder and face him man to man, I'll go and see that him and Andrew don't get no unfair advantage."

He could tell that Finis was not strong for such a notion, but Luke was not one to read minds and faces very well. Luke declared, "And I'll be with you too, Finis. Ain't much they can do with three of us standin' together."

Isaac grunted, remembering the long-ago fight in Tennessee. The two Lewises had won.

Finis was caught between his two younger brothers. With obvious misgivings he said, "I ain't afraid of him, if that's what you-all are thinkin'. I ain't afraid of nobody. I reckon it won't hurt nothin' to go down and talk to him. When the talkin's done, we'll see what happens."

Isaac smiled inwardly but did not let Finis see it. Chances were that nothing would happen, for the Lewis brothers would be too much on their guard to allow Finis the kind of advantage he would want before he would make any attempt on Michael.

Finis seemed to be stalling for time, licking his lips nervously as he looked down toward the field where the Lewises worked, each following a plow behind a large ox. "Now, don't you-all lag behind. You stay right up beside me, because we ain't go no idee what them Lewises are apt to do."

Isaac said, "One thing they *won't* do is to shoot first. So you don't have to worry unless you fire at them. Then you probably won't have *time* to worry."

Finis gave him a look of anger, tinged with fear. "I swear, little brother, sometimes you just don't sound like a Blackwood."

If Finis had any hope of catching the Lewis brothers by surprise, that hope was quickly dashed. Long before the Blackwoods reached the field, Michael and Andrew Lewis had walked to the end of the freshly turned rows and stood waiting, rifles cradled in their arms. Isaac chilled a little, looking at those weapons. He hoped Finis or Luke would not do something stupid, for he would be forced to try to defend them.

Finis halted a dozen paces from the Lewises. Luke went a little farther, then backed his horse nervously as he realized he had put himself in front of his older brother. Isaac reined up a little short of both. He felt Michael's gaze touch him for a brief moment before returning to Finis. It was clear that Michael regarded Finis as the spokesman and, if it came to that, the primary target. Michael said, "Finis." Not *howdy,* or *hello,* or even *what the hell do you want here?* Just *Finis.* A man could put any meaning he wanted to that, or no meaning at all.

Andrew did not speak. Clearly, Michael was the spokesman for both Lewis brothers.

Two hundred yards away, Isaac saw a movement at the double cabin. A slender woman stood in the dog-run, the breeze gently moving her long skirt. She also held a rifle. He remembered their brief conversation with her several days ago. She had shown them no fear, he remembered. She had remained on the dog-run the whole time, not more than a single step from a rifle she had brought outside and leaned against the log wall. He remembered too that she had an odd way of talking, some kind of a foreign-sounding way of speaking her words. Isaac wondered if these foreign women had been taught to shoot. He wondered if she was a good enough shot to hit a man at this distance. Maw could. Inasmuch as this was Michael Lewis's wife, he thought it likely that she could too.

Finis said, "We already come once. You was gone."

"I'm here now," Michael replied flatly. "If you've got business with me, let's get it done."

Finis glanced fretfully at his brothers, one on either side of him, as if he were half afraid they might not be there.

Luke blurted, "Your damn right we got business. Tell him, Finis."

Finis gave Luke an irritated look that said to keep his mouth shut. "We come a long ways, Michael. You-all with them guns, you look like you're afraid of us."

Michael's voice had a cutting edge. "I'm never afraid of a Blackwood as long as I'm lookin' at him. I just don't want him gettin' behind me."

Isaac had learned years ago to tell when Finis was lying. His voice shifted to a higher than normal pitch, and he talked faster. He began talking faster now. "We never come to do you no harm, Michael. The things that happened, they was a long time ago. We just come here lookin' for a new home."

"It's Stephen Austin who parcels out the land. I got nothin' to do with that."

"He says we got to have a recommendation. You could give us a recommendation, Michael."

Isaac frowned, wondering about the direction of the conversation. Finis had already given up on obtaining land in Austin's colony, and surely he entertained no hope of an endorsement from the Lewises. Isaac suspected Finis was stalling for time, hoping for some opportunity to grab the upper hand. From the determined look in the cold blue eyes of the Lewis brothers, Isaac judged that they could stand here until the snow fell and never give up any advantage.

Michael's voice kept its edge. "I couldn't give *you* a recommendation to old Scratch himself, Finis. If that's what you come for, you've put some good horses to a long trip for nothin'."

Finis muttered a little. He raised the stub of an arm. "It was you done this to me. Crippled me for life, you did. I figure you owe me somethin'."

Michael's hand tightened on his rifle. "Mine wasn't the first shot. And I fired from the open. You fired from ambush."

Isaac remembered that Michael had boldly faced the whole Blackwood family later the day of the shooting and delivered the same declaration. It had made no difference to the Blackwoods then. It made no difference to Finis now.

Finis said, "This is a nice-lookin' place you got, Michael. Good-lookin' woman over yonder, and I seen a young'un too. I ain't got none of that. I ain't likely to ever have none of that. I can't work the land like a man that's got two arms. And you have any idea how a woman looks at a man that's just got a stump of an arm? Turns their stomachs, it does."

Michael said nothing. But Andrew challenged, "It ain't the arm that turns their stomachs, Finis. You ever take a bath? You ever shave so you can get a good look at yourself?"

Isaac could see his brother's ears reddening, a twitch beginning around his eyes. When that happened, Finis sometimes lost what good sense he otherwise had. Isaac said nervously, "We're gettin' nothin' done here, Finis. Let's be goin'."

When Finis showed no sign that he had heard, Isaac reached out and gripped his good arm. "Come on, Finis. Let's git."

Finis angrily shook loose. "Shut up, Isaac. We ain't leavin' here till we've took care of business."

Michael said, "We've *got* no further business, Finis." He shifted his rifle from a cradled position to the ready.

Finis was seething. "There's a lot of things could happen to a man, Michael. That fine cabin of yours, it could burn down some night with you in it, and that woman, and that button too. Your stock could all turn up dead, and your fields could burn off just before the harvest. There's lots of things could happen to an unlucky man."

Andrew had followed Michael's lead and had his

rifle aimed loosely somewhere between Luke and Isaac. Michael's was pointed straight at Finis. Isaac felt a deep chill and wondered if Finis was so enraged now that he could not see what was fixing to happen to him—to all of them.

"Finis," he pleaded, "for God's sake—"

Luke declared, "We can git them both, Finis."

Isaac's lungs ached from holding his breath. His hands were slick and wet on the stock of his rifle. He felt death in the air, strong as the tingle he sometimes got from an electrical storm. If firing erupted, he had no choice. He had to try to defend his brothers. A protest stuck in his throat. He wanted to cry "No!", but it would not come out.

He saw a movement in the timber down by the river. Horsemen, a lot of them. He tried to tell Finis, but his throat was too tight.

Luke saw them too, turning his head abruptly in their direction. "Finis," he shouted, "looky yonder! Indians comin'!"

It was not Indians, Isaac realized. It was soldiers, fifteen, no, more like twenty of them.

Finis tore his attention from Michael, but Michael's gaze never left Finis for an instant. He asked his brother, "What is it, Andrew?"

Andrew turned. "Mexican soldiers, Michael." He showed a semblance of a smile. "The officer in charge, I think maybe he's our old friend Zaragosa."

Isaac looked at his oldest brother. He saw rage turn to consternation and consternation to fear in Finis's eyes. Finis swallowed hard. He lowered the rifle to his lap. Defeat was in his voice. "Them soldiers is friends of yours, Michael?"

Michael's gaze was still riveted to Finis. "One of them, anyway."

Luke was near panic, for he had heard stories from Paw about Spanish soldiers shooting American prisoners ten years ago. Spanish—Mexican—to him they were all the same. He pleaded, "Let's run, Finis, before they git us."

Relief helped Isaac find his voice. "They'd catch up to us before we went a mile."

Finis mustered a semblance of nerve again. His voice scolded. "Michael, what kind of an American *are* you? You got a wife that talks funny. Now you got some Mexico soldier friend comin' to save you."

Isaac would not tell his brother for fifty dollars in United States gold, but he had a strong notion it was not the Lewises those soldiers were fixing to save.

8

Michael Lewis decided finally that the Blackwoods were no longer a threat. Dread of the soldiers was plain in their eyes, especially Luke's. Michael remembered from old times in Tennessee that Luke had never been very fast in the head. He had a streak of cruelty broader even than Finis's, but he was easier to scare. Michael was a little surprised to see relief in Isaac Blackwood's face. He had always considered Isaac the smartest of the bunch but badly misled by his older brothers. He would like to give Isaac the benefit of the doubt, but he could not overlook the fact that he was, after all, a Blackwood. The taint in the blood might be diluted some—maybe his mama had met a traveling man—but it was still there.

Michael turned half around to see what the soldiers were doing. They had paused at the cabin. Marie stood in the open dog-run, pointing toward the field and gesturing with both hands. Her easy command of Spanish had been handy on those rare occasions when soldiers or Mexican officials came around. Michael had learned enough Spanish that he would not starve to death for want of communication should he somehow become stranded in Mexican territory, but he doubted that he could hold down his end of any complicated conversation. Andrew had been an easier learner when it came to languages. Michael attributed that to his being more sociable. Andrew could horse-trade more easily with the occasional Mexican entrepreneurs who came through the colony to buy or sell livestock.

Zaragosa doffed his hat, bowed in the saddle, and turned away from Marie. He started toward the field, his troops following. Michael felt the old chill that uniformed soldiers always gave him, even though this time they had come at a most opportune moment.

Luke's voice trembled. "They fixin' to shoot us?"

Michael thought that might not be a bad idea. But Andrew seized upon the moment as a chance to guarantee the Blackwoods' good behavior. "Not if you do just what they tell you. But raise an eyebrow wrong and they're liable to blast you right off of your horse."

Michael doubted that. However, the Blackwoods seemed to accept it as gospel fact. Michael would not give them comfort by denying his brother's words.

Zaragosa rode directly to Michael and Andrew, reining his shiny black horse up beside them, facing the Blackwoods. He held a long flintlock pistol that looked heavy enough to club a man to death if the shot missed. It was not pointed directly at any of the Blackwoods, but it might as well have been for the fear it put into Luke Blackwood's eyes. The soldiers fanned out in a ragged line on either side of the lieutenant as if to cut off any notion of flight by the three brothers. Zaragosa spoke a greeting to the Lewises in Spanish. Michael brought himself to answer, "*Buenos dias,* Zaragosa." He liked Zaragosa the man, but the uniform aroused chilling old memories that could easily get in the way of friendship.

Andrew said something a little more complicated than *Buenos dias*; he enjoyed using his Spanish.

The officer turned to a young corporal who sat on a bay horse beside him. He talked rapidly. The young soldier in turn translated into a clipped, strongly accented English while Zaragosa fastened a stern gaze upon the Blackwoods.

"My lieutenant says you will dismount from the horses. You will place your rifles upon the ground."

Finis did not comply. His brother Isaac said curtly, "Better listen at him, Finis. Or ain't you counted them?"

Finis swallowed and pulled his gaze from the officer. "Damn you, Michael, you've always had the devil's own luck."

Michael replied, "I don't know if it was our good luck or yours, them comin'. Either way, you'd best listen to what the soldiers say. I've seen what they can do. So's your old daddy."

The young soldier translated Michael's words for the lieutenant's benefit, though Michael sensed that Zaragosa understood most of it. The lieutenant nodded gravely as if to reinforce Michael's dark warning.

Isaac dismounted, laying down his rifle and gripping Finis's reins with his big-knuckled right hand. "Come on, Finis. Ain't no show for us now but to do what they tell us."

The young soldier listened to the officer a moment,

then asked of Finis, "You have land in Esteban Austin's colony?"

Finis sat slumped in defeat and did not reply. Isaac did it for him. "No, we just now come out of Tennessee."

The soldier translated, then came back with, "The lieutenant, he says it is better you *return* to Tennessee. People who make trouble, there is no room for them in Texas."

Finis grumbled, "We got a right."

The soldier's face flushed with sudden anger. He did not wait for his officer to reply. "You are *americano*. You have no rights in Texas but those our government gives you. Here, the lieutenant is the government. He says you do not stay."

Finis lost what little momentary bluster he had managed. He dismounted as ordered and laid his rifle carefully on the green grass. Luke followed his example, trembling. The officer spoke, and a soldier gathered up all three weapons, carefully blowing the powder out of the pans as a precaution.

The officer turned back to Michael and Andrew, taking time now to shake hands. Michael steeled himself a little and looked directly into Zaragosa's friendly brown face, trying to see only an old acquaintance and not the uniform. It was difficult to shut out the other soldiers. Their presence, welcome though it was, rekindled the painful memory of the day Spanish troops had killed his father and the other men who had ridden with him. Michael felt his mouth going dry. He was not much of a whiskey-drinking man, but at this moment he could have done good service with a jug of Kentucky squeezings.

Andrew evidenced no such reservations. He

grinned like a fox stealing grapes and said how glad he was to see Zaragosa and his men. Andrew asked, "Whichaway you headed, *amigo*?"

The young interpreter answered, "We go to San Felipe de Austin, then up to Nacogdoches. The lieutenant says we will take these men with us and see that they leave Texas."

Isaac Blackwood asked carefully, "You sayin' we're your prisoners?"

The lieutenant replied through the interpreter, "Let us say you are our guests. We would be most hurt if you did not remain our guests all the way to the Sabine River."

Luke glanced woefully at his older brother. "The Sabine? Ain't that the one we swum over gittin' out of Louisiana? That's a powerful long ways."

Andrew put in, "A long ways. Too far for you to be a-comin' back." He narrowed his eyes. "Was they to catch you tryin', they'd shoot you like as not, and throw you into a bush belly-up like they'd do a snake."

Andrew had always been one to spread the butter good and thick, Michael thought. Michael's own inclination would have been to tell them that if they came back *he* would shoot them like snakes. But in the stifling presence of the soldiers he kept his mouth shut.

He was gratified to see fear stark and cold in Finis's eyes. Cruel, cold-blooded though he might be, Finis Blackwood was a coward, like his daddy before him. Old Cyrus Blackwood had betrayed his fellow Tennesseans to the Spanish military to save his own skin. He bore the stain of Judas. Finis was cut from the same shoddy piece of cloth. Michael did not think Finis would try anything foolish now, not with so many Mexican soldiers ready to cut him down. And Luke would not do anything unless Finis put him up to it. He had no initiative of his own.

Isaac? Michael was not sure what to make of Isaac. He saw no fear in Isaac's eyes; only an odd sort of relief that left Michael puzzled. He surmised that Isaac's heart had not been totally committed to this little sashay in the first place.

Finis grumbled, "We still ain't settled nothin', Michael."

"There's nothin' left to settle. Looks to me like the soldiers have taken care of it all."

"Maybe. And maybe you'll see us again sometime. Me and you still got us an accountin'."

"You better write it *paid* and forget about it, Finis."

Andrew invited Zaragosa and his soldiers to camp and be the Lewises' guests. Michael flinched. He would be pleased to host Zaragosa, but all those troopers, looking so much like the men who had slaughtered the Tennesseans on an open prairie so long ago— He closed his eyes and tried to shut out the insistent image that kept coming back.

Zaragosa eased his fears. He had never gotten down from the big black horse. Through the corporal he said, "I much regret that I must decline. Many hours remain of the daylight, and we would wish to be much nearer San Felipe before night. We would visit Esteban Austin in the morning. It is yet a long way to Nacogdoches."

Michael did not give Andrew a chance to argue. He said, "We understand. It's probably best that way. The farther you take the Blackwoods away from this place, the better we'll feel."

Zaragosa spoke for himself. "There is old trouble here?"

Michael gritted his teeth, glancing at the Blackwoods, then at Zaragosa. "You remember the wretch who betrayed my father to the soldiers?"

Zaragosa nodded grimly. "I remember." The royalist zealot Lieutenant Armando Rodriguez had ordered Zaragosa to shoot both the wounded boy Michael and the cringing old Cyrus Blackwood. Zaragosa had disobeyed at considerable peril to himself.

Michael pointed his chin toward the Blackwoods. "That was the daddy of these men here. The blood ain't improved a bit."

Zaragosa's interest quickened as he studied the three brothers. He acknowledged the family resemblance.

Isaac Blackwood appeared saddened. "Then it's true. Paw always swore that what you said was a lie."

Michael replied, "Ol' Cyrus swore a lot."

Isaac pondered. "Then this here soldier saved Paw's life, and yours."

Michael shuddered, remembering how close it had been. "He did."

Finis raised his stump of an arm. "It's a damn shame he didn't kill you. I'd still be a whole man."

Michael gritted, "You never was a whole man, Finis. Even before you made me shoot you, you was a moral cripple."

Zaragosa drew the conversation to a close. He nodded affably to Michael and Andrew. "Now we must go. *Adiós, amigos.*" He touched spurs to his black horse and reined him eastward. His troopers closed around the Blackwoods and followed.

Finis turned in the saddle and shouted back. "It ain't over, Michael." A soldier prodded him with the muzzle of a musket.

Michael heard Isaac say, "Better hush, Finis."

He thought there might be hope for *one* Black-wood.

Neither Michael nor Andrew spoke until the soldiers and the Blackwoods had gone several hundred yards along the tree-lined river. Andrew gave an audible sigh of relief. "Not to complain about your shed, Michael, but maybe now I can afford to go home and get a good night's sleep in my own bed."

Michael lowered his rifle to arm's length. He had not realized he still held it cradled in his arms as if for quick duty. "Surely you wasn't afraid of them Blackwoods. The worst day we ever had, we could've taken care of ourselves against such as them."

"I expected them to sneak up and try to shoot you in the back."

"They never could shoot very straight."

Andrew shrugged. "Even a blind hog'll find an acorn once in a while." He looked back toward the cabin. Marie still stood in the dog-run, watching, though she had put her rifle away. With a touch of regret he said, "I only regret that I can't stay around here and eat at Marie's table. It's back to my own cookin'."

Michael thought his brother had put on a few pounds in the days he had spent here, helping watch for the Blackwoods. Like just about every bachelor Michael had known, Andrew had done himself proud when he had a chance to eat in a woman's kitchen. "No use bein' in a hurry about it. We'd just as well finish the day in this field, and let Marie fix supper for you."

Andrew was still looking toward the cabin. Michael saw something in his brother's eyes that bothered him. It appeared there every time Marie was in sight. If it had been someone other than his brother—Michael said, "You know what's the matter with your cabin, don't you?"

"The matter? Ain't nothin' the matter with it. The roof's tight, and the walls are chinked good and proper."

"It's too empty. Needs a woman in it. There's bound to be a likely young lady someplace, just waitin' for you to fetch her a bouquet."

"Marie's been tellin' me the same thing. But women are even scarcer around here than money."

"If a man can't catch fish on his own side of the stream, he goes where the fish are hungry and bitin'."

Dryly Andrew replied, "It's a long ways from here to anywhere. And I got mighty little for bait. You can't swap a bundle of winter pelts for a woman like you'd swap for coffee and beans. Even if you could find one."

"You've got a land claim. You've got a future. That's all I had when me and Marie got married. It's still all I've got, except for her and the baby. She don't complain."

"She never would; Marie's special. You could hunt for ten years and not find another like her."

Michael frowned. He had long sensed that his brother was drawn to Marie. He was convinced it was not a personal thing, especially. It was just the natural attraction of a man to a woman, any woman, when he lived alone. Michael told himself it was nothing that need ever worry him. The situation would resolve itself when Andrew found a woman of his own. If he found a woman of his own.

Andrew seemed uneasy with this subject and changed the conversation's direction. "This was one time that seein' soldiers didn't seem to upset your liver too much."

That was easy to say, Michael thought; Andrew couldn't see the tension they had aroused within him. "Zaragosa was with them. Anyway, if they hadn't showed up we might've had to kill that whole bunch of Blackwoods. They wouldn't be worth the aggravation." Michael looked up at the afternoon sun. "Let's see how many more rows we can get planted before sundown."

He fed the animals in the fading light of the spring evening before seeing to his and Andrew's own supper. It had always been a cardinal rule among the Lewises that the welfare of their livestock was the first order of business. A man could miss a few meals without dire consequences, but if his animals went hungry he might find himself afoot, or with nothing to pull a plow.

Andrew went to the cabin to fetch the wooden milk bucket, carrying an armload of firewood in for Marie as he went. Michael frowned, watching. It was a good thing Andrew didn't stay here all the time; he would have Marie too spoiled to live with.

Returning with the bucket, Andrew said, "I'll leave Ol' Boss with you till your cow freshens. That boy needs the milk a lot more than I do." He put some feed in the trough and sat on a handmade wooden stool, setting the bucket beneath the cow's udder. The cords bulged on the backs of his hands as he rhythmically set about the milking. It was a job Michael had never found to his liking, though he had done it often enough. It was like following the ox and the plow, a necessity but hardly a pleasure. He would rather be out in the forest, hunting fresh meat. By contrast, Andrew seemed to enjoy the task. They were brothers and had been close all their lives, but there were some things about Andrew that Michael would never understand.

Michael observed, "Ol' Boss always stomps at the bucket when I try to milk her. She gets along a lot better with Marie."

Andrew shook his head. "That's just an excuse so you don't have to milk her yourself. You'd better take good care of Marie. You'd never find her like again."

"I don't intend to ever look."

Zaragosa glanced back once before the Lewis cabin dropped out of sight behind him. He had been tempted to accept Andrew's offer and camp the night on the river. It would have been pleasant to spend a few hours in the glowing company of Michael's wife Marie, for she reminded him considerably of his own Elvira. He found himself missing his wife terribly, though he had been away from her only three days. He would be fortunate if he got back to her within three months. When he returned from this mission he would give serious thought to her father's offer of a place on the family farm. Soldiering was all right for a bachelor, but it involved too much traveling for a man who had a family. This trip made him realize how much he was tiring of it.

He would have liked to have listened longer to Marie Lewis's lively version of Spanish. It had a little of the intriguing accent that came from the relative isolation of her forebears in northern Texas and Louisiana, and perhaps just a trace of the French influence imposed by her father. Marie and Elvira would get along nicely, he thought. But it was unlikely they would ever meet, for the social and cultural division between the Mexican town of Bexar and the American colonies to the east was like a great stone wall that could be climbed from neither side.

He felt this same alienation even from the two Lewis brothers, though he had known and liked them for several years. It was a pity, for he would prefer to be a closer friend. Language was just one of the barriers that stood between them.

The three Blackwoods seemed, by the tone of their voices, to be quarreling among themselves. The young Corporal Diaz, the interpreter, dropped back to listen discreetly. Presently Zaragosa nodded for him to come forward. He asked, "What is the disagreement between them?"

"The two are blaming the young one. They say he could have shot Miguel Lewis from a distance and spared them all this trouble. He is saying they were wrong to come here at all."

"So long as they quarrel among themselves perhaps they will not give us trouble."

"I do not think they will give us trouble anyway. They are frightened of us, especially the two. They speak of their father and what happened to him."

"Perhaps I should have followed my orders ten years ago and killed him. The world would not have mourned the loss."

Diaz considered a while before he asked, "Those two named Lewis—they are really your friends?"

Zaragosa shrugged. "I once saved the life of the one named Miguel. Years later, he and the brother did me a great service in return. Yes, they are friends, as much as any *americanos* can be friends to one of us."

Diaz frowned. "It is hard to see *any* of them as friends."

Zaragosa was a little surprised. "You have lived among them, have you not? I understood that is how you learned to speak English."

Diaz nodded. "My family had a farm not far from Nacogdoches. The Lieutenant Rodriguez decided my father was disloyal to Spain. We had to flee into Louisiana. We lived among the *americanos* until Mexico freed itself from the tyranny."

"Surely you must have made some friends among them."

Diaz pondered darkly. "We lived among them. We worked among them. But friends? Never. We were much too different."

Zaragosa thought he understood, but he asked, "How so?"

"The language, the customs. And the Americans never seemed to have enough of anything. If they had one horse, they wanted two. If they had two horses, they wanted four. If they had a hundred hectares of land, they wanted twice as many. I never could understand their hunger."

"Whether we like it or not, they are among us now."

Diaz shook his head. "Not if the choice were mine. We have made a mistake, sir, letting them come into Mexico. Wait. Watch. They remain Americans. How long do you think they will be content to live under Mexican laws instead of their own? Even Miguel Lewis who is your friend—did you see how he looked at the rest of us? He does not like us."

Zaragosa said, "That is your imagination." He

knew it was not; he had seen the look in Michael Lewis's eyes. But he thought he knew the reason for it; he thought he knew the memories that haunted the Tennessean, for at times they haunted Zaragosa as well.

Diaz turned and looked back with a dark frown at the Blackwoods. "These and their kind will keep coming no matter what we do. The day will come when we will regret that we ever let the first American stay in Texas. The day will come when we will have to go to war with them and take Texas back. Or we will lose it."

Zaragosa turned his gaze back toward the river. Diaz had struck a painful nerve, for the same thought had troubled Zaragosa from time to time. He changed the subject abruptly. "As I remember, there is a nice spring a few miles farther on, which affords fresher water than we can get from the Colorado. We will find it and camp there tonight."

PART 2

THE PRICE OF HORSES

9

Andrew had observed with misgivings that Michael was becoming increasingly ill at ease, confined since spring and into the summer to cabin and field and the limited distance which his cattle roamed in their casual grazing along the river. Michael betrayed his restlessness in the way he would sometimes halt whatever he was doing and stare off into the distance, usually westward. One day Andrew found him standing beside the river, the empty wooden bucket in his hand. Michael gazed wistfully upstream, toward the unknown land where the Comanches roamed free. Andrew felt a jolt as he realized how much Michael resembled their father Mordecai, and how often he had seen this look in Mordecai's eyes. Usually it was just before he left on an extended trip to God knew where.

Andrew deemed it prudent not to speak of it openly, but he thought Michael would understand his meaning. "You got a wife here that needs you, and a baby on the way."

Michael stiffened, as if surprised that Andrew had read his mind. He tried to deny what had not even been said. "The corn and the cotton are hoed out good. Marie's been needin' some stuff. I been thinkin' about ridin' down to San Felipe."

San Felipe was to the east. Michael was looking westward.

Andrew pondered the possibilities. On the one hand it might relieve some of the pressure if Michael did go to San Felipe and get away by himself for two or three days. But on the other Andrew suspected he would not be content with a trip so short. The limitless and mostly unexplored land that was Texas spoke to men like Michael in ways other men would never hear. Two or three days could stretch into two or three weeks, even two or three months; it often had with Mordecai. And a trip started eastward toward San Felipe could easily turn back upon itself, ending up to the west instead, perhaps even to search out the headwaters of the Colorado River. Of late, Michael had spent a lot of time contemplating the swift-flowing waters.

Many things could happen to Marie while Michael was gone, and few of them good. Andrew lied, "I been thinkin' about goin' to San Felipe myself. Whatever Marie needs, I can fetch it back."

Michael's narrowed blue eyes flashed with quick resentment. "You don't trust me to come home?"

Andrew's voice took an edge of its own. "You'll come home. The only question is: when? I know you, Michael."

"No you don't. You're a farmer at heart. I've had to force myself into that mold, and it's a damned tight fit. You don't know how it binds on me to be tied to one place and not be able to move around free."

"What about Marie? She's tied down too. How long since she's been any farther off this farm than over to the Willets'?"

"She don't have the need. She's a woman. It's in her nature to build a nest and stay there."

"But not by herself. You ain't a free man anymore. You've got a responsibility here." Andrew squared his shoulders. "If anybody goes to San Felipe, it'll be me."

Michael's eyes were narrowed almost to the point of being closed to conceal his full resentment. "When I started to Texas from Tennessee and you tagged along after me, I had a good notion to chase you back. Maybe I ought to've done it."

"Maybe you could've done it then. You couldn't do it now. You need me here to keep you pointed in the right direction."

"I don't need you tryin' to mind my business," Michael declared sharply. He turned away from Andrew and stepped off several angry paces before he stopped. He stood a minute, his back to Andrew. Then he turned again, grudgingly resigned. "Marie'll have to tell you what she's needin'. Can't be much because we got mighty little money to buy anything with."

In Austin's colony, most negotiations were done through barter rather than in coin. All the honest coin for seventy miles along both the Colorado and the Brazos rivers probably would not fill a demijohn.

Andrew tried to smooth over the bad feelings. "I'll bring Ol' Boss down here before I leave. Marie and little Mordecai could probably use the milk."

"No need," Michael said stiffly. "Our cow's givin' more than enough."

Andrew shrugged. "Then I'll just turn her calf out with her till I get back." He paused, then said hopefully, "No hard feelin's?"

"I wouldn't go so far as to say that." Michael walked back to his shed, picked up a hoe and strode stiffly off toward the field, leaving the water bucket empty. Regret weighed heavily upon Andrew as he watched, but he contented himself in the conviction that what he had done was best for Marie. He could only hope that Michael would eventually realize it was for his own benefit as well.

Andrew had always considered Marie beautiful, and she had never been more so than now, her dark eyes sparkling with the anticipated joy of another birth. Her stomach, normally small, was beginning to expand some, but she managed to move with a certain ease and grace. If she had slowed any in her work routine, Andrew was unable to discern it. Watching her bustle about the kitchen, trying to keep up a busy show of normalcy, he felt a melancholy longing to take her into his arms and hold her protectively. This made him cautious about getting close. As much as possible he kept a nervous distance, at least half the width of the room. If she knew, she gave no sign. But he wondered, how could she not know?

He told her, "Michael asked me if I'd mind goin' to San Felipe. Said there's some things you're needin'."

"*You* are going?" She seemed a little surprised. "I thought Michael—" She smiled thinly then, and the smile said she knew. Andrew had never been a good liar. "Thank you, Andrew. I have much dreaded the day he would go."

Andrew felt some repair was needed. "He wasn't hard to talk out of it. He knows he belongs here with you."

"I would not tell him he should not go. That he must know for himself."

"He knows. Otherwise I couldn't've convinced him so easy."

"I suppose," she said, though her eyes betrayed doubt. "He tries, but he cannot help being as he is. And I would be much wrong to try to force him."

Andrew was eager to change the subject, for discussing Michael's restless nature was as futile as complaining about the hot, humid summer winds that forced their way inland from the Gulf and sometimes left him gasping for a good breath. "What all you needin' from San Felipe?"

"Very little. A Mexican woman is there, a midwife. She puts together a mixture they say helps ease a woman who is"—she searched for a modest way of saying it—"in the hope. I think she would trade some of it for a ham from our smokehouse. It should cost no money."

It pained Andrew to see Marie do without most of life's conveniences. He wondered sometimes what Marie's father, old Baptiste Villaret, would say if he could see how his daughter lived in this rough cabin of oak logs, hands raw from hard work, her few clothes patched and faded from wear and washing. She shunned little niceties that she once had taken for granted, protecting her precious little money for those few things that were absolute necessities. If he knew, the prosperous old French merchant would probably drive a team of good horses to death getting here from Louisiana as quickly as he could. But then, he and his wife had pioneered in their own time; they had not always had the comfort they enjoyed now. Each generation made its own way, invented its own life.

If Andrew were in a hurry, unmindful about the welfare of his mount and the pack horse that carried some winter-cured hides for barter, he could reach the seat of Austin's colony in less than half a day. He took his time, however. He could sympathize with Michael's cooped-up feeling. He had some of the same symptoms, if considerably less severe. Both men had spent many long weeks getting the crops up, properly hoed, and on the way toward harvest. He watched for any new arrivals who might have broken out their first land this spring and summer while he had been too busy with his own place to know what anyone else was doing. The sight of a new farm, of a new chimney sending its friendly smoke skyward, always brought him a sense of satisfaction. It pleased him to see the land becoming populated. He liked knowing he had neighbors close by. The more the better.

By contrast, Michael fretted helplessly when he saw the prairie sod broken and trees cut down. He had favored this land the way it was the day he had first arrived. Sometimes Andrew wondered if Michael did not begrudge even the trees downed for the cabin he shared with Marie and the boy Mordecai. It was certain that Michael saw his field as a necessity and not a joy.

They were brothers, but on this basic issue they sometimes argued. Given his chance, Andrew sometimes thought, Michael would probably move to the moon. There nobody would crowd him.

It was in his mind to spend the night at the cabin of the Willet family, a few miles east of his own place. Old Man Lige Willet could talk the bark off of a tree, and that was what Andrew needed right now, some congenial socializing with people he liked, people beyond just family. They called him Old Man Willet, though in truth he was probably no older than his middle forties. That was old by the standards of the Texas colonies, for this was a young man's province. Breaking out new land, opening a new empire, was young man's work.

The Willet place was larger than either Michael's or Andrew's, for Willet had a sizeable family and qualified for a larger block of land. One of his sons had come of legal age, expanding the family holdings. For a man who loved to talk and played the fiddle better than anyone Andrew had ever heard, Lige Willet was nevertheless about as hardworking and knowledgeable a farmer as Andrew had ever known, perhaps as good as his own Uncle Benjamin back in Tennessee. His fields were clean, his rows straight as a new pine plank fresh from the sawmill. He had even found time to set out an orchard. Willet was going to be a most popular man in two or three years when those trees began bearing fruit enough to make a neighbor's journey worthwhile. Andrew suspected that was the main reason for the orchard in the first place; Willet loved company.

He expected to find Lige in his field, for it was just midafternoon. Several hours of daylight were left for righteous labor before the farmer put the day's due behind him to go in for supper and a leisurely hour or two of talking and fiddle playing to pass the evening. That was the Lord's reward for a day's work well done, Willet always said.

However, Andrew found only the oldest son Zebediah in the field, hoeing out a fine stand of corn.

One of the youngest boys, a towhead named Daniel, leaned against the fence. At his feet was a wooden bucket with a tin dipper floating in it. The boy had brought fresh water to his older brother.

Andrew raised his hand and spoke jauntily to the older Willet boy. "You're doin' the work of two mules, Zeb. That'll make an old man out of you."

Zeb was always a serious one, in strong contrast to his jovial father. He nodded and leaned for a moment on the hoe, wiping his sleeve across his forehead. The sleeve was almost the only part of his shirt not soaked with sweat. "Good day to you, Mr. Lewis. If you're lookin' for Papa, he ain't here. He's gone over to help some new neighbors raise them a cabin."

"New neighbors?" Andrew's interest was immediately aroused. "Whichaway?"

Zeb pointed eastward. "Couple of miles down the trail toward San Felipe. Ain't hardly no way you can miss it. Folks' name is Nathan."

Andrew dismounted and walked up to the boy at the fence. "You got enough water to spare me a drink, Daniel?"

The boy, about seven or eight, had a grin that looked wide as a barrel hoop. "If I ain't, I'll go fetch another bucket." He was like his father; the more people around him, the better he felt.

Michael took a long drink of water from the dipper, then sipped a little more while he admired the standing corn and told Zeb what a good job he and his father were doing. Young Daniel pointed enthusiastically. "Papa traded and got me a pony. He's out yonder if you'd like to see him."

Zeb said with mild rebuke, "You oughtn't to pes-

ter everybody who comes along about that pony,
Daniel. They ain't all as interested as you are."

Andrew caught disappointment in the boy's eyes.
"I'd be tickled to look at him. I been thinkin' about
findin' a pony for Michael's boy Mordecai. He'll
pretty soon be gettin' big enough to learn how to
ride."

He tied the pack horse to the fence and motioned
for the boy to swing up behind his saddle. They rode
off in the direction Daniel pointed. A little east of
the family's sprawled log cabin they came upon half
a dozen horses grazing. Daniel said proudly, "That
there is him, the sorrel one."

The pony was of a nondescript nature, looking
like a scrub out of a wild mustang band. Andrew
praised him nevertheless, and the boy beamed
proudly. Andrew said, "I didn't know you-all had
this many horses."

"Papa done some tradin' with an old man who
come down from Louisiana. Him and the old man
went over to the new neighbors' place this mornin'
to see if they'll be needin' any horses."

"What old man was that?" Andrew asked.

"I disremember his name. Just an old man with
gray whiskers. Papa traded him some pelts and
stuff. You ever seen a prettier pony?"

"Don't reckon I ever did."

He returned the boy to the field and retrieved the
pack horse. He waved his hand at Zebediah, who
had worked his way far down a row. Andrew then
set out eastward in an easy trot that would not tax
the animals. It was in his mind that if he came across
the old man from Louisiana he wouldn't mind trading his brown mount for a better one. Trouble was,

he probably had nothing much to offer for boot. Texas was big and fresh and beautiful and new but almighty stingy with its material blessings.

In a place where last spring he had ridden across an open grassland prairie, he found a family just starting the raising of a log cabin. They had evidently lived out of their wagon until they got their field broken and planted, which showed they had their priorities in order. Their crops appeared late, however. That meant they would go into fall praying for a late frost so they would not lose the corn before it could reach maturity.

Andrew knew the people had spotted him when he was still three hundred yards away, for a man stopped chopping and trimming a pine log that lay on the ground. He waved his hat as a sign for Andrew to come on in. There had been times and places when the first thing a man did upon seeing a stranger was to fetch his rifle, just in case. Andrew surmised that these folks came from a civilized country.

He recognized Old Man Willet a hundred yards or so before he reached the cabin. Willet, a broad-shouldered, broad-hipped man of some two hundred pounds, walked out to meet and greet Andrew. "Come on in here, Andrew Lewis, and meet these good folks. We need one more strong back, anyway, to help us lift them logs up where they're needful."

Like his young son Daniel, Lige Willet had a grin wide as a barrel hoop. Andrew could not conceive of his having an enemy anywhere in the world. Willet was a red-faced man with an unruly shock of rust-colored hair curling out from under an old black hat that had probably been new twenty years ago. Andrew swung down from his horse. He endured the crushing grip of the man's ham-sized hand and the breath-taking slap of that same hand across the middle of his back. "Miles Nathan," Willet declared in a happy voice loud enough to carry back to his own cabin, "I'd like you to meet Andrew Lewis. Him and his brother Michael are your neighbors a ways on up the river."

"Howdy," Nathan said. He drove the blade of his ax into the end of a log and left it there. Like Willet, he was a large man with a ruddy, deeply creased face that easily broke into a broad smile. He wiped the back of a big hand across his sweaty face and walked forward, extending the other hand. "If Willet vouches for you, you're mighty welcome at our house. I can't say *in* our house because we ain't got it finished yet."

If any bones in Andrew's hand remained uncrushed after Willet's grip, they fell victim to Nathan's, strong enough to choke a bear. This was a lonesome country where no man remained a stranger long.

Nathan made a broad sweep with his hand. "This here is my family."

Andrew took off his hat in deference to a bonneted woman in her thirties. Nearby stood a girl. He guessed her at twelve to perhaps fourteen. Some shy of marrying age, he thought, then wondered why such a notion had even come into his head. He said, "My sister-in-law Marie'll be tickled to hear we've got some new neighbors."

Nathan said, "We knowed there was folks up thataway, but we been too busy to come callin'. Didn't get our seed planted till late. If we don't make a crop, we're apt to have us a mighty long, thin winter."

Andrew nodded, remembering. The same thing had happened to him and Michael and Marie their

first year. They had managed to survive largely
on wild game. Now the hunting had already been
compromised because the land was becoming more
densely settled. What the Lewises had done, these
people might not be able to do. Well, he and Michael would not let them suffer. Nor would the Willets. They would share if the need came; that was
the way people did in a pioneer country like this.
Andrew looked at the children, ranging in age from
two or three—about the size of little Mordecai—up
to the girl. By the time they got grown, this land
would see a lot of changes.

Andrew had to stare wishfully for a moment at
the wagon. The Nathans were fortunate to have it,
for wagons remained a luxury in Austin's colony.
They were difficult to transport the long distance
overland and prohibitively expensive to ship to the
Texas coast by sea. Most people packed their goods
on horseback or on mules, or they built a log sled,
like a raft on skids, often difficult for horses or oxen
to pull. Andrew and Michael had little hope of acquiring a wagon for a few years yet.

He figured the Nathan family would be mighty
popular around these parts. Sharing with neighbors
was like an eleventh commandment, and a lot of
people would want to borrow that wagon.

Mrs. Nathan's face was half hidden by the long
bonnet that cast a shadow over her features, but
her rough hands bore ample evidence of a life of
hard work. Her eyes betrayed no complaint, and her
smile was broad. "I'll fix you men some coffee," she
said, and turned back toward the canvas-covered
wagon. "Come along, Birdy, and stoke up the fire
a little."

Andrew decided to bide a while with this good

company. He pitched in to help shape the logs for the cabin wall, answering Nathan's urgent questions about the land, the seasons, the best ways of coaxing a good crop out of the soil. Andrew assured him that Willet was the best man to advise him. "He's the best farmer on the Colorado River," he said. "Me and Michael, we come over to his place and take lessons from him."

Willet beamed, enjoying the kind words.

Andrew stopped once to catch his breath. He could hear the ring of an ax somewhere in the woods. Someone out there was felling more trees for the cabin.

Nathan said, "Willet tells me you've had very little Indian trouble."

"None, really," Andrew replied. "We been lucky. The folks down on the Gulf've had some bad dealin's with the Karankawas. Some I know up this way have been visited by the Wacos and the Tawakonis. Mostly they just steal horses if they get the chance. But I wouldn't much like them to catch me out all by myself, with no rifle."

Willet shrugged off the discussion of Indians. "I ain't even seen one the whole time I've lived here. The only rifle I've got stays at the house where my wife can use it to defend her layin'-hens from the varmints. Was I you, neighbor Nathan, I'd worry more about wolves than about Indians. They'll make short work of your chickens and then go after your calves."

Nathan nodded in satisfaction, watching his wife pour part of the contents of a pot into three cups. "They told us in San Felipe that this'd be a good place to put our roots down, but it's a comfort to hear it from people who've lived here a while."

The "coffee" was, as Andrew suspected, a substitute made from parched corn. It occurred to him to wonder if anybody had ever planted coffee beans here. He thought he might try. There were probably twelve good reasons why it wouldn't work, but he would find them all before he gave up. Parched corn made a poor drink, though he assured Mrs. Nathan that it was the best he had had since leaving Tennessee. It was not always a sin to lie to one's neighbors.

He saw a movement at the edge of the wood, in the direction from which he had earlier heard the ax at work. He saw a big workhorse dragging a log. Behind, holding to the long reins, trudged a rail-thin man whose stride bespoke considerable age. Andrew squinted, trying to see him better, for something in the man's movements seemed familiar.

"Who is that?" he asked.

Willet turned to look. "That's an old feller who come down with some horses to trade for whatever we might have that he could sell in Louisiana. I swapped him some of last winter's pelfry catch for three horses. Ain't very good horses, but they can all walk."

Andrew nodded. "Daniel showed me his pony. What's the old man's name?"

Willet glanced at Nathan. "Eli's his first name. I disremember if I even heard his last."

Andrew's heartbeat quickened. "Pleasant?"

"Yeah," Willet said, "he's a pleasant old feller, for a horse trader."

"That too, but is his name Pleasant? Eli Pleasant?"

Miles Nathan nodded. "That's right. I remember him tellin' me. You know him?"

"I'd know his hide in a tanyard."

Willet remarked, "A skinny hide it'd be. Ain't much body inside it."

"Maybe not, but there's a heart in it as strong as a lion. I've told you about him, Lige. He was a friend of my father's, and he brought my brother Michael back from the gates of hell."

He walked out toward Eli Pleasant, then in his eagerness broke into a run. The workhorse pulling the log shied away. Eli Pleasant sawed on the lines and commanded, "Whoa there! Whoa now!" To Andrew he shouted, "You, farmer, don't you know better than to run at a horse thataway?"

"And you, old man, have you plumb lost your eyesight that you don't know me?"

"My God!" exclaimed Eli Pleasant. He dropped the lines on the ground and strode forward to meet Andrew. They threw their arms around one another and danced a jubilant little jig.

When they were done, Andrew stepped back for a good look. "I swear, Eli, you ain't got a day younger."

"And you, little brother Andrew, you ain't learned a damned thing about horses."

10

Andrew picked up the lines and started the plow-horse to pulling the log again. Eli walked alongside him, more than willing to yield the heavy work to a much younger man. He asked eagerly about Michael and Marie and how many children they had. "Always thought the world of your brother," Eli said warmly. "And I promised Ol' Man Villaret that I'd visit his daughter and his grandchildren if I was to find the place where you-all had settled at."

"They could easy have told you in San Felipe," Andrew pointed out. "Austin has a map on his wall."

Eli shook his head. "Me and Mr. Austin, we got a difference of opinion. The Mexican government has some kind of a notion that I ought to pay duty on whatever I bring into Texas. Austin, he'd see that I went to a Mexican *calabozo* if I was to let him lay hands on me. So I taken roundance on San Felipe."

Eli Pleasant was by trade a smuggler. Long ago he had begun making a career of smuggling trade goods into Spanish Texas from Louisiana, defying the customs officials, and had smuggled Spanish goods back into Louisiana. When Mexico became independent, he had seen no reason to change his occupation, for it was regarded as a necessary and honorable one by the settlers who benefited from it. This ancient trade was condemned only by the officials. Eli had never been particular what government he cheated out of its revenues.

Andrew decided there was no hurry about his getting to San Felipe and back home. The longer he took, the more time Michael would have to get over his resentment about the spoiling of his plan to travel. Andrew found himself enjoying the company, the easy camaraderie that went into cutting and shaping the logs and raising the walls of the cabin. And Mrs. Nathan knew her way around the cookfire. The Nathans were Alabama people. Mrs. Nathan's cooking reminded him of his mother's.

She voiced her anticipation of being able to move into the cabin and cook on a real hearth after all these months living out of the wagon. "It'll be a blessin'," she said. "Almost like we'd never left home."

The American colonists who had come into Texas had brought their old ways with them and had tried to duplicate in this new land the customs and the atmosphere they had left behind them in the old. Thus Texas had as yet developed few characteristics that were specifically its own. It was, in the main, still a rough copy of the Southern states.

Mrs. Nathan said, "The only thing lackin' now is a preacher to help us offer proper thanks for all the Lord has given us. Been a long time since we've been to proper services."

Ministers were about as scarce as real money in

the colony, but Andrew said, "If I happen across one, I'll send him to you."

At night they sat around the dying fire and talked of old times back in Tennessee and Alabama and, in Lige Willet's case, Kentucky. After listening to Willet relate for an hour all the glories of the bluegrass country, Andrew wondered how he had ever brought himself to leave it.

Eli Pleasant related his dark memories of the trip he had made to Texas with Andrew and Michael's father and an eager group of Tennesseans, seeking wild horses to take back and sell to farmers. Michael, fifteen then, had followed behind, joining the group when they were too far from home for his father to send him back. After they had captured a sizeable bunch of Texas mustangs, the chronically quarrelsome Cyrus Blackwood defected in anger. Captured by Spanish soldiers, he betrayed the rest of the band to save himself. Eli missed the slaughter because he had ridden out to recapture some runaway animals. Finding Michael lying wounded among the many slain, he carried him to a Mexican family for first treatment, then spirited him out of Texas to recover in the Louisiana home of the Villaret family. It was then that Michael and Marie had begun a friendship that years later led to marriage.

"Mean times they was," Eli said gravely. "I hope we never see their likes again."

Andrew observed, "We're under Mexico now instead of Spain. It's different."

The dancing light of the fire made the age lines look terribly deep in Eli's bewhiskered face. "Maybe."

They raised the walls the second day with the help of two bachelor neighbors to the east who came drifting in. The roof was well along when Andrew decided on the third day that the Nathans had more help than they needed. "I reckon I'll get on down to San Felipe," he said to Eli. "You just follow the river west and you'll come to Michael's place. Him and Marie'll be tickled to see you."

Eli shook his hand. "If you happen into Mr. Austin, I'd as soon you didn't remember me to him. I ain't as fast on my feet as I used to was."

Andrew promised the Nathans that he would stop by on his way back from San Felipe and perhaps eat the first meal cooked on the hearth in their new cabin. Then he set off to complete the trip he had started three days earlier. He was two hours on the trail when he encountered a trio of settlers, a father and two sons who said their name was Mann. Their home was up on the Brazos River. Quenton Mann, the elder, rode a mule. Harlan, the older of the sons, rode a young gelding that seemed not yet well broken. The other rode a black mare Andrew thought was old enough to have carried George Washington. They were looking for some lost horses, they said. They showed Andrew a set of tracks they had been following. The tracks led southward.

"Looks pretty clear to us that they was stole," said the father. "They ain't never showed any inclination to leave home. All we got left to ride is these three. They're just one notch better than bein' afoot."

For a fleeting moment Andrew thought of Eli and the horses he was trading in the colony. He quickly dismissed that notion and felt a little guilty over entertaining it at all. Eli skirted along the edge of the customs laws, but he had never been regarded as a thief. The Austin colony had suffered little from thievery, thanks to Austin's careful selection of the people he accepted as settlers. This was the sort of thing Andrew would have expected from the Blackwoods, but they had been escorted out of Texas. Another thought occurred to him. "You-all ever have Indian trouble up your way?"

The father glanced uneasily at his sons. "That possibility has crossed our minds."

"If it was Indians and you found them, what would you do?"

The father shrugged. "See how fast a mule and a wore-out old horse can run."

Andrew wished them luck and watched them for a few minutes as they proceeded southward, following the tracks.

His first move in San Felipe was to find the Mexican midwife and trade her the ham he had brought from Michael's smokehouse for the preparation Marie hoped would ease her pregnancy discomforts. He rode then to the store and traded the proprietor the hides from his pack horse for a few supplies.

He seldom visited the settlement without paying a courtesy call upon Stephen Austin, without whose self-sacrifice and sometimes painful negotiations with the authorities none of these Americans would have been allowed to settle in Mexican Texas. He found Austin looking harried and overworked as usual. After some casual small talk about Michael and Marie and crop prospects up on the Colorado River, Andrew mentioned his encounter with the horse-hunting Manns. It was the first Austin had heard. He said, "It is possible that some of those blackguards who have illegally settled the redlands up against Louisiana have come down here to see what they can steal. Or it could be Mexican outlaws from the south. But most likely the horses simply strayed. I will make some inquiry and see if anyone else has had losses."

He gave Andrew a moment's frowning study. "I realize you are isolated and do not see many people out where you live. But I wonder if you have heard of any discontent, any stirring against the government?"

It was a question Austin asked almost every time Andrew saw him. "Nothin' of any consequence."

"If any should arise, I hope you will do what you can to stifle it before it spreads. Such a thing is very dangerous for our position here in Texas."

As Andrew prepared to go, Austin said, "If you are not in a hurry, I hear a rumor that there is a minister about, and he plans to hold services tonight out at the Hawkins farm."

"Are you goin'?"

"I cannot. Under the laws of Mexico, only Catholic services are allowed to be conducted here. As *alcalde* it would be my duty to take legal action should I witness any violation."

"But if you know about it—"

Austin smiled. "I know nothing. One hears rumors about many things. One cannot waste his time running after every rumor." It was not always the letter of the law that counted in colonial Texas; it was the appearance of law.

It occurred to Andrew that he might talk this minister into riding out to the Nathans' place. A visit from a man of the cloth would please Mrs. Nathan almost as much as moving into the new cabin. Marie would probably enjoy such a visit as well, though her French and Spanish upbringing had given her the faith officially sanctioned by Mexico. "I believe I'll go. A little churchin' wouldn't hurt me too much."

He stopped a while to share some catfish at the invitation of the village blacksmith who, when not busy, liked to walk down to the river and cast a line into the deep waters. Andrew asked directions to the Hawkins farm. It was west and a little south, not far off the trail he customarily used. On the way he met several settler families, some afoot, some on horseback, a couple in wagons, all traveling in the same direction. The Catholic church periodically sent a priest into the settlements to do marryings, baptisms, and conduct mass, and occasionally Protestant ministers clandestinely made the rounds, but these happenings were irregular and unpredictable. Given any notice at all, they usually drew a large and grateful crowd.

It was dusk when Andrew arrived. He estimated that close to a hundred people were gathered around a double log cabin. Because the summer weather was beneficent, and the cabin much too small for so many, the services were being conducted outdoors. The minister stood in the open dog-run, his back to Andrew. A large gathering crowded in front of him. Andrew could see that he was baptising several babies of varying sizes, born since the last clerical visitation. A large black-bound Bible sat on a chair beside him, but he did not need it. He was reciting the Scriptures at length by heart. The voice was deep and strong and reassuring. It also sounded somehow familiar.

Andrew tied his horses out away from the services, among those of the earlier arrivals, and strode around toward the front of the cabin to join those already in place. He heard the minister declaring, "Now we have come to join these couples in holy matrimony in the presence of the Lord and the sight of this company." Andrew wondered idly if any of the babies belonged to one or more of the three couples he saw standing before the dog-run, awaiting marriage ceremonies. Probably not, but such a thing was by no means unknown in isolated settlements where the Lord's messengers seldom came. The minister now had the Bible in his left hand and his right hand uplifted. "You will repeat after me—"

Standing on the far edge of the crowd, Andrew could not see the minister well. The man was shrouded in the gloom of the roofed-over dog-run and the gathered dusk. But he felt he had heard that voice before, or one very much like it. The minister exhorted the couples to be true to one another and to the Lord's covenants, to go forth and multiply and fill this pagan province with true believers. "It is your mission, and that of your descendants, to take this new land and bring it to full blossom, to make it an empire that will shine forevermore in the glory of Him who sent us here."

Andrew thought Mrs. Nathan would enjoy hearing that message.

The marrying done, the minister gave a short prayer, then told the congregation, "If you good people will forgive me, I must pause for a bit of supper to rebuild my strength so I may properly deliver the urgent message of salvation I have brought for you tonight. May the Lord's countenance shine upon you and bless you, and now let's eat."

Most of the people had brought food, and they began carrying it forward, placing it on a long, crude table assembled from split logs in front of the cabin. This would be a community supper, the participants contributing because few farmers in the colony could afford to host so many people out of their own limited resources. Andrew felt a little guilty that he had nothing to put on the table. The little stuff he had bought at the store was for Marie, not for himself. It mattered little, though. He knew he was as welcome here as if he had brought a side of beef. As a whole, the Old Three Hundred and those who had followed them were a gregarious and generous lot.

This, he thought, might be his chance to get close to the minister and ask him to visit the settlers out on the Colorado. He awaited his turn, for many people had crowded around. The man's back was to Andrew. When the well-wishers momentarily thinned, Andrew called, "Preacher, could I talk to you?"

The heavyset minister turned. Andrew sucked in a surprised breath and held it. A chill shuddered through him when he saw the black patch over one eye. He declared in revulsion, "Fairweather!"

The minister's jaw went slack as he stared at Andrew. He tried to speak, but in his surprise no words came. He grabbed at the big black Bible to keep from dropping it to the ground.

Andrew became conscious of several people staring at him and the black-clad minister. He said, "Maybe we'd better walk off out yonder a ways where we can talk in private."

Fairweather looked him over suspiciously. Andrew said, "I'm not armed. My rifle is on my horse."

Fairweather stammered to the people who watched, "If you will excuse me, please, this young gentleman and I have some unfinished matters to discuss."

When they were out of earshot, Andrew said, "I thought they were finished a long time ago. I figured by now somebody had killed you."

"The Lord has been kind to me since our last meeting."

"Kinder to you than to them around you, I would imagine. What kind of swindle are you tryin' to pull off here? You're no more a minister than I am."

"I am no longer the same man I was when last you saw me."

Andrew gave him a dark study, trying in vain to read whatever was behind the man's one good eye. "You look the same to me. You were nothin' but a trail pirate. You used that preacher disguise to put us off our guard so you could rob and murder us on the road to Texas. If you ever worked for anybody besides yourself it was for Satan; it sure wasn't for the Lord."

He knew that the man's name was not even Fairweather. He had assumed that name, taken from a real minister he had robbed and very possibly even killed. But Fairweather was the only name Andrew knew him by.

Fairweather said, "I will admit that in those evil days I was not what I appeared. But I underwent a great revelation after my parting with you and your brother. Like Saul on the road to Damascus, I was blinded by a miracle, and then I could see as never before."

"You was blinded by a bullwhip in the hands of a woman you turned over to your gang of cutthroats to be raped and killed."

"And a just retribution it was. It took the loss of one eye to open the other to the path of righteousness."

Andrew sniffed. "Righteousness! You've just figured out a new way to rob people, is all. Your words are as bogus as them weddin's you just performed. Nobody ever ordained you to be a preacher."

"I need no man's ordination. I took mine from the Book, wherein reposes all truth."

Andrew began to wonder. He put little stock in sudden reformations, but it was just barely possible that the old fraud had used the Bible so long as a device for larceny that he finally had come to believe his own preachings. "If you're lookin' to take up a big collection from these folks, you're in for an awful disappointment. There's not enough cash money in this crowd to buy a demijohn of Kentucky squeezin's."

"There are rewards far greater than money could buy. I carry the Word so that I might earn that great reward for my soul when it comes time to depart this world of care."

It's a damned shame you didn't depart it a long time ago, Andrew thought. But he saw that these people believed. It would be cruel to rob them of their pleasure in a rare opportunity to hear someone deliver the Word in tones as persuasive as Fairweather's. "Tell you what: I'll stay around and listen to your preachin', and maybe I won't tell anybody what you really are. But there's a catch to it."

"And what might that be?"

"I want you to tell them before you start that you don't want any of their money, that you ain't goin' to take up any collection."

"That, young gentleman, is a heavy test of my sincerity."

"I can't offer you any better. If you won't do it, I'd advise you to leave right now. Otherwise, they just might stone you to death, like in the Book."

"Money is the root of all evil, my young friend. I have no need of it. I shall take up no collection."

"Fine. Go get your supper and then give these good folks the best sermon you ever preached. I'll be listenin'."

"Do that. You may find yourself uplifted."

Andrew watched with a frown as Fairweather turned away from him to the warm reception of the crowd. Either the man had truly reformed or he had become an even bigger fraud than Andrew remembered.

Andrew ate skimpily, not wishing to abuse hospitality when he had brought nothing to the table but his appetite. He noted that Fairweather suffered from no such compunctions but ate heartily and enjoyed the attention of the people who thronged around him. Andrew wanted to give him the benefit of the doubt but remembered all too well his and Michael's encounter with the bogus minister on their way to Texas. Twice the man had tried to kill them. He had also tried to appropriate two wagonloads of whiskey belonging to a woman teamster named Sally Boone. But her prowess with the whip had been his undoing. The skill that enabled her to knock a fly off the nigh leader's ear let her take out Fairweather's eye.

The supper done and the crowd quieted, Fairweather offered a prayer, then launched into the Biblical story about Saul and the road to Damascus.

Andrew suspected that was for his benefit. Fairweather talked about the blinding of Saul, who had been a scourge to the Christians, and his redemption as a true believer under his new name of Paul.

Fairweather's name change had come long before his conversion, if indeed there had been one.

Andrew saw that the people were swept up in the glory of Fairweather's message, and after a while he began to feel the magnetism himself. Some of the doubt still clung, but he began to feel that the weight of evidence was swinging over to Fairweather's side. If he was not sincere, he was the best playactor Andrew had ever seen.

The meeting broke up, finally. Some of the crowd began leaving for home. Others would camp the night and go home in the daylight. Fairweather, of course, was offered the Hawkins' bedroom in the double cabin. Andrew sidled up to him just before the minister retired.

"That was a pretty powerful load you dumped on the folks."

"It is written that the good shepherd always feeds his flock."

"You got any other flocks to tend in these parts?"

"Where the spirit beckons, I follow."

"There's some folks up on the Colorado River that would appreciate hearin' you. I'll take you tomorrow."

Fairweather was surprised again. "I thought you were the doubting Thomas."

"I am. I still got my doubts that you know the Master, but you do know the Word, and that's what the folks want to hear."

"I shall be ready."

Andrew lowered his voice. "Just one thing, Fairweather. One false move and I'll do to you what you tried to do to me and Michael. I'll shoot you, and tell God you died."

11

As was his custom, Andrew left his blanket at first light, but he found the Reverend Fairweather not inclined to early rising. Fairweather said, "The Lord provided the night so we could sleep. It is still night."

"That rooster yonder don't agree with you."

"Man was given more reason than a rooster. When the good folks start fixing breakfast, I shall be up and giving praise for the new day."

In fact, Fairweather gave praise several times. Many people who had camped set about building small fires and fixing their own meager breakfasts rather than impose upon the hosts. Fairweather arose when the first smell of frying ham reached him. He went from camp to camp, fire to fire, blessing the food, partaking liberally as it was offered to him. Andrew judged that he had eaten enough to kill an average man. But when the farmer Hawkins walked out onto the dog-run and bade the minister come in to breakfast, Fairweather obliged him.

Andrew itched to be saddled up and gone, but Fairweather had a parting sermon for those who had stayed over. He would not be rushed. He exalted the glory of sharing. He spoke of the angel who visits unaware and promised to be back on this circuit before long. Everybody pressed around, wanting to shake his hand one more time. Andrew despaired of their ever getting started. But eventually they set out upon the trail. Fairweather looked back over his shoulder at the people behind him, preparing to return to their homes refreshed in the spirit.

"There is a great joy in such fellowship."

"And some possibility of a bellyache."

It felt strange to Andrew, riding with a man who once had sought to rob and kill him and Michael. He wondered what Michael would say, though Michael's opinion would not alter Andrew's actions one way or the other. Except for Fairweather's eating like a starved wolf, Andrew could not see that the man had abused these folks' hospitality. If he left them feeling better for his coming, what was the harm? And far be it from Andrew to deny a similar comfort to Mrs. Nathan, who felt that a new home needed a minister's blessing. People who left everything behind them to come out and settle a wild new land deserved whatever consolation might come their way.

He had forgotten how many farms lay between San Felipe and the new place settled by the Nathan family. Fairweather insisted upon stopping at each one to extend his best wishes, inquiring if there was any spiritual need he might help satisfy. A ride that should have taken a few hours under normal circumstances stretched through that day and into the next. Fairweather resisted Andrew's efforts to push him along. "One does not rush the message or the messenger."

Suspicion gnawed at Andrew although the people along the way seemed to accept Fairweather without questioning his claim to speak for higher authority. He knew the Book backward and forward, it seemed. He must have done a lot of reading in it since Andrew and Michael had first encountered him on the trail to Texas. At that time Andrew had smelled a skunk when Fairweather spoke of Jonah in the lions' den. He seemed to have his stories straight this time, though Andrew by no means considered himself an expert on the subject.

He found the Nathans' roof finished and ready to be tested by rain. Mrs. Nathan was beside herself with joy when she saw Fairweather dismount. She recognized his calling by his black suit and the Bible which he took from his saddlebag before Andrew had a chance to introduce him. Bachelor neighbors Joe Smith and Walker Younts, who had helped raise the walls and work on the roof, were still hanging around. They probably enjoyed Mrs. Nathan's cooking too much to hurry back to their own places. Andrew suspected that both were also interested in the girl Birdy; their eyes followed her constantly. By Andrew's standards she was still underage, but scarcity on a frontier made girls a much-sought-after commodity. They tended to marry early. A rose hardly had time to blossom before it was plucked.

Lige Willet had gone home. Family men had responsibilities.

Andrew was surprised when Eli Pleasant walked out from the cool shade of the dog-run to shake his hand. Andrew said, "I thought you'd be gone to Michael and Marie's by now."

"Wasn't no hurry about it. These here are pleasant folks. I don't think I've et better since the time I set my feet under your mama's table back in Tennessee." Eli glanced toward the woman. "Miz Nathan is almighty tickled that you brought a reverend with you."

Andrew frowned. "I hope she won't find reason to regret it."

"Any reason she might?"

"His name is Fairweather. You've heard me and Michael speak of him."

Eli rubbed his chin, studying the minister speculatively from afar. "I don't remember you sayin' anything good. But maybe havin' a bad reverend is better than not havin' any reverend at all."

"I hope so. I never saw a black horse turn white before. I'm afraid a little rain might wash the paint off of this one."

"Then we'd better help him pray for sunshine."

Fairweather did his duties as if he were being paid. He blessed the new cabin, he blessed the family, he blessed the field and the livestock, and he blessed the big meal Mrs. Nathan set on the newly hewn pine table.

One of the Nathan youngsters let curiosity get the better of his manners. He asked what had become of the eye covered by the patch. Fairweather gave Andrew a quick glance across the table. "I once allowed myself to gaze upon wickedness, and the eye was taken for penance. You have two good eyes, my young gentleman. Take care that they look only upon what is worthy in the sight of the Lord."

"Amen," said Mrs. Nathan with a questioning glance toward the bachelors whose attentions had been devoted to her daughter.

The sound of horses' hoofs intruded upon the meal. Nathan got up and went to the door, casting a quick gaze upon his rifle over the new mantle but not moving toward it. "Three men have just ridden in with a dozen or so horses."

Andrew made his excuses to Mrs. Nathan and followed Nathan outside. Eli Pleasant trailed behind them. Fairweather did not pause in his good work at the table. Andrew recognized the Mann father and two sons he had met on the trail to San Felipe. They were riding better horses this time. The younger of the sons sat hunched in the saddle. As the horse turned, Andrew saw a bandage wrapped around the young man's arm. The father and the older son pushed the horses through the open gate of Nathan's pole-pen, dust swirling around them. The son stepped down from his horse and pushed into place the poles that served as a gate. Quenton Mann turned and raised his hand in greeting. He looked haggard and worn and worried.

"Any of these horses belong to you folks?" he asked.

Andrew stepped forward, and Mann recognized him. "Seen you down yonder a ways, didn't I?" He pointed his chin eastward.

Andrew nodded. "Looks like you found your horses."

"Ours and some more. Hoped you folks might know who the rest of them belong to."

Eli walked up to the boy whose arm was bandaged. He took hold of the bridle reins. "Son, you look mighty hard used. I see the blood in that wrappin'."

The father spoke for him. "He got an arrow in his arm. Me and Harlan, we pulled it out. Good lady named Willet on a farm over yonder cleaned the wound and wrapped it for him."

Alarm began to rise in Andrew. "You took these horses away from Indians?"

Mann demonstrated his story with much movement of his hands. "One Indian. He was holdin' them while the rest of the bunch was off somewhere, probably lookin' for more horses to steal. We come on him sudden and taken him by surprise, but he was quick as a panther puttin' that arrow in my boy's arm. I shot him before he could take another one out of his quiver."

"Kill him?" Andrew asked anxiously.

"Stone cold dead."

Andrew pressed, "What about the rest of the Indians?"

Mann shook his head. "We didn't figure it'd be smart to stay around and wait for them. We just gathered up all the horses there was and pushed them away from there as hard as they would run."

Eli asked, "You know what kind of Indians they was?"

"Got no idee. The one we saw was tattooed a right smart."

"Waco, more'n likely," Eli said.

Andrew's anxiety continued to build. He gave Eli a quick, searching look. The old smuggler's eyes were narrowed with concern.

Andrew said, "They'll be wantin' revenge for the one that was shot. If they follow the trail of the horses—"

Eli nodded. "They'll come to the Willet farm sure as hell."

Andrew found his hands shaking. "And it's just a short ways on over to our places, Michael's and mine. They could hit there just as easy."

Mann was apologetic. "We never intended to cause trouble for other folks. We just went to get our horses back. And I couldn't just sit there and let that Indian finish killin' my boy. I had to shoot him, don't you see?"

Andrew said, "We see, but I doubt them Indians will. Eli, I've got to hurry and warn Michael and Marie."

Eli's furrowed old face was solemn. "And I'll git myself over to Willet's as fast as I can. He's so easy-goin' he may not realize the danger he's in."

Fairweather had sensed the excitement and wandered out to see what it was all about. "Anything I can do?" he asked.

Andrew said, "If you've really got somebody up there who'll listen to you, you can pray for a bunch of innocent folks."

Fairweather told Eli, "Friend, I'll ride with you over to the Willet farm. If the Indians do come by, those good folks'll need all the fighting men they can get."

Andrew frowned. "I didn't think you were armed."

"I am armed with the power of the Word. I've also got a pistol buried deep in my saddlebag. One never knows when he may encounter a heathen."

"You'd be the one to know about heathens."

Andrew did not take time for good-byes. He quickly threw the saddle on his brown horse and put him into a run, leaving the pack horse behind. He looked back once. Eli and Fairweather followed far behind him, but he did not wait. Their trail was shorter than his.

He kept the brown horse in a lope as much as he dared, slowing him to a trot frequently to give him a chance to recover his wind. His imagination ran wild and free. Andrew had never been in an Indian fight or seen the aftermath of a raid, though he had heard about them often enough as a boy in Tennessee. Mordecai Lewis had been an Indian fighter, leaving home and family several times that Andrew could remember to join an expedition of rescue or revenge. His descriptions, when he returned, were graphic and terrifying. Those descriptions played through Andrew's mind now as he imagined himself finding Michael's cabin ablaze, Michael and Marie and the boy slaughtered. He left the longer trail that would have taken him by the Willet farm and cut straight across toward his own. In his anxiety he almost ran the brown horse to the ground. He forced himself to slow, though it was painful. He would be of no help to anyone if he killed the horse and could not reach the farm in time.

He kept watching for smoke. Once he thought he heard shooting, and he pulled the horse to a stop so he could listen. Now he heard nothing. He chastised himself. He had to put a bridle on that wild imagination.

The brown horse was lathered with sweat when Andrew pushed him at last over the final hill and saw Michael and Marie's cabin below. Everything looked normal. The only smoke was rising from the chimney. He felt a little foolish as relief rushed over him like a tide. All those old Indian stories—he had let them run away with him.

Nearing the field, he saw Michael standing amid the corn, hoeing weeds. Andrew started waving his hat. Michael paused, started to go back to hoeing, then reluctantly walked out toward the fence to meet his younger brother. He offered no welcome. Andrew knew Michael still resented his taking the trip away from him.

Michael said, "You stayed gone long enough. Thought maybe you went all the way to Nacogdoches instead of to San Felipe."

Andrew felt a little tremor in his voice. "I might've stayed a little longer, but an emergency's come up."

"Emergency? What kind?"

"The kind that wear feathers in their hair."

Michael's resentment was quickly shoved aside. His eyes widened. "Where at?"

"Maybe here, before long. I think you'd better lay down the hoe and get up to the cabin. They'd make short work of you if they caught you out here in the open. They won't be as apt to rush a cabin that they know has got armed men in it."

Michael picked up a rifle he had leaned against the rail fence, and he left the hoe in its place. "How'd you come to know all this?"

Andrew explained it to him as he rode on up toward the cabin, Michael striding along beside him. Michael exclaimed, "You say Eli is in the country? I'd give a pretty to see that old man again."

"You will. He said he'd be comin' along. But right now he's over to the Willets', lendin' a hand in case the Indians come by there."

Michael said with concern, "We've never had any Indian trouble out here to speak of, a little horse and mule stealin', is all. Except for the Karanka-

was down on the coast, they ain't killed hardly anybody."

"We've never killed any of *them* before."

Marie had seen them coming. She waited on the
dog-run, smiling her pleasure. "It is good that no
one is angry now," she said, misreading the situation. "It is not good here when you argue."

Michael said, "Whatever argument we've got, it
has to be set aside for a while. We have somethin'
bigger to worry about."

Andrew said, "Don't you be gettin' scared, Marie,
but there's a chance Indians may be comin' this way."

Marie looked anxiously toward the kitchen door.
Little Mordecai came out. "How do, Uncle Andrew?"

Michael said quickly, "Mordecai, you'd best be
stayin' in the cabin."

Marie gathered the boy into her arms. Andrew
wondered if she ought to be lifting him in her condition, but it was not his place to say anything, and
Michael didn't.

Andrew thought of something. "Where's your
horse, Michael?"

Michael seemed surprised that he had not thought
of the horse. "I saw him grazin' down by the river a
little while ago." He pointed northeastward.

Andrew said, "I'd best find him and bring him up
here where we can watch him. The reason the Indians are out and about is to pick up horses."

Marie put in quickly, "If you see the cow,
Andrew—"

The boy said, "Indians? Are we goin' to see
Indians?" He seemed eager rather than frightened.

Andrew swung up onto the brown horse and
headed quickly for the river. From one day to the

next, even one part of the day to the next, there was no telling where Michael's bay horse might graze. He was a free roamer. But he seemed to have a strong preference for one particular place downriver a mile or so from Michael's cabin. Andrew supposed it had something to do with the soil there, and the flavor or nutrients it put into the grass. He reined the brown in that direction, his senses keened. He was very much aware that the horse might not be the only thing he found.

He had traveled only a short way when the bay came running toward him. Andrew reined up, and the horse passed by him, eyes rolling in fright. The animal kept running, headed toward the cabin as if something were after him. Perhaps something was. Andrew's blood seemed to have ice in it as he held up a moment, staring hard in the direction from which the horse had come. He saw nothing. But a strong premonition made him shudder. He turned and followed the horse toward the cabin.

He remembered that Marie was concerned about the milk cow, but he decided it would be prudent to let the cow take care of herself. She was a creature of habit. Come milking time, she would amble in on her own. Indians had no use for cows except once in a while to butcher one for the meat, as they would do with a buffalo. They saw no pride of property in a cow.

The bay had entered the pen of its own volition and stood with its neck over the fence, watching Andrew's return. Instinct had made it turn to a place of safety when frightened. Michael was on his way from the cabin to the pen. He shut the gate behind the bay and waited for Andrew to ride up.

He asked, "What did you do to my horse? He came runnin' in here like the day we heard a big cat over in the timber."

"He ran by me the same way. I got a feelin' he saw somethin', and it wasn't a cat."

Michael asked no more questions. He bridled his bay horse, which trembled in fright. He patted the animal gently to calm it. "I been thinkin'—we'd better tie the horses up against the cabin, just in case. Worse come to worst, we can put them *in* the cabin."

"Might get a little crowded in there."

"Better crowded than left afoot."

Andrew was startled to see Marie walking toward the river with a bucket in each hand. He dropped his reins and hurried down to intercept her. "You've got no business leavin' the cabin. There's no tellin' where them Indians might be."

Calmly she said, "The buckets are nearly empty. Should they come and stay a long time, we will need the water."

"I'll fetch it. You better get back yonder to the boy."

It struck Andrew that many people, and not just women by any means, would be in panic at the thought of Indians somewhere near. Marie's mind was on the practical considerations. She said, "We will also need milk. You did not see the cow?"

"To tell you the truth, I didn't look none too hard."

She said pointedly, "If it were men who had the babies, you would know the cow is more important than the horse."

Andrew watched as she turned and walked back

toward the cabin. In spite of the tension, he found himself chuckling.

If I ever find a woman for myself, he thought, *she'll have to be a lot like Marie.*

12

The emergency took precedence over other considerations but did not eliminate them. Andrew was aware that Michael's resentment still simmered quietly beneath the surface. *Well, hell,* he thought, *if that's the way it's got to be, then it'll just be that way.* He went out to the dog-run and took a seat where he could watch most of three directions including the front of the cabin where they had staked the horses. Michael said nothing. He took up a position at the other side of the dog-run, his back to Andrew. He watched the opposite side of the cabin and westward, where the trees along the river stretched away into the horizon. West was his favorite direction, as it had always been their father's.

After a time Andrew was compelled to turn and look at him. By way of a peace offering he said, "You didn't miss much."

Michael only grunted.

Andrew said, "They've had aplenty of rain over east. The early-planted crops are lookin' good. May be late gettin' the rest of them into the ground, though. Mud."

Michael did not even grunt.

Andrew reflected that a certain amount of stubbornness went with being a Lewis, especially the oldest Lewis. It had been that way with their father. It would probably be that way with little Mordecai when he got old enough to assert himself over his younger brother or sister, whichever Marie turned out to be carrying.

He felt he ought to try once more to explain. "Like I told you, the shape Marie's in, I didn't figure you ought to be goin' off and leavin'."

"I'd say that's a decision for me and Marie to make."

"For you *and* Marie. Didn't look to me like you'd asked her one way or the other."

"If you'd go find you a wife of your own, you wouldn't have time to be tellin' me what-all to do about mine."

"I oughtn't to have to tell you. You ought to know."

"You don't understand how it is with me. Nobody could understand except maybe Papa. He was the same way."

"It got him killed, and left Mama a widow."

Andrew decided that further argument might only lead to a fight. He felt awkward, for over the years the two brothers had seldom traded cross words. He sealed off the subject by commenting, "Seems kind of hot, even for this time of the year." It wasn't really that hot, but it was something to say, better than silence.

Michael grunted.

Andrew decided to let silence prevail. He watched

the line of trees that bordered the river on its easterly flow. That, he judged, would be the most likely point of approach should Indians come. They would hardly want to ride in from the open country that stretched beyond the field, for they would be seen far away. They would want to use the cover of the timber as long as possible, then, likely as not, come charging up from the nearest point, hoping to catch the Lewises unready. That was the direction from which the bay horse had come running. Andrew strongly suspected the raiders had tried to take the horse and he had run away from them. That meant they were probably down in that direction somewhere. He could only hope they were well on their way northwestward, back the way from which they had originally come. That would likely make them Wacos, as Eli had said, or possibly Tawakonis. From what Andrew had heard, these were kindred tribes which lived, hunted, and did some limited farming along the Brazos River far beyond the Texas settlements. It was claimed they were much less nomadic than, say, the Comanches, and even lived in lodges made of grass. They were not given to perpetual war as the Comanches seemed to be against the Spanish and the Mexicans, but they were not reluctant to raid and to fight against such other tribes as were considered enemies. That they had raided little in Austin's colonies was fortunate for the colonists. Like the Comanches, they were perhaps still trying to figure out just what kind of people these Americans were.

The Manns, father and sons, had shown them what kind of enemies the Americans could be.

Andrew sat for perhaps two hours, enough that his rump was beginning to feel sore and his back ached. Changing positions seemed not to help much. He got up and stretched, then walked a little to stir his blood into better circulation. He saw Michael's bay horse jerk its head around, its ears pointed eastward. Little Mordecai's spotted dog, which had appeared to be asleep beside Andrew on the dog-run, raised up and looked around.

Horsemen appeared on the rim of a hill, in the direction of the Willet family's place. Andrew felt a quick chill. His voice was husky. "Michael! You better come look."

Michael was there in an instant, peering in the direction Andrew's finger pointed. Andrew asked, "Look like Indians?"

Michael flexed his fingers nervously against the stock of his long rifle and was a minute in answering. "No, looks like white folks to me. Best I can count, there's eight of them."

With his fingers Andrew stretched the skin around the edge of his right eye, a trick he had found gave him a moment of improved vision, though to hold it long had an adverse effect. "If I'm not mistaken, one of them is Eli Pleasant. Looks like the horse he was ridin', anyway."

"Eli!" Michael exclaimed. Eli had always been good news.

Marie had heard their quiet speculation and ventured out onto the dog-run. But when the boy Mordecai tried to follow her from the kitchen, she shooed him back through the door. "Then the Indians are already gone, you think?"

Most of the riders stopped at the top of a rise. Only two came ahead. One was Eli Pleasant. The other—

Andrew had not found Michael in a mood for listening much, so he had not told him about the Reverend Fairweather. "That's Eli on the left," he said. "You'd best gird yourself up for a little kick in the belly when you see who's with him."

Michael recognized the man and whispered a word under his breath that he never spoke in Marie's presense. So far as Andrew knew, she would have no idea what it meant. He would like to think she had been sheltered more than that. "Fairweather! Or whatever his name is. How come somebody hasn't killed him by now?"

"Don't you be takin' a notion to do it yourself. He's got folks convinced that he's the holiest man since John the Baptist. I'm kind of wonderin' myself. Maybe he's changed."

"Only if you can change a wolf into a sheep."

Any other time, Eli Pleasant would have swung to the ground and pumped Michael's hand until his arm felt ready to come off at the shoulder. But he sat on his horse, his face grave. "You folks all right here?"

Michael responded to the old man's somber mien. Quietly he said, "We're doin' just fine, Eli. Mighty glad to see you." He walked out and extended his hand. He pointedly ignored Fairweather.

Eli took Michael's hand, but there was no joy in his eyes at their reunion. "I'd be tickled to see you too, Michael, if things was different. But them folks back yonder"—he jerked his head, indicating the direction from which he had come—"they ain't passed so well. There's been killin' done."

Andrew tensed, glancing back at the alarm in Marie's face. "Who's dead?"

"Lige Willet, that helped us raise the cabin for the Nathan family. It was done before me and the reverend got there to warn him. Willet was out plowin' his field, and they come upon him unawares. His boy Daniel was out there ridin' a pony I'd traded them. The Indians taken him along."

Marie asked urgently, "And what of Mrs. Willet? What has happened to her?"

"She's all right, except she's been left a widow. The rest of the family was close to the cabin. They seen what happened but was too far to help. They got inside and bolted the doors. The Indians come up close, but they decided not to go against the walls. They rode off takin' all the Willet horses, and the boy cryin' for his mama."

Andrew remembered the eager boy he had carried behind him on his saddle just a few days earlier. And he remembered the jolly face, the jovial stories told by Lige Willet. He felt like crying a little himself. He pointed his chin toward the horsemen who waited at a distance. "Who's that yonder?"

"Willet's bigger boy Zeb, and Mann and his oldest son, and Nathan and some others. We follered the Indian's trail. They didn't miss your place by more'n a mile or so. Probably crossed the river right down yonder, just beyond that rise where you couldn't see them."

Andrew shuddered. He hadn't seen them, but Michael's bay horse had. The Indians had been in too big a hurry to try to chase him down.

Michael said grimly, "We'd ought not to be standin' here wastin' time. I'll fetch me some powder and shot, and I'll be goin' with you."

Andrew saw Marie's face fall in dismay. He turned on Michael in a flush of anger. "No you won't. I'll go. You stay here and take care of your family."

Michael flared even more swiftly. "When're you goin' to quit tryin' to tell me what to do?"

"When you start doin' what you ought to without me havin' to tell you."

Michael glared, then strode toward his staked bay horse. Andrew started after him in long, angry steps. Michael took the reins. Andrew grabbed them up near the bit. "Marie needs you at home. So does that boy. You're not goin'!"

Michael's eyes narrowed, his cheeks flushed red. "Andrew, I ain't hit you since we was boys. But I'm fixin' to now if you don't turn aloose of my horse!"

Andrew only half heard Fairweather's voice. "Gentlemen, this is not a time for quarreling. There is a young boy yonder in the wilderness, crying out for rescue."

Michael grabbed Andrew's wrist and tried to twist it, to free the rein. Andrew fought back, shoving his brother up against the bay horse, which sensed the anger and began to strain heavily against the stake that held him.

Marie stepped between them, shouting as Andrew had never heard her before, "You will stop fighting, both of you. I will not have it. I will not!"

Andrew countered, "You can't stay here by yourself."

Eli declared, "She won't. They're gatherin' up all the womenfolks and young'uns from around here and takin' them to the Willet place. It's got the best protection. There'll be a wagon along here pretty soon to fetch Marie and the boy."

Marie said, "That is best. Mrs. Willet will need friends to be with her. There we will be safe enough."

Eli added, "The Indians appear to've already gone

away from here anyhow. Probably tryin' to get back to where they come from as quick as they can."

Andrew backed away from Michael, but his blood still ran hot. He faced Marie. "His place is here with you. No tellin' when we might get back."

Marie touched Michael's arm and turned to look into her husband's face. "Michael's place is where Michael feels he needs to be. He will do what must be done. You are both needed, so go now. The boy and I will be all right."

Andrew felt a little chastened. He sensed that Marie did not really want Michael to go, but it was to be expected that she would back her husband. She would put on a brave face and make Michael feel that the idea had been her own. He would not leave this place carrying a burden of guilt.

She looked off toward the river and pointed. "The cow comes up to be milked. Her we will tie behind the wagon and take with us. There will be other children at the Willets' besides Mordecai. They will need much milk. But the chickens—the chickens will have to take care of themselves."

She walked into the cabin with Michael, her arm around him. When Michael came out in a minute with his powderhorn, a leather pouch, a sack of food, and one rolled blanket, she did not come with him. Michael did not look at Andrew, but he said to Eli, "She's busy gatherin' up stuff to be ready when the wagon comes. She'll give you a proper greetin' the next time."

There had been no greeting at all for Fairweather. He said, "God be with all who live in this house."

Michael gave him a surprised glance but made no comment. He set the bay horse into a long trot toward the riders who waited farther on. Andrew was busy tying his blanket behind his saddle and had to spur hard to catch up.

The other horsemen saw them leave the cabin and moved on down toward the river, passing out of sight. Michael altered his direction to compensate, for he had taken the lead without asking. The men were watering their horses when Michael, Andrew, Eli, and Fairweather reached them. The new settler Nathan was there, and the elder Mann along with the son Harlan who had not been wounded. The bachelor farmers Smith and Younts were there, and young Zebediah Willet, his face dark with pain and anxiety and hatred. He looked much older than the twenty or so that he really was. This country could age a young man fast.

Michael knew all of them except the newcomer Nathan, who quickly introduced himself. "It's a bad time, a bad time," Nathan said. "I had not thought to encounter Indian trouble. We had just gotten settled."

Andrew rode up beside Zebediah Willet and placed a heavy hand on the youth's shoulder. "I'm mighty sorry, Zeb."

The answer came in a voice strained almost to breaking. "I seen it, Andrew. I seen the whole thing. I was just too far off to be any help." Tears threatened in his eyes.

"There's no way we can bring back your daddy. But if there's any chance atall, we'll bring back your little brother. Seems to me like you'd ought to go home now. You'd be a big consolation to your mother."

"I can't. If you'd seen them, if they'd carried off your brother, you couldn't stay home either."

Andrew glanced at Michael. "No, I reckon not."

Michael wasted no time. "This is their trail, I take it?" He nodded toward a mass of horse tracks on the riverbank.

Mann said, "They crossed here. Couldn't've been more'n maybe two, three hours, goin' by the sign."

Andrew flinched. That would have been about the time he had gone hunting Michael's bay horse.

Michael put his horse into the water. The Indians had chosen a fording place that required the animals to swim only a few moments before putting their hoofs on the riverbed. Andrew knew of a better place a little farther downriver, but he supposed the Indians were not that well acquainted with this part of the country. The Wacos' normal range was along the Brazos, not the Colorado. Michael turned once to see if everyone was following. Andrew pushed in just behind him. He glanced back. Fairweather, bringing up the rear, hesitated a minute before hitting the water on his big black horse.

Folks who talk about Heaven all the time are not usually in a hurry to get there, Andrew mused.

It quickly became apparent that this party had no real leader. Everybody was together by common consent, but sooner or later they would face a situation that demanded quick decisions; there would be no time to stop and take a vote.

Michael remarked to Eli, "They've sure left a clear trail."

Eli shook his head. "For now. They're wantin' to get as far from this place as they can, in a hurry. A little later on, when they think they've got time, they'll take the trouble to cover their tracks. Then they'll disappear like smoke. They'll be hell to trail unless we catch up to them before that."

Michael looked around to see if anyone would

claim leadership. He pointedly avoided Andrew. Most of the men seemed to be looking at Eli, seemingly assuming that because he was by a wide margin the oldest, his experience would make him the logical choice. Eli felt the pressure and quickly demurred.

"Michael, these ol' eyes ain't as good as they was. But yours was always sharp, as I remember."

Michael hesitated, waiting to see if anyone would challenge his leadership or express a preference for someone else. No one spoke, least of all Andrew. Whatever his disagreements with his older brother might be in regard to family responsibilities, he had confidence in Michael's ability to carry this burden. Michael had more of their father in him than Andrew did.

Michael said, "Let's be gettin' on about the business, then." He turned the bay horse and led off at a trot. Andrew half expected someone to protest the slow pace, but no one did. This trail was so broad and plain that they could have followed it in a lope. But that abuse would run their mounts into the ground in a few miles. Even if they were fortunate enough to overtake their quarry before that, the Indians would probably outrun the pursuers' tired horses.

Andrew saw impatience in the eyes of young Zeb Willet, but the youth accepted the necessity of the slower pace without complaint. No one else spoke of a desire to push harder, though most probably wished they could. Andrew took the lack of argument as a promising sign; these were frontiersmen who knew what they were about, or at least were willing to put their faith in a leadership that knew what it was doing.

Andrew looked back once, wishing he could see the cabin, wishing he knew that someone had arrived with that promised wagon to take Marie and the boy to a place of greater safety. Like Zeb Willet, he had to accept some things on faith. If Michael was concerned—and Andrew thought certainly he must be—he gave no sign. He kept riding, his gaze shifting between the distant horizon and the tracks on the ground. Andrew could only guess what his brother was thinking. He thought it likely that Michael was remembering a time when he himself had been young—though not so young as the captive Willet boy—and had faced death in a strange land at the hands of an implacable enemy. Someone had come to Michael's rescue. It was time now, if it could be done, that Michael lead the way to the rescue of a boy much like the youth he once had been.

13

The sun dropped behind a thin line of reddening clouds to the west, then below the horizon. In the half light that lingered, Michael pushed the bay horse into a lope for the first time, trying to use whatever time remained. The pursuit would have to stop soon because of darkness, and the horses could rest then.

Though Michael had been in most ways a better woodsman and hunter than Andrew, it had been Andrew who excelled in following a track, whether of a tiny fox or rabbit or of a horse. Somehow this was one phase of their father's teachings that had come easier to Andrew than to his older brother. It had always scratched like a piece of gravel in Michael's craw that in this one occasionally vital area he was outdone. Andrew had been watching the tracks, the occasional scattering of horse manure, and gauging for himself how long they had been there. So far as he could tell they were keeping up with the Indians' pace but not besting it any. He did not voice his opinion to Michael. If Michael wanted it, he would surely ask for it. And to speak discouragingly in Zeb's hearing would be cruel.

Zeb occasionally lapsed into bitter self-recrimination. "Papa never was one to give much thought to the bad things that could happen, but *I* should've known. When the Manns brought those horses by our place, I should've guessed that the Indians would be trailin' them. I seen Daniel ridin' off on that new pony and could've stopped him. But I never once thought—"

Eli reined in beside the young man. He had a voice that could cut like a razor when the need arose, but it was soft and comforting now. "Ain't no more use in you blamin' yourself than for me to blame myself for tradin' your daddy that pony in the first place. You wasn't brought up in an Indian-fightin' country. Wasn't no way for you to guess what they'd do."

Zeb knotted his plow-hardened fists. His voice was raw. "I just wish I could kill them all! I will, if I get the chance."

Eli frowned. "I wouldn't be studyin' on that too much, boy. If a man lets hate get ahold of him, it robs him of his judgment. The only thing for you to be thinkin' about is gettin' your little brother back. Them Indians, they're just followin' their nature, like a wolf or a catamount."

"But Papa never done anything to hurt them. He never hurt anybody in his life."

"Just chance, boy. It's like a storm. He was standin' there when the lightnin' struck. Wasn't nothin' personal in it. And it didn't make no difference how good a man he was. To them he was just another white man, and a white man had killed one of theirs."

The elder Mann heard and looked back. He declared defensively, "I didn't kill just to be killin'. I killed to save my own boy."

Eli grunted. "Seems like there was bad luck all the way around. Been lots of people died in Texas just for hard luck. It's the damndest hard luck country ever I seen."

For others perhaps, but Andrew began to wonder if Michael considered this incident bad luck. Times, when Michael glanced around, Andrew saw exhilaration in his brother's eyes. This was Michael's element, this expedition across a new country; he was glorying in the adventure of it. Andrew remembered that look in his father, many times. And he remembered the sadness that always came into his mother's eyes because of it.

Darkness came. Andrew tried to guess how many miles they had traveled. The last good look he had taken at the sign, he had doubted they were showing much if any gain on the Indians. Michael drew rein at the bank of a stream and waited for the others to come up even with him. "We'll lose the tracks if we go any farther tonight. All we can do is wait for daylight."

Zeb Willet demanded, "What do you think those Indians are doin'?"

Michael frowned. "They'll probably ride half the night, puttin' in all the distance they can. But they know their direction. They're not havin' to follow somebody's tracks."

"We know their direction too. They ain't changed it much. We could keep goin' the same way. Come mornin', we'd be that much closer to them."

"But like as not we'd stray off the trail, and we'd waste a lot of time tryin' to find it again."

"More time than we'll waste waitin' here for day-light?"

Michael had to shrug, for he had no answer to that.

Zeb declared, "You-all can stay here if you want to, but I'm goin' on if I have to go by myself."

Andrew pointed out, "You may be able to keep goin' all night, but your horse can't. What if you came upon the Indians with your horse all give out? Even if you got ahold of your brother, you couldn't get away with him. They'd run you down in a hurry."

Eli Pleasant seconded Andrew's statement. "There's a time to be bold and a time to be patient, son."

Zeb wavered but did not give in. Michael said, "We'll split the difference, Zeb. We'll stop here and rest a while; the horses need it. We'll fix ourselves a little supper, get some sleep, then be up and travelin' a long time before daylight."

Eli put in, "Them Indians'll stop eventually and take their rest. Might be we'd catch them by surprise in the early mornin'." He stressed the word *might,* so Andrew knew he thought it unlikely. Andrew considered the chance very remote that they would overtake the Indians this near the settlements. If this party caught up to them, it would almost surely be much farther up into the higher reaches of the Bra-zos River, where few white men had yet traveled. But to voice that opinion would not help now. He kept it to himself, knowing that most of the men probably shared it.

Zeb Willet capitulated. "All right. But I'll be watchin' the stars. Two hours past midnight, I'll be travelin'."

Michael promised, "And we'll be with you. Let's

water the horses. Then we'll build us a small fire low against the far creek bank where the Indians can't see it if any of them are hangin' back watchin'. We can all use a little supper."

Andrew had no provisions with him, for he had not been home. But the other men had brought bread and parched corn and some cured meat from the Willet place, and Michael had picked up a deer ham when he had gone into the cabin for his blanket, powder, and shot. He did not offer it to Andrew, however. Andrew ate a little from Miles Nathan's ration. They all drank a little parched-grain coffee.

Michael had avoided looking at Andrew, but he must have felt Andrew's gaze fixed on him. Defensively he demanded, "You been wantin' to say somethin'. Say it."

Andrew spoke quietly, for this was no one else's business. "I look at you and all I can see is Papa all over again, always ridin' off to some new country, lovin' every bit of it."

Michael frowned. "You think I like what happened back there to Willet and his boy?"

"No, but you like what's come after, the chase and all. You look like a man who's just been let out of jail."

"A man can't help bein' what he is."

"No. But I'd like it better if you didn't like it as much."

The horses were staked to graze atop the creek bank. Andrew took first watch, by the horses, while the other men rolled out their blankets and tried to fall asleep. Eli was snoring within a few minutes. Andrew had heard him say once that in his line of business he sometimes had to do without sleep for extended periods, so it was useful to be able to take as much of it as he could when the chance came. He looked at eating in the same way, something he had learned from his frequent association with Indians: eat all you can when you can, because there is no way of knowing how far away the next meal may be.

He listened to the sounds of the night, the insistent chirping of a bird, possibly calling for a mate with which to share a nest, a feeling Andrew knew also from time to time. He heard a wolf howl not far away, a call quickly answered from some distance. He felt an involuntary chill run up his back. He had no fear of wolves, but hearing them reminded him that he had ridden beyond the bounds of the colony he knew, into a part of the country he had not seen before. It had not looked different particularly, but knowing he had never been there imparted to it a sense of mystery. There was always a feeling that over the next rise, the next hill, might wait something totally alien.

Such a challenge was like strong drink to Michael; he thrived on it. But Andrew preferred the known to the unknown.

He heard a quiet voice. "Reckon them are really wolves?" Zeb Willet had come up to join him.

Andrew whispered accusingly, "You're supposed to be gettin' some sleep."

"You know I couldn't. I'd just as well stand all the watches. Even if I *did* close my eyes, I'd probably dream about what happened today. Maybe I'm even a little afraid to go to sleep because I don't want to see it all again. You think they're wolves? I've heard that Indians signal each other by makin' sounds like animals."

"Papa used to tell me the same thing. But I think

those out yonder are just what they sound like. They're lonesome and tryin' to get together."

Willet was silent for a few thoughtful minutes. "I want you to tell me the truth, Andrew. What do you think are the chances we'll bring Daniel back?"

Andrew wished the young man had not asked him. But since he had, Andrew would not lie. "I'd say it's a chance, but not a big one. Like Eli said, they're not botherin' right now to try and hide their trail. They're movin' fast to get way off out into their own country. But once they feel like they've put enough distance behind them that they can afford to slow down, they'll cover their tracks. We'll have a hard time of it then."

"If we don't get Daniel back, what'll happen to him?"

"I've never had any experience with Indians myself. I hear that if a boy shows a lot of fight they'll sometimes take a likin' to him and try to make him into a warrior."

"He was fightin' them right enough. I could see that. I just wish I could've been down there to help him."

"Him, they just took prisoner. You, they'd've killed."

"Like they did Papa." Zeb's voice went grim, the hatred coming through again.

Andrew said sternly, "If you don't get some rest, you'll fall out on us tomorrow. You go back yonder and lay down."

Mann's son Harlan came, after a while, and relieved Andrew of his duty. Andrew lay down on the edge of his blanket, drawing the rest of it over him. He lay with his eyes closed, still hearing the wolves talking to one another in the distance. The last image that came to him was Marie's.

He felt a hand on his shoulder and came suddenly awake. Eli Pleasant said, "Best be gittin' up, Andrew. It's time."

He smelled the faint aroma of parched grain being boiled as a substitute for coffee, down below the creek bank. He arose, rolling his blanket. Remembering, he looked around quickly to be assured that Zeb Willet had not carried out his threat and ridden on. To his query, Eli said, "Zeb's down yonder fixin' him a little bacon on a stick. Wouldn't be a bad idee if you done the same. No tellin' when we'll eat again."

It was still just as dark as when he had given up his watch and taken to his blanket. He saw not a sign of light to the east except the brilliance of stars. He looked at the Big Dipper for the time and knew it was about halfway between midnight and daylight. "It don't take long to spend the night," he commented.

Eli grunted. "For a man in my occupation, this is the best time of the day."

Fairweather gave thanks for the quick breakfast they bolted down. So far as Andrew had been able to tell, Michael had not spoken a word to the man, nor did he give any sign that he intended to. Michael was long at remembering and short at forgiving. Fairweather had a lot to be forgiven for.

They saddled their horses in the light of the stars and by unspoken common consent followed Michael as he set the course in the darkness. He heard one of the bachelors, Walker Younts, express a worry that they were going back the way they had come. Some people never learned a sense of direction. Andrew's had always been good, and Michael's was even better. Andrew knew Michael was leading them the right way. He started to say so but decided that if Michael wanted to be defended, he could do it himself.

Eli whispered urgently, "You better hush up, Younts. Voices travel a long ways in the night."

Andrew wondered if Eli was concerned about the Indians or about Michael.

Daylight found them many miles farther to the northwest. But it also found them off the trail, the very fear Michael had expressed. He said, "It may not be far, but then again it might. We'll just have to split up and find it."

Andrew suggested, "Why don't I angle off to the northeast and Eli to the northwest? The rest of you can keep on travelin' the way you're goin' so you don't lose too much time. One of us is bound to find it." He saw that Michael was about to come up with an argument; he probably preferred to go himself. Andrew quickly turned off and started northeastward, not giving his brother time to change the plan. He looked back in a minute and saw Eli headed off at an opposite angle. Michael motioned with his hand, and the other men resumed travel in the direction they had begun.

Andrew put his reluctant brown horse into a fast trot, for he had more distance to travel than Michael and the main body. He had ridden perhaps half a mile when he came upon the trail, as plain as it had been last night. It still led northwestward. Andrew saw a slight rise in the ground ahead and put the brown into a lope. He stopped there, saw the rest of the men at a considerable distance and waved his hat, hoping they would see him. They did not at first, but he kept waving. Shortly they stopped. One man went riding off northwestward, probably to find Eli, while the rest rode toward Andrew. Michael, always in the lead, gave him a wordless glance, looked a moment at the tracks, then turned to Zeb Willet.

"I reckon you were right. I'd hazard a guess that we've gained on them a little."

Andrew doubted that, but he supposed Michael was trying to make Zeb feel better. God knew he had little enough to feel good about.

Fairweather said, "I prayed for the trail to be plain. The Good Lord hears the pleas of those who believe."

Michael gave Fairweather not a glance. Michael believed in the Lord, but he had no faith in Fairweather. He said, "We'll be ridin', then. Eli and Walker can catch up to us in their own good time."

The two riders were an hour or so in rejoining the others. Eli glanced at the tracks as he pulled up beside Andrew. "Reckon how far ahead of us they'd be?"

Andrew looked around for Zeb. He did not want the youth to hear. Quietly he replied, "The better part of a day, I'd make it. They've got to stop sometime, or we've got to do a lot of catchin' up." He tried to read Eli's eyes for some sign of the old man's thoughts. Eli was a woodsman, and his judgment in matters of this sort was better than Andrew expected his own ever to be. But Eli's eyes were half closed, hiding whatever thoughts lay behind them. Andrew took no comfort.

They came at length to a wide forest of pine and oak and a tangle of undergrowth that made travel slow for a while. The tracks indicated some confusion among the Indians as they picked their way through it. Andrew surmised that they had struck it in the darkness. The trail led to a spring-fed creek. Charred remnants of wood showed that the Indians had built a couple of small fires here. Andrew held his hand low over one set of ashes but felt no warmth. Carefully he dug his fingers in, hoping to find some remnant of heat to indicate that the fire had not been out very long. He was disappointed, for the ashes were cold.

Michael asked no questions. Andrew's face evidently told him all he needed to know. Michael said, "Looks to me like they slept here." Several patches of grass were flattened where men had lain.

Andrew saw many moccasin tracks. After a bit he found a few tracks much smaller than the others, tracks that indicated the heel of a boot or shoe. He beckoned Zeb Willet and pointed. "They still had the boy with them here."

Zeb knelt and placed his hand over one of the tracks, as if he might thereby feel something of his brother's presence. He looked up hopefully. "That's a good sign, wouldn't you think? I mean, if they've brought him this far without killin' him, chances are they don't intend to kill him at all."

Andrew glanced at Eli for support. Eli said solemnly, "Likely as not, they figure on tradin' him. These Wacos, they're tradin' Indians. They swap with the Comanches for buffalo meat and hides, and sometimes horses. They occasionally trade captives too. They're like some white folks I know; they'll trade in anything that'll fetch a profit."

Zeb's eyes narrowed. "They'd trade off my brother?"

"There's other Indians that might take him for a slave. There's white folks who don't care how they get rich. They might buy him and make him work for them. Boy that age, he'll forget in a few years where he come from. I've seen some that couldn't even remember their daddy's and mama's names. All the slaves ain't black."

Zeb's jaw was set hard and grim as he stared at Eli. "They won't do that to Daniel. I'll find him or die."

Andrew said, "Let's don't talk about dyin'. Let's just find him."

The country began to take on more of a rolling, hilly aspect, frequent thickly wooded patches interspersed with the open meadows. In these, the heavy shade from the trees prevented grass from growing, and the thick matting of old leaves on the ground sometimes showed little sign of the Indians' passing. More than once, Michael was stopped cold. Andrew and Eli would ride forward, quietly taking over the search for the trail without being asked. Andrew suspected Michael would not request his help unless it came to a matter of life and death. The rest of the men would hold back without being told, for they respected Andrew's and Eli's abilities as trackers. Presently either Andrew or Eli would find enough of a trace to show they were on the right path, and the pursuit would proceed.

Andrew found it remarkable that no evident friction developed between the men. The nearest thing to harsh words came from the elder Mann when his son suggested that they ought to turn back and see to the wounded brother they had left at the Nathans'. The father said sharply, "This trouble started with us, even if not by our intention. We'll stay and see it through."

The two young bachelors, Smith and Younts, rode

close to Miles Nathan most of the time. First one and then the other asked him questions about his daughter Birdy. Nathan told them he was sure his daughter would appreciate their concern over her welfare, but she was much too young to show that appreciation in any tangible way. Andrew suspected he was wondering what kind of son-in-law one of them would make, a few years hence.

Fairweather rode in silence most of the time, just now and again requesting the Lord's favor when they encountered difficulty picking a path through one of the heavy thickets or tangled forests that blocked their way.

"This'll never be a fit country for civilized men," Quenton Mann declared. "I don't see how even the savage endures it."

Fairweather commented, "The Lord never meant for man to find life easy. He tests us at every turn to see if we are worthy."

Miles Nathan said, "This country is just waitin' for good men with axes and plows to come and make it blossom as the Lord intended."

Michael had spoken little, but he turned in his saddle and declared with an intensity that bordered on anger, "Lots of people seem to know just what the Lord wants without askin' Him. I ain't heard *Him* say to come in here and cut down His forests and plow up all the land. He must've had a purpose for it the way it is or He'd've made it different."

Nathan was taken aback. "I thought everyone understood that our mission in life as Americans is to go forth and tame the wilderness and bring it into the productive service of civilized mankind. That is why I brought my family to Texas."

Michael said curtly, "I never understood it that way atall. I like the looks of this country just the way it is."

Eli put in, "Then you'd better take a good look at it, because it won't stay this way long. I've seen it in other places: the forests go down, the houses go up, and the prairie goes under the plow. Almost makes me glad I'm such an old fart, because at least I've seen most of it the way it used to be. By the time you're my age there won't be none of it left."

"Progress," Nathan said. "Time does not stand still."

They came, in time, to a stream where the tracks seemed to disappear. They led off into the water but did not come out on the far side. Eli said, "Well, they've decided to start hidin' their trail. They probably figure they've put a lot of distance between them and the settlements, and they can afford the time to cover their tracks." Without waiting for Michael to make it official, he looked at Andrew. "Well, boy, I reckon it's a job for me and you. I'll go upstream. You go down."

Andrew glanced at Michael, who gave him no sign one way or the other. Andrew took the absence of a negative indication to be approval of sorts. As he turned downstream he heard Michael say, "Everybody had just as well rest their horses. We're apt to be here a while."

Andrew rode slowly, his gaze fixed intently on the north bank. He deemed it unlikely that the Indians would have turned south again, though that possibility could not be discounted entirely; they had a fox's cunning when it came to confounding their enemies. He had ridden a mile, perhaps nearer two, without seeing anything. Suddenly the brown horse jerked its head up and poked both ears forward, alert. Andrew drew rein and held his breath while he raised his long rifle up from his lap, ready.

For a minute he stood still in the stream, seeing and hearing nothing. Then a sound came to him, the sound a horse makes when it grazes, cropping off the grass. He held his breath again, listening hard. The sound continued, unhurried and undisturbed. Gently he walked the brown up out of the water and onto the north bank. He dismounted quietly, tied the horse, then crouched low and began making his way toward the sound. He kept to the timber, letting it screen his movement. He came in a minute to a small clearing. The first thing he saw was the disturbed ground leading up out of the stream. Someone had dragged a branch over the sand, obviously trying to rub away the tracks. But the surface had a brushed look and was still damp from the water the horses had dripped as they came up onto the bank. A few more hours and it would have been difficult, perhaps impossible, to see.

Andrew's blood went to ice. He stiffened, his hands cramped on the rifle. Forty feet ahead, a dark-skinned Indian boy sat leaning against a tree. For a moment Andrew thought the boy was looking at him. Then he realized the lad did not see him. He was asleep.

14

Andrew puzzled over this unlikely development, catching an Indian asleep, his horse staked out to graze. This was a lad in his teens, not the full-grown warrior Andrew would have expected. And to find him this way! This was not the omnipotent Indian vigilance he had heard legends about as long as he could remember.

The boy appeared to be alone. He was dressed only in a breechclout and moccasins. A small leather medicine pouch was suspended from his neck. It moved up and down with the steady rhythm of his breathing. His face was heavily tattooed.

This was the closest Andrew had ever been to an Indian, not counting the tame ones he used to see back in the Tennessee settlements from time to time. He had to stare and wonder. A boy! That he had been a member of the raiding party seemed likely. Probably he had been left here to watch for pursuit. Had he been vigilant he would have heard Andrew coming and could have hurried forward to warn the others. But he was merely a boy, not a warrior grown. If the others had left him here as a test of his manhood, his qualification to become a warrior, he had failed the test. Eternal vigilance was too much to expect of such a youth. The ride had been long, and he had been tired. He had probably put forth his best effort to remain awake, but the demands of nature would not be denied.

Andrew pondered what he should do. Some men would simply kill the boy in his sleep and declare good riddance. They would say that a dead Indian boy would not grow up to kill settlers and prevent the taking of tribal lands that had been too long in the pagan service of savages. Certainly that would be the easiest thing, for the boy was vulnerable. But Andrew gave that notion no more than a moment's passing consideration. An alternative would be to take the lad prisoner. But what would he do with him once he had him?

He decided to do nothing except retreat and leave the boy lying where he was, undisturbed. He returned quietly to the brown horse, mounted, and rode once more in the direction from which he had come.

He found most of the men stretched out on the ground, taking their rest while they could. As Andrew rode up, Michael asked with his eyes. They had quarreled, and pride would not let him speak the question aloud.

Andrew nodded. "I found the trail. It's headed just about due north. Found somethin' else, too."

Zeb Willet came quickly to stand beside Andrew's horse. "Sign of my brother?" he asked eagerly.

"No, but I found an Indian boy asleep over yonder. I figure they left him to watch and see if anybody was comin'. He was just too give out to stay with the job."

Michael had to speak to him then. "What did you do to him?"

"Nothin'. Left him just like I found him."

"He'll flush like a quail when he sees us. He'll probably beat us to wherever the rest of them are goin', because he knows where that is and we don't."

Andrew frowned. "You know I couldn't just kill him."

Zeb Willet's face clouded with hatred. "*I* could."

Miles Nathan argued, "If we captured him, maybe we could get him to tell where they're takin' your brother."

Andrew argued, "How? I doubt that even Eli can talk the Waco language."

Michael said, "He can talk with signs, though. Just about all Indians can understand that." He turned to Joe Smith. "You'd better ride upstream and fetch Eli. We'll go on and see if we can catch that Indian. You-all find us."

Uneasiness stirred in Andrew. Likely as not somebody would become over eager and shoot the youngster. He argued, "That boy probably wouldn't tell us anything if we burned him at the stake. I know which way the tracks were goin'. All we have to do is circle north and find them. The boy don't need to know we ever even came by."

Michael seemed to give serious consideration to his argument, but some of the others did not wait. Zeb Willet got on his horse. Quenton Mann and his son followed suit, then Miles Nathan and Walker Younts. Nathan said, "It's a chance," and turned to go with the others.

Shrugging, Michael got on his bay horse. He

jerked his head as a signal for Andrew to come along. Michael spurred out to circle the men and take the lead. He motioned for them to slow down, for they had put their horses into a lope. "He'll hear us comin' for a mile," he warned. The men eased their mounts to a walk, though Zeb Willet was reluctant. Andrew could see that the young man was keyed to a nervous pitch.

They had ridden a mile and more when Michael raised his hand to signal a halt. He turned, searching out Andrew. "How far now?"

Andrew pointed. "Just up yonder, past that bend in the creek." He looked around anxiously. "We don't have to kill him."

Michael was the only one who offered any acknowledgment. "We'll take him alive if we can."

They crossed over the stream to the north side and proceeded in a slower walk, the horses' hoofs making little sound on the mat of old decaying leaves and the thin scattering of grass upon the stream's higher bank. At length Andrew said, "We're gettin' close. I'd say maybe a hundred yards."

Michael nodded. "All right, me and you and Walker'll circle around past him, then come back on him from the other side. The rest of you give us a couple minutes, then come ahead. Everybody remember, we want to take him alive. You can't find out much from a dead Indian."

Andrew felt his pulse quickening as they made their arc, carrying them past the point where the boy should be. He heard a horse nicker. It could have been the boy's, or it could have been one of the others, becoming aware of the Indian pony.

Michael declared, "That spilled it. Let's go!"

They were too late. Before Andrew could see

anything, he heard shouts, then the boom of a gun-shot. The shouts subsided. He and Michael and Walker Younts broke out into the small clearing where he had seen the boy. The young Indian lay twisted on the ground, a small pool slowly spreading from beneath him.

Michael declared, "I thought I said—" He stopped then, staring at the elder Mann, bent over in his saddle. An arrow protruded from his leg, above the knee.

Zeb Willet exclaimed, "I had to do it. He put an arrow into Quenton, and he was goin' after him with a tomahawk. I had to do it."

Mann's son Harlan cried, "Paw!" He rode his horse up close and grasped the shaft of the arrow to pull it out. His father cried in pain and grabbed his son's hand, pushing it away.

Michael said, "We got to get him down off that horse and see what we can do for him." He dismounted quickly. Andrew and Walker Younts stepped to the ground and reached up to help Mann down from the saddle. Mann gritted his teeth but had to cry out in agony as he swung his leg over the horse. Andrew and Younts eased him to the ground.

Young Mann declared almost in panic, "Paw's bleedin' to death."

Andrew said, "He needs to bleed to wash away the poison. But that arrow's got to come out." He glanced around to see if anyone would volunteer.

Quenton Mann, cold sweat breaking across his face, looked up expectantly at his son. "It's your place to do it for me, Harlan. We're family."

Harlan trembled, eyes brimming with tears. "I can't."

Andrew said, "I'll do it, Quenton."

Mann's voice took on a stern edge, through the pain. "No, Harlan'll do it. He's got the strength. He's just got to work himself up to it."

Miles Nathan took a small tobacco pouch from his pocket. "Here, Quenton. Somethin' for you to bite down on."

Mann took it. "Come on, son. Let's get it over with."

Harlan's shaking hands grasped the shaft. He closed his eyes for a moment, gathering his nerve, then jerked. Quenton bit down hard on the leather pouch but screamed in spite of that. Andrew thought for a moment that Mann was going to lose consciousness. Blood welled from the wound.

Harlan stared at the arrow shaft in white-faced dismay. Its bloodied end was bare. "The head didn't come out. It's still in there."

No one spoke for a minute. Quenton Mann shuddered in shock, his breathing rapid and heavy.

Michael said, "It's got to come out. It'll fester in there till the whole leg mortifies. He'll die." He brought a skinning knife out of its scabbard on his belt.

Harlan Mann protested, "You can't. You'll kill him."

"It's got to be done."

Harlan demanded, "Did you ever cut an arrowhead out of anybody before?"

Michael conceded that he never had.

The Reverend Fairweather stepped forward. "I have. Arrowheads, bullets. In my former occupation I was called upon many times." He took the knife from Michael's hand. "Somebody should build a fire. We need to cleanse the blade. While we wait, I shall consult with a higher power." He turned away, walking off to the edge of the timber and standing with his head bowed.

Michael stared at him in disbelief while Andrew and Younts quickly struck up a spark with flint and steel and built it into a small fire.

Zeb Willet had turned the young Indian over onto his back. The eyes were open and staring, but they no longer saw. Zeb said over and over, "I had to do it. I just had to."

Fairweather held the knife blade into the flames for a minute, then said, "It'll take a couple of you to hold him." Andrew took Mann's arms, Younts the legs. Harlan held his father's hand.

Mann screamed when the blade entered the wound, and he almost burst free from Andrew's firm hold. Then he slumped, suddenly limp. Harlan cried fearfully, "He's dead."

Fairweather shook his head. "No, lad, it's just the Lord's mercy. He has allowed your father to fall unconscious so that he feels no more of the pain. It is no easy life He had given us on this earth."

The blood flowed freely, and Fairweather had to work by feel rather than sight. Andrew watched the one-eyed man sweat nervously as he probed, finding the arrowhead, almost getting it, losing it, then getting it again. Slowly, gingerly, he worked it upward with the tip of the blade.

"Hurry," Harlan cried. "He'll bleed to death."

"Hush, lad," Fairweather said. "Trust."

The arrowhead floated out on a sudden fountain of blood. Fairweather caught it in his fingers and held it up for all to see. He let the wound bleed a little more for cleansing, then said to Younts, "You'll find some bandaging cloth in my saddlebag. Fetch it for me, please."

Andrew looked at him in surprise. "You brought cloth to make bandages?" Such an idea had not even crossed his mind.

Fairweather replied, "Experience, young gentleman. One rarely ventures upon a mission of this kind without seeing the spilling of blood. My former life was not without its useful experience."

Eli Pleasant and Joe Smith rode up about the time Fairweather got the bleeding slowed. Fairweather said to Harlan, "Son, I have one more harsh duty to perform before I bandage this wound. I do not think you want to see it. Please, take your leave for a few minutes."

Harlan stared at him in doubt but accepted and walked away. Fairweather said, "Andrew, your powderhorn, please."

He uncapped it and poured black powder around and into the wound, then handed the horn back to Andrew. "Flint and steel, please." He struck a spark. The powder flared. Quenton Mann went into a spasm and screamed again. Andrew smelled burned flesh and felt his stomach turn.

Eli edged up close to Andrew. He had lived a hard life and had seen many bitter things, but this sickened him too, a little. Andrew said tightly, "If it was me, I think I'd sooner just die."

Eli grunted. "You say that now, but if you was in Mann's place you'd want all the help anybody could give you. Whatever Fairweather may be otherwise, he knows about doctorin'."

Michael said, "Damned rough butcher, if you ask me."

Zeb Willet knelt again beside the young Indian. A tear ran down his cheeks into soft, youthful whiskers. He said in a breaking voice, "I thought

I wanted to kill them all. But this is just a kid. He's not a whole lot older than Daniel. And I killed him."

Michael placed a hand on the youth's shoulder. "You wasn't given a choice. If he'd've killed you he wouldn't've sat up all night worryin' about it. Fortunes of war—"

Eli commented, "The boy was probably left behind to prove he could be trusted as a warrior. He went to sleep, which he shouldn't've done. But he put up a fight, so I guess he went out as a warrior sure enough."

Andrew looked at Quenton Mann, who had regained consciousness and was struggling not to lose it again. "Odd the way things turn sometimes. It was Quenton who killed an Indian down yonder and started everything to happenin'. Now, out of everybody here, it's him the kid puts an arrow in."

Miles Nathan remarked, "Three people dead, two wounded, one carried off. All for a few horses. Where's the sense of it?"

Eli declared, "There ain't no sense to it. That's just the way life is. But everybody wants to live it as long as they can. I expect Zeb's little brother is scared to death he's fixin' to lose his. We'd better be gettin' on about what we come for."

Harlan said, "Paw can't ride. And we can't just leave him."

Quenton Mann declared in a hoarse voice scarred with pain, "Like hell you can't. You have to. Just leave me a little food and my horse. I'll lay here till I get to feelin' better; then I'll start for home."

Harlan argued, "I'll stay with you."

"No, son, they'll need everybody. You'll go with them and tote your load. You've got my part to do now as well as your own. Go, and see that you do a good and proper job of it."

Joe Smith and Walker Younts dragged the Indian boy's body to the stream and caved off a section of steep bank to cover it.

Eli started dragging up dry deadfall timber and piling it where Mann could reach it. Nathan and Zeb helped him. Eli said, "That boy ain't buried very deep. The smell of him is liable to draw wolves. Come night, Quenton, if you ain't travelin' by then, you'd better build yourself a good fire to keep them away. They'll take the scent of your wounded leg and see you as meat."

Mann nodded grimly. "I'll be all right. You all go get that young'un back."

The men mounted their horses and prepared to go. Harlan hugged his father. As Harlan turned to leave, Quenton reached out and gripped his son's arm for a moment. "Go, son, and do your duty."

15

The going was slow, and at times Andrew almost despaired. He remembered what Eli had said at the beginning, that a time would come when the Indians would seem to have disappeared. It was as if they had been swept up into the clouds. The trail, what there was of it, had grown cold. Often the searching party lost it and hunted for hours, finally finding some vague sign like horse droppings or old moribund grass stems bent and broken by hoofs. Andrew kept watching apprehensively a slow buildup of clouds to the west. Rain would wash away whatever little hope they still had of following the trail to its conclusion.

Andrew sensed restiveness in most of the party, even in Michael. Other men might already have admitted defeat and turned back. If any of these harbored such feelings, they were silenced by the driving determination in young Zeb Willet. The darker the prospects, the grimmer the set of his jaw became. Andrew was reminded of stout-hearted dogs back in Tennessee, trained to work cattle. They would grab a recalcitrant animal by the nose. The harder the cow fought, the deeper the dog's teeth bit in. The dog almost invariably won. Zeb avoided making a challenge of it, but he made it clear by his attitude that if the others turned back, he would go on alone.

Without exception, every man on this expedition came from a frontier heritage, a history of generation after generation moving farther out into the wilderness, each in its own time. That heritage was a driving force which impelled them onward now, not seriously considering abandonment of one of their own to continue a solitary quest that would probably result in his death. And somewhere out yonder, a frightened boy was probably looking back, wondering if anyone was coming for him. Everyone knew, and no one spoke of giving up.

The food they had brought was rapidly being depleted. There was no question of hunting, though they saw deer as well as smaller game, and on the open prairies now and again a few buffalo. The sound of a gunshot would racket far, they had no idea what the distance might be to Indian ears. They began stretching the food that still remained, eating berries when they found them. They paused to fish in the occasional stream they came across, usually with indifferent results. It was not a generous land to men who dared not use their firearms.

"Beautiful country," Michael enthused. "You ever seen prettier, Eli?"

"Mighty wild," Eli replied with reserve.

"That's what makes it so beautiful."

"If I was a younger man, maybe I could appreciate it more. And if you wasn't a man with a family—"

Andrew grinned. Eli could say it aloud without arousing Michael to a heated defense. Andrew could not.

Michael said only, "I wasn't talkin' about movin' here. I was just talkin' about the look of it."

"Somebody'll come along after us and settle. Then others'll come in behind him, and first thing you know it'll all look like San Felipe."

Andrew saw nothing wrong with that. San Felipe was a right nice place, with prospects. A hundred years from now there was no telling how big and important it would be.

The first sign that they might be nearing an Indian village was close-cropped grass and the tracks of many horses. Eli recognized the implications before Andrew did. In his smuggling operations he had often traded with Indian tribes in the region north and west of Nacogdoches. Eli knelt, careful about his rheumy knees, and examined the grass. Andrew dismounted and knelt with him, eager to learn.

Eli said, "They grazed their pony herd here yesterday or maybe the day before. They don't let their horses graze too far from the village. Afraid some other tribe'll run them off."

"Whichaway is it apt to be?"

Eli kept looking until he found the tracks moving in a definite direction. "They just loose-herded the horses to graze. But here's where they gathered them up and started drivin' them. Yonderway. Yonderway's the village. Where we find it we'll find a river or a creek, or at least a good clear spring. Indians are like the rest of us: they got to have water."

Andrew felt his pulse quickening. He looked up at Michael, still in the saddle, and saw exhilaration in his brother's eyes.

Zeb Willet said excitedly, "That's where Daniel is, then."

Eli held up his hand as a sign for caution. "Likely, boy, most likely. But where exactly? We got to know for certain before we can do anything. We can't just ride in there and tell them to give him to us. And if we get the camp stirred up, like as not they'll kill him out of hand just to keep us from gettin' him back. No, sir, we got to be as sneaky as coyotes about this thing. And patient."

"It's hard to be patient, knowin' we're so close to him."

"Your mama has already got enough to cry over. Let's don't be hasty and give her more grief." Eli studied the landscape. He pointed to a wood, lying half a mile to the east. "Michael, if you say so, we can hide ourselves over yonder till dark. We're out in the open here. There's always a danger some Waco'll come ridin' over the hill and see us."

Michael accepted the suggestion with a nod. Eli and Andrew remounted. Andrew kept looking back over his shoulder as they rode to the thicket, expecting any minute to see Indians appear. The riders made it into the deep shadows of the timber without being discovered.

Eli said, "Close as we are, we better not be buildin' a fire. The smell of smoke can carry a long ways."

Michael replied ruefully, "We got damn little left to cook anyway."

The men unsaddled their horses to give them a chance to rest. Zeb Willet did not. He trembled in excitement. "I can't just wait here, knowin' I'm so close to Daniel. I want to go scout around and see what I can find."

Michael said sternly, "You'll find an arrow, and we'll have to try and explain to your mama how come we lost both of her boys." He unsaddled Zeb's horse, leaving no room for argument.

Most of the men sat or lay down to rest. Andrew tried, but he found himself almost as nervous as Zeb. He studied the timber, a random mixture of almost every kind of wood he had seen grow in Texas. "Odd," he said to Eli, "how we'll go along and have long stretches of open prairie, and then we'll run into thickets like this on ground that otherwise looks the same."

Eli nodded. "Seems to be like that over the biggest part of Texas that I've seen. Must be the soil that makes the difference. Ain't always clear to the eye, but there's somethin' in part of it that likes to grow trees, and somethin' in other places that likes to grow grass. Me, I'm like the deer and the wild critters; I take it as it comes and don't ask for reasons."

"I'm wonderin' how far these woods reach to the north. You said the Indian village has got to be on a river or creek or somethin'. Reckon these woods reach to the water?"

"They might."

"And just about anywhere you find a river or a creek, you'll find timber. I was just thinkin' that if me and you was to follow this forest north, we might find cover to hide us all the way to the village."

"Nighttime, we won't need cover. The dark'll do that."

"But in the night we may not be able to see where

they're keepin' that boy. If we would watch in the daytime, maybe we could see him and know where to go for him tonight."

Eli considered for only a moment, then pushed stiffly to his feet. "I've rested up already."

Zeb had been listening. "I'm goin' with you."

Andrew had rather he didn't, but he realized the young man could not be denied. "You know the odds are against us. You know the woods may run out, or if they don't, we would watch that village all day and not see Daniel. I'm wonderin' if you're ready to handle that kind of disappointment without doin' somethin' that'll get you killed. Us too maybe."

"I'll be all right. You just give me a try."

Michael saw them saddling their horses and came to find out what they were about to do. Andrew did not answer. Eli explained, cagily making it sound like his own idea, for Michael would have rejected it had he known it was Andrew's. Michael said, "I'll be goin' with you."

Eli shook his head. "These other men look to you to lead them. With you gone they might get restless and do somethin' foolish. Besides, the fewer of us go, the less likely it is that we'll be seen." He swung into the saddle, giving Michael no time to think of a rebuttal. "You-all ready?"

Andrew and Zeb fell in beside him. "Ready."

They moved off quickly, leaving Michael standing there trying to think up reasons to counter Eli's explanation. They worked their way through the timber with some difficulty, dodging low limbs that threatened to drag them from their horses and briars that tried to snare and hold them.

Andrew said, "This'd be mean travelin' in the dark."

Eli responded, "In the dark we won't have to."

As Andrew hoped, the wood extended over the hill and down the other side. Without ever leaving it, they came in an hour or so to taller, bigger trees that lined a clear-running river. Eli glanced at Andrew. Words were not necessary, but his eyes said it: *Your hunch was right.*

They rode upstream, for judging by the horse tracks they had found earlier, that was where the village had to be. It was not necessary for anyone to say they had to be especially watchful or careful. After a little while Andrew heard something to the west and reined up, standing in the stirrups to listen. It came again, the distant barking of a dog, answered by another. Eli's gaze met his for a moment and confirmed his feeling. *We're getting close.*

Andrew began to watch Zeb with some apprehension. He was still concerned that young Willet would forget himself and do something rash. But Zeb managed to contain whatever feelings might be building inside, threatening to burst into the open. Andrew touched his arm. "You goin' to be all right?"

Zeb nodded, not speaking.

They rode another hundred yards, then Andrew saw something move and made a quick gesture with his hand. The three riders drew into the heaviest timber they could see. A tattooed young Indian rode his horse down to the river and paused to let it drink. He carried a deer in front of him.

Eli whispered, "They'll have somethin' to eat in his lodge tonight."

Andrew's stomach growled, reminding him how little he had eaten. "I wish we were on friendly terms. I'd like some of that myself."

When the horse had drunk its fill, the Indian crossed the river and then followed its bank westward. Eli said, "Now we know the village is yonderway, and on the other side."

They heard more noise as they proceeded, more barking of dogs, the distant shouting of children at play. At length they spotted the pony herd, scattered at some distance on the south side of the river. So far as Andrew could see, it was being held by just two riders.

"Boys," Eli said. "That's a job they turn over to the young'uns to teach them how to be responsible. Unless they're lookin' to be attacked. In that case, they send the good warriors out."

"Then they're not lookin' for us," Andrew said, taking comfort in that. "They didn't expect anybody would ever trail them this far. Maybe nobody ever has."

Zeb declared, "Maybe nobody has ever had to try and follow a stolen brother before."

The smell of smoke began to reach them, becoming heavier as they rode slowly and watchfully. Sometimes it carried the scent of roasting meat, which only added to Andrew's discomfort. He saw then the round, grass-thatched huts which he had been told were a mark of the Wacos. Horseback tribes farther west used tepees, covered with buffalo hides, but these were Indians who stayed put, more or less, and built lodges for comfort and a degree of permanence.

Eli nodded toward a dense thicket and dismounted. Andrew and Zeb followed him as he led his horse there and tied him. Eli said, "From here, we'd best go afoot, and be careful as if we was rabbits prowlin' around a wolf's den."

The smoke seemed to drift into the thicket and settle there like fog. Andrew's nerves were drawn tight as a fiddle string. He studied Zeb, wondering if they had indeed made a mistake bringing the youth along. Zeb's eyes were wide with excitement. Beads of sweat were rising on his face. His whole body trembled. "Zeb, maybe you better stay with the horses."

"No. I've come to see, so I'll see."

They worked carefully through the wood, stopping often to listen for any change in the sounds, any sign of discovery. At the least, Andrew expected a loud reception from the village dogs. But the wind, such as it was, blew in their favor. It gave them the smoke, but it also kept their scent from reaching some sharp-nosed cur.

Eli was a couple of paces in the lead. He motioned quickly for Andrew and Zeb to drop, and he flattened himself to the ground. A moment later, two young boys appeared upon the creek bank, splashing their horses across with happy yelps and proceeding out of sight. They both looked about the age of the one Zeb had killed on the trail. Remembering young Willet's early declaration that he wanted to kill them all, Andrew worried. But though Zeb watched the boys with keen eyes, he gave no sign that he contemplated anything foolish. He had killed once; he seemed not eager to do it again.

Eli waited a couple of minutes to see if any more might be coming along. Satisfied, he pushed to his feet and went on. Andrew and Zeb followed, crouching to present as little profile as possible.

Presently Eli beckoned them to come up even with him. He had found a vantage point from which they could observe most of the village and yet be screened by the low, thorny vegetation. "It's a good place to watch from," he said. "I just hope there'll be somethin' to see."

The thing that caught Andrew's eye was a field, or perhaps a succession of gardens, in which corn grew much like his own at home, and melons and squash and the like. Several women stooped over the plants, pulling weeds. He thought he could enjoy one of those melons right now.

The village was a random scattering of grass-covered huts, their shape and general appearance reminding him considerably of beehives. The grass was sun-bleached, well-weathered. That, and the lush field, told him that though this might be a warrior society, these people were not nomads. Studying the huts, he realized they had one door to the east, another to the west. That could be useful information if they determined in which one the Willet boy might be held. He saw smoke curling from the tops of a few huts and wondered how the Wacos could have a fire inside without its catching the dry grass ablaze and sending the whole structure up in flames. He saw women scraping deerhides and cutting meat into strips for curing in the sun. Men lounged in the shade of the trees or the grass huts. Children played, rolling hoops made of willow switches, much like children in Tennessee, or around San Felipe.

Andrew looked in vain for sign of Daniel Willet. "Where *is* he?" he demanded after a long, silent wait. His voice had an edge of desperation about it.

"Patience," Eli counseled. "He's in one of them huts, I'm thinkin'. But which one, there ain't no tellin'. And we can't go pokin' in every one of them to find out. Just keep watchin'."

In the west, clouds built, dark and ominous. Much of the day Andrew had watched them and worried that a rain might come and wipe out the tracks. It did not matter now, for the tracks were no longer an issue. The clouds boiled up and covered the sun, and suddenly the air had a little of a chill about it. A distant rumble of thunder told him a spring storm was building to the west.

The rumble brought several men out of their huts to look. One hurried over to where some boys were practicing marksmanship with small bows. His hand movements suggested that he was giving brisk orders. The marksmanship contest broke up, and the boys scattered. Presently Andrew saw several of them start carrying firewood into the huts. He remembered the many times he had hurried to replenish the supply of dry wood for his mother in the face of a threatening rain. It struck him that in many ways these Indians were similar to his own people.

Zeb Willet grabbed Andrew's arm. In silence, he pointed, his face suddenly ashen. For a moment Andrew was puzzled, searching the village for whatever had caught Zeb's attention. Then he saw. Three boys had come out of a hut, followed by a man. The man wore only a loincloth, as did two of the boys. But the third wore shirt and trousers, ribboned and torn. That boy paused, looking back at the man in some confusion. The man pointed toward a pile of wood, then back to the hut. The two Indian boys shouted at the other one. At the distance Andrew could not distinguish their voices from others originating in the camp, but he suspected by their attitude that they were derisive.

Andrew glanced at Zeb. "Daniel?" he whispered.

Zeb nodded grimly. Movement in his throat suggested he was too choked to speak.

The boy reached down to pick up a stick. One of the Indian boys already had one, and he struck Daniel across the back. Daniel spun around, grasping his stick in both hands, swinging it hard. He connected against the Indian boy's head. The Indian boy went down. The other boy ran up and jumped on Daniel, knocking him to the ground. The two rolled in the dirt, punching at each other. The man stood for a minute, watching, then moved in to break up the fight. He pointed to the clouds in the west, then to the wood again. When Daniel stood back in an attitude of defiance, the man picked up the fallen stick and shook it threateningly at him. Daniel surrendered, after a minute, and began gathering wood. The boy who had been struck picked up another stick and moved toward Daniel with a vengeance, but the man cuffed him and put him back to the task at hand. The three boys carried an armload of wood apiece into the hut.

Eli grunted in satisfaction. "Well, at least we won't have to go knockin' on everybody's door tonight."

Zeb agonized, "I don't know how I can leave him down there another minute."

"You've got to. He's taken it this long. He can take it a few more hours. The boy's got a lot of fight in him."

Andrew said, "So've the Indians. Ridin' in there may be easy. Ridin' out could be a little meaner."

Eli grunted agreement. "If you come up with a better notion, I expect we'll all be ready to hear it. For now, though, I believe we've seen about enough. We better be gettin' back to the others."

16

Andrew let Eli and Zeb do the talking. He stood back and watched Michael's face as the old man and the young one described the village. Michael frowned deeply, listening. He asked, "Are you sure you can find the right hut? They'll look alike in the dark."

Eli said, "The one the young'un's in has another behind it, raised way up off the ground. They got food stored underneath. I hear tell they make the young girls sleep up there on the high floor with the ladder taken down so the boys can't get to them. I doubt as it works very good. In my day it wouldn't've."

Zeb declared, "It don't matter how dark, I'll know which one Daniel is in. I'll feel it."

Michael gave him a glance that spoke more of sympathy than of belief. "I'd a lot sooner go by seein' than by feelin'." He looked back at Eli. "You said those huts look like beehives. They'll buzz like beehives too, the minute we go in there. We're apt to have the whole tribe down on us before we can get out."

Andrew felt a nervous itching along his backside. A vague idea had come to him as they were riding back along the river. He hesitated to bring it up for fear Michael would automatically reject any idea of his. But perhaps he could plant the seed and let Michael believe the idea had been his own.

"Eli," Andrew said, "somethin's bothered me about them grass huts. How can they build a fire inside without burnin' the place down?"

Eli explained, "They put the fire right in the middle, with stones around it and a hole in the roof for the smoke to go out. They don't let the fire get too big. One good spark could put them out of house and home in a minute."

Michael's eyes brightened. Andrew saw that the seed had sprouted. Michael turned away for a minute or so, staring off into the distance. Then he announced, "It just come to me how we can get their attention away from the hut where they're keepin' the boy. We'll set off a couple of huts on the far side. While they're all rushin' to try and stop it, we'll run in and grab Zeb's brother."

Eli said, "Seems to me like that's what Andy Jackson used to call a *dy*-version."

Miles Nathan declared, "Whatever you call it, it sounds good to me."

Zeb Willet said, "I'm with you, Michael."

Michael frowned at Andrew. "I'm surprised you didn't think of it yourself."

Andrew suppressed a smile. "I don't have your experience."

Michael looked to the west, where the sun had

dropped below the horizon and a heavy cloud was rapidly bringing night's darkness upon the woods. A rumble of thunder shook the ground. He said, "If it sets in to rainin', that accidental fire is apt to be hard to start."

Andrew turned to the man with the eye patch. "Then, Reverend, looks to me like it's time you prayed for dry weather."

They waited for full dark. Lightning was flashing to the west when they started. Michael led them out of the timber, but only far enough that they could ride unimpeded by the tangle of trees and the clutching of briars. They were always near enough to the wood that they could quickly pull back into its protective cover. Andrew worried that the bright flashes of lightning might give them away if anyone was alert in the village, or guarding its perimeter.

Eli tried to ease his mind. "Indians don't seem to've ever caught the white man's likin' for guard duty, unless they've got a strong feelin' there's an enemy about. Most of the time they don't bother with settin' up a watch. They just turn that over to the dogs and go to sleep."

The men fell silent. Though they rode in a body, each was alone with his own somber thoughts. In a while they reached the place where the village's horses were loose-herded on an open patch of grassland. Andrew watched for guards in the occasional flash of distant lightning. He saw none, but he knew there must be one or two, at least, preventing the horses from straying away in the night. They probably had little thought of attack by an outside enemy.

Walker Younts said, "This thing all started with

the Wacos stealin' horses. It would pay them back good and proper if we was to run away with that whole herd. They'd be worth a fair dollar back in the settlements."

Michael replied, "They'd slow us down and get us caught up with. We're here to get that boy back, and nothin' else." He paused. "What's more, if we can get away without havin' to kill any more Indians, it'll help our chances. Kill one of them and they're liable to hound us all the way home."

Harlan Mann pointed out, "We killed and buried one already, the one that wounded Paw."

"They ain't missed him yet. Chances are they'll never know what come of him."

Reaching the river, the riders moved along its south bank until the smell of smoke began to mix with the pleasant hint of rain on the breeze from the cloudy west.

"Wind's still on our side," Eli noted quietly. "If we're careful, maybe we won't stir up the camp dogs."

The breeze carried a faint sound of singing. At least, Andrew guessed it was singing. To his ears it was discordant, unlike any music he had known.

Zeb worried, "I hope that's not a scalp song or somethin'. You don't reckon they're fixin' to burn Daniel at the stake?"

Eli reassured him. "I never heard of these Indians doin' such as that. If they intended to kill him they'd've done it at the start, like they done to your daddy." He pointed. "I expect this is a good place for us to cross the river. Village is right up yonder."

They eased into the water and let their horses drink. Done, they moved up over the north bank and halted. This was very near the spot from which Andrew and Zeb and Eli had watched earlier. Andrew could make out the vague outlines of many huts. Some had a faint glow from fires built inside, though most looked dark. A few outdoor fires made tiny pinpoints of light. Andrew studied the scene a minute, then pointed. "That's the hut where they had Daniel."

Zeb and Eli agreed.

Michael was silent for a time, concentrating his thoughts upon the village. "Where's the door?" It was too dark for him to see that kind of detail.

Eli said, "These huts have generally got two doors, one on the east and one on the west. The back door faces this side."

"Then we ought to be able to go in without havin' to be exposed to the center of the camp. Now, if somebody could sneak around yonder and touch off a couple of the huts on the far side, it'd draw the attention over that way."

Younts volunteered. "That's a good job for me and Joe."

Eli said, "I'll go and stand guard while they do the honors."

Michael accepted. "Try not to let anybody see you. It'll be better if they don't realize they've been invaded. Get the fires started, then h'ist your tails back to here. This is where we'll leave the horses."

Michael looked at Zeb Willet. "We don't want to make any mistakes in the dark and find out we've carried off some Indian boy instead of your brother. You want to go with me into the hut?"

Zeb nodded grimly. "That's the only way I'd have it."

Andrew declared, "Two won't be enough. I'm goin' in with you." His voice was firm. Michael frowned but did not disagree.

Fairweather said, "That still leaves three of us."

Michael yielded him a quick, distrustful glance, then said to Miles Nathan, "I want a good responsible man to stay here and hold onto the horses. If any of them was to get away from us, we'd be in a bad fix."

Nathan nodded assent. "You can depend on the reverend and me."

Michael did not seem to care whether Fairweather assented or not.

Fairweather said, "I will ask the Lord's hand to guide you."

Michael ignored him. Andrew, however, said, "We'd take that kindly."

Harlan Mann asked, "What do you want me to do?"

Michael said, "You'll go with us halfway and stand guard to make sure nobody cuts us off from gettin' back to the horses."

Andrew's pulse quickened as Michael dismounted. Michael said, "All right, Eli, you-all get started. We'll wait till the village is in an uproar, then we'll go in."

Eli beckoned Younts and Smith with his chin. "*Vámanos,*" he said, using Spanish without giving a thought to whether they understood. In seconds the three riders were swallowed up in darkness. Lightning flashed, but Andrew could no longer see them.

Michael handed his reins to Nathan. He looked at Andrew and Zeb. "No shootin' unless there's no way around it. We don't want to pull anybody's attention away from the fire."

Andrew could see Zeb's hands visibly trembling as he handed his reins to Fairweather. "Steady," Andrew said. "With luck, we'll be away from here pretty soon." But he could feel his own hands shaking a little, and cold sweat broke on his forehead. He stared at the quiet hut which they had targeted, and he wondered how many people inside might be inclined to fight. He wiped his wet palms against his trousers.

Michael gave him a critical study. "Maybe *you* better stay and help hold the horses."

Andrew retorted, "You won't have to be lookin' back, wonderin' where I'm at. I'll be in front of you."

"Not too far in front. That's like bein' by yourself."

Crouching, the three moved away from the river, closer to the edge of the village. Somewhere to the north a dog barked, and other dogs picked up the call. Andrew was heartened to see that they aroused no particular interest among the villagers. One man stepped out of a hut and spoke threateningly. His dog stopped barking, but others did not.

Michael raised his hand. "Far enough. We'll wait."

The wait seemed an hour long. Andrew began wondering how long it would take three men to circle the village on horseback and start a fire.

Zeb was having the same thoughts. "Reckon they got caught?"

Michael said, "We'd be hearin' a lot of excitement. Things are pretty quiet."

Andrew could hear the singing continue from a hut somewhere away from the perimeter. He began to wonder if setting one of these grass structures afire might be more difficult than it sounded.

Then, on the far side of the village, flames began to lick up the side of a hut, and they burst suddenly atop a second hut nearby. A woman screamed, and children shouted. In the glow Andrew saw people running from the two huts. Within moments, excited voices were raised all over the village. Against the growing flames, he could see people hurrying in all directions. They poured out of other huts, some running toward the fires and some away. The west wind picked up sparks and then firebrands. A third hut began to burn.

Zeb raised up, ready to go. Michael touched his arm. "Wait a minute. We need to allow time for Eli and them to get back. When we leave this place, we'll want to be leavin' fast and not have to wait for nobody."

Andrew's mouth was dry. He was glad there was no need for words, because the tightness of his throat might not have let him speak. He sensed that Michael was counting under his breath. At last Michael whispered, "Let's go."

Andrew was two paces ahead when they reached the back side of the hut. He could hear children's voices inside, and a woman speaking excitedly. The man or men in the hut had probably gone to help fight the fires. At least Andrew hoped so. The door was of woven grass, much like the rest of the hut. He grasped it and pulled. It came free, without a hinge. He rushed inside and for a moment felt blind in the darkness. The interior smelled heavily of smoke. The only light was a faint glow of coals in a stone circle at the hut's center.

Zeb Willet cried out, "Daniel, where're you at?"

A surprised answer came in a boy's thin voice. "Over here!"

Andrew saw him lying on a blanket or a hide—he could not tell which. The boy tried to jump to his feet but could not. His hands and feet were bound, and he was tethered to one of the tree-limb braces that made up the hut's framework. A woman screamed. Other children cried out in their surprise and terror. A boy, larger than the others, rushed toward Daniel with a knife in his hand. Andrew tripped him and grabbed up the knife as the boy sprawled. He pitched it to Zeb and put his foot gently but firmly on the back of the boy's neck to hold him still.

Zeb rushed to his brother. The blade flashed a reflection from the coals as he severed the tether and swept Daniel into his arms.

Michael said, "Let's get the hell out of here!"

Andrew motioned for Zeb to leave first, carrying his brother. The woman dashed out the hut's front door, shouting, leaving the children behind. Andrew saw several pairs of bright eyes staring at him in fright from around the circular wall of the hut. He said, knowing they would not understand him, "You-all go back to bed." He lifted his foot from the bigger boy's neck.

Michael stood at the east door through which they had entered. He made an impatient motion with his hand. "Will you hurry the hell up?"

Andrew went out ahead of him, just in time to see an Indian man come running around the hut, grabbing at Zeb and the boy Daniel. Zeb turned quickly away, shielding his brother. Andrew saw a knife in the Indian's hand. He ran toward him, shouting a challenge. The man whipped around to face him. Andrew parried at him with the barrel of his rifle. The Indian stepped quickly aside, avoiding the thrust, then was on Andrew like a wildcat.

Caught off balance, Andrew tumbled and fell backward. The Indian was on top of him in an instant. Andrew let go of his rifle and used both hands to grab the Indian's wrist. The man was bigger and stronger. Inexorably, despite Andrew's best resistance, the knife blade was forced down toward his throat. He smelled the warrior's hot breath in his face. He felt the point bite into his skin.

A dark form appeared above him. Michael swung his rifle and struck the Indian a solid blow across the side of the head. The man went limp, and Andrew quickly rolled out from under him. He grabbed the knife from the loosened fingers. He considered plunging it into the Indian's throat, as the warrior had tried to do to him.

Michael said curtly, "I wish you wouldn't do it, but if you're goin' to, hurry up."

The impulse waned. Andrew struck the Indian's knife in his belt and picked up his rifle. "Wouldn't be any gain in it." He moved into a trot, following Zeb and the boy back toward the river where Nathan and Fairweather held the horses. Michael followed closely. Behind them, the village was thoroughly aroused, fighting the fires, trying to prevent their spread. So far as he could tell, no one except those in the hut and the one who had jumped him knew that outsiders had passed so near.

Harlan Mann fell in behind them, providing a rear guard.

Fairweather exclaimed as he saw the boy in Zeb's arms, "The Lord be praised."

Only then did Zeb pause to cut the rest of the rawhide thongs that bound his brother. Daniel clung tightly to Zeb's neck, but he did not cry.

Andrew asked, "Daniel, are you all right? They didn't hurt you?"

The boy declared, "They beat on me some, but I hit them back, every chance I got. The one you tripped, he was the worst. I'd like to go back and hit him with a stick."

Fairweather said quietly, "Vengeance is mine, sayeth the Lord. Be content, my young friend."

Daniel plainly did not understand what he meant.

Eli, Younts, and Smith rode up. Eli saw with satisfaction that the rescue had been made. He nodded toward the village. "They'll be lucky if half the place don't burn, the way the wind is gettin' up. I reckon they're too busy to be huntin' us for a while."

A bright flash lighted the entire village, and the ground shook to the power of the thunder. Michael said, "It's fixin' to rain, and that'll help them. We'd better be a long ways from here if they decide to come lookin'."

Zeb Willet mounted his horse, and Andrew boosted Daniel up behind him. Michael paused a moment to be sure everybody was in the saddle, then he heeled his bay horse into a run. The rest followed his pace. Their escape route led them past the horse herd. It would be easy to cut off several and drive them along, but Michael made no such move. Escape was the primary consideration now.

Daniel pointed. "My pony's out there. They stole him."

Eli said, "You just hang onto your brother and ride like an Indian. I'll git you another pony someday."

They ran the horses as long as they dared. Michael slowed his bay to a trot and looked back to be sure none of the party had fallen behind. Giving Zeb and Daniel a look of satisfaction, he smiled for the first time. "Zeb, I wish we could've taken time to get your horses back."

Daniel's arms were around his older brother. Zeb patted the small hands. "I've got what counts. For this, I'd walk the rest of my life."

Michael pulled around to Andrew. "Looked to me like you were havin' a little trouble back there with that big Indian and his knife. Did he cut you?"

Involuntarily Andrew's hand went to his throat. In the excitement he had put it out of his mind. It stung a little, where the knifepoint had driven into the flesh. "It was a long ways from the heart," he said. "It'll heal."

Michael grunted. "You didn't want me to come on this little sashay atall. I expect you're glad now that I did."

Andrew wanted to admit that he was. But he still felt that he had been right. Michael's proper place had been with Marie. But where was the point in saying that now? He made no answer.

The rain started, suddenly and with a vengeance, lashing at them as the lightning split the night skies and thunder made the earth shake beneath the horses' feet. Andrew trembled at the chill and felt concern for the boy. But Zeb wrapped a blanket around his brother and kept riding. "After all he's been through," Zeb said proudly, "a little cold rain ain't goin' to bother him much. He's a fighter. Papa'd be proud—"

Andrew said, "He'd be proud of both of you."

The water ran in rivulets down the gentle hills. Eli looked back, then down. "Whatever tracks we left behind us, this'll wash them away. I doubt them

Wacos'll come after us in all this rain. If they commence later, they'll have a hell of a time findin' a trace to start on."

The riders came to another heavy wood, where tall pines formed an almost solid canopy overhead. This did not stop the pounding rain from coming through, but it slowed the force. Michael said, "We'll rest the horses and wait out the storm."

Fairweather suggested they all kneel and offer up their gratitude for safe delivery from the hands of their enemies. Hats came off, even in the rain. Andrew thought the loudest *Amen* came from Zeb Willet.

The men huddled in sodden misery beneath the trees, the cold offset somewhat by the warm success of their venture. Andrew sat on his heels, his back against a pine, and listened to various ones recount their personal memories of the raid on the village. Younts said, "Ol' Joe here, he was so nervous he kept droppin' his flint. I thought he never was goin' to get a fire started."

"Ain't so atall," Joe Smith countered. "It was him that couldn't hold onto his flint. I got my fire started and had to go and help him with his. And I was the one had to blow on it to keep it goin'; he was plumb out of wind."

"*You* ain't never been out of wind," Younts declared.

Nathan Miles laughed aloud. "You-all both done yourselves proud," he said. Andrew suspected either one of them would be welcomed as a son-in-law, provided they didn't try to start soon. Birdy was young yet, even by frontier standards.

Michael said, "Everybody done themselves proud." He brought his glance painfully to the one-eyed preacher. "Fairweather, I'll always remember what you did to us years ago. But I won't forget that you held up your part here, and more."

Fairweather acknowledged the faint compliment. "I have never asked even the Lord to forgive me for my past life. I have only asked for mercy."

The rain stopped at daylight. The men had little food left except for some jerked venison. They gave that to the boy. The parched grain substitute for coffee was gone, but the wood was so wet they probably could not have started a fire to boil it anyway. Hungry, tired, chilled, no one had to say anything about going home. Michael tightened the girth on his saddle and mounted the bay horse. The other men silently followed suit.

Andrew was aware that they were retracing more or less the route they had taken on the way north. He guessed, but didn't ask, that Michael wanted to find the place where they had left Quenton Mann, to be sure he had managed to get on his horse and start home alone. They struck the river a little west of their original crossing and rode downstream. Andrew recognized the place where they had had their quick skirmish with the Indian boy. He knew the tree under which they had left Mann after the arrowhead had been removed from his leg. Mann was gone.

Harlan Mann nodded in satisfaction. "I reckon Paw got to feelin' stronger. He'll be home by now, with Maw takin' care of him."

The rain had washed away whatever tracks Mann might have created. The river was on a slight rise, its waters an angry brown. But it was no obstacle to men on their way home from a long and bruising expedition that had challenged their endurance. They crossed over and set out southeastward, the way they had come. Andrew guessed it was upward of noon when he saw a horse standing several hundred yards ahead of them, beneath an oak tree.

Michael held up his hand as a signal for everybody to stop while he tried to decide if a lone horse out there so far from civilization suggested any threat. "Anybody see somethin' that I don't?" he asked.

No one had anything to contribute. Michael proceeded after checking his long rifle and pouring fresh powder into the pan.

When they were within a couple of hundred yards Harlan Mann said tightly, "That looks like Paw's horse. Yes sir, I believe it is."

A little nearer, Andrew could see a man lying on the ground.

"Paw!" Harlan exclaimed, and set his horse into a run. The rest of the men followed but never caught up to him. When Andrew got there Harlan was on the ground, kneeling before his fallen father. He saw at a glance that the wounded leg had swollen far beyond its normal size, and blowflies had found it. The stench made his stomach turn.

Michael dismounted quickly and handed his reins up to Zeb Willet. Andrew did likewise. Eli stayed in the saddle but looked down sadly. "Is he dead?"

Andrew felt for the man's pulse. He saw Mann's eyelids flutter. Mann blinked a few times, trying to see. He picked out his son and painfully brought him into some focus. "Harlan?"

"It's me, Paw. I'm here."

"I tried to wait. But the leg—" His voice trailed off. "Tell your mama—"

That was all he managed to say. The pulse weakened gradually, and finally it was gone. Mann had waited for his son. Once Harlan had come, he had no strength left for holding on any longer.

Andrew said, "I'm sorry, Harlan."

Fairweather spoke a quiet prayer.

Young Mann bit his lip. "Will you-all help me put him on his horse? I'll take him home now."

Fairweather watched as Mann's body was tied securely to his saddle. He said, "I'll go home with you, son. Your mama will feel better if there's somebody to read the words over him right and proper."

The others sat on their horses and watched with bowed heads as Harlan and Fairweather started their solitary journey, angling almost due east toward the Mann home on the Brazos.

Nathan Miles mused soberly, "Two dead on our side and two dead on theirs. Kind of evens everything up, don't it?"

Nobody spoke for a minute. Finally Eli observed, "This Texas, it has a world of promise. But it sure asks a hell of a toll."

They were a tired, bedraggled, bewhiskered, and hungry group as they limped in finally to the Willet farm. Andrew's shoulders were slumped. His backside felt numb from the long, weary ride. They had managed to shoot one deer on the way back, a small doe that was more flavor than substance and certainly not large enough to satisfy everybody's need. They had given the boy the best of it.

During the trip he described his treatment as a captive of the Indians. Often he had been confused because he did not understand their language, and they tended to whip him when he did not respond as they wished him to. "Most of the time I didn't know what they wanted me to do. And even when I knowed, I acted like I didn't. The one you was wrestlin' with, Andrew, he acted like he was wantin' to make a slave out of me. One time when he hit me, I got ahold of his hand and bit him good."

His face saddened. "I never did know which one it was that killed Papa."

Zeb hugged his brother. "It don't matter anymore. Gettin' you home to Mama and them is all that counts now."

Fatigued though they were, the two young Willets seemed to gain new strength as they came in sight of the spread out, comfortable-looking log structure Lige Willet had built for his family on the farm which was to have been his home into his old age, a place to watch his children grow up and to raise the grandchildren who would have brightened his final years. Andrew felt a catch in his throat, looking at the place, at the field which Willet would never harvest again, at the young orchard from which he would never taste the fruit. It had always been a joy to come over here and sit a spell with the Willets and their brood. It would never be the same again. He felt the loss more now than when he had first heard of Willet's death.

He saw a number of horses being herded on grass a quarter mile from the house, guarded by two riders still unwilling to discount the threat of Indians. The horses belonged to the settler families who had gathered here for mutual protection.

Several wagons stood near the shed. Lige Willet had not owned one.

The riders were seen long before they reached the cabin. More than a dozen people poured out onto the dog-run and into the open yard, waiting. Daniel cried, "Yonder's Mama."

Zeb could not restrain himself. He heeled his horse into a run, carrying him and Daniel in ahead of the others. Andrew blinked as he recognized Mrs. Willet, hurrying out to meet her sons. Zeb handed the boy down to her. She clasped him in her arms as if she would crush the life from him. Zeb slowly dismounted. When she looked up at him, he went to her, and the three of them stood there, holding to one another. At the distance Andrew could not hear if anything was being said. He doubted that words were necessary.

An excited crowd gathered around the Willet family, offering congratulations for the boy's return. Miles Nathan went to his own family, his wife reaching out for him. The two bachelors, Younts and Smith, gave their full attention to the Nathan girl, Birdy.

Andrew saw Michael's eyes brighten and a smile break across his whiskered face. Andrew followed his gaze, though he did not have to; he knew who Michael had been searching for. Michael put the horse into a trot and moved to meet Marie. She advanced beyond the others and stopped to wait for him. Andrew watched as Michael jumped to the ground and swept Marie into his arms. The boy Mordecai grabbed his father's legs and held tightly.

Only Andrew and Eli remained on their horses, on the edge of the crowd but somehow not a part of it.

Eli must have read the emptiness in Andrew's face. He said, "It's hard goin', sometimes, bein' a bachelor."

Andrew looked away, his eyes burning. He had never felt more alone.

PART 3

THE FREDONIAN REBELLION

17

In later years the incident would be remembered grandiosely as the Fredonian Rebellion, and some would claim it was the earliest glimmering of the Texas revolution against Mexico. It began with a brashly confrontational Kentuckian named Haden Edwards, one of many land *empresarios* who attempted to bring in American settlers and establish colonies in Mexican Texas after the pattern set by Stephen F. Austin. Most failed, but few did so with the bluster and bitterness and legacy of official mistrust that marred Edwards's brief career as an empire builder.

The fault was not his alone. Much of it was rooted in the inefficiency and carelessness of bureaucracy, granting him lands upon which others had prior claim, including Mexican citizens who had lived there for generations, peaceful Indians who considered it theirs by birthright, and even Americans who claimed squatters' rights by virtue of having survived years of futile efforts by the Spanish and

Mexican governments to push them back across the Sabine River.

Andrew had little inkling of the future trend of events when he encountered Edwards's brother Benjamin that summer. He did not go often to Michael's cabin, for the rift that had broken between them had not healed. He would not have gone at all had it not been for his need to look in occasionally upon Marie and the boy Mordecai. He kept himself busy on his own place and tried not to dwell upon the loneliness of it. Eli Pleasant had stayed only a little while, then drifted back toward Nacogdoches and his own place just across the Sabine in Louisiana.

One morning, working in the field, Andrew caught a movement on the horizon and stopped the blue-speckled ox. He wiped sweat from his forehead and eyes and squinted. He saw a lone rider, evidently a stranger, because Andrew did not recognize the mount. He knew every horse between here and San Felipe, just about, and could identify them from farther away than he could identify their riders. The horseman was coming from the direction of San Antonio de Bexar, the Mexican capital of Texas.

He's had him a right smart of a ride, Andrew thought.

He wondered at first if this might be Stephen Austin, for Austin often traveled to Bexar to conduct business with representatives of the Mexican government. But as the distance lessened, it was evident this was a larger man than Austin.

The rider was well-dressed for a man on the road, though dusty and trail-worn. He did not look at all like a farmer. Andrew took him for a lawyer. The man stared with much interest at Andrew's cabin, at his field, at the ox in the yoke. He spoke in a manner that indicated a better education than Andrew's. "I must say, I am glad to see sign of civilization. I had feared for some time I had lost my way."

"You're on the right way if you're headed for San Felipe," Andrew assured him. He strode forward and offered his grimy hand. "Name's Andrew Lewis. If you'll give me time to unhook the ox, I'll go with you to the cabin and fix us a bite of dinner."

The man dismounted and accepted the hand, dirt and all. "Benjamin Edwards. Perhaps you have heard of my brother, Haden Edwards?"

Andrew shook his head. "I don't get away from this place much. If you asked me who is the president of the United States, I might get it wrong."

"My brother is an *empresario*, like Stephen Austin. No, not like Austin—better."

It occurred to Andrew, now that he thought about it, that Eli had said something to him about an Edwards who was making a claim to land around Nacogdoches. If he remembered right, Eli had said there was trouble over the titles. But it would be impolite to bring up such a disagreeable subject with a chance passerby. He said, "The fare won't be fancy, but it'll be fillin'. I left a pot of beans on the coals this mornin'. And there's venison."

They went to the pens first, where he forked a little hay to the ox and slid a bar into place so the animal could not leave. If the visitor did not stay long, Andrew could get a lot more work done in the field before dark.

While he fried venison in the little fireplace, he asked about conditions in Bexar, a place he had always found somehow fascinating.

"Poorest town I ever saw in my life," Edwards replied distastefully. "Mexicans mostly, and no real cash money among the lot of them. They think poor and they live poor. What they need is some good American energy to bring that place to life."

Andrew shook his head in mild disagreement. "Always seemed an agreeable bunch of people to me. I've gotten along with them well enough."

He saw that Edwards's feeling was deeply held. It was bad form to argue with a guest, especially when he saw so few of them. He put the food on the table, asked a quick blessing, and told Edwards to help himself. Edwards fell silent, putting away two men's share of the venison, beans, and rough-ground corn-bread. The trail from Bexar was long.

At last Edwards pushed his chair back from the crude table and rubbed his stomach in content-ment. "Plain and humble fare, my friend, but filling enough to do me until I reach a better place."

"Glad you liked it," Andrew said with irony, for the visitor's mild disparagement had not gone un-noticed. The beans should have lasted Andrew three or four days. They wouldn't now. He said, "If your colony is up at Nacogdoches, what brings you all the way to Bexar and San Felipe?"

"The stupidity of government," Edwards declared sternly. "They gave us our grant, and now they say there is difficulty over titles. There are squatters on our land who resist our efforts to move them, and the central government has been no help. On the contrary, it has been a major part of the problem. I went to Bexar to apprise the authorities of the true situation and to let them know exactly where my brother and I stand." His face creased with remem-bered indignation. "I told them most forcefully that an agreement is an agreement. Sometimes, however, these Mexicans are like children. One must take a firm position with them, show them that an American is not to be trifled with."

Andrew felt a stirring of concern. Edwards's manner told him the man had done a lot of telling and very little asking. As little experience as Andrew had had with Mexican authorities, he knew their pride did not respond well to lecturing by a foreigner. Lecturing had never been Stephen Austin's style, one reason he had gotten along so well. He was a diplomat. Had he not been, no American would now be in Texas legally. And perhaps not illegally either. Stirred up, the Mexicans, like the Spanish before them, had a most severe manner of dealing with trespassers upon their ground. Somewhere up toward Nacogdoches, Mordecai Lewis's unmarked grave bore silent testimony to that fact.

Frowning, Andrew asked, "Just what was it you told the authorities?"

"I told them they had granted my brother that land, and if the central government did not expel the interlopers, we would do it ourselves without their assistance."

"The Mexicans don't appreciate bein' talked to like that."

"By the eternal, sir, they listened with rapt attention."

"I'll bet they did," Andrew said dryly.

Edwards stiffened. "You find fault with me, sir?"

"There's people in Mexico huntin' for any excuse to get rid of all us Americans that've taken up land on Mexico soil. Every time Austin deals with them, he acts like a man walkin' on eggshells. Feller like you goes to stirrin' them up, he's apt to make trouble for all of us."

"I did no more than stand up for my rights—mine

and my brother's. If I stepped on any sore toes, they should not have been stuck out in the way. I am going now to San Felipe to apprise Mr. Austin of what has been done and said. If there is to be trouble, I shall expect him as an American to stand with us."

It was in Andrew's mind that Austin would not be pleased by this report. But Austin was plenty capable of speaking for himself; Andrew had no need to speak for him.

Edwards walked to the door and gave Andrew's farm a long study. "We have better land at Nacogdoches, and much closer to a civilized country."

"I've seen it," Andrew replied. Edwards could take any inference he wished from that. "I'm satisfied right where I'm at."

"And are you satisfied with Austin? He is much too thick with the Mexicans to suit me."

"I count him a friend of mine."

Edwards put on his hat. "Very well. Time will tell which of us is right. I am obliged for the meal, sir."

"Welcome any time," Andrew replied, though he hoped the next visit would not be soon.

He watched Edwards ride toward Michael's cabin and made a dry, humorless smile as he thought how much better meal the man could have eaten if he had gone there first and had sat at Marie's table instead of Andrew's. Well, he probably deserved about what he got.

He put the yoke on the ox and took him back to the field. He tried to put Edwards out of his mind but could not. He kept remembering Austin's concern over keeping friendly relations with the Mexican authorities. The American settlers in Texas could look to no one but each other for help if the radicals in Mexico gained enough influence to try to put them off of the land.

A few blustering bullies like Edwards could spoil the fragile alliances that held American Texas together and bring catastrophe down upon everyone.

18

Ever since he had seen the surveyors, Isaac Blackwood had expected trouble. The Blackwood family had been squatters for generations, so they dreaded surveyors as they dreaded Indians. The lawyers would not be far behind, and eviction was sure to follow. It had been that way since Grandpap's time, way back in the Appalachians.

Finis had taken up his rifle to kill the surveyors, and Luke backed him, as always. Isaac had argued that missing men draw searchers, and it was hard to hide a killing, especially that of several men. Finis had maintained that they could throw suspicion onto the Cherokee Indians who lived in the general vicinity. Isaac had managed to convince him that the Cherokees were regarded as civilized, and the authorities in Nacogdoches would not long be fooled.

"All right," Finis had raged, flapping his stump of an arm, "but there'd better not be no striped-britches son of a bitch come and try to run us off of our place. I'll kill him deader'n a skint mule."

It wasn't much of a place to be run off from, Isaac thought. He said, "I don't know why anybody'd want to come here when there's so much better land to be had."

The Mexican soldiers who had captured them at the Lewis farm had conducted them first to Nacogdoches for examination by the civil authorities, then to the bank of the Sabine. The troops had waited in ominous silence while the Blackwoods swam their horses across to Louisiana. Isaac would have been content to squat on the Louisiana side, where the laws at least were American. But Finis had his hard head set on Texas and satisfaction from Michael Lewis. He could not do it sitting on the east side of the Sabine in Frenchman country. They had waited until nightfall, then sneaked back into Texas in the dark of the moon.

So now they bided their time at a place they had found abandoned on a small creek in a clearing in the midst of a heavy East Texas piney wood. Isaac surmised that some squatter before them had built the small cabin and had broken the ground for a field little larger than a garden. He had probably been driven out by Spanish or Mexican soldiers. Or perhaps simply by starvation. The field seemed to grow rocks better than it grew anything Isaac had planted.

It had one virtue, however: proximity to the Sabine River and quick escape into Louisiana in the event Isaac's brothers followed their natural propensities for mischief and a hasty departure for the United States became necessary.

He paused to lean on the hoe and wipe a sleeve across his face to stop the burning sweat from trailing down into his eyes. The tall, green cornstalks rustled around him, intercepting much of the breeze that might have blown cool through his half-soaked shirt. He looked about for his brothers. Luke sat in the shade beside the log cabin, sagging on a rough bench like a sack of cornmeal. He looked all tuckered out, but he was just lazy. He had spent perhaps half an hour helping Isaac hoe weeds out of the corn, then had quit the work.

Isaac did not see Finis anywhere, but he had a good notion his oldest brother was in the cabin, and not alone. Once Finis had found a woman who would tolerate him, he was rutting like an acorn-fed boar. They had discovered neighbors a few miles to the south, squatters like themselves who had no official sanction to be in Texas but probably were unwanted anywhere else. Or perhaps they *were* wanted, by one sheriff or another. Among their numerous brood was a plump and red-headed daughter Nelly, twenty years old, not much for looks but a fair-to-middling cook and housekeeper, and perfectly willing to take up with Finis Blackwood. Her folks had seemed relieved to see her go, though they had acted a little put out that no money went with the deal. They had made no fuss about the lack of clerical blessing. Mentally Nelly was on about the same level as Luke, certainly no bragging point. What made her attractive to Finis was that she seemed perpetually in heat.

Finis had first claim, but when he was in a better than average mood he lent her to Luke. When the two happened to be gone off hunting, Nelly would rub up against Isaac. Sometimes he resisted and sometimes he accepted her invitation. He was not proud of it. But he had been doing most of the work around here and getting damned little of the pleasure. Finis owed him.

With all the planting being done, it seemed a foregone conclusion that a crop would sprout one of these days, and nobody would know whose it was.

From the corner of his eye Isaac caught a movement at the edge of the wood. He paused only a moment before dropping his hoe and trotting to the end of the row where he had propped his rifle against a log. He saw three horsemen. They wore no uniform, so at least they were not Mexican soldiers. But strangers always had a way of bringing bad news.

First the surveyors, then the lawyers. It had been that way forever, seemed like.

He trotted to the cabin, shouting at Luke to wake the hell up and grab his rifle. He pushed open the cabin door and, as he expected, saw Finis on the bed, all tangled up with Nelly. "What the hell?" Finis grumbled. He was not embarrassed; embarrassment was not in him. He was simply irritated at the interruption.

"You better git your britches on and fetch your rifle. Looks like we got company comin'."

"Who is it?"

"I don't know. But you can bet they ain't here to bring us no money."

Nelly tried to cover herself with the blanket as Finis quit the bed. It didn't matter. Isaac had seen all there was, more than once. He went outside and took up a station in front of the cabin, rifle cradled across his arm.

Luke moved up beside him. "I can pick off one of them, and you can git another. Finis'll git the last one before he makes the timber."

Isaac frowned. "Shootin' at people is the way Finis lost that arm, or have you forgot?"

The three riders were not lawyers; they were too sun-browned and weather-creased to have spent their lives in a courtroom. But Isaac figured no lawyers would get out this far from the settlements anyway; they would send somebody who worked cheaper. These three had the dour look of lawmen Isaac and his brothers had encountered all over Tennessee, carrying out the orders of the landed gentry and merchant class.

The biggest among them leaned forward in his saddle, his gaze running from Isaac to Luke to Finis, who had finally come out with britches unbuttoned and no shirt or boots. The rider said, "You folks just passin' through here, I hope?"

Finis shook his head. "I was hopin' the same about you all."

"We represent Haden Edwards, who has permission of the Mexican government to settle eight hundred families. He has posted legal notice in Nacogdoches that all who have a prior claim are to present proof to him of their legal presence here or vacate the region immediately."

Isaac said, "We ain't seen it. We ain't been to Nacogdoches."

"I have a copy of his order if you want to read it." He reached into a saddlebag. Luke quickly hoisted his rifle to his shoulder. The man paused in ill-suppressed alarm. "I'm just goin' after the paper, is all."

Isaac said, "Stand easy, Luke."

Luke paid him no attention, looking instead to Finis. Finis said, "Let him, Luke. We can kill him afterwards."

The document looked official, but Isaac had never

made much sense out of such things. Finis and Luke could not read at all. Isaac said, "A man can write down anything he wants to. That don't make it so. We found this place. Wasn't nobody usin' it. We claim squatters' rights."

The man gave him a long, cautious stare. "There's no such thing. You have no right to be on this property."

Finis spat, tobacco juice trailing back into his rough black beard and shining in the sun. "We got a right. We got it right here." He shifted his rifle to his shoulder and took aim at the man on the horse. "You want to come a little closer and see?"

The man glanced at the riders on either side of him for reassurance. Neither had moved. His face flushed a little. "Mr. Edwards is fully prepared to take the case to the Mexican authorities. You will find yourselves in court."

Finis grunted. "We been in court before. Ain't never been no judge's hammer come down as hard as the hammer on this rifle."

The horseman pulled up on his bridle reins. Isaac saw fear in his eyes, a fear that was more than justified. If Finis took it in his head to shoot, he would. He had never been one to dwell upon consequences. Isaac wanted to tell Finis to back off a little, but that might have seemed a weakening of their stand, giving strength to the visitors. He knew if Finis killed this one, he and Luke would have to finish the other two. They could not let any of the men leave here alive unless all three did.

The rider had trouble speaking. He finally managed, "Might I inquire you gentlemen's names?"

Knowing Luke would blurt it if he did not speak quickly, Isaac said, "It's Smith."

The man did not believe. "Half the squatters we've found are named Smith."

Isaac nodded. "We got a lot of kinfolks. Now, you-all have more than wore out your welcome. The trail you used comin' in here is the best one to use goin' out."

The three riders glanced at each other and seemed to agree that they had business elsewhere. The spokesman turned his horse half around before he declared, "There will be more to this."

Isaac said, "If I was you I'd forget how to find this place."

As the men rode away, Luke lowered his rifle, but Finis still held his aim, bracing the long barrel with his stump of an arm. Isaac reached out and pulled the muzzle toward the ground. He grunted at the effort, for Finis was surprisingly strong. Isaac had often wondered where he got it; certainly not from hard work.

Finis grumbled, "I got a mind to kill the son of a bitch. He ain't out of range yet."

"Then we'd have to leave anyway. What's the sense in that?" He knew the way to deflect Finis's attention from the three riders was to draw it to himself. He gave Finis a quick study from his tousled black hair down to his bare feet. "Hell of a sight you are. Wonder they didn't laugh theirselves to death."

Finis scowled. "Ain't nobody laughs at me. Not but once."

Isaac pointed his chin toward the tiny field. "The corn needs hoein', and I can't keep up with the weeds all by myself. Why don't you put the rest of your clothes on and come help me?"

"Ain't much I can do with one arm."

Isaac let sarcasm creep into his voice. "I expect Nelly'd disagree about that."

Finis looked quickly toward the cabin, as if he had forgotten she was there. "I'll be out directly. But don't expect me to do much." He went back into the cabin.

Isaac turned to Luke. "What about you?"

Luke's mind was not on the field. "Finis is with her right now."

Isaac shrugged with a sense of futility and let his gaze go back to the three horsemen, disappearing where the trail turned into the woods.

They would be back. Maybe not for a week, maybe not for a month. He wondered what he would do when they returned, for there would probably be more of them next time. Damned place wasn't really worth fighting over anyway. But fight he would, if it came to that, because he was a Blackwood. And he would probably lose. Because he was a Blackwood.

19

Isolation and attention to what he considered more important matters kept Andrew Lewis from hearing much about the increasingly brittle situation around faraway Nacogdoches, or giving much thought to the little he heard about the growing conflict between old settlers and new ones the Edwards brothers brought in to place upon land others regarded as their own. The fall harvest kept Andrew busy, for he had no rich man's implements, no slaves, to help him gather the fruits of his summer's labor like he had seen on large places downriver. He gathered his corn crop the poor man's way, using a long, sharp knife as he slowly worked along row after row of ripened stalks. He hoisted each canvas bag upon the brown horse's back just before it became too heavy for him to lift alone, toting it up to his log shed for storage. At such a time he dreamed of acquiring a wagon someday. The produce of his garden likewise required hand labor—his own—for he had no money to hire help. Always before, he and

Michael had combined their efforts for those tasks too large or too heavy for one man. But this time he did his work alone. The old quarrel still stood between them like a patch of briars. Neither knew how to take the first step to cut a path through the thorns without losing some of the Lewis dignity and pride.

Of more import was Marie's delivery of her second child. It happened, appropriately, just as the crop harvest began. Andrew kept finding excuses to go to Michael and Marie's cabin to look in upon her, even if it was no more than whittling some sort of toy for little Mordecai. Michael would acknowledge his presence with a strained civility and find business elsewhere. The new neighbor, Mrs. Nathan, came over to provide midwife services. By the look of her, Andrew judged that she would be needing a return of the favor before winter was out. But her condition was no hindrance to her hustling and bustling about, ordering Michael and Andrew to the chores she needed done.

A woman of considerable stature herself, she kept worrying aloud about Marie's small size. "I had a cousin once, little bitty woman like Marie, married to a big strappin' feller like Michael is. Baby come, it taken after its papa. Too big for such a little woman. Died givin' birth, she did. Died hard."

Michael pointed out that this would be Marie's second; she had had no particular difficulty delivering Mordecai. But Mrs. Nathan kept talking about her cousin until she had Michael and Andrew both in a cold sweat. As the ordeal began, Andrew kept water boiling in a pot over coals in the fireplace while Michael held little Mordecai on his knee and tried to explain to the worried boy what was the matter with his mother and why they needed that bossy woman in the house.

Andrew poked nervously at the fire during the interminable wait, thinking of Mrs. Nathan's cousin and the thousand things that could go wrong. At last he heard a tiny cry from the bedroom, a cry that lasted but a moment. His mouth dry, Andrew stared intently at Michael and listened hard, fearful.

"Must be a boy," Michael said, his shaky voice betraying his own apprehension. "Lewis boys don't cry much."

Mrs. Nathan entered the kitchen, wiping her hands on a towel. She held the men in painful suspense a minute, then smiled. "Michael, she wants you to go in now. She'd like to show you your new daughter."

Michael stared at her as if he did not quite believe. "Daughter? You sure it's not a boy?"

Mrs. Nathan grinned. "After several of my own, I think I can tell the difference."

Andrew slumped, the tension flowing out of him. Damn Mrs. Nathan's stories. He wanted to grasp his brother's hand but waited in vain for a look that might seem an invitation. He took little Mordecai as Michael eased his son down from his knee. He said, "Lewis *girls* don't cry much either."

The boy had seen few other children. His had been a world of adults. All the talk had been about his getting a new brother to play with. He did not understand why he had been given a sister instead. "I don't know what we need her for anyway."

While Michael went in, Andrew held Mordecai and tried to explain that a little sister was just the same as a little brother except different.

"What do you mean, different?" his nephew wanted to know.

Mrs. Nathan was no help. She slumped exhaustedly at the table, drinking parched-grain coffee and smiling benignly at Andrew's stumbling efforts.

Michael came back into the kitchen presently, his rugged face aglow. Any momentary disappointment had already been put aside. "Marie wants Mordecai to come see the baby. You'd just as well come too, Andrew, long's you're here."

Marie was drawn and tired, but her black hair was freshly brushed, and her dark eyes were shining as she turned toward the tiny figure lying beside her. "Look, Mordecai. This is your sister."

The boy seemed less than impressed. "She looks kind of old."

Andrew ached to put his arms around Marie. He put them around the boy instead and said, "She'll get younger."

"She can't have my bed."

"Time she gets big enough to need it, I'll build you a larger one." His anxiety for Marie returned, for she appeared wrung out and frighteningly vulnerable. "The baby looks fine. But how about you? You've had us scared half to death."

"I feel like getting up from here and singing."

He touched her hand, then quickly drew away, but not before he saw a flicker of reaction in her eyes.

Michael sat on the edge of the bed, reaching across the baby to hold his wife's hand. Little Mordecai looked with suspicion upon the new arrival. He crawled up on the side of the bed and drew close to his mother. She hugged him to give his assurance.

Andrew felt like a fifth wheel on a wagon. He withdrew to the door but paused to look back at the three people—four now—who were most of his world. "It strikes me, Michael, that me and you, we'll be Tennesseans as long as we live. And Marie'll always be from Louisiana. But them two little 'uns, they're born in Texas. What does that make them?"

Michael gave the question a moment's thought. "Texicans. They're the startin' of a whole new tribe."

Marie was up the next day, getting around far sooner than Andrew thought she should. She took up most of her accustomed tasks, leaving little for Mrs. Nathan. Andrew waited for Michael to register disapproval. When he did not, Andrew admonished her, "Our mama always laid up for a couple, three days, takin' her rest. You oughtn't to be on your feet yet."

Marie acknowledged his concern with a soft smile, then shrugged it off. "I have been long enough in bed. There is much work to be done."

He said, "That's what Mrs. Nathan came here for."

Marie exaggerated a frown. "But she is in a delicate condition." She put an end to the discussion by pointing toward a wooden bucket. "I need some water, Andrew. Would you mind?"

Carrying the empty bucket down to the riverbank, Andrew wondered if Marie and Michael ever argued; he had never heard them. He thought it would be interesting sometime, for he could not conceive of either giving up to the other. If they were ill-matched in size, they were well-matched in wills.

They did not even have a proper argument over a name for the baby, though they had strong and differing opinions. Michael wanted to name her Patience, after his and Andrew's mother in Tennessee. Andrew thought that was a splendid notion, but he did not interfere. Marie, because of her French-Spanish heritage, was torn between naming her Angeline, for a beloved French aunt who had graced Marie's childhood in Natchitoches but had died in a fever epidemic, and Cristina, from the Spanish side of her family. They compromised, joining the names and calling the baby Angeline Cristina Patience Lewis.

Andrew remarked, "Poor kid's apt to grow up slump-shouldered, carryin' the weight of such a name."

Marie kissed the baby on the forehead. "Most Spanish names are much longer."

Michael squared himself to his full six feet. "Just so she remembers that her last name is Lewis."

Being around Marie had been a constant reminder to Andrew of the emptiness of his own cabin. Now that she had the baby, the feeling was even more acute. Andrew found that he could abide being by himself only a few days at a time. Then he had to ride down to Marie and Michael's place, ignoring Michael's cool and calculated silence for a chance to talk with Marie a little and bounce the boy Mordecai on his knee. He would watch with a helpless hunger as Marie moved about the cabin, cooking supper in the fireplace, caressing her new daughter.

He had long sensed that Marie understood how he felt about her. In her relationship with him there was always a sisterly affection, but there was also a vague uneasiness, an invisible line which she had drawn and over which he dared not step. Her dark eyes would silently tell him when he came dangerously near that line, and he would back away.

The baby was about three weeks old when Marie broached a subject she had mentioned several times before. Michael was out at the shed milking the cow. Marie watched Andrew stack an armload of freshly cut wood beside the fireplace, then motioned for him to take a chair. Andrew argued that he had some more wood to be fetched in. But she nodded again toward the chair, trouble in her eyes. Andrew sat.

Marie pulled up another chair and stared at him for a silent moment before saying, "You'll very soon be finished with the harvest. There will not be much for you to do in the winter except trap, and pelts will bring but little money. I think a good idea would be for you to go away a while. See something different. Go visit Nacogdoches or Natchitoches."

He suspected what she was working up to. It would not be the first time. "You're wantin' me to bring home a wife."

"I did not say that. But if it be in God's plan, why not?"

If he traveled three thousand miles he would not find a woman who would measure up to Marie. He would never be free to tell her that, not in words, but she could read it in his eyes if she so chose. He said, "I've got mighty little to offer. It's a hard life for a woman out here so far from the settlements."

She shook her pretty head. "It is a good life. I am happy. Michael is happy. This country will grow, and our children will grow with it. Find the right woman, Andrew, and she will be happy too. You should have your own family. You should be raising your own sons of Texas."

Andrew frowned. He thought he could read her mind: if he had a woman of his own, perhaps he would be less drawn to Marie; perhaps the awkwardness they felt toward each other would disappear. With it, perhaps, would go the barrier that had arisen between him and Michael. But he was not ready. "Sometime, maybe. Not yet."

The trouble was strong in Marie's eyes. He thought they might even hold a touch of fear. "There is something else. Michael is restless again. He says nothing, but he stares to the west with that look, that look from his father. One day he will not be able to stop himself, and he will ride away to see what is out there. If he knows you will be here to watch over us, he will feel free to go."

Andrew nodded, thinking ahead of her. "And if I was gone, he'd have no choice except to stay."

Her black eyes begged him. "Please, Andrew. He might die out there as your father did, so far away that not even God would know where he was. I do not want him to go. But he will, if you do not."

Andrew rubbed his rough hands together and tried in vain to think of a good argument. It was useless. He would walk barefoot across a bed of hot coals if Marie should ask him to. He said in resignation, "I remember your old daddy. A merchant to the core. He could sell an ox-yoke to a muleskinner. Looks like he raised his daughter the same way."

Michael returned from the cow pen, fresh milk steaming in the wooden bucket. Marie gave Andrew no chance to equivocate. She declared, "Andrew is going to make a trip. He is going back east to find a wife."

The warmth of embarrassment rushed to Andrew's face. "I'm just goin' to visit around a little, is all."

Michael set the bucket on the floor. Andrew saw

momentary disappointment in his brother's blue eyes. Michael was realizing that Andrew's absence would force him to give up any notion of exploring, at least for now. The disappointment passed, after a bit. Michael did not speak directly to Andrew; he seldom did, these days. He said, "I been tellin' him all along that he needs somebody to share that cabin. I'm glad he's finally decided to listen to me."

Andrew glanced at Marie. She smiled with the guileless face of an angel come to earth. He said in resignation, "I always listen to good advice."

He approached the journey without relish, feeling that the decision was not his own; he had been pressured into it. He kept putting it off until winter's cool breath was in the morning air. One day Michael came to him and said, "If you ain't goin', then I think I'll make a little ride out west a ways. There's some country I been wantin' to take a look at."

Andrew replied, "I was figurin' on leavin' tomorrow."

He packed the necessaries into a canvas bag and hung them off of the saddle, his blankets tied behind the cantle. The brown horse looked dwarfed beneath its burden, but it was more bulk than weight. Andrew gently pinched the baby's fingers, then hugged little Mordecai and Marie.

Michael watched him soberly and in silence.

Marie asked, "How far will you go?"

"Ain't figured, for sure. I expect I'll make a turn over by Nacogdoches, and maybe as far as Natchitoches."

Michael broke his silence. "You could go all the way back to Tennessee, see Mama and them."

Andrew shook his head. "Not until we can all go together and let Mama meet her grandchildren."

Marie said, "There will be some of yours by that time, perhaps."

Andrew frowned. "You-all are expectin' an awful lot of me. I tell you, I ain't lookin' for a wife. I'll be comin' back by myself."

Marie's eyes were wistful. "If you see my mother and father, tell them—well, you will know what to tell them."

"I'll tell them you're happy. That'd be no lie."

He gave Marie a brotherly kiss, feeling awkward about even that, then swung up on the brown horse. He started to pull away but glanced back. "I'll be comin' home by myself," he declared again.

He set out downriver, feeling as if he were being sent on a fool's errand. He had about as much business making this trip as a mule had going to a dance.

He stopped for a short visit at the Willet place, where he was pleased to see little Daniel looking fit and happy and none the worse for his experience with the Indians. He did not tarry long, because the memory of Old Man Lige Willet hung over him like a cloud. Mrs. Willet hugged him several times, telling him repeatedly how grateful she was for his part in bringing Daniel home. "I didn't do any more than the others," he demurred.

"All of you did more than Christian duty called for," she declared. "I pray for each one of you every night."

He stopped next at the Nathans' new cabin. Mrs. Nathan, her stomach pushing out more and more noticeably, wanted to know all about Marie and the baby. And she had advice for Andrew. "While you're a-travelin', it sure wouldn't hurt you none to keep your eyes open for a likely young woman. There's bound to be one somewhere just a-waitin' for an eligible young bachelor like yourself to come along."

Andrew figured she had been talking to Marie. Women saw romance in everything, seemed like.

Miles Nathan took a practical view of the matter. "Makes good business sense to me. Austin'd give you a right smart bigger grant of land if you was to come back harnessed up double."

"I'm just goin' to visit some old friends. Findin' me a life's companion never once crossed my mind."

"Be sure and sample her cookin' first. Beauty fades away"—Nathan glanced uneasily at his wife—"but good cookin' is a joy forever."

That kind of joy, at least, was in plentiful supply around the Nathan place. He noticed that Walker Younts was there, and Walker put away a hearty meal. But Andrew doubted that food was Walker's primary reason for coming. He was hanging on the girl Birdy's every word, every flutter of her eyelashes. Andrew wondered where Joe Smith was. He was not paying adequate attention to his interests if he was letting Walker steal a march on him.

Departing after eating more than good judgment would have suggested, Andrew carried some of the leavings at Mrs. Nathan's insistence so he could make another meal or two out of it along the trail.

She stood in front of her cabin and shouted one last bit of advice as he rode away. "Remember what I told you about my cousin. Find yourself a good sturdy woman that won't have any trouble bearin' babies."

He seriously considered bypassing San Felipe, the headquarters of Austin's colony. He figured he would probably get more matrimonial advice there, some of it like as not from Stephen Austin, still a bachelor himself and therefore probably an expert on someone else's need for a helpmate. Rumor was that Austin had seriously planned marriage himself to a likely young lady but had been too busy with his colony to invest the time and energy necessary to a successful courtship.

On reflection, Andrew decided a visit to San Felipe might be time well spent before he started the northward leg of the trip. Isolated at his and Michael's farms, he had heard but little of recent events. Nacogdoches and Natchitoches could both have burned to the ground or been wiped out by a fever epidemic without his knowing anything of it.

He was half surprised to find Austin there. The *empresario* was gone from San Felipe much of the time, traveling often to San Antonio de Bexar and even as far as Mexico City—on business for his colony. The wear was showing, for he appeared to have aged ten or fifteen years. His was a pace Andrew did not envy. It was probably easier being a farmer.

He found Austin distracted, seeming to pay little attention until Andrew mentioned that he planned to travel north to Nacogdoches. Austin's eyebrows went up. "Are you aware of the explosive situation which has developed there?"

Andrew shook his head, surprised. "No."

"The entire region around Nacogdoches seems on the brink of a revolt. Haden Edwards and his brother have tried to force old settlers as well as recent squatters from their land and turn it over to their own colonists. There has been a great deal of resistance and protest. Now the Mexican government has canceled the Edwards grant and ordered him to leave Texas. The last word I have is that he is resisting. He has even been recruiting Americans to join him and hold his colony by force if necessary."

Andrew whistled. "I'll bet the Mexican government ain't none too pleased about that."

"The situation reinforces those Mexicans who have opposed the American colonies. If it goes to an extreme, it could result in the eviction of all of us from Texas."

"You've got lots of friends in Mexico City. You can make them see that Edwards and his kind don't represent most of us."

"I try. But it may require us to do more than talk. It may require our joining the Mexican government in moving against the Edwards brothers."

Americans against Americans. The thought brought a bitter taste to Andrew's mouth. "It won't set well with a lot of folks."

"Neither would our eviction."

Andrew had gained the impression that those in Mexico who opposed allowing Americans into Texas were a minority voice, that a majority saw the American colonists as a stabilizing influence in a land but thinly settled and eternally subject to the terrors of Indian depredation. He had not given serious thought to what he would do—or what Michael would do—if anybody were to try to force them off of their land. Even the government of Mexico—

"Our roots are too deep now," he said. "We couldn't leave."

Austin's voice was grim. "When you remove a tree from a field, you do not dig it up by the roots. You simply chop it down. You have never seen anything of the Mexican army except a scattered few troops. You have never seen it as I have, deep in the interior of the country."

"Is it big enough to drive us out?"

"More than that. It is big enough to chop us to the

ground and leave us lying in pieces. All it needs is the will, and a strong leader who hates Americans."

Andrew shuddered in premonition. He could see himself and Michael standing shoulder to shoulder in defense of their land, and being cut down like wheat under a scythe. "Anything I can do to help?"

"I receive only sketchy and contractory reports. You could quietly look around Nacogdoches and determine the true situation. That would help me decide upon our best course."

For the first time Andrew began to see a broader purpose in his journey beyond pacifying his brother and sister-in-law, and preventing Michael from going on the roam. This was a more sensible mission than looking for a wife.

Austin said, "My fervent hope is that the Edwards brothers will recognize their position as untenable and simply leave Texas. That would save all of us some grief."

Andrew remembered his brief meeting with Benjamin Edwards. He had not been impressed. "They're probably already gone."

"Let us hope so. That would be the best news you could send me." Austin brightened. "And while you are there—"

"You too?"

Austin shrugged. "Would that I had the time myself. There is not much comfort in this life for a bachelor."

Because Nacogdoches had become a gateway into Texas for American immigrants traveling overland, Andrew found the trail considerably better marked and worn than the last time he had ridden it. He met several travelers, occasionally one or two but more often small family groups, all wanting to visit a while and ask questions about Austin's colonies or others in the Texas interior. Andrew was glad to oblige, for he had little opportunity to see many people beyond his own small circle. And most of these immigrants brought real coffee.

He took the opportunity to ask them what they had seen or heard in Nacogdoches. The only agreement he found was that trouble was astir. What kind and whose responsibility it was varied with the teller of the story.

He remembered that the limited rural settlement in the Nacogdoches region, aside from scattered illegal squatters, was within a relatively short distance of the old Spanish fort town. The old Spanish royalist government had distrusted its citizens and actively discouraged settlement in isolated regions away from official scrutiny. That Mexico had finally turned to revolution and won its freedom from Spain was proof that the official misgivings had been well-founded.

He sensed that he was approaching Nacogdoches when he saw a dim trail leading off the main trace, meandering into the tall pines whose thick foliage sometimes blocked the sky from view. He followed it and came to a small farm. It was deserted. A few abandoned chickens, wily enough not to be caught by predators, scratched for food around and amid the gray ashes and blackened ruins of a log cabin. A couple of domestic hogs came out of a flattened log pen and grunted expectantly at him, wanting to be fed.

"What happened to your people?" he asked aloud.

Whatever, they had obviously departed in a hurry to have left even this little. People in Texas wasted not of the mite they had, for want was always close at hand.

Vaguely disturbed, he returned to the main trace and came, after a while, to another trail which circled around a dense piney wood and out of sight. He realized he was probably too far from Nacogdoches to reach there by night. Clouds boiling up from the east threatened a cold and rainy night. If he could find a farm and some friendly folks, he might at least sleep on a porch or under a shed, in the dry. He set the brown horse upon the track and in a few minutes was pleased to see a reasonably new cabin of logs, this one still standing. Livestock pens and a shed sat out beyond the cabin, and a small field beyond that, reaching to the edge of a pine forest so thick that he could not see twenty feet into it.

"Brown horse, you may even get a little hay tonight."

He saw a milk cow inside the pen, though the gate stood open. She was eating hay someone evidently had pitched onto the ground for her from a fenced-off stack just out of her reach. As at the other place, chickens scratched around the yard. But here he could see grain lying on the ground. Someone had just fed them.

"Hello the house!" he shouted. It was poor manners to ride up to a cabin unannounced. It could also be hazardous.

No one replied. He saw no sign that anyone was around. That seemed odd, the chickens and the cow having just been given fresh feed. He shouted again. The door stood half open, but no one moved or answered. He dismounted, looped his reins around a post, and walked up to the door. "Anybody at home?"

He looked back over his shoulder toward the shed, puzzled. "I'm comin' in," he said, and pushed the door the rest of the way open.

He saw a quick movement. In a dark corner a girl crouched, eyes wide with fright. She made a little cry and covered her mouth with her hands.

He raised his arms as a sign that he meant no harm. "Don't be scared," he said in the gentlest tone he could muster. His voice quavered a little, for he had been startled almost as much as the girl. "I didn't come to hurt you."

His eyes accustomed themselves to the darkness of the cabin, and he realized the girl was Mexican. She probably did not understand what he said. He struggled to repeat in Spanish. She still crouched against the wall, her eyes big and dark and frightened like those of a small rabbit caught in a corner. For a fleeting moment she reminded him of Marie.

Not for all the world would he willingly see Marie frightened this way. He began backing toward the door. He told the girl in Spanish, "It will be all right. I am leaving."

Something poked hard against the middle of his back. A man's voice declared in Spanish, "You will not leave yet. Raise your hands."

Andrew felt the breath go out of him. Even before he turned, he knew he would be facing a rifle. And holding the rifle was a young Mexican whose black eyes glittered with threat.

Andrew tried to speak but had to clear his throat.

"You do not need that rifle. I am not here to hurt anyone."

"And you *will* not. Not tonight. You are my prisoner."

20

Andrew chilled as he read desperation in the young Mexican's black eyes. A frightened man might squeeze the trigger without intending to. Andrew had to ponder his Spanish, for he had never used it enough that it came without an effort. "I am your prisoner if you say so. But I am not your enemy. Turn your rifle away from me, *por favor*."

The young man seemed to consider the proposition, but Andrew could almost smell the fear emanating from him. The girl said in a frightened whisper, "Careful, Carlos. Careful."

Andrew's arms began to ache from holding them high. "I have to let my arms down. I will do it slowly."

"*Very* slowly," Carlos said, "and back away from me a little." The rifleman took a backward step of his own, far enough that Andrew could not easily grab the weapon. Andrew had no such foolish intention; it would probably get him killed.

He said, "I am just a traveler. I mean no one any harm."

Carlos seemed to want to believe him, but distrust was not easily put aside. The girl kept her back to the rough log wall, far beyond Andrew's reach.

The man demanded, "Where do you come from?"

"San Felipe de Austin."

"You swear you do not come from the *hermanos* Edwards?"

"I do not know the Edwards brothers." That was not entirely true. Benjamin Edwards had visited briefly at Andrew's farm some months ago. But it was no great stretch of the truth to say that he did not *know* him. "I am from Austin's colony."

Carlos stared hard, as if trying to see beyond Andrew's eyes and into his soul. The girl moved cautiously in a broad circle, trying to inch closer to Carlos while remaining well beyond Andrew's reach. Her first fear had eased, but her eyes remained suspicious. The young man asked, "What do you think, Petra?"

"He might be telling the truth. I do not want you to kill him."

"That might be safest."

"No. If he *is* one of them, they would stay after you like wolves until you are dead, perhaps until we are all dead. And if he is *not* one of them, the Father *Dios* would condemn us both."

Carlos demanded of Andrew, "If you are not one of them, why do you come into this cabin like a thief?"

"A thief would not shout three or four times, asking if anyone was here. And those people you are afraid of—I do not believe they would either."

The girl acknowledged with a nod. "He did call out. You must have heard him."

Andrew argued, "Look, my name is Andrew Lewis. I only wanted a dry place to sleep tonight." After this hostile encounter, he would as soon sleep in the rain.

The young man seemed almost convinced. "Do you know anyone who would speak for you?"

Andrew had spent no time around Nacogdoches. The only name that came readily was Lieutenant Elizandro Zaragosa. That brought a flicker of recognition to the young man's eyes. As an afterthought Andrew mentioned Eli Pleasant. "Eli lives on the other side of the Sabine, but he trades in Texas a lot."

Carlos's eyes narrowed. "You know the old man Pleasant?"

"I do." Andrew wondered if he had helped or hurt himself. Eli had many friends on the Mexican side of the Sabine River, but his various activities had left him enemies, too.

The girl moved closer, studying Andrew intently. He tried not to blink; she might take that for a sign he was lying.

She said, "The old man Pleasant has been good to us, Carlos."

In the gloom of the corner, where he could see little detail except her dark, fearful eyes, she had looked considerably like Marie. The light was better where she stood now. Andrew saw that the resemblance had been more than superficial. Petra was slight, like Marie, and her animated black eyes were much the same. Her complexion was a bit darker, more olive, than Marie's. He felt ashamed that he had given her a fright. He would not have wanted anyone to frighten Marie this way.

The tension began to drain from him, for he perceived in Carlos's eyes that the danger had passed. The rifle barrel sagged, pointing toward the hard-packed dirt floor. Carlos said, "I take you at your word that you are a friend of Pleasant."

Andrew tried to smile, but the tension had not drained that much. He raised his hand to chest level. "I have known him since I was that tall. I have not seen him in a few months."

"No one sees Pleasant unless he wishes to be seen. That is why he has lived to become an old man."

Andrew felt weakness in his knees after looking into that rifle barrel. He slumped into a rough-hewn chair. It struck him that the cabin had largely been stripped. He saw no pots, no pans, no utensils on a rough shelf over the table. A wooden bedframe had no blankets, no goatskin, no cornhusk pad. It was getting on toward suppertime, but the fireplace was cold.

"They must have looted this place."

The girl shook her pretty head. Her voice was sharp. "They would have. This was our own doing, to save all we could from the thieves. They would take our land and everything. But our father lived and died on this land, and our grandfather. The king gave it to them. Now come those American filibusters who say it is theirs."

Andrew could not help staring, for she looked so much like Marie. "I heard in San Felipe that the Mexican government ordered the Edwards brothers to leave Texas."

Carlos said, "The government is far away."

"It has soldiers in Nacogdoches."

"They are too few against so many. So we band together in groups to protect ourselves and wait until the government does something. *If* it does something."

Andrew glanced from the man to the girl and back. "You do not look like a very large group to me, just you and your wife."

"My sister," Carlos corrected him. "This place is mine. We come here only to feed the chickens and the animals I could not take with me. Then we return to our family and our friends."

"Where are they?"

Suspicion flared again in the young man's eyes. He did not answer.

To repair the damage Andrew said quickly, "It is just as well that I do not know." He frowned. "South of here I saw a farmhouse burned."

The girl said sternly, "The land does not burn. It will still be ours when all these land-stealing *extranjeros* are gone."

Andrew warmed to the spirit in her voice, the angry fire in her eyes. It was what he would have expected from Marie. He wanted to distress her no longer. "If you are finished with me, I will be on my way."

Carlos asked, "To where?"

"To Nacogdoches."

Carlos's suspicion showed again. "What would you do there?"

"See what is happening, then report back to Stephen Austin. He is concerned."

"Do you think he would help us?"

"He wants no trouble with the Mexican government. I believe he will help you if he can." Andrew decided it was time to be riding, before Carlos took it in his head to disbelieve him again.

A distant rumble of thunder gently shook the cabin. The girl said, "You would be caught in the rain. Go with us. It is not far."

Carlos gave her a quick and questioning glance. She said, "I want to believe him. There may be someone who will know him and can say if he tells the truth. The old man Pleasant was with us last night."

Andrew brightened. "Eli? I would ride far to see him."

Carlos considered for a long moment before nodding. "All the work is finished here. We can leave now."

At dusk they broke out of the timber and came to a farm, a small open place in the midst of a dense pine forest. It was typical of many old Mexican farms he had seen in Texas; limited, providing for subsistence but nothing more. These were a people traditionally poor, used to little and asking little more of life than enough to eat and a place to live. Central to the farm was a cabin, the oldest part small and darkened with age. Additions had been made periodically, evidently to accommodate a growing family. Andrew saw a set of log corrals, the timber dark and sagging with its years, and a couple of sheds, all built of material cut and dragged from the woods which encroached upon the farm on all but one side and darkly threatened to overwhelm it.

He counted three wagons, which he assumed belonged to refugees. The place had some appearance of a military camp, for several tents clustered around the cabin. He counted three Mexican-style picket *jacales,* evidently put up to provide temporary shelter against the winter for some of the people banded together here. A couple of women cooked over outdoor fires. A light breeze drifted the pleasant aroma of pine smoke toward him, reminding him that he had eaten but little. From things Carlos and Petra had told him on the way, he knew Petra shared the old cabin with her mother, the Moreno family matriarch, and brothers and a sister younger than Carlos. Their father had been murdered by a Spanish loyalist officer many years ago, before Mexican independence. The rest of the people here, aside from the Morenos, included old Mexican settlers and some recent American squatters, assembled for mutual protection against a common threat.

Their situation reminded him of an occasion during his Tennessee boyhood when settlers had massed in the face of Indian danger. He remembered that he had worried more about the hazard of so many guns in the hands of careless people than about the Indians. The only casualty he recalled was a convivial leatherstocking—friend of his father Mordecai—who imbibed freely of corn whiskey and shot off his toe.

Andrew looked back over his shoulder toward the storm cloud. He could hear an occasional rumble of thunder and wondered if there was shelter enough for all these people to sleep dry. If they didn't, he couldn't ask to.

A tall, heavy-shouldered American of perhaps forty strode forward to meet the three riders. He carried no rifle, but his huge hands looked strong enough to provide a considerable persuasion. Andrew wondered if he might be a blacksmith by trade. "Who have you brought with you, Carlos?" the man asked in a Spanish better practiced than Andrew's.

"He says he is from the Austin colony at San Felipe. He says he knows the old man Pleasant. We wanted to see if Pleasant will speak for him."

The big man shook his head. "Eli is gone. He rode to Nacogdoches to see what is happening there." His dark gray eyes fastened upon Andrew with a measure of hostility. He shifted to English. "What's your name?"

"Andrew Lewis. Carlos has the right of it. I've got a farm out west of San Felipe."

"Maybe. Or maybe you're hopin' to get a farm out west of Nacogdoches by workin' for Haden Edwards and his bunch. You ever know an old feller called Tolliver Beard?"

The name sounded vaguely familiar, but Andrew could not remember why. "Not that I can recall."

The man looked back over his shoulder and jerked his head. Another who resembled him enough to be his brother walked out carrying a rifle. "You'll pardon us if we don't quite trust you to be tellin' us the gospel truth. We been lied to by several that was slicker'n goosegrease. Wouldn't be the first time that Beard has tried to send a spy into this camp."

The second man raised the rifle. He did not point it directly at Andrew, but was close enough. Andrew took a chill. He declared, "I've got nothin' to give you but my word. I can see that ain't enough. So I'll trouble you folks no longer and just be on my way."

The big man quickly stepped forward, grabbing Andrew's reins up close to the brown horse's mouth. "You've seen enough to have a good idea how many of us there is. Beard and the Edwards brothers would probably be tickled to know that. If you was to leave here, you just might go and tell them."

The man with the rifle moved in and motioned for Andrew to dismount. The muzzle now was aimed at Andrew's chest. But Andrew did not move from the saddle. It was in his mind that on horseback he still had a chance to cut and run. Afoot, he would be helpless.

The girl made a protest in Spanish. "Please! We think he tells the truth." She looked frightened, indication enough to Andrew that he also had reason to be. These people had been pushed hard, and they were strongly inclined to push back.

The girl pleaded, "We did not bring him here to be killed."

"You should not have brought him here at all. You have put this whole camp at risk."

Andrew said dryly, "Not as big a risk as mine. Why don't we just leave everything the way it is till Ol' Eli gets back?"

"We have no idea how long that might be. Eli does what he wants to, when he wants to. We may not see him for a week."

From beneath a shed a voice shouted, "Ain't you goin' to shoot him?"

Andrew thought he knew the voice. He wished he did not.

The big man answered, "Shootin' a man don't come easy."

"Depends. With some, it ain't hard at all."

The speaker stepped out of the shed's gloom and into the fading light of evening, his hands in his pockets. Andrew felt a mixture of apprehension and shame, as if he had foolishly stumbled into an enemy's camp.

Isaac Blackwood said, "What do you reckon, Andrew Lewis? Reckon I ought to tell him to go ahead and shoot you?"

Foreboding was like a knot in Andrew's stomach. "Wouldn't surprise me if you did, Isaac. Wouldn't surprise me if your brother Finis shot me himself."

The big man glanced at Isaac in surprise. "You know him?"

"Ever since back in Tennessee."

Andrew was not sure that such a statement from a Blackwood would be accepted as a recommendation; not if these people knew much about the Blackwoods. He said quickly, "We never was friends."

Isaac gave Andrew a long moment's contemplation. "Looks like you need a friend right now, Andrew. Even if it's just me."

Andrew had to swallow his resentment. "I'd be obliged if you'd tell them who I am." He sat in a nervous sweat, waiting for Isaac's words either to free him or to condemn him.

Isaac took his time, letting him stew. "What Andrew told you is the truth. He's got a farm in Austin's colony. Me and my brothers, we been there." He looked straight into Andrew's eyes without blinking. "Him and his brother Michael, they run us off. Said they'd shoot us if ever we come back."

The man who held the rifle let it sag to arm's length. The big man turned loose of Andrew's reins. He said, "I'm surprised that you'd speak up for him, then."

Isaac shrugged. "Surprises me a little too. But I

guess in a time like this, all us Tennesseans got to stick together."

Andrew thought of his brother Michael, and how it would gravel him to learn that the Lewises owed a debt of gratitude to a Blackwood. He saw the big man wipe cold sweat from his forehead and realized the quandary he had been in. Andrew had sweated some himself. He dismounted from the brown and forced himself to extend his hand. "No hard feelin's."

The big man stuck his hand out. "And none with me." Andrew winced under the crushing strength of the grip. "Name's Simon Wells. Hope you'll pardon us for bein' suspicious, but that Edwards bunch burned out me and my family and my brother. If the Morenos hadn't taken everybody in, we'd all of us be in a bad fix."

Gratitude toward Isaac Blackwood did not lessen Andrew's misgivings. He could not believe the Blackwoods had any land to lose. "What are you-all doin' here, Isaac?"

Isaac's eyes were steady; he did not give an inch. "We'd found us a little place, me and Finis and Luke. That bunch out of Nacogdoches, they come up on the cabin while me and Luke was off a-huntin'. They taken Finis and Nelly by surprise. Time me and Luke seen the smoke and come a-runnin', the deed had been done. So we come here and joined up with these other folks that've been mistreated the same way."

Andrew wondered who Nelly was. "I reckon I owe you, Isaac."

"I reckon you do. But I ain't decided *what* you owe me. I'll think of somethin'."

Andrew had no doubt of that. He turned to the Mexican brother and sister who had brought him here. Her eyes reflected confusion; she had understood little or none of the conversation in English. She had seen only that the threat had passed. In Spanish he assured her, "It is all right now. This man"—he nodded toward Isaac—"knows me."

He saw doubt in her eyes. She asked, "You are friends?"

He suspected she had already formed an opinion of the Blackwoods. He said, "Not friends. But we know each other."

She gave him a fleeting smile that looked like Marie's. "I am glad you are not friends. That one seems not too bad, but his brothers?"

Andrew warmed to her. For a moment she was not a stranger named Petra; she was Marie.

Isaac puzzled. He did not know Spanish. "What's she sayin'?"

"She's just askin' if I'd like to eat supper with her and her folks."

Simon Wells arched an eyebrow.

21

Andrew sat on the cabin porch, listening to Simon Wells recount the settler's grievances against the Edwards brothers, but his primary attention was not with Wells. He watched the girl Petra move about the cabin, helping clean up after a simple family meal to which she and her mother had invited Andrew. He had shared it with Petra, Carlos and his wife, two younger brothers named Ramón and Felipe, a sister named Juanita, and the old *señora*. The Moreno family had eked out a living in the region for generations, farming in a small way, raising a few cattle. The oppressive final years of the Spanish government had been a brutal trial, taking the life of Petra's father, forcing her brothers to assume the burdens of manhood years too early. Many of their relatives had been driven into exile in Louisiana because of their real or imagined opposition to the crown. To have endured all that, only to be subjected again now to possible loss of their venerable land claims, had been a cross they were unwilling to bear without stiff resistance.

Wells conceded, "We can't rightly blame the Edwards brothers for all of it. Way I've been told, Haden Edwards spent a lot of time and money and work down in Mexico earnin' the right to bring settlers into this part of the country. But the Mexican government is new and big and clumsy. One part ain't got the first notion of what another part is up to. One side grants rights and another takes them away. They don't trust each other, and it's sure as hell they don't trust Americans."

Andrew could hear Petra and her family in the cabin, speaking Spanish among themselves. Some of the talk was so rapid that its meaning was lost on him. He pointed his chin toward the door. "There's the biggest trouble of all: we don't understand one another. Us Americans, we come out of a different upbringin'. We get throwed together with the Mexican people, and all anybody can see—them or us—is the differences. It was probably a mistake for us to've come into their country in the first place."

"But we're here now," Wells said firmly. "This is our home too, and we ain't noways about to leave." Wells stopped talking. He seemed to wait for Andrew to make some comment, but Andrew was silent, watching through the door. Wells turned to see Petra kneeling before the fireplace, poking up a blaze. "There's good folks amongst these Mexicans, even if we don't always understand each other."

Andrew grunted agreement.

Wells smiled. "Some don't hurt the eyes none either."

Andrew felt a little like a boy caught at mischief. "She just reminds me of somebody, is all."

"You a bachelor, Lewis?"

"Never had a chance to be otherwise. Livin' way

out past the settlements don't allow for much social life."

Wells said, "My wife's Louisiana French. But if I was a young bachelor in Texas I might be lookin' to marry a likely Mexican girl. It'd set a man up better with the government."

"I'd be more concerned about how I set up with the girl."

"But if you had the girl and the government both feelin' generous towards you, it'd be like a double patch on your britches, wouldn't you say?"

Petra rose and turned, her eyes catching Andrew looking at her. She smiled self-consciously and turned quickly away. His face warmed.

Wells studied him. "She was scared to death that me and my brother was fixin' to shoot you."

"The same idee crossed my mind."

"We wouldn't have; that was all bluff. I had a feelin' she'd've walked in front of the rifle to stop us."

Andrew blinked. "Why?"

Wells shrugged. "I ain't been married but twenty years, and that ain't near long enough to figure them out. But I'd guess she's took a likin' to you."

"She don't talk English, and my Spanish is barely passable."

"There's worse things in this world than havin' a woman that can't talk to you."

"I didn't come here lookin' for a wife."

"I wasn't either, when I met mine. But a man that don't grab a good opportunity when he sees one is liable to sleep in a bachelor's bed the rest of his life. It can get godawful cold here in the wintertime."

Andrew pushed to his feet. He removed his hat and stepped into the doorway. Petra smiled Marie's smile, and watched him with Marie's dark eyes. He said in Spanish, "I am grateful for the good supper. Now I will be saying good-night."

Petra said, "But you will stay until the old man Pleasant comes back?"

"No, I will be going on to Nacogdoches in the morning. Austin will be waiting to hear from me."

Petra's smile left her. "I—we thought you might remain with us a while."

"I wish I could. It would be a great pleasure."

"At least you will visit us on your way back to San Felipe?"

"I will look forward to it."

Petra started to extend her hand, glanced uneasily at her watching mother and drew it back, clasping both hands at her waist. "As we will."

Andrew stepped backward onto the porch, nearly stumbling over a rough-cut board.

Wells said, "Careful, Lewis, or you'll lose your balance."

Andrew could have told him he already had.

He hoped the storm cloud might go around, but it did not. The thunder became louder, and lightning flashes told him he had better hunt for a dry place to sleep. He found the first shed already sheltering all the men who could crowd beneath it. He dreaded the second because he had seen Isaac and Luke there. But he saw no choice other than to bed down in the rain.

Isaac watched impassively as Andrew brought in his blanket and sought out a place on the ground not already taken. "Careful. You might get contaminated, breathin' the same air as us Blackwoods."

Andrew frowned. He saw only Isaac and Luke. "Where's Finis?" He thought it a good idea to know the whereabouts of all three.

Isaac jabbed his thumb in the direction of a

canvas-covered wagon near the shed. "Him and Nelly, they got their own accommodations."

Andrew had seen Nelly, an amply fleshed girl who did not seem to have all of her buttons sewed on tight. "Where'd you-all manage to steal a wagon?"

Luke took offense and stepped menacingly toward Andrew, but Isaac caught his brother's arm and pulled him back. "You Lewises always did look for the worst. We figure we had the wagon comin' to us. Them fellers that burned us out, some of them was travelin' by wagon. We convinced them it'd be good for their health to walk back to Nacogdoches."

Andrew conceded, "I can see a certain justice in that."

Isaac smiled thinly. "Glad we can agree on somethin'."

Andrew was a long time in going to sleep. He had little concern about Isaac, but it was worrisome lying so near Luke, who had never been known for good sense. Grunts and groans, both male and female, emanated from the wagon. They were disturbing to say the least of it. After a time Andrew complained to Isaac, "Don't Finis know everybody hears, or does he just not give a damn?"

Isaac said in a resigned tone, "I hope you don't have any notions about makin' them stop. You'd have to fight Nelly as well as Finis."

Andrew turned over in his blankets and tried to block the couple from his consciousness. But they made his thoughts drift unwillingly to the girl Petra, and sleep was as elusive as a doe in the woods.

Nacogdoches had grown in recent years, since Mexican independence had encouraged many of the refugees from Spanish oppression to come back, and since American colonization had turned the piney-woods town into a resting place and supply point for overland travelers bound toward Austin's and other colonies. It was still dominated by an old stone building which had variously been courthouse and military headquarters in Spanish times. But a great many new buildings had gone up, mostly of logs because timber was plentiful and required little haul. Horses and cattle grazed around the outskirts. Andrew's eye was caught by the numerous wagons, and he wondered if all the newcomers were so rich.

As he rode up the street it was apparent there was some unusual excitement in the town. Men gathered in small huddles, talking earnestly, some of them shouting, some arguing, most seeming to be having themselves a high old time. Several staggered, obviously drunk. One man waved a bottle and whooped loudly with almost every uncertain step.

A large man in a long black coat clutched a Bible and protested at the top of a voice that Andrew found familiar, "Awaken, brothers. This is no time to indulge ourselves in drink and debauchery. It is a time to counsel with the Lord, to beg Him for His guidance and mercy."

If anyone besides Andrew heard him, no one gave any sign.

The man turned, and Andrew could see the black patch over one eye. The other eye lighted with recognition, and he hailed Andrew. "Welcome, my young friend. You seem sadly out of place here among the Philistines."

"Howdy, Fairweather. How's the collections comin'?"

"I subsist. That is all I ask for. That is about all this land provides for anyone."

"Looks like a lot of excitement in town."

"The devil has found many idle hands here for his workshop. Were I you, I would not tarry any longer than it takes to water your horse. Seeds of violence are being sown here today. The harvest will be briars and thorns."

Andrew frowned. "What seeds are they plantin'?"

"Seeds of sedition, of rebellion. They are declaring themselves independent of all law except their own. I am about to depart this wicked place before God and the Mexican government hurl down a thunderbolt and destroy it. I would strongly advise that you leave with me."

"I can't, not yet. I've got a job of work to do."

"Then watch yourself. You could find more trouble here than you found in that Waco village." Fairweather turned and walked toward the stone building, his large Bible tucked under the arm of his black coat.

Andrew saw a dozen or so men clustered around a flagpole at the front of the old structure. He watched two of them raise an unfamiliar flag of red and white. It was not Mexican, not Spanish, not American. He rode the brown horse up closer. On the flag he made out the words "Independence, Liberty, and Justice." As it reached the top of the pole, men cheered. Some waved their hats, and a couple fired rifles into the air. Fairweather raised the Bible above his head and exhorted them to prayer, with the same lack of results as before.

Two buckskin-clad men came up and stood beside Andrew's brown horse, watching with much interest the commotion around the flagpole. One held a long rifle, the other a jug. The man with the jug said, "Never seen it to fail. Try to celebrate a happy occasion and a preacher'll show up to sour the whiskey."

Andrew asked, "What's the happy occasion?"

The man with the rifle looked up, his face furrowing. It was a young face, stubbled with whiskers. His gray eyes held a challenge. Andrew thought perhaps he had seen the man before. He immediately took him for one of those who turn mean when they get drunk. The red veins in his eyes made it appear likely that he was drunk a lot. "You don't know? Where you been, anyway? The moon?"

"It seems that far. Where I've been, you don't hear much. What's that flag?"

"Why, my friend, that's the flag of the Republic of Fredonia. This community has just declared its independence from Mexico and the United States and the whole damned world!"

"That don't sound legal."

"Anything's legal if you can make it stick." The man patted the rifle's long barrel. "We're the boys that can make it stick."

"There's Mexican troops stationed here. What're they goin' to say about it?"

"Ain't enough of them to say anything. If they was to try, we'd hoe them down like weeds in the field. We'll be sendin' them packin' pretty soon, back to Bexar. And hell, we may decide to go down there and take Bexar too." The whiskey was loud.

The other man unstoppered the jug and raised it for a long drink. He passed it to the rifleman and laughed. "Here you go, Jayce Beard. Better oil up your goozle some more before you start marchin' off to Bexar. It's a fur piece."

Beard. Andrew had heard the people at the Moreno place speak the name. He thought he had heard it somewhere before, as well. He studied the face, and he remembered. This was the young ruffian who had angrily bumped into him one day in front of Stephen Austin's office in San Felipe. An older man had been with him, his father. What had been his name? Tolliver, that was it. Tolliver Beard.

Jayce's Adam's apple bobbed up and down as he held the jug high. He wiped the back of his hand across his mouth and lifted the jug toward Andrew. "Better have a snort, moon man. The celebration is a-fixin' to commence."

Andrew shook his head. "If I was you, I'd wait and see what the Mexicans say before I celebrated too much. And I expect Stephen Austin will have some notions on it too."

"Stephen Austin has got nothin' to say about it. Haden Edwards tried to get him to help us, and he wouldn't raise his hand."

"He may raise it now."

The man with the rifle began to frown deeply. Suspicion crept into eyes glazing from the whiskey. "I thought you just now rode into town. How come you to know so much about what Austin's goin' to think?"

"I can guess."

The other man's face had clouded. He pushed in close beside Andrew's left stirrup. "Where'd you come from, stranger? Louisiana?"

Andrew considered lying to them but decided against it. When he had to lie to such as these, it would be time for him to slink off into a hole. "I just came up from San Felipe."

"Then you're a spy!" shouted Jayce Beard. "A damned stinkin' spy!" He turned and yelled to the men at the flagpole. "Come a-runnin', boys. We got ourselves a spy!"

Andrew tried to pull the brown away, but the man with the jug grabbed the reins and held them. Andrew saw three or four men come running from the direction of the stone building. He tried to bring up his rifle, but someone grabbed its barrel. Rough hands gripped him and began trying to pull him down from the saddle. He struggled to hold on, to spur the brown and break free. He felt himself being dragged off the horse's left side. He clutched at the pommel but could not hold it against all that angry strength. Falling, he kicked his left foot free so it would not hang in the stirrup and perhaps break his ankle. He struck the ground with an impact that took the breath from him. He felt himself being dragged between two log buildings.

He heard Fairweather's voice. "Gentlemen! Gentlemen! I implore you not to resort to violence. It is an abomination in the sight of the Lord." No one paid any attention to him.

"What we goin' to do with him, Jayce?" someone demanded.

"Take him to Ben Edwards and see if he wants to hang him. But we're fixin' to stomp on him a little first."

Jayce had uncommon strength as he hauled Andrew to his feet. His breath was foul. He pushed Andrew up against a log wall and drove a huge fist into his stomach. Andrew lost what little breath he still had. He tried to shout a protest, but the cry was choked off in his throat by another blow. He bent and felt a fist strike his face, driving him half around and slamming his head against the log wall. He tasted blood warm and sticky and tinged with salt. He sensed more than saw the men gathered around him, two or three joining Jayce and his friend at the beating, others cheering them on. Lightning flashed before his eyes, and he felt himself trying to retch.

Gradually he seemed to go numb, hardly feeling the blows to his ribs, his stomach, his face. He sensed that he was sinking to the ground, that he was looking at the men's boots from close up.

He heard an angry roaring voice and saw a tall, angular shape pushing between the men semicircled around him. He felt a boot strike him in the ribs, but the impact was dull, without pain. He saw the quick movement of a long-barreled rifle and heard it swish as it swung with a mighty force. He expected it to crush his head open, but it did not. He heard a cracking sound and a cry of pain. A man sprawled on the ground beside him. Through a red haze he recognized the bloody face of the man called Jayce. His eyes were rolled back.

He heard that angry voice again. "Now the rest of you-all had better step back, because I'm just on the point of losin' my temper." The voice had the crackle of age, but it carried an authority that would make a prudent man stop and take notice. Andrew sensed that his antagonists were backing away.

The voice raged, "You there, drag that son of a bitch away before I take a notion to hit him again. And any of you wants a taste of what's in this barrel, you just make a false move towards me or that boy."

Apparently their curiosity was limited, for nobody made any such move. Someone grabbed Jayce's feet and unceremoniously dragged him off through horse droppings that happened to be in the way.

The voice demanded, "You, preacher, you fetch that brown horse over here. And you two, you lift that boy up onto him. Careful now, you hear me? I'm fixin to get mad in a minute. When I get mad I even scare myself!"

Andrew felt strong hands raise him up from the ground, then lift him into the saddle. He tried to find the stirrups. Fairweather guided first one boot into place, then the other.

"All right, now, back away from him, all of you."

Andrew blinked. He could see the men, though they seemed to sway backward and forward. It was like looking at them through a fog. He got a grip on the pommel of the saddle, for this would be a poor time to fall to the ground. The preacher took the reins at the bit and led the brown horse out into the dirt street. Andrew dimly saw the tall man climb stiffly upon a horse of his own, then turn back and take the brown horse's reins. Andrew blinked his eyes clear. There in front of him, gaunt as an old wolf but defiant as an old badger, sat Eli Pleasant, ten years older than Methuselah and still as tough as the first time he had ever shaved.

Pleasant said, "Thanks, Fairweather, for comin' and fetchin' me." To Andrew he said, "I declare, seems to me like I am everlastin'ly havin' to come and drag you Lewis boys away from trouble. Between you and Michael, you've probably worried ten years off of my life."

22

Andrew felt his throbbing eyes swelling shut. After a while he could see through little more than a slit in his left and less in his right. He clung painfully to the saddle, knowing that if he loosened his hold he would fall like a sack of corn. Old Eli rode in front, setting an easy, plodding pace, leading Andrew's brown horse. Andrew was apprehensive over possible pursuit, but Eli showed not a whit of concern, humming a discordant little tune that grated on the ears. He had probably thrown a healthy scare into that bunch with the crazy-old-man look in his eyes, his raspy voice carrying a threat of hellfire that the preacher Fairweather might have envied. If any of the crowd were personally acquainted with him, they had probably counseled the others that Eli Pleasant was a good man to leave alone. He was a quiet old codger when things went his way, but he could be aroused to fight like a sore-footed bear. He had survived long years in the outlaw country of western Louisiana, making his living smuggling goods in both directions across the border at considerable risk to life and liberty. He was not one to be intimidated by anything or anybody small.

Eli's voice was gentle now. "We're fixin' to come to a little stream, just yonder a piece. You'll feel better when you've got all that blood washed off of your face."

The water was freezing cold. Its first rude shock set Andrew to trembling. But it eased the fever in his battered face, at least temporarily. He could see a bit better, too.

Eli fetched a bottle and bade Andrew take a long drink from it. It warmed him all the way down, though Andrew knew its warmth was but temporary. When it passed he would probably be colder than ever. Eli eyed him critically. "You ain't pretty. I wonder what you done to get them boys back yonder so riled up."

"They thought I came here to spy for Austin."

"Did you?"

Andrew considered a moment. "I wasn't lookin' at it in quite that way."

"If you was in their boots, how would you look at it?"

"Like they did, I reckon. That don't make me hurt any less."

"Always try to look at a thing through the other man's eyes. At least you'll have a better idee what to expect from him. Come on, we'd best be goin' if we don't want to ride all night."

"Where you takin' me?"

"To some friends of mine. Same place I carried your brother Michael the time he was wounded and your daddy killed. They're pretty good at takin' care of hurt folks. They've had a-plenty of practice with their own."

As the sun went down, the evening turned cold. Andrew hunched painfully in the saddle, shivering. In the darkness, with his vision impaired by the swelling, he had no idea what direction they traveled.

Eli talked on. "Them boys in Nacogdoches ain't ready to start listenin' to reason; they're havin' too much fun. But they'll wake up some mornin' with their heads hurtin' and their stomachs all soured, and they'll know it ain't no easy thing to run your own country. I'd say the hell with them, except they're liable to get Mexico riled up and spoil Texas for all of us. I'll bet there ain't a hundred fifty, maybe two hundred Fredonians if you was to put them all in one wad. The Mexicans just need to set back a little while, then come marchin' in some mornin' when the boys are sick of one another. Like as not, there won't even be no fight to it."

Andrew grunted. He feared Eli was not taking his own advice, that he was not seeing the incident through the Mexicans' eyes. "I've got to get the word back to Austin."

Eli sniffed. "The shape you're in, you'd be to New Year's gettin' there. The news'll reach Austin in due time."

"But I promised him—" Andrew realized he was making no headway with Eli. The old man was selectively deaf; he heard only what he wanted to hear. Andrew felt his body slowly going stiff, the soreness settling all the way to the bone. He gritted his teeth and resisted complaint until finally he lost his grip on the pommel and felt himself sliding forward over the horse's shoulder. He tried in vain to make his numbed fingers grasp the brown mane. He struck the ground with a dull thump. The impact hurt all the way to the ends of his fingers and toes.

Eli dismounted and knelt. "World's come to a hell of a pass when a Lewis can't even stay on a horse. Bust anything?"

Andrew groaned. "Feels like everything's busted."

"Got to give them boys credit: they don't settle for halfways. We'd just as well make a dry camp. Looks to me like you're used up. Next time you go to talk politics, you'll first take the measure of them you're talkin' to."

Andrew offered no argument. Eli staked the two horses while Andrew struck flint and steel, trying to spark a fire in a wad of dry grass. He hurt too much, and Eli had to complete the job. Andrew rolled up in his blanket and tried to get warm as the blaze slowly built in a small pile of deadwood. Eli voiced regret over not having anything to fix for supper. That was the least of Andrew's concerns; his jaw was too sore for chewing, and his stomach was too riled to accept food if he could have forced it down.

Eli said, "I wasn't worried about *your* supper; I was thinkin' about mine. I ain't et since breakfast."

Andrew huddled close to the fire, trying to absorb all of its warmth. He said, "The one that started it all, I heard somebody call him Beard."

"That was Jayce Beard. He's got a mean streak in him but damned little sense to go with it. Tolliver Beard, his old daddy, is the one you really got to watch. He's just as mean but a right smart faster in the head. It's his notion that he can take over a fat lot of land under Haden Edwards's new rules. And he's got the determination to do it if somebody don't put a stop to the Fredonians. I know that old bastard from Louisiana. He's like a dog that, once he gets ahold of a bone, he don't turn it loose."

The cold and the constant hurting kept Andrew from going to sleep for a long time. He hoped the two men Eli had struck with his rifle barrel were feeling a similar misery. When he finally managed to nod off, his dreams carried him to Marie's kitchen, warm and snug and smelling of a hot supper cooking on the hearth. He played with little Mordecai and watched Marie rock the baby in a cradle Michael had built. He could not tell if Marie was talking French or Spanish or English; he only knew that her voice tinkled like a silver bell.

Once his dream altered a little. Instead of Marie, he saw the girl Petra. Then it was Marie again, or perhaps not. He found he could not tell them apart.

He awakened to see a cold winter sun rising in the east, all light and no heat. Half frozen, he shivered and tried to sit up. He made it on the third attempt. Through a blur he watched Eli saddling the horses.

Eli studied him critically. "Your face is speckled with blue welts, and them eyes appear to be swollen nigh shut. Do you feel any better than you look?"

"Damn little," Andrew admitted. He struggled slowly to his feet, swaying. Eli led the brown horse up to him, and Andrew steadied himself by leaning against the saddle.

Eli gave him a careful boost up. "I've seen beef hangin' on a hook that looked better'n you do. Wouldn't surprise me none if you've got a rib or two broke. But we still need to ride a ways if you can make it."

Andrew gritted his teeth. "I can make it."

He soon reconsidered that declaration of confidence, though he was determined not to retract it.

Every step the brown horse made was like the blow of a Fredonian's fist. Andrew broke a dry twig from a tree and stuck it between his teeth, clamping down on it when he felt like making a cry. He did not want Eli to see the extent of the pain. It had been part of Mordecai Lewis's teaching to his sons that a man never complained; he took whatever was his lot and made the best of it.

Andrew began recognizing landmarks. He sensed Eli's destination long before they reached it. His swollen eyes made out the shape of the log cabin, the nearby sheds, the wagons and tents and *jacales* close around. "I've been here," he said. "Some of these folks thought I was a spy for the Edwards brothers."

Eli chuckled. "I never thought about it before, but all you Lewis boys have got an honest face. That's more'n enough to make folks suspicious in a country like this."

Word of their coming preceded them. People emerged from the tents and sheds to watch their approach. Andrew saw the three Blackwoods standing beside their wagon. Finis had his one arm around the waist of the plump girl Nelly. Her startled gasp at the sight of Andrew's face told him how bad he looked. Finis hollered at Eli, "Did you do that to him all by yourself, old man? I'd've been glad to come and help you."

Eli ignored him, and Andrew tried to. That was difficult, hearing the pleasure in Finis's voice at Andrew's misfortune. Finis declared loudly, "I swear, Andrew, this is the first time I ever thought you looked good."

Luke Blackwood laughed.

Andrew had no strength to respond, but he

mentally set Finis's remark on a back shelf in his memory, to be called up for review at some appropriate time in the future. He sensed someone following him and turned his head painfully. Isaac Blackwood trailed him afoot. Isaac's two older brothers stayed behind.

Several people had come out onto the tiny porch of *Señora* Moreno's cabin. The girl Petra made a small cry and hurried forward, lifting her skirt so she could run. She spoke to Eli as she passed him, then stopped beside Andrew's horse. "What has happened to him?" she demanded in Spanish.

Eli replied that Andrew had disagreed with some men in town over a matter of politics and had failed to persuade them to his line of thinking.

Petra called for her brothers to help her lift Andrew down from the saddle. Carlos gently edged her aside and took hold. Andrew managed to swing his leg over the horse, but he would have fallen had the strong hands of Carlos and Ramón not held him. He swayed drunkenly and bumped hard against the brown. The animal shied away from him, almost making him fall despite the efforts of the Moreno brothers. Isaac Blackwood lent them a hand.

Andrew wanted to tell him to go back to his brothers Finis and Luke, but at the moment it was expedient to accept help from any quarter. At least Isaac was not laughing at him.

Isaac said, "Must've been some of the Edwards people."

"It was," Andrew managed.

"Some of the same ones that burnt us out, I expect. Same ones that've got all these folks forted up here. What're we goin' to do about it?"

Eli put in, "Andrew tried talkin' to them. You can see how much good that done."

Isaac said tightly, "I was thinkin' about somethin' stronger than talk."

Andrew took a quick though blurry look at the people gathering around, eager to know what was happening. "There's a way too many for this little bunch to whip."

Isaac shook his head. "I know we can't do that, not without some extra help. I was just wonderin' how we might go about gettin' that help."

Andrew said, "Austin."

Isaac asked, "What about Austin?"

"Austin has got to know what's happened. I've got to go and tell him."

Eli snorted. "I didn't think I'd even get you *this* far. It'll be some days before you go anywheres."

Andrew grudgingly admitted to himself that Eli was right. "Then you go tell him."

Eli shrugged. "Not me, boy. Austin never did approve of my business activities. Was I to go down into his bailiwick, he just might take it in his head to turn me over to the Mexican authorities in Bexar. It'd tickle them to have me for their permanent guest."

Petra cried out, "Are you men going to keep him standing out here all day? Bring him into the house."

Isaac said quickly, "Austin's got no quarrel with me. I'll go. What you want me to tell him, Andrew?"

Andrew stalled. Surely there must be somebody here more responsible than a Blackwood to carry the message; Simon Wells, perhaps. But Isaac allowed him little chance to argue. He took Andrew's right arm, and Carlos took the left. Together they half carried Andrew into the log cabin. Isaac kept talking. "This ain't no time for holdin' old grudges. Me and my brothers, we got an interest in this thing too. Even bigger'n yours, because there ain't nobody burned you out yet. Now, what is it Austin needs to know?"

As they eased him onto a rough wood-frame bed with rawhide stretched beneath a cornshuck mattress, Andrew reluctantly told what he had heard about the declaration of a Fredonian republic. "If Austin can get word to the Mexican authorities about it before they learn from their own people, maybe it'll help keep them from seein' us all as rebels."

Isaac declared, "I don't much give a damn what the authorities think; they're a greasy-lookin' lot to me. But I'd admire to see them land thieves in Nacogdoches get their due for what they done to us. So I'll carry your message to Austin." He turned toward the door but stopped. "Never thought me and any of you Lewises would ever take the same side in a fight. It'd spoil Finis's supper for a week if he was to know I done you a favor, Andrew. So if he asks, you tell him you tried to stop me but couldn't."

Andrew *would* have stopped Isaac if he had known how. He tried to raise a protest with Eli, but Eli had already gone back out the door and was talking earnestly to Isaac, telling him what he knew of events in Nacogdoches.

The last thing Andrew saw was Petra's sympathetic eyes as she laid a damp cloth over his face and gently told him to lie still.

A small blaze in the fireplace made the cabin pleasantly warm. Andrew gradually lost his chill and drifted off to sleep, though the pain momentarily awakened him every time he moved. When at last he came fully awake, he knew by the faded light that the weak winter sun was almost gone. He opened his eyes as much as he could. The blurred images confused him at first. He thought he saw Marie sitting in a handmade wooden chair. That made no sense; there was no reason for her to be here.

"Marie?" he asked incredulously.

Petra's voice told him he was mistaken. "Who?"

He blinked, trying to clear his vision. "Sorry. I woke up and thought you were somebody else." He realized he had spoken in English. He repeated in Spanish.

She said, "You slept a long time. Do you feel better now?"

He was not sure. He tried to raise up, but he felt as if he were bound by rawhide. Every muscle in his body seemed paralyzed. He lay back, defeated.

She touched his face with her small, warm hand. He remembered old times at home in Tennessee, when he had been ill or hurt, and his mother's hands felt as if they had a healing power. Petra's touch was like that, soothing, strengthening.

She said, "Your face is still fevered. Now that you are awake, I will bring another wet cloth. That will draw out some of the pain and the heat."

He could have told her that her hand had the same effect. He said simply, "Thank you."

He felt with his right hand and confirmed what he already knew, that his face was swollen and cut and sore in a dozen places. He felt his nose, wondering if it might be broken; it hurt enough. Those damned Fredonian patriots might have killed him if Eli Pleasant had not shown up. He doubled his fist in remembered anger but quickly relaxed it when a sharp pain jabbed his knuckles.

Petra brought the wet cloth and carefully laid it across his face. Her hand rested a moment on his cheek before she drew it away.

He felt a cold draft as the wooden door opened, then closed. His eyes were covered, but he could hear boots scuff across the packed-earth floor. Eli Pleasant's voice was solicitous. "Girl told me you finally come awake. For a while I was afraid we might have to organize a buryin' party."

"You may yet. There's a whole army of little demons hammerin' away inside of me."

"Naw, it takes a heap of killin' to put a Lewis under the ground. Remember, I've seen some mean ones try."

"They might've done it this time if you hadn't been there. I owe you, Eli."

"I'll mark it down in my ledger. Someday when I'm an old man I may want to come and live with you."

"Someday? You're already old enough to've helped raise George Washington. You can come and live with me now; I'd be obliged for your company."

"You don't need an old man sharin' your cabin. What you need is a young woman. Have you taken a good look at that girl Petra?"

"My eyes've been swollen to where I can't hardly see."

"When they get unswelled, you open them good and wide. Was I a couple years younger, I'd be interested in her myself."

"Everybody keeps tryin' to get me harnessed up. I don't remember hearin' that *you* ever got married."

"I never stood up in front of no preacher, but a man is meant to share his blessin's. How do you think I learned to talk Spanish so good, and French too?" Eli paused. "Your Spanish could stand some improvement, boy. While you're laid up healin', you ought to work on it. I got a feelin' that girl'd be a willin' teacher."

"I'll be up and leavin' here as soon as I can."

"What for? Austin'll be bringin' help, more'n likely. You'd just as well stay here and wait for him. Besides, if that bunch in Nacogdoches decide to do mischief out thisaway, these folks'd need all hands. They could use a Lewis's help."

Andrew mused, "I hadn't thought of it like that. You'll be here too, won't you?"

"I'm fixin' to go back into Nacogdoches. Takin' care of you made me run off and leave some unfinished business."

"That bunch that jumped me, they'll know you. No tellin' what they might do."

"Ain't no swamp rats got the guts to bother Ol' Eli. Ol' Tolliver Beard has knowed me from way back. He knows I got some rowdy friends that'd stove their heads in. Besides, in Nacogdoches I can see what's goin' on. Out here, all I can do is guess."

Andrew was still trying to argue with him when he heard the old man's feet shuffling across the floor. Eli had never been given to lengthy arguments. He just went ahead and did what he wanted and let the devil take the hindmost. He acted as if he had Lewis blood in him.

Andrew shivered from the chilly draft as Eli went out.

He heard Petra's concerned voice. "Are you cold?" Her hands pulled the blanket up tighter around him, and they stayed longer than was necessary, touching his shoulders.

"I am all right," he replied in Spanish. He considered a moment. "Did you hear what Eli said?"

"He spoke in English. I do not understand English."

"He said my Spanish is not very good."

"It could be better," she admitted ruefully.

"I could improve it. But I need someone to talk with."

"When you first awakened you called me by someone else's name. Marie. Your wife, perhaps?"

"I am not married."

"Your sweetheart?"

"I have no sweetheart."

"But the way you called her name—perhaps she is someone you *wish* were your sweetheart."

"Nothing like that. Marie is married to my brother. When I saw you, I thought you looked like her; that was all."

He thought he heard her release a pent-up breath. Her voice sounded like a smile. "Ah—then, Andrew Lewis, I think I would like talking with you—to improve your Spanish."

She did not get the chance, not for a little while. He felt the cold air again as the door opened. He recognized Finis Blackwood's sullen tone. "Andrew Lewis, what did you go and talk my little brother into doin'?"

Andrew could not see him; the damp cloth still covered his eyes. "I didn't talk him into anything."

"Well, he rode off for the south and said he was carryin' a message to Austin. Your message. What right you got to be sendin' a Blackwood off to do your errands?"

"Fact is, I told him I didn't want him to go. I wanted somebody else."

The tenor of Finis's voice began to change. "You mean he went agin your wishes?"

"He did. I'd've rather had anybody go besides a Blackwood."

Finis was silent a moment, thinking it over. "Well now, that puts a whole different complexion on it. You don't trust a Blackwood to do anything right, is that what you're sayin'?"

"That's about it."

Finis chortled in triumph. "Then damn you, you're fixin' to see somethin'. He'll deliver that message to Austin and do it better'n you could've. He'll show you high and mighty Lewises."

He left the door open as he went out. Petra hurried to close it and returned to Andrew's bedside. "I do not wish to speak against your friends, but that one I do not like."

Andrew smiled, though the effort was painful. It pleased him to know she was a good judge of character.

23

Petra brought Andrew some of the family's meager supper from the cooking place on the hearth in the next room. Though he tried, he managed to put down only a little of it. Petra worried, "How can you live if you do not eat?"

"Maybe tomorrow," he said apologetically.

She set the spoon in the plate and the plate in her lap. "It seems strange. I remember when the old man Pleasant brought another Lewis here a long time ago, just as he has done for you. Your brother had been shot by the federal soldiers. I was only a girl then, and had much fear because I had seen their officer murder my father. But my mother and brothers said we should take care of Miguel Lewis because we were all on the same side.

"We won that fight. Now you are here, and we are on the same side in another."

"You'll win this one, too."

She touched his hand. "With your help. That is why you must get well."

Some time after dark, Petra's brother Ramón—younger than Carlos—came into the tiny room and undressed, folding back a blanket on the other small bed.

Andrew felt a twinge of guilt. "I have taken someone's place here."

"Felipe. You are in Felipe's bed."

Felipe was a third brother, the youngest.

"Where will Felipe sleep?"

"Out there." Ramón jerked his head toward the door. "Under a shed."

"He will be cold. I am not so badly hurt that I should force Felipe to sleep outside."

"It will be cold in here too, once the fire dies out. Do not concern yourself. Felipe and his friends will tell wicked stories half the night. He will not notice the cold."

"I do not like being a burden."

"We did not consider your brother a burden. His enemies were our enemies. The men who hurt you would do the same to us if they could."

Despite the reassurance, Andrew lay awake a long while after Ramón had begun snoring. As the cabin's chill closed in and he pulled the blanket tightly around him, conscience made him think of Felipe lying out yonder under a shed, a raw winter wind cutting him to the bone. That was above and beyond hospitality.

Next morning, sore and aching, Andrew arose when Ramón did. With some difficulty he managed to get into his clothes, waving off the young Mexican's offer of help. Gingerly he felt his face, knowing it was still puffed and discolored. He asked, "How do I look?"

Ramón grimaced. "You do not want me to tell you."

Andrew nodded. That was answer enough.

Ramón broke into a knowing smile. "If I were you, I would lie in bed and let my sister wait upon you. It is not a privilege she often gives to anyone, certainly not to Felipe or me."

"I am not an invalid."

"One should accept blessings whenever they come. We do not receive many in this world."

Petra, her short, stocky mother, and a sister younger than Ramón were in the cramped area which served as kitchen, eating place, and sitting room for the Moreno family. Petra's dark eyes widened with misgiving when Andrew stepped into the small room. "You should not be up," she declared.

"I am all right."

"You should look at yourself. No, you should not. The shock would be bad for you."

"It is better that I am up and moving. People die in bed."

Petra insisted, "Ramón, talk to him."

Ramon shrugged. "I cannot hold a rifle on him."

Señora Moreno said, "He is a grown man. You will learn that grown men do not listen well, especially to good advice."

Ramón grinned at Andrew. "I told you Petra enjoys being nurse to you. You should not be so eager to give that up."

Petra blushed. "Ramón—"

Younger brother Felipe, fourteen or fifteen years old, walked in from outside, blanket wrapped around his shoulders. He shivered from the cold.

Andrew said, "Look at Felipe. Next she will have to be nurse for *him*. I have been a burden long enough."

Petra's eyes softened. "But you are not, Andrew Lewis. We are glad to have you here."

Andrew thought Felipe looked less than enthusiastic. His face was a chilled blue. "I will not take Felipe's bed another night. I will find a place for myself."

Petra glanced at her mother for support. "There is no need. We can make room here somewhere. Perhaps in the kitchen. It has often served for sleeping in the past." Her eyes pleaded. They had the same look as Marie's when Marie had asked him to make this trip so Michael would be obliged to remain at home.

He demurred. "The inconvenience—" It was much more than the inconvenience. The way Petra's fingers clutched his arm—

After breakfast he went outside. Several young men huddled around a fire just beyond one of the limb-covered sheds. A couple of them moved to make room for him. A chunky young bachelor farmer whose name he remembered as Dick Johnson rubbed huge hands together briskly. "You don't look too good, Lewis. Was I you, I'd stay in that nice warm cabin as long as I had the chance. I do believe this was the coldest night we've had."

Andrew asked, "Where'd you sleep?"

Johnson pointed his chin toward the shed. "Another night like this and we're liable to all freeze to death. Then Ol' Man Beard and the Fredonians can just walk in and take everything."

Andrew stared toward the several flimsy picket-style *jacales* various ones had built for shelter. "If three or four of us worked together, it wouldn't take long to build somethin' like that."

A man named Pete Bradley frowned. "And live like a Mexican?"

"They're warmer'n *we* are."

Johnson rubbed his hands again. "Well taken. How do we start?"

Bradley said with misgivings, "I don't believe us Americans can build one. It takes a Mexican to rightly do that."

Andrew had visited in a number of these crude *jacales* around Bexar. Their walls were of upright pickets, the lower ends of tightly fitted branches set into a shallow trench, the tops tied together, the roof a thick set of branches topped by sod. The walls were mudded inside and out to turn the wind. There was even a mud fireplace, poor to look at but functional. A tentative shelter at best, a *jacal* was nevertheless better than sleeping cold beneath an open-ended shed.

He found the exertion helped draw out the soreness and speed the healing process. The black-and-blue marks gradually faded from around his eyes, along with the swelling. He remembered that when anyone among the Lewis children had complained about the burden of labor and asked what they were going to receive for it, their father Mordecai would declare, "Work is its own reward. It clears the mind and heals the body and makes a man wise."

Andrew had always harbored reservations about the wisdom gained by working endless rows of corn, chopping out weeds with a hoe, but he had accepted the rest of the axiom.

Carlos and Ramón gave advice and often pitched in to help with shovel or ax or mallet as the *jacal* began to take shape. Despite his dark predictions that the work would come to naught, Pete Bradley put his thin back into the project. A wiry young man, in contrast to Dick Johnson's fleshy build, he seemed never to tire. And never to stop worrying about failure.

Somehow the pair, Johnson and Bradley, reminded him of the two young bachelors, Younts and Smith, who were courting Miles Nathan's daughter in the Colorado River settlement.

Finis and Luke Blackwood idly watched with a superior air. Finis taunted, "Won't be nothin' but a damned hovel. Fit for Mexicans, maybe, but not for a white man."

He changed his mind when he saw it finished and found it snug and warm and dry inside. He loudly declared that he and Luke could build a better one. Finis contributed mostly orders and ill temper; Luke did the sweat labor. After they finished the structural work they put too much heavy earth cover on top against the advice of Carlos Moreno. Finis declared that he had never met a Mexican who could tell him anything worthwhile.

A hard rain added the weight of all the water that soaked into the sod. About dusk it brought the *jacal* crashing down upon a surprised Nelly and Finis and Luke. Hefty Nelly shook clenched fists and told Finis her opinion of him and all his ancestry while rain washed rivulets of mud out of her hair. He, in turn, cursed Luke with a magnificent command of Tennessee backwoods maledictions. Luke, having no one to whom to pass it on, picked awkwardly through the wreckage, trying to rescue his soaked blankets.

Andrew thought it was probably the first time he had laughed since he left the farm on the Colorado for his ride to Nacogdoches.

Petra was more inclined toward sympathy. Standing on the small porch, watching the Blackwoods chase each other aimlessly through the rain, she said in a half-scolding manner, "It is a shame to laugh at the misfortunes of others."

That only caused Andrew to laugh the more. "Not when you know the Blackwoods." His laugh was contagious, for her frown turned unwillingly into a faint smile. She hurried into the cabin, but not before he heard her break into laughter.

Her laugh was like music. It reminded him of Marie's. His own laughter ended, and he began to feel hollow inside.

It was a long way back to the Colorado River.

The men who had gathered for mutual protection at the Moreno farm had established a military-style schedule of guard duty to help prevent any surprise attack by the Fredonians. After a couple of days of mending, Andrew insisted that he take up his share of that responsibility. Pete Bradley was dubious about his beginning so quickly. "It won't work," he predicted. "Shape you're in, you might not stay alert. Might even fall asleep, like Luke Blackwood does. Takes one man to watch out for Luke and another to watch out for whoever might come."

"I can tote my own load," Andrew insisted.

Dick Johnson accepted Andrew's offer without voicing any reservations. "Me and you can stand watch together. I like your sand, Andrew Lewis."

Andrew suspected Johnson wanted to be on hand to add his own weight in case Andrew was not up to the responsibility. But he accepted the man's friendship with gratitude. "Dick, if you ever get tired of these piney woods, I'll be glad to put in a word for you with Austin. There's good land to be had along the Colorado."

Johnson shoved his hand forward. "Couldn't ask for no better'n that."

Pete Bradley worried, "I hear you can't grow nothin' down there, hardly."

After some days Andrew began to feel that all this guard duty was wasted. The nearest thing he saw to outside intrusion was a few white-tailed deer poking their way out beyond the edge of the woods to browse late in the evenings. By day, those refugees who had left livestock elsewhere would ride out to see after them, making it a point to be back before dark. They always went well-armed. Carlos was among them, usually taking Ramón to help him. Since their scare with Andrew at Carlos's place, Petra had not been going. She said that was Carlos's choice, not hers. But she appeared content to remain at the home place. It seemed to Andrew that almost every time he looked around, she was somewhere within sight, hanging clothes on a line, feeding the chickens, gathering the eggs, sweeping the ground in front of the cabin. And she always had that smile— Marie's smile—when he caught her looking at him.

It warmed him, yet made him vaguely uncomfortable. In an odd way that he could not comprehend, he felt disloyal to Marie. It did not help to remind himself that Marie belonged to his brother and always would. He tried to look away from Petra's smile, but that too was difficult.

Half of the men were away seeing after their livestock the morning old Eli Pleasant came spurring in. Andrew, sharing a casual guard duty with Dick Johnson on the trail that led toward Nacogdoches,

saw Eli coming and walked out to meet him, dropping his long-barreled rifle to arm's length. He perceived a basic contradiction between Eli's calm face
and the fact that he had run the horse until it was
lathered with sweat despite the winter chill. But Eli
seldom let anything excite him much, at least not in
a way that it showed.

"Welcome, Eli."

"I may be welcome," Eli declared, "but I doubt
as them behind me will be. You-all better be gettin'
yourselves ready to receive company." He delivered
the message with about as little emotion as if he had
announced that the west wind was getting up.

Dick Johnson's ruddy face quickly became agitated. "How many's there goin' to be?"

"Enough to go around," Eli replied casually. "I
hope all the men are in camp."

"They're not," Andrew admitted. "Half of them
are gone out to tend their stock."

"Them that's left had better get up on their tippy-
toes, then," Eli said. "Them Fredonians ain't far behind me. Ol' Tolliver Beard is in the lead of them.
He's got it in his mind to take this place for his
own."

Andrew said, "We'll rouse up all that's here."

Eli nodded his satisfaction. "Reckon you could
rouse up a cup of coffee for me? And a bite to eat
wouldn't hurt my feelin's none. I left a mite too
early for breakfast."

Johnson stayed to watch the trail while Andrew
went to the Moreno cabin with Eli. Eli's message
brought anxiety to Petra's eyes. "What will we do,
Andrew?" she asked urgently.

"Stop them," he replied, not giving her time to
ask more questions for which he would have no an-

swer. He turned the old smuggler and his appetite over to the mercies of Petra and her mother. He beat a piece of steel bar against a big iron ring hanging from the edge of the porch, a device *Señora* Moreno had used for years to call her menfolk in from fields and pasture. In a minute Andrew counted just five men standing anxiously in front of him. He regretted that two of those were Blackwoods; a man had to accept what he could get in a pinch. The womenfolk gathered too, standing beside or behind their men. Andrew tried not to betray his uncertainty as he relayed the message Eli had brought.

"How many's there goin' to be?" demanded Simon Wells, whose brother was among those gone to see after their own affairs.

"Fifteen to eighteen, best Eli could tell. He didn't stay around to call the roll."

Pete Bradley's gloomy face went into deep furrows. "That's two apiece, just about. Looks hopeless to me."

"Depends on how much you think of your homes."

Bradley said gravely, "They'll whip us, maybe kill us."

"There's one way to avoid that. Everybody could hurry up and pull out before they get here. Just turn it over to them without a fight."

Simon Wells stiffened. "The odds is poor, but they ain't impossible."

Andrew could see anger building in the men's faces, and courage, too. They glanced at one another, borrowing determination.

Wells said sternly, "Andrew, your farm is down in Austin's colony. But ours are here, and we ain't leavin'."

"Then what're we standin' here talkin' for? Let's get out yonder and fix for company."

The men scattered to tents and *jacales* and sheds for their rifles and ammunition. Shortly they were back, faces flushed with excitement as they took count. There were Simon Wells and the youngest Moreno boy, Felipe. There were Finis and Luke Blackwood. There was lean Pete Bradley, who shared a *jacal* with Andrew and Dick Johnson. Johnson waited out at the guard post on the trail. With Andrew himself, that made seven.

Eli stepped from the door of the Moreno cabin, a cup of parched-grain coffee in his hand. "I got nothin' better to do," he mumbled around a mouthful of food.

Eight. Andrew frowned at Eli. "You sure? Things might get awful uncomfortable for you in Nacogdoches if you help us."

Eli shook his head. "The string's about to play out on them boys. I figure Austin and his bunch are apt to be here pretty soon. Any business I got in Nacogdoches can wait a while."

The women embraced their men and cautioned them not to get themselves shot up. Andrew saw deep concern in their faces, but he was pleased that he saw no panic. Petra started to reach toward Andrew, then stepped back. "Be careful," she whispered. He did not hear the words; he read them on her lips.

As they hurried up the trail to join Dick Johnson, Andrew waited for somebody to assume the leadership. No one took hold of the reins. "All right," he demanded after a short wait, "we've got to have a plan."

Bradley declared fatalistically, "I don't see where a plan'll make up for the way they got us outnumbered. They're goin' to whip us anyway."

Simon Wells countered, "You're right, Andrew. What's your plan?"

Andrew felt a quick annoyance. They had been sitting here for weeks expecting just such a contingency, and they had no plan designed to meet it. They had a far greater stake here than his; in fact, he could argue that he had none at all. Yet they expected him to lead them. He almost wished Michael were here.

He looked around hurriedly for a place to set up a line of defense. "We've got to take all the advantage we can to offset their numbers."

Wells looked at the others, then back at Andrew. "If you have an idee, let's hear it."

Andrew looked to Eli for help, but Eli just stared back, his eyes calm and trusting. "You're ol' Mordecai's son. I expect you can handle it."

Andrew wished he could be that sure. He felt like a pack mule under the sudden and heavy burden of responsibility. He wondered if he could carry it. "We need to scatter out where we can give ourselves some good cover. Just up yonder there's a fair amount of timber fallen down alongside the trail."

Felipe volunteered in Spanish, "It fell in a twisting wind last year. We were afraid we would lose the cabin also."

Andrew said, "That's damned little of a plan, but it's all I've got."

Eli grunted. "It'll serve." His long legs began striding toward the fallen trees, their leaves and needles just brown remnants lying beneath the dried and skeletal branches. The other men followed him.

Andrew quickened his step to catch up to Eli. It occurred to him that he could not have moved so easily a week ago.

Eli gave him a long glance. "I still see a blue mark on your face. Otherwise, you look like you've healed up."

"It's been long enough."

"Good nursin' probably didn't hurt you none. You thought any more about that girl?"

That Andrew had thought a good bit more about her than he wanted to was none of Eli's business. "We got more important things to be thinkin' about."

"Them boys from Nacogdoches'll come and go in a little while, but a good woman'll stay with you."

They reached the place where Andrew thought they could put up the best defense. He waited a moment, glancing first at Simon Wells, then at Pete Bradley, waiting to see if anyone would assume some leadership. No one did. He pointed to one side of the trail, then the other. "Let's scatter out behind that deadfall stuff, about half of us on one side and half on the other, to where we'll catch them between us. Maybe it won't even come to shootin'. But if it does, let's be careful we don't hit our own people on the opposite side of the trail."

Bradley fretted, "If they was to rush by, we couldn't stop them all. Most of them'd get on past, and they'd be down there amongst the women and children before we could reload to fire a second shot."

Andrew said, "I figured to hold them right here."

"How? The trail is open."

"Time comes, we'll close it."

Eli's face twisted. "I already rescued you Lewis boys once apiece. You fixin' to make me do it again?"

"I hope not. But we've got to let them see that our intentions are serious."

As Eli had told them, they did not have long to wait. Andrew heard the sound of horses' hoofs from within the woods, where the trail bent out of sight beyond the outer fringe of timber. The others heard it too. They knelt behind their protective piles of downed trees to present little target. Andrew remained on his feet. As the riders burst into sight in the fringe of pine and scrub he knew they spotted him instantly. He took a rough count; seventeen or eighteen. One more or less didn't make much difference. He saw several rifles pointed at him. The pit of his stomach felt as if it carried thirty pounds of lead, but he forced himself to stand still. When the lead riders were thirty or forty yards away, he stepped out into the trail and set his feet solidly upon the ground, a little apart. He thumbed the hammer back and cradled his rifle in his arms.

The horsemen reined in. Several formed a solid line, facing Andrew. He hoped they could not smell his apprehension. *He* could. It was like the nose-tingling smell lightning sometimes left in a spring thunderstorm. He gripped the rifle hard to keep his hands from trembling.

He heard himself say, "You fellers ain't welcome here." The voice did not sound like his own. He thought he should have said something more authoritative, like, *Stop or I'll shoot!*

He picked a blocky, gray-eyed, gray-bearded man in the center as the probable leader. The dour old man confirmed his judgment by demanding, "You ain't one of the Mexicans who claims this place. Your face ain't brown enough."

Andrew's gaze swept quickly over the men in the front line, the ones he thought most likely to move against him first. He recognized Jayce Beard, who had led the beating in town. He discerned some facial resemblance between Jayce and the older man who led the party. The gray-haired one was the Tolliver Beard he had been hearing about, the one he had encountered once in San Felipe.

Andrew was pleased to see a long dark streak across Jayce's nose and cheek where Eli's rifle had clubbed him.

"Mornin', Jayce," he said. "Remember me?"

Jayce had already recognized him. He scowled bitterly. "You're that spy we caught. If you don't move out of our way we'll finish what we started."

Andrew's words spilled without conscious thought on his part; he did not know where they came from. "Might cost you considerable. Ain't much free in this life."

The gray-haired Tolliver Beard was impatient. "I'll handle this, son." He focused his attention on Andrew. "We have come to claim this property. We find the title faulty and the claim null and void under the laws of the Republic of Fredonia."

"I'm a farmer, not a lawyer. Seems to me like generations of plowin' and plantin' mean more than a piece of paper."

"We are not here to bandy words. We have come to take this property. We will do so peacefully if possible. We will use force if we must."

Andrew drew a long breath of winter morning air. It seemed to steady him. "Well now, Mr. Beard, you might be able to do that. Then again, maybe not. Before you start tryin', I feel like you ought to meet some folks who don't agree with you." He glanced to the left-hand side of the trail, to the pile of deadfall timber there. "Felipe Moreno, would you stand up?"

Felipe did, slowly, raising an old musket that probably had originated in Spain.

Andrew said, "That's Felipe. He's the youngest of the Moreno family who own this land. That gun he's got there, they call that an *escopeta*, I believe. Ain't much to look at, but it can blow a hole in a man big enough to let the wind whistle through him." Andrew turned to the other side. "Simon Wells, I wish you'd show yourself."

Wells rose. His long rifle was pointed at Tolliver Beard. The hard look in Wells's eye told Andrew that he had encountered Beard before.

Andrew said, "Now, Simon, he's got a wife and family down yonder. I don't know how many of you fellers are family men, but those that are, you know a man don't stand back and let somethin' happen to his family without he puts up a fight."

Andrew switched his attention back to the left. "Dick, would you and Pete please stand up? I want to introduce you." They complied, their rifles aimed into the riders. Andrew said, "I saw Dick Johnson shoot four squirrels the other day. Hit all four of them in the head so as not to spoil the meat. But there was five squirrels in all. He flat missed one of them. Maybe you'll be lucky, and he'll miss again.

"Pete Bradley, now, he don't claim to be a great shot. Says he has to get close. But he's close now, wouldn't you say?"

Tolliver Beard's face gradually flushed. His voice

went deep, but Andrew thought he detected a slight rattle of uncertainty in it. "There's twice as many of us as there is of you. You couldn't get us all."

"That's a fact," Andrew admitted. "Best we could do would be to get half of you. You sure you want to find out which half?"

The men from Nacogdoches began to stir uneasily. The rest of the defenders rose up on both sides of the trail. They had the horsemen boxed. One of the invaders said, "Beard, I don't like this one bit."

"Shut up. Can't you see he's tryin' to bluff us?"

Andrew said, "Sure, I'm tryin' to bluff you. If we all fired a volley, half of you would still be alive to go on down yonder and take over the camp. Trouble is, you don't know which ones that'd be. I can only guarantee that you won't be amongst them, Beard. And neither will your little boy Jayce."

Jayce said, "Papa, we goin' to stand here and let them do us thisaway? We can take them." It was probably imagination, but Andrew thought the bruise on Jayce's face had darkened with his anger. His eyes were getting a little wild.

Andrew said, "I haven't finished introducin' everybody yet. You probably wouldn't like them—I don't—but there's the Blackwood boys over yonder, Finis and Luke. Finis ain't too good a shot. He tried to kill my brother one time but hit my uncle instead. He'd probably miss whichever one of you he aimed at and hit somebody else. You never can tell about Finis."

Several of the Nacogdoches men began pulling their horses around. Tolliver Beard called out to them in anger, "We come here to do a job. You ain't fixin' to let him scare you off, are you?"

They didn't answer him, but five started riding

away. Two more watched them uncertainly, then turned and set out after them in a trot. Andrew sucked in another long breath and slowly let it go. He found his hands still sweaty on the rifle, but they were steady now; he did not have to grip so hard.

He waited until Beard got through mumbling under his breath, then said, "That changes the odds some, but there's still more of you than there is of us. Three or four of you might still make it through to the camp."

Jayce was sweating now despite the winter's cold. He had spotted Eli Pleasant among the defenders. He tugged at his father's coatsleeve and pointed. "That's the old man everybody's been tellin' about, the one who laid that rifle over my head. He ought to be amongst the first ones we get, Papa."

Tolliver Beard said grittily, "That's Eli Pleasant. He can shoot the wings off of a bumblebee. If you've got a lick of sense, you'll leave him alone."

One of the Fredonians who remained said, "Looks to me like we'd better leave them all alone, Tolliver."

"You goin' yellow on me too?"

"Not yellow. But I can't help wonderin' what good a piece of this land is goin' to do you if you're buried under it, and some of us layin' there with you."

Beard's eyes blazed. "Get out of here, then. Get the hell away from me."

The man did not tarry long. "I'm obliged you see it my way. Anybody comin' with me?"

Four of them did.

Andrew waited to see what Beard might do. Beard stood his ground. Andrew said, "I believe you might want to take another count."

Beard began to slump. When he dropped his gaze

to the ground, Andrew knew he had won. He relaxed a little.

Jayce Beard cried, "Papa, you ain't fixin' to give in! We come here to take this land away from those damned Mexicans, and by God we're goin' to take it!"

Andrew tensed again. He did not like the wild look in Jayce's eyes. He said, "If you-all want to go catch up to your friends, I guarantee you none of us will shoot at you. But stay here another minute and I can't promise what anybody'll do. Especially Finis."

Tolliver Beard said in resignation, "Come on, son."

Jayce gave Andrew a gaze that could have burned bark from a tall pine. "You son of a bitch!" His hand moved, and Andrew instantly brought the muzzle of his rifle into line with the man's chest. Jayce screeched like a panther and came spurring, a pistol in his hand.

Tolliver cried, "No, Jayce! Come back!"

But Jayce drove straight at Andrew, his right arm extended, the pistol leveled at Andrew. Andrew caught one quick breath, then pulled the trigger. He saw the powder flash in his rifle's pan, then felt the hard shove against his shoulder and watched the black smoke billow. Jayce's pistol went off. The ball smacked harmlessly into the earth, for Jayce was already falling from his horse. He pitched to the ground almost at Andrew's feet. Andrew held his breath, his mouth dry, his heart pounding. He made no effort to reload the rifle.

Tolliver Beard sat a moment in shock and dismay, then cried, "Jayce! Son!"

That brought Andrew out of his trance. He drew a deep breath, choked a little on the remnant of powdersmoke, then knelt and felt for a sign of life in Jayce. He found no pulse.

He looked up at the old man. He said in anguish, "I didn't want to do that."

Beard's voice was thin and raspy. "He's dead?"

"He oughtn't to've rushed me. I didn't go to kill him."

Jayce's horse had run by Andrew. Felipe Moreno caught it and brought it back. He bent down and confirmed Andrew's finding. "He is dead," he said in Spanish.

The other men from Nacogdoches held back. It had probably sounded easy in town; just go out and throw a scare into those people and run them the hell off. A gunfight had not sounded like much over a bottle of whiskey. But it was different now in the cold light of a winter sun, one of their own lying here dead in a small pool of his own blood. The Fredonians looked on from a safe distance, stiffened by shock.

Tolliver Beard rode slowly forward. He was careful not to make a threatening move with his rifle, because the settlers' rifles were all aimed at him. They would cut him to pieces if he showed a real threat to Andrew. He said thinly, "Jayce was headstrong, but he didn't deserve bein' murdered."

Defensively Andrew said, "I didn't murder him. I shot him because I had to."

The man's eyes brimmed with tears. "Would you kindly lay him across his horse so I can take him home?"

Andrew put his rifle down against a weathered log and, with Felipe's help, placed Jayce across his saddle. The horse did not like the burden. Andrew handed the reins up to the old man.

Beard's eyes had taken on fire. "What is your name?"

Andrew told him.

Beard said, "I got a boy to bury, and the mournin' to do. But I'll be seein' you again, Andrew Lewis. And they'll be buryin' you the way I've got to bury my son." He turned and led the horse away. The other Fredonians parted to give him room, then closed around him. Shortly they had disappeared into the tall pines.

Andrew felt as if he had a thousand needles sticking into his flesh. Eli Pleasant handed him his rifle. He said, "Wouldn't hurt if you keep that loaded from now on."

"He won't be comin' back right now."

"But he *will* be comin' back sooner or later, or layin' in wait for you someplace. I told you, I know that old man. He's swore to kill you, and he'll do it or die tryin'."

"One killin', and that has to lead to another? I didn't want any of this." Andrew looked at his hand, trying to see the blood. There was none, but he was sure he could feel it anyway. He rubbed the hand against his leg as if trying to get rid of it. He wanted to cry out, but he held it back. He turned, his eyes afire, and started down toward the cabin.

24

Dick Johnson remained behind to watch the trail. Like Pete Bradley, he had no worried women-folks to report to. The rest walked back toward the cabin and the tents and the *jacales,* where they could see the women and children waiting in the open yard, fearful for what the gunshot might have meant.

Andrew felt sick at his stomach. He wanted nothing so much right now as to be back home on the Colorado, to put this incident as far behind him as he could.

Most of the men had little idea how he felt; they were too jubilant over their turning back the Fredonians. That a man had died seemed not to matter a great deal. That man, after all, had been a land thief, on the other side.

Pete Bradley was almost dancing in unaccustomed euphoria. "I knew we could do it!"

Simon Wells said with admiration, "Andrew, that

was mighty slick, the way you counted us off one by one and bluffed all that bunch."

Andrew did not feel like talking, but he replied, "I learned that from my brother Michael one time. No matter how many people a man has got with him, he feels all alone when he looks at a bunch of rifles and knows one of them is probably pointed straight at him."

Felipe, youngest of the defenders, hurried ahead to give the first account. By the time the others reached camp, the women had a fair picture of what had happened.

Petra stood with hands clasped just under her chin. As Andrew neared, she took a couple of steps forward, her dark eyes soft with sympathy. "You are all right, Andrew?"

He stopped. He came near calling her Marie by mistake. "I killed a man," he told her painfully.

"I know." She extended her hand. "Come. Come into the house. I think I can find you some whiskey."

He followed her. *Señora* Moreno followed both of them, but only with her eyes. She remained outside with her youngest son Felipe.

In the cabin, away from the others' sight, Petra turned. She threw her arms around Andrew and buried her face against his chest, sobbing in relief. "Oh, Andrew, Andrew. I was so frightened for you."

He stood awkwardly, not knowing what to do with his hands. So he let nature tell him, and he put them around Petra.

He shared a meager supper with the Moreno family. Through the meal he tried not to see but could not escape the tug of Petra's gaze. He gave up after a bit, pushing the food aside. His stomach was still in turmoil. He excused himself from the table to walk outside and wrestle with his confusion in the chill of dusk. Shortly Petra came out onto the small porch, a thin shawl over her shoulders. Her eyes searched, lighting when they found him. "Where are you going, Andrew?"

"Just walking a little, taking some air."

She came down into the yard to join him. "I would like to walk with you."

"Where?"

"It does not matter. Along the creek, or up the trail."

Reason warned him to find an excuse, but reason left him when he looked into the dark eyes so much like Marie's. "People might say it would not be proper."

Her eyebrows arched. "You would not do anything improper, would you?"

"Would you want me to?"

She slipped her arm beneath his. "I might."

Señora Moreno came onto the porch. She watched them with concern but made no move to follow.

They walked arm-in-arm beneath a darkening winter sky. A bend in the creek took them out of sight of the cabin and camp. Large trees on the bank extended their branches almost far enough to intermingle with those on the other side. Petra asked, "Do you have such a pretty creek on your farm?"

"I have the Colorado River. It is much wider. The trees cannot reach across."

She said, "I have not seen even the Sabine River. I never have been far from this place in my life. Where you live, does the land look much like this?"

"It's sandier. The trees are not so tall, and in most

places not so dense. I think we get less rain than you do."

"I get tired of the rain sometimes, and the mud. I wish I could see your country, Andrew. It must be beautiful."

He shrugged. "Any place looks good if it is yours."

Her fingers tightened on his arm. "You look good to me, Andrew. I wish I could know you were mine."

He wished he knew some way to answer. He mumbled something that made no sense.

The air had turned from a light chill to very cold. She shivered and drew closer to him. He said, "We should go back."

"I wish I never had to go back. I want to be with you. Put your arms around me and I will be warm enough." Turning, she raised her own arms.

He hesitated, then embraced her. Her arms went around him, and she pressed her face against his chest. He bent to rest his cheek against the top of her head, her soft hair. He felt her body convulse and sensed that she was sobbing.

"Petra." He touched her face with his hand, trying to lift her chin so he could see her. He felt the wetness of a tear.

"No," she protested quietly, "do not look at me now. I feel foolish, crying like this. But I keep thinking how easily you might have been killed."

"I wasn't. There is nothing to cry about."

"It is not the first time I have cried for you, Andrew. You have not known—"

"I have known," he said uneasily. "But you shouldn't. There is no reason."

"There is reason. I love you, Andrew."

"You don't even know me. I have not been here long enough—"

"I know you. I feel that I have known you all my life. I feel that I have waited for you since I was a little girl. Can you not feel something like that for me?"

He floundered, trying to find an honest answer that would not bring pain. "I do, but not the kind of feeling you need."

"Do you find me ugly, Andrew?"

"No. I find you very pretty. But love has to come from more than that."

She clung fiercely. "I would go anywhere with you, Andrew. I would do anything you want of me, just to be with you. There would not even have to be a priest if you did not want that."

"I would not shame you, Petra. If I felt that strongly, I would want a priest too. But—" There was no painless way to tell her. "Do you remember the day I awoke and mistook you for someone else? There *is* someone else. Yes, I am drawn to you, Petra, but it is because you remind me of her. The feelings I have for you are not honest, because when I look at you I see her. When I hold you, I am holding her. You deserve much better."

"I would be content with that, if that was all there could be. But there could be more. I could teach you to love me."

Holding her, he felt a rising warmth, an intoxicating desire to take her, here and now. He brushed his cheek against her face and found it almost hot to the touch. He felt light-headed, as if he had been drinking. He sensed that he could lay her down upon the dry grass, and she would not resist. In the heat of the moment he toyed with the temptation, nearly crushing her in his arms. But the moment passed, and reason forced him back from the edge. To do such a thing to Marie would be unthinkable. And Petra, to him, was another Marie.

He pulled away from her as far as she would let him, for she still clung to his arms. "What is the matter, Andrew?"

"Nothing. For just a minute there—We had better go back before we make a bad mistake."

Her eyes brimmed with tears. "It is my fault, Andrew. I have made a fool of myself. I will not do it again."

She squeezed his arms once more, then broke free and ran back toward the cabin. He followed, confused and frustrated but grateful that he had found willpower to retreat.

She brushed past Eli Pleasant with her head down, giving no sign she had seen him. Eli stared after her, then turned toward Andrew, the question in his eyes.

Andrew said shakily, "Don't ask me, Eli. I wouldn't want to lie to you."

"Wouldn't do no good if you tried. It don't take a man of education to read what you've both got writ all over you."

"Don't be jumpin' to any notions, Eli. Ain't nothin' happened."

Eli glanced toward the cabin, where Petra had closed the door behind her. "Pity. Looks to me like she'd've been ready, and you too."

"But I ain't proud of it. Any other pretty girl'd affect me the same, like as not. I just ain't been around enough of them to know for sure. And I figure she ain't been around many men, outside of family. She's put me up as a hero or somethin'. I never been a hero in my life."

"Waitin' around for true love to find you, you'll

keep sleepin' cold and all by yourself. True love probably don't even know where Texas is at. Take what's offered to you and don't ask too damn many questions. I never did."

"It wouldn't be fair to her."

Eli shrugged and turned away. "Then you'd best pray for Austin and his bunch to turn up quick and give you a reason to leave here."

Andrew did not go so far as to pray for that eventuality, but Austin turned up anyway, three days after the encounter with the Fredonians. The approach of a large armed force aroused apprehension among many in the Moreno farm encampment, fear that the Fredonians might be returning in massive strength. Though he did not dismiss that possibility, Andrew thought the direction, from the southwest, was unlikely for invaders out of Nacogdoches. He saddled his brown horse and rode out warily, hoping to identify the riders at a distance that would not put him in peril. He determined that they were a mixture of civilians and Mexican soldiers. Fredonians would not be traveling with the military, except perhaps as prisoners.

Relieved, he rode boldly on. He soon recognized Isaac Blackwood riding at the head of the column, guiding it toward the Moreno farm. Beside Isaac rode Stephen Austin, and beyond him a dark-skinned Mexican officer whose dusty but braided uniform bespoke considerable rank. Following, Andrew was pleased to see, came a long column of armed Texas colonists and, separately, what appeared to be a couple of companies of Mexican soldiers. Most slumped wearily in their saddles;

the road had been long. Several rifles were brought to bear on Andrew as he approached. He held his breath until Austin and the officer sent back orders for their men to stand easy.

Isaac Blackwood nodded at Andrew but did not extend his hand. He said dryly, "Well, Andrew, I see my brothers ain't killed you yet. I hope you ain't killed them."

Andrew flinched at the bitter memory. "No, I didn't kill *them*."

Austin shook Andrew's hand. He looked thin and tired, but that was nothing new. "It is good to see you, Andrew. I assume things here are as Isaac Blackwood represented them."

Andrew gave Isaac a brief study but withheld judgment. "I don't know what he represented, but the Fredonians sent a bunch out three days ago to try and take this place."

"I would assume you did not yield it to them."

"We—I—had to kill one of them. They ain't tried again." Andrew's gaze ran down the long, strung-out column, making a rough count. "Goin' to be hard to catch them by surprise. A bunch like this won't be easy to hide."

Austin nodded. "We have not tried to make a secret of our coming. We want them to know. If they are not of strong resolve they will have time to retreat to Louisiana, and we will have no need of a fight."

"And if they are resolved to stand on their ground, you've got enough men with you to push them off of it."

"That is our reasoning. Will you go with us into Nacogdoches?"

"I reckon that's what I've been waitin' here for."

"Very well. Isaac has told me about the Moreno farm. We will camp there the night to rest the men and horses, then proceed in the morning." Austin scrutinized him closely. "Isaac spoke of injuries. You appear well mended."

"Us Lewises have always been fast menders."

Austin smiled. "Which reminds me, there is another Lewis with us, somewhere down the column."

Andrew stiffened. "My brother Michael?"

"The same. I think you will find him with one of the soldier companies."

"Soldier companies!" Andrew was surprised, for the sight of soldiers always seemed to upset his brother. Soldiers much like these had slaughtered his father and the Tennesseeans who had come to Texas with Mordecai and Michael a long time ago.

Austin said, "He has been riding with an officer, an old friend, I believe."

Andrew nodded. "That would probably be Zaragosa."

"Yes. A good and honorable man, from what I know of him. Proceed, Isaac."

Andrew pulled out of the line of march, nursing a growing resentment. His initial relief at seeing Austin and the column had turned sour. He waited to let the column pass by him rather than ride down to meet Michael. Any pleasure he might take in seeing his brother was more than counterbalanced by his strong old conviction that Michael belonged at home on the farm with Marie and the children. He had no business coming way to hell up here on an adventure that had some potential for leaving Marie a widow. Andrew's rising anger was near a boil by the time he spotted Michael riding beside the officer, Lieutenant Elizandro Zaragosa, and a younger

Mexican soldier Andrew remembered seeing on the Colorado the day the Blackwoods had come to call.

Michael recognized his brother and pulled out of the column, trotting his horse until he reached Andrew. He seemed about to extend his hand, which surprised Andrew a little, then he withdrew it, which was no surprise at all.

"Well, little brother, looks to me like you're in one piece after all, far as I can see."

Andrew's voice was crisp. "What the hell are you doin' here? The only reason I came myself was that I tried to make you stay home with Marie where you belong."

Michael's eyes flared in quick response to Andrew's challenge, but he seemed to try to hold the anger from his voice. "Now wait just a minute, little brother. I knew why you came up here. Believe me, I taken it to heart. I didn't want to leave Marie, but she insisted. Isaac brought word that you was hurt, and she was anxious about you."

Andrew was dubious. "She sent you?"

"She sure as hell did, or I wouldn't've come. You don't seem to know, Marie's a grown woman, and strong. She takes care of herself mighty good. When she says *go* and really means it, I go. And another thing, I taken her and the young'uns over to stay with the Nathan family till I get back. Miz Nathan's fixin' to have her baby. Marie and the young'uns are as safe there as at home. Probably safer. You think I'd just go off and leave them?"

"Wouldn't be the first time. You sure you didn't come here just because you saw this trip as some kind of a lark?"

Michael's face twisted with pain. He turned in the saddle and looked back toward the approaching Mexican troops. "You think I enjoyed it, bein' amongst all these soldiers? I've had a cold chill all the way. Every time I look at them I remember what happened to Papa. But I gritted my teeth and came on because of you. And because Marie wanted me to."

Andrew's anger began to ebb. "Maybe I spoke too quick."

Michael gave him a critical study. "You sure them fellers didn't club you across the head and addle your brains a little?"

The last of Andrew's resentment faded away. "I wouldn't be surprised." He extended his hand, and Michael took it.

Zaragosa rode up smiling, his teeth very white against several days' trail growth of black whiskers. He greeted Andrew in Spanish and said he was glad to see him looking so well; he had thought he might find him otherwise. He turned to the young soldier who rode with him. "This," he said, "is Corporal Diaz. He speaks much better the English than I."

Diaz nodded with a quiet reserve, not offering to shake hands. Andrew thought he saw distrust in the dark eyes. He chose not to force the issue by extending his hand and pressuring Diaz into shaking with him. *What did I ever do to him?* he thought.

Michael asked, "You got any brothers, Elizandro?"

"Several. They are far from here."

"Kind of wish right now that I was far from here myself. I come all this way to rescue my brother from God knows what, and he jumps into the middle of my back."

Zaragosa seemed uncertain, afraid he had blundered into a family argument. "He does not seem to have drawn any blood. And did I not see you shake hands?"

Andrew said quickly, "We did. It was nothin'. Let's just forget about it."

Michael agreed. "We can't be fightin' amongst ourselves. We'll likely face the Fredonians tomorrow."

Andrew noted, "Austin hopes they'll pack up and leave town before this column gets to Nacogdoches."

"That'd be a pity. I ain't had a good fight in so long, I was almost glad to see Isaac Blackwood."

Zaragosa put in, "I hope Austin is right. I have seen enough trouble, enough fighting, to last me forever."

Michael frowned. "That's an odd thing for a soldier to say."

"Who knows better than a soldier what the cost of blood is?"

Andrew shuddered. "There's others that know."

Such a large column would have swamped the Moreno farm had it attempted to camp around the cabin. Austin and the Mexican commander selected a place down the creek, where the men could attend to their necessities without concern over the sensibilities of the women. Andrew took Michael up to the cabin. "You recognize this place?" he asked.

Michael said gravely, "I wouldn't forget it if I lived for a hundred years. Was it not for those kind folks, I'd've been dead a long time ago."

Michael stared with interest at the tents and temporary *jacales* the refugees had put up. Andrew saw his brother's face twist at sight of Finis and Luke Blackwood standing beside their wagon. Isaac was already there. Finis held his good arm possessively around Nelly's expanding waist.

Michael demanded, "Where'd a snake like Finis ever find him a wife?"

"He hasn't married her."

"He'd better, the way her stomach's pushin' out. How'd the Blackwoods come to be mixed in here with decent folks?"

"These people couldn't afford to be choosy. They needed all the help they could get."

"I'd've been choosier than *that*."

"You'll have to admit that Isaac took it on himself to go to Austin and tell him what was happenin'."

Michael's eyes narrowed. "Not out of pure human kindness. He was workin' on somethin' for himself—and his brothers."

Andrew missed a step. "What?"

"You'll remember that Austin wouldn't let them stay in his colony the first time they tried. He didn't like their looks. You reckon he could refuse them now? He's obligated."

Andrew felt suddenly foolish. "I never thought about that."

"Just goes to show which is the smartest of us, little brother. It was the first thing that came into my mind."

Señora Moreno waited on the porch. Petra stood beside her, hands clasped nervously at her waist. When Andrew's gaze met hers, she quickly looked away, pain in her eyes.

The older woman did not wait for Michael to be introduced. Recognizing him, she stepped down from the porch and opened her arms. She hugged him tightly, tears on her cheeks. Michael responded with embarrassment at first, then melted into the spirit of the reunion. He struggled with his Spanish. "I have never forgotten your face, Mrs. Moreno." His voice quivered. "I owe you my life."

The dark-faced woman backed away and looked up at the tall Michael Lewis with approval. "You owe God your life. We are but His servants. You grew into much of a man, Miguel." She glanced at Andrew, then back to Michael. "I see much of your brother in you."

Michael tried to break the solemn spell with a forced smile. He glanced at Andrew for help with his Spanish. "Tell her I can't help it. Our old daddy marked us all."

Señora Moreno declared, "You will have supper with us, both of you." It was not an invitation; it was a command. Andrew was about to decline as gracefully as he could, for he knew how uncomfortable it would be, sitting at the table with Petra. But Michael spoke quickly, "Of course we will."

Michael turned his attention to Petra. He bowed in a style brought from Tennessee and enlarged upon after exposure to the courtesies of Mexican people in Texas. His Spanish was slower and more awkward even than Andrew's, but he managed to work his way through it. "I remember a little girl. She looked at me with fear and stayed behind her mother."

Petra avoided Andrew's eyes, concentrating her attention on Michael. Her voice was subdued. "I had not seen an American before. And your wound frightened me. I thought you would die, as my father had died. I am glad you did not."

Michael said, "So am I."

Petra let herself glance for just a moment at Andrew. He met her gaze, and she looked away again. Michael seemed to notice, for he looked from one to the other with a question he did not put into words.

He went through an emotional reunion of hugs and *abrazos* with the Moreno brothers, Carlos and Ramón, one of whom long ago had helped Eli Pleasant with the wounded Michael while another had gone up the trail to watch out for Spanish soldiers. Felipe stood back. He had been too young to remember much.

Someone mentioned Eli's name, and Michael demanded, "Where is that old reprobate? I have looked forward to seeing him."

Carlos shook his head. "The old man Pleasant did not wish *Señor* Austin to see him. There is some difference between them. And he is not much liked by the military. He said he remembered some business left unfinished in Louisiana."

Lieutenant Zaragosa came in a while, along with the young soldier Diaz. They both received a warm welcome from the Moreno family. Zaragosa had done what he could to shield them from persecution as rebels in the final years before freedom from Spain. Diaz had grown up not far from here; his family had fled into Louisiana to escape that same persecution.

The visit lasted long after supper. Andrew sat back and let Michael do the talking for both of them. Not once did he catch Petra looking at him. Now and again he felt the strong gaze of Diaz, however, and he puzzled over the young soldier's hostility.

As Andrew and Michael walked in darkness toward the *jacal* Andrew had been sharing with Dick Johnson and Pete Bradley, Michael said, "Grand folks, the Morenos. Grand people."

Andrew knew the problem his brother sometimes had in dealing with Spanish and Mexican people; the ghost of Mordecai Lewis always seemed to stand between them. "It doesn't bother you that they're Mexicans?"

"They had nothin' to do with what happened to Papa. The same officer who killed him murdered their daddy too."

Andrew could only nod agreement, for his mind lagged behind, in the Moreno cabin.

Michael said, "That girl Petra— There's somethin' about her— All night long I had the feelin' she looks a little like somebody. I just can't figure out who."

Andrew almost stumbled. He looked back once and swallowed. "I guess just about everybody looks like somebody else."

25

Ever the pessimist, Pete Bradley worried aloud all the way to Nacogdoches. "They won't give up without a strong fight. There's some of us ain't comin' out of this alive."

Dick Johnson finally got enough of it. He said, "Maybe you'll be lucky, Pete, and just get shot in the head. That's the only place in your body that a bullet won't penetrate."

But there was no fight, hardly even a scuffle. The arrival of Colonel Ahumada and Stephen Austin's column in Nacogdoches was anticlimactic, as Austin had hoped. The Fredonian movement had dissolved ahead of it. Those loudest in their denunciation of Mexican authority retreated across the Sabine into Louisiana. Most others who had attached themselves to the Fredonian cause met the troops without hostility or arms and expressed a hope for leniency and understanding. As the column marched into the old Spanish town, most of the populace cheered, relieved to see the last of the abortive rebellion. The most pressing concern for the military was the Cherokee Indians, some of whom had allied themselves with the Fredonian movement out of frustration over the government's slowness to follow through on promises of secure land grants. To reassure the Cherokees, Ahumada dispatched an old filibuster named Peter Ellis Bean, survivor of a Spanish massacre not unlike the one which had taken Mordecai Lewis.

Virtually the only blood spilled was that of two Cherokee leaders who had taken up the Fredonian banner. Their chief put them to death as a show of loyalty to the government of Mexico.

To Lieutenant Elizandro Zaragosa that seemed more extreme than justice called for, given the evident hopelessness of the Fredonian cause from the beginning. But he could not recall when anyone over the rank of colonel had ever asked his opinion.

"A pity," he told the young corporal Diaz. "This has been a farce, too ridiculous for anyone to have to die over it, don't you think?"

Diaz shrugged. As an enlisted man, he was unaccustomed to having anyone over the rank of private ask his opinion. "One never knows why the Indians do what they do."

Diaz was riding with Zaragosa and a small detail of troops from house to house as interpreter to be certain none of the army's orders were misunderstood by the English-speaking settlers. A one-eyed preacher named Fairweather rode with them, trying to ease any lingering apprehensions the people might have, and explaining in his own way that the government meant no harm to those who meant no harm to *it*. Diaz was a little dubious about having the minister along, for he was Protestant, and the law decreed that the only religion here be Catholic. But Zaragosa was a realist. The Americans would come nearer listening to one of their own. Besides, from what Zaragosa could ascertain, Fairweather held no real authority to preach. He had no diploma, no church sanction, nothing but a big black Bible and an ease with words. For all Zaragosa knew, the man might be a charlatan. But at least he seemed to help in this situation; the Americans listened to him and understood what he said.

It appeared to Zaragosa that Americans understood what they chose to understand. They pleaded ignorance when the message went against their pleasure.

Diaz agreed with a dark frown that betrayed his antipathy for the entire race. He could speak freely in Spanish, for Fairweather knew only English. "They understand more than they admit, these Americans. They are a selfish and scheming lot." That he had lived among them while his family was exiled in Louisiana, avoiding persecution by the Spanish royalists, had left the young man unaccountably bitter, the lieutenant thought.

Zaragosa said, "One does not condemn the many for the sins of a few."

"The many envy the few. They would all do the same were they not fearful for their lives and their possessions. They put much value in possessions, these Americans. And they would possess all that belongs to someone else if they were but given the chance to take it."

"Did they ever take anything from you?"

"Much. Those blackguards in Louisiana set upon us soon after we crossed the river. We thought we were safe because we had left the Spanish soldiers behind us. We did not know that worse waited on the American side. They took the little money we had, and our horses."

Zaragosa said, "You were in the neutral strip. It has always been infested with outlaws; ours as well as theirs."

Diaz shuddered. "My sister was a girl much like the Moreno's Petra. They carried her away screaming."

Zaragosa felt a chill. He had not heard this before. "Did you ever find her?"

"Much later, in Natchitoches. She wandered there when they were done with her. She was working in some American woman's household. She did not want us to see her. She was with child. From which of those demons, it was impossible to know." Diaz clenched his fist. "God was merciful. When time came for delivery, He took both her and the child."

Zaragosa nodded his sympathy. "I understand."

"The Americans did not understand. They saw we were penniless and without hope, so they put us to work in the fields like their black slaves. They worked us hard and paid us little and fed us even less. My father was much ashamed. He said it would have been better had we died fighting the Spanish. But he died in a cottonfield, carrying a sack with the black men. I came back to Texas and fought the Spanish so what was left of my family could return and live where they belonged, in peace."

Zaragosa wished for an adequate way to express his compassion. But he also had to express his reservations. "Surely you must have known a man named Guadalupe Lucero. Like you, he fled to Louisiana because the Spanish hellhound Rodriguez put him on the death list. Rodriguez murdered some of Lucero's kinsmen like the old Moreno, trying to make them betray Lucero. I was there. I saw. Lucero lived among the Americans, but he did not hate them. He had many friends like the Lewis brothers, Michael and Andrew. He did not confuse the good with the bad."

"I have no wish to offend you, sir, but I have seen that you count the Lewises as your friends also."

"They once saved me from Rodriguez. I was privileged to return that favor."

"You may one day regret that you did, sir. They may seem to be your friends now, but a time will come when they will see you only as another Mexican to be robbed of whatever they wish to take from you."

"I cannot believe that."

"Why are we in Nacogdoches, sir? We are here because some Americans decided to take land that belongs to Mexico. They will try again. They will keep trying until their numbers are so large that they overwhelm us. Then they will take it all: Nacogdoches, San Antonio de Bexar— Who knows? They may go all the way to Mexico City."

Zaragosa vigorously shook his head. "There are many good men among them. They will not let that happen."

"It will happen. And when it does, your friends the Lewises will be there with the rest, seizing whatever they can take." Diaz's eyes pinched with resentment. "Did you not see the one named Andrew, and the way he looked at the girl Petra? And did you not see her eyes? I think he has already taken her, as those others took my sister."

"Imagination," Zaragosa countered briskly. "The Lewises are not that type."

"They are Americans. We have seen only the

beginning. They will yet take everything we have. As soldiers we will have to fight them. And we will probably lose."

Zaragosa shook his head. "I will not be fighting ever again, at least not as a soldier. I am going to leave the army and become a farmer."

Diaz said with regret, "That would be a waste, sir."

"Not to me. I am separated too often from my family. My father-in-law is sickly and asks me to take over his farm. My wife wants me to do it. I have given it much thought."

"We will need you, sir, when the fight comes."

"There will be no fight, Diaz, not with the Americans."

"They are not like us and never can be. We are not like them and should never wish to be." He looked at the minister Fairweather with eyes that betrayed his hostility. "Yes, lieutenant, we will fight."

Like Austin, Andrew was gratified that they had not had to fight to enter Nacogdoches. He sensed that Michael harbored a little disappointment, however, for a good scrap would have capped this little venture away from the boredom of the farm on the Colorado River. Andrew had to smile when Pete Bradley cockily declared, "Cowards, the lot of them. I figured they'd turn tail and run when they seen us comin'."

Dick Johnson called Bradley's hand. "I thought you said they were liable to kill us all."

Bradley vigorously shook his head. "When did I ever say that? You must've been listenin' to somebody else."

Andrew was relieved that a diligent search of the town revealed no trace of old Tolliver Beard. Like many of the others, he evidently had fled eastward into Louisiana, from whence he had come.

Michael was not quite so pleased. "It'd've been better if we could've caught him. I'd feel a lot better knowin' he was in a Mexican prison someplace and not roamin' around out yonder somewhere waitin' for a chance to kill you."

"It's a long way from Louisiana to the Colorado River. He won't know where to find me."

"The Blackwoods found us, didn't they?"

The two older Moreno brothers had joined Austin's column, leaving younger brother Felipe behind to watch over the rest of the family. Carlos and Ramón rode with Andrew and Michael, Johnson and Bradley now, carrying their search through the town and out into the countryside. The Morenos' main interest had been in finding Tolliver Beard and impressing their disapproval upon him in some memorable way. They accepted failure philosophically. Ramón said, "Your brother is right, Miguel. We seek after birds that have flown the nest, while we are tied to the ground."

Carlos spoke what was truly on his mind. "There is nothing more for us to do here. I would like to go home."

Carlos was a married man with responsibilities. Andrew thought Michael should feel the same way. He looked hopefully at his brother. "Ramón's right. Marie'll be wonderin' and worryin'. You'd ought to be gettin' home to her."

Michael's eyes softened at mention of his wife's name. His righteous indignation seemed to fade. "We ought to go tell Austin before we take our leave."

They found Stephen Austin looking very concerned for a man who had won a victory without
firing a shot. The *empresario* sat in the old stone
fort building, frowning over a lengthy report he was
writing. Though the papers were upside down from
his side of the table, Andrew could see that Austin
was composing in Spanish, probably giving a full
report to the authorities in Mexico City. He smiled
at the Lewis brothers, seeming to read their minds.
"You have my permission."

In truth, they did not need it. Neither was an
enlisted member of the militia. But Andrew said,
"Thank you." He nodded toward the papers spread
in front of Austin. "At least you can tell Mexico that
the whole thing was a little of nothin'. It wouldn't've
raised a wave in a coffeepot. Most of the people
around Nacogdoches are glad to see the Fredonians
go. The Americans who've settled in Texas are a
faithful lot."

Austin's face pinched with concern. "I know that,
and you know it. But except for Colonel Ahumada,
the officials of Mexico have not seen it themselves. I
am afraid they will read a great deal more into this
little insurrection than was ever here. Those who
have always distrusted us will tell them the worst.
And I fear the officials will be inclined to listen to
them."

"But in the end they always listen to *you*."

"Up to now," Austin said darkly. "Up to now." He
looked beyond Andrew and Michael to the door, to
the four men who waited outside. "The Morenos
will be going with you?"

"Yes, sir. I expect the people camped around the
Moreno farm will be packin' up and leavin' for their

own homes. Carlos and Ramón want to be there to tell them *adiós*."

Michael said dryly, "And they'll want to be there when the Blackwoods leave, to be sure they don't take away more than they brought with them."

Andrew felt he should probably salute or something, inasmuch as Austin was an officer of the volunteer colonist militia, but he did not know how. He said simply, "Come see us when you can," and started for the door.

Austin called, "Andrew, Michael, there is one thing more."

Andrew turned. He did not like the reluctance he saw in Austin's thin face.

Austin said, "Michael, you mentioned the Blackwood family. I have already gathered that you and Andrew have no great love for them."

"You have good eyes, sir."

"Nevertheless, I owe Isaac Blackwood a debt for having come to report to me about the Fredonians. So I gave him a letter for my assistant Sam Williams in San Felipe. The Blackwoods will receive a grant of land."

Andrew swallowed. "Not close to ours, I hope."

"The choice is theirs."

Andrew saw steel come into his brother's eyes. He gritted his teeth and grabbed Michael's arm, hustling him out of the room before he could say something he might someday regret.

Michael trembled with anger. "He don't know what he's done."

"He did what he thought he had to do."

Michael's body was rigid as he mounted his horse. He kept a stony silence and avoided looking at anybody. Dick Johnson arched an eyebrow and asked, "What's got into him?"

Pete Bradley said, "Must've been bad news. Ain't but little happens around here that ain't bad news."

Carlos and Ramón were too polite to ask questions. Michael took the lead as they started upon the trail that led southward from town. At length he grumbled, but not loudly enough that Andrew could understand.

"What did you say?"

Michael kept his gaze fastened upon the trail. "Just said I'm sorry for all the times I had a good excuse for shootin' a Blackwood and didn't do it."

Carlos took the lead, for he was a married man whose wife awaited him anxiously and would be demonstrative in her relief that nothing unpleasant had befallen him. Pete Bradley and Dick Johnson argued good-naturedly about which had been most apprehensive. They still reminded Andrew a lot of the bachelors Younts and Smith. Michael was moody and silent, brooding about the Blackwoods. Andrew found himself riding along with his head down, thinking about Marie, about Petra; sometimes it was hard to know which image came into his mind.

Ahead, from down the trail, he saw a flash. In the split second before the rifleball snarled past his ear, he recognized Tolliver Beard, smoking rifle braced against a heavy pine tree. Then, before anyone seemed able to react to the surprise and begin to move, Beard was on his horse and racing away through the pines. Andrew sat, frozen.

Ramón and Carlos, Johnson and Bradley went spurring into the timber after Beard. Michael reached out and grabbed Andrew's shoulder. "You hit?"

It was a moment before Andrew was able to answer. His mouth was suddenly bone dry. "I'm all right. Just taken me by surprise, is all."

"That the man we all been huntin' for?"

"He is. I reckon he decided not to go to Louisiana."

Michael said gravely, "It don't look that way." He checked the powder in his rifle's pan.

For a few minutes Andrew could hear the sound of horses moving in the forest, plunging through the underbrush. Then the woods went quiet. There were no shots, so nobody had caught up with Beard. Andrew regained composure enough to step to the ground, where he might make less of a target if Beard circled back.

It was the better part of an hour before the four men returned empty-handed. Dick Johnson said apologetically, "We seen him once or twice, way off in the timber. Never got close enough for a shot. Last we seen of him, he was movin' in the direction of Louisiana."

Pete Bradley worried, "But he won't go there. He'll come back, Andrew. He'll come back and kill you, sure as hell. Maybe kill all of us."

Michael Lewis gave Andrew a long, concerned study. "I think it's high time we got back to our own part of the country, little brother."

Andrew dreaded stopping at the Moreno farm because he did not know what he could say to Petra that would not add to the hurt he had already caused her.

The six horsemen found the refugee camp breaking up. A few families had already gone. Felipe

Moreno came to the shed to greet his brothers as they unsaddled their horses. He was disappointed at the report that they had not been able to exact retribution upon Beard or his followers.

Andrew missed the Blackwoods' wagon. Felipe said, "They were the first to leave."

Michael asked, "Did you count your chickens?"

Felipe grinned. "I watched them load their wagon. There was almost a fight between Finis and Simon Wells over the rightful ownership of a saddle. Everyone knew it belonged to Simon. Isaac made Finis leave the saddle here."

Andrew observed, "Isaac is pretty honest, for a Blackwood."

Michael snorted. "He just knew they couldn't whip the whole camp."

The older Moreno brothers walked toward the cabin. Carlos's wife hurried out to throw her arms around him. Mother Moreno hugged Ramón. Petra came out onto the porch, her gaze touching gratefully upon her brothers, then searching out Andrew. Her eyes held to his for a moment, until he flinched and looked away. When he glanced up again, she was hugging her two brothers who had ridden away to war. She and the rest of the family—except Felipe—were grateful they had not found one. Felipe had wished for blood.

Johnson and Bradley went down to their *jacal* to start gathering up their few possessions. Andrew and Michael stood back from the old cabin, not intruding upon the Moreno family's reunion. Petra pulled away after a minute and came down from the porch. She walked toward Andrew, her dark eyes steady. She stopped two paces short of him.

"I am glad to see you, Andrew. I am glad no one was hurt."

"Petra—" He stammered in confusion. He had expected her to cry, or to shout at him, or simply to turn away in silence. He had not expected this calm, controlled reception.

He said, "We'll be riding on, Michael and me."

"But you will take bread with us first."

He floundered, trying to find words. "We had better not. It's a long way back home."

Michael put in, "Much too long for us to leave here on an empty stomach. We accept your invitation, *señorita*, with thanks."

Andrew could have kicked him.

Señora Moreno said, "Petra, we must start cooking. These hungry men must eat." Petra gave Andrew a moment's quiet and inscrutable study, then turned and followed her mother into the cabin. Andrew watched the door and felt somehow empty.

Michael said, "That girl still makes me want to think of somebody. I just can't figure out who."

Andrew started to tell him she looked a little like Marie, but he was not sure how steady his voice would be. He decided to let Michael figure it out for himself. "I'll go and water the horses," he said.

The meal was punishment to Andrew. He had to sit across the table from Petra and try not to look at her, for seeing her stirred feelings of guilt. He excused himself from the table as soon as he could and walked out to the corral where the horses had been unsaddled and given a little grain. He bridled and began saddling the brown. Hearing footsteps, he turned, expecting to see Michael. Petra stood at the gate, watching him.

While he tried to think of something to say, she took the initiative away from him. "I'm sorry," she said.

He blinked, surprised. "*You're* sorry? It's me who has something to apologize for."

"No, I threw myself at you. I had no right. I have had a few days to think about it and to see that I have caused embarrassment to you."

He stood slump-shouldered, trying to come up with a response.

She said, "I just wanted to let you know I am ashamed of myself. I promise you nothing like that will happen again."

Before he could speak, she walked back toward the cabin. She met Michael, who tipped his hat and turned to look at her a moment before coming on down to the corral. He gave Andrew a quiet study before saying, "Seems to me like you're in an almighty hurry to leave here."

"I thought you'd be in a rush to get home, with Marie waitin' and all."

"I reckon. But I have time to tell folks a decent *adiós*."

"I've said my good-byes. If you're ready, let's ride."

"You sure you ain't leavin' anything undone?"

"Nothin' I can think of."

Riding away, crossing the creek, he stopped once and looked back at the cabin. He thought he might see Petra standing on the porch, watching, but she was not there. He hunched a little and spurred to catch up to Michael.

They rode south in silence a while. At length Michael said, "As I recollect, you was aimin' to come back from this trip with a wife."

"That was your idea, and Marie's, not mine."

"Maybe so, and not a bad idea, either. Couldn't you find a suitable woman?"

"I got kind of busy."

"Not *that* busy. You was at the Moreno farm a right long time. Seemed to me like I seen somethin' in that Petra girl's eyes whenever she looked at you."

Andrew swallowed. "You've got too much imagination."

"Or maybe you've got none atall." Michael gave him an accusing look which Andrew tried to ignore by calling attention to the fact that a little green was beginning to show at the base of the old dry grass. Spring would be coming pretty soon.

Michael was not so easily distracted. He said, "I finally figured out who that Petra girl reminded me of."

Andrew thought, *She looks like Marie. You ought to've seen that from the first.*

Michael said triumphantly, "I don't know how you missed it. She looks a little like our sister Heather, back in Tennessee."

They angled across the country, bypassing Austin's San Felipe because they had no particular business there. They crossed the Brazos River and in due time struck the Colorado at a ford a little way below the Nathan farm, where Marie was supposed to be. It was not a river that could be crossed just anywhere a man wanted to unless he was prepared to swim. And it was a little swollen, indicating that rain had fallen upstream, a harbinger of a favorable spring season.

"Water looks cold," Michael said, standing his horse on the bank and looking at it.

"A little muddy too," Andrew agreed. It often was, in varying degrees. That was why it bore as a name the Spanish word for "reddish."

Michael dismounted and began peeling off his clothes. "Then our dirt won't hurt it much. I ain't goin' home to Marie without I bathe first. She's got notions about such as that. Comes from the French side of her, I reckon."

Andrew dropped his roll on the ground and sought out a chunk of Marie's lye soap, made in a washpot behind her cabin. It had been used sparingly on this trip because the winter weather had not been conducive to bathing often or long. It was good for removing dirt, but sometimes it took skin too. He pitched the soap to Michael, who caught it, took a deep breath, and stepped out into the edge of the river. He let out a whoop. "Cold, did you say? It may be comin' spring out on the land, but it's still winter in the water."

Andrew finished stripping to the skin, then plunged in. The initial shock was enough to take his breath; but once he had shivered away the first chill, the water became bearable. Michael handed him the soap. He shaved the best he could with the cold river water and the lye soap, and without a mirror. His face burned as if he were peeling the skin from it. He suspected he probably was, in places. Done, he handed the razor to Michael and climbed out of the river, shivering while the wind dried him.

"Hell, ain't it?" Michael declared, "the things a man'll do for a woman?"

Andrew thought of Petra Moreno. "You'd know better than I would. I don't have one."

"Your fault, not mine."

Dressed, they crossed over the shallow ford. Michael grinned in anticipation. "Marie'll be tickled to see us. She'll put the big pot in the little one tonight. I've been hungry ever since we left the Morenos' place."

Andrew took that for a favorable sign. Maybe Michael had the roaming worked out of his system for a while.

"Can't hardly wait to see the young'uns," Michael exulted. "Till you get some of your own, little brother, you can't know how they pleasure a man."

Andrew frowned. He didn't see much chance for having any of his own, not in the near future.

They were all keyed up for a reunion at the Nathan place, but they were disappointed. Miles Nathan met them in the yard and invited them into the cabin to see the new Nathan baby. Andrew noticed that the two bachelors, Walker Younts and Joe Smith, were sitting together on a rough bench in front, staring glumly off toward a meadow. There the girl Birdy walked with a boy who appeared to be nearer her own age, or at least not so much older as Younts and Smith. Squinting, Andrew recognized Zeb Willet.

Nathan grinned. "The path of true love is indeed a thorny one, full of pitfalls."

Mrs. Nathan was already at the fireplace, fixing something for the family to eat. She said, "Michael, your Marie is a fine midwife. I just wish you'd look at my new baby girl."

Michael tried to show a great interest, but his disappointment showed more. "Where'd Marie go?"

"Home. There was some folks come by in a wagon and offered her a ride, so she tied her milk cow on behind and went with them. Said she had a heap of work piled up and waitin', and a garden that'd soon need plantin'. You-all are stayin' for dinner, aren't you?"

Michael said, "Couldn't eat. Ain't hungry. Much obliged, but we'll be ridin' on."

Andrew was gratified to see his brother so eager to return to Marie. Maybe it would be a while before he got restless enough to want to leave again.

Other times, coming home after a long trip of solitary exploration, Michael had gone in nervously, guilty about having left, guilty about having stayed so long. For this trip he had had a solid excuse, and no apologies were necessary. He was singing as they came upon a roan cow with his brand burned on her hip. She pulled away distrustfully from the horsemen, but not before Andrew saw that her sides bulged. Michael observed happily, "Looks like she'll be freshenin' pretty soon." The Lewis fortune was growing, one crop, one calf at a time.

Andrew nodded. "Looks to me like you've got just about everything a man could want."

They rode up over a small roll in the land, and Michael's cabin came suddenly into view, half a mile away. "Come on, Andrew," Michael chortled. "I can already taste that cornbread."

Andrew saw a wagon sitting near the double cabin. It was covered with canvas. "Looks like you've got company."

Michael nodded, puzzled. "Reckon who it could be? You don't suppose some of our folks from Tennessee—?" He tapped his spurs against his horse's ribs.

Approaching the cabin, Andrew began to suspect that he knew the wagon. He decided not to voice his suspicions. If he was right, Michael would find out all too soon.

He was right. He saw a man on a wooden bench leaned back against the log wall, lazing in the sun. The man got up and slowly stretched himself, then strode forward. He had only half of his right arm.

Finis Blackwood said, "Welcome home, Michael Lewis."

26

Michael dismounted stiffly. His jaw was thrust forward belligerently as he confronted Finis Blackwood. "I've run you off of this place once already, Finis. What're you doin' here?"

Finis was looking more like his shiftless old daddy every day, Andrew thought. His beard was black and unkempt and showing traces of tobacco juice. He had old Cyrus Blackwood's half contentious, half whining way of meeting a challenge. "Why now, it was your missus herself that invited us to stay. We wasn't figurin' to impose, but when she seen Nelly's delicate condition, she wouldn't have it no other way. Good woman you got there, even if she does talk a little funny."

Andrew found dark humor in Finis's description. Nelly was indeed pregnant, but hardly delicate.

Michael said firmly, "I'll expect you to be gone in an hour, Finis, and I never want to see you on my land again."

"Well now," Finis replied, his back stiffening a little, "might be you'd want to ask your missus about that first. Strikes me as a woman with notions of her own, she does."

A boy's voice cried, "Daddy!" Little Mordecai hurried out from the open dog-run, opening his arms for his father. Michael turned away from Finis and leaned down to catch his son, sweeping him up into his arms. He and the boy hugged each other fiercely.

Andrew watched, wishing.

Marie stepped out then, wiping her hands on a rough homespun cotton towel. "Michael!" She started to run to him as Mordecai had, then glanced at Andrew and Finis and caught herself. Andrew felt suddenly guilty, feeling that he was compromising the couple's rightful joyous reunion. Michael embraced his wife while still holding onto the boy.

"How's the baby?" he asked.

"Fine. She's fine. It is good you have come home."

Michael turned, staring balefully at Finis. "I'd sure have to agree with that. You know who this man is?"

She had to know, for the Blackwood family had often been discussed around the Lewis family hearth, along with droughts and grasshoppers and fever epidemics. She said, "They are in need. Nelly is in the hope."

Michael responded dryly, "Damned little hope, tied to such as Finis. Did she tell you they ain't even married?"

Finis put in, "We're married, Michael. Found us a preacher named Fairweather and done it all proper and legal. Man gets more land if he's got him a wife."

Andrew had to turn away and grin. He doubted

that Fairweather's services carried any legality; he was self-ordained. But that was a problem for the Blackwoods to work out. And Austin.

Michael said sternly to Marie, "I told Finis to pack up and be gone from here before dark."

Marie pulled back to arm's length. Her voice took on a strength she had always possessed but did not often bring into the light. "And I told him they could stay until they get a cabin up."

Michael protested, "Maybe you just don't realize what kind of people they are."

"A woman in her condition should not live in a wagon; *that* I realize. Until they have a cabin, she will stay with us." Her tone carried a finality that Andrew would not have wanted to argue with.

Evidently Michael did not either. He turned resentfully upon Finis. "You've got yourself some land already?"

Finis nodded, triumph in his eyes. He raised his good hand and pointed eastward. "Yonder, a ways down the river and on the other side."

Andrew took some little comfort in the fact that they would at least be across the river.

Michael glanced at Andrew, his eyes flashing anger. "I thought Texas was far enough away—"

Finis gloated. "We'll be your neighbors again, Michael, just like back in Tennessee."

"You may live here, but you'll be no neighbor of mine, not in a hundred years." Michael lifted the boy up onto one shoulder. "I'm goin' in and see the baby."

Marie said, "She's not in the bedroom. I let Nelly have that, and Finis. We sleep in the kitchen."

"Damn!" Michael declared, and stomped into the cabin.

Marie stared after him, her dark eyes a little hurt. They reminded Andrew of Petra's.

He said, "Hello, Marie. Remember me?"

She gave him a sisterly hug. "I am sorry, Andrew. It was not as I wished. I did not know he felt so strongly."

"You know now." Andrew watched as Finis retreated to the bedroom side of the double cabin. It was discomforting to think of him and Nelly profaning that place which had been graced by Marie and Michael's love.

Marie glanced in that direction a moment, and Andrew wondered if the same thought had come to her. She probably would not admit it, but she might have found reason by now to regret her hospitable nature.

He said, "The sooner the Blackwoods are off of this place, the better."

"I could not turn the poor woman away."

"We can't run them out of the country. I reckon they've got a legal claim to stay. Best thing to do is to get some of the neighbors over and raise them a cabin as quick as we can. Till we get that done, I'll give them the borrow of mine."

"I could not ask that of you, Andrew."

"I'm doin' it on my own. I don't want to see an argument come between you and Michael."

"And what of the argument between *you* and Michael?"

"We sort of lost it somewhere along the way. Did you really send him along with Austin, to see about me?"

"I did."

"You're too generous a woman, Marie."

She smiled. "And you are a generous man, Andrew Lewis, to give up your cabin to the Blackwoods."

"I'm just hopin' to keep Michael from doin' murder. I'll bring my stuff over here and sleep in the shed."

"When the Blackwoods leave, you can sleep in the kitchen."

That would not give Michael and Marie the privacy they needed, especially since Michael had been away a while. "The shed'll be fine."

She smiled again. He suspected she understood his reason. "For you and Michael, I will fix a big supper tonight."

"I'd be much obliged."

She started to turn away but stopped to study him thoughtfully. "I had hoped you would not come back alone."

Looking at Marie, he remembered Petra and felt a tug of regret. "A man can't force some things. They've got to come natural or not at all."

She touched his hand, and warmth arose in him. But as he looked into her lively eyes he found he was seeing Petra, not Marie. She said, "Sometimes nature needs help."

She left him standing there awkwardly holding the brown horse's reins. He heard the sound of wood chopping out behind the cabin. He tied the horse to a post and walked around to the back. There he saw Isaac Blackwood, ax in hand, cutting pine logs and branches into firewood. A goodly supply was neatly stacked near the cabin.

Andrew asked, "Did you cut all that yourself, Isaac?"

Isaac turned, wiping sweat from his face onto his sleeve. "Not all of it. There was already a little here

when we come. I figured I'd ought to do somethin'
to help earn our keep."

Andrew wondered. This was not like the Blackwoods he remembered, certainly not like Finis or
Luke. It was the first time the middle brother had
come to mind. He asked, "Where's Luke?"

"Down by the river, tryin' to catch some fish. He
never was much of a hand with a choppin' ax."

Or anything else, Andrew thought. He pointed.
"That's my cabin you see up yonder. I'm goin' to
lend you-all the use of it till you get a cabin of your
own put up. Or maybe two cabins, seein' that Finis and Nelly are married now. It'd be kind of awkward, all of you sleepin' in one."

"Wouldn't be the first time." Isaac frowned.
"Nelly may not look like much, and she's not as
smart as some, but she's a woman. We're goin' to do
right by her. She's goin' to be a mother bye and bye."

"To Finis's baby."

"Maybe. But I'd like to think it just might be
mine." He rubbed his arm across his face. "That surprise you, Andrew?"

"Can't say as it does. I'd think the young'un'd
have a better chance in life bein' yours than bein'
his. But how'll you ever know?"

"I'll know. I'll look at it, and I'll know."

Andrew bent over and reached for a piece of
wood. "I'll be carryin' this into the kitchen for you."

Andrew made a horseback round to the nearest
neighbors, including the Willet family, the Nathans,
the bachelors Younts and Smith, and set a day for
them all to gather at the Blackwoods' place to raise
a cabin. He knew he should be breaking out his field

in preparation for the spring planting, but it was more important to get the Blackwoods out of his cabin and far enough away that he did not have to look at them often. He and Michael and Isaac felled and trimmed trees, dragging them up to the site where two cabins were to be erected. Finis pleaded helplessness because of his crippled condition. Luke did not plead at all; he just went to the river and fished.

The saving grace in the whole situation was that the claim was a full three miles downriver and on the opposite side. The river was a barrier of sorts, psychological if not physical, so maybe the Blackwoods would not venture too often to its south side. Andrew and Michael agreed that Marie had better take a close count of her chickens every day for a while. There had always been plenty of four-legged varmints skulking around, looking for a chance to grab them, but the Blackwoods introduced a new dimension to the need for vigilance.

Michael was in a dark mood while they prepared for the cabin-raising. "It goes against all that's sacred and holy to be puttin' forth this amount of sweat for such people as that," he complained to Andrew. "But Marie wouldn't have it no different. I hope the day don't come when she regrets that kind heart of hers."

"That's one of the things that makes her special," Andrew replied. "Maybe you don't know how lucky you are to have her."

"I do know. Otherwise I'd be doin' somethin' else than choppin' timbers for the Blackwood family."

Cabin-raising was usually the occasion for a community party in colonial Texas, and some effort was made in that direction for the Blackwoods.

The womenfolk brought food, and some made new clothes for Nelly to wear during her indisposition. The men brought their building tools, their teams, and somebody brought along some bad whiskey that had never seen Kentucky. Finis and Luke got a lot more interested in the whiskey than in the building project, and they became considerably more of a hazard than a help. Isaac stayed sober and did much of the heavy lifting. By dusk, two cabins were standing where there had been but grass before. There would be much finishing-out to do, but the major work was done.

Normally it would have been time for everybody to cut loose and celebrate, but Finis and Luke got into a terrible row that ended with each of them trying to beat the other's brains out. Watching disgustedly, Andrew thought it a hopeless cause; neither had enough brains that anybody would notice if they *did* get knocked out. At least now he should be able to move back into his own cabin, though he might have to let it air a couple of days first. He had noticed a long time ago that horses hated to move in where hogs had moved out.

There were times, usually when he least expected it, that a sudden violent image would explode in his brain, and he would find himself confronting the memory of the day he had been forced to shoot Jayce Beard. He would awaken suddenly in the middle of the night, shouting at Jayce to back away. He would find himself in a cold sweat, shaking.

He began to understand how old dreams of a Spanish massacre could still sometimes haunt his brother Michael. Always, after the image of Jayce, he saw the vengeful eyes of old Tolliver Beard, and heard Beard's promise to kill him.

It was a long way to Nacogdoches, and farther even to the Louisiana line. He felt some safety in that distance. The old man had tried once to kill him and had missed. Chances were he had given up and had gone back to Louisiana to nurse his grief, Andrew told himself. But Michael had a colder view of the world and its violence, for he had seen more of it than Andrew.

"From what I heard about that old man, he meant what he told you," Michael warned. "It might be a week, it might be a month, it might be a year, but the day'll come when you'll look up and see him. And you'd better not let him catch you unprepared."

As Andrew had stayed close to Michael earlier, when they had reason to fear the Blackwoods, Michael kept close to Andrew now, watching always for a stranger. They worked together as they plowed their fields, as they handled their few cattle, as they hunted wild game for the table. A rifle was never far from reach by one or the other.

Andrew wearied of the watchfulness and was inclined to forget, but Michael was not. And one day as they were planting corn, Andrew saw Michael stop abruptly, his attention riveted to the east. Sweat ran into Andrew's eyes and stung them, so he had to wipe them clear before he made out the vague shape of two horsemen.

"That wouldn't be Beard," Andrew said. "There's two of them."

"He might've brought help," Michael replied, stepping across the plowed rows and picking up his rifle that he had leaned against the rail fence. Andrew had left his own weapon at the end of the field. He set out in a trot across the soft ground to fetch it.

By the time he had retrieved the rifle, Michael had joined him, waiting by the fence on the lower side. A rail fence always made a good rest for a rifle if a man needed to take careful aim.

But Andrew saw no threat. In fact, one of the riders was slumped forward in the saddle, as if hurt or sick. The other began waving his hat and hollering, long before he was in good hearing range. Andrew turned his left ear to the sound but could not make out the words. When the two riders were close enough, he recognized one. "It's Isaac Blackwood. The other one, I can't tell."

Michael sucked in a long breath. "It's Eli Pleasant. It's Eli, and there's somethin' the matter with him!"

He vaulted over the rail fence and hurried toward the horsemen in a long-legged stride that Andrew found impossible to catch up with.

Eli was bleeding. He had his right hand pressed against his chest, but blood seeped out between his bony old fingers. His grizzled face was ashen.

Michael reached him first, grabbing the old man as he seemed about to slip out of the saddle. He steadied Eli on the horse, then turned furiously upon the other rider. "Isaac Blackwood, if you-all've done this—"

Isaac quickly shook his head. "I was out a-huntin'. I heard a shot and found Eli on the ground. I wanted to take him to our place—it was closer—but he wanted to come to you."

Eli raised his head. He seemed to have trouble seeing, because he looked at Michael and called him Andrew. "I had to come tell you. It's Tolliver Beard."

Andrew felt the bottom drop out of his stomach. "He's here? He shot you?"

Eli nodded. He tried to say something more, but the words were unintelligible.

Michael said desperately, "Let's get him to the house. He'll die sittin' on that horse."

Andrew bit his lip. To him, it looked as if Eli would die no matter where he was. He took the reins while Michael swung up behind Eli to hold him in the saddle. Isaac motioned for Andrew to get onto his dun horse, behind him.

Michael called for Marie, and she was waiting at the dog-run as they rode up. Andrew slipped off of Isaac's horse and helped Michael lift Eli carefully down from the saddle. The old man gasped as he was moved. Marie's face whitened, but she held the bedroom door open while the brothers carried Eli in and laid him gently on the bed. She shooed the boy Mordecai back to the kitchen so he would not see.

Michael said desperately, "I'll need a sharp knife, and hot water and some cloth for bandages. We've got to get that bullet out of him."

Eli raised his hand as if to wave Michael off. "Too late for that," he said. "He put it in too deep." He grimaced in pain, and cold sweat broke across his forehead. For a moment Andrew feared he was gone. But Eli opened his eyes. He blinked, trying to see. "Which one is Andrew?"

Andrew said, "I'm here, Eli."

"He's come for you, Andrew. I heard, and I tried to get here first. But we run together out yonder—"

Andrew's throat tightened. He had a hard time speaking. "You oughtn't to've, Eli. We've both been watchin' for him. He wouldn't've caught us by surprise."

Eli rasped, "Missy—where's Marie?"

"Here, Eli."

"Seen your papa. Your mama too. They said tell you—" He began to cough blood.

Marie took his hand and held it tightly. "It's all right, Eli. You don't have to talk now."

Eli quit coughing. Andrew took a cloth and wiped the blood away from his mouth. Eli tried to focus on him. "Watch him, Andrew. He's a mean old man. He'll—"

The voice trailed. For a moment Andrew heard nothing except Marie's quiet sobbing. Then Eli spoke once more. "You Lewis boys—you're goin' to be the death of me yet."

With that, he was gone.

Michael folded the old hands carefully across Eli's chest. Andrew wiped the blood from Eli's face the best he could, then pulled the boots from Eli's feet.

Isaac stood back quietly. He had known Eli but briefly at the Moreno farm. He said, "I'll go tend to the horses and leave you folks with him for a spell."

Nobody replied, so Isaac walked quietly out the door and onto the dog-run. He stopped dead still. Something about his manner made Andrew look up.

"Andrew!" Isaac said, his voice a little strained. "He's out here."

Andrew knew before he asked. "Beard?" He felt that cold chill in his stomach again.

"I expect so. He looks like the description. He's just standin' out here beside his horse, like he's waitin'."

Michael said in a low voice, "Let him wait. I can draw a bead on him from the window."

Andrew gritted his teeth. He picked up his rifle and checked the load. "No. I've got to do this myself.

It was me he came for. It was me Eli died for. It's for me to finish."

He gave his brother and Marie a long study. He saw raw fear in Marie's eyes. He said, "Isaac, you'd better come back in here."

Isaac complied. He said, "He's got a look in his eye that I've seen in a bear's, just before he charged. He's got a rifle, and he looks like he knows how to use it."

Andrew glanced once more at Eli. "I know he does."

He took a deep breath and stepped out onto the dog-run, rifle in his hands, in a ready position.

Old Tolliver Beard's eyes were as Isaac had said. They were like eyes Andrew had seen in a boyhood nightmare.

Beard's voice was deep and grim. "I've come to have my vengeance, Andrew Lewis. Blood for blood. Are you prepared for eternity?"

Andrew made no answer; his throat was too tight. No answer would have changed anything.

The old man betrayed himself. He narrowed his eyes just before he brought the rifle into position to aim. That was edge enough for Andrew. He leveled his own rifle, saw the man's broad chest over the sights and squeezed the trigger. He saw the flash of the pan just before Tolliver's rifle belched fire. He saw Tolliver stagger backward.

Something struck his head with the force of a sledge. He felt as if his brain had exploded. He was driven back, stumbling, falling hard upon the ax-hewn floor of the dog-run.

27

Andrew's return to consciousness was slow and painful. His first awareness was that his head ached as if someone were driving a hammer against his skull. He drifted in and out of vague dreams in which he relived the shooting of Jayce Beard, and he saw the vengeful old man standing in Michael's yard, cursing him, raising the rifle to his shoulder. The dream would fade, and he was back at the Moreno farm, sitting with Petra or walking with her along the creek, holding her and not wanting to let her go. Then Petra would disappear and Jayce would come again, with the hard-eyed old Tolliver Beard. Andrew would go through the shootings once more. Sometimes he saw Eli Pleasant, sometimes he didn't. There was something strange about Eli—

He sensed that these were only dreams, but they were so real that he went through the rush of all the old emotions as each came and went and transformed into something else. He became aware of light, eventually, and slowly opened his eyes. He found his vision was blurred. Something seemed to be crushing his head. He raised his hand and found a bandage there. He saw the vague, thin figure of a woman sitting in a chair, and he was back at the Moreno farm, as he had been after the beating in Nacogdoches.

He called, "Petra?"

The woman rose and came to his side, and he realized he was lying on a bed. The voice said, "It's Marie." A hand touched his cheek. "You do not need to move. You just lie there." Through a haze he could see her move to the light, where he discerned the fuzzy outline of a door. She called, "Michael!"

The voice was Petra's, or seemed to be. But why would Petra be calling for Michael? His confusion frustrated him. How did he get back to the Moreno place?

Michael spoke then. "You finally comin' alive, little brother? Me and Marie, we began to wonder if you ever would."

"Marie? What is Marie doin' at the Moreno farm?"

"This ain't the Moreno place. It's our house, mine and Marie's. That shot kind of churned your brain, looks like."

Andrew closed his eyes, for the light hurt them. Gradually it began coming back to him, a little here, a little there. He remembered about Tolliver Beard.

"Beard!" he exclaimed. "What happened to Tolliver Beard?"

Michael said, "He's dead. You got him square through the heart. The way it looked to me, you fired a second before he did. Your bullet hit him just as he pulled the trigger. Else he'd've shot you plumb center instead of layin' a bullet up against your skull."

Andrew could not remember that part of it. He remembered the old man bringing his rifle around. He thought he remembered himself, squeezing the trigger; he wasn't sure.

Michael's voice was grim. "At least you paid him for Eli."

Eli. Andrew had forgotten. Eli was dead. Old Eli, friend of their father. He had saved Michael's life, and probably Andrew's as well, pulling him away from that mob in Nacogdoches. Now he was dead. Painfully Andrew said, "Nothin' would ever pay for Eli."

He opened his eyes again, though the light hurt them. He could discern Michael standing over him, Marie by his side. Or was it Petra? Everything was so blurry he could not tell. "My eyes. Somethin's wrong with my eyes."

Michael said, "I'm not surprised. That rifle ball cut a crease along the side of your head. It was bound to affect somethin'. But you've got the hard head that comes with bein' a Lewis. It'll probably be all right in a day or two."

Andrew tried sitting up. The pounding intensified, and he had to drop back upon the pillow. Marie's voice spoke. "You lie still now, Andrew. You should not too soon get up." The words were English, so this had to be Marie. Petra did not speak English.

He said, "First time in my life I didn't know where I was at."

Marie said, "Or who was with you. You called me Petra."

Odd, he thought. That other time, he had been with Petra, and he had called her Marie.

He said, "Michael, we got to do somethin' about Eli."

"Isaac has gone to fetch the neighbors so we can

give him a fittin' funeral. I thought we'd bury him up on that hill yonder where he can watch over us. Wasn't for him, we wouldn't none of us be here."

"What about Tolliver Beard?"

"We'll bury him on the other side of the river, where we don't have to look at the place, and a long ways from Eli."

Andrew remembered something Eli had said after Quenton Mann's death. He said huskily, "Texas. It sure does take a toll."

He was unable to walk up the hill for the funeral. Young Zeb Willet put him onto his own horse and rode double with him to the place where neighbors had dug the grave. There was no preacher, so Miles Nathan delivered the eulogy. Michael stood beside Andrew so Andrew could lean upon him for support when his legs weakened. His vision was better but still blurred. He saw Marie as if she were wearing a veil, and she looked for all the world like Petra Moreno.

Days, Michael was in his field, planting. Andrew felt he should be at his own place, doing the same, but he lacked the strength. That blue-speckled ox would be getting fat, not having to work. Then one day all the neighbors came back together, and they stayed long enough to plant a good part of Andrew's field for him. They had no sooner finished than a good rain began, assuring that the seeds would sprout.

Texas. It could take away with one hand, but it could turn around and give so much with the other.

Until his strength returned, Andrew remained with Michael and Marie and the two children. Earlier, he would have liked nothing better than to be close to Marie this way. Now, somehow, things had changed. He could look at Marie without wishing she were his. He looked at Marie and saw someone else.

One day he watched Marie hanging out the family's clothes on a line Michael had strung for her. His vision had cleared; it had returned to normal now, except when he looked at Marie. Finished with the clothing, she walked up and stood before him with a willow basket in her hands.

She asked, "Do you think you can ride a horse?"

"I suppose I could. Why?"

"Just now you watched me, but you did not really see me. You looked beyond me, to somewhere else. Somebody else."

He felt a stirring of surprise. "I didn't know it showed."

"Always it has shown, ever since you came home from Nacogdoches. I was not sure, but when you called me by that girl's name, then I knew."

"Petra?"

"Petra. Michael has told me about her. You are a sick man, Andrew Lewis. You will not be well until you go and get her."

"I hurt her, Marie. She might not come."

"I think she will come. I think all you must do is ask her. Must I get Michael to put a saddle on your horse?"

Andrew pushed to his feet. "I reckon I'm strong enough to saddle my own horse."

He left at daylight. The first day's ride found him still weak, and he had to stop several times to rest. The second day he did better, and the third day he stopped only because the brown horse needed rest. He found himself pushing the animal harder and harder with each day that passed.

The pine trees seemed taller and denser. His excitement built as he remembered landmarks that told him he was getting closer to Nacogdoches. He came, finally, to the narrow road leading into the timber that hid the Moreno place. He put the brown into an easy lope, a pace he had resisted until now. He broke out of the timber and saw the sprawling cabin, the shed, the corrals. He saw the field, where Ramón and Felipe were working their oxen. They recognized him and waved, and they halted their plowing. Andrew waved back but did not stop, for he had not come to see Ramón and Felipe.

He saw her then, in the garden, wielding a hoe. The old mother was there with her. It was *Señora* Moreno who saw him first and pointed. Petra turned, her dark eyes wide with surprise and joy.

Andrew swung down and almost leaped over the rail fence in his eagerness, but he managed to get control. He tied the horse and walked to the open gate. *Señora* Moreno came out to meet him. She gave him a hug, looked back with a smile at Petra, then walked toward the cabin without once turning to see.

Andrew stopped and stared at Petra from a full two paces. "Petra. You do not know how beautiful you are."

She blushed and looked down self-consciously at the stained old dress she wore for the garden work. "You should not surprise me so. I must look terrible, so dirty and all."

He moved a step closer. "You are the most beautiful sight I ever saw in my life." He wanted to reach for her, to sweep her into his arms, but there were things that had to be said. "I made a mistake, Petra. I told you that when I looked at you I kept seeing someone else. Well, I have seen her now, and when I looked at her, all I could see was you. All I wanted was to come back and see you again."

"So now you see me, all ugly and dirty. Is it worth so long a ride?"

"It will be much shorter going back, because I will be taking you with me."

She stared at him with some trepidation. "I would like that, Andrew. But one thing is bothersome: you are American, I am Mexican. Some people say the two are much too different; life together may not be easy."

"*Texas* is not easy. But it is worth the struggle."

She came to him, and he took her into his arms. She said, "Then let us make the struggle together."

Forge

Award-winning authors
Compelling stories

· ·

Please join us at the website
below for more information
about this author and other great
Forge selections, and to sign up for
our monthly newsletter!

· · · · www.tor-forge.com · · · ·